## *Midnight ir*

A sexy, mesmerizing read. *...ic Covers)*

A storming good read. Deliciously seedy. Darwin Porter's evocation of the modern (and gay) Deep South would shock Aunt Pittypat but not Rhett Butler or Scarlett O'Hara.         *(Angles)*

Profoundly moving, tragic too,    but also consistently, rapaciously funny in its send-up of the South—Savannah in particular.     *(Fab)*

An undeniable pleasure. Stylish and fun entertainment that gets down and dirty in the deep old South.         *(Inferno)*

A great, sprawling, tragic, comic work of art.         *(Outrage)*

An immobilizing thriller.         *(La Noche)*

A portrait of madness that's compelling, disturbing, and scary. Darkly comic, darkly tragic. Triumphantly fascinating.     *(George S. Mills)*

Carnal. Glamorous. Relentless. To what ends will people go to grab a life for themselves? To great lengths. Even murder. *(La Trova Roma)*

A glittering thriller. A rush of gorgeous, agile exposition. Better than snorting coke.         *(Queer Biz)*

Darwin Porter continues to be outrageous. Surely there is something here to offend everybody!         *(Lothian)*

If you're not already a Darwin Porter addict, this novel will make you one.         *(La Movida)*

Read this book and you'll know why the author can never go back to Savannah.         *(X-TRA)*

A dark and gritty read that never disappoints.         (Use-it)

# To our readers:

*From the Georgia Literary Association.*

In 1981, in Savannah, a sought-after male prostitute was murdered in the home of the city's wealthiest and most controversial antiques dealer. As he bled to death on an expensive oriental carpet in one of the city's most lavish mansions, steamy Georgia suddenly got even hotter.

Some of the dramas that unfolded were celebrated in a book (known today in Savannah simply as THE BOOK) and a subsequent film treatment that rocked the state. In the aftermath, Savannah emerged as one of the touristic meccas of America, and its souvenir trade boomed.

In 2000, celebrity biographer Darwin Porter, bestselling author of *Frommer's Guide to Savannah,* and a resident of the state at the time, crafted his own spin on Savannah and THE BOOK that had brought the city such instant fame.

The result is **Midnight in Savannah,** which we proudly present to you in its third printing. It's intended as a tribute that's more controversial, more satirical, and more eccentric than any coverage that the city has ever received before or since.

It's also a distinctive work of art in its own right, an artfully brutal saga of corruption, greed, sexual tension, and murder, highlighted by the eccentricities of the Deep South.

Despite its inordinate fame, Savannah still retains its allure and many of its mysteries. But this book, better than any that has preceded it, might provide you with a key to some of the implications of sexual life in the Old South. And it will do so with a languorous decadence that you'll remember long after you finish the final pages.

Best wishes, and happy reading
**The Georgia Literary Association** *and*
**Blood Moon Productions**

*First there was THE BOOK, the one that exposed the sexual priorities of Georgia's <u>steamiest</u> city.*

*Now there's <u>Midnight in Savannah,</u> a decadent novel that tells a whole lot more.*

*This is the Savannah of today: Gay, straight, and transgendered, presented with affection and verve by Darwin Porter, The Georgia Literary Association, and Blood Moon Productions. Scandal is no stranger in Georgia!*

# <u>*Midnight in Savannah*</u>

*by Darwin Porter*, bestselling author of *Butterflies in Heat, Blood Moon, Rhinestone Country, Hollywood's Silent Closet, The Secret Life of Humphrey Bogart, Katharine the Great* (a biography that exposes what Hepburn wanted to forget), *Howard Hughes: Hell's Angel, Brando Unzipped,* and many of the *Frommer Travel Guides.*

COPYRIGHT 2000
BY PORTER & PRINCE CORPORATION
ALL RIGHTS RESERVED
Fourth Edition Published in the U.S. in September, 2006

ISBN No. 0-9668030-1-9
Cover photo and graphic design by Russell Maynor

# The players in this drama are as bizarre as The Old South itself.

Any similarities between them and most living or departed persons is purely coincidental:

## PHIL HEATHER

An extraordinary lookalike for Montgomery Clift, this classically handsome young man shares that actor's penchant for doom. Glamorous yet vulnerable, he's full of masculine grace and charm luring those who would both love him and seal his fate.

## LULA CARSON

As eccentric and vibrant as the Gothic creations on the pages of her novel, she's married to a male beauty "too incredibly handsome and virile" not to be desired by the lustful men and women he encounters. Capable of the wildest infatuations for members of either sex, Lula— much like her role model, Carson McCullers--lives in a world of her own creation.

## TANGO

During her childhood in the backroads of The South, the devastatingly alluring Tango learned what white boys did to "yaller gals" when they caught them late at night. Wanting to be white herself, she captured the attentions of enough blond-haired white boys that she was eventually hailed as "The Queen of Savannah."

## LAVENDER MORGAN

"The Life of the Party" and the toast of continents, Lavender Morgan is a celebrated courtesan who seduced some of the richest and most famous men on earth. With her looks fading, she uses her fat checkbook to buy only the finest in male flesh.

### DANNY HANSFORD

"A walking streak of sex," Danny is for sale to the highest bidder, either male or female--it doesn't matter to him. He knows he has beauty that most men dream of possessing only in their wildest fantasies. That body can be yours, if you don't care about the price.

### TIPPER ZELDA

Evoking such tragically doomed figures as chanteuse Libby Holman or Judy Garland, this has-been singer desperately clings to her reputation as the darling of café society, long after that big-spending and hedonistic crowd had gone with the wind. A torch singer *par excellence*, she has the cobra's sting.

### JASON McREEVES

This sexy, virile stud was rivaled in Savannah only by Danny Hansford. Lula Carson always said, "What God didn't give Jason in the head was more than compensated for with what he packed down below." Jason could never make it as a male prostitute, because he thinks that loving is something you give away for free.

GEORGIA
LITERARY
ASSOCIATION

# www.BloodMoonProductions.com

This book is dedicated to the city of Savannah
and to Danforth Prince

It was published with a bequest from

www.BloodMoonProductions.com

# Chapter One

The persistent ringing of a telephone was at first only vaguely heard by Phil Heather. It'd been a long night. When he did manage to open his eyes, he wasn't certain where he was. Some vague memory of checking into a Florida Keys motel stirred in his brain. He was in Marathon.

Sitting up in bed, he reached for the phone on the nightstand. Its ringing had also brought a stirring of the body next to him. Phil decided he'd take the call and deal with the body later.

His horror every dawn was in confronting the strange body in bed with him, a trophy, as always, he'd picked up on his nightly rounds. Who or what would it be this time? Sometimes he was pleasantly surprised but most often not. He feared that after fifteen Scotches his judgment about male flesh became seriously impaired.

"Yeah," he said into the phone, not really wanting to know who was on the other end.

It was Jerry Wheeler, the producer of the film, *Butterflies in Heat*, that Phil was supposed to be writing. "I'm glad I got you before you headed down for Key West this morning."

"Jerry," Phil said as if remembering who he was for the first time, even though they'd known each other for more than fifteen years. They'd met in a bar in West Hollywood. After a night at the Château Marmont, they decided not to become lovers but friends instead. They were too similar in physical type to fall in love. "How did you know I was here?" Phil asked.

"Did you forget? You called last night and left a message on my answering machine. You sounded drunk."

"I was just rehearsing in case they ever remake *The Lost Weekend*. What change of plans?"

"My backers here in New York have decided to set the film in Savannah instead of Key West."

"But the setting is a tropical island. The whole story screams Key West."

"Forget it! It's going to be Savannah—and that's that. This is not a democracy. You don't have a vote."

"But Savannah's been done. Haven't you heard of *Midnight in the Garden of Good and Evil?*"

"It's precisely because I've heard of *Midnight* that we're going to do the film in Savannah. The town's hot now. Maybe we can capitalize off some of the fame of the place and the book. Reflected glory, you might call it."

"But I've already rented a cottage in Key West for the season," Phil said. "I've even paid for it."

"I'll get a friend of mine from San Diego to sublease it from you. He wants to go to Key West for a few months. Besides, I've arranged for a small house for you in Savannah. You'll love it. I've misplaced the address but I'll give you the number of the caretaker."

Getting up nude from the bed, and still not daring to look at the creature he'd hauled in last night, Phil went over to a writing desk and retrieved a ballpoint pen. Back on the phone, he diligently copied down the number as he realized he had a headache so alarming that death itself would be preferable. He always woke up with a headache in the morning, especially when nervous producers called with a change of plans.

"You'll have a phone installed in a few days, and I'll call every day and have you read me what you've written," Jerry said.

"What fun." Phil rubbed his aching head. "It'll be like school, with teacher grading me."

"I'll grade you all right, and you'd better not fuck up this screen play. Need I remind you that you've written five screen plays in the past seven years, and not a one of them has been produced."

"But I got paid. Forty thousand was the smallest paycheck. One-hundred was the largest."

"The fee just got smaller. Remember I'm paying you only twenty-five thousand."

"Don't remind me."

"You're just not commercial enough. You always insert too many gay characters. Do you think young kids in Indiana want to spend their fast food money watching some faggots cavort on the screen?"

"Then why did you hire me for *Butterflies?* It's pretty gay."

"For the first time we really want gay characters. You're perfect for the job. The narrator in *Midnight* appeared like a closet case. You didn't know if he was straight, transgendered, gay, or a neuter, although I certainly have my own private opinion about that. Clint Eastwood in the film made him straight, and even hired his daughter as our hero's love object. What shit! We won't do that. We want to have a gay old time in Savannah. Go where *Midnight* dared not to go."

"I'm your man. But couldn't you spare a few more dollars? What if word gets out I'm writing screen plays for twenty-five thousand dollars?"

"Word is already out. If you don't pull this one off, you're finished on the coast."

"I still have my annuity. You know, of course, I'm from a rich family."

"I know. You've told me enough times. A family who hasn't allowed you to come and visit in a decade after that last scandal. That was a bit much—even for you."

"We all make mistakes."

"Some more than others," Jerry said. "At any rate, you know Savannah. You grew up near Savannah. You're a Georgia boy. You're familiar with the milieu. Personally I can't stand Southerners, except yourself, of course."

"So it's good-bye Key West. Hello, Savannah."

"You'll love Savannah. Just try not to audition the local football team all on the same night. One at a time. Remember that: One at a time."

"You'll be proud of me. We'll light up the screen. I'm already rehearsing the speech I'm going to give on Oscar night."

"A bit premature, my pet. When we speak again, I want to know you're installed in Savannah and writing frantically. If I don't produce something to make some money soon I'm going to be back pumping gas in Santa Barbara. That's how I got my start. This hot shot from Beverly Hills pulls in one day. Thinks I'm cute. Grabs me and tosses me in his car and the next morning I wake up in a palatial mansion. But he's dead now and I'm saving the rest of that story for my memoirs."

"I'll ghost write it for you. But you've got to agree to tell everything. Leave out no detail regardless of how sordid. Even that scene in the men's room in downtown Los Angeles. When you went down on Rory Calhoun."

"I don't know about that—we'll see. Oh, incidentally, I've announced in the papers we're shooting *Butterflies* in Savannah. The press release I sent down included an eight by ten glossy of you. That means you'll be getting some interesting phone calls. Maybe some requests from guys who want to play the hustler in the film. You audition them before me. Save only the best ones for me. I don't want to mess up my mouth with the small fry. After all, I had a father with a ten and a half inch dick. I don't like to settle for less."

"As Mae West always said, if you arrive in town, don't keep it a secret. I had hoped to be more anonymous in Savannah."

"Honey, that glossy I mentioned is even going to be on the frontpage. The publicist who sent your picture to Savannah thought you bore an amazing resemblance to Monty Clift. In fact, she asked me if you were the son of Montgomery Clift. Could you imagine Clift ever fathering a son?"

"Some things defy the imagination."

"Do a lot of guys you pick up think you're Montgomery Clift's son, or at least a relative of the Clift family?"

"Jerry, I hate to tell you, but most of the guys I pick up don't even know who Montgomery Clift was. Only one ever made the connection. He said, 'You remind me of some long dead movie star. Montgomery Clift. Wasn't he the lover of Elizabeth Taylor, even though I heard he was gay?'"

"What do you expect when you cruise kindergartens? I had a trick last night who had never heard of Greta Garbo. Imagine, a queen not knowing who Greta Garbo was!"

"They've only heard of the great Joan Crawford because of that God damn book by her daughter. I hear the bitch is running a B&B somewhere in Idaho, or some such place. Who knows? Who cares?"

"Let's get all this movie nostalgia behind us and get on with our own film. The publicist thinks you're a real good-looking guy, but I told her to forget it. You don't swing that way. I also told her that you and I had bumped pussies in the night. I haven't seen you in a few months. I hope you still have that great body—even at thirty—and haven't gone to seed."

"If I have such a great body, and I still do, why did you kick me out of your bed after only one night?"

"You fell an inch and a half short of the standard set by my father, and you have dark hair. As you know better than anyone, I'm famished for blonds."

Phil heard rumblings from the bed. He had to end this conversation with Jerry. "Talk to you soon." After saying good-bye to Jerry, Phil finally put off the inevitable. He looked over to confront the strange body in his bed, noticing that they'd rented a double instead of the usual twin beds.

There was movement under the sheets as the head turned. It definitely looked male. Phil hadn't been so drunk he'd picked up a woman. It was impossible for him to imagine he'd ever get that drunk.

The young man turned over. With trepidation, Phil gazed upon the face for the first time today. He almost let out a gasp.

He'd won lottery!

The strawberry blond kid staring back at him—unlike everything else he'd picked up for the past bleak seven months—was Adonis. A bit young, but Adonis nonetheless.

"I do believe I have encountered Sleeping Beauty," Phil said.

The boy cast a mischievous grin. "I was told that Sleeping Beauty was supposed to be woke up with a kiss—not some God damn phone ringing."

"Let me oblige." Phil leaned over the young man's body to kiss his perfectly formed and rather full lips. They looked succulent.

But when Phil was only inches from the boy's face, his hair was yanked violently, his head forced downward. The boy pulled back the sheets to reveal a perfect golden torso.

"Not my lips, faggot," he said. "That's not where I want to be kissed. Suck my cock!"

*****

The Savannah sun was shining into the bedroom of Lula Carson, a light so brilliant it sent its rays under the bed to awaken her. Unable to sleep and haunted by demons, she'd retreated here last night to hide under her bed. Since she did this often, she'd even placed a quilt her mother had made under the bed to provide her some comfort when she was forced to flee here from the world.

Last night had been worse than most. Her dreadful failure at medical school came back to haunt her. She'd never aspired to be a doctor. Her family had wanted her to go into the medical profession. She'd never been able to hook her mind around physics, chemistry, and mathematics. Yet her family had insisted she study at Athens even though her heart wasn't in it. They'd invested their entire life savings in her schooling.

A kindly doctor, sensing she wasn't suited for the same career, had taken her to a local hospital one afternoon, leading her through a ward of patients dying from horrendous causes—everything from screaming babies with AIDS to crippled and gnarled old women who prayed for death and asked doctors to administer something to take them out of their misery. The antiseptic smell alone had made her want to puke.

It was when he'd taken her downstairs through a dank corridor and into an underground room that she'd confronted the most horrible scene of her life. He'd showed her an autopsy table holding what might have been a man at one time. The raw cuts on his body had made the corpse look like he'd been butchered as in some human sacrifice. The nausea of excrement, blood, and death had overcome her. She'd fainted. The sight of that bloody body had come back to haunt her last night. She'd awakened screaming and had reached out for Jason, finding that he'd escaped their bed in the middle of the night.

The phone at her bedside table was ringing. She crawled out from under the bed, although her back was in great pain, and stood up to answer the phone. It might be Jason. Perhaps he'd had an accident.

It was Tom Caldwell, a distant cousin of hers who worked for the Savannah police department. "Lula, I'm out at the Shady Oaks Motel. You know where that is. Jason's here. We've subdued him but he's in one of the motel rooms. Naked as a jaybird. Won't put on his clothes and yelling and cursing. The manager wants him arrested, but I've convinced him that you can subdue Jason. Just take him out of here and put him to bed."

"I'll be right there, Tom, and thanks for calling." She hung up and quickly put on a pair of shorts and a seedy looking blue blouse. She went out the back door, hoping her car would start. It often didn't.

Within twenty minutes, she was pulling into the parking lot of the Shady Oaks. Tom rushed over to her. "Glad you're here. He's in room eight. One of my men is in there with him now."

She didn't need to be told what room Jason was in. She could hear him. She opened the unlocked door and walked in, telling Tom's partner that she could handle the situation. The police officer looked with disgust at Jason, then left the room.

Completely nude, Jason cowered in the corner. Upon seeing her, he became strangely quiet. She looked around the room for his clothes, finding a pair of blue jeans on the floor. She picked up the jeans and tossed them to her husband. "Here, put these on."

"I don't have my underwear," he protested.

"God can only imagine where your underwear is. Put on the jeans without underwear, and let's get out of here before you're arrested."

As he rose up from the floor, she couldn't help but be mesmerized by his male beauty. He had almost beige hair and was incredibly handsome. At twenty-two he was at the peak of his male beauty and virility. In fact, everything about him looked like perfection itself, including his sculptured body. If only his mind weren't so fucked up.

He put on the jeans and tried to stuff his ample load in as best as he could before zipping up. "I can explain everything."

She handed him his T-shirt. "I don't want to hear what happened. You know you're incapable of telling the truth. You'd just make up a lie. I don't want you to overtax your brain this early in the morning."

"I'm sorry," he said, reaching to kiss her.

She backed away. "Save your kisses. My job now is to get you home without you going to jail." She peered out the window of the motel. "Tom and his partner have gone. You don't owe this motel any money, do you?"

"I paid when we checked in."

"I won't ask who 'we' was. From the look of this room, it must have been some real rough trade. I don't want to think about it. At least you don't look bruised."

"I'm okay now. Something came over me—I don't know what— and I just started yelling my guts out."

"Let's go home."

On the way back to their double house with its shared front porch, he was silent. Neither wanted to speak of last night. She didn't want to revive her nightmare, and she certainly didn't want any biographical details of Jason's encounter last night.

"I've got some good news," she said. "The landlord came yesterday."

"Are we behind in the rent?"

"Not quite. He said he's renting the house attached to ours. We'll have to share the backyard and the front veranda, of course."

"What's good about that? We'll have no privacy. You can practically hear everything going on next door."

"It could be worse. I feared a family with screaming kids might be moving in. But it's going to be a fellow writer like me. Phil Heather is his name. I was told he's from Georgia like us—not a damn Yankee."

"What does he look like?"

"How in hell do I know what he looks like? I've never met him." She looked skeptically at her husband. "His looks don't matter. He's here to write something—not be distracted by you. Which means I don't want you lying nude out on that chaise longue in the backyard. He needs to concentrate on his writing and not spend all day glaring at that thing between your legs."

"We don't even know if he's gay."

"No, we don't, and for all of our sakes, I hope he's a straight arrow. But if he's gay, I bet you'll be the first one to find out."

The rest of the short drive, and even the rest of the morning, proceeded slowly in silence.

*****

All through the night the old bogey man seemed to lurk around the darkened apartment, waiting to scare Tango if she closed her eyes to get one wink of sleep. The bed was the most comfortable she'd ever known, but it still didn't bring any shuteye to her. Ever since she'd learned what white boys liked to do to a "yaller gal" like herself, she'd never been able to sleep alone. She needed the comforting arms of a blond white boy around her—no other type would do. They had to be blond and blond all over. The biggest turnon for her was a boy with blond pubic hair. She felt that was the most delectable sight in the world. She'd gone and bought this mattress last week, but realized now she'd be short when it came time to pay the rent which was due in a few days.

All her hard-earned money had gone into that mattress and even that wasn't enough to lure Danny Hansford to her bed last night. He'd left the club just as soon as they had finished their last dance. She ran up the alley chasing him, but he turned and yelled at her. "Get off my back!" He'd informed her that he had another engagement. That was all she was likely to learn about what he was up to last night—that is, if he came home at all. Sometimes when they weren't working at the club, he'd be gone for days. When he came home, he never explained where he'd been.

As she lay on this comfortable mattress, she remembered the many nights her mother had made a bed of pine straw for her as they slept out in the open field, wandering the backroads of South Carolina trying to find house work. But few homes wanted to hire a woman with a "yaller gal." The black families shunned them. As one stern old woman said to her mama, "Listen, black bitch, all that youngin' of yours do is advertise that you've laid in sin with a white man. Why, she's almost white."

When they'd wake up in the morning, her mama would leave her alone to search the fields for something to eat. She often returned with a stolen melon and maybe some fruit. After a breakfast of that, they'd be on their way.

Tango swore back then she'd have a real home one day and a real bed to sleep in. For breakfast, she'd have her favorite food—sideback and cornbread and all the creamy milk she wanted to drink. As she got out of bed this morning in Savannah, she realized she had the bed, even if it was empty. But one look in the refrigerator told her there was nothing to make for breakfast, only a half empty bottle of coke and it had gone flat.

Still groggy from lack of sleep, she stumbled into the bathroom and peered at herself in the mirror. Without her wig, she looked too masculine. Her own hair was closely cropped, and she could never get it to behave right. That's why she always wore a wig when she went out on the street. A red wig. She never wore any color of wig but red.

After her shower, she stood looking at herself in the full length mirror. Her skin was almost golden. But there was something wrong with the picture. She didn't like the sex the mirror revealed. She felt it made her look obscene, and she'd spent most of her life trying to hide her dick. She loved dicks on other men, especially Danny's, but she hated one on herself. It looked like some disgusting gut protruding from the bottom of her belly.

When she did her shows, she'd learned all the professional tricks to conceal her goodies. Men didn't come to her show to see her dick. They came to see her female beauty in all its glory.

In those tight white pants he wore on stage, Danny showed enough dick for both of them, maybe even enough dick for three men. If somebody in the audience wanted to see the outline of a male dick, let them look at Danny's. He certainly didn't mind flashing it. In fact, he liked to flash it so much he visited every latrine he could whether he had to go or not. He once told her it was a big thrill for him to see the reaction of other men when he stood at a latrine. "I get the most interesting offers that way," Danny always said. "Sometimes when I head for the men's room, as many as four or five guys will trail me in there for the unveiling."

It was Sunday morning, and she was going to Clary's Café for breakfast. She still had twenty dollars in her purse, and that would be all the money she needed. The rent wasn't due until Friday, and there was still plenty of time for Danny and her to raise it. She feared she'd have to come up with all the money herself since Danny spent all his money on drugs, especially coke. That boy loved his cocaine, and he could hardly get through a day without the drug.

Before she made her appearance on the street, she'd have to spend at least an hour, or maybe two, in front of her dressing mirror. She never knew if she'd encounter fans on the street, and her public always expected her to look beautiful regardless of the hour.

Tango was known for her beauty. The club owner, Matt Daniels, told her she was the most beautiful woman who'd ever set foot in Savannah. She liked hearing that. What she didn't like was his calling her into his office every chance he got, unzipping his pants and demanding to be serviced. She didn't like his stubby dick, and the cheesy taste of it made her want to throw up, but she wanted to keep her job. Besides, she'd read this was how Marilyn got her start, and that one went on to become a tragic but legendary figure, so Tango accepted the fact that kneeling before the disgusting club owner was all part of being in show business.

As she sat before the mirror transforming herself into Tango, she recalled how understanding her mama had always been about her wanting to be a girl. They never talked about it. Her mama had possessed such great intuition she just seemed to know her son wanted to be a girl. Although Tango at birth had been named Haskell Hadley Yett, her mama had taken to calling her Pearl. Her mama had once worked for a white woman in Columbia who had a pearl necklace, and her mama had always dreamed of owning a pearl necklace herself, but had died long before such a dream could ever come true. She'd died alone and in poverty, having never seen more than twenty dollars at one time in her whole life. Years later when she learned to dance, Tango had discarded the name of Pearl for her present name which completely suited her act. She was, along with Danny, a tango dancer.

"This is one yaller gal that's going to become the toast of Savannah," Tango said out loud to the empty apartment. Even as she said that, she knew there was another piece of "toast" that was going to get burned—her rival, the black drag queen known as The Lady Chablis, named after a bottle of wine. Even though Clint Eastwood had cast The Lady Chablis as herself in the film, *Midnight in the Garden of Good and Evil*, Tango felt she could have done a much better job. Sitting in a movie theater, she'd cringed every time Eastwood had directed the cameras to turn on The Lady Chablis.

"Look," Tango had said to Danny in the seat beside her at the first screening of the film. "Chablis is old and she's ugly—and she has really bad teeth. I don't see why no white boy would be attracted to her unless they were looking for an old black mama."

Tango truly believed that any blond-haired white boy, when faced with a choice of her or The Lady Chablis, would haul Tango away into the night.

"She might think of herself as the Empress of Savannah," Tango said to the mirror, "but that's one black drag queen that's about to be dethroned." Tango applied an extra heavy coating of lipstick. "Tango's in town now, and Savannah is too small for two black divas. The Lady Chablis had better pack her gowns, her sagging tits, and fallen ass, and head for Columbia or some place. There's room here for only one empress."

Just as she was making these pronouncements in the mirror, she heard the key in the door turn. She could literally feel her heart beating. "Make it Danny," she whispered to herself. "Let it be Danny. It's got to be Danny. Oh, Lord, let it be!"

*****

At the maid's knock on her door, a stirring of life came to the body of Lavender Morgan. She'd been daydreaming peacefully about the old days. She was sailing the high seas on the yacht of Onassis and spoon-feeding caviar to an aging and decrepit Sir Winston Churchill. The knock on her door, the aroma of fresh coffee, and the faint light in the room brought her back to the reality of her life in Savannah.

Her maid, Norma Dixie, served her coffee and pulled the draperies all the way back, and in general tidied up the room. Not a word was spoken. Lavender always demanded a period of two hours of silence at the start of her day. She couldn't be confronted with one irritating problem, with one annoying voice, until well into the day. She was thankful when Norma left.

She didn't need people in the mornings, only in the afternoon and at night. To her, people before noon were a nuisance. Her rich and powerful lovers around the world always understood that she was not a morning person. Her real reason for being alone in the morning was that it took hours and hours to create the illusion of beauty she planned to reveal to the world. Now at seventy-two that beauty took longer and longer to expose.

The truth was, she was not a beautiful woman. She'd never been beautiful. As a little girl, she'd actually been an ugly duckling—and chubby too. But with artful makeup and the right clothes, she managed to cover every flaw, until the world, especially the press, always called her beautiful. In time it didn't matter if she were actually beautiful. The illusion had obviously sufficed.

Her wisest choice was in her insistence that all her clothes be in shades of lavender. Even on the grayest day, she moved through a landscape with such striking color that no one ever stopped to notice the insecurity or even the fear that might be reflected in her face. They saw her dyed blond hair, her colorful attire, her jewelry, but never her. She didn't want anybody looking too deeply at her.

She'd been privy to the secrets of some of the world's greatest men, but she'd never told them hers. In spite of an offer at least once a year, she didn't plan to write memoirs. The idea of writing memoirs was absurd to her. She'd devoted her entire life to concealing her escapades. Why reveal those in a book? She'd once discussed the subject with her lifetime friend, Jacqueline Onassis. Mrs. Onassis informed her she'd never write her memoirs either, in spite of frequent offers.

As she sipped her morning coffee and surveyed her lavender-colored room, she pondered what outfit she'd wear today. It would certainly be lavender, because she owned clothes in no other color. She wasn't called Lavender for nothing. Actually, as too many people knew, her real name was Priscilla. Her mother had never really wanted to have a baby, and Lavender was convinced that naming a little baby girl Priscilla was an act of hostility.

When people had nicknamed her Lavender, she'd welcomed the new appellation. It seemed to fit her much better. She was convinced that she could never have captured the heart of some of the world's most famous and richest men if she'd kept the name of Priscilla.

She stretched her nude body in bed. Putting her unfinished coffee down, she let her hands travel across her not altogether fallen breasts. She fondled her thighs, remembering how smooth they'd once been. She'd been as famous for her shapely legs as Marlene Dietrich. Today she no longer appeared in any clothing that was not floor length.

When she'd seen a published photograph taken by the paparazzi as she was getting off a plane in London, she decided never to show her legs in public again. That day was over. The more of her body she kept covered, the more glamorous she looked. Today she showed only her face to the world, and even that face had been carved by a surgeon sculptor in Geneva. She'd undergone the world's most expensive facelift.

As she slowly got out of her bed and headed for the combined bath and dressing room, she felt weary. She feared each day upon awakening that she'd be unable to create the artful mask that completely warpainted what she planned to show to the world.

There would be callers today, as always. The bachelors always came for tea. They usually brought friends. Increasingly she was becoming the fag hag of Savannah. She always preferred to be called "the Empress of Savannah," an appellation she'd carried for years. Lately she'd been hearing reports that some dreadful black drag queen was referring to herself as the Empress of Savannah too. Lavender wondered if she could consult a lawyer about this encroachment upon her title.

She had plenty of lawyers. There seemed no end to the estate battles she was involved in. She was certain that as her funeral cortège made its way to the cemetery, various nerdy looking men would be there attempting to serve her corpse with subpoenas.

There would be no society ladies at her afternoon soirées. The corpulent Savannah society ladies in their flowery print dresses and blue rinse always shunned her. They'd ridiculed her as a little girl when she'd grown up here and attended a local school, and they ridiculed her now when after a fabled life she returned to her parents' home to die.

These ladies used to refer derisively to her as Miss Scarlett O'Hara. Lavender knew why she was shunned. The women feared she'd take their husbands away from them. After all, she'd captured the husbands of some of the world's most famous couples. These men never married her, but she'd become their mistress instead. Never more than one at a time. When she was the mistress of a man, she was always faithful to him. They were never faithful to her, but she knew that men were incapable of being faithful. It was biologically impossible for them.

As she headed for her shower, she dreaded the early part of the afternoon before the Gucci carpetbaggers arrived to entertain her in her salon at four. Right after breakfast, which she always demanded to be served at noon every day, she'd have to deal with her attorneys on the phone in New York.

That dreadful NBC, which had broadcast libel about her private life for forty years, was set to give her that network's ultimate shock. They were preparing an hour-long special on her life to be broadcast in prime time. She had to try to block the broadcast with every legal means at her disposal. The program, and even now the idea of it made her shudder, was to be called *The Last Great Courtesan of the 20th Century*.

\*\*\*\*\*

His mind reeling from drugs, Danny Hansford was only vaguely aware of Tango's face buried between his legs. He'd come back to the apartment wanting sleep—not sex. He'd had all the sex he could handle, at least for the day. When night fell, he might feel differently on that subject.

Right now his mind drifted off to the night just past. He'd made one-thousand dollars, the most money he'd ever seen at one time in his eighteen-year-old life. It'd been easy money, too, and he expected there was a lot more cash where that came from.

It had all begun at Whitefield Square, that verdant park centered around a gazebo and named for the Rev. George Whitefield who in 1738 succeeded John Wesley as the Church of England's minister to the Georgia colony. That was a long time ago. Today that square belonged to Danny Hansford. It was his turf, just as it had once been the private cruising grounds of the first Danny Hansford.

That Danny Hansford was depicted in *Midnight in the Garden of Good and Evil*. It was the story of Danny's murder by the antique dealer, Jim Williams, that formed the major plot in the book, *Midnight*. All today's trinket-peddling merchants in Savannah were getting rich off a dead hustler who'd never known money in his short life and who now rested in the cemetery.

What a lot of Savannah didn't know was that a new Danny Hansford had arrived on the scene. From all accounts, the new Danny was better than the original "streak of sex"—better looking, blonder, more talented, and far better hung, according to all reports from eyewitnesses who could speak with authority.

It didn't matter to this new Danny that his name wasn't really Hansford. It wasn't even Danny. He'd been born Jeff Broyhill in Clinton, Georgia. How could he go anywhere in the world with a name like Jeff Broyhill? He firmly believed you didn't have to accept the name you were assigned in life but had the right to take any name you wanted. He wanted the name of Danny Hansford. That was his role model.

Reading about the first Danny Hansford had lured him to Savannah in the first place. He'd heard that many locals were terribly disappointed when Jim Williams had shot the original Danny. He was known as great sex, and many prominent members of Savannah society, both male and female, had not had a chance to sample Danny's wares. They'd felt that Jim Williams had deprived them of the opportunity of enjoying sex with Danny by shooting the boy. Fortunately for those disappointed souls, the new and better Danny was going to treat them to a far better time than his role model ever could.

Danny Hansford hadn't died. He lived on in the body of Jeff Broyhill.

With her full lips and sensual mouth, Tango was a great cocksucker. In spite of his initial lack of interest in sex, Danny was nearing climax. When his explosion came, he held her head down and erupted, then turned over in bed, hoping to get some sleep now that she'd had a taste of him.

Before drifting off, Danny recounted his meeting Steve Parker at Whitefield Square. The man had been there for the past three days, and had seemed to be carefully studying Danny. At first Danny feared the stranger might be a cop. He'd made no attempt to approach Danny, and Danny always insisted that the john come to him. He never made the first move. "If he wants to swing on what I've got, let him make an offer," Danny said under his breath.

On the third day the same strange man had showed up again and had stood outside his car, leaning against the fender, observing Danny, just watching and waiting.

The stranger was starting to make him nervous. Finally, Danny had decided he had to do something. He'd headed across the square to a public toilet at the other end. Before entering the door to the men's room, he'd glanced at the man with a wicked leer. He'd gone inside the foul-smelling toilet and had stood at the public urinal.

Danny didn't need a scriptwriter to tell him what was going to happen next. In minutes, the middle-aged, balding man had taken a position at the urinal next to Danny, although the stranger didn't unzip his pants and had made no pretense that he had to go.

"That sure is a big one," the stranger had finally said, looking down at Danny. "It sure looks like it needs a workover."

Danny flipped his cock a few times, causing the man to audibly sigh. Danny's only response had been to stuff himself back in his jeans and head for the door. Back on the square, the stranger had caught up with him. "There's fifty in it if you'll go back to the motel with me."

Danny had looked at him with disgust. "Those prices, even in Georgia, went out of fashion twenty years ago. One-hundred bucks and that's only for a blow-job—nothing else. Don't ask me to fuck you because you're too old, ugly, and fat."

The man had seemed insulted by that remark and had appeared on the verge of walking away. But after he'd looked down at Danny's crotch, he'd changed his mind. "Okay, it's a deal," the man had said. "Get in my car. But for a hundred dollars, you'll have to come in my mouth and let me lick your balls and tongue your ass."

"Whatever turns you on. You don't want me to use a rubber? Aren't you afraid of getting AIDS?"

"I've sucked off a thousand Georgia boys," the man had said. "With this fat gut of mine, do I look like I have AIDS? AIDS is the thin disease. Besides, only faggots get AIDS. I'm a married man from Valdosta with a wife and two kids. That hardly makes me a faggot."

Danny had sighed and had gotten into the car, even though he'd been convinced by then the man was an idiot—not smart at all.

The familiar session back in the motel had gone uneventfully. The man who claimed his name was Steve Parker had been like all the others—just another cocksucker. Except this one had wanted to taste and lick everything. Danny had smoked a cigarette and had hoped the ordeal would end soon. He had to dance at the club with Tango that night, and he needed plenty of sleep before going on.

When it was over, Steve had turned over the hundred-dollars. "With what you've got between your legs, you should be on film. I make films for private collectors in Georgia. Nothing really public. No national magazines or shit like that. Just private collectors. Usually married men like myself. Some are from Japan. On business in Atlanta."

"I ain't making no gay film," Danny had said.

"Who said anything about gay? I want to film you and this cute little female hooker I met. I think the two of you would be dynamite together. There won't be anything gay in it. Most of my customers don't like films about gay sex. They like to watch real men in action with real women."

"I don't know."

"There's five-hundred dollars in it for you, and it will take only about two hours. This hooker is great sex too. Real beautiful with big tits. It'll be a chance for you to show what you can do in front of the camera. Some of my Jap business clients in Atlanta will really go for you. They can't get your type back home where the men are hung like a small piece of okra."

"I could do that." Danny's enthusiasm for the idea had grown by the minute. "I sent Clint Eastwood a nude photograph of myself trying to get cast as the hustler in the *Midnight* film. But he didn't even reply. Maybe I sent it to the wrong address."

"Forget that now," the man had said. "Will you do it?"

"Okay. But you'll have to give me a thousand dollars."

"That's a lot of money."

"I've got a lot of cock, and have you ever sucked off a guy as good-looking as me?"

"My son is good looking."

"Do you give him blow-jobs?"

"Sometimes. He's a football player. He's straight. But he likes blow jobs."

"Skip the biography. One thousand dollars or no deal."

"It's a deal."

Lying in the bed with Tango, Danny could hardly remember the film he'd just shot. There hadn't been much of a script. Steve Parker hadn't lied about the hooker's looks. She'd been gorgeous. And the thousand dollars looked real. He'd hidden it in his shoe. He didn't want Tango to find it. She'd rush out and spend the money on a new gown.

The mattress felt good to Danny. It just might be the best mattress he'd ever slept on. He'd not known many good beds in his life. In the days and weeks ahead, he was going to sleep in some of the finest beds in Savannah.

He was certain of that, just as he was certain that he'd never grow old. He'd be just like Marilyn Monroe who knew enough to check out before she turned into an old hag. Danny was determined that the world would remember him as forever young.

There was so little time remaining in his short life and so much to do.

\*\*\*\*\*

Even now she couldn't believe it as she read the morning paper. She was back for the season and had opened in Savannah at the Blues in the Night Club. But Tipper Zelda had been upstaged by a mulatto tango dancer and her teenage dancing partner who wore white pants so thin and so tight he might as well have appeared nude on the stage.

They were supposed to be her supporting act—not the stars. Almost the entire night club review was devoted to their charm and their talent. They'd also gotten most of the applause. In the review, she was assigned a final paragraph.

"Ms. Tipper Zelda, our longtime favorite torch singer, headlines the show. She usually returns to Savannah in November for the winter season, and has never appeared here in hot, hot August. But her road show tour was canceled because of lack of audiences, and she's back at the mike again, as big and busty as ever. Last night when she did her classics, 'Moanin' Low' and 'Body and Soul,' it was easy to understand why Tennessee Williams once called her 'the sound of a siren in heat' and Noel Coward viewed her as 'the chili to my con carne.'"

And that was it. When had the star of a show been reviewed in the last paragraph? Another reviewer had concentrated on her declining physicality. "Tipper Zelda was never a pretty woman except for a brief period in her youth when she was dating Montgomery Clift. Today she rivals Rosemary Clooney in weight and is as blousy and dumpy as Shelley Winters. Tipper's dyed red hair is out of control as if she just stuck her finger into a live electric socket. A cotton mill worked overtime making enough fabric for her dress, and no makeup artist, regardless of how skilled, can fill the deep crevices in her face. As one member of her flamboyantly attired, mostly male audience said last night, 'Tipper has been around longer than the clap. She got her start at The Last Supper.'"

Even though she'd been a world class headliner, the darling of fading café society, some of the younger reviewers didn't even know what a star she'd been. No members of Generation X came to her concerts. Her appeal was totally lost on the young. Except for the aging bachelors who usually came to the club in the entourage of Lavender Morgan, Tipper's audiences were dwindling. How much longer could she hold on?

She threw the newspaper on the floor and got out of bed. Her raven hair always stuck out in the morning as if she'd received electric shock, and she could not bear to face herself in the mirror until she'd made some coffee.

As she sat in her garden in a flimsy nightgown covering her corpulent body, she sipped her coffee and took in the sight of her flowers, all of which needed watering. She had to let the gardener go. Her funds were as low this morning as her spirit.

Her life could have been so different now. She could be enjoying a comfortable retirement like Lavender Morgan if fate hadn't dealt her a cruel card. For one brief five-month period in 1963, following Taylor Zachory's fatal shooting, she'd been the heiress to a fortune of thirty million dollars. Even today, thirty million is a lot of money, but in 1963 it was a fabled fortune.

It had all been hers until Taylor's family had discovered that prenuptial agreement that even she had forgotten she'd signed. She must have been drunk when Taylor got her to sign that on the day before her wedding. He'd always put papers in front of her to sign. She never knew what she was autographing. She'd been tricked. Those millions had disappeared from her control, and she'd ended up with twenty-five thousand dollars instead. What a letdown.

Long before it made headlines around the world, her romance with Taylor had gone so promisingly. When Taylor had proposed after having met her in a night club and having known her for only two hours, she'd giggled.

"With my name of Tipper Zelda and your name of Taylor Zachary, we have the same initials. If I do agree to marry you—and that is very uncertain at this point—we could save money."

"How do you mean?" he asked.

"Don't you get it? TZ and TZ. We wouldn't have to change any of our monogrammed towels. Tipper and Taylor. The names seem to go together."

A knock on her door interrupted her thoughts about Taylor. Heaving herself up from her chair, she made her way to the front. Opening the door, she confronted Lavender's chauffeur with a hand-written invitation. After the driver had gone and she'd shut the door, she tore open the invitation.

"Now that you're back in town," Lavender had scrawled in her bad handwriting, "and in between murders, why don't you join the boys and me for tea at four today?"

*****

After hours and hours of tedious driving through the state of Florida, Phil at last neared the Georgia border, retracing the same route he had so recently traversed. He had found it hard saying good-bye to his strawberry blond, Chris Leighton. Although he'd demanded that his cock be sucked and had treated Phil rather roughly, Chris mellowed over breakfast. He wasn't the tough hustler he was pretending to be—rather a sweet Georgia boy, not well educated but a first-rate beauty. And unspoiled.

After his third fried egg, Chris had confided that he acted tough and mean because that was what he thought Phil wanted from him. "I aim to please," Chris had said, downing a second glass of V-8 juice. He had an amazingly hearty appetite.

Before Chris had finished his second cup of coffee, Phil had fallen in love. That was not unusual for him. Sometimes in the course of only one week, he fell in love three times. Every man he took to bed with him he tried to turn into Mr. Right. But after thirty years of auditioning, Mr. Right never showed up at his doorstep. He'd been eager to go to Key West, as he knew the town was crawling with good-looking boys. But, as he also knew from previous experience, Savannah was also filled with good-looking boys. They were not quite as available as those in Key West so he'd have to work a little harder.

Maybe it was just as well Jerry had announced his assignment in the newspapers, and that his picture would be widely viewed. Maybe a lot of good-looking boys in Savannah would want to meet a bigtime script writer who might cast them in a movie and make them an overnight sensation. It was a good line. When he got to Savannah, he'd see how far he could go with it.

In the motel parking lot in Marathon, Phil had lost all cool and confessed his love to Chris. Phil had wanted to take Chris to Savannah.

"Hell, man," Chris had said. "I've spent my entire life trying to get out of Georgia. Why would I want to go back there? It's Key West for me. That's why I took up with you in the first place. Because when you picked me at that truck stop, you said you were going to Key West."

Pleading his case a little too strongly, Phil in a desperate move had offered Chris the role of the blond hustler, Numie, in *Butterflies.*

"I've already got an offer from a bigtime movie producer who lives in Key West," Chris had claimed. "I got his number from a friend of mine. He wants to audition me for a really big part."

"What, porno?"

"Don't knock it. Stallone got his start in porno. *Italian Stallion*."

"I saw that film. I'd retitle it *Italian Pony*."

"Shit, man," Chris had said. "Since you're not driving all the way to Key West, I've got to get on the road and hitch a ride."

In desperation, Phil had given him his only means of contact, the name of the caretaker in Savannah. Jerry had been so stupid he didn't even know the address of the house where Phil would be living. Somewhat reluctantly Chris had taken the phone number. "I don't think I'll be needing this," Chris had said.

"You never know. Things might not work out so well with this bigtime movie producer in Key West. You might end up getting used and abused. I don't know if you know this, but some of these producers demand that a trick allow himself to be fist-fucked."

"Like hell, man. Any man who tries to stick anything up my ass is going to end up in the morgue."

"I'm just warning you."

"I can take care of myself. No one messed with me in my hometown. One time three of the biggest boys in school ganged up on me, and I beat the shit out of every one of them. No one fucked with me ever again."

"I know you're big and strong. I like that in a man. Please call me. I'll always be there for you." As Chris started to walk away in the parking lot without a word, Phil called after him. "How about a good-bye hug?"

"Shit, man, in the fucking parking lot? Do you want someone to see us and think we're a couple of queers?"

"I've done more than hug in a parking lot."

"I'm not into this crap. I think you got your money's worth out of me."

"I got more than my money's worth. You were worth every penny. So great I want to adopt you and take you to live with me forever. I don't know when I've tasted a lollipop as good as yours. Talk about an all-day sucker." Phil reached into his wallet and handed Chris another two-hundred dollars. "Here you might need this."

Chris took the money, stuffing it into his tight jeans. "It's just a loan, man. I'll probably be making so much money in the next few months I could lend you big bucks."

"I'm sure you will," Phil had said, feeling forlorn.

"Let's face it: I'm one hell of a lot better looking than that shitface, Leonardo DiCaprio. A faggot name if I ever heard one. Also, he's got a lousy body, and I've got a great body. Rock hard all over, and I mean all over. I also read the blond shithead might star in *Titanic*, but he's not Titanic under the belt. When those producers cast me, they can even do nude shots. I bet I can make millions for those guys out in Hollywood, especially if they let me dance. I'm a dancing fool."

"I'm sure you will. One day I'll be able to tell everybody that I knew Chris Leighton before he became a big star."

A frown crossed the boy's brow. "You won't tell anybody on the *National Enquirer*, will you? I mean just how well you knew me."

"It'll be our secret."

"I mean, when I'm dating all those bigtime chicks in Hollywood, and I'm the stud of California, and all the stupid little teenage girls across America are setting up fan clubs for me, I don't want word to get out that I let some faggot suck me off in a Marathon motel."

"My lips are sealed." He'd stood for a long time watching Chris head for U.S. 1. With a sigh, Phil had gotten in his car and headed back north up the Florida Keys toward Georgia, humming about the man who got away, even though he was no Judy Garland.

The Georgia border had seemed like the end of the world until he finally crossed the state line. On an impulse as he neared the cut-off going east into Savannah, he stayed on the main road. He wouldn't appear in Savannah until Monday morning. He wouldn't have a phone until then any way, so Jerry couldn't reach him if he wanted to.

He was heading to his hometown of Darien (population 1,736). Even though he was no longer welcomed at the plantation, one door had always remained open to him—that of his Aunt Bice. Considering her own notorious past, Aunt Bice made few moral judgments about others. When she'd first learned that he was gay, she was reported to have said, "I can understand that. Who wouldn't like to suck cock?"

Phil felt a little depressed today. He was bitterly disappointed he couldn't work in Key West this autumn, and Mr. Right, otherwise known as Chris Leighton, had just walked out of his life in that

Marathon motel parking lot, no doubt heading for the den of some Key West pervert where the boy would be turned into a sex slave.

Aunt Bice was the tonic Phil needed on this overcast Georgia day. As he neared the ancestral grounds of his childhood, his spirit lifted. Spanish moss and great-armed oaks made him nostalgic for this southern coast where he'd grown up. The summer sun was a fiery furnace, hot enough to cook the brain and boil the blood, but he was glad to be back anyway. As he neared Aunt Bice's dilapidated antebellum house, a golden light seemed to pierce the sky followed by sweet and cooling rain. He viewed this as a good omen.

A dream of love lifted his soul and inspired his heart to thump with joy. He was overcome with a glorious feeling, almost one of rapture. He knew—just knew in his soul—that some heart was beating for him in Savannah. Mr. Right waited for him there.
Love waited for him in Savannah. He just had to go and claim it.

So strong was his feeling about this, he even whispered to the breeze as he got out of his car. "Your lonely nights will soon be over."

*****

The tedious work on *The Tireless Hunter* was going very badly for Lula Carson in the hot, sticky Savannah afternoon. If Jason and she could only afford air conditioning, but she'd been given only a ten-thousand dollar grant to write her novel. Much of that money was already spent and she didn't know where any more was coming from.

After she'd quit medical school, her family had cut her off from all support. Jason seemed incapable of holding down a job. He'd be all right for a few days, and then his crazy period would begin. At that time, he was likely to do anything. When he was gone for long periods of time, she dreaded to hear the ringing of the phone, fearing Jason had gotten himself embroiled in another disaster.

Steeped in the writings of Freud and D.H. Lawrence, she continued to slave over her novel, fearing it would be "too perverse" for the average reader. But was she actually writing for the average reader? Her mentor, an aging playwright, said she wrote with "the tongue of angels." It was inspiration like that that carried her forth into the day and into her writing.

She feared Jason secretly resented her writing. Once in a rented house in Columbus, he'd burned what she felt was her best chapter, forcing her to recreate it, although she suspected the second version was not as good as her original inspired text. Jason had claimed her writings must have gotten in with some newspapers he was using to start a fire, but she never believed him.

Lula missed literary companionship, and she hoped that this new writer moving next door would turn out to have a kindred spirit. She needed someone to talk to. Jason wasn't interested in writing. He was interested only in sex, which he pursued day and night when he was not in bed sleeping off the ravages of some past escapade.

Even now she had no explanation as to why she'd married Jason McReeves. Her father had warned her that there was "something odd about that boy—not natural somehow." Her only response to her father was to give him her strong opinion that "all love from the human heart is natural. It is hatred that is unnatural. Cruelty to others is unforgivable."

Although she had dated Jason in high school, they had been more like brother and sister to each other. She didn't know if he had turned to others for sex, and she hadn't wanted to know either. Right after high school, he'd enlisted in the army and was stationed at Fort Benning. She thought she'd never see him again until he showed up unexpectedly at her doorstep in Columbus. He'd proposed marriage. His army service had lasted only five months. He offered no reason as to why he'd been discharged. She did not press him for details. All he ever said on the subject was, "The Army is not for me. I'm not the military type."

Even now when she should be concentrating on her writing, she was thinking of Jason. He was still asleep in the next room in their battered old bed. She always told people the bed had been rescued from a bordello in New Orleans. Actually, she'd picked it up at a flea market in Augusta. She did not believe that when one told stories, one had to be historically accurate. As a good Southerner, she knew that tales told to people were for the sake of entertainment—not total truth. If one had to embellish certain details to make a better story, she saw that as perfectly acceptable. She knew John Berendt had done that in *Midnight in the Garden of Good and Evil.* Although peddled as non-fiction, he had embroidered the facts and changed the sequence of events—even physical appearances—to make a better narrative, or to conceal identities.

If one could do that in a "non-fiction" book, she didn't know why she couldn't do that in everyday conversation with people. She realized most people led a boring life, and she felt duty bound to bring some entertainment to them. She was shocked when she'd moved to Savannah to learn how many people she encountered had never been to New York. She had lived in New York for five months, and she got a lot of mileage out of that experience in detailed stories of the wickedness that went on there—the drugs, the prostitution, the violence. She'd related that on at least three different occasions she'd seen people murdered on the street.

She hadn't gone to any of the fancy places in New York and couldn't tell about that, but she'd explored the lower depths. She arrived in the city wearing a pair of dirty tennis shoes and had left the city with only that pair of shoes. If the shoes were good enough to walk through the red dust of Georgia, she figured they were just fine to carry her through the dirty, garbage-littered streets of New York.

Her aunt had given her an old fur coat which she'd pawned immediately upon reaching the city. She was not a woman to wear the hide of slain animals. She loved animals—in fact, cared for them even more than she liked people. A plain cloth coat would do for her.

Almost every day of her life she'd asked herself why she'd married Jason McReeves. She didn't know the answer to that other than she'd immediately felt some bond with him. He'd seen beauty in her where others hadn't. The girls she'd gone to high school with taunted her, claiming she looked like a "freak," that she was "queer looking" or "a bit weird — maybe a whole lot weird."

She'd never followed any styles and always wore the same pair of blue jeans or a simple blouse, washing them every Saturday so that they would be ready for school come Monday. "The last place in the world I will ever visit is a beauty parlor," Lula was always proud of saying. She did her hair herself. She knew that any fool could maintain straight black hair and bangs. She cut it herself, sometimes not always evenly. But such silly vanities didn't seem important to her.

What was important was writing this great novel that she was pursuing, a venue that would lead to incredible fame. She dreaded this upcoming fame. She'd read stories about the price celebrities paid, and she feared she and Jason weren't prepared to bask in the limelight. Tipper Zelda and Lavender Morgan had known great fame, but in each case it had led to humiliation and defeat for them. She feared the American public only built you up to tear you down.

Even the President of the United States wasn't immune. He might be the most powerful man in the world, but few figures in public office had had to withstand the humiliation that man had faced, the exposure of the most intimate details of his life. She shuddered at the prospect that some media types would explore her own background, much less that of her husband's. She had a lot of secrets, and she knew that Jason had so many dark skeletons in his locked closet that he dared not open the door for anyone to look in, certainly not her.

She respected Jason's dark closet, just as he respected hers. Maybe he didn't really believe that she had to go to Atlanta every so often to read from her work in progress to the committee that had granted her the ten-thousand dollars. She knew that Jason knew that the committee was in New York and not Atlanta. But he never challenged her. She didn't ask what happened in the Shady Oaks motel last night, and he wouldn't ask what she did on her next trip to Atlanta. She once confided in a friend that she and Jason had a "gentleman's agreement" about matters pertaining to the pursuit of one's heart.

"If you follow your heart," she had written in her book, quoting one of her characters, "you don't know where it will lead you, but you must always be prepared for the surprises that await you there."

At times she regretted that God had spent so much time in creating and giving Jason such a long and thick penis and hadn't concentrated more on imbuing him with a lot more talent and brain power, maybe even some emotional stability. In many ways she felt that Jason was the victim of his own penis. She believed that if he'd been born with a small dick, life would have gone easier for him. But having a penis as big as his had led to one disaster after another. Once people, men or women, had learned of the size of Jason's penis, they'd pursued him. It was as if they had to have it, if for no other reason than to find out if it were as big as everybody said.

Jason was not ashamed to pull off his clothes in front of anybody. He took every chance he got to strip jaybird naked. He was obviously proud of his possession and wanted to share it with the world. She could understand that. What else did he have to dazzle the world with? She had writing talent, her own special kind of genius. Jason had none of those things. There was little humor and definitely no talent there. She'd gotten him three jobs since coming to Savannah, and he'd been fired from every one of them. The word was now out: No one in Savannah would hire Jason. The only profession he seemed suited for was that of a male prostitute, but she knew in her heart that Jason would not be good at that. He was too loving and kind and would give it away for free, forgetting to charge. That was the way he was.

She sighed. Savannah was moving deeper and deeper into its afternoon, and no words were getting written. It was hard for her to concentrate on the imaginary problems of her fictional characters when her own problems seemed more important and overwhelming.

Once when she was a little girl, she excelled at tree climbing. She'd conquered the tallest oaks in her neighborhood. The towering elms near her house were perfect for her feat. One day with Jason she'd climbed the tallest oak on a neighboring plantation. She'd always seen the oak when passing by the property but had never dared go onto the land to climb it. The owner of the plantation, Jeb McBush, shot at anyone, man or woman, trespassing on his property.

Climbing the stately oak was important to Lula, but not risking her life. One day when her mama told her Jeb had died, she called Jason, telling him that the day had come when she was climbing that tree. All Jeb's family, even the servants, would be at the funeral. The tree was hers to conquer.

Lula led the charge up the tree and had made it all the way to the top branches with Jason behind her. But at the very top, she'd lost her nerve and had clung desperately to the tree, afraid to begin the long descent. She'd cried out for help, and Jason had been there for her. In a very soft and subdued voice, he'd demonstrated every step of the precarious descent. When she'd become afraid, he'd soothed her.

Once on the ground, she'd laughed nervously, concealing her embarrassment at the sudden fear that had overcome her. It was the fear of the unknown. She'd made Jason promise that he'd never tell anybody that the champion tree-climber of Columbus had lost her nerve.

When Jason had been discharged from the army at Fort Benning, and had returned to Columbus to propose marriage to her, she'd remembered how he had helped her down from that great oak. That more than anything was why she'd agreed to marry him. That same night when he'd taken her to the moving picture show, he had confessed later over a hamburger that he had certain "proclivities." She did not need to know what those proclivities were, as she felt that was Jason's secret. She did not believe in harshly exposing the secret heart and hidden desires of other people. That's why she hated Ken Starr and viewed him as the most dangerous man in America.

That very night, she'd even gone so far as to confess that she too had certain "proclivities." Jason had remained silent at her confession and had not asked for more information. That had convinced her that she'd made the right decision in agreeing to marry Jason.

She did not expect to enter into a conventional marriage. Right from the first, they'd agreed they would have no children. Both of them had a contempt for breeders, and felt there were already enough children in the world, many of them abandoned and starving. It would not be a marriage that even her parents could understand. But she'd been really touched by the way Jason had coached her out of that tree. If she climbed too high in life, achieved too much fame and became paralyzed at her own celebrity, maybe Jason would be there again to help her as she began her descent.

*****

With a belly full of Danny Hansford cream, Tango was ready for her day. God, that white boy tasted good. She'd been sampling the cream of white boys or white men since she was nine years old, but nobody made cream quite as delectable as Danny's—and so much of it too. Sometimes when they were home alone and didn't have to appear at Blues in the Night, she had that boy three and four times in one day. Each load he delivered was just as creamy and thick as the one before. She called him her cum-making machine.

She'd once worked in Atlanta with a fellow black drag queen, Dominique, who was very political. She hated all white people and couldn't wait for the day when black people took over this country. "What are you always chasing after those pasty-faced blond white boys for?" she'd repeatedly asked Tango. "They look like they popped out of the oven not even baked yet."

"Those you go around with aren't just baked, child, they are burnt. You don't just like black, you like blue-black. Haven't you ever heard of golden brown like me? I'm the most beautiful color of all."

"You, gal, are some mongrel caught between the races. At times in the right spotlight, you ain't got no color at all. The men in the audience think they are looking at a white girl up there shaking her ass at them."

When Dominique got a cause, she wouldn't let go. Night after night at the club Dominique proclaimed the glory of black dick. "I've been to bed with a few white boys," the black diva had claimed. "Gal, they weren't enough to mess up my mouth with. The average white boy even when fully hard extends for three inches or four at the most. The average black man has six inches—and that's soft, baby. When fully erect, at least nine and often twelve. I've even known thirteen on one guy who was only a teenager."

"Child," Tango had said impatiently, "you'd better get another ruler and take new measurements. There are white boys walking around out there who can match any nigger stud you claim to have had. When white boys have got it, they've got it!"

"Maybe one out of a million," Dominique had sneered.

"Then I've been one lucky gal. I keep running into that one out of a million."

One night and after constant urging, Tango had agreed to go to a straight bar with Dominique, catering mainly to blacks where the ratio was three men to every woman. "You'd better watch it, child," Tango had cautioned her. "Two drag queens are likely to get beaten up in a straight bar."

"You think I don't know what I'm doing, gal? I've been going to straight bars ever since I was sixteen. As gorgeous as this pussy is, no one has a clue that I'm a boy. Even I don't think I'm a boy. It's so small you can't even see it anyway."

"Surely during sex they find out."

"I have my ways to hide that," Dominique had claimed. "I'm a rear door girl. Even the few who have found out didn't let it bother them too much. I have learned that straight men who really like to fuck aren't gender specific. Any black hole in the night will do, baby."

"I'm not so sure." Even though a bit fearful, Tango had agreed to go. She'd just broken up with her white boy friend, Nick Corman, and had been feeling lonely and depressed. She'd dressed up in her most fetching white dress and had approved mightily of her own looks. "I look like a real woman," she'd said to herself in the mirror. She'd known that no black diva in America looked quite as luscious as she was. She was beautiful with perfect skin, and no one could deny her that. Her mama had been a plain and ordinary woman—not pretty at all. Tango had always known she'd never gotten her looks from her mama. She'd wished that her mama had saved a picture of her real daddy. Tango had always believed his pretty boy genes had dominated over that of her mama's. "That must have been one gorgeous man," she'd claimed repeatedly to herself. Sometimes she wondered if he were still alive today. She thought if she ever met him, he'd be proud of the star she'd become. "He'd have to approve of my looks," she constantly said to reassure herself.

It had been after one o'clock in the morning when a taxi had pulled up at the Red Light Bar which used to be a private members-only place when it was called The Tongue Club. It had long since opened its doors to the general public. As Tango had emerged from the taxi with Dominique, she'd heard the loud music blasting away. "This place don't reach its peak until three o'clock," Dominique had assured her.

The moment Tango in her white dress and Dominique in her red dress had entered the crowded room, they'd immediately become the center of attention. Black guys had started hitting on them even before they'd had time to order their dainty cocktails. Tango disagreed with Dominique on most issues but on one thing they concurred. "Ladies" didn't order beer in bars but requested sissy drinks like a Pink Lady.

Within moments after entering the club, Dominique had been surrounded by three guys, leaving Tango to fend for herself. At least for that part of the evening, luck had been on her side. As she'd placed her drink order at the bar, a man introducing himself only as "Sam" had taken the seat next to hers. He hadn't possessed the blue-black skin so preferred by Dominique. Although not as white as Tango, he had lovely brown skin and had been remarkably handsome, showing off a splendid physique in a tight-fitting T-shirt and even tighter jeans.

"I've never seen you in here before," Sam had told her. When the bartender had presented the drink and the bill, Sam grabbed the check. "This lady's drinks are on me." He'd turned and smiled at Tango, flashing the most perfect set of white teeth she'd ever seen, and she'd seen some beautiful teeth on men in her time.

"Thank you," she'd said demurely.

Sam had seemed like a real gentleman, and she'd trusted him. After surveying the rough trade in the bar, she'd thought she had captured the prize. She'd also liked his honesty. Right at the beginning, he'd told her that he was a married man with two kids, and that his wife was out of town. "I'll be up front and honest. God don't like liars. I'm lonely. I'm horny. I'm out for fun. I know how to treat a lady nice. Come mañana we'll go our separate ways—and no harm done."

Tango had not been certain where Dominique had disappeared. She'd just vanished into the night, leaving Tango alone with Sam. Tango had long ago decided that was not a hardship. Sam had grown more charming and appealing by the minute, especially after she'd switched from a Pink Lady to gin martinis, all of which he'd paid for. Gin had always made her wild and impulsive. An hour later had found her in Sam's battered car driving back to her apartment in midtown.

Once they'd entered her apartment, Sam had dispensed with preliminaries and even foreplay. She'd found herself trying to swallow him whole, and he'd held her head down forcefully, penetrating her throat. At first she'd fought against gagging, but had breathed through her nose and had begun to open up to Sam. Perhaps Dominique had been right about black boys, at least their penile measurements. But even as she'd sucked Sam, she'd realized that he didn't count in the contest. She had suspected that he was just as much white as he was black.

Oral sex hadn't been enough to satisfy Sam. When he'd demanded more, she'd claimed she was having her period. That hadn't stopped him.

"I'm a fucker, baby," he'd proclaimed. "Blow jobs are just warm-ups for me. My wife has to take it two or three times a night, even when she screams and begs me to get off her. That is just music to my ears. It goads me on." He'd placed his strong fingers at her neck, tightening hard, choking her. No longer was he the kind and considerate gentleman she'd met in the bar. He'd looked at her violently. "If one hole is not open to me, Sam will find another one." He'd tossed her over, ripping down her panty-hose. The penetration had been quick, searing, and violent.

He'd churned her guts turning them into tapioca, and he hadn't advocated lube, or even a quick feel-up. Wave after blinding wave of pain had overcome her, as he'd pounded forcefully into her. Her nerve endings had seemed in red-hot torment. At some point when her guts were being ripped endlessly apart, he'd reached under to feel her in front. That had been a major mistake. Unlike Dominique, she wasn't that small, although she'd always kept her goodies artfully concealed. But Sam had been no fool. Even though she'd suspected he'd never felt up many boys in his life, he'd known a dick when he'd encountered one.

Without warning, he'd yanked violently out of her, hurling her body over and ripping off her red wig. He'd attacked her clothing, tearing and shredding, before hitting her face violently. "You fucking faggot!" he'd shouted at her. "God, I hate faggots." His fist had pounded into her face. She'd tasted her own blood, knowing he'd loosened her two front teeth. "I'll kill you, you God damn cocksucking queer. Trick me, you faggot." He balled up his fist and had knocked her face so violently and powerfully she'd welcomed the all encompassing blackness.

Bleeding and seriously injured, she'd come to in about an hour, calling for an ambulance. A week later and with two new front teeth, she'd asked Dominique to drive her to Savannah. Sam had threatened to hunt her down and kill her if he ever heard she was appearing at another club in Atlanta. At some point in the bar she'd foolishly told him she was a "cabaret entertainer."

"Good luck, gal," Dominique had said, letting her out near the waterfront in Savannah. "Got any money?"

"Not much," Tango had said.

"Sorry I can't lend you any. I got just enough money to buy enough gas to get back to Atlanta. I'll see you back in Atlanta some day when all this blows over. Gals like us can always count on the tenth one we meet being a little bit crazy. It's happened to me."

"Thanks for the ride." Tango had gotten out on the cobbled streets and wandered for hours looking for a room to rent. She had only two dresses in her suitcase. Dominique had promised to send her the rest as soon as Tango had earned enough money to have her wardrobe shipped from Atlanta to Savannah.

Tango had found a tacky little room in a bad section of town costing only twenty-five dollars a week. After all the money she'd spent at the hospital and at the dentist, she'd hardly been able to afford that. Paying medical and dental bills had wiped out practically everything she'd been able to save after three years of working in clubs.

She'd brought a white dress—almost identical to the one she'd worn in the bar where she'd met Sam—and a purple gown with her to Savannah. It was the purple dress she'd donned when she'd headed for The Tool Box where management often hired drag queens to perform on Friday and Saturday nights.

As she'd walked into that bar, she'd spotted the world's most beautiful white boy dancing go-go style on the bar, wearing a sequin-studded jockstrap of almost transparent material that left little to the imagination. He was not only beautiful, but blond. She'd never been the marrying type, but right at that moment she'd decided then and there that that white boy was going to become her husband.

No sooner than she'd sipped the first of her Pink Lady, than she'd learned that the dancer's name was Danny Hansford.

"That's not his real name," the bartender had assured her. "But that's what he calls himself."

Within minutes, Danny was shaking that ample jockstrap right over her face. It was only inches from her luscious scarlet-painted mouth. His body had been sweating profusely, and beads of perspiration had dripped down. She'd imagined some of that golden nectar had fallen into her drink, sweetening her Pink Lady.

A steely determination had crossed her brow. Whatever Tango wanted, Tango got. And right now, and maybe forever more, Tango wanted Danny Hansford.

*****

Deep into her third drink of the afternoon, Lavender sipped her brandy and surveyed the sea of bachelors in her parlor. If she counted right, and without glasses she couldn't be certain, ten—or was it twelve?—bachelors had showed up for tea today. Her black maid, Norma, had already danced the shag with one of her guests. Norma had then entertained this room of faggots with her rendition of "C'mon and Get It, Honey." She'd shaked, rattled, and rolled and had everybody laughing until Lavender signaled that was enough.

Before she was forced to become a maid because of age and her alarming weight, Norma claimed she'd been a headliner in Harlem. "My place was called Norma's Room, and all the big stars came to hear me perform. Lena Horne. Louis Armstrong. In fact, honey, many of those high-time niggers stole my material. They repackaged it and made millions that rightly belonged to me."

What Norma left out of her autobiography was that at the age of sixteen she'd been operating a Harlem bordello whose advertising slogan was, "There is no human desire we can't satisfy, honey."

Lavender knew Norma had been a whore and had procured young girls—or even young boys—for her customers, but she'd always felt that Norma's claim as a show business great was far-fetched. If Lavender ever learned the truth, she'd probably discover that Norma had been a stripper or something trashy like that.

Norma could exaggerate so that it was entirely possible she could take an appearance as a stripper in some cheap after hours dive and turn it into a show business legend in Harlem. Lavender suspected she'd never learn the truth about Norma. The maid could reinvent herself night after night. At one time she'd even claimed that she was the maid to Mae West who'd left her controlling interest in an apartment house in Los Angeles.

"What happened to the apartment house?" Lavender had inquired.

"I let some sweet-talking, muff-diving brown skin nigger with a sugar dick talk me out of it." At that point Norma had turned on the vacuum cleaner, and Lavender never heard the rest of this far-fetched tale.

When Norma had applied for a job as a maid with Lavender she could only list one reference and that was Mae West. "I'm sorry my one reference is dead," Norma had said. "But it's all I've got to put down."

Lavender had hired her on the spot because she needed a maid. Because of Lavendar's reputation for being a difficult employer, other women in Savannah didn't want to work for her. After Norma's first day on the job, she appeared to have no experience at all, but Lavender kept her on, hoping she'd learn by doing.

The bachelors were always amused by her Mae West stories, which differed radically from all published accounts. Norma, in fact, maintained that the late star was not a woman at all, but a drag queen. If pressed, Norma would then elaborately describe Mae West's "tiny dick" which Norma claimed she'd seen on repeated occasions.

The only time Norma had grown suspiciously silent on the subject of Mae West was when the drag queen, Craig Russell, had arrived in Savannah for a sold-out performance. The bachelors were eager to bring Craig and Norma together to exchange Mae West stories. But Norma had been very sparing of Mae West details when she'd met Craig and was even a little vague as to when she'd worked for the fabled movie star.

Norma increasingly alarmed Lavender. More and more Norma was upstaging her. Lavender knew the boys had come to hear her tales of encounters—often a close encounter—with the rich and famous. But even after her song-and-dance routine, Norma would enthrall her guests with stories that happened in her night club—read that, alleged night club.

"White folks used to go to Harlem in those days," Norma was telling the amused bachelors who appeared captivated. "Lana Turner visited whenever she was in town. Lana would have a few drinks and by midnight she'd be in the men's room servicing some of our more well-endowed customers. Lana always told me not to send any black stud with less than ten inches back to her. She demanded ten or ten plus—or else that stud would never know Lana's luscious red lips."

Lavender decided to interrupt. "Why don't you check everybody's tea to see if they need a refill?"

Norma looked crestfallen and went to the bar to start replenishing drinks. Even though Lavender invited the boys over for tea, no one ever drank tea. Bourbon and branch water was the drink of choice. Lavender had a strict rule in her house. She never served water with those bourbons if that water had run through a pipe. She always had her driver go back to the branch at her ancestral home in central Georgia and fill large containers of the branch water she'd drunk as a child. She stored this water in the cottage in back of her property and always demanded that it be served at her parties.

She was convinced that drinking water run through pipes had destroyed the Roman Empire. Cancer might claim her but she was determined she wasn't going to die by drinking bad water piped in from God only knows where.

She'd also understood, and this had been confirmed in that awful book, *Midnight in the Garden of Good and Evil*, that one of the local rednecks carried a vial of poison around that was so lethal that if dumped into the city's water supply, it could kill most of Savannah. She wasn't taking chances. Even when she went to clubs, she had one of her escorts carry a thermos of bottled branch water with her to sweeten her bourbon.

The photographer, Gin Tucker, Savannah's Truman Capote clone, took the seat next to her. The town's most venomous gossip, Gin seemed to coach Lavender in the telling of her stories. Of course, he'd heard them all before. But the bachelors were always having house guests, often from New York, so there was usually somebody in attendance who hadn't heard her tales of the seduction of the high and mighty.

Even for people who didn't see well, Gin always stood out in a crowd. He wore suits colored in lime green with pink accessories. "I'd wanted to wear white but Tom Wolfe has always laid a claim to that. I didn't want people to think I was imitating Tom Wolfe, the most untalented writer I've ever read. His lips are too thin. I never trust a man with thin lips. Thin lips don't do a God damn thing for me."

Wispy and effeminate, Gin spoke in a high-pitched voice. He'd descended from one of Atlanta's finest families. From reports Lavender had heard, that family was happiest when Gin stayed down in Savannah. "I feel at home here and I feel safe," Gin had told her. "I've gone into all the bars and I've never been beaten up. Besides, after midnight everybody turns gay in Savannah."

Lavender wasn't certain about that. It seemed like a gross exaggeration, although from her experiences since her return Savannah was increasingly gay. It hadn't become Key West yet, but it seemed to be headed in that direction. She realized, naturally, that she couldn't draw conclusions based on her circle of acquaintances. She never mistook them for friends. She called the bachelors her "caddies." Their job was to carry her purse, order drinks for her, and keep her amused. She never confused her court jesters with friends. Over the years her real friends had either deserted her or died. They were always men. Women never liked her. Lavender felt in her heart that all the women she'd encountered in life were incredibly jealous of her.

Lavender listened to the silly little queens and the gossip which usually consisted of who was going to bed with whom. Enjoying another brandy, Lavender could easily remember what her former lovers had talked about. They were involved in events that would shape the course of history. She'd heard and been told things about what was going on in the world that the press even today had never uncovered. She found it amazing what age did to a woman. She'd gone from such a lofty plateau to her present one where she was reduced to listening to the bedtime stories of Savannah's gay colony. She only pretended to be interested. Except for Gin and a few others, she couldn't remember the names of most of these boys any way. She called them "darling" or "sugar," and that seemed to suffice. She didn't like their habit of always kissing her since she didn't know where their mouths had been before. She especially didn't like those lip kissers. But she'd never voiced any objections and pretended to go along with the social customs foisted upon her.

Seeing that everyone had had their final drink, Lavender summoned Norma and privately ordered her to go over to Tipper's and see why she wasn't attending tea after having been invited. Lavender felt the polite thing to do would have been to call and cancel if she couldn't make it. Lavender always became infuriated when one of her invitations was turned down.

Norma had complained of the intense heat but reluctantly agreed to walk over to Tipper's whose home was only three blocks away.

With Norma, her dancing, and her wild nights in Harlem stories out of the way, the spotlight shifted back to Lavender. Gin was urging her to tell the story of her affair with John F. Kennedy. There were at least three bachelors in the room who hadn't heard it.

"Kennedy always said he was never finished with a woman until he'd had her three ways," Lavender told her admiring audience. "I can vouch for that. He was a man of his word."

Gin led the chorus of laughter. One of the bachelors from New York piped up. "I've been dying to ask and no one ever told me. It must have been enormous. Was it all that big?"

"I'd say five inches at the very top," Lavender said, "and that's being mighty generous. JFK was no LBJ."

A hush seemed to fall over the room. It was as if she'd destroyed a national monument, or at least one of their legends.

"Except for LBJ, most presidents in modern times have had small dicks," Lavender claimed. "Richard Nixon, Jimmy Carter, and especially Bill Clinton. I haven't gone to bed with any of those men, and I wouldn't have wanted to any way. But they've been observed. The truth is known about them. Many world leaders, good or bad, have had small dicks. Napoléon's a classic example. Hitler, or so I'm told, had the smallest dick of all, and only one ball. But many German women—not only Eva Braun—found him immensely appealing. A sexual fantasy actually. Over the years I have found if a man has enough power and money his dick size didn't matter. Money and power make up for dick size. Don't you agree, Gin?"

Gin looked flustered. "No, not at all. To me, dick size is everything. I could go to bed with the ugliest man in the world if he had a big dick. I always look at the crotch first, then the face later."

"In my day, we used to call men like you size queens," Lavender said.

"Sugar, we still do," Gin said. "No one ever came up with a more graphic appellation than that. And speaking of size, we're inviting you to the Blues in the Night."

"Yes, I've heard that Tipper is going on again tonight. Her road show went bust. I invited her for tea but the bitch didn't show up. I view that as a slap in the face since we are her only fans. If it weren't for us, Tipper would have no audience."

"Gawd, we've heard Tipper Moaning Low a million times," Gin said. "I never liked the damn song anyway. Tipper's headlining, but the real stars are a black drag diva named Tango and her partner Danny Hansford."

"Danny Hansford?" Lavender asked, puzzled. "But he's dead. Wasn't he the hustler Jim Williams shot?"

"That was another Danny Hansford," Gin said. "This guy uses the real Danny's name, and the stories I could tell you about the real Danny Hansford. This new Danny is a tango dancer. He appears in the club without his shirt and wearing the tightest white pants ever sewed onto a white boy. My dear, there is meat for the poor there. Wait until you see it. I'm photographing him early tonight with his partner. Publicity stills for the show. But I'll be able to snap some unrehearsed pictures on the side. I'll let all of you see them."

"I don't have any other invitations, so I'll attend the next performance with you," Lavender promised.

"We'll reserve a table and call you with all the details," Gin said. "And, sugar, I know you don't like the world to know you're blind as a bat, but you really should wear glasses for this show."

"It sounds like fun—I'll be there if I ever forgive Tipper for not showing up to tea or responding to my invitation."

At six thirty the boys always filed out of her house. That was a house rule. Nobody stayed after six thirty. She never knew what the boys in Savannah did after six thirty and before their appearances later in the evening at the clubs, and she didn't want to know either. There were many things she didn't want to know, believing that ignorance about such matters was bliss.

Slowly Lavender made her way up to her bedroom. When Norma got back from Tipper's, Lavender wouldn't ask the maid to prepare her a light supper. She'd retreat without food but with her brandy to her bed where she felt the most comfortable these days. In fact, she'd given serious consideration to going to bed and staying there for the rest of her life. She'd need all the rest she could get before going out to a night club.

At her age there were no more rich men to seduce, no more benefactors giving her money and jewelry. What she'd accumulated would be it. There would also be no more rejections from lovers. Murrow, Agnelli, and Rothschild had all rejected her. They'd either gone back to their spouses or married fresher and more innocent women.

She felt her life was dwindling down to a few precious years, maybe only a few months. One couldn't be sure. She'd always defined herself through the eyes of her men. But all the men were gone now. Many were dead. Those who lived preferred to spend their declining years in the arms of other, younger women. Lavender knew she could no longer compete. Not knowing where to go, she'd come back home to Savannah where her career as a woman had begun.

When she'd arrived, there had been no welcoming party. No invitations. After a few weeks, Gin Tucker had showed up on her doorstep unannounced. She didn't know who he was but she was lonely for company and had invited him in. Gin had announced that he was the world's greatest photographer, far better than Richard

Avedon at his peak. Gin claimed recognition had eluded him because of the rampant homophobia in the world.

From that meager and unpromising beginning, Lavender had become den mother to the town's growing number of bachelors. Gin had invited clusters of them over to meet her and to welcome her to Savannah. She felt these men were driven by curiosity more than love of her legend. In some way she suspected they hoped to learn her secret of capturing the world's most desirable men. But that she would never divulge to them. Back in her heyday she'd used men such as Gin as social secretaries and bus boys—nothing more. She had real men in her life then and didn't need these bachelors for companionship. Today the boys had become her only companions. She fully expected them to be at her bedside on that final day when she'd retire from the world for good.

*****

Danny stood in front of 429 Bull Street in the hot Savannah afternoon, contemplating the facade of Mercer House where his idol, the real Danny, used to go to fulfill the sexual desires of the rich faggot antiques dealer, Jim Williams. On the square in front, Danny looked up at the window where the scene of the crime took place, but the lavender shutters were always drawn, and he could only imagine the life that must have gone on here back in the days when Williams gave his legendary Christmas parties, inviting the cream of society one day, followed by another night party "for gentlemen only."

Every day as Danny came to the square to stand here, he envisioned the shooting that occurred in Williams's study. Did Williams murder the real Danny? Or was it self-defense? No one would know for sure, and it would always remain a mystery. Danny was dead, and Williams died of a heart attack in 1990 in the very same room where he'd killed Danny. His body was found behind his desk in the exact spot where it would have been discovered in 1981 if Danny had shot at him and hadn't missed.

The house had endless intrigue for the new Danny, although he'd never been inside. He dreamed of going inside one day, even if he had to break in. It was inhabited by Dorothy Williams Kingery, Williams's sister, and she'd allowed Clint Eastwood's film crew access to it—for a price, of course. Danny didn't have Eastwood's money to buy his way into the house but he had to come up with a way to get inside. He feared if he tried to break in, he'd be arrested. It was such a compelling desire that he was going to take that chance. Not today, nor even tomorrow, but one of the nights to come he was going to sleep an entire night in Mercer House, the way the real Danny had done.

Danny didn't need a jury to tell him that Williams was guilty of murder. In his heart, Danny knew that Williams had killed the young hustler. After all, Williams had been found guilty twice, though each conviction was overturned. A third trial of Williams on a charge of murder ended in a mistrial. Finally, far removed from the intrigues of Savannah, Williams became the first person in the history of Georgia to be tried on a charge of murder four times. At his fourth trial in the city of Augusta, he was finally acquitted and allowed to go free, even though he didn't have that long to live.

Danny adjusted the crotch of his too tight jeans and pulled out a cigarette, lighting it without taking his eyes off Mercer House. As long as he stood here, sometimes for hours at a time, he never saw anybody leave the murder house, although he knew it was inhabited.

Sometimes he'd close his eyes and could still hear the squealing wheels of the real Danny's black Camaro, as he careened into Monterey Square. "The kid likes to hot-rod it all over the place," one old-time Savannah man told him. "The way he would whip around the squares of Savannah in his Camaro made me run for cover. I figure Danny was trying to kill me or himself. The way he drove, I think he had a death wish. No young guy would drive like that who wanted to live on this planet much longer."

Danny had heard that the long-dead young hustler had a "cocky strut," and that was the very walk Danny himself used as he made his way across sultry Savannah in the August heat.

His blond hair was just as blond as the real Danny's, even thicker and blonder if eye-witness accounts could be believed. His trim, muscular body had to be just as fine a specimen as the real Danny's was, maybe even better. In one department he knew he had Danny beat. A trick he'd turned when he first arrived in Savannah had employed the stud services of the real Danny on more than one occasion. After his first night with the new Danny, the faggot had told him that he had the real Danny beat by at least two good inches. "Jim Williams always told the bachelors of Savannah how well endowed Danny Hansford was. What if Jim Williams had ever had the chance to meet you? He would have choked on it. I don't think Williams could have handled it."

Thrilled at the revelation, the new Danny set out the next day to have some T-shirts made. The real Danny wore a T-shirt that said, "Fuck you!" Although the old Danny was his idol, the new Danny didn't want to imitate his role model that closely. Instead Danny went to an outfitter and ordered ten T-shirts, each one asking the provocative question, "Think you can handle it?" That T-shirt lead to more offers than anything else he'd done in his whole life, including hanging out on street corners waiting to get picked up.

When he finished his cigarette, he lit another. He smoked and drank all he wanted, and snorted all the coke he wanted too. His body was perfection itself, almost as if a sculptor had created it, instead of his mother. People he talked to claimed he was ruining such perfection by abusing his body. What he didn't tell them was that there was no need to take care of his body. He wouldn't inhabit this body for that long. Ever since he was a little boy, he always knew he'd die young and leave a beautiful corpse. He wouldn't be around long enough to die of a long, lingering lung cancer.

He didn't plan to commit suicide. That would be too easy. The man who was to murder him was out there somewhere. He was going to be shot just like the real Danny was. Right now he didn't know who was going to kill him, but he'd know the person when he met him. In his heart, he'd always understood that it would be impossible to flee from his executioner. That would be like running from Death itself. How stupid! There was no place on the planet or even the universe where you could hide out from Death. When Death wanted you, he'd find you, regardless of where you were.

This afternoon Danny felt that his executioner wasn't even within the city limits of Savannah. But Danny knew he'd be arriving soon. He could just feel it in his bones. When he met this man, Danny would face him squarely and play out the drama that both of them were destined to act out. Danny suspected his would-be executioner wasn't even a violent person. When they'd meet, it would be immediately understood that they had a role to play in each other's lives. Although Danny would know immediately what his part was, his murderer wouldn't be aware of the drama that was unfolding, or even of his role within it. Such knowledge gave Danny a slight advantage in the form of being able to determine the circumstances and the time of his own death.

Whoever it was that was coming to Savannah to kill him wasn't yet aware that the spirit of Jim Williams had already inhabited his body. The reincarnated Danny, living within the sculpted body of Jeff Broyhill, knew that both the old Danny and the restless spirit of Jim Williams were still engaged in a to-the-death struggle. The very fact that Jim Williams had died of a heart attack, and not by means of a bullet, meant that Williams had escaped without paying for his crime. There had to be another murder, perhaps even a double murder, a final cleansing and decisive act that would release the souls of earth. The spirit of the old Danny, reincarnated in its new, beautifully formed body, would never leave this earth until he had paid Williams back.

The new Danny shuddered to think what awaited him. It was ghoulish, the idea of participating in his own murder. But at this late stage, any resistance offered by Jeff Broyhill was increasingly feeble against the obsessive and grimly determined soul of the late Danny Hansford.

At first, from the remote isolation of Clinton, Georgia, Jeff hadn't understood what was happening to him as conflicting egos raged within his hunky body. Until his body had actually been consumed by the spirit of the dead Danny Hansford, he had never even heard of Jim Williams, and had never thought a lot about Savannah, either. Some mysterious force had compelled him to read *Midnight in the Garden of Good and Evil*. Up to then, Danny hadn't read an entire book in his whole life, preferring hot-rod and weight-lifting magazines instead. *Midnight* was the first. A lot of it, he just skimmed through quickly. He wasn't particularly interested in the parties and social struggles of society ladies, Georgia football games, or the restoration of Savannah. He had wanted to read only about Jim Williams and Danny Hansford. When he'd drained from the book every piece of information about them he could, he still didn't understand the primal appeal of what he was told had altered the economy of the city forever.

Eventually, as if directed there by some mysterious and hypnotic force, he moved to Savannah, making a living hustling in the same haunts, using the same strutting walk and the same sense of smoldering defiance that he attributed to Danny Hansford. Then, as if pulled toward her by a mysterious guide who by now he had begun to view as his destiny, he met "The Haitian Venus" in the form of Erzulie, a voodoo lady. Only after a dialogue with her did he fully understand the implications of what he had become, and the role he would play in the inevitable conclusion of the Williams-Hansford tragedy.

He had wanted to meet with Erzulie this afternoon, continuing what had become almost a daily meeting. But she had had to rush off to Atlanta to put a spell on a drug dealer who was causing trouble for her son. She wouldn't be back until tomorrow.

Danny glanced at his watch. He took one final look at Mercer House, vowing that he'd be back. He wouldn't always be outside looking in. At some point during his short life, he'd be a resident in that house, if only very temporarily.

Right now he was late for an appointment. He had to meet Tango at the studio of the photographer, Gin Tucker. Tucker was to take pictures of them as tango dancers to use for publicity stills for their night club act.

Danny threw his still-lit cigarette on the square. "Tucker will probably be a faggot," he muttered to himself. "Why are they always faggots?"

*****

Tipper sat in her courtyard patio awaiting the arrival of Norma Dixie who had called earlier that she wanted to come over for a drink. Tipper knew that it was in her own best interests to have responded to Lavender's invitation to tea, but she'd gone ballistic at the invitation. How dare Lavender invite her over and write "between murders" on the invitation. It was an insult that could not be overlooked.

In the fading light of the afternoon when the most ferocious of the August heat had cooled, Tipper tried to become more reasonable. She needed Lavender and all her bachelors to attend her performances. They, in fact, made up a good part of her audience, as increasingly she was failing to attract any new fans. Her road show had proven that.

She knew that Lavender firmly believed that it was Tipper who had killed her first husband, Taylor Zachary. Tipper had heard

Lavender quoted on many occasions. "To my dying days," Lavender had always proclaimed to her bachelors, "I think Tipper killed Taylor. That was no suicide. Tipper fired that fatal bullet into poor Taylor's head." Many bachelors privately confirmed to Tipper that Lavender had "dined out" on the story, using her version of the alleged murder to enhance her own allure at dinner or cocktail parties.

Tipper had had nothing to do with the other three men in her life who had been found dead under mysterious circumstances. The press had dubbed her the "Black Widow," and that dreadful appellation had stuck. It'd been a terrible coincidence that these men had died under suspicious incidents. Tipper always viewed it as a cruel twist of fate that she'd been singled out to play the fatal role of widow. Selecting the right men to marry had not been one of her major accomplishments in life.

She always felt she would have had a far bigger career had Taylor not been shot on that fatal night. Her recordings were increasing in sales, her fans growing, before that night. The suicide of Taylor—more often labeled murder—had become one of the most sensational cases of the 60s. It had all the ingredients for a ripe, delicious story: A rising singing star and her handsome young husband, the heir to a tobacco fortune.

They were two beautiful and glamorous people caught in a web of unexplained circumstances. Tipper had read a recent book called *America's Ten Most Unexplained Murders*. The story of Taylor's death was widely featured in this libelous work. The author more or less had named Tipper as Taylor's murderer, discounting all suicide theories. There were only two people who knew what had actually happened on that long-ago night in Winston-Salem, North Carolina. One of the witnesses, Peter Paul, Taylor's lifetime companion, was dead. Tipper was the only one left who really knew the truth of that night, and she'd never confided the actual circumstances to anyone.

At the sound of the doorbell ringing, Tipper got up and walked through the house to let Norma in. Tipper had long ago learned the standard Savannah greeting, "What will you have to drink?" Tipper had known Norma long enough to anticipate her answer which was always the same—a rum and coke.

As the women sat in the patio sipping their cool drinks, Norma told her what she didn't want to hear. "Miss Lavender is really mad that you didn't come to tea or at least call and turn her down."

"You know, of course, what that invitation said?"

"That between murders crap." Norma sighed, slouching down deeper in the chair with her rolls of fat. "That was mighty insulting— I know that."

"But I guess I'd better go and write her a little apology. If Lavender and her bachelors don't show up at my club, I would be unemployed. God knows I need the money. I just got a notice from the bank. I'm three months behind in my mortgage, and they're making threatening growls."

"I know, honey. Money was always my problem too. I never had enough. I certainly didn't get money from Miss Mae West—at least not while I worked for her. That bitch liked people to work for her for free."

"But I thought you told me Miss West left you an apartment house."

Norma looked startled, as if she'd forgotten revealing that. "Guess I've got no sense today. But that was when she died. When she lived, she gave me nothing. A salary of fifty dollars a week, and she wanted me to be in constant attendance day and night. We're talking Monday through Sunday with no time off."

"The temperamental Miss West must have been but a warm-up for Lavender. I hear the cow has gone through five maids since arriving in Savannah."

"That's right. I'm number six on her list. The others just couldn't take it."

"Well, I've got to take it. Eat humble pie and kiss Lavender's butt."

"She's planning to come to your club tonight. But I think those bachelors want to see that new tango dancer, Danny Hansford, more than they want to see a class act like you."

"I think you're right. I don't know why that God damn Danny doesn't just whip it out and show it hard to all the faggots in the audience. That's what they want to see anyway."

"And that black drag queen, that Tango gal, is a disgrace to my race. If my son in Atlanta dressed in drag, I'd kill him. I love white drag queens, white gays, but I could never stand black queens!"

"I know. Tango looks so much like a woman I have to remind myself that it is actually two men up on that stage performing a sex act they call a tango. I don't call it a theatrical performance. I call it sexual intercourse on stage."

"What are you going to do about it?"

"I've just called the owner of the club, a sleaze, Matt Daniels. He's coming over here. He should be here any minute. I'm informing this scum that I will not go on tonight with this drag act. Imagine me appearing on stage with a nude man—well, practically nude—and a black drag queen. I've always been a class act, drawing the finest audiences. Now this!"

"Be careful, honey, threatening that Daniels. I hear he's a real son of a bitch. You don't want to find yourself out of a job—not with all those mortgage payments you've got to face."

"I know but I'm going to stand up to him anyway. Even though the wolf is at my door, I have my pride. Great stars have great pride, as Norma Desmond said."

"Who is Norma Desmond?"

"Gloria Swanson in *Sunset Boulevard*. You should know that. Your buddy, Mae West, turned down the part, claiming none of her fans would believe her as a has-been. My darling Monty Cliff turned down the Joe Gillis role."

"Oh," Norma said, looking slightly miffed. She never liked people knowing more about Mae West than she did.

Tipper got up and poured Norma another drink. Norma always liked a drink "for the road," especially when she was driving, although she'd walked over today. An awkward silence had fallen over the patio.

"Before I go, you'd better write that little suck-up note to Lavender. That will smooth over things. That way, she and her bachelors will come to your club tonight."

"Okay, I'll do it." Tipper got up again and walked toward the front of her house, as Norma waddled along behind her. At her desk, Tipper hastily scribbled a note of apology to Lavender, then sealed it and handed it to Norma.

Norma tucked it into her ample bosom as she prepared to face the sidewalk again. "I'd better be going. I wish I could see you tonight. But I never get invited with Lavender and her bachelors."

"Bachelors," Tipper said with a slight disgust in her voice. "That's what they call them in Savannah. A polite term. We used to call them faggots."

"Yeah, but we try to be polite in Savannah."

"For some reason not clear to me, these gentlemen homosexuals have always been my fans, and invariably my escorts. I think I fulfill some maternal need in them like Judy Garland did. My fans have always been weak, vulnerable men. They used to be young. Now they're not so young. I used to date these callow homosexuals because I could dominate them. I think I liked to dominate men more than I liked men to dominate me. That's why I've always been involved with weak men. I think I wanted to be the man in the relationship."

"Not me, sugartit. I didn't go for men who stuck their dicks in other men. With me, I wanted men to plug me. And the bigger their plugger, the better it was. It took a lot of man to fill me up."

Tipper reached and kissed Norma on the right cheek. "Memories," she said affectionately, patting Norma's other cheek. "That's all you and I have now. Those gentlemen callers haven't come knocking on our doors lately, now have they?"

"They're out looking for some young stuff. Not that I blame them."

"Marilyn warned us in her song that we all lose our charms in the end."

"We should have taken Marilyn's advice and got those rocks," Norma said. "Back when the getting was good."

"Too late to worry about that now." Tipper showed her to the door. After a final kiss on Norma's cheek, Tipper was about to shut the door when the newsboy arrived with the afternoon paper.

She scooped it up and carried it to her library where she'd sit and read it until Matt Daniels arrived. She put the paper in her armchair and went over to the bar to mix herself another drink. She didn't want to get too drunk before her performance tonight, but she thought one more drink wouldn't be lethal.

Putting on her glasses, she opened the paper, ignoring the headlines about Bill and Monica. That story didn't interest her at all. What caught her attention was a story at the bottom of the page, announcing that a Hollywood scriptwriter, Phil Heather, would be moving to Savannah temporarily where he planned to write the screen adaptation of a novel, *Butterflies in Heat*, which would then be filmed in Savannah. Having another film crew in Savannah so soon after the departure of Clint Eastwood's gang filming *Midnight in the Garden of Good and Evil* didn't interest her as much as the photograph accompanying the story.

It was of Phil Heather, the scriptwriter. She stared long and hard at the photograph. It was as if long-dead Montgomery Clift had returned to earth. The resemblance to Monty was so amazing that at first Tipper suspected the newspaper had made a mistake and had run a before-the-accident picture of Monty instead of Phil Heather's picture. Although she immediately detected the differences in the two men's faces, she was fascinated by the similarities. Two remarkably handsome men—no, not handsome, beautiful really. Did Monty father a son she never knew about?

Breathing deeply, Tipper decided she had to meet this man. The paper didn't announce where he'd be living, but some of Lavender's bachelors would surely know. They learned and knew everything going on in Savannah.

Montgomery Clift had been the unrequited and tragic love of her life, and they'd lived out a destructive relationship that had been doomed from the beginning. With the arrival of Phil Heather in Savannah, Tipper believed that Monty had come back to re-create their time together and to live it as it should have been lived without the tragedy.

"Could it be?" Tipper asked herself out loud in the privacy of her library. Was a chance at happiness possible for her even at this late date? She stared at the picture, completely mesmerized by it. Phil Heather, she just knew, was going to play a major role in her life.

She held the newspaper up to her lips and kissed Phil's picture. "It's going to work this time, Monty. I just know it."

Her private moment was rudely interrupted at a pounding on her door. "God damn it, Tipper," Matt Daniels called from the door stoop. "Your fucking doorbell isn't working. Open up the door!"

The reality of Matt Daniels destroyed her private magic. She got up and walked quickly to open the door. Even the prospect of facing a sleazeball like Daniels didn't dampen her spirit. She was still filled with the aura of Phil Heather's photograph. Was F. Scott Fitzgerald wrong when he said there were no second acts in American lives? Was God granting her a second act?

# Chapter Two

In the cool, cool of the evening, Phil Heather sat on the back veranda of his Aunt Bice's home. Even though in exile from his family plantation, he was always welcome here at the home of a woman who called herself "the only liberal in this part of Georgia." The fiery furnace of the summer sun had simmered down, and a few evening breezes from the sea graced the meadow out back where forget-me-nots and violets grew.

The wind was like a mother's love, although his mama died young and he didn't remember what her love was like. All the maternal love he'd ever received in life was from Aunt Bice. Here he sat in the bosom of Dixie, thinking he might be out cruising the bars of Key West tonight if it weren't for the success of that book, *Midnight in the Garden of Good and Evil.* God he hated its author, John Berendt, and he didn't even know the man.

Aunt Bice came out onto the porch carrying a small tray of drinks, her customary bourbon and branch water. She always put a sprig of fresh mint in the drink. "Just like you like it," she said, setting the drink down in front of him. Actually he hated fresh mint in drinks but he always pretended it was his favorite way to enjoy a libation.

At eighty-five, and dressed in her classic purple, Aunt Bice sat down in a wicker chair and lit her fifth cigarette of the evening. Amazingly, she'd never died of lung cancer, and she'd been smoking since she was fourteen. There was still the elegance of regal beauty in her features, although time and liver spots had taken a toll. Her blond hair was now a dirty-looking yellow gray, and she no longer bothered to spend time in beauty parlors. "Why waste the money?" she'd always said. "The kind of man I could attract at my age I don't want."

"I've always felt a certain affinity for gay men," Aunt Bice was saying between deep lung-filling puffs on her cigarette. "Damn cigarette. I never liked new fangled cigarettes. I don't know why I gave up rolling my own."

"What do you mean, 'feeling an affinity for gay men?'" he asked. "Of course, you've always been gay-friendly, unlike the rest of the State of Georgia."

"We're in the same boat," she said. "When a straight woman is old, no one wants her. The same with a gay guy. Old straight men can always find somebody. After forty the white boys stopped knocking at my door. I was able to switch to good-looking black men then. A black man will fuck a blond woman even if she's past forty. But by the time you've reached fifty, you'd better start putting cigarettes in your mouth instead of something bigger." She raised her glass of bourbon. "It also helps if you drink a lot. Bourbon passes the night away. That and my memories."

"I know what you mean. As you know, I'm thirty. I think I have another five good years. After that, I'll end up taking what I can get. For the type of guy I go for, thirty-five is about as far as they'll go. To some of the kids I pick up, I'm already a daddy at thirty."

"Has it ever occurred to you that while you're still in your prime, you should marry some hot little number—blond like you like them? Hopefully, ten inches. You could even settle for nine, or else be satisfied with eight and a half if he's good looking enough. Personally, anything under nine never interested me very much."

"I've met a lot of guys. But it never seemed to work out. Three months and that's about it for my relationships. I usually come home, find a note, check the apartment to see what they've stolen, and then I'm out the next night making the rounds seeing what I can pick up."

Aunt Bice sat back in her wicker chair and sighed. "You're a good-looking boy, Phil. A spittin' image of Monty Clift. I would think some Monty Clift admirer would have grabbed you up and taken you home by now."

"I know, I know," he said, taking a hefty swig on his bourbon. "Maybe I drink too much. Maybe I'm too self-centered. What kind of fool am I? Never to have fallen in love."

In the softening twilight, Aunt Bice turned her regal head and stared deeply at Phil, illuminated in the yellow glow of her porch light. "You did fall in love—and that's why you can't go home again."

"I remember it well. Ten long years have passed, and I vividly recall the last day I spent under my daddy's roof."

"It was your sister's wedding day. I was there. Everybody important in this county was there. You were a naughty boy. A real naughty boy. You certainly ruined that wedding. The one thing you should never do at a wedding is run off with the groom."

"But he was only seventeen years old. God, what a beauty. My sister even then was thirty-seven. Why did she want to marry Terry Drummond in the first place? He was obviously gay."

"I know. The marriage would never have worked out. But Bleeka doesn't believe that. She still accuses you of destroying her one chance for happiness. Today she stays in her room most of the time. Won't come out. She watches TV all day and eats boxes of chocolate. If you think she used to be fat, you should see her now."

"I didn't mean to fall in love with Terry. He was so nervous before the wedding he spilled his drink on his tux. I had a jacket to spare. He went upstairs with me to my bedroom. He removed his jacket. I found his shirt was soiled too. Off came the shirt. That was the most luscious chest I'd ever seen in my life. I had to taste it. I had to suck those nipples."

"Stop, you're turning me on. I know the feeling. I once met a married man at a wedding—not the groom, thankfully—and I just had to have him. I succeeded in getting him too. Back in those days I could have any man I wanted."

"After I'd plowed it to him, he told me he'd fallen in love with me and didn't want to go through with the marriage. He also told me he found Bleeka fat and disgusting. In the year and a half we lived together, he never told me why he'd agreed to marry Sister Woman in the first place."

"It was all too obvious. His parents were behind it. They wanted him to marry into the Heather money. If a fat girl came with the prize, he would have to grin and bear it."

"But that is no way to go into a marriage."

"Who are we kidding? Many marriages are launched just that way."

"At any rate, Terry and I had a blissful year and a half. In looking back, it was more blissful for me than for him. One day he left me. He'd met the owner of a motel in Mobile, and off they went to check in guests at the damn motel. That's the last I ever saw of Terry Drummond, my would-be brother-in-law."

"Why don't you go to Mobile? Hunt the little stud up. He must be mighty tired of that motel owner by now. He's ripe for the picking. He would be only twenty-seven now. Do you have the address of the motel?"

"I know where it is. In fact, I was the sucker who introduced Terry to the creep in the first place. At a gay party in Fort Lauderdale. He was a married man. A wife and two children."

"A classic gay profile."

Phil finished the rest of his drink and decided he needed another one. This time he got up and went inside to make the drinks, returning to the porch to notice Aunt Bice had lit up again.

"What are the chances you and me can drive up the hillside tomorrow and see Big Daddy? Even Sister Woman if she's forgiven me."

"Not bloody likely. But I think your Daddy is wanting to see you again. I'll go over there tomorrow. I'll tell him you're in Savannah writing that screenplay. It will take some doing but I think I can get you an invitation some time during your stay in Savannah. We hope to see a lot more of you. Will you invite me down?"

"As many times as you want. I'd welcome the company."

"It's a deal. I'll talk to Hadley tomorrow. Sister Woman may even come around, although I'm not sure. Fat girls hold grudges for decades. But you are Hadley's son. It's been ten years. He's mellowed a bit but not that much."

"At least he's sent me that thirty thousand every year. Sometimes I didn't need it, but a few years I needed it desperately. Really damn glad to get it. Of course, I wish he'd up it to fifty or more."

"Dream on. That's all you're going to get." She sampled the drink he'd poured, finding it just to her liking. "When I die, which is going to be sooner than later, you're going to get this antebellum spread of mine. If the termites stop holding hands, it will fall down. But it's yours. I can see you right now forty years from now sitting out on this very same porch, sipping bourbon and watching the twilight creep over you. I won't be here, but wherever I am I'll be thinking of you. Looking down and protecting you."

"Thanks," he said. "That's why I love you so much."

"I'm not a rich woman. Other than this property, I've got about four hundred and fifty thousand. That's yours too. One or two of the things I own might be very valuable. You'll find out. Hadley's got five million. When he dies, I don't know if he's going to give it all to Bleeka or divide it between the two of you."

"You've never seen his will?"

"Not since he had a new one made a few years back, I've always pleaded with him to be fair to the both of you. After all, you're his son."

"Thanks for looking after me. Hell, no one in this world has done that but you."

"I love you, boy, and I always will. Ever since I used to change your diapers, I've loved you. When your mama died, I tried to be a mama to you. In fact, I suspect you've used me as a role model."

"What do you mean?"

"Chasing after men all the time."

He laughed. "You taught me well."

"Let's just sit here and watch the night come upon us."

"Great idea. I've got to leave in the morning for Savannah. As soon as I get set up there, I'll come for you. I'll drive up and get you."

"I can still drive a car," she said. "I'm known as the terror of the highway. The cops always stop me. I use the same line on 'em. I tell them I'll give them a blow-job if they won't give me a ticket. That wins them over every time. Unfortunately, they don't take me up on my offer."

"You're a dear. My kind of woman."

"There's a woman I want you to meet in Savannah. I know she'll take to you. Probably adopt you."

"What's her name?"

"Lavender Morgan."

"I know of her. I heard she's screwed every important man in the world. There's a new book coming out on Prince Philip. It details in lurid description his affair with Lavender. I already heard about a story that's in that book. Prince Philip, or so it is alleged, was dating Princess Elizabeth. She was considering marrying him. But they'd never made it together. One night in a garden he unzipped his pants, took her hand and guided it inside his fly. He told the princess, 'Marry me and that's what you're going to get.'"

"I can't wait to read the book." Aunt Bice sighed deeply. "I'll call Lavender in the morning. Once you get into her good graces, Savannah will be yours. You'll have great success in Savannah if you don't meet a native. Hang around only with the new arrivals. They call them Gucci carpetbaggers. They're a lot more fun. Old Savannah society won't take too much to a gay young man in town writing a screenplay called *Butterflies in Heat*. I just know it."

"I think you're right. This Lavender sounds like a blast."

"You've got to be careful to never be alone with Lavender. She must be all of seventy-two but her hormones are still working."

"Tell her I'm gay."

"That never stopped Lavender Morgan."

Aunt Bice reached for her shawl and put it around her to ward off the slight chill in the air. She gazed out over her darkening garden. The sky was a deep purple black. "Welcome home, Phil."

"It's good to be back." He closed his eyes before getting up to fix the next round.

The windows in the kitchen were open. As he poured more bourbon and branch water, he heard Aunt Bice singing, "*Down in the vall-lee, hear the wind blow...*"

***** 

The pounding she was taking from Jason churned her inside. Lula felt she was bleeding, but she'd anticipated the rape. Every time Jason had one of his encounters the night before, he sexually attacked her the following morning. She supposed it was an attempt to prove he was straight after all.

She'd screamed in pain at Jason's initial intrusion. He was just too big. As much as she needed him and wanted him in her life, having sex with him was something to be endured, never enjoyed. She uttered a strangled cry and prayed that he would soon be off her. She didn't think she could hold out much more, as he hammered harder and harder, faster and faster.

Jason rocked together with her in a feverish embrace, as he continued his assault, plunging deeper and deeper into her until she felt she was going to split from the impact. Finally, it ended in a gasp as he thrust hard into her for the final time, then pulled out abruptly, snapping his head back and spewing his cum all over her chest. His eyes closed, Jason fell back on the bed, as she rushed to the shower. She was definitely bleeding.

An hour later, as Jason slept, she walked the still hot streets of Savannah even though darkness had come. She found herself dreaming of the days when her adolescent heart wandered the streets of New York, looking up at the distant skyscrapers and feeling the snow peppering her face. That was the year she'd read all of Chekhov, Tolstoy, and Dostoevski, but decided they were not for her. She'd forge her own statement. Before Christmas of that year, she'd conceived of the plot for *The Tireless Hunter*. She would be no Tennessee Williams, Truman Capote, or William Faulkner. Her literary voice would be uniquely different from those men.

In spite of her tiny, boyish figure, she knew in her heart she'd be a giant of a literary figure, no doubt celebrated before she turned twenty-three. The vibrant, Gothic characters she was creating would capture the imagination of the world. Just as her own life was one of her own making, so was she creating this imaginary world where she could control the actions of the characters and their destiny. She liked that, as she'd never been able to control the events in her own life. Writing gave her a power she'd never possessed before. Her friends, the deep and true ones, were not in Savannah or anywhere else for that matter. Her real friends were those she could conjure up in her dreams and put on paper. This imaginary world was the one she truly inhabited, not the cruel real one. On paper she could be as colorful and outlandish as she desired. In real life, people challenged her stories and doubted their truth. But on paper, truth was what she said it was. No one could challenge fiction. They could attack her characters and her writing, but that was all they could do. Even if critics said her characters were unreal, they were real to her.

To her horror, she spotted Gin Tucker coming toward her. Whenever possible, she tried to avoid him but they seemed on a collision course.

At first she and Gin had been friends, but there was professional jealousy there even though she was a writer and he was a photographer. They were naturally competitive. She'd become infuriated when Gin had told half of Savannah that, "I have more interesting ways to spend my evenings than in the company of the self-centered Lula Carson. Instead of *The Tireless Hunter,* she should call her novel *The Boring Hunter.*" Such remarks had bitterly angered Lula. Their lives at present touched very infrequently, as Gin preferred to spend his evenings in the entourage of Lavender Morgan.

Nonetheless, when she encountered Gin she always engaged in friendly banter, the way her mother had taught her to do back in Columbus, the way Southerners often do with each other, especially around people they hate.

To her, Gin Tucker existed in the twilight world between the sexes—neither male nor female. Below the waist he had a sturdy, rather masculine build with strong legs. But above the waist he was thin and willowy, as if a breeze might blow him away. His butterscotch hair was cut in bangs. His head was big and a bit handsome, but it was a youthful beauty that was quickly fading. The grotesque older man that he was surely to become was emerging rapidly in his features.

"As I live and breathe," he said, with just a touch of mockery in his voice. "It is the great Lula Carson out walking the streets of Savannah and alone. If I were married to that Jason I'd be home paying homage to him. The word about town is that he's got the biggest dick south of the Mason Dixon line."

"Those are just stories spread about Jason," Lula said. "Actually he's quite small—not enough for you to even bother with. I hear you're still the reigning size queen of Savannah."

"The bigger the better I always say. I don't like to criticize God, but I always wondered why he made people so fleshy. If I had been God, I would have distributed the flesh more evenly. Put more meat into the dick and less into the gut."

"Some day when you get a chance to be God, I'm certain you can remedy that situation." Excusing herself, Lula tried to walk on as she had a secret rendezvous with Norma Dixie and she didn't want to be late.

But Gin, standing on legs as firm as a Shetland pony, blocked her way. "How is that world class masterpiece coming? I'm dying to read it."

"It's moving along nicely. It's going to be a great book. I expect I'll receive a lot of literary awards."

"No doubt all of them will be deserved too." That tone of mockery had come into his voice again. "It is that book I want to talk to you about. I must photograph you for the dust jacket."

"You know what bad pictures I take."

"Sugarpie, I can take a sow's ear and turn it into the smoothest of silk. Give me a chance. I will charge you nothing if that's what you're worried about. I come from a rich family and I dabble in photography only as a hobby."

"I know you come from a rich family. All of Savannah knows you come from a rich family. So you don't have to remind me of that. I come from a poor family. I have only three-thousand dollars left from my literary grant, and the money is going fast. When it's gone, I don't know what I'm going to do to make a living. That's why my book has got to be a big success. It's my only chance. I can't depend on Jason to help me make a living."

"My, oh my," he said. "It sounds as if the wolf is at your door. I'd loan you some money but I have a hard and firm rule. I never lend money to dear friends."

"I understand. Saving the money to pay your hustler bill?"

"Now, now, my pet. Let's don't get catty. All of us have our little eccentricities. Need we go into the tales I've heard about the great Lula Carson?"

"There's no need."

"Back to that dust jacket," he said, wincing and suddenly appearing very business like. "I have come up with a great idea. I want to take a photograph of you that would make the world forget that decadent picture Truman Capote posed for on the jacket of *Other Voices, Other Rooms*. That became a literary scandal. When was it? Back in the forties—or something. Decades before I was ever born. I want to capture you in that same pose. Except it'll be female and you'll be even more southern decadent than Capote, if such a thing is possible."

She paused, taking him seriously for the first time. "That's not a bad idea. Not bad at all. In fact, I think I actually like it. As much as I loathe calling attention to myself, I think I must give in to the demands of the marketplace. Why write a book if you don't want people to read it? And how are they going to know to read it unless you capture their attention and imagination?"

"Then you'll do it?"

"I'll do it, and thank you for thinking of it. I'll call and make an appointment to come by your studio."

"That's great. Don't worry about what to wear. I'll provide the outfit."

"I'm sure you will."

"Then we have a date," Gin said. He kissed her on both sides of the cheeks, as she tried to ignore his gin-foul breath.

Fleeing from Gin, Lula hastened across a Savannah square. She was eager to be cuddled in the arms of Norma Dixie.

*****

As Tango crossed the square, she spotted Lula Carson going the other way. Lula never came to her Blues in the Night club, and Tango always envied her, wanting to meet her, but never having had the chance. If there was one thing in all the world Tango wanted more than Danny Hansford, it was Lula's husband, Jason McReeves.

She'd once spotted him at Tybee Island on the beach. He was by himself and scantily dressed in the thinnest of white bikinis. She'd been bored all day at this rickety-tik amusement park with its corn dog stands and putt-putt golf. Earlier when she thought she could tolerate no more video arcades and airbrushed T-shirts, she was about ready to head home.

Then Jason McReeves appeared and she was spellbound. Until Jason walked into her vision, she'd never known that God had created such a perfect man before. She recognized him at once. Only last week his picture had been in the paper.

Jason had been arrested for disorderly conduct. He'd staggered drunk into Mrs. Wilkes's Boarding House where long lines had formed outside waiting for such Southern classics as black-eyed peas and collards. Jason had gone to the front of the line. He wasn't after cornbread and taters but had wanted to take a leak. When he'd been ordered to go away, he'd taken out his dick and pissed right on the sidewalk in front of the out-of-towners with their guidebooks, some of them clutching copies of *Midnight in the Garden of Good and Evil*. How Tango wished she'd been there that day. Even though Mrs. Wilkes's family didn't really know how to cook a decent pot of collards, Tango would have eaten the whole pot and drunk the pot liquor too just for one glimpse of Jason doing his unveiling act.

From all reports, it was some show. One woman later told a Savannah reporter that the only nude "private parts" of a man she'd ever seen in her life were those of her husband, and Jason had "ten times more than her husband had."

At the beach and closely observed by Tango's hawk eye, Jason went over to a stand to order some beer. Tango followed close behind, planning to take the bar stool next to his. Before she got there, a fat lady in a chartreuse bathing suit and wearing purple sunglasses grabbed the stool before she could claim it. The cheeks of her fat ass had spilled over both sides of the red-upholstered stool.

Before his beer was served, Jason signaled the bartender he'd be right back. He'd headed for the men's room. For the only time in her entire life, Tango wished she'd been Haskell Hadley Yett again and not dressed as a woman. As Haskell she could have followed Jason into the men's room but didn't dare go in there dressed as Tango. She'd feared she might have been arrested although legally she was certainly entitled to use any men's room she wanted.

When Jason came out, he'd taken his seat at the stool with the fat lady and had quickly drunk his beer. From out of nowhere, Lula Carson had emerged, wearing a pair of blue jeans and a simple blouse. She'd said something to Jason, and he'd frowned but had apparently agreed to follow her to the car.

Tango didn't understand why Jason would be attracted to a boyish woman like Lula. She didn't seem to have any figure at all— no breasts, no beautiful hair, no pretty white teeth. She wore no makeup and didn't seem to care about her appearance at all. Lula was completely unsexy. Tango had also recognized Lula from her picture in the paper. Lula was said to be writing the great American novel. The story accompanying Lula's picture in the paper claimed that she'd been awarded a grant to write this book, and she was living in Savannah with her husband, Jason.

Tango didn't know what Jason did for a living, or even if he did anything. Jason didn't look like the type of man who had to work. Tango was certain that half the women in Savannah—and the men too—would gladly support Jason just to have him around the house.

She thought Danny Hansford was terrific. But Danny was only eighteen and hadn't quite filled out his body yet. Jason must be all of twenty-three, and he stood tall and proud at the peak of his male beauty and virility. Jason was already the man that Danny could only aspire to become.

When faced with a blond boy or a blond man, Tango had always gone for the man. Boys were fun to fool around with, but sometimes a woman needed a real man to work her over.

Tango suspected that Gin Tucker knew everybody in town, probably Jason. Once at Gin's studio, she planned to make discreet inquiries about Jason, find out where he hung out, what scene he was into. She just had to meet him. In her secret heart, Tango believed that if Jason really focused on her, he'd be captivated by her. She turned on men in all walks of life. Why not Jason? To her, he'd looked ripe for the picking. One thing she didn't understand. How had he managed to pack such an ample load into such a thin bikini. That bikini had looked to her as if it were stretched to maximum endurance.

Thoughts of Jason vanished as Tango wrapped her mind around the business of the night.

She'd left Danny asleep in the bed with her new mattress. Originally she had wanted him to come with her to Gin's studio but he'd claimed he needed one more hour's sleep. She'd set the alarm for him and also planned to call him twenty minutes before Gin was ready for him to make sure Danny was up and awake. Tango had met Gin several times but Danny had not been introduced. She planned to be with Gin and Danny at all times during the photo shoot. She just knew that Gin would be captivated by Danny, and she had to protect her interests in the boy and keep him from the clutches of the town's most notorious white faggot.

Gin had wanted to photograph her for one hour, Danny for one hour, and spend the final hour shooting the two of them together in provocative poses from their tango dancing.

Two blocks from Gin's studio, Tango detoured out of her way a block to pass by Blues in the Night. Upon reaching the club she noticed to her astonishment that the marquee had been changed. Yesterday the sign had said, "Tipper Zelda singing nightly. Also appearing: Tango and Danny Hansford." Today the sign read, "Appearing nightly: Tango and Danny Hansford. Also appearing, Tipper Zelda."

Tango couldn't believe this. Matt Daniels had given her star billing over Tipper. A big time star like Tipper wouldn't take to this at all, and Tango feared her top billing on the marquee would be short lived. She planned to be here first thing tomorrow morning with her camera. She just had to get a picture of this marquee. She didn't know when she'd ever be headlining a show again, and she wanted to capture this moment on film so she could treasure it forever.

Tango glanced at her watch. She was late for her appointment with Gin but she could hardly bring herself to leave the front of the club as her name up there thrilled her.

Now she knew why Matt Daniels wanted pictures of Danny and her. He was planning to give them the star treatment. Tango believed that Savannah was coming to watch her act with Danny. The town surely had grown tired of Tipper and her stale old act that hadn't added a new number since Eisenhower was president.

At Gin's studio she rang the bell. When there was no answer and after a long pause, she rang it again.

Through the door she heard Gin's wispy voice, "Coming, coming!"

Wearing a straw hat inside his house, and clad only in a pair of white shorts and a T-shirt, Gin threw open the door. Seeing only Tango, he looked disappointed. "Where is that divine Danny Hansford?"

"He'll be here in an hour," Tango said as she was ushered inside. "He wanted another hour's sleep, and he thought you could do the solos of me first."

"Oh," Gin said, still looking disappointed. "Very well," he finally agreed, tottering off toward the rear of his town house, trailed by Tango.

"I couldn't come to the door right away," Gin said. "I was just saying good-bye to one of our local football heroes. He'd agreed to let me take a mold of his dick. It's a super one. It'll make a great dildo. All the queens in Savannah will want one. Maybe I'll even give one to you." He paused, then looked back at her and smiled demurely. "Of course, in your case I suspect you don't need a dildo. You have your own live-in dildo—that succulent Danny Hansford."

*****

Lavender sat on her back veranda, trying to digest the news she'd received from her attorneys in New York only an hour ago. Even now as the full impact of the news settled over her, she couldn't believe their claims. How could a woman who'd inherited one-hundred and fifteen million dollars from her octogenarian statesman husband be broke? There was no way. The only conclusion was that someone had stolen her money, no doubt the attorneys managing her estate.

She'd been told to put her Maryland summer retreat, Willowbanks, up for sale with an asking price of three and a half million dollars, even though she was unlikely to get that. Much of the history of the Democratic Party in modern times had taken place at Willowbanks. If only the walls could talk. She'd entertained Jack and Jackie there, carried on an insipid affair with Adlai Stevenson whom she suspected was gay, and had invited Bill and Hillary for a weekend there shortly after he was elected president.

She was told she'd have to take out a mortgage on her New York condo and her house in Georgetown. Those two mortgages would bring her another two million. She'd also been told to sell her private plane for one and a half million and to unload her vacation home in Barbados. It stood next door to the home of the late Claudette Colbert, and Lavender used it only one month a year. Her husband, Roland Morgan, loved Barbados but Lavender had always detested the place. At least with Barbados behind her, and Colbert dead, she would no longer have to endure that dreadful island or the unwanted lesbian attentions of the aging Colbert.

From her associations with the rich and powerful, Lavender always knew that you could be wealthy on paper but cash poor. Of her so-called fabled fortune, only twenty-five million was liquid. Everything else was tied up in stocks and bonds or real estate. After tax the estate brought in only one-million a year. With all her real estate, all her bills, all her attorney's fees, plus her contributions to the Democratic Party, she was spending some two and a half million a year. Her husband had specified in his will that from her personal reserves every year she was to distribute certain benefits to his two sons and one daughter by his previous marriage. These benefits ate up most of her one million earnings, leaving her only three-hundred thousand dollars, hardly enough to carry the burden of her various staffs.

To make matters worse, the heirs were suing her, demanding a settlement of fifteen million which they alleged belonged to them in lost earnings since the death of their father in 1984.

Long known as a spendthrift, Lavender had always been able to raise money in the past. When she was young and beautiful, money had come in the form of gifts from her lovers with names like

Niarchos and Agnelli. As she'd aged, those contributions to her welfare had dried up as her lovers had turned to younger women.

Over the past few years, Lavender had made some unfortunate choices. She'd borrowed heavily against the estate, at one point taking out an eight-million line of credit from Morgan Guaranty. She needed this for living expenses at the time. She'd followed that with other substantial lines, until her annual interest bill alone was nearly seven hundred and fifty thousand.

"What are the exact charges against me," Lavender had demanded to know.

Her attorney, Clifford Willkie, said it was "for negligence and breach of fiduciary duty."

"Those greedy little bastards!" Lavender had shouted into the phone. "After all I've done for them."

"You're in big trouble, Ms. Morgan," Willkie had told her. "We are only now beginning to digest the extent of your losses when Mortimer Cutler ran your estate. He made one bad decision after another."

"I thought I could trust him. After all, he was once Secretary of the Treasury. His job was to protect the treasury of the United States. I thought he could at least look after my meager millions."

"But he was eighty-nine years old before death finally claimed him," Willkie said. "His dying saved him from jail. He's got so many law suits filed against his estate that it may be 2020 before the dust settles."

Lavender sighed. The entire world seemed to be conspiring against her.

"We've got to begin a survey of your marketable securities," Willkie had told her. "I know it's going to be painful, but selling is the order of the day." He paused. "Even the paintings."

"But you know how important my paintings are to me."

"I know how hard it is, but we're in serious do-do, as George Bush would say."

"I hate that wimpy shit," she'd said. "Don't ever mention George Bush to me again."

"We are making discreet inquiries to sell your *Mother and Child* by Picasso for twenty-five million. There were no offers at that price. Even when we lowered the price to sixteen million, there were still no offers. I think we have to offer it to Sotheby's or Christie's for auction."

"I'd never auction anything at Christie's," Lavender had said. "They fucked me over in 1966, and I've never forgiven them."

"Well, Sotheby's then. Can we have that Picasso shipped to New York? We need to put it in a vault in our headquarters on Park Avenue."

"I guess, but I want to live with it a few weeks longer."

"I heard Savannah with all that humidity and torrid heat is rotten for paintings."

"Savannah is even more rotten for broken-down old courtesans," Lavender had said. "I don't care to discuss money any more tonight. I'll call you when I'm up and about tomorrow." She put down the phone, not able to bear one more bit of bad news.

As the night shadows of Savannah enveloped her, Lavender was tempted to call Gin and cancel the evening's entertainment. She feared she couldn't put on a public face even for a night club table. She knew that the society ladies of Savannah abhorred her, viewing her as no more than a rich whore. But they always held a begrudging respect for her. If you're rich, Southerners will forgive you for everything, even incest. But if word leaked out that she was facing bankruptcy, she would be a total cast-off. She prayed that the people investigating her life for that television biography would not plunge into the waters of her financial problems. Being called a whore on TV was one thing. Being called a bankrupt whore was another matter.

If only she'd made the right decisions in her life. As long as she'd had men to protect her, she'd been fine. It was when she was cut off from the men in her life that one bad decision led to another. There was no one she could trust. Only herself.

That was a sobering reality. Once at a party in New York, Bette Davis had told her, "Old age isn't for sissies." Bette was so right about that. If Lavender died now, she could escape humiliations coming her way. But she lacked the courage to take her own life.

She knew she should be getting made up if she was going to face an evening with the bachelors. They always expected to see her looking dazzling in one of her lavender gowns, which she suspected they really wanted to wear themselves. But she could not bring herself to leave her veranda. She'd sit here a little longer, remembering a greater day when she was the toast of two continents.

With bitter irony she reviewed other tragedies in her life when she'd been defeated and bankrupt before. She'd rallied then and made a comeback. Bill Clinton wasn't the only one who was the comeback kid. Lavender Morgan would stand up to her accusers and face the demons squarely. It might be her last hurrah but it would be a spectacular climax to a celebrated life.

*****

A call came in from Matt Daniels, asking Tango to come to the Blues in the Night Club for a "conference." He said he was at Tipper's and would be at the club soon. Gin had already taken the joint shots of Danny and Tango going through their routine. He asked Danny to remain behind in his studio for some solo shots. At first Tango had been reluctant to leave Danny alone in the studio with Gin, but Matt was demanding that she meet him at the club. She told Gin and Danny she owed that "white man a big favor for giving us star billing."

Alone at last with Danny, Gin seemed to be devouring his body like a succulent morsel he was about to consume.

Shirtless, Danny was clad only in the tight white pants he wore to dance the tango at Blues in the Night. He felt it would just be a matter of minutes before Gin put the make on him. He was going to turn him down and tell him to back off. Although many devouring mouths had descended on him, those petulant lips of Gin Tucker repulsed him as few men had. Maybe he wasn't a true hustler in the sense he could take on all comers the way the original Danny Hansford had done. When a john was ugly and revolting, Danny had often been able to relish in the narcissistic delight he felt at inspiring someone to such rapture. He got off on the fact that a john was getting off by having a rare chance at a body such as Danny's. Worship of Danny brought its own kind of thrill, causing him to eventually reach climax.

But there was something in the smirk on Gin's face, something in his prissy mannerisms, that turned off Danny completely.

Following the dual shot with Tango, Gin asked that they take a break. He offered Danny a beer which he accepted. Sitting opposite

Gin at a small table, Danny asked, "People tell me you knew the real Danny Hansford. If that's true, what was he really like?"

Gin licked his lips and reached over to pat Danny's hands. "People are always asking me that. It was such a long time ago. I was much younger then. Far more attractive. In fact, I was the most beautiful boy in Savannah."

Danny smiled, finding it impossible to imagine that Gin was ever beautiful, much less the most beautiful boy in Savannah.

"In fact, I was a bit of a celebrated beauty. I have no idea why I was patronizing the town hustler. Back then I could have any man I wanted." He sipped his favorite gin and eyed Danny with coy amusement. "In fact, Gin can still get her man if she wants him badly enough."

The threat was not lost on Danny. "I'm sure you were a regular femme fatale. But come on. Tell me what the real Danny was like."

"Oh, well," Gin said, seemingly bored with the subject. "That streak of sex was highly overrated. I mean people claimed he was the greatest lay in Savannah, but that doesn't say much for who else they were laying."

"He was no good in bed?" Danny asked eagerly.

Gin paused. "Oh, he was okay, but I've had better." He looked over at Danny's crotch. "And bigger."

"I heard he was well endowed."

"It wasn't something you'd turn down in a gay bar. Danny Hansford's dick, following his untimely demise, has become legendary in Savannah. I once heard a queen at the Tool Box say that she could vouch for the fact that it was thirteen inches long. The truth is less spectacular. Maybe eight inches on a good night. Fairly thick. As I said, nothing you'd turn down but not something you'd write home to mama about either."

"People sure talk about those inches of his as if he were the Second Coming or something."

"I know. That's what happens when you die young and at your peak. That's why Marilyn Monroe is such a legend today. She didn't stick around long enough for people to see her age. If she were alive today, she'd be working a cocktail lounge on some back street in Vegas or getting some queen to ghost-write her memoirs, 'My Life with the Kennedys.' There's a lot to be said for dying young."

"I'm going to die young," Danny said. "I just know it."

"That's not an ambition I'd set for myself if I were you." Gin poured some more gin into his drink, although he was already completely intoxicated. "I don't know why you want to use that old Danny Hansford as a role model. I mean, he was murdered. He wasn't that special anyway. A piece of Southern white trash. He had no talent. No ambition. I don't think he ever accumulated more than twenty bucks in his pocket at one time."

"People say I could have picked a better role model. But all of us have our destiny. I have to follow mine."

"That's very melodramatic but probably not practical in life's terms. With what you've got, you could be a star all on your own under your own name. You don't need to take Danny's name. Be yourself. You are the sexiest stud ever to hit Savannah—not Danny Hansford. Unless you've stuffed those breeches of yours, it looks to me like you've got Danny's legendary eight inches—but soft. God knows how high one would have to go to climb the mountain when you're fully erect."

"Dream on, guy. I came here because I was sent by Matt Daniels. He wants publicity shots. You and me getting it on wasn't part of the deal."

"I'm not asking for sex," Gin said. "At this point in my life I'm more of a voyeur anyway. The publicity shots are one thing. But I might like to hire you to do some private modeling for me. I pay the best prices in town. Would you consider it?"

"I'll think about it," Danny said, leaning back in his chair and opening his legs wider to give Gin a better view. "You mean, strictly posing?"

"Strictly posing," Gin said. "No funny business."

"You pay well?" Danny asked. "I mean I charge top dollar."

"And well you should with what you've got. I wouldn't cheat you. You could make some real big bucks if you'd also agree to let me make a mold of it."

"You mean, a dildo?"

"Why not? No one would know it was you. You could make real big bucks." He eyed Danny with a smirk. "Those bucks would buy a lot of cocaine."

"I'll think about it," Danny said. "I'm not sure."

"Honey, you practically used to dance nude at the Tool Box. I don't know why you're being so shy. You've got nothing to be shy about."

"I said I'd think about it." Danny glanced at his watch, an expensive gift from a john he'd met one night in Atlanta. "Man, I've got to get to the club. I'm almost late now. We should have allowed more time."

"Come back tomorrow afternoon. Any time. I'll be sober then. Right now I need a little beauty nap. I'm taking a very rich lady and a big crowd of admirers to your club later tonight. Put on a big show for us."

"I will."

"Will you be here tomorrow?"

"Maybe—maybe not," Danny said, getting up and reaching for his shirt. "Gotta go now."

Gin's words were slurred. "And could we talk about my other offer tomorrow after we've finished the publicity stills?"

Danny looked down at the drunken man. "We'll talk about it—that's all. I'm very expensive."

"Don't worry about money," Gin said. "I come from a very rich family."

"I come from a very poor family. We weren't even dirt poor. We were so poor we didn't own dirt."

Gin looked up at him and reached out to him but his arm seemed suspended in midair before falling beside his body again. "I have a feeling you're going to be a big star. I mean really big. Far bigger than Tom Cruise."

"Do you really believe that?" For the first time Danny's feelings toward Gin changed. Maybe he wasn't so repulsive after all. At least he knew a star when he was in the presence of one. A man who could judge talent like that couldn't be all bad.

It was only after he'd left Gin's studio and was rushing to get to Blues in the Night that reality descended on Danny again. For a few brief moments he'd allowed himself to get caught up in Gin's fantasy about future stardom for him.

Only now did he remember the awful truth: He wouldn't live long enough to become a star.

*****

Matt Daniels, owner of Blues in the Night, sat in Tipper's living room, deep into his third bourbon. Up to now he'd said nothing she wanted to hear, and she didn't expect their meeting was going uphill from here. At three-hundred pounds, he wore the same white suit he always did. He never seemed to change it or have it dry-cleaned. As best as she could, she tried to ignore the sea of yellow urine stains at his crotch. The role model for Daniels was Colonel Tom Parker, but she was definitely not Elvis. Actually, Daniels looked more like Sydney Greenstreet than Colonel Parker.

"I want you to cancel that drag and sex act," Tipper demanded. "I won't perform tonight if you don't. I mean, you can use that group from Atlanta that looks and sounds just like Peter, Paul, & Mary did in the 60s. They could be my warm-up act. Then I could come out Moanin' Low."

"Dream on, big tits! When you get to the theater tonight, you've got a big surprise waiting for you. Wait until you see the marquee. The new stars of the show are Tango and Danny Hansford. They're the ones bringing in the business. If you want to continue to work at my club, you're going to be their warm-up act."

Tipper's throat went dry and she gasped for breath, not believing she'd heard this sleazeball correctly. She tried to say something but couldn't formulate words. The room had grown unbearably hot, as she'd turned off the air conditioning system to save money which she didn't have. She couldn't pay old bills, much less run up new ones.

"I'm through with your club," she finally managed to say. "Get out of my house."

"That I will gladly do," he said. "Except it'll be my house soon. Larry down at the bank said you're behind in your mortgage, and they're thinking of repossessing. I'm going to buy it from the bank— nice house."

"You son of a bitch!"

"That's true. Mama was just a cheap whore. Her problem was she forgot to charge."

"Just leave. Get out."

"Not before we discuss the three-thousand dollars you owe me. I gave you that advance last season, and you never paid it back. I was to take it out of this season's pay on installments of three-hundred a week. I want my money, and I want it now."

"I'll pay you your god damn money. Now get out."

Daniels heaved his hefty body from the chair and made his way to the door. "Keep all the silver polished," he called back to her. "I don't want to have to pay some nigger maid to do extra dusting when I claim all the goodies."

At the slam of the door, she collapsed in her chair. She sobbed and sobbed some more. But there were no tears flowing. Instead of providing release, her sobs seemed to lodge in her throat.

There had to be a way out of all this. She'd taken an inventory of all she had left in the world. Maybe there was something she could sell. So much of what she'd owned was now gone, but there were some trinkets left, gifts from admirers of long ago. She still had that diamond and sapphire ring Monty had given her. That would be worth something. She had some letters Elizabeth Taylor had written Monty. Maybe some collector might be able to peddle them. She had that letter Martin Luther King wrote her to thank her for financing his trip to India. Surely that would be worth something. Tomorrow she thought she might call Coretta personally and discuss it with her. After all, Tipper had provided money for the Kings when they didn't have any. Perhaps their charity could go to her now that she needed help.

She also had love letters from Martin, but for the moment— subject to change—she'd keep those locked away.

Since she wasn't going on tonight, she might as well get drunk. There were so few pleasures left.

After pouring herself another drink, she slumped down in her chair. No sooner had she settled in than the phone rang. She figured it was that sleazeball, Matt Daniels, calling to apologize and beg her to appear tonight at his club. After all, Lavender and all the bachelors would be there, demanding to see her perform.

She picked up the phone to hear the voice of Frank Gilmore, the owner of Shocking Pink, a night club. He told her that Emma Kelly, the songstress dubbed "The Lady of Six Thousand Songs" by Johnny Mercer, wanted three weeks off. "Would you fill in for her?"

"How did you know I was free to accept an engagement?" Tipper asked.

"Word travels fast in Savannah. I just spoke with Matt Daniels. He told me you and he had called it quits. He's a shit anyway."

Even though Tipper had a completely different style from Emma, Tipper was jealous of the local sensation. Of course, Tipper had been a far bigger star than Emma ever would be. But the acclaim she'd received since the publication of *Midnight in the Garden of Good and Evil* had been extraordinary. In the book, Berendt had devoted an entire chapter to this songstress. Every night, fans at the club brought the book up to Emma to autograph as if she'd written it herself.

"Well, what about it?" Frank asked. "The pay's good. Better than Daniels was paying you."

"I don't know. The idea of filling in for someone. Since when does a big star fill in for a lounge entertainer?"

"Many big stars have filled in for lesser stars. All the big names except Sinatra and a few others end up in the garbage heap sometime."

"I'm not in the junkyard yet, and I resent that."

"Do you want the job or not? If you don't, I've got this trio that sounds just like Peter, Paul & Mary in their golden years. So, what about it?"

"I'll take it."

"Come over tomorrow at ten, and we'll make the arrangements. You've got to sign a contract."

"I'll be there. Could you make it ten-thirty? I need time to get ready."

"No, ten." He slammed down the phone.

She poured herself another drink and went to sit in her garden. There an hour or two drifted by. She'd lost all sense of time. The night sounds of Savannah as heard in her garden always enchanted her. It made growing old more graceful. Young people never had time to sit and listen to the sounds of a summer garden.

She wanted another drink but was just too tired to get up and go after it. In the old days she was always surrounded by young men only too willing to pour her drinks. Even at her age, Lavender still held that lofty position. Having money made all the difference in the world.

Before midnight, Tipper had made a steely resolve. More important than all her trinkets, she possessed the most valuable gift of all. Her own life story. For years publishers had clamored for her to sign a contract for her memoirs. After all, she was the famous "Black Widow" of the tabloids. A notorious "singer of sin songs" who had married four young men, all of whom had died under mysterious circumstances. No case was more sensational than the death of Taylor Zachory. He was not only a handsome prince charming but the owner of tobacco millions. The other men had been poor and didn't create quite the sensation Taylor did upon his death one summer night long ago.

Up to now she'd never given interviews about her marriages or the untimely deaths of her husbands. The younger generation couldn't care or didn't even know who she was. But a lot of older fans remembered her. She felt there remained great interest in her story if shopped around to publishers in New York.

She sighed and lifted herself from her chair, feeling wobbly on her feet. All of a sudden she knew in her heart who could ghost-write her story for her. Phil Heather. He was a writer. He was coming to town. He looked like Monty Clift. Without knowing anything about this young man, she knew he would be ideal. She'd always followed her intuition, and she knew that intuition would serve her well in picking Phil as her writer. She would tell the sordid story of a tragic life to Phil Heather and give him the job of making the world buy it, but it would be strictly her version.

*****

Aunt Bice had gotten so drunk he had to carry her to bed and tuck her in. That left him drunk too but still wide awake and eager for adventure. Gay young men in small Georgia towns didn't have many options unless they had built up a regular clientele of married men who came to call. "What the hell!" Phil said out loud in the parlor as he searched for his car keys. He'd find a local bar. In Georgia that wasn't always easy but he knew of one place where he used to get lucky on occasions ten years ago. It was called Bootleggers. Maybe it was still in business.

As he drove toward Bootleggers, hoping he'd taken the right direction, his eyes were blurring. But his need for adventure was so strong tonight it compelled him to go on. Somewhere there must be some fun waiting for him in all the Golden Isles off the southern coast of Georgia. Surely it wasn't all great-armed oaks covered with Spanish moss.

With wry amusement, Phil realized he was the end of a dynasty. When he'd arrived in these parts, Jehosat Eastwood Heather had founded a dynasty. He'd grown rich as an indigo and rice shipper in Savannah. With some degree of accuracy, Phil realized they were still living on Jehosat's money. Jehosat had built the antebellum house in which his father, Hadley or Big Daddy, still lived, along with Sister Woman, the increasingly morose Bleeka.

Hadley would be dead soon, and Bleeka would probably overdose on chocolates one night. Even years ago she'd shown a tendency toward diabetes. He didn't think a box of chocolates a day had contributed to her general state of health. Hadley drank so much his liver must have long ago quit crying out for help.

Phil knew that left only him as the last scion of the Heather clan. He didn't expect to carry out the line. Fathering children wasn't exactly how he saw the future. Aunt Bice was very kind and gracious to draw up a will giving him her house and money when she died. He appreciated that, as he dearly loved his Aunt Bice.

But what he wanted sometimes more than sex itself was to see himself installed one day as the lord and master of the Heather mansion, Belle Reve. That might come sooner than later. Each day that went by, Sister Woman and Big Daddy proceeded with the mass destruction of their own bodies. For all he knew, there might be a joint funeral. They might decide to go at the same time. That way, it would save the Angel of Death the trouble of having to call twice at that plantation. But who would be its inheritor?

Belle Reve belonged to Phil just as much as it belonged to Big Daddy and Sister Woman, although they were in control now. But the way Phil saw it, it rightfully belonged to the sole survivor of the Heather clan. He was sure that was how Jehosat would have wanted it.

Over the years there had been much sacrifice to keep Belle Reve. Its most crucial hour came in 1864 when General Sherman's looting, butchering, and burning troops headed here enroute to Savannah.

The minny balls the Yankee soldiers had fired on that long ago day into Belle Reve's white columns could still be seen. The antiques had been burned for stovewood, and the windows were broken for the sheer sport of it. But, according to legend, the house was saved by Jehosat's son, Jehosat Eastwood Heather II. Everyone said he was "too beautiful to be a man." The portrait that still hung in the Heather library seemed to confirm that.

If tales the old folks told could be believed, Jehosat no. 2 is said to have offered his shapely Confederate bottom to these bearded, dirty, and horny Yankee soldiers from some godforsaken, frost-bitten northern bog. His wife, Maude, wasn't even in consideration to play such a role. Jehosat no. 2 had married a stern, matronly woman who'd eaten too many pancakes all her life. Not even the horniest Yankee soldier could be inspired by her.

From all reports, Phil's succulent bottom did the trick and saved Belle Reve. After sampling the rosy delights of what was reputedly Georgia's most beautiful man, two Yankee soldiers practically swore an affidavit that they would never lie with a woman again.

One Yankee soldier, Adam Conray, apparently liked Jehosat's bottom so much that he stayed on at Belle Reve for the next thirty years, never going on with Sherman's troops to Savannah and never returning to his wife and children on the northern bog.

Jehosat's wife didn't raise any objections to this strange new Yankee man under her roof. From what she'd told relatives, she was relieved that Jehosat would never be coming to her bed again. She'd viewed having to endure penetration from a man as preferable only to death itself.

This mating of the invading Yankee hun with a golden boy of the aristocratic south paid off. Belle Reve was not only saved but went on to prosper in the Reconstruction era when many other landowners lost everything.

The Yankee officer is said to have liked beautiful things, especially one Jehosat Eastwood Heather II, and also antiques. Even though his men had burned the Heather family heirlooms, Adam in time found better and more valuable ones. In the 1870s he had money to spare. Southerners still left with anything Sherman's troops didn't destroy or cart off were only too eager to sell to Adam to pay off the tax man.

All the beautiful furnishings in Belle Reve today came about through the acquisitions of Adam, a Yankee. Adam died in 1903 in the arms of Jehosat. Jehosat himself died two years later, apparently having grown morose and then ill after his beloved Adam's death. Jehosat's wife, Maude, survived in the house until 1920, an increasingly alienated and bitter old woman.

As Phil neared the bar which was still there waiting for him ten years later, a steely determination came over him. He was a Heather, the last of his line, and he belonged at Belle Reve, offering his bottom, like Jehosat II, to any good man who wanted it. If installed at Belle Reve, he'd be carrying on in the Heather tradition. It would take some scheming to get back into the good graces of Big Daddy and Sister Woman after having run off with Terry Drummond.

But Phil knew he was blessed with a devious mind. If there were some scheme out there the human mind could devise, he would think of it. Winning over Big Daddy and Sister Woman would be the challenge of a lifetime but he was determined to do it. He had to. How else could be reclaim his rightful heritage?

He paused before entering Bootleggers. If anything, the place had grown shabbier than he remembered it. But the music was just as loud as ever. In fact, it seemed to him the same music was playing. Maybe they still had that same jukebox from the 50s. He bet he could still find Paul Anka records on it.

He stood outside the bar and sucked the night air into his lungs. Of two things he was certain: Belle Reve belonged to him, and if there were one good-looking man in this straight bar tonight, he was going to make off with him under cover of darkness.

*****

After a violent attack by Jason, Lula always sought the comfort of suckling at the breasts of Norma Dixie. Lula could lie for hours at a time, licking Norma's breasts. Encased in the warmth of the big, sagging tits, she could relive the only happy time she'd known in her life: When she'd been raised by Nellie Bullis, the family's black nanny. Even though Nellie had a baby of her own, she always gave Lula first dibs on her milk. Lula imagined it was chocolate. Even today she drank only chocolate milk, never white.

"Now, now," Norma said, comforting her and stroking Lula's hair, as the young woman sucked her nipples. "It'll be okay tomorrow. I'll rub some of my special salve on it like you like it. It won't be sore forever."

"But it hurts so much," Lula said. "When he enters me, it's like he's splitting me open. I don't know why women pursue men so. They can keep their dicks in their pants for all I care."

"Honey, I'll try to explain it to you sometime. You're always complaining how big they are. Or at least how big Jason is. I've got another complaint. They were always too small for me. I never met a man who could really fill me up to my complete quota. Usually when they were completely in, I'd ask 'em, 'Is that all we've got to work with?'"

"Oh, Norma! You're such a sex maniac. When I married Jason, I thought we'd have more of a spiritual union. Not so much sex. I thought he'd turn elsewhere for sex."

"From what I hear, Jason turns plenty of other places for sex."

"I think that's how it should be. I don't think a man and wife should be monogamous. That's not what I want in a marriage. After all, we must go where our hearts lead us. To deny the human heart other emotional entanglements is wrong. What I want in a man is loyalty, not sexual fidelity. The Queen of England has always understood that in her marriage to Philip. You can do a lot worse in using the Queen of England as a role model."

"I'm sure you can," Norma said, continuing to stroke Lula's hair. "I never used the Queen of England as my role model. Somehow Her Majesty and I just didn't seem to move in the same circles. Unlike Lana Turner, her Royal Highness never once came to my night club in Harlem. But Princess Margaret showed up one night. Ever since that night, I was tempted to call Norma's Room, Royal Norma's Room."

"Princess Margaret showed up? Really?"

"Really, child. When she was younger, that white girl loved black dick. I had a friend who came to New York from St. Vincent. He said that the Princess used to have a black boy friend down there named Basil. All the white women were after Basil. From what I heard, Basil must be the black version of your buddy, Jason."

"I see nothing wrong with that. In my novel, *The Tireless Hunter,* love is color blind. How can one stop to think about what color a person is if your heart is telling you to love?"

"I never thought much about that. When it came to men, I always stuck to my own kind. I figured it was safer that way. I was talking to this white gay boy one night, and he told me that even when he was stationed in the Far East, he never went to bed with Orientals. He said their genitals were too small. I told him I never went to bed with white men because I'd heard the same about them. Of course, your Jason is an exception, I'm sure."

"I like the tender side of men—not their genitals. But most men are afraid to display their tender side. They think the world wants only to see their violent side. I abhor violence in all forms."

"I don't mind a man getting a little violent when he's pounding me. That way, I know he's really getting off on it."

"Oh, Norma," Lula said, caressing her breasts and snuggling in. "I can't believe we are so far apart on so many issues, but so close together in so many ways."

"Opposites attract."

"I guess so. But I'm always searching for the kindred spirit. That's why I'm looking forward to living next door to Phil Heather. He's that writer I told you about. Although there's a wall between us, Jason and I will actually be living in the same house with Phil."

"Do you know anything about this Phil? If he's gay, you'd better keep Jason away from him. That Jason can zero in on a size queen faster than anything I've ever seen, and I've seen plenty."

"Even if Phil is gay, I bet he doesn't measure a man by the size of his genitalia. As a writer, he surely has better values than that. I'm sure he is far more sensitive."

"Honey, if he turns out to be a Southern white faggot, I can virtually assure you he'll be a size queen. Have you ever met a Southern white faggot who wasn't a size queen?"

"Can't say that I have. But I keep hoping."

"Some day." Norma cradled Lula in her arms, the way Nellie used to. Norma always sang to her at this time, the soft, soothing words of an old black spiritual of a mama putting her baby to sleep for the night.

Lula closed her eyes and felt totally protected and safe in the arms of Norma. Lula was sorry that people had to grow up and face adult responsibilities and challenges. If she'd had her wish, she would have remained in the nursery forever. Babies were protected there and taken care of. They didn't have to think for themselves.

She knew in her heart that this would be her last summer on earth to lead an anonymous life. With the publication of *The Tireless Hunter*, she feared she'd be sucked into the world of fame and celebrity. What would happen to Jason in this whirlwind? He already felt threatened by her writing talent. How could he handle her fame?

He'd be known as Mr. Lula Carson or at least Mr. Carson. No one would know his own name or even care. She'd be invited to all the chic literary cocktail parties. Jason would be there only as her escort. No one would want to talk to him except to ask him questions about her.

Jason's ego was fragile enough the way it was. Being married to a celebrated international writer might be more than he could take. When Jason felt threatened, he struck out against the world.

Without her being aware of it at first, Lula realized Norma had finished her song. "Now, child, I've got to pull myself out of this chair and get that special salve for you. I'll rub it all around your pussy like you like it. It will heal your wounds. Maybe if this Phil is gay, he'll be right next door and could relieve you of some of your marital duties."

"I doubt it. Jason likes violent sex. I'm sure Phil doesn't. I just know Phil will be more like me."

Later, as Lula lay nude on Norma's bed, the soothing salve brought comfort to her. Norma made her feel whole again.

After kissing Norma good-bye and heading back across the square, Lula was looking forward to a quiet evening at home with Jason. She might read to him some pages of *The Tireless Hunter*, even though the power of the book might threaten him. Perhaps he could not tolerate her portrait of him. She'd better keep the book from him.

"A writer must write about what she knows," she always told Jason. "My job as a writer is to take my actual experiences and make them universal so that people all over the world will identify with the problems I had growing up."

"I'm not so sure." That was all Jason ever said. He didn't seem to be sure about anything in life.

When she got home, all the lights were off. At first she thought Jason might be sleeping. But after she'd searched the house, she realized he'd gone for the evening. She didn't know where he went. Obviously out on another one of his nocturnal adventures. She never understood exactly what Jason was searching for. Maybe himself.

She knew that like Jason, she too was condemned to be a wanderer on this earth.

Suddenly, her vision became impaired. A blinding headache descended, and there were stabbing pains at her temples. She felt she was going blind. Quickly she made her way to the bedroom and crawled under her bed. The demons wouldn't find her here. She'd hide under the bed until morning, and only then would she get up to face the world.

*****

The need for Gin Tucker's pictures of Tango had grown more urgent by the minute. At Blues in the Night she'd just come from the office of Matt Daniels. He wanted new publicity pictures of Tango and Danny right away. She'd rather forget what he'd made her do. Instead of that distasteful act, she wanted to concentrate on her new-found stardom. Tipper Zelda was out of the act. Tango was the new star. Tango, of course, and Danny Hansford.

Before coming into the club, she'd stood for fifteen whole minutes looking at her name outside. If only her mama had lived to see this. Tango always knew she'd be a star but it had seemed like some distant thing, not something that would immediately happen to her. Like a great flash of lightning in the sky, stardom had descended upon her. She'd have to start acting and behaving differently, and she wasn't altogether certain just how stars behaved.

As she wandered into the main arena of the club, she spotted the bartender setting up and polishing the glasses. The first customers wouldn't start coming in until about an hour from now, so she had plenty of time. She was tempted to call Gin Tucker's studio to see how the shoot went with Danny. But on second thought she decided against that. She didn't trust Gin Tucker alone with Danny for one minute, and didn't want to think about what might have happened once she'd left the studio.

At the far end of the bar she spotted one lone customer dressed in white pants and a white shirt opened to the waist line. She figured if a man had a golden chest like that he might as well show it off. Why not? As she eyed him in the distance, she felt he looked like Danny Hansford's older brother—that is, if Danny had an older brother, and he didn't, at least not any older brother she'd heard about. With Danny, you could never be sure.

On a second glance, she realized that she was looking at Jason McReeves, her dream man. To her knowledge, he'd never been in the club before. She found herself breathing heavily at the sight of him.

He looked so all alone, so forlorn. Unlike that day at the beach, here was her chance to meet him. She resisted the impulse to rush over and throw herself in his arms. Stars didn't do that.

She wasn't sure how Madonna went about meeting men. Jason might walk over to her, but perhaps he was nearsighted and didn't even see her.

She decided the best course of action was to stroll by Jason as if she had some urgent business up front. She was glad she was already clad in her black and white tango dress. Nothing made her look quite as alluring as this tight-fitting dress.

As she walked toward Jason at the other end of the bar, she knew in her heart she moved with more grace and rhythm than any woman ever could. Sometimes she felt a man impersonating a woman could be more feminine than an actual woman. Tonight she felt all woman. Not merely the mock.

As she neared Jason he turned and smiled at her. It was a smile so winsome, warm, and welcoming that she felt she'd died and gone to drag queen heaven. Not only had she just received the first star billing of her life, but her fantasy man was smiling at her.

"Are you real?" Jason asked. "Or is this some little star who just fell out of heaven?"

She stopped only feet from him, placing her hands on her hips and appraising him with a come hither look. "What you see is what you get. Welcome to our club. You're our first customer of the evening."

"Thanks," he said. "I don't go to night clubs very much. I go to bars when I have some money for beer. But this is the first actual night club I've ever been in in Savannah."

"Don't make yourself a stranger." She signaled the bartender. "From now on, his drinks are on my tab." Seated next to him, she could almost smell him. He was so fresh and clean, with such beautiful blond hair. Jason was the type of guy who always looked like he'd just emerged from his bath.

"You are about the prettiest gal I've ever seen." He raised his beer to toast her as the waiter sat a club soda in front of her. "No, I take that back. You *are* the prettiest gal I've ever laid eyes on."

"Are you a specialist in beautiful women?" she asked, raising her club soda in a toast to him.

"I'm a specialist in beautiful people. It was your picture outside that I took a liking to. I just had to come inside and see if anyone in person could look as beautiful as that picture."

"Do I measure up?"

"You're much more beautiful than any stupid picture. Your skin—it's perfect. I think you'll go on and become a big star. Even bigger than Diana Ross."

"That's pretty big. If I become a star like that, I'll have to leave little old Savannah and go to New York. Maybe Hollywood. Who knows?"

"You'll make it one day. I have this gut feeling."

"Thanks for the encouragement. Are you staying for the show?"

"I'd love to. I've never seen anyone dance the tango before."

"You'll like it."

"It's nice of you to offer to buy my drinks tonight. Otherwise, I couldn't stick around. I never have much money for beer. I'm married to a woman writer, and she's doing this masterpiece. It'll make her rich and famous. But in the meantime we don't have much money to live on."

"It must be boring sitting around all day and listening to someone at her computer."

"It is. I've tried a job or two but nothing worked out. I'd forget to go to work or else if the day were pretty enough I'd just take off and go my way. I want to be a free spirit but I need money for that. Making money is something I don't know anything about."

"Making money is the hardest thing we have to do in life. With your looks, I don't think you'll have any trouble making money."

"I don't exactly know how my looks translate into money."

"A pretty boy never has to go hungry." She looked deeply into his eyes. Without really knowing it at first, she'd fallen madly in love with Jason. "I hope you won't misunderstand, but I think I can help you."

"I don't know how," he said.

"I can't really talk about it here in the club. But I think you and me have got a lot more to say to each other. I'd like to meet you tomorrow."

"That would be just fine with me. Lula writes all day on that damn novel of hers. I've got nothing to do but sit around the house."

"Why don't you meet me in front of the club? Say around two o'clock tomorrow afternoon. We could go for a drive. Talk things over. Something tells me I could become very important in your life. We could be great for each other."

"I hope that's true," he said. "But we'd have to keep our meeting a secret."

"I was just going to ask you to keep it secret too. It would be a private rendezvous. Two souls meeting each other and discovering each other."

"I'd like that," he said.

"I'd like it too. Thank you for calling me a pretty girl. Even a star needs that reassurance. I'd like to return the compliment. You are the best looking white man I've ever laid eyes on. And the sexiest."

"If you think I'm sexy with my clothes on, you should see me with my clothes off."

"I don't think any sight in all the world would thrill me as much."

A yank of her arm spun her around in her pivoting bar stool. She confronted the steely blue eyes of Danny Hansford.

"Get back to your dressing room, black bitch," he said, yanking her from the stool. "Stop annoying the customers." He glared at Jason before turning to stalk away.

She blew Jason a quick kiss with a promise of tomorrow and trailed after Danny, hoping he wouldn't beat her up before she had to go on to face her newly found public as the star she always wanted to be.

*****

In his tight-fitting white pants, a shirtless Danny Hansford was deep into his dance of the tango before Lavender Morgan realized she was falling in love with him. Even as this thought became increasingly alarming to her, she felt powerless to check the impulse. It couldn't be happening—not to her. She knew she was much too smart to fall in love with anybody at any time. She'd told some of the richest and most powerful men in the world she'd been in love with them. But she'd lied. If she'd loved anybody, it was herself, never a mere man. Men were toys to be played with and used for your amusement—nothing more.

She shuddered at the spectacle of herself. She was old enough to be Danny's grandmother. How could she be falling in love with him? She doubted if he were even twenty years old.

As she watched Danny move his sexy body about the club, she seemed to be reliving the Blitz in World War II London. She was far younger than Danny when she'd first fallen in love. Her mother had already died two years after giving birth to Lavender, and she'd been brought to London by her father who was a diplomat representing American interests at the Court of St. James's. From early morning until late at night, the air-raid sirens sounded in her ears. She'd almost grown used to them.

After a night of bombing, she'd walk through the rubble of London streets in the morning, looking at the huge craters. One morning she'd stood in horror taking in the sight of her favorite department store, John Lewis's, reduced to rubble. In spite of it all, Londoners went about their business, patronizing the shops, sunning themselves in Green Park. Young British women strolled arm in arm with American soldiers stationed in London. To some of them, it didn't matter if those soldiers were black.

It was one day while strolling through Green Park watching the other lovers that Lavender had almost collided into a handsome young man in his lieutenant's uniform. Corn fed and from the great American plains, Karl Andersen was like a walking, talking fantasy of a man, from his deep blue eyes and golden blond hair to the end of his big feet which carried around six feet two inches of the best packaged male flesh she'd ever seen in her life.

From the moment she'd first spotted Karl, it wasn't a question if she were going to bed with him. It was a question of when. When he'd spoken to her, he had even more charm. His voice was deep and husky, very compelling. It seemed to pull her closer to him like a magnet. She'd wanted to listen intently to his every observance regardless of how trivial. When Karl said it, it no longer was banal but some acute and deeply penetrating observance. He was wearing a leather jacket, and she could almost smell the man behind it. It was a clean, refreshing smell that evoked soap and scrubbing with a touch of cheap after shave lotion that on Karl smelled like the most intoxicating of perfumes.

In spite of her worldly aura, she was still a virgin until she'd met Karl. For the past two years, she'd been eager to surrender that virginity. She was waiting for the right man. In her heart she knew that Karl was the man to deflower her.

The seduction had come in her bed-sitter three hours later. It had hurt her at first, but Karl had been so loving, gentle, and reassuring that she'd found the pain not only tolerable but had been delighted when it gave way to the most exquisite pleasure she'd ever experienced in her life.

Even on that long ago afternoon, she'd realized she might know many other men in her life but none would ever occupy the place in her heart that Karl did. She'd dug her fingers into his back and had bitten his ear. He'd caused her such ecstasy she couldn't stand it at times. She'd screamed out his name as he'd plunged deeper and deeper into her body where no man had ever gone before.

Days later when she'd learned that Karl had a young and pregnant wife waiting for him back in Kansas, she hadn't stopped loving him. Knowing he would be hers for only a short time made her moments with him all the more precious.

She'd licked his entire body, savoring the taste of him. She'd become even more devouring when she'd learned his wife didn't do any of these things to him, and he'd obviously relished all her oral work over his perfectly sculpted body. That had led her to the conviction that his wife didn't fully appreciate the treasure she'd married. A man like Karl was the type you brought gifts to. He'd told her that people, mostly men, were always coming on to him, and he'd been flattered at their attention, never treating anyone rudely, even when he'd turned down their offers. He'd told her that he'd known he was going to bed with her the first moment he'd spotted her in the park. "I wasn't a child molester until I met you," he'd said. There was a magic and chemistry between them that grew day by day and even intensified when word came in that he was soon going to be shipped out to an unknown destination.

Their last night had been the most thrilling she'd ever known and would ever know again with any man. They'd lain for hours in each other's arms, savoring each other's bodies, before the dawn that held out every possibility that it would be the last they'd ever face together. When she'd told him good-bye that morning, she'd known in her heart it was the final farewell.

It was eight months later than an old army buddy had called on her at her bed-sitter. He'd confirmed what she had known all along: Karl had died in action.

As the days and weeks had passed before her, she'd relived every experience with Karl. She'd felt a compelling need to imbed each of his memories deeply into her brain. There would be times in the years ahead when she'd need the memories of the happy moments. If they lived within her heart, she could draw upon them like checking money out of a bank.

Her mind blurry from drink, Lavender looked up at the stage. Danny and Tango were taking their bows. Their act for the evening was over. As Danny stood in the spotlight, taking a solo bow, she realized that Karl had come back to her. Danny's resemblance to Karl was amazing. It was as if he had stepped intact from 1942 into her life again. If it's true that every man has a twin on this earth, Lavender knew that Danny was Karl's twin. Maybe it was an even closer bond. Maybe Danny was Karl himself returning to recapture the love of her life, a love that had been brutally ended by the destruction of the war.

When Gin Tucker had stopped applauding wildly, Lavender gently touched his arm and whispered in his ear, "Please go backstage and invite that divine young man to our table. I want very much to meet him."

"He's a little young for you," Gin had said with a smirk. "Don't you think?"

"Dear heart, when I was twenty-five I fell in love with a man of eighty-two. It was one of the most abiding and passionate affairs of my life. Age is to be transcended, not morbidly dwelled upon."

"I understand," Gin said. "Coming up: One Danny Hansford delivered to one Lavender Morgan."

She watched as Gin disappeared backstage. She smiled at the bachelors at her table and joined them in a champagne toast. She was breathing deeply. "Think youth and beauty," she told herself. She'd always been able to project youth and beauty even when she'd lost both. She prayed her old seductive powers would not desert her tonight when she needed them more than ever.

With his shirt on, Danny Hansford was approaching her table trailed by Gin. As he got closer and closer to her, Lavender grew more convinced than ever that it was not Danny but Karl walking toward her the way he did on that faraway day in Green Park in London.

"Your skin is just like a pretty peach," Karl had said. "A peach I'd like to take a bite out of."

Those words were still echoing in her head as she reached to shake the firm, masculine hand of Danny Hansford.

*****

As Danny Hansford looked into the face of Lavender Morgan seated across from him, he felt she was the oldest woman he'd ever known except for his grandmother back in Clinton, Georgia. He suspected that Lavender had a good ten years on his grandmother. He was amazed, though, at how she'd artfully concealed her age behind perfect grooming and make-up. This was obviously a high-class lady, and he'd known very few of them.

"That sure is pretty hair you got," he said to Lavender. "Purple hair, it looks good on you."

"The hair is lavender," she said, "not purple. Purple is an entirely different color."

"I was never good at identifying color," he said. "I call everything red—not scarlet or all those other colors that red is called."

"I like that," she said. "It means you don't like to put up with a lot of nonsense. A back-to-basics kind of guy."

Danny looked away from Lavender to survey the sea of faggots she had brought with her to the club. When Tipper was the star of the show, she always catered to this table, so Danny felt he had to do the same. He guessed that that was the price of stardom, although he could think of eight million other places he'd like to be right now.

He was flattered when Gin came backstage to summon him up front. Tango was miffed that she wasn't invited too. She blamed it on racism. But Tango blamed everything on racism. If enough people didn't show up at Blues in the Night, she blamed that on racism too instead of lack of audience interest.

"What made you decide to become a tango dancer like Valentino?" Lavander asked.

"Who is Valentino?" he said.

She looked askance. "He was a great silent screen star who died young. A legend, really. The great lover."

"I've never seen a silent movie. In fact, I've never seen a movie in black and white except that old *Psycho* movie. I see movies only in color, and I like a lot of action in my films. If there's no action I get up and walk out. The most boring film I ever had to sit through, and I was doing it only for a friend, was *Midnight in the Garden of Good and Evil*. They should have had a lot more action in that film."

"You mean perhaps like the burning of Savannah the way Atlanta was burned in *Gone With the Wind?*"

"Yeah, that would have made it a great movie. The way it came out, there was too much talk. Also, The Lady Chablis was too old and ugly. Tango should have played the part."

"Your friend Tango is very beautiful. Lovely skin."

"I'll pass along the compliment," he said. "I sent Eastwood a picture of myself hoping he would cast me in the part of Danny Hansford. I could have done a better job than that psychotic fart they cast in the role. He wasn't even sexy and couldn't act either."

"I truly agree that you could have made a far better Danny Hansford."

"Thanks," he said, accepting the beer the waiter offered him. "Of course, if I had gotten the part, I would have insisted on a far larger role. They would have had to beef up my part. I don't do walk-ons."

"I think Eastwood made a big mistake not casting you and Tango in the parts. It would have been a box office success, I'm sure, instead of a bomb."

"I'm real disappointed in Eastwood. I think he's getting old and senile." No sooner were the words out than Danny realized he'd made a mistake. If Eastwood were old and senile, what did that make Lavender? He quickly moved on, hoping she wouldn't take offense at that remark. "I've been turned off by Eastwood for a very long time. Ever since I saw him in a pair of jockey shorts in a movie. I always thought he was such a big man. But, Christ, there was nothing but a concave in those jockey shorts. Don't they have a set director or somebody out in Hollywood to stuff jockey shorts when they have actors who need to rely on padding?"

"If they don't, they should. But that is obviously not your problem."

Danny leaned back in his chair, "If you got it, don't keep it a secret I always say." He downed more of his beer preferring it from the bottle instead of from a glass. "My, God, where are my manners? You'll think I've had no raising. You asked me how I became a tango dancer, and we rambled off on all this other talk."

"I was curious," she said. "I don't know many young men today who dance the tango."

"I've always been a good dancer. You could just show me the routine, and in minutes I'd have the steps down pat. It's a talent I have. I was dancing professionally in Savannah when Tango spotted me. She'd always loved the tango. I'd never even heard of the tango until I met her. She asked me to go into show business with her. In just two weeks of rehearsals, I learned to dance the tango and I've been doing it ever since. We even had this guy from Argentina come to the club. There are a lot of tango dancers in Argentina." He looked over at Lavender. "That's a country somewhere in Central America."

She smiled indulgently. "I know. It's even much farther south than Central America."

"I know it's down there some place. That's where Evita came from. Did you see Madonna play Evita in the movies? Talk about no action."

"I didn't see the movie but I knew the actual Evita."

"You did? I'm impressed. You're not making this up, are you? I mean, Evita was really famous."

"I actually knew her. One of my former companions had a great deal of business one time with Argentina. We went to Buenos Aires often."

"That's something else. I never thought I'd be talking to someone who knew the actual Evita. Of course, until I saw Madonna play the part, I'd never heard of Evita, but I'm told she was very well known."

"She was the most famous woman in South America."

"Is it true she was a hooker?" he asked.

"That's true. Before she became a saint. But everybody has to get started someway." She looked at him provocatively. "Even you."

There was a long period of silence between the two of them. He looked into her eyes and saw they were filled with desire. He felt so uncomfortable under her gaze he wanted to run. But then he decided any hustler worth the name would not flee from the presence of a woman as rich and powerful as Lavender Morgan. Everybody in

Savannah talked about her. She had millions. In fact, she was the richest woman in Savannah, and he knew she wanted him. He guessed he could make love to her but the lights would have to be turned off. With the room dark, he could imagine Lavender as young and beautiful. That he was fucking her in 1942 and not 1998. If she wanted him, she'd have to pay and pay a lot. But at the same time he suspected she wasn't used to reaching into her purse and pulling out five-hundred dollars to give to a young and well-endowed hustler. That wasn't her style. He'd have to find another way.

He was the one who finally broke the silence and eye contact between them. "If I look a little disappointed tonight, I am. I've been sad all day."

"What's the matter?" she asked.

"I saw this big motorcycle on display today. Purple, just like your hair. I wanted it more than I've ever wanted anything in my life. But I don't have that kind of money. Even though I'm a star here at the club, I don't make much money. Matt Daniels is one cheap bastard. I'd do almost anything to get that motorcycle. You see, I don't think I'm going to live a long time. So if I want something, I've got to have it now. I can't think about years ahead because I don't have those years."

"You're young and obviously healthy. What makes you think you're going to have a short life?"

"This voodoo queen told me everything. She said there's a curse on my head. She's trying to break the curse but she said the curse is more powerful than any of her magic."

"I'm very sorry to hear that. You look like the kind of young man who, at least potentially, could bring delight to women or men for decades to come."

"I know. But I won't be around. If a woman or a guy wants to enjoy what I've got to offer, they've got to go for it now."

"Do you mean that?" Lavender leaned over and gently caressed his arm. "I bet you could bring pleasure to a woman that few men ever could."

"I can make a woman feel like she's died and gone to heaven."

Lavender sighed. "The trouble with getting older—at least for some women—is that the desire doesn't die. It does for some women but not for all women. Some women are just as much in need of love when they're older as when they're young."

He looked at her with a sexy smirk. "Why not carry on and enjoy yourself to the very end? That's what I always say."

"Danny, I don't have much experience in what we're negotiating right now. All my life I've been the recipient of gifts from men. But I think the time has come for me to reverse the roles. When a man wanted to seduce me, he gave me a painting, diamond necklace, even an apartment in Paris. I rarely accepted perfume. I was not for sale for a bottle of perfume regardless of how expensive. Perhaps I need to learn a lesson from all the men in my life."

"What are you getting at?"

"What do you say to the prospect that you could be riding that motorcycle tomorrow morning?"

"I'd say that was a pretty good prospect. I'd do a lot of things to be riding that motorcycle."

"It's yours."

"You want me to go home with you tonight?"

"There is nothing on earth I'd desire more," she said, stroking his arm, her hand riding higher to feel its muscle. "There's just one thing I insist on."

"What's that?" he asked, a frown crossing his brow.

"The motorcycle has to be lavender—not purple, and you've got to take me for a spin on it tomorrow."

*****

The name of the late night dive was Harlow's Box but someone long ago had crossed out the "w" and made it a "t." Ever since then the club had been called Harlot's Box. It was where the performers of Savannah, both black and white, gathered after two in the morning when most of the bars and clubs had closed for the night. These show business people, mostly country and western singers, needed a place to unwind before heading back to their dreary rooms, trailers, or small apartments before the dawn.

When Norma Dixie had called Tipper to invite her out, she had gladly accepted. She didn't want to be alone at night with her memories. Although already drunk before Norma came to pick her up, Tipper decided to go anyway. She recalled the nights when Monty and she could drink for days on end, never taking food at all, seeming to get all the nourishment they needed from alcohol.

It was amazing. She'd been less than an hour between jobs. She'd walked out on Matt Daniels only to have Frank Gilmore immediately hire her. She fully expected that her arch rival, Emma, might never return to Shocking Pink after Tipper made her debut. When the fans heard Tipper singing "Moanin' Low," they would clamor for her every night. Tipper fully expected her three-week gig to stretch on throughout the winter season. Emma would just have to find work in another club.

At a table at Harlot's Box, Tipper and Norma were surrounded by admiring fans, in this case two black drag queen divas, one hustler, and two good ol' boys who used a young Johnny Cash as a role model.

"Norma tells me that you personally knew Dr. King," one of the black divas, Maybelle, said. "Is that true? You're not just a name dropper are you?"

"I knew both Martin and Coretta very well," Tipper said in a slightly slurred voice. "Coretta and I are still friends. Back when I was making a lot of money and my records were selling well, I occasionally made grants. I was always a champion of the civil rights movement."

The other black diva, Laurie Mae, more masculine than the first one, said, "I heard you had a lot of money. Owned Lucky Strike or something."

"Not quite," Tipper said. "But I was well off. I liked the way Martin espoused nonviolent resistance. I knew he greatly admired Mahatma Gandhi and wanted to visit India and meet some of his followers who were still alive. I personally wrote a check to Martin for five-thousand dollars. Martin and Coretta went to India where they spoke with Nehru and other leaders in the movement for Indian independence. They lived on my five thousand during the month they spent on the subcontinent. There Martin became more convinced than ever that nonviolent resistance was the most potent weapon for blacks to use in the civil rights movement in America." Tipper took a hefty swig from her drink and leaned back in her chair. "You might say I financed the early civil rights movement in America."

Norma sighed. She'd heard the story too many times and was anxious to change the subject, although the black divas were obviously impressed. The good ol' boys looked as if they could care less.

The hustler looked bored too. After Tipper had finished, he looked over at the black divas. "Which one of you pussies has any money tonight? I'm selling it if you can pay for it."

The more masculine black diva, Laurie Mae, hawkeyed him carefully. "I pay by the inch, stud. Ten dollars an inch. How much would a session with you cost me?"

"Eighty-five dollars. You'll have to pay five dollars for that final half inch."

"It's a deal," Laurie Mae said, getting up and reaching for his hand. After excusing herself, she headed for the door with her newly acquired hustler in hand.

"You always take me to the classiest joints," Tipper said affectionately to Norma.

"You've spent too much time with all those café society folks you're always talking about. 'Bout time you got out in the real world and met some down-home people."

One of the bubbas got up and asked Norma to dance. In spite of her massive weight, Norma could still move with a certain grace across the floor. Tipper always found it amazing. Norma certainly proved that fat gals can still dance and do a lot of other things. As she watched Norma take over the floor, Tipper smiled indulgently. Being with Norma always made her feel better in spite of how bleak the night. "There's not much time left on this earth for any of us," Norma always said, "and I'm gonna make the most of what time I got left."

At the end of her dance, Norma and her good ol' boy received loud applause. Huffing and puffing, and sweating profusely, Norma came back to the table and plopped down.

"You really know how to shake it, sugar," Maybelle said.

"I sure can, honey," Norma said. "That's what a real black woman can do. As for you, you're merely the mock."

"Now, now," Tipper said, reaching over to stroke Maybelle's arm. "Norma didn't mean that. Actually, she's very gay friendly."

"I'm gay friendly, but I never took much to nigger men dressing up like women," Norma said. "I figure whites laugh at us too much as it is. We don't have to put on a dress to have them make fun of us some more."

"Fuck you!" Maybelle said. "This is a free country. If I want to be a woman, that's what I'll be. In fact, I'm thinking of having the dirty little thing snipped off and becoming a total woman."

"You do just that, nigger gal. At least you'd fool a lot more men that way."

"Shut your face, Norma," her white dancing partner said. "When I can't get some real pussy, I fuck some boy ass, black or white. I prefer them dressed up like a woman. I sure don't want to go to my trailer park with a man. The more sissy they are, the better I like it. In fact, I'm considering taking Miss Maybelle home with me tonight and letting her know what a pussy stretcher some white men can be."

Maybelle giggled. "I'd like that a lot. I never did know how to say no to a white boy."

"My son comes down from Atlanta every chance he can get," Norma said. "Wait till you see him. That's what a black boy should look like. He dresses well. He's good-looking. Very masculine. I hear he drives half the women in Atlanta crazy. My son is a real man."

"I can't wait to try him out," Maybelle said. "But first it looks like I got a date with this sexy Johnny Cash clone over here."

"You got that right, baby. But I've got to warn you. Once I get in the saddle, I ride all night."

Maybelle giggled again. "I'm getting up and heading for the powder room. When I get back, I want to see you at the door waiting for your tamale."

Tipper had had enough of Norma's friends and was suddenly anxious to end the evening. She had to look her best for that meeting with Frank Gilmore at ten in the morning. She reached over and rubbed Norma's sweaty cheek. "It's been a great evening," she said. "Very educational." Remembering something, she turned to Norma. "You never told me you had a son."

"I don't talk about him much, but I'm real proud of him. I'll let you meet him the next time he comes to Savannah."

"I'd like that," Tipper said. He sounds real nice. What's his name?"

"I call him Domino. That's his real name. His daddy always liked to play dominoes and I named our son after the game."

"Domino Dixie. That's a name you can remember. What does he do?"

"He doesn't always tell me much about his business. Likes to keep everything secret. But I know he's in show business in some way. I think he books acts in Atlanta. Yeah, that's right. He's a theatrical agent."

"I wish he could book me into a gig. After my new gig at Shocking Pink, I don't know where I'm going to perform."

"Something will turn up," Norma predicted. "It always does for God's youngin's."

"I hope so..."

Norma looked at Tipper rising on wobbly legs. "Do you want this big fat mama to drive you home?"

"No, it's not far. I think I'll walk. I need the night air."

On her way home she always passed by Lavender Morgan's town house where she would look up to see if Lavender's light was still on in her bedroom upstairs.

Tonight the bedroom lights were out. She figured that Lavender had gone to bed, probably deciding to cancel her reservations at Blues in the Night when she'd learned that Tipper wouldn't be appearing.

Stepping back in the shadows, she spotted Gin Tucker's car pulling up at the gateway to Lavender's home. After feigned kisses and a promise of a drink tomorrow, Gin let his passengers out. Lavender stood on the sidewalk with a young man. On closer inspection, Tipper realized to her horror that the young man was Danny Hansford. She'd recognize those tight white pants anywhere.

That betraying bitch Lavender had gone to the club after all. Not only that, she'd invited one of the stars of the show back home with her. Tipper wondered if the jealous Tango knew where her boyfriend was tonight.

Tipper watched as Lavender mounted the steps to her town house and inserted the key. Within moments the old hag had disappeared inside the house with her succulent morsel of teenage male flesh. Tipper shuddered to think what grotesque scene might occur within Lavender's house tonight.

Looking at the house for a long time past the moment when the chandelier was turned on in the parlor, Tipper turned and walked toward her own home. As much as she wanted to condemn Lavender, she knew she never could. Lavender could always control her.

Lavender had been a guest in her home in Winston-Salem on that night when Taylor Zachory was killed. Lavender publicly blamed Tipper for the death but offered nothing specific. It was just a vague accusation designed to amuse her bachelors at Tipper's expense. Lavender had never told the real truth of what happened that long-ago night, and for that Tipper was grateful. Lavender knew too much and could reveal plenty, the most incriminating of details. But so far Lavender had maintained a steely silence about the actual events that took place on that night. Tipper hoped Lavender would go to her grave and never reveal what she knew.

Holding her head high, Tipper walked proudly into the Savannah night. The words she'd told her last interviewer at the close of her most recent show in Chicago came back to her. "I suppose you've heard all those wicked stories about me. Well, I've lived my life as it came and I've done bloody marvels with a bad hand."

# Chapter Three

Aunt Bice was too hung over to get out of bed to fix his breakfast, so Phil kissed her good-bye and promised to see her again real soon. In the clear light of day, he headed south to Savannah before the scorching heat of the August sun burned too deeply into everybody's skin. He didn't know where he'd be living. He had only the telephone number of a caretaker. He prayed he'd written down the number correctly, and he also hoped the caretaker was home. He didn't want to wait around for six hours in the burning sun.

Last night at Bootleggers had been a complete dud. The bar was filled with men and a few women. But the men were of the sort that Phil wouldn't even consider on the darkest, drunkest night. In fact, they were so bad that if faced with a choice he thought he would prefer a woman. That was how desperate the scene was there.

Since he'd been drinking all night, he'd left the bar a few shades less than sober at two in the morning, staggering to his car. The road had been a bit of a blur, and he'd hoped he'd taken the right turn to Aunt Bice's house. At one point he'd found himself dozing, as his car had veered dangerously into the left lane. He'd come around only to see a flashing dome light in his rear-view mirror.

"Oh, shit!" he'd said, pulling over into the graveled yard of a gasoline station that had long ago closed for the night.

The two cops had taken a long time getting out of their squad car. Phil hadn't known what he was supposed to do. He'd wondered if he were to get out first and go to them. But he'd feared he might stagger on the way to their car.

Finally, one of the cops had gotten out of his car and had headed toward Phil's vehicle. He'd been a highway patrolman.

Upon closer inspection of the patrolman, Phil had realized that this was the type of man he'd been searching for at Bootleggers and hadn't found. His dark brown hair was curly, and he had a hard-chiseled body and a good-looking face. He appeared to be no more than twenty-three. The cop's eyes glittered appraisingly as he peered into Phil's car. "I'd say you were driving drunk if I didn't know better. Let's see some I.D."

Phil had reached into his wallet and pulled out his driver's license. The cop had scanned it closely. "Heather. You aren't one of the Heathers who live in that big house on the hill?"

"I'm Hadley's son. Do you know him?"

"Everybody in these parts knows Big Daddy. You must be his gay son that people are always talking about."

"I'm his son."

"Gay son, I heard. Are you denying you're gay?"

"I'm not denying anything."

"I hear you gay boys are great cocksuckers, much better at it than women. Is that true?"

"Some are better than others."

The patrolman had studied his driver's license for a few more seconds, then handed it back to Phil. "I'm sort of new around these parts. I'm from Macon and I don't know a lot about the way things are done here. I'd better check with my partner." He'd walked back to the squad car and had said something to the man inside.

In moments, the other patrolman had gotten out of the car and had approached Phil's vehicle. "Hi, Phil, welcome back home."

Phil had looked up into the man's face, not recognizing him at first. He was much larger than the first patrolman, a tall, rugged blond that stood about six feet four.

"Do I know you?" Phil had asked.

"Do you know me?" The man had grabbed his groin. "You used to swing on this big old thing. Don't tell me you've forgotten. I'm Brian Sheehan."

"Brian!" Phil had opened the door and slid out from behind the wheel. "I didn't recognize you at first. You're bigger somehow."

"Bigger all over," Brian had said. "Ever since you left town— Christ, that must have been ten years ago—I never found anybody who could suck cock like you. All the guys on the team said that. We're all married now, but if you come back here to live all the guys would come to visit you—that's for damn sure."

"I'm glad you appreciate my talents." Phil had smiled provocatively at him. "Wait until you sample them now. I've had ten years of experience under my belt. Learned a lot of new tricks."

"Did you learn those tricks up in New York and out in California?" Brian had asked.

"I did indeed."

"That figures. I hear the perverts up there and out in Los Angeles will even stick their tongues up your ass. You never used to do that to me."

"I didn't know what I was missing," Phil had said, moving closer to Brian and resting his hand on the man's strong, firm arm. "Since I knew you, I have perfected those skills too."

"Fuck man, you're getting me hot. I'm recalling all that sucking you used to do. You could swallow it all. No one's ever been able to do that since you left town. My fucking wife gets three inches in her mouth and starts to puke. What fun that is!"

"I don't want to get taken in for drunk driving. Could I show you a little fun in the back seat of my car? Maybe after I finish you off, you'd invite your friend to come into the back seat with me. What's his name?"

"Jeff. But I don't know if he goes that route. I'll have to check with him."

"At least you'll go for it."

"Will I ever!" He'd walked back to the squad car and had said something to Jeff. In minutes Brian was back, crawling into the back seat of Phil's car. Once inside he'd pulled down his pants and slipped his white jockey shorts down to his knees. "Come on in, Phil. This big lollipop is just waiting for you."

In the rear of the car, Phil had crawled in after him. He'd reached for Brian's cock, before his fingers had slipped below to weigh the fullness of his balls. "That's some cock. Even better than I remember. I hope your wife knows how lucky she is."

"It's too big for her."

Straddling Brian's legs, Phil had opened his mouth wide and guided the throbbing prick to his lips. He'd let out a soft moan as Brian had pushed forward into the narrowing passage of his throat. Phil no longer gagged like he used to. With all his experience, he'd become far too skilled as a sword swallower to do that. As Brian's eager prick had scraped across the roof of Phil's mouth, he'd descended even farther until the light brown pubic hair of Brian's groin had ground against his nose. As he'd sucked voraciously, Phil had massaged Brian's balls, removing his mouth occasionally to lick and tongue them. At one point he'd descended lower, reaching that virgin rosebud of Brian's. Brian had squealed like a pig as Phil's tongue had entered him. Brian had grabbed Phil's hair, holding him into position as he'd feared at any moment he was going to pull away. "I'm going to cum," Brian had shouted.

Quickly Phil had descended on the pulsating prick again and just in time, as Brian had exploded in his mouth. With his firm hand, Brian had held Phil between his legs. Phil had taken advantage of the opportunity to lick up any final drops coming from Brian. Finally, Brian had released him.

"God, I wish you'd move back to Darien. I need that every day. I've really missed you, man. I've got to report back to duty. But I wish we could go to a motel room somewhere. I need to be worked over from head to toe, and I bet you're just the kind of guy to do it."

"I'd like nothing better. I'm going to be living in Savannah. I don't know the address yet until I get there. But could I have your number and call you? I'd like you to slip away from your wife and kids for a weekend. Come to Savannah. I'll show you a good time, I promise."

"You got yourself a date." Brian had pulled up his jockey shorts after Phil had planted a good-bye kiss, then had gotten out of the car, zipping up his pants. He'd reached into his pocket and had written down his phone number for Phil. "You call me now, you hear?"

"I can't wait." Phil had looked back at the squad car. "What about Jeff? Does he need some relief tonight?"

"I guess he does but he's a little shy. He once told me that he'd heard that gays only go with guys with big dicks. I think he's a little worried that he doesn't measure up."

"It's okay," Phil had said. "My mouth fits all sizes."

"I don't think so," Brian had said, kissing him on the cheek. "As a matter of fact, I think I'd be jealous. I'd rather keep you for myself."

Brian had walked back and said something to Jeff before returning to Phil's car. "Get in," he'd ordered Phil. "I'm driving you home. I always wanted to see the Heather mansion anyway."

"But I'm not living there," Phil had protested. "I'm staying with my Aunt Bice. Do you know her?"

"Hell, yes, I know her. I once pulled her over for speeding. She must be a hundred years old. Do you know what she did?"

"Offered to give you a blow-job."

Brian looked puzzled as he'd gotten behind the wheel of Phil's car. "How did you know?"

"I know my Aunt Bice." Phil had gotten in the front seat on the passenger's side, as they'd headed down the road, with Jeff trailing them in the squad car.

"I hope that was some welcome home present I gave you," Brian had said.

"It was. I won't wash out my mouth for days. Christ, Brian, you're even better looking than you were in school. I bet if some bigtime movie producer saw you, you'd be hauled off to Hollywood at once."

"A lot of people say that to me. Do you remember? I played a few parts in school plays."

"You were damn good too. In fact, I'm in Savannah writing a screenplay right now. It's called *Butterflies in Heat.* You'd be perfect for the lead. When the producer comes down from New York, I think I'll introduce you two guys. Who knows what fireworks might happen."

"You mean that? Or, are you just bullshitting?"

"It was just something to say at first. But on second thought I'm deadly serious. The part calls for someone like you. You'd be surprised. There aren't many guys out there who look like you at all. You've got what it takes."

"It's all yours, baby," Brian had said. "Any time you want it."

Thoughts of Brian faded quickly as Phil's car crossed the city limits of Savannah. He both anticipated and feared the adventures awaiting him here.

*****

After a night under the bed, Lula Carson emerged into the new light of day to find Jason had returned from a mysterious night out. He didn't come to the bed all night. Once he'd sexually assaulted her, she would be free of his attacks for a number of days until he wanted to prove his manhood again. He lay sprawled nude on their living room sofa, sleeping off what she just knew was a drunk. He must have discovered the house money she'd withdrawn from the bank and had gone out on a drinking binge.

In the kitchen she looked into the empty sugar bowl where she'd stored one-hundred dollars, finding it completely empty.

Jason had never known money before, and he felt if he had any money he had to spend it right away. The day they were married, he'd confessed to her he had only three dollars in his pocket. Thank God her literary grant had saved them from starvation.

When his parents had divorced, Jason even as a little boy had to fend for himself. Since thirteen he'd managed to support himself some way, some how. She'd never known for sure, and Jason never liked to talk about what he'd done as a teenage boy. She knew that he'd disappeared for a few years. He'd told her that he'd done a number of odd jobs, bumming around the South. Once, or so he'd claimed, he'd driven a truck for a bootlegger in Wilkes County, North Carolina. Eventually he'd enlisted in the army, and was stationed at Fort Benning, but something had gone seriously wrong there. She was overcome with the fact that she knew very little about the husband she'd married even though they had known each other for years and had been playmates. Jason forever remained a mystery to her.

Lula surveyed her kitchen this morning. It was a mess. Neither she nor Jason were trained in the domestic arts. On the floor rested every pan they owned, each containing charred food she'd thoughtlessly allowed to burn on the stove. She'd hope that by soaking the pans they'd come clean, but they didn't. The burnt remainders of failed suppers clung tenaciously to the bottom of each pan.

She sighed and headed for her coffee-maker. A cup of strong black coffee was all she wanted any way. She was filled with a tremulous excitement. She wasn't sure but she expected Phil Heather to move in this morning. The place was already furnished so moving in would be easy for him. He'd probably arrive with just a suitcase of clothing and his computer. She wondered how far he'd gotten into his screenplay and was anxious to talk to him soon, but didn't want to appear too forward. She'd have to arrange to meet him discreetly in the rear garden.

The garbage truck was due today, and after finishing her coffee she set about rounding up the trash. She hated household chores, and became very aggressive about them, wanting to bring an end to them as soon as possible so she could begin work on *The Tireless Hunter*. She rounded up the garbage in the house and emptied the containers in the cans outside, while singing the Funeral March from

*Götterdammerung.* As she slammed the lids shut, she fantasized it was the clashing sounds of cymbals and kettledrums accompanying her voice.

After she'd finished with the garbage, Lula sat in the courtyard she'd eventually share with Phil. She contemplated her day. That hundred dollars Jason had stolen from the sugar bowl would have to be compensated for in some way. The money was running out too quickly, and she desperately wanted to finish her novel before it was all gone.

Even though both of them loved creamy butter, she'd have to switch to lard to save money. Instead of the thick brown bread they liked, they'd buy the pasty white stuff. Somehow she'd figure out a way to save. Maybe Phil would be tempted to cook out in the backyard at the unused barbecue grill. If he did that, she and Jason would appear around suppertime, and maybe he'd offer them some barbecue. Both Jason and she loved barbecue, but she never made it right. She always burned the meat instead of charcoaling it.

Impulsively she'd gotten up from her chair when she'd heard the paper boy toss the morning paper in the yard next door. She always stole the paper from the frontyard of her neighbors and read it before they got up. Mr. and Mrs. Purley never seem to get out of bed until way past noon. Apparently, they spent every night drinking until late. She always folded up the paper neatly and returned it to their frontyard, so they were never the wiser. She was pleased at how thrifty she was. That way she could keep up with the news and not actually have to subscribe to the paper. When she became rich and famous, however, she was going to subscribe to all the glossy magazines. If she got time later, she'd draw up a list of all the magazines she wanted to subscribe to. There were so many of them. Making such a big decision would be tough.

On the frontpage of the paper was a picture of John Berendt, announcing that he was going to be making an appearance at a local bookstore signing copies of *Midnight in the Garden of Good and Evil.* He had these autograph signings frequently, although he'd actually written his bestseller years ago. But he still appeared to sign autographs. Everyone in Savannah who could read had already devoured the book. But thousands of tourists arrived daily, and many of them purchased copies. She didn't know if people actually read the book once they'd bought it. She suspected that many of these arriving visitors actually bought the book as a souvenir. They wanted it autographed by somebody. If the author himself wasn't available, which was most likely, they got the songstress Emma Kelly to autograph it. Even The Lady Chablis autographed copies of the book, although Lula had heard that she'd written her own memoirs and probably preferred fans to purchase her own book instead of the one by Berendt in which she was featured.

Looking at her watch, Lula noticed that Berendt's signing was at ten o'clock in a location about eight blocks from her house. It was already ten minutes before ten, and Lula decided if she left now she could make it.

Not bothering to dress up, and wearing only sandals, jeans, and a simple blouse, Lula headed for the bookstore with her own dogeared copy of the *Midnight* book. It wasn't actually hers but belonged to the library. She'd checked it out three months ago and had never bothered to return it. She didn't like the book at all, but she'd keep that news from Berendt. Instead of literature, she'd dismissed the book as gossip.

It had depicted a side of Savannah that held little interest for her. The antiques dealer, Jim Williams, was long dead and gone before she'd arrived on the scene, and the murdered Danny Hansford wasn't the kind of man she wanted to meet. Although black drag queens held a certain fascination for her, she could not imagine herself hanging out with The Lady Chablis. The woman seemed too self-centered for her. Lula preferred gatherings where she was the center of attention, not some black diva.

Although her obvious reason for going to the Berendt signing was to get the author's autograph on his famous book, she had an ulterior motive. She didn't really want his autograph. She'd want the autograph of Tennessee Williams and most definitely William Faulkner, but not Berendt. Her secret reason for attending the signing was to observe how a famous author handled it. She knew that in months she would be in Berendt's position, signing copies of *The Tireless Hunter*. She'd observe him very closely, watching how he signed copies of *Midnight,* perhaps looking over his shoulder to see what he actually wrote. Did he write any message or did he sign only his name? She needed to know all these things.

At the bookstore the lines were long. Savannah was crawling with tourists today, and seemingly each of them had purchased a copy of *Midnight in the Garden of Good and Evil.*

She had plenty of time, even though she felt guilty that she wasn't at home working on the next scene in *The Tireless Hunter.* But instead of getting in the line right away, she positioned herself a few feet in back of Berendt. That way she could observe his every move and witness up close how he greeted his fans. When the crowds finally dwindled, she'd go to the back of the line and get Berendt's autograph herself.

The lines moved slowly, and Berendt appeared to be a gracious author but rather closed off and impersonal. She noticed him perspiring heavily. That wasn't surprising since the Savannah August morning was exceptionally close, and Berendt was dressed in a suit with a white shirt. At least he hadn't worn a tie. He looked as if he'd gotten off a plane from New York and hadn't fully adjusted to the summer ferocity of Savannah's impossible climate. To her, Savannah was always too fiercely hot or too bitterly cold. There never seemed to be an in-between time.

In person Berendt appeared much as he did in the book. He seemed to relate to the public in a polite manner but never gave much of himself. It was as if he were saying, "Yes, I wrote that book. But your buying it doesn't give you a right to know anything about my personal life."

Lula certainly had learned very little about Berendt's personal life from reading the book. In the book he'd seemed like a voyeur, reporting on the outrageous antics of the characters of Savannah, but never once telling you much about himself. She wondered if she should use him as a role model, zealously guarding her privacy from her future fans.

When the line finally dwindled, and enough tourists had purchased their daily quota of *Midnight in the Garden of Good and Evil,* Lula had gone to the end of the line. She'd ripped out the envelope with the library card. She certainly didn't want Berendt to realize she was giving him a library copy to autograph.

When she actually came face to face with him, she detected Berendt wasn't well. He was perspiring even more heavily and kept putting his hand to his throat as if finding it hard to breathe in the stuffy bookstore where the air conditioner had failed—that is, if they had an air conditioner.

"Mr. Berendt," she said. "I just loved your book, and I'd like you to autograph it." She'd adopted a rather exaggerated voice with a Georgia accent, because she felt that such a voice lent more sincerity to her insincere words. She found it difficult being a fan to anybody else's work but her own.

"Thank you," was all Berendt managed to say without making eye contact with her.

"Please make the dedication to Lula Carson," she said. "That's L-u-l-a." She giggled. "I'm sure you know how to spell Carson."

For the first time Berendt made eye contact with her, but his gaze was blurry. Maybe he was coming down with summer flu. After all, God knows how many people from how many God forsaken places had been breathing their germs on him.

"I'm going to be a great writer myself," she blurted out.

He looked up at her again but said nothing.

"Maybe just as famous as you, although I'm not doing it for the fame. I'm completing a novel called *The Tireless Hunter*. Remember that title. Two hundred years from now my novel will be read by half the world. No doubt it will still be a bestseller on the moon and maybe on some other planets as well."

This time he looked her directly in the eye although he didn't say anything. His face indicated he felt she was some kind of nut. She stopped talking at once, realizing how foolish she must appear before him. She'd gone and embarrassed herself as she so often did.

Berendt returned her book. He hadn't dedicated it especially to her. She looked at his autograph with disappointment. He'd simply signed the book, "John Berendt."

"I didn't want to dedicate a page to you personally," he said. "That way, when it's eventually returned to the library, it will not look like anybody's personal property."

She felt her face redden until she knew she must look like she had scarlet fever. Somehow he'd detected it was library property and not her own book. She felt mortified and didn't know how to excuse herself from this awkward moment. With her head held low, and avoiding eye contact with him, she sheepishly took the copy back from him.

All of a sudden he slumped over the little desk placed there for him by the store managers. Then he raised himself up suddenly as his hands darted to his chest.

She screamed, alerting the attention of two women staff members who rushed over to Berendt. He seemed to be having a stroke.

"Get an ambulance," Lula called out to no one in particular. A woman at the cashier's desk picked up the phone and dialed somebody.

Sensing something was terribly wrong, one of the beefier women pushed Lula aside and ordered everybody back.

All the customers were being ordered from the store. A space was cleared around Berendt. Lula was stepped on twice before she finally made it to the sidewalk. She was there with the rest of Berendt's fans when an ambulance arrived. Two attendants rushed inside the store with an emergency stretcher and came out in minutes carrying the body of the author. At first Lula thought he might have died until she detected movement on the stretcher.

As the ambulance pulled away, with its siren blasting, Lula confronted a portly woman with stringy hair in a jogging suit. She was clutching a copy of *Midnight*. "I saw you talking to Mr. Berendt like you knew him," she said.

Lula smiled at her. She didn't mean to say what she was about to, but she said it anyway. "Oh, yes, we've been friends for years. I live in Savannah. In fact, I gave him a lot of the background on Savannah that he used in his book."

"That's wonderful," she said. "But I think I could have done without the part about the black drag queen. That was a little much. After reading the book I have one big question to ask, and I bet you know the answer." She paused in the hot late morning air. "That is, if you'll come clean with the truth."

"What do you want to know?" Lula asked, watching the ambulance disappear around a corner carrying this world famous author whose life now appeared in great danger. Lula then looked again at the woman who was sweating just like Berendt had done before his stroke. "What was your question?"

The woman seemed to have lost her nerve and didn't want to ask it after all. Finally she blurted out, "Is John Berendt gay?"

*****

Sitting in front of the Blues in the Night club, in a battered old car borrowed from Matt Daniels, Tango checked her appearance in the rear-view mirror. She'd never looked more gorgeous. Marking time with her left high heel, she tapped a tune on the floor of the car. *Niggah gal, you're gonna get all my cash tonight.*

She wondered if Jason would be on time for their rendezvous. Her strappy red shoes were those fuck-me kind that Joan Crawford used to wear in 1945. Tango wore a tight swingy dress in flaming scarlet. Once she'd applied her lashes and lipstick, she'd put on the dress which seemed to lift her silicone breasts like a bra.

Tango had always looked to movie goddesses for inspiration. She might be wearing Crawford fuck-me shoes, but she'd chosen the Rita Hayworth look for her wig, letting a wave fall just across the eye on the left side. Was that really Rita Hayworth or the 40s screen goddess, Veronica Lake?

She knew if she'd let her own natural hair grow, instead of keeping it closely cropped, that she'd also have beautiful hair and didn't need the damn red wig. She credited her white daddy's genes for her beautiful straight hair as her own mama had nothing but peppercorns on her head.

She still dreamed of meeting her daddy, and when she didn't have anything else to do she wrote to everybody in the phone book in a little town called Hollywood, South Carolina. Her mama hadn't told her the name of her daddy. But she'd discovered an old letter buried in her mama's possessions when she died. It was from a Duke Edwards with an address of Hollywood, South Carolina. After a little detective work, she'd learned that he was no longer at that address or even in that town.

Tango had sent for a phone directory of Hollywood, and she was writing everybody in town to see if they knew of a Duke Edwards or what had become of him. She had already worked herself through the Hs. So far, she'd received only three letters, two from a family named Edwards. Each letter writer had assured her that Duke was not part of their family. Both had settled in Hollywood apparently long after Duke had left town.

In spite of her disappointment at the mail, or lack of it, Tango had not given up. She figured that a man as charismatic as Duke Edwards must surely have left an impression on somebody.

Apparently he was quite a womanizer, with a penchant for black girls. Surely there must be some woman in town who remembered him and knew what had happened to him. She planned to keep on writing those desperate letters.

Thoughts of Duke disappeared suddenly when she spotted Jason heading toward the club. He was wearing a pair of blue jeans, far too baggy for her taste, and a white T-shirt that showed off the muscles of his finely sculpted chest. In the bright light of day, he looked like the golden boy of her dreams. He searched the front entrance of the club and started to head to the door until she called out to him.

"Your mama's over here." She signaled him to get in. "Let's go for a spin."

In the front seat with her, he took his marblelike arm and gave her a squeeze. Even getting into the car Jason moved his body with precision and perfection. Just over six feet, blond, blue-eyed, and muscled, Jason was her dream of a man. And unless he'd stuffed that bikini that day at Tybee, he was all man. Maybe enough for three men all in one ample package.

"I sure loved that tango dancing," he said as she drove toward the outskirts of Savannah, having no particular destination in mind. "That was hot, hot, and hotter."

"I'm glad you liked it. I love dancing the tango. Learned it from a former partner of mine. I took to it like a duck to water."

"That boy—that Danny Hansford. He looks like me a few years ago. Is he your boyfriend?"

"You might say that. He's very jealous so let's keep our little thing a secret."

"Honey, as I'm sure you'll find out, little thing is not the word you'd use for me." He was breathing sexily.

"Those are the truest words ever spoken by a white man." She appraised him appreciatively. "I guess you're not opposed to cheating on your wife?" she asked.

"Lula and I have an open relationship. I don't ask her where she's been, and she doesn't ask what I'm up to."

"I like that in a marriage. Personally, I don't plan to get married. I like to play the field. Imagine me being married and faithful to my husband. Then a blond God like you walks into the club. Out the door go those marriage vows."

"Let's face it," he said, moving closer to her in the seat. "You and I were instantly attracted to each other. You're one pretty girl."

"I see you don't mind crossing the color line."

"I'm not prejudiced if that's what you mean. I've never gone out with a real black person. More coffee colored like you. In fact, you don't look like black at all. You could pass for Puerto Rican."

"Thank you. Like Michael Jackson I never wanted to be born black. I've always thought of myself as white. I don't date black boys."

"Frankly, I think it's bad to get hung up on one type. That sort of limits your chances in life."

"I can't help it." She looked down at the package of cigarettes in the seat between them. "Light me one of those things, sugar. You do smoke, don't you?"

"If there's a bad habit out there, I do it. I smoke, I drink, and I like to fuck."

She giggled. "I bet you're good at that."

"Not as much as you'd think. People often complain that I hurt them, make them bleed, shit like that."

"Tiger, you've met your match. I've never met a man yet I couldn't do the joy ride with."

"I'm looking forward to this, but it's not going to happen today."

She looked crestfallen and disappointed. "Why not, sugar?"

"Believe it or not, I'm a bit old-fashioned around women. I don't do anything on the first date except some heavy kissing. I like to know a woman a little bit before we get really intimate. It's better that way."

"I hope you don't wait too long, because my honeypot is itching for you."

"Maybe on the second date I can be had."

"Let's make that second date tomorrow afternoon. Same time."

"It's a deal."

She pulled the car into the parking lot of The Grits Cafe. "I don't know about you but I'm starved. Haven't had any food since yesterday afternoon."

"I could sure use some ham and grits. Lula starves me to death. She can't cook worth a damn. She's burned every pot in the house."

Over ham and grits, Tango cast a steely eye on this beautiful but somewhat innocent golden boy in front of her. "In the club you seemed to really appreciate beautiful women like this gorgeous pussy before you. I've seen your wife. She's very charming, I'm sure, and I hear a great writer. But..." She hesitated.

"You mean she's not pretty." Jason leaned back, licking the butter from his lips. "I know that. I didn't marry Lula for her beauty. I admire her talent. But more than that she's a kindred spirit. I always wanted to have a tomboy sister more than I wanted a wife. Lula seemed to understand me. I've been condemned by about everybody who knows me. It seems I get into a lot of trouble. But Lula is always forgiving. She knows how flawed I am but she overlooks that. I like that in a woman."

Tango toyed with a piece of salt ham, deciding not to eat it after all. For the first time all afternoon she didn't know what to say to Jason. She wanted to say many things to him, share many secrets with him, but right now she didn't dare. There was one important issue between them. She didn't know if Jason understood that she was really a man. Surely he would find out sooner than later. Maybe someone at the club had already told him. After all, Savannah was but a small village and people gossiped. She didn't know how to approach the subject. She sipped her coffee and eyed Jason suspiciously. "So, you're a devotee of beautiful women."

"I like beautiful people, at least as bed partners. When it comes to friends, I don't much care what they look like."

"Or wives."

A slight resentment crossed his brow. "I already explained about Lula."

"I didn't mean anything by that. I'm sorry."

"It's okay." He resumed eating his grits.

"I noticed you said you liked beautiful people—not just beautiful women."

"I like beautiful men too. They don't have to look just like me. They can be dark haired, short, or tall. It doesn't matter to me."

"Are you bisexual?"

"I don't believe that sexual attraction should be limited. My gut feeling is that if you meet someone and you're attracted to them, it doesn't matter what sex they are."

She sighed with relief. At last that was out in the open. Even if Jason found out she was a man, he wouldn't panic the way that guy had done in Atlanta. "Let's drive down to San Simon," she said, signaling the waitress for the check. "Maybe go for a walk on the beach."

"I'd like that."

In the car with Jason again, she drove for a long while in silence, letting the breezes from the water blow into the car. "I think I'm falling in love with you."

He didn't say anything at first. Finally, he spoke in a low, husky voice. "I know that."

Impulsively she swung off the main highway and turned down a little secondary road that seemed to lead to nowhere. After a mile she braked Matt's car in the lot of an abandoned filling station that the main highway had passed by.

The moment she parked the car, she was in Jason's arms, kissing and fondling him. When she kissed him, he probed her mouth with the most delicious tongue she'd ever known. She wanted to kiss and suck every inch of his body, savoring the smell and taste of this delectable man. She reached between his legs, fondling his rapidly expanding cock. "My God, you're fabulous. I can't believe the size of that thing." She resumed kissing him with more fever than before. I've got to have it. Let me sit on it." She fumbled for the zipper of his jeans.

Suddenly, he got out of the car walking rapidly toward the woods.

Adjusting her dress, she followed him, nearly tripping on the gravel in her too high heels. "What's the matter, sugar? We were going fast and furious there."

"Too fast and furious for me," he said, turning around, his cock seeming to want to burst forth from his jeans. "I told you I want to slow this down a bit. I'm used to one-night stands. That's all I've ever had since I've been married to Lula. With you, I sense it could be so much more. I want to take you to bed. Maybe tomorrow afternoon. But what I'm afraid is I won't want to go back to Lula once I've been intimate with you."

"That's the most flattering turn-down I've ever got," she said, moving close to him and gently kissing his sweet red lips. "Mother fucker, I like the taste of you."

"Will you do it my way?" he asked, backing away from her.

She stood letting the breezes gently blow her wig. In the distance an orange and silver U-Haul approached, whizzing past. She couldn't see who was driving. On both sides of the highway, pines made a shaggy curtain impossible to see beyond or into. "Right this very moment," she said, "I want to get into that car with you and drive all the way south to Florida and never return to Savannah and our lives there."

"That's a mighty tempting offer," he said. "But I think we're going to get in that car and head back up the road to Savannah. That's where we belong right now. Tomorrow afternoon we'll know more about where we're going."

"You're right, sugar. I got a little carried away back there in the car. But you're the type of guy a red-blooded all-female kind of Niggah like me can get really carried away with."

"I'm just a man. It's just flesh."

"What a beautiful package it is."

"C'mon," he said. "It's getting late. Let's hit the road."

She moved closer to him and reached to taste his sweet red lips again. He descended on her, tongue and all. "You're my kind of woman," he whispered in her ear as he broke his grip on her lips.

Back at the car, he turned to her to give her a final kiss before getting in. "When I was growing up, women like you were forbidden fruit."

Opening the door and sliding in behind the wheel, she turned to him as he got in on the passenger side. "I'm more forbidden and more fruit than you know." She turned on the ignition, spun around, and zoomed toward Savannah, carrying that town's most desirable hunk of male flesh.

*****

It was already afternoon, and Lavender Morgan still hadn't risen from her bed of passion. Norma had long ago brought her her morning coffee, but Lavender still remained in bed, not wanting to leave the intoxicating aroma of the sheets where Danny Hansford had lain with her all night.

As she reached to run her fingers over his smooth ivory skin, he'd bolted toward the bathroom. "That is one bubble-butt," she'd said to herself. His back muscles were clearly defined as in a Grecian statue, and he had long legs that looked almost sculpted. She'd lain with men all over the world, often misshapen, but she'd never known a man, except one, who matched the physical perfection of Danny. He was so easy to fall in love with.

Last night Danny had stripped in her bathroom and had emerged into her chamber fully nude. To disguise her age, the lights in her bedroom were soft and forgiving. She always preferred pink lights when seducing a man. She felt that pink, almost lavender, light, made her look more alluring.

His youthful body had thrilled her. He was an adorable blond angel. The bulging of his biceps and his boyish grin had stirred a lust within her she hadn't known in years. He'd looked just like Karl did when he'd first pulled off his clothes in her bed-sitter in London during World War II.

There had been a hint of hunger hidden deep in Danny's green eyes, and he'd made her feel desirable again after all these years. A raw sexual scent hung in the air. He'd moved his supple body closer to her, knowing the mesmerizing effect it must have on her. He'd been like a panther on a jungle prowl.

As he'd stood over her bed, a salacious smile had crossed his face. Up close to her she'd made out the size of his cock for the first time. It had been astonishing, at least three times the size of JFK's. It was long, thick, and uncut. "The boy also has balls," she'd said to herself. Even if some of the men she'd known in her past were well hung, their testicles had often been small. She'd wanted both Danny's cock and testicles to be large, and Danny hadn't disappointed her. She'd planned to spend the night licking and devouring this young man. For all she knew, Danny Hansford might well be the last man she'd ever know in a long parade that had topped the two-thousand mark by the 1980s. After that, the seductions had dwindled into nothingness.

Danny had made her feel young and beautiful again. For one brief moment she'd erased the other two-thousand men in her life and had imagined that Danny was Karl come back again to deflower her, to take her virginity and make her the woman she was destined to be.

When Danny had turned out the light, she'd been grateful. Even in the soft, forgiving glow of lavender spots, she'd preferred the darkness considering what she had had planned for him.

In that darkness, he'd found her, bringing his red lips to her and kissing her. As his tongue had entered her devouring mouth, it was warm and wet. She'd sucked on it voraciously as if by doing so she was draining the very youth from this boy and injecting that vitality into her own tired veins. He'd flicked his tongue along the backs of her teeth, as his hands had traveled lower to caress and twist the nipples of her ample breasts.

Even though only a teenager, Danny had moved over her body with a sexual skill far beyond his years. She'd known the moment he'd entered her bed that she was not the first woman he'd seduced. He had a technique far greater than many men she'd known who had been bedding women for forty years.

Suddenly, he'd moved from on top of her and had lain in the soft bed on his back. That had been her signal to begin the feast of the night. She'd wanted to taste, suck, lick, and savor every inch of this delectable body, and that's what she'd done. She'd begun at his ears, probing with her tongue as deep into their cavities as she could. There had been no part of his throat that she hadn't licked and caressed before going on to enjoy the aromatic taste of his armpits. He'd been dancing the tango that night and had sweated profusely. Licking his armpits and swallowing all the flavor she could scoop up there, she'd been delighted to find that he hadn't showered. She hadn't wanted to taste bar soap but the full flavor of this young sex God.

There was no part of him she didn't savor, especially the succulent nipples on his hairless chest. If she'd ever had a son, and hadn't had all her children aborted, she would have wanted that son to be just like Danny. Even as she'd licked him and tongued every inch of his chest and arms, she'd imagined what it would have been like, washing and bathing her baby boy. She'd imagined that she would have been an uninhibited mother, kissing her baby's penis as she dried it, watching it grow bigger and bigger every day.

Avoiding his cock, which was rock hard now and standing up straight in the air when she'd felt and measured every inch of it, she'd descended with her tongue on his legs. Karl had liked her to lick and suck his tasty long legs before he demanded that she suck and nibble every one of his toes. Danny's moans had told her what she'd wanted to hear. He'd obviously liked this particular form of love-making.

Without being told, he'd known what to do next. He'd turned over presenting the target she'd wanted to taste before enjoying the main offering. She'd worked her tongue toward his tight rosebud, pulling his cheeks apart with her hands to gain greater access to this hidden delight. His sphincter had loosened under the voracious probing of her devouring tongue. She'd inserted herself as deeply into him as she could, causing him to moan and squirm. Her nose had squashed against his tender flesh, and she'd eaten him out. He'd had the most delicious flavor she'd ever known. Even this afternoon, she couldn't remember how long she'd remained buried in this most secret part of a man. It had formed a memory in her mind that she'd treasure forever.

Finally, when he'd been able to take it no longer, he'd pulled her hair, demanding that she service him from the front. She'd licked up and down his cock, momentarily deserting the tasty treat to lick his savory nuts. She'd loved the strong taste of him and the sweat of his balls. It was a nectar to her. She'd then wrapped her fingers around the thick base of his cock and flicked her tongue across the sensitive rim of the crown, teasing him.

But he'd had enough of her fun and games and had demanded his release by taking her by the hair of her head and forcing her all the way down on his cock until her lips had touched his blond pubic hairs that were amazingly like Karl's. He'd had great staying power in spite of his young age, and she'd known that he was determined that she lick, suck, and taste him until she'd had her fill. But nature's demands had taken over at one point. Suddenly, without warning, he'd erupted inside her mouth.

She'd pulled back slightly to be able to taste and enjoy the flavor of him. His cum had been the sweetest she'd ever known. At first she hadn't dared swallow it, wanting to rub the flavor around in her mouth to enjoy it. Only the crown of his cock was in her mouth, and she'd kept her lips glued to him to taste any final drops that might emerge from his body. As she'd enjoyed the taste, it reminded her of Karl's cum. She'd always felt that Karl's cum had a slightly almond taste to it. So did Danny's. Perhaps Danny was Karl come back to love her after all.

As she'd swirled the cum around in her mouth, she'd recalled the taste of the semen of so many other men. JFK's always had a slightly lemony flavor, not really to her liking, and Ed Murrow's vaguely tasted of nicotine. Aly Khan had the flavor of cognac, and Frank Sinatra had no flavor at all but was of an unusual consistency like unflavored yogurt.

Immediately after his release Danny had fallen asleep. At three o'clock he'd descended on her to her great joy. This time there had been no subtlety or foreplay. He'd kicked her legs apart to give him greater access, and she'd been wide and eager for the invasion. He'd charged forward, plunging deep within her. She'd shrieked in joy, feeling he was exploring a depth within her never reached by another man except Karl. His strokes had been quick, almost cruel, ripping and tearing at her flesh. But she'd welcomed this young sexual warrior in the middle of the night, wishing that so many other men had felt like this. Only Karl had fucked her like this. Her mouth had gaped open in a slight pain followed by the most exquisite pleasure. She could feel Danny's soft blond pubic hair rubbing against her, and it had given her such a thrill of delight. She'd reached for his bubble-butt, pulling him into her, wanting to make sure that she got every thick, pulsating inch of this athlete.

Before his finale, he'd lifted her right leg up in the air, granting him more access to his target. He'd reamed and twisted inside her with the hardest, biggest dick she'd known since Karl died. Her mouth had clenched hard in a grimace of agony and pleasure as he'd taken her over the top before collapsing on her, not withdrawing right away. In the final moment, he'd descended on her neck, biting it hard. She didn't care if he made her black and blue. She'd wear the assault as a badge of honor and not attempt to cover up the mark with a scarf.

Finally, he'd fallen off of her. He grabbed her hair again. "Lick me clean," he'd ordered before drifting off into sleep again.

Now as Danny stood before her, wearing only the skimpiest of briefs, she reached into the drawer of her night table and removed five one-hundred bills. She inserted those bills into his briefs, fondling his cock once more, amazed at its size and thickness even though soft.

"I've already called the motorcycle place," he said. "They've got what we want in stock. What say I come back at four and we go over there?"

She sat up in bed, trying to look as alluring as possible. "You promised to take me for a spin."

He looked down at her. "Don't you know by now that I'm a man who lives up to his promise?"

"With all my heart, I know that."

He bent over and kissed her long, hard, and passionately, inserting his tongue. Then suddenly he'd disappeared, leaving the room almost without her noticing he was gone.

She was too happy to talk to those lawyers in New York. She didn't want to hear about a dwindling money supply. Regardless of what those lawyers said, she knew she had plenty of money, at least enough to get her through life in the grand style she demanded. She was determined to give Danny anything he wanted. Jim Williams, at least according to *that* book, had been very cheap with the real Danny Hansford, not even giving him a twenty-dollar bill when the hustler wanted one. She was determined not to make such a big mistake with the second Danny Hansford.

The motorcycle would be the first of many gifts. By this time next week, she fully expected that Danny would have moved out of his place with Tango and would be living here with her, while Norma waited on him.

Lavender sat up in bed. She didn't have much time, and she wanted to make herself especially alluring this afternoon for her motorcycle ride. Since she didn't know what to wear, she would have to call Gin Tucker. This effeminate little man was certainly no Hell's Angel, but she remembered once that he told her that Marlon Brando, while visiting the summer cottage of Tennessee Williams on Cape Cod, had invited Gin to go for a motorcycle ride. Gin also claimed that they'd later stopped by a sand dune where he'd gone down on Marlon. "Frankly, I think he should be known as *Miss* Brando instead of Mr. Brando. There wasn't enough there to mess up my mouth with."

Lavender wasn't even certain that Gin had ever met Marlon Brando, but it made a good story nonetheless.

All she knew this morning was that regardless of what she wore on that bike ride, the clothes had to be lavender in color.

There was another more personal thing she had to ask Gin. Except for liquor, she'd never used drugs in her life. She'd never even snorted coke when it was freely available at all the chic New York society parties she'd attended, or the gathering of the Hollywood greats in Los Angeles in the 70s. But she was smart enough to know that if she were going to retain the love and affection of Danny Hansford, she'd have to get Gin to pick up a supply of cocaine and pot. To her, heroin was a vicious drug and she wouldn't allow it in her house. But she didn't see anything wrong with a little pot or some coke to snort. Danny would like that.

Knowing he could always find a constant supply of drugs, she fully expected he'd come over more often and be tempted to linger. She just hoped the drugs wouldn't have a debilitating effect on his sexual drive, as she heard they so often did. The idea of a diminished Danny Hansford didn't excite her at all. In the days and weeks ahead, she was going to demand more and more sex from the boy.

He was the true streak of sex, and she planned to enjoy him to the fullest.

\*\*\*\*\*

In Lavender's living room, Danny stood for minute after minute, staring at the Picasso painting, *Mother and Child.* Until last night he'd never heard of Picasso, but Lavender had assured him Picasso was the most famous artist in the world. She'd also informed him that this painting was valued at twenty-five million dollars.

"How could any piece of shit like this be worth that much money?" Danny asked himself out loud. He wasn't even an artist and didn't even know how to draw, but he was certain he could do a better job than Picasso. Right then and there he decided that Picasso was gay. He felt all artists were gay. He'd met two artists in his life—both faggots, both men who had wanted to paint him in the nude. He bet if he ever met Picasso he would find out that he was just like Gin Tucker. Picasso would probably want Danny to pose nude too. He just knew that.

Suddenly he became aware of a presence in the parlor. He spun around to stare into the stern face of a black mama. She looked like Hattie McDaniel in *Gone With the Wind.*

"What are you staring at, white boy?" she asked.

"Who in the hell are you?" he asked.

"I'm Norma Dixie, the one who brought you coffee this morning. I'm the domestic engineer for Miss Morgan, and I say you're looking at that painting a little too long for comfort. You see, I'm also head of security around here."

"If you're so God damn smart, black bitch, you saw whose bed I was in this morning when you brought that awful coffee. You don't even know how to make coffee the way I like it. I'm going to show you one time—and that's it. You'll learn to make coffee around this house like I like it, or you're out the door."

"What gives a pasty-faced white fart like you the gall to start ordering me around? And watch who you're calling black bitch. You wouldn't be the first white boy I've beaten the shit out of!"

"Don't start something with me, you broken down old whore." He cast her a defiant smirk. "Lavender has told me plenty about you."

"Don't call me a whore. You're the last person that should be making that charge. It's like the pot calling the kettle black. You should be ashamed of yourself for taking advantage of a senile lady old enough to be your great-grandmother."

"I'm not taking advantage of nobody. When Danny Hansford gets paid, he delivers the goods. I've got something hanging between my legs that drives both women and men crazy. And once they get a taste of it, they come back for seconds."

"You think you're so special, don't you? To me, you're nothing but special shit."

He moved menacingly toward her but she stood her ground. "I'm telling Lavender how you talk to me. If you want to keep this maid's job, you're going to learn some respect when I come in the door. Just for treating me like you just did, I'm going to smear my shit all over the toilet bowl and yell for you to come and clean it up."

"You little bastard!"

"I'm not little, fat mama. I'm big. I'm known as the biggest stud in town."

Norma glared at him. "You should not get Miss Morgan's hormones rising. Old women like that should let those sleeping dogs lay where you found them. You shouldn't go stirring up unnatural lusts in the poor old thing. When I saw the two of you in bed this morning, I thought it was the most disgusting sight I'd ever seen, and I've seen some pretty awful things in my day."

"That's tough shit. You're going to be seeing a lot more of me in the weeks ahead. In fact, I'm considering moving in tonight."

"There's no place in this house for a male whore like you."

"Don't you think that's for Lavender to say?"

"Miss Morgan don't know her own mind. Any woman who would go to bed with a teenage boy like you don't know her own mind."

He groped himself. "Lavender has had a sample of this, and she can't get enough of it. It was all I could do to escape her bed this morning. Like I didn't give her enough last night, she wanted more of what I've got this morning."

"You seem mighty proud of yourself."

"I got a lot to be proud of."

"Honey, I've seen guys in Harlem that would make you look like Princess Tiny Meat."

"Cut the shit! I'm known for having the biggest dick in Savannah. Just ask anybody."

"The biggest dick in Savannah is attached to one Jason McReeves."

"Who in the hell is that? Jason? Sounds like a faggot."

"He's all man. You can trust me on that. Every time he goes to bed with his wife and rams that pussy stretcher of his into her, I have to treat her with my special salve. He's so big he makes her bleed. Have you made any woman bleed lately with that little sausage of yours? Hell, in my heyday in Harlem I wouldn't go to bed with no man who had less than fourteen inches."

"You're lying, bitch. You're just trying to put me down."

"Bullshit. I have a son in Atlanta. His name's Domino. His cock, or so his girl friends tell me, is about twice the size of yours. Of course, I'm guessing but those tight pants of yours don't leave much for the imagination. My son even has to have special jeans made for him with extra room for his goodies."

"Like hell, you say. If I ever meet up with this son of yours, I'd win the contest. We'd stage it at the Tool Box and let the faggots put up their money. May the best man win."

"I'm out of here. I got more things on my mind and more things to do today than talk dirty with some white boy."

"Do you know how to cook?"

"What are you talking about? I'm the best cook in Savannah. I was the personal high-class chef for Miss Mae West of Hollywood."

"Who was that?"

"Do you mean to tell me you've never heard of Mae West? She was the biggest star of all time. She saved Paramount from bankruptcy."

"She must have been long before my time because I never heard of her. The only oldtime stars I know were the ones in *Gone With the*

*Wind.* Clark Gable as Rhett Butler and Janet Leigh as Scarlett. I take that back. I did see a movie on TV. It was *Psycho* and starred Janet Leigh. It's the only black and white film I ever saw. Janet Leigh looked different in *Psycho* than she did as Miss Scarlett."

"So much for your movie knowledge. You don't even know the names of the stars in movies you see. No wonder you've never heard of Mae West."

"I know plenty, bitch. I know who Clint Eastwood is."

"Big fucking deal. You know who Clint Eastwood is. You should go on *Jeopardy.*"

"Before you got off on all this Hollywood kick, I asked you if you know how to cook."

"I'm celebrated for my recipes."

"Good, then hustle your fat black ass off to the kitchen and rustle me up some pancakes. When I get to the kitchen, I want you to be wearing a red bandanna too. I don't want no nigger hair to get into the pancake mix."

"White boy, until Miss Morgan comes to her senses and kicks you out of this house, I've got to take your shit. Just remember this, I'll be the one packing your bags and kicking you out the front door. You haven't been kicked until I've plowed my shoe into your white ass."

"Until that great day comes, you'll do as I say. Danny Hansford can't be replaced because I'm unique. I'm practically the toast of Savannah. Old, fat black maids like you can be replaced in an hour. Savannah is full of 'em."

"I'll have you know I was voted Miss Harlem of 1956."

"Do you know how long ago 1956 was? The only thing I know about the 50s was what I learned watching Michael J. Fox in this movie, *Back to the Future.* From what I saw, I wouldn't have liked the 50s at all."

"No wonder. A hustler like you would have ended up in jail, no doubt."

"I've got to go buy a motorcycle. Get my breakfast and be quick about it."

Without saying another word, Norma in a huff turned and waddled out of the room.

He turned his eyes to that Picasso again. There were eight other paintings in the parlor, not just the Picasso. He bet they were valuable too. Not as valuable as the Picasso, but worth millions as well. He didn't know one of these modern paintings from the other. They all looked like the work of grade school children. Several depicted women but the artists got their shapes all out of line. Any artist who drew women like this must be the same as that faggot Picasso. They couldn't even draw, yet the world appraised their paintings at millions. He just knew the Picasso was the most valuable. When a john like Lavender was trying to impress him, she would obviously call attention to the most valuable painting. She pointed out only the Picasso, not the others.

He surveyed the living room. Here he was standing in an art gallery—well, practically—with paintings worth millions of dollars. There was no security guard except a fat black mama. Someone could break into Lavender's house one night and make off with all these paintings. Every one of them. He bet some art gallery up in New York would pay millions to acquire works like these. If the Picasso were worth twenty-five million, then maybe the other paintings were also worth a combined twenty-five million. That was a total of fifty-million dollars. That was more money than he could ever think of spending in one lifetime, much less a lifetime as short as his.

He wasn't even sure what he would buy for fifty-million dollars. The most expensive thing he'd ever wanted in his life was this car he'd read about. It had been bought by some Saudi sheik for sixty-five thousand dollars. Even if he bought the car, he'd still have plenty of money left over once the sixty-five thousand had been deducted from the fifty million.

"Come on in," Norma said, reappearing at the door. "I've mixed up a pancake batter for you. I've also made you some real coffee, and don't tell me you don't like it. Also would you like me to put some bananas and rum into that pancake mix?"

"That sounds like you're after my heart." He appraised her with a steely look, deciding it was better to befriend her than make her an enemy. He might need her cooperation in the weeks ahead.

"C'mon and get it, then."

Before she could head back to the kitchen again, he called out to her. "I've been thinking. I could well imagine you were Miss Harlem of 1956."

For the first time this afternoon, she smiled and beamed at him. "You could?"

"Your tits must have been fantastic. I mean, they're great now and everything. But back then you must have been a five-alarm fire."

"I was hot stuff. All the men were after me. Harry Belafonte fell in love with me. Chased me all over Harlem. Louis Armstrong was after me. A lot of white men wanted me too, even a former mayor of New York. But I never went that route. I think birds of a feather should flock together."

"I don't buy into that. I don't see color when I look at somebody."

"I've heard about you and that boy, Tango."

"Tango is a girl. Don't you ever let her hear you call her a boy. She'd claw you blind."

"Well, I guess if anybody in Savannah knows the true sex of Tango, it's Danny Hansford." She wasn't as hostile now, as she turned and waddled toward the kitchen, trailed by him.

"Over pancakes," she said, calling over her shoulder, "maybe you'll tell me why you're taking that dead hustler's name, Danny Hansford. Why don't you go by your own name and be your own man—not follow in someone else's shoes? Especially someone who was a piece of white trash who ended up shot."

"But Danny Hansford put Savannah on the map. Before he lived and died and before that book came out, no one in the world had ever heard of Savannah. He made the city."

In the kitchen she reached for the rum bottle. "I suppose you think we should go and erect a memorial to him, or some such shit."

Seated at the table, he accepted a cup of freshly brewed coffee from her. Actually he'd liked her coffee when served in Lavender's bedroom. It was, in fact, the best cup of coffee he'd ever had in his life. His mama back in Clinton always used instant. He reached for the bowl of sugar, measuring a total of four tablespoons into his coffee.

"You sure do like it sweet, sugar," she said.

"Tell me," he said, watching her mash up a banana for his pancakes, "does this Mae West still live in Savannah? Maybe you'll introduce me to her sometime."

"If I'd introduce you, it'd be in the graveyard. Mae West is dead. But if you're going to live here with Miss Morgan, I'll show you some of Mae's films."

"Was she a great actress?"

"The greatest of them all. Meryl Streep, Emma Thompson, and all those other white bitches can't act at all. Mae would have shown them how to do it. I was an actress myself. In fact, I tried to get Clint Eastwood to cast me in the movie. I could have played the voodoo queen."

Danny wanted to reveal two things to her but decided against it. First, he wanted to tell her he too tried to get cast as the hustler in the film. He also wanted to tell her about his involvement with Erzulie, the local voodoo queen of Savannah. But he felt he'd better keep these confidences to himself for the moment. Both revealed failure, and that was not the image he was trying to convey.

"Lavender's buying me a motorcycle this afternoon. I'm taking her for a spin."

Flipping her pancakes, Norma almost missed her beat. "Did I hear that right? You're getting Miss Morgan on a motorcycle? At her age?"

"You heard right. When Lavender Morgan met Danny Hansford, she just moved into the fast lane."

"That's one old lady who'd better look out and see that some big diesel truck ain't also barreling down that same lane. You and Miss Morgan might end up crushed flatter than this pancake here."

"But what fun we will have had." He ate his breakfast in silence as Norma fussed over him. The day was his but he faced a lot of problems. What was he going to do about Tango? How was he going to let her know there had been a slight change in his living arrangement?

"What the hell," he said loud enough for Norma to hear but mainly to himself. Scarlett O'Hara in *Gone With the Wind* knew how to postpone things like that until tomorrow. So could he.

The five-hundred dollars felt good in his jeans. In fact, the one-hundred dollar bills seemed to be burning a hole in his pocket until he could spend it. The motorcycle would feel even better under his ass.

And the millions from those paintings would provide a spectacular finish to a life that had been disappointing up to now.

*****

Looking her most glamorous best, Tipper showed up at Frank Gilmore's office at the Shocking Pink nightclub exactly at ten o'clock, although she preferred a later appointment. Before going into his office, she went into the nightclub's women's room and double-checked her make-up. She'd had a troubled night's sleep and didn't think she looked her best. Except for a brief time in her 20s, she'd never looked really good and had to artfully conceal her imperfections with makeup. She was also prematurely wrinkled which she blamed on too much time in the sun.

Imitating Lavender, she'd worn her most flamboyant suit, itself a kind of shocking pink in honor of the nightclub's name. In fact, she was going to suggest to Frank that she appear in shocking pink every night as a gimmick. Perhaps he'd advance the money so that she could have two or three gowns made.

She was especially nervous this morning, because Larry had called at eight thirty, just as she was stepping from her bath. He was the man who handled her account at the bank. Lately she'd given him trouble instead of business. Larry had not only demanded the last of the mortgage payments, but had sadly informed her that her last three checks had bounced.

Three merchants in town, including her local grocery store, claimed they were going to take her to small claims court. She felt desperate this morning, and was hoping that Frank would cover the checks for her that bounced. She could warn him that if he didn't, news of this would get in the papers and it might hurt business at his club, if the patrons knew that his star entertainer bounced checks.

She knew this was not a good way to start off a relationship with a new club owner, but she also knew that Frank had money. He not only owned this club but he also ran three successful restaurants in Savannah. His family, or so she was told, owned a hotel on Myrtle Beach, the redneck Riviera, that was a "cash cow." Frank always drove around town in expensive cars with a young companion.

Checking her appearance for one final time, she adjusted her makeup and headed for Frank's office. She noticed that during the day the air conditioning was turned off. This was an especially hot morning in Savannah, and she feared her make-up would run.

MIDNIGHT IN SAVANNAH / 127

In the office, stacked with magazines and unopened mail, she spotted a couple who looked exactly like Peter, Paul, and Mary from the 60s. The tall girl's blond hair was just as Mary used to wear it when she was mouthing the words of "I've got a hammer."

At first Tipper felt it necessary to introduce herself but decided against it. The group looked at her as if she were a threat. Until the contract was signed, she realized she had no firm deal with Frank. Maybe he was considering these Peter, Paul, and Mary clones as a possible replacement for Emma until the songstress returned.

Frank's secretary was a young man who looked like Johnny Ray, that crying singer of the fifties. She suspected that this man didn't even know who Johnny Ray was. He also had Johnny Ray's nervous mannerisms, and seemed so intense he looked as if he might explode at any minute.

"I'm Tipper Zelda," she said, introducing herself. She'd deliberately lowered her voice because she didn't want the clones to know who she was. Glancing over at her, they were staring intently back at her, but said nothing.

"Frank's not here," the young man said. "I'm Dale Evans. I'm his secretary."

"Dale Evans?" Tipper laughed, trying to break the tension in the air. "You mean Dale Evans as in the wife of the late Roy Rogers. Queen of the Cowgirls?"

"I'm glad you find that amusing." Dale looked a bit bitter. "I've been the butt of jokes all my life. At school they used to call me the Queenie Cowgirl. I didn't like that at all."

"I'm sorry. Of course, I know Dale is also a man's name. There used to be a movie star in the Fifties called Dale Robertson. Real handsome guy. I met him one night at a party in Hollywood. Fell for him at once. But I think he preferred the Sandra Dee type to me."

"How Fifties!" Dale said with a bit of a smirk. "If you come to work for Frank, you'll find I'm not like Dale Evans at all. She's a vicious homophobe just like her squinty-eyed cowboy husband was. They were the only celebrities who came out and defended Anita Bryant when she attacked gays back in 1977 in Miami."

"My," Tipper said, feeling awkward. "You certainly know your gay history. Where were you in 1977?"

"I was five years old, but I read all about what happened in this magazine called *Stonewall*. I always tell Frank that if he ever hires a homophobe singer here, even for a temporary engagement, I'm out of here. You're not a homophobe, are you?"

"Not at all. When I had some money, I always contributed to gay causes. Black causes too."

"That's good," Dale said, "because Frank won't hire phobes. There's enough hatred in the world without giving our money to them. They've got most of it anyway. They use it to oppress us the way that God damn neo-Nazi senator, J. Hue Dornan, does. I hear he's coming to Savannah to make a speech. He's the guy who sponsored that law outlawing same-sex marriages. Of course, he's deep into his fourth divorce."

"I read about that, and I'm sorry. I believe that anybody can marry anybody he wants to."

"I'm glad to hear that. Frank and I certainly believe that. Unfortunately, Frank's family doesn't agree. They won't even let me visit their place in Myrtle Beach. I talked to Frank's mother the other night. She told me that it's all right for faggots to live in Savannah, although she thinks all of them should be rounded up and shipped to Key West. She doesn't want a one of them remaining in the State of Georgia. She definitely doesn't want me to come to Myrtle Beach. She said she's talked to the mayor there. They want to keep Myrtle Beach faggot free. Not like Atlanta. Everybody's gone gay in Atlanta."

"I don't think you'd like Myrtle Beach. I've never been there but it doesn't sound like a place I'd like to visit. I'm not much into beach resorts."

Dale looked really disappointed. "I'm very sorry to hear that, and I hope you'll change your mind."

"What do you mean exactly?"

"Frank and I are going to open a gay bar with cabaret in Myrtle Beach. Just to defy the locals, his family, and the rednecks. A sort of in-your-face move on our part. If you go over here, we were thinking of hiring you to headline the opening show. It'll be a sensation. With you as our star, we'll get a lot of publicity."

"I see." She felt the oppressive heat of the office. She glanced over again at the clones. They were still staring intently, still taking in every word.

Dale also seemed aware of their eavesdropping presence for the first time. "Let's step inside Frank's office where we can talk more privately."

Mercifully Tipper discovered that Frank's office was air conditioned because she felt her make-up had already started to run. Inside the office, she took the chair Dale offered her in front of Frank's empty but cluttered desk.

"Considering that it's the opening of a club, I definitely would reconsider my position on Myrtle Beach," Tipper said. "Perhaps it's not as bad as I've heard."

"I'm glad you see it my way." He smiled at her, then went around and sat at Frank's desk, putting his feet up as if imitating Darryl Zanuck in the Thirties. There was an awkward silence in the room.

"Where's Frank?" she managed to ask.

He ignored her question. "I know you have a gay following. Of course, it's nothing compared to what Judy Garland had. Did you know her?"

"Quite well. She once spent a nervous few days at my place up north. She was on the verge of a breakdown."

"I also heard you were involved with Montgomery Clift. He was gay, wasn't he?"

"I've always made it a point never to discuss Monty's sexuality."

"I see. Still trying to keep him in the closet after all these years."

"It's not that," she stammered. Dale made her feel unglued.

"Do you really want to know where Frank is?"

"Of course, we had an appointment. I'm a star. I'm sure you've been around star entertainers before. You know stars don't like to be kept waiting."

"Don't be a smart ass with me. I'll tell you exactly where Frank is. He's working right now on your behalf. He's at the bank meeting with Larry. He's covering three checks of yours that bounced. One from the owner of a grocery store. Word travels fast in Savannah. The guy from the store called here claiming he was going to take you to court unless his money is taken from your first paycheck. While at the bank, Frank is also paying off your back mortgage payments, so they won't repossess your house. But you've got to be good for the next payment. I can't have Frank spending all his money on you when he's promised me a new winter wardrobe. He's going to take me to New York. I've never been there, and I want to look gorgeous. He's going to take me to all the fancy places."

"I'm very embarrassed you found out about my temporary financial difficulties. I'm planning to sell some things. I'll have money soon."

"That's great but in the meantime my darling man is putting up all our hard-earned cash for you. So you'll owe us a big favor. Are we willing to admit that?"

"I'm grateful."

"We'll see how grateful when Frank gets here."

"I don't understand. You're talking in riddles."

"You want me to spell it out."

"Spell what out?" she asked.

"After Frank finishes paying off your debts at the bank, he's going over to Blues in the Night—God, what a tacky club—and pay off Matt Daniels that three-thousand dollars you owe him. Matt is also threatening to attach your salary."

"The son of a bitch! After all I've done for him."

"As I said, don't you think you'll owe us a big favor after all this?"

"What do I have to do? Go to bed with both of you? Turn you straight?"

"That's disgusting. The idea of going to bed with a woman is the filthiest thing I've ever heard of. I hear it smells like rotten cheese."

"Do you mind if I smoke?" she asked.

"Go ahead."

She reached into her purse and pulled out a cigarette, lighting it.

When he saw her blowing smoke in the air, Dale said, "I hear you used to own Camel cigarettes."

"Something like that. My first husband was a tobacco baron."

"I'm glad we finally got around to the point. It's your first husband I want to talk about."

"I never mention him. Sorry."

"Today we're going to mention him. He was murdered, wasn't he?"

"He was killed. But I remember nothing. I've drawn a complete blank on the day he was shot. I think it was a suicide, but I really don't want to talk about it."

"I'm afraid you must. We're not only going to talk about your first husband, Taylor Zachary, but we're going to talk about your second husband, Derek McKee. He was murdered too. And your third husband, Richard Olken. Murdered also. And your fourth and final husband, Dan Luskin. Also murdered."

"No one has ever determined that they were murdered. It's true all of them died under mysterious circumstances. But hardly murder. At any rate, I was not involved in their deaths, despite lurid speculation to the contrary."

"I'm glad to hear that. Then you won't object to the way my Frank and I plan to bill your act?"

"Bill my act?"

"Frank is rushing to have your costume made. He ordered it the moment you agreed to fill in for Emma. It'll be ready at two o'clock this afternoon, and is it ever stunning. I've seen it. In fact, you might say I designed it."

"What kind of costume? I was thinking of appearing in some shocking pink night gowns. Very tasteful. Very elegant. Setting a high tone for the club, because I attract only the best people."

"Let's hope you attract people regardless of their social credentials. As long as they've got money."

"What is this costume?"

"It's called Black Widow fantasy. You'll come out dressed as the notorious Black Widow. Everything black. The only color will be a red spot. One spot of red symbolizing blood. The local newspaper has already provided us with pictures of your four husbands. I should say four late husbands. We want Gin Tucker to take a picture of you in the costume. You'll be at the center of the action with pictures of your four husbands surrounding you. They were all handsome, thank God, and they all died young. It'll be a show business sensation. All the locals will come. Out of curiosity if nothing else. All the tourists will want to see the notorious Black Widow spin her magic. I'm sure the papers will pick up on it. My God, faggots will even fly in from New York to catch the act. Could you imagine what a queen like Rex Reed might write about the show?"

Even though air conditioned, the office had become oppressive to her. She crushed out her cigarette on Frank's desk and fled toward the door.

"Come back," Dale called after her. "You owe us too much money to run out."

Out on the street she was breathing so heavily she felt she'd collapse. In the blinding heat she became disoriented. She wanted to go home but wasn't certain for a minute where that was.

"Monty!" she called out to no one in particular. Maybe he'd come like a guardian angel to save her. If only Phil Heather would get to town. Phil was Monty. She just knew that. Only Phil Heather could save her at this point.

*****

Not knowing where his new house was, Phil Heather dialed the phone number of the caretaker, his only link to his new living arrangement Jerry Wheeler, the producer of *Butterflies in Heat*, had given him. Phil didn't even know the name of the caretaker. The phone rang eight times, and Phil was about to give up and go have lunch before calling again. On the ninth ring a groggy Southern voice answered, "What the hell!"

"This is Phil Heather. I'm the writer Jerry Wheeler arranged to rent a house for. Are you the caretaker?"

"Just a minute here," the molasses voice said. "What is this caretaker shit?"

"I didn't mean to offend you."

"All you northern queens come down here and think the South still has slavery. I'm no fucking caretaker. You probably think I'm a nigger. You got that wrong. I'm the whitest man in Georgia. There's not one bit of nigger blood in me."

"Well, whoever you are, are you handling the arrangements for my house?"

"I might be and I might not be."

"Exactly what is that supposed to mean?"

"What is this? Some court of law? Are you the type of creep like Bill Clinton, saying it all depends on what you mean by is?"

"I'm not like Bill Clinton. We have different tastes in sexual partners."

"I'm glad to hear that. If there's one thing I can't stand, it's Clinton. I think he should be given the electric chair for what he did to Monica Lewinsky."

"Don't you view that as severe punishment?"

"Not at all. In fact, if he's not jailed for his high crimes and misdemeanors, I plan to take the train to Washington and shoot him. I'll go down in the history books. I'll be even more famous than Lee Harvey Oswald."

"I'm sure you will."

"Don't interrupt me. I ain't finished yet. You've got to come over to my place and take a look at my bedroom. I've plastered it with pictures of Linda Tripp."

"You mean Monica?" Phil said.

"Don't tell me what I mean. I mean Linda Tripp. She's the only good thing that came out of this whole mess. I think I'm in love with her. Know what?"

"What's that?" Phil asked not really interested and definitely convinced he was talking to a nut.

"This didn't come out in Starr's investigation but I know it's true." Bill Clinton titty fucked Monica Lewinsky. I just know it. Every night, I grow to believe more and more that he titty fucked her."

"About my house..."

"Would you shut up until I'm finished talking? You Yankees have the rudest manners."

"I'm not a Yankee. I'm from Darien. You know Darien. Right up the road."

There was a long pause. "I know Darien. Don't you ever mention Darien to me again. I was arrested there. This cop claimed I went to this playground where these little schoolgirls were playing and that I pulled out my dick and started jerking off in front of them."

"I don't know why he'd go and say a thing like that," Phil said, growing exasperated in the stifling Savannah heat.

"He said that because he was a faggot, and he took one look at me and wanted to suck my dick. He was just fantasizing about me jerking off. He wanted me to jerk off on his face so he could swallow my cum."

Phil began to think that if this man held the key to his new home, he'd never get in it. When Phil didn't say anything, the caretaker went on.

"Linda Tripp is one good-looking woman. If there's one pussy I'd like to eat in all of America, it is Linda Tripp's. I can just taste it now. I bet it's the real overripe kind, the way I like it. I like to eat a woman's pussy after she's been laying on the beach all day at Tybee. I like it filled with flavor, don't you?"

"I'm not so much into smells. I like my bed partners to shower."

"That's because you don't know what's good. I could bury myself in Linda's pussy and slurp the day away."

"You didn't introduce yourself."

"I'm Arlie Rae Minton, son of the Old South. I'm mighty proud to be from Dixie. We Confederates know how to eat pussy. You Yankees just stick your sissy tongue in a bit and pull back in horror. We Southern boys can dig into pussy and eat it out all night. When I finish with a woman, I bring her over the top three times and leave her so dry she has to stick a hose up there to lubricate her walls again."

"I'm sure you're very talented."

"Wouldn't you like to go down all night on Linda Tripp?"

"As a matter of fact, I wouldn't. I find her disgusting. I think she's an ugly piece of shit. No doubt psychotic. She's a shaggy dog from hell. A miserable fat cow."

For a long time Arlie Rae didn't say anything. At first Phil feared the caretaker was going to hang up.

"I see that politically you're a left-wing communist. If there's anything I can't stand, it's a left winger. You say you're a Southerner. But how can you be from the South and not like Linda Tripp? I bet nearly every boy in Dixie goes to bed at night dreaming about eating Linda Tripp's pussy."

"God help them." Phil glanced nervously at his watch. "Could you let me in my house? I really need the afternoon to move in and get adjusted. I've got to go to work in the morning."

"I see you don't want to talk about Linda Tripp. The address is 24-26 West Charlton Street. Don't go to 24. That's where that dyke Lula Carson lives. Go to 26. I'll meet you there."

"How do I find the place? I'm at..."

Arlie Rae slammed down the phone.

Outside the phone booth, a helpful local, a weather-beaten man in his 70s, gave Phil directions to reach the house. Introducing himself, Jeb Davies said he was going right near there and he'd direct Phil. In Phil's car, he said that West Charlton Street was a fine address. "A Yankee boy like you could have done worse." The man went on to tell him that the houses on West Charlton Street were built as an investment by Daniel Robertson between 1812 and 1857. "That was before the war of Northern Aggression," the old man said.

On the street of Greek Revival townhouses, Phil seemed pleased that Jerry had gotten him a house here. His own home was part of a two-frame building which the old man said was constructed about 1845, another investment for Daniel Robertson. The twin houses looked almost Federal in style. Getting out of his car, Jeb asked if he could spare five dollars. Phil gladly gave him the money.

It was almost an hour before Arlie Rae showed up. Seeing him coming toward him on the porch, Phil realized that he felt distinctly uncomfortable in the presence of Arlie Rae. He looked like a thirty-year-old Peter Lorre. But Arlie Rae in person was even more Southern cornpone than over the phone. He wore a Confederate baseball cap and a dirty T-shirt with a faded Confederate flag on it.

Arlie Rae was so skinny he appeared almost skeletal. He only looked like Peter Lorre in the face. He didn't have that actor's body. Arlie Rae looked like he'd never had a square meal in his life. He was smoking rather violently, sucking in the smoke as if it were not regular tobacco but pot.

He stopped a few feet from Phil, looking him up and down with a skeptical eye. "A pretty Yankee boy if I do say so myself. You'd better watch your step around Savannah. Some nigger men, especially if they've had a few drinks, will grab you one night and pump nigger dick into your tight white asshole. All nigger men have fourteen-inch dicks so you'll be bloody before morning. They'll have to take you up to the hospital to sew you up."

"I'll be careful."

"Well, this is the house. But before I unlock the door and show you around, I've got to ask you a personal question. Are you a faggot?"

"That's very personal."

"I've got to know. I'm not going into that house with you alone if I know you to be a faggot. For all I know, you'll go inside that house with me and grope me."

"I promise I won't. You're very safe with me."

"I had this faggot grope me one time in a men's room. He asked me to take out my dick so he could suck it for me. I was a bit horny that day so I obliged him. When I get it hard, it doesn't even measure up to three inches. When he saw me fully erect, he got up off his knees and laughed in my face. 'That's no dick,' he said to me, 'that's a pussy. It looks more like a clit than a dick.' I'm the last man that faggot will ever laugh at. I pulled out my pocket knife and slashed his face. He still goes around with the scar today, and he didn't go to the police either. I've got to warn you. If I go into that house alone with you, I've still got that knife."

"Hell, Arlie Rae, if anything, I'm afraid to go into the house with you."

"It's okay as long as you don't make a pass at me."

"I won't bother you. Just let me in the house."

"You never really answered my question. Are you a faggot?"

"Not at all. I like beautiful women. Really beautiful women."

"Are you married?"

"No, I'm divorced—in fact, divorced twice," Phil lied. "If I can find a young Grace Kelly or a young Jackie Kennedy, I might get married if they'd have me."

"Maybe they won't have you. I find that women are just like faggots: They like men with big dicks. Is your dick as small as mine?"

"Not from what you say. It's more than three times your size and extremely thick."

"Thick!" Arlie Ran his tongue along his lips. "That's what women like. A thick dick. I can't give 'em what they want. That's why I developed this talented tongue. I've even had women turn down men with big dicks to sample some of my tongue action."

"I'm sure they're amply rewarded."

"I hope you're not telling me a big lie about the size of your dick. Because I'll find out sooner than later."

"How do you propose to do that?"

"I'll let you in on my secret. It's like giving you fair warning. At night I visit certain houses. Not everybody has all the drapes pulled or the window shades down. You can see a lot of what is going on at night. The darkness protects me. When I come upon a scene I like, I jerk off. Then I get home and go to bed. Of course, I've got Linda all around me. I lie on the bed nude while Linda's eyes are everywhere. I don't know about Linda but at least Monica didn't fall for a big dick. Jennifer Flowers said in *Penthouse* that Clinton has a small dick."

"Most presidents in modern times, as best as we can tell from gossip, have had small dicks. With one exception, of course."

"Who was that exception?"

"LBJ."

"A fucking Democrat! If there's one thing I hate more than faggots, it's a fucking Democrat. When the Southern Republicans really take over this country, there may be some concentration camps set up in the Middle West. I know a lot of people bad-mouth Hitler, but he had some progressive ideas."

"Please, Arlie Rae, I really want to go inside."

Arlie Rae stood at the door and somewhat reluctantly inserted the key. "I'm going to let you in this house, but God knows what type of perversion is going to take place inside once you get installed."

Once inside the hot, stuffy house, Phil took in the parlor, finding it fully furnished in a Victorian style.

"I've got to warn you," Arlie Rae said. "Stay away from your neighbors next door. Lula Carson lives there. She's a writer too. She lives with her husband, Jason McReeves. Both of them are perverts."

"I'll run away at the sight of them."

After showing him around the house, Arlie Rae said he had to go. "I'm really hungry. It's a hunger that even corn bread and collards can't satisfy. I want to eat some pussy if I can find me a girl that looks like Linda Tripp. I'll eat her out all afternoon. It's hot and it's humid, ideal pussy-eating weather in Savannah."

"Sounds like fun," Phil said, disguising the mockery in his voice.

"Wanta come with me?"

"I've got to move in. Get my phone hooked up, shop for some groceries, restock the liquor cabinet. The usual."

At the door Arlie Rae handed him a set of keys. "Remember what I warned you. Don't commit any perverted acts here. 'cause I'll be right at one of the windows watching and taking it all in." With that he turned and passed through the doorway.

For a long moment Phil watched him go before deciding he'd keep the draperies pulled and the shades down if he were going to live here.

*****

Several hours had gone by, and twilight was approaching. Lula Carson figured that she'd waited long enough to introduce herself to her new neighbor, Phil Heather. She'd seen him come onto their shared porch, and she'd wanted to rush up and meet him right away. But when she'd spotted him with Arlie Rae Minton, she held back. Whenever possible, she went to great lengths to avoid Arlie Rae.

Every town as big as Savannah has to have a fully blown nut. Arlie Rae fitted that bill. In spite of her reservations about him, she still treated Arlie Rae with great respect, knowing that he no doubt would go down in the history books as a famous figure when he assassinated Bill Clinton. It would be a dubious kind of fame, yet at least he'd immortalize himself. She fully expected the world would long remember both Arlie Rae and herself: Arlie Rae for killing Clinton and herself for writing *The Tireless Hunter.*

Two problems had presented themselves to her all afternoon. In the heat of the day she had no solution to either of them. Since she couldn't afford air conditioning, all she could do during the most intense heat of the day was sit around and die, waiting for the cooling effect of twilight. First, she was concerned about the proper way to greet Phil Heather, as she suspected this was going to become one of the most important friendships of her life, and she desperately wanted to make a good first impression. The next problem that troubled her was what she was going to do to follow up the inevitable fame and success of *The Tireless Hunter.* Her newly acquired fans would be holding bookstores under siege waiting for her next opus. The sad truth was that she didn't have one single idea for another novel to follow *The Tireless Hunter.* Not even a clue as to what to write about.

Through the curtains she'd spotted Phil leave his house and head for his car. He'd returned an hour later carrying some groceries and liquor. She was thankful that he was a drinking man. She never trusted a man who didn't drink whiskey. She viewed whiskey as the drink of the earth, and she felt both men and women should consume as much of it in one day as was needed and required. Whiskey made the pain of living a little easier. She didn't think one should drink until one fell down on the floor, as Gin Tucker had been known to do on more than one occasion.

She wondered where Jason was. His comings and goings were so mysterious. But she never wanted to inquire about what activities he was engaged in. She strongly felt that the secrets of the human heart should remain known only to the owner of that heart. How that heart beat and where it beat, at least in her view, need concern no one but the owner of that heart.

Through the screen door of her kitchen, she heard activity on her patio. She looked out to see Phil Heather walking around inspecting the courtyard with a drink in his hand. She decided right there and then this was the ideal time to meet him. She never liked introducing herself during the blinding heat of the day. She firmly believed that appearances were so much more dramatic at twilight.

She checked her hair in the mirror in the hallway, deciding it was no use to do anything with it. She felt that as a writer Phil would be interested only in her spiritual side, and her actual physical appearance didn't matter.

Opening the screen door, she emerged onto the back veranda, looking down at Phil in their shared patio. "As I live and breathe," she said in her most dramatic theatrical voice, "it's Montgomery Clift in the final reel of *A Place in the Sun*. Which role can I play? Shelley Winters or Elizabeth Taylor?" She brushed her hand into the oncoming night. "Don't answer that. I already know."

"I hope my life works out better than Monty's," he said.

"I do too," she said, walking down the steps and extending her hand. "You're the spittin' image of him. I'm Lula Carson, and I'm the spittin' image of nobody. When I was born, they broke the mold."

"I'm Phil Heather. As is rather obvious, I moved in next door." After shaking her hand, he released it quickly. "And don't worry. I don't plan to throw liquor parties with lots of wild women running screaming through the house."

"If you did, Arlie Rae would love you. He'd be right outside the window, taking everything in."

"Is that so? So he's a real Peeping Tom? I thought he might be saying that to spook me out."

"Not at all. Just raise your shades at night and there will be the beady little eyes of Arlie Rae taking in all the action. Everybody knows and tolerates Arlie Rae. In fact, I know a couple in Savannah who deliberately leave the lights on and the curtains open. They claim that knowing Arlie Rae is out there waiting makes it all the more exciting for them."

"Whatever turns you on."

She sensed he was uncomfortable in her presence. In her nervousness, she felt she'd blurted out all the wrong things, giving him a bad impression. "I hear you're adapting the screenplay for *Butterflies in Heat*. The only part in that book I could play is the role of Anne. She falls for the male hero, a big good-looking blond who's got something everybody in town wants. The story of my life."

"How does that parallel your life?" Phil asked, offering her a drink from his bottle of bourbon. She willingly accepted, telling him she liked hers straight.

"I married Numie, the hero of your screenplay. Wait until you meet Jason, my husband. He looks just like the guy on the cover of the book."

"I don't mean to be offensive," Phil said, "but the guy on the cover of *Butterflies* is wearing a wet T-shirt and sporting a ten and a half inch hard-on."

"We'll have to make the part bigger for Jason."

"I'm not sure what that means."

"We'll have to add another inch and a half, maybe two inches. I've never actually measured."

"You must be married to a hell of a man!"

"I am. Forgive me for being so presumptuous but it comes as a way of warning you. Jason doesn't know if you're gay or not. Come mid-morning he'll be lying stark naked out here in the courtyard. He'll put on a full display for you. If you are gay, and for your sake I hope you're not, you won't get a word of that screenplay written. You'll be staring at nothing but Jason."

"That sounds like a lot to stare at."

"Since your sexual preference is going to determine the course of our living together, I have to do something I don't normally do. I have to ask you something. Are you gay?"

Phil smiled at her as he sipped his drink. "My God, I've met only two people in Savannah and both of them asked me my sexual preference."

"I know how rude that is. But in the case of our living arrangement here, it's imperative that I know."

"I told Arlie Rae I liked beautiful women because he was such an obvious homophobe. But I'll tell you the truth: I like beautiful men instead."

She sank back in her chair, feeling relieved. "I'm glad that's out in the open. This will help me a lot."

"I don't see how my being gay can help you."

"My, I'm getting forward. Like a wanton slut. It must be the bourbon. Pour me some more, please. If you're gay, you might relieve me of some of the burdens of satisfying my husband's overwhelming sexual desire. He needs someone day and night paying homage to that thing of his."

"Are you suggesting that you might actually want me to go to bed with your husband?"

"The idea has occurred to me."

"I might not be attracted to him."

"If you're gay, and unless you like only black men, you'll be attracted to Jason. I never met a gay man or a woman either who wasn't attracted to Jason. He's the sexiest man south of the Mason-Dixie line."

"He sounds formidable."

"Maybe you'll tailor the role of Numie, the hustler in your screenplay, to allow Jason to play the part."

"He sounds eminently qualified. In his case he sounds as if he doesn't have to act. Just turn the camera on him and let him do his magic."

"Jason is very mesmerizing. But enough about him. I want to talk about us. I'm a writer too."

"What kind of writer?"

"I'm a novelist. I have this grant to write a book which I call *The Tireless Hunter.*"

"I see." He seemed hesitant, not knowing what to say next. Finally, he said, "What's it about?"

"It's about the timeless wanderings of the human heart."

"That sounds like a mighty strong plot."

"When you're not working on your own screenplay, perhaps you'll read my first chapters and let me know what you think. My book will become a masterpiece. It will bring me fame and glory by this time next year. But more than that, it'll be read by generations from now. Years from now when the one hundred most significant novels of all time are compiled, *The Tireless Hunter* will surface near the top of the list."

"I like a writer with confidence."

"It's more than confidence. It's my destiny."

They were interrupted by the sudden appearance of Jason in the patio. He'd taken off his white shirt and had wrapped it around his golden neck. As Lula took in the appearance of her husband, she tried to imagine what Jason must look like to a gay man. He must be a fantasy, the type gay men dream about but rarely possess. She felt honored that she could present her newly acquired friend with the gift of her husband. She just knew that Phil would appreciate her all the more after she'd made such an offering.

"Sorry, I've been gone all day, Lula," Jason said. "I fell asleep in the park and just woke up now."

"Come on over here, my darling man, and meet our new neighbor, Phil Heather. We're practically going to be living together."

Phil rose immediately to extend his hand to Jason. But Jason paused, taking in Phil's face in the dim light.

"I don't believe it," Jason said. "You're Montgomery Clift returned from the dead. He was my favorite actor. I saw *Red River* a dozen times, and I've seen *A Place in the Sun* thirty times."

"Phil is the son of Montgomery Clift," Lula said. "Born after Monty died."

Phil appeared confused, as if wanting to correct something she'd said. But after a moment's hesitation, he said nothing. "I adore your wife," Phil said. "I'm sure I'll feel the same way about you too, neighbor."

As Jason reached to shake Phil's hand, Lula turned to her husband. "Phil's gay."

"In that case I won't shake your hand but give you a kiss instead," Jason said.

"I'd like that," Phil said. "With Lula's permission."

"You have my permission," Lula said. "Jason has the sweetest mouth in Georgia."

In the twilight Jason stood close to Phil, moving toward his mouth. "Do you want tongue or not?"

"Tongue, please," Phil said in a deep husky voice.

Lula turned her back to the men. "While Jason is kissing you, you have my permission to feel between his legs. Find out for yourself that I didn't exaggerate."

*****

Jason looked younger, blonder, and more of a beautiful hunk than Tango had remembered, as he approached her borrowed car parked in front of Blues in the Night. He carried a bouquet of flowers which he no doubt stole from someone's carefully cultivated garden. To her, stolen flowers were more romantic than those bought at a shop or stall.

"Here, beauty, flowers for my lovely," he said, smiling at her and offering his bouquet through the car door window.

She took them and blew him a kiss. "You look good enough to eat." She sniffed the flowers. "These flowers smell real nice, but I don't think they smell half as good as Jason McReeves, especially before he takes his Saturday night bath."

"How did you know we used to bathe only on Saturday night?"

"Sugar, I grew up in the South too." She smiled at him again, then smelled the flowers once more. "Get in. I have an afternoon planned for us."

As she headed for a condo she'd rented on Tybee Island, the sky was overcast. It didn't look like afternoon at all, but a palette of gold, flame, and purple, the kind of Georgia sky you often see at sunset, not in the mid-afternoon. Up to now Savannah had exploded in a blast of white-hot heat that had seared the city, tearing at its face. All day Tango had felt her throat was parched but she was convinced that Jason's semen would lubricate it. She noticed that he was sweating, his white shirt clinging to his body. Already she could anticipate the salty taste of him. She'd lick those armpits as clean as a baby's butt after a bath.

In the car sitting so close to him, she shivered with an involuntary twitching of her muscles. It seemed her rosebud was already anticipating the massive penetration it was going to get later in the afternoon.

As they drove along, she kept checking her appearance in the mirror. She needed all the reassurance she could get. People told her that her face lacked the rotundity of the pure Negro. She had high cheekbones and a nose that was a bit small—not broad with wide nostrils like her mama. Her lips were thick but not unduly so. Most men claimed they were luscious after she'd put them to work on a man's most sensitive areas. Her row of evenly spaced white teeth contributed to her beauty, and she brushed them sometimes eight or nine times a day. Her eyes were velvety soft and brown like those of an antelope. All she lacked was creamy white skin like Jason's. Her skin was creamy but more of a light copper brown. If only she could meet Michael Jackson and learn his secret of going from black to the palest of light browns.

"I hope you're not going to hold out on me today, sugar, like you did yesterday afternoon," she told Jason.

"I'm not holding out at all. It's just I have this rule about the first date with a woman. This is our second date. We know each other now."

"I don't know you well enough," she said. "I know what your mouth tastes like but there are a lot of other things I'm dying to taste too."

"Honey, just think of me as a great big banana split," he said.

"I ain't never seen a banana the size of you, unless that was a snake I was feeling in your pants yesterday."

"It's all me. The day I was born, or so I've heard, the nurses at the hospital were astonished. Had never seen anything like that on a newborn baby. Of course, I've grown some since then. I don't think I'll disappoint you."

"I don't think you will either." As she approached the Crab Shack at Chimney Creek, she eyed Jason. "Did that Lula Carson feed you today?"

"Not a damn bite. There wasn't even some cereal in the cupboard."

"We'll pull in here and order the seafood platter. They have the most delicious fat crab which they make into the most delectable cakes. And wait till you taste their fresh shrimp. I hope you like fried seafood."

He looked at her in astonishment. "Is there any other way?"

Finding a wooden table outside, they ordered beer and drank it from the bottle, taking in the other diners in their bathing suits and sandy feet.

"This food tastes really off the boat," Jason said, smacking his lips.

She took in the view at the bend in the creek. "This is Lowcountry at its best. I couldn't imagine living anywhere else."

She said nothing for a moment, and neither did he. With Jason, she felt she didn't have to blabber a lot. She just enjoyed being in his presence.

He was devouring some okra fritters. "I'm firmly convinced, only the people of Savannah know how to make okra fritters." At the end of his meal, he ordered another beer and licked the grease from his succulent mouth. He leaned closer to her. "Have you got a place for us? With real nice clean sheets?"

"I sure have. For the rest of the summer I've rented a condo at the Tybrisa Beach Resort. It's very comfortable but a bit basic. I'm making good tips now at the club, and I can afford it. Only yesterday I couldn't even afford to pay the rent on my apartment in Savannah. Now the money's starting to come in."

As she drove him there, he leaned back in the seat, rubbing his belly. "I've always liked Tybee Island. Of course, the faggots who come down from the north hate it. Gin Tucker wouldn't be caught dead here. But to me it has a real down-home feeling. A Georgia boy can feel at home here."

"It seems like one great big beach party to me," she said. "Of course, today I'm bringing my party to the island. I don't need to go looking for one."

"No fayrer or fytter place," he said.

"What in hell are you talking about, sugar?"

"That's what the explorer Ribaut wrote when he first saw the Lowcountry."

"You literary types," she said, pretending a disdain she didn't really feel.

"I'm more the romantic type than the literary type. Perhaps tomorrow afternoon we'll go for a typical Lowcountry walk. Let's pray for a mild afternoon. A stroll along a sandy path, with Spanish moss hanging from the oak trees. Me holding your hand. The afternoon light filtering through the trees, making you even more beautiful than you are."

"Stop it, white boy. You're making me fall in love with you too quick."

"That would be a strange new sensation for me," he said. "No one has ever loved me before."

"Doesn't Lula love you?"

"Lula is self-enchanted. She wants a companion in me, not a lover."

"I can't imagine men and women not falling in love with you. My God, you're a fucking fantasy."

"Men and women have wanted to go to bed with me. Men and women have not wanted to love me."

"I guess I'm in an awkward position, sugar. Right now all I can think about is going to bed with you, too."

"That's okay. Isn't that what lovers are supposed to do?" He leaned over and kissed her on the cheek.

The simple kiss was so thrilling to her it almost burned her cheek. If a little kiss could do that, she wondered what a closer encounter with Jason might do. No doubt set off a five-alarm fire.

An hour later, fantasy became reality on the white sheets of her newly rented condo. Jason did not disappoint. He was more man than she'd ever dreamed of before, making Danny look like a mere schoolboy.

When she'd had him fully stripped, she'd taken off her own clothes as she was proud of her breasts even if she had to create them for herself with no help from Mother Nature. She modestly retained her red bikini underpants. A girl didn't have to reveal all.

With him spread before her on the bed, she attacked his neck and shoulders, wetting him down thoroughly. Her skilled fingers wandered his massive hairless chest, tweaking his hard, passion-tipped nipples. His body was hard and lean and fit for all the purposes to which she would put it. This was a young blond hunk in his prime.

As her fingers slipped below to fondle, tease, and measure, she knew Jason had been right. He did not exaggerate. It was incredibly long and thick, and as she sucked his tongue in her devouring mouth it seemed to grow even larger. She reached below to fondle his ballbag, finding it was among the biggest ever. It was going to be hard enough getting just one of those delicious orbs in her mouth at one time, much less two. When she'd finished sucking his tongue, her own tongue traveled southward, enjoying and savoring his sweat of the day, licking all the salt from the surface of his body.

Under her probing tongue and at the mercy of her worshipful hands, he shivered in anticipation of even more fun and games.

At long last her wet red lips locked around the thick head of his penis. Inch by powerful inch she began to ease down on it. Her jaws were stretched but she was determined to have every stiff bit of it, all the way to the blond pubic hairs, even if it went to the bottom of her throat.

His cock started to swell, stiffen, and thicken all the more. It was one fat slab of meat. Thank God she'd been practicing night after night on Danny to prepare herself for this massive invasion. His hips were rocking instinctively upward, driving the thick tool deeper and deeper. As she took him, her fingers enjoyed the satin softness of his ass. She was determined to spend a good part of the afternoon, licking, sucking, and devouring that treat.

But now a more urgent mission consumed her. She made it, finally reaching the final inch of his cock and enjoying the pubic hairs tickling her nose. She stayed on him as long as she dared, before coming up for air. Her throat sucked in the air before she plunged down on him again, working her talented lips up and down. He was moaning now as he continued to force feed her inch after thick inch. He penetrated a part of her throat that was still virgin, and she'd been worked over by experts.

As he neared his climax Jason seemed out of control. She feared for a moment her face would risk whiplash he was impaling her so. She felt his ballbag contract as he slammed into her, pounding against her chin. His moans and grunts of pleasure were growing louder and louder.

When his eruption came, it was a blast so powerful she felt he was blowing her head off. Her lips swallowed only the head, licking, slurping, and demanding every drop which she gulped down as fast as he produced it. She saved the final wad in her mouth to savor for taste. It was ambrosia.

As he lay panting on the bed, she traveled his body, lapping her way up past his belly button to gnaw on his hairless tits. She slipped up to lick the sweat from his armpits, inhaling their musky man-scent. She then gave both of his ears the best tongue-lashing of their lifetime.

With her belly full of his cum, she squeezed and tugged at his heavy balls. She was a great expert on the stallion flesh of white men, and Jason was her triumph of all times. His broad shoulders and flanks, his butt, and the track of his spine—everything fell victim to her sensitive fingers with their rapine touch.

"Honey," he whispered, rubbing her neck and shoulders. "I'm a fucker. That was an appetizer. I've got to have a lot more to satisfy me. I want some pussy."

At first panic came over her. As his fingers felt for her, she interrupted them, taking them in her mouth instead to suck and devour every one of them. "Sugar, sometimes a gal is having her period. But there's another part of me that's ready and rarin' to go. If truth were known, I'm more of a rear entry gal anyway."

"That suits me just fine," he said, as his long fingers searched for her rosebud. "I like it better back there anyway."

"I'm gonna sit on it even if it plunges all the way to China."

"Even though you're just a tiny little thing, I've got to get all of me up in you. I've got to."

"I want you there," she said, reaching below to fondle and weigh his balls. "We gotta drain these big things dry before I send you back home."

"Home is going to be where you are. I'm in love with you. Sometimes I think I have quite a gay streak in me. But this afternoon, you convinced me I'm straight after all."

\*\*\*\*\*

Gin Tucker seemed to know where everything was for sale in Savannah, and what to buy at any time. "Savannah hardly lives up to Truman Capote's description of a city," he'd once told Lavender.

"What do you mean," she'd asked.

"Capote said a city was a place where you could buy a canary at three o'clock in the morning."

"I'm not looking for a canary, but I need an outfit that I can go riding with Danny on a motorcycle. I also need that pot I asked you about. The cocaine you can deliver later in the evening."

After she put down her phone, she realized how convenient it was to have Gin in her life. His family wasn't quite as rich as he told everybody. Even if they were rich, his family kept the money to themselves and didn't send much of it to Savannah for Gin. Lavender had lost count of the "loans" she'd paid to Gin. Of course, she never expected to get one of these loans paid back. The advantage of lending Gin money was that he was always at her beck and call at any time of the day or night. Gin knew everybody in Savannah and was good at 'fixin' things, as he always put it.

By five o'clock that afternoon her riding outfit had arrived. At least it was the right color: lavender. But she wondered if she'd sweat too much wearing vinyl in the hot August afternoon. After she'd tried on her outfit, she was delighted to see that it fitted. Gin knew the size of everything, especially cock sizes. She suspected he went around with a tape measure.

Surveying herself in the mirror, she was surprised at how youthful she looked. She felt Danny's semen was like an elixir making her young again.

Adjusting her hair before putting on a lavender-colored leather baseball hat, she was interrupted by the ringing of the telephone. Picking up the receiver in anticipation of it being Danny, she was disappointed to hear that it was only her old friend, Bice Heather.

"Bice, you old whore, I don't have much time to talk," Lavender said. "Did you get arrested in a men's room and you need me to post bail?"

"I no longer work the turnpikes. I'm calling about my nephew, Phil Heather. The writer."

"Oh, yes," Lavender said. "I read about him in the paper. He's coming here to do a screen adaptation of *Butterflies in Heat.* That's great. Gin gave me the book to read. I think I'm perfect for the part of Leonora de la Mer, the dress designer."

"You speak to my Phil. I'm sure he'll have the producer cast you in the part. Personally I think you'd be terrific."

"Thanks, I will. If I hadn't entered another profession, I think I might have become an actress."

"Darling, you were an actress all your life. Pretending what great sex all those decrepit men were. All the while you were thinking about how much money they had and not their dicks."

"You do know me, don't you?"

"I didn't call to discuss our notorious pasts. I called about Phil."

"How can I be of service?"

"He just called me. He's got a house there. It's joined to the house Lula Carson shares with her husband, Jason McReeves."

Lavender grew chilly at the mention of Lula. "Lula and I know each other. We're not exactly kissin' cousins if you know what I mean. She's not my type."

"Phil even knows his phone number. He'll have service tomorrow. Perhaps you'll call him and introduce him to your bachelor friends."

"I might. Is he gay?"

"He's had as many men as you and me combined." Aunt Bice coughed into the phone. "No, I take that back. Nobody on earth has had that many men."

"Is he good looking? It helps in Savannah if you're good looking. We don't need any more ugly boys around here. We've got enough home grown ones of our own."

"Wait until you see him. He's the spittin' image of Montgomery Clift."

"You're making that up."

"I swear it. You'll be amazed when you see him."

"If Phil looks like Montgomery Clift, that old hag, Tipper Zelda, is certain to fall for him. She's still carrying a torch for the real Monty, although I don't understand why. I heard Montgomery Clift had the smallest dick in Hollywood. Tipper's husbands, especially Taylor Zachory, were legendary for their endowments."

"Maybe Tipper was engaging in lesbianism when she was with Monty."

"Maybe." Lavender lit a cigarette, wishing Aunt Bice would get off the phone. "I have an idea. You'll have to call Phil and get him to agree to it. I need a label for Phil. You know, something to pique the interest of the bachelors. How old is he?"

"About thirty."

"That's perfect," Lavender said. "I can claim that Phil is the son of Montgomery Clift. Born around the time of Monty's death. That way, Gin and his faggots will be only too interested in meeting Phil and inviting him to all their parties."

"That's wonderful. I'll speak to Phil tomorrow when he gets his phone hooked up and get him to agree to it. He's a great party animal. He'll view it as a joke and play along."

"Fine." Lavender crushed out her cigarette on her vanity ash tray. "Now give me that number and I've got to go." As Aunt Bice gave her the number, Lavender wrote it down with a gold pen given her by Lyndon B. Johnson.

"You call him now, you hear," Aunt Bice said.

"I'll call him," Lavender promised. "Even though I'm a bit busy these days. I have met the most divine creature. I've fallen in love. He's a tango dancer and looks a bit like Guy Madison."

"Honey, you and I may be the only people in the world who know who Guy Madison is. Phil knows who Guy Madison is. Even as a little boy, he used to pin up 1940s pictures of Guy Madison in the bathroom."

"Then I'd better not introduce your Phil to my Danny. Danny is divine. He's only eighteen—maybe seventeen. What do I care? You won't believe that thing he's got stuffed in his tight jeans. He worked me over last night like I've never been worked over." She hesitated. "Except once. Long ago."

"You mean London, 1942. That married boy Karl you're always talking about."

"Danny is like Karl in so many ways."

"I really envy you. I wish some eighteen-year-old was in my broken down old brass bed. I don't think I've been worked over by a teenager since Lincoln was in the White House. Don't you think he's a bit young for you?"

"Hell, no. Danny might be my Last Hurrah. I'm taking full advantage. I'll confide something to you. I think his semen has the power to make me young again. I've swallowed it only once and already I look five years younger."

"That's incredible. Do you really think so? If you do, you could bottle it and send me a cocktail?"

"That's disgusting. It has to be consumed fresh for the best results."

"When I come down to Savannah to see Phil, I've got to meet this Danny. At least I can live vicariously."

"I'll see to it. Just to show him off, I'll insist he wear his tightest white pants. Or maybe I'll put a sheer white bikini on him so you can see him when he emerges from my pool. You won't believe it."

"That's reason enough to come to Savannah. That and to see Phil."

"I'll call your Phil tomorrow afternoon and introduce him to the queens of Savannah. Rehearse him on the Monty son thing."

"I will and thanks, Lavender. You've always been there for me."

"Gotta go now." The moment Lavender put down the phone, it rang again.

It was Danny and he was angry. "My God, you must have been talking on the phone for hours. I've called nine times."

"Sorry, an old friend from Darien called."

"Forget it. I'm at The Crystal. You worked me over so much I could eat a horse. Meet me here right away. My cycle will be ready in an hour."

"I'm already dressed so I'll taxi over."

"And don't forget your American Express card. They already know you're paying."

"Is it lavender? Have you seen it?"

"Hell, yes I've seen it. It's a light purple. I guess you could call it lavender. I'm not sure I know exactly what color lavender is. Sounds faggy to me."

"It is, darling, I'll be right over."

For reassurance, she looked for one final time in the mirror, wondering if she'd applied too much make-up. She decided at her age you couldn't apply too much make-up. She was thrilled. In spite of all her financial difficulties, and potential lawsuits, she felt young and alive. Danny Hansford had done that for her.

She was even eager for the motorcycle ride to be over so she could take him to her bed again and suck, lick, and devour every inch of his delectable golden flesh. Tonight, and for every night in the foreseeable future, she was going to go to sleep with the cock of Danny Hansford in her mouth.

*****

By the time Lavender, dressed in her lavender riding outfit, walked through the door of the Crystal Beer Parlor, Danny had already consumed a seafood gumbo, some fried oysters, and a cup of chili. God, he was hungry today. Having to satisfy the libido of half the pussies in town took a lot out of a man, even a young man.

As Lavender approached his booth, he looked up at her and smiled the hustler smile, not believing even now that he'd been able to make love to her. He must need money real bad to have done that. When he sold off her paintings, he was going to make a vow to himself—no more mercy fucks. With millions in the bank, he'd spend the rest of his short life doing just what he wanted to do. He'd select the people he wanted to make love to. No more bald and middle-aged men. No more over-the-hill broads on their last legs.

"What kept you?" he asked. "You took so long I finished eating already. Also, where in hell did you get that purple number you're wearing?"

"Gin Tucker got it for me."

"That figures." Danny didn't bother to disguise the sarcasm in his voice.

"With that purple cycle and your purple outfit, we'll look like two freaks going through town."

"It's not purple—it's lavender. There's a big difference. And we'll look terrific."

As she eased into the seat with him, he cautioned her, "I hope you're not hungry. I already called for the check. I want to get out of here before that place closes."

"I'm not hungry, and we can go." As the waitress appeared, Lavender reached into her bag and handed her a platinum American Express card.

"I've got to warn you," Danny said. "I've had a lot of gumbo and chili too. With you riding behind me, I hope we don't get a downwind."

"Don't worry," Lavender said, waving her hand in the air. "A blast from you would be like ambrosia. The wind will blow it away in a second. No one will know."

Within the hour after leaving the beer parlor, the lavender motorcycle—thanks to Lavender's credit card—belonged to Danny. He'd never felt such pride of ownership about anything in his life. What he wanted to do right now was ride the damn thing with the wind blowing through his hair. No helmet. He hated helmets. He cursed himself for agreeing to take Lavender for a ride. He wanted to be alone following the highway wherever it led him.

Instead of heading out of town for the open road, Lavender wanted to be taken to Gin Tucker's house.

Danny sneered at her. "About the last thing I want to do right now is visit that pissy old queen."

"While they were checking my card, I called Gin. He's got a big surprise waiting for us."

"His kind of surprise I don't want."

"You'll love it. Don't tell me you're opposed to taking a few drugs?"

He smiled that hustler smile again. "That Gin Tucker is a man after my own heart. Let's get the hell over there."

He wanted the ride on his newly acquired cycle to last longer but they were at Gin Tucker's house in minutes. As they rode through town, Lavender had clung to him like he was a rope and she was dangling over a ten-thousand foot cliff.

In Gin Tucker's living room, Danny reluctantly accepted the Budweiser Gin offered. Both Gin and Lavender preferred gin with tonic. "My, oh my," Gin said, appraising first Danny, his eyes settling in far too long for a thorough scan of the boy's crotch. He then turned to Lavender. "This motorcycle drag really becomes you," Gin told her. "You don't exactly look like Marlon Brandon in *The Wild One*, but..." He paused as if he had nowhere else to go with his thought. It was obvious he was already deep into his gin lineup for the afternoon. "Did I ever tell you I once had Marlon?"

"Yes, yes!" she said rather impatiently. "Many, many times."

"Well, forgive me," Gin said, seemingly offended. "If I can sit through one more tale of your seduction of JFK, surely you can hear about the time I had Marlon."

Danny interrupted. "Let's forget this 800-pound piece of mumbling blubber. Who in the hell would ever want to go down on Marlon Brando?"

"Well, of course," Gin said, a little defensively. "When I had him, he was a lot younger and thinner. In his prime, actually." He seemed to drift for a drunken moment, lost in some long forgotten escapade that may never have happened except in his imagination.

"I hear you've got a surprise for us," Danny blurted out. He was anxious to escape from the presence of Gin Tucker even if he had to take Lavender with him.

Gin looked at Danny through blurry eyes. At first he didn't seem to comprehend what Danny was talking about.

"That little bag of goodies we talked about earlier," Lavender said, bringing him into focus.

"Oh, that!" On wobbly legs, Gin rose and headed toward the rear of the house. "Come with me, Danny. "I've just had the stuff delivered. It's on my table out back. I don't want to touch the shit. I prefer gin myself. I want you to examine it and see if it's the right stuff before I pay the dealer. I mean for all I know, the pot might be oregano, the cocaine baking powder."

"Gladly," Danny said, getting up, casting a quick glance at Lavender, and heading past the stairs and down the long hallway that led to the back of Gin's town house.

On the table in the kitchen rested a bag of pot and another plastic bag of cocaine. He smelled the pot before pouring some of the cocaine on the kitchen table where he snorted it up his nostrils. "All this shit is real stuff," he said, looking up at Gin. "Pay the fucker."

As Danny gathered up the drugs, Gin reached out and enclosed his fingers around Danny's left arm, holding it in a tight grip.

Instinctively Danny pulled away. "What in the fuck do you want?"

"I want your answer about that dildo proposition I made to you. You said you'd get back to me." He stood back, waving his hands in the air. "Well, here I am. What's your answer?"

"I don't know," Danny said hesitantly. "I guess it'd depend on how much you paid."

"Two-thousand dollars and that's my final offer."

Danny looked Gin over carefully. "All I'd have to do for that is have you mold a dildo of me. No sex or shit like that."

"None. Maybe let me snap a few pictures and that's that. It would only take an hour or two. The easiest money you've ever earned."

Danny thought for a second, warming to the idea. He'd be leaving the world soon, and it might be a fitting present to leave behind his most precious possession. With that dildo in mass production, both men and women would be getting fucked by him for years to come. In a way that dildo might offer him immortality. With that dildo, no one could dispute his sexual prowess the way they questioned that of the real Danny Hansford.

He looked up at Gin and smiled. "Okay, I'll do it. When do you want me to come over?"

"Eleven o'clock tomorrow morning."

Danny smiled again. "I'll be here." Stuffing the drugs into his jacket, Danny outpaced Gin getting back to the living room and Lavender. She was pouring herself another gin. At first he thought it might be too risky taking her on a bike ride in her condition. She looked drunk, not as much as Gin, but nonetheless very intoxicated.

"C'mon, babe," he said. "I got the stuff. Let's go for a ride."

At the door, Gin was reaching for his straw hat. "I'm going out for a late afternoon promenade in Savannah. Perhaps along the riverwalk. Just to see what's going on in this town." On the steps to his town house, he paused to admire the motorcycle, as Danny helped Lavender into her seat.

"Why don't you take me for a ride some time?" Gin asked Danny. "I'd love it. Did I ever tell you about the time Marlon took me for a ride on his cycle?"

Gin's words faded from Danny's ears as he headed through the streets of Savannah toward the open highway, carrying Lavender with him. Her fingers dug into his chest, possessing him.

As the hot air of the late afternoon blew into his face, it became a cooling breeze, and he knew in his heart that in his short life no one would ever possess him. That is, no mortal person.

Only the trapped spirit of the real Danny Hansford lived within him, and even now with the highway before him he knew that that Danny was demanding to escape.

*****

The pounding on her door and the pounding inside her head would not go away. Tipper pulled back the draperies and peered out. Standing in her porch light were Frank Gilmore and his companion, Dale Evans. Dale was holding a large box.

"Come to the door," Frank yelled into the night, loud enough for all her nosy neighbors to hear. "We know you're in there, Tipper."

"Listen, bitch!" Dale called out in his shrill voice. "We paid your fucking bills! Let us in." He pounded on her door even harder than before.

It was late at night, and Tipper feared Frank and Dale would wake up the entire neighborhood. She had to let them in. It was better that way. Very reluctantly, she turned on the light in her living room and headed for the door. She opened it only wide enough for both men to enter one at a time.

"What kept you?" Frank said, barging past her and heading uninvited to her living room. "We're here to talk show biz." Carrying the big box, Dale trailed his lover and boss.

Once in the living room both men plopped down on her sofa, Dale tossing the box on her coffee table.

With all the grace she could summon, she entered the living room, crossing in front of them and seeming to glide into a winged armchair across from them. She had no intention of offering them a drink or showing Savannah's famed hospitality at all. "And how may I be of assistance to you gentlemen?" she said, sounding like Melanie in *Gone With the Wind*.

"Dale..." Frank hesitated and reached over and patted his younger companion on the knee. The men exchanged smiles. "This sweet boy here claims that while I was covering every bad check of yours all over town, even paying the mortgage to keep a roof over your head, that you stalked out of my office when my little sugartit here..." He turned and smiled at Dale again. "God, this tender young boy has got the sweetest tits in all of Savannah."

"I'm sure he does," she said, disdainful of the pair. "I was asked to exploit my past. In fact, I think in that damn box is a Black Widow costume. You guys are asking me to trade off my past. All the tragedies I suffered."

Dale glanced quickly at Frank as if seeking encouragement, then turned with a certain controlled ferocity to Tipper. "Fuck the tragedies you suffered. Wasn't it the other way around? It seems to Frank and me that your husbands suffered the tragedies. All of them were murdered. Four in a row!"

Tipper gasped. In spite of mountains of tabloid newspaper print, she'd never been confronted this directly in Savannah with murder. "My husbands were killed, all under circumstances never fully explained. Suicide, perhaps. One doesn't know. I certainly don't know or remember."

"You already told me you don't remember a thing about the day Taylor Zachory was found shot," Dale said. "That's God damn convenient."

"Yeah," Frank butted in. "Shoot someone and then not remember a thing. Pretty God damn convenient like sweet Dale here said."

"Convenient or not, it was the truth," she said. "No jury convicted me."

"Yeah," Dale said sarcastically. "There was no trial—that's why you weren't convicted. I researched your life in the library this morning. I'm up on all the details."

Tipper rose swan-like from her chair and headed for her liquor cabinet where she poured herself a stiff drink, deliberately not offering one to her unwanted guests.

"You go on there, sweet boy of mine," Frank said, running his fingers through Dale's hair. "Tell the bitch what you know."

The downing of the liquor giving her renewed courage, Tipper turned to face her accusers again.

"That second husband of yours, Derek McKee, was found stabbed to death on a beach in the Florida Keys," Dale said. "They never found out who stabbed him. Was it you?"

"Hell, no! I was desperately in love with Derek. He was much younger than me. He looked like a young Dolph Lundgren. I called him my Viking God. Derek loved me too. But every now and then he liked to sneak off and find himself a young Cuban boy. He always liked Latinos. I understood that need in him, and although I warned him of the dangers, he was still compelled to sneak off with these slimy hustlers."

"A hustler is out to get a john's money," Dale said. "Your husband's money was found intact in a beach bag near his body. He also wore an expensive gold bracelet given to him by you. There was semen found in his mouth. With all the goodies intact, it didn't appear like a robbery. Your whereabouts at the time of his murder weren't known."

"I'd gone for a long walk on another isolated part of the beach while he indulged in his sordid little affair."

"Move on," Frank urged Dale. "Ask her about Richard Olken. How he died."

At the mention of Richard, Tipper felt her whole body shudder in painful memory. "I was working in Hollywood at the time," she said, "making one of my few films. In this one I played a torch singer. Richard and I lived in a lovely house high, high in the Hollywood hills. Richard had been drinking that night. We had a terrible fight. I screamed for him not to, but he ran out the door and got into our car. We had a convertible. He started the motor and pulled recklessly out of the driveway. Within two minutes he'd lost control of the car. It went over the embankment. The car exploded killing him." She gasped for breath.

"There was a suggestion at the preliminary inquest that the brakes on that car were tampered with," Dale said.

"That's ridiculous. The car had burst into flames. How could the police prove such a fantastic charge? I was desperately in love with Richard. Why would I want to harm him?"

"That's for you to know and for us only to guess," Frank said. He patted Dale's knee again. "Go on, sugartit. There's more."

Before Dale could present another accusation, Tipper interrupted him. "Dan Luskin was my fourth and final husband. I almost loved him as much as I loved Montgomery Clift. Perhaps not that much, but almost. Dan was a wonderful man, much younger than myself. He had certain tendencies which I overlooked. But I loved him desperately."

"All your husbands, apparently, had certain tendencies," Dale charged. "Didn't you ever marry anyone straight?"

"I can't be blamed if the men I married also had to have another form of love to satisfy them. All I could do was provide an understanding heart."

"Tell the truth, Tipper," Frank urged. "Dan Luskin was poisoned."

"Yes, he was," she said, "but I didn't do it. I don't know who poisoned him. We had met Jackie Kennedy at a party. She'd told us about this wonderfully decadent place in Haiti. We went to Port-au-Prince for a second honeymoon. It was everything that Jackie said it was. We were having a glorious time at this resort until Dan was found poisoned one night."

"Why didn't you ship his body home?" Frank asked. "Why did you have him buried in Haiti?"

"He loved the country so," she said. "It seemed the right thing to do. The local authorities insisted that bodies be buried right away. I was estranged from Dan's family."

"It was that very family that got his body exhumed and an autopsy performed," Dale said in a most accusatory manner. "If they hadn't gone through all the legal channels, it would never be known how Luskin died."

"It was intensely investigated," Tipper said. "No charges were ever filed against me."

The oppressive heat of a Savannah night had consumed the room. It was not ventilated. All of them remained silent, as if not knowing where to go from this point on.

Tipper turned her back to the men and faced her liquor cabinet. She poured herself another stiff drink. She belted it down the way she'd seen Joan Crawford kill a vodka once at 21 in New York. Finding renewed courage in the liquor, she turned around to face Dale and Frank. Her head was exploding with memories of her dead husbands. With her high-heel shoe she kicked the box on her coffee table. It fell to the floor, opening to reveal the Black Widow costume. She glared first at the costume, then at Frank and Dale. "If you're not out of this house in one minute, I'm calling the police."

Frank stood up first, staring first at Tipper with unconcealed hostility, then at the dress on the floor. He reached for Dale. "C'mon, boy. We're getting out of here."

Dale rose to his feet confronting Tipper. "You'll hear from us. Frank's spent a lot of money bailing out your ass. You'll hear from us."

She heard the door slam. They were gone from her life but she knew not for long. She stood for a long moment in the oppressive heat. Her breathing was irregular, as if coming in gasps. Slowly, very slowly, she began to remove all her clothing, even her underwear, letting each garment fall to the floor.

When she was completely nude, she stooped over and retrieved the Black Widow costume. At first she held it away from her body as if the costume were contaminated and radioactive. Sighing in defeat, she clutched the gown to her bosom before surrendering to it and using it to cover her body.

As she tried on the gown, she noted how beautifully it fitted her body. It was as if this gown could provide a protective shield for her. With the gown fully fastened on her, she walked deliberately and slowly to the full-length mirror in her hallway. There in the dim light she took in her vision for the first time.

Staring back at her in the mirror was the ferocious Black Widow herself.

# Chapter Four

No sooner had his phone been installed than Phil called his highway patrolman, Brian Sheehan, in Darien. With all Phil had going on, he didn't need a married man in his life to complicate matters. But the memory of his recent backseat lovefest with Brian lingered, that and the taste of Brian's sweet juice when they were teenagers. He'd remembered once asking Brian to run away to Florida with him, but Brian had always insisted he was straight, and Phil hadn't seen much future in sticking around Darien, especially when Big Daddy had disinherited him, planning to give everything to Sister Woman.

Phil called the police station in Darien, but was told that Brian had the day off. He then dialed the other number Brian had written down. The phone was answered by a woman with a pronounced Southern accent. "I'm Joyce," she said. "I'm his old lady. Who's calling?"

"Phil Heather, an old classmate of his. I'm nearby and I thought I'd look up my buddy."

"Phil Heather!" she screeched into the phone. "Brian talks about you all the time. Said he ran into you at Bootleggers the other night and you invited all of us to come to Savannah to stay at your new place."

Phil was taken aback. He must have been drunker than he remembered. He didn't recall inviting all the Sheehan family, only Brian.

"Brian's in the shower right now soaping up that big old thing of his."

Phil gave her his address and phone number. She muttered something. "Brian was going to drive me and the kids—we have two boys, John and Henry—to Tybee Island today. Maybe we'll stop off and take you with us."

"I'd love to but..."

Joyce yelled something at someone at the front door. "There's a package for me. I pray it's our new bathing suits. Gotta go now. We'll catch you later. Don't leave your house this morning. We'll be there as soon as Brian finishes soaping himself." She yelled to someone that she was coming. "See you later, sugar," she said into the phone, letting out a little screech before slamming down the receiver.

Even as he put down the phone and made himself some coffee, he couldn't believe that the Sheehan family would show up at his doorstep. He suspected Brian would dump the wife and kids at Tybee, then slip off to see him later—that is, if he showed up at all.

Forgetting about Joyce and her piercing voice for a moment, Phil placed a call to New York, where he got Jerry Wheeler's message service. He left his new Savannah phone number for Jerry and fully expected that he'd hear from the producer before the day was out, demanding to know what progress, if any, he'd made on the screenplay, *Butterflies in Heat.*

At this very moment, Phil didn't have a clue as to how to begin the screenplay. He was tempted to begin the film as in a hazy dream, a man awakening from a deep fog after a restless night spent on a beach on the Florida Keys. The camera would slowly move up the lead character's legs, clad in blue jeans, coming to rest on his crotch on which a butterfly was sewn.

Phil had installed his computer in an upstairs backroom overlooking the courtyard which he shared with Jason and Lula. If there was one man who could make him forget about Brian, it was Jason. As he worked this morning, he kept glancing out the window, hoping Jason would go for a sunbath in the courtyard. But so far there had been no stirring of life from next door. Lula and Jason must be sleeping late.

Phil was going to give his Aunt Bice another hour or two to pull herself together after no doubt another drunken night. He wanted to speak to her about setting up a meeting with Lavender Morgan. Since the screenplay was to be set in Savannah, he wanted to get connected to the town in some way, the way that John Berendt had done when he wrote *Midnight in the Garden of Good and Evil.* Phil fully expected he could achieve greater authenticity for his screenplay by moving around at night getting to know the local characters. Although years had gone by since the publication of Berendt's so-called non-fiction book, Phil fully suspected that there existed in Savannah background characters even more intriguing than any found in the Midnight book.

So intrigued was he in trying to capture the opening sequence of *Butterflies in Heat* on his computer that an hour or even more time must have gone by before he became aware of angry voices next door. Lula and Jason were having one hell of a fight. He couldn't make out what they were saying, but it was clear from the sounds that both of them were bubbling mad and not giving a damn about what the neighbors thought.

A few minutes later he heard the back door slam. The fight was over. As he peered out his window, he could see Jason, clad only in a pair of shorts, storming up the driveway toward the street. So much for his plans to invite both of them over for lunch.

He'd truly wanted to get to know them better, especially Jason, although Lula intrigued him as well. How many women had he known who would invite a gay man to feel between her husband's legs on their first meeting? Any woman that liberated fascinated him. Even now he could taste Jason's lips on his. Jason offered him the feel of a lifetime. That was a heavenly package Jason carried around, and Phil was eager to open that package and explore its contents more fully. Hadn't Lula already given him permission?

A loud knocking on his front door jerked him out of his reverie about Jason. Even though he had a doorbell, someone was banging. As he raced down the steps, thinking it might be Jason, he heard a kid screaming, followed by a woman's screeching reprimand. The voice he recognized as belonging to Joyce Sheehan.

With trepidation, he opened the door. There he confronted Brian's smiling, happy face. He was wearing a red bathing suit that definitely revealed he was a man of considerable bulk. He was holding one of his sons in his arms. The other boy was tugging at his mother's new bathing suit. Joyce was very overweight with a pasty skin covered in parts with red blotches. Before he could say anything, Phil took in the family portrait in disbelief. Why do some of the handsomest men marry the world's ugliest women?

"Phil, baby, so glad to see you, old buddy." Brian and his son came right in through the door before Phil could even invite them in.

"I'm Joyce," the big woman said, whacking the other son in the face when he defiantly kicked her leg. "This is Henry. He's been cutting up all morning and is gonna get his ass whupped."

"Glad to meet you," Phil said, standing back to let them in. "I didn't expect to see you guys so soon."

Joyce grabbed Phil's arm. "We're supposed to bring some sandwiches, and Brian won't get paid for another two days. You got anything I can make sandwiches out of?"

"Yeah," Phil said. "I picked up some supplies in town yesterday."

"That's great," Joyce screeched before heading to the kitchen and his refrigerator without an invitation.

"I hope you don't mind our dropping in like this?" Brian said, putting his other son to rest on the floor. The boy was too big to be carried around. "This is John, by the way."

"Hi, John," Phil said, deliberately lowering his voice.

John stared long and hard at Phil before turning to his father. "He's even prettier than you said, Dad. I can't believe it. Most girls in the world ain't as pretty as this guy." He turned back to stare into Phil's face. "You're something else, mister."

Henry had already run into the kitchen where Phil could hear him loudly demanding that Joyce make him a sandwich too.

"I want one too," John called out, racing into the kitchen to join them.

After they'd gone, Brian leaned closer to Phil. "The other night was just foreplay," he said. "Tonight I've got some deep plowing to do."

Before Phil could say anything, Brian rushed out onto the front porch and retrieved two suitcases and what looked like a laundry bag.

Back in the foyer he handed one of the suitcases to Phil. "Here, old buddy, help me carry this up the steps." He bounded ahead of Phil going up the stairs.

Phil followed lugging a suitcase. Everything was happening a little too quickly for him.

At the top of the landing, Brian turned to him. "Which is your bedroom?"

Phil motioned to the room on the left. Brian put his suitcase inside the door. He took the laundry bag and peered into the next bedroom. "This is a big guest room. Joyce and the boys can sleep in here. I'll share your bedroom." He turned and winked at Phil. "Hey, I gotta take a piss." He headed toward Phil's bedroom, leaving the door open. "C'mon in," Brian called after Phil, "and shut the door. I've got to ask you a big favor."

Phil came into his bedroom and closed the door behind him. In the bathroom where that door stood open he could hear Brian pissing loudly into the toilet.

"For God's sake, where are you?" Brian called from the bathroom. "Come in here, I've got to ask you something."

Phil came into the bathroom, noticing that Brian had turned sideways to piss, offering Phil an unobstructed view.

"It ain't nothing you haven't seen before," Brian said, elaborately shaking himself. He then stuffed himself back into his bathing suit. "It's hard to fit it all in," he said to Phil.

"That bathing suit should be a bit bigger or you should be smaller."

"That's not likely to happen," Brian said, winking at him again. "Especially not when I'm around you. It just grows and grows."

"What's the favor?" Phil asked. Now that Brian had stuffed himself back into the bathing suit, Phil knew it wasn't going to be that favor.

"You gotta watch the kids today. We had promised to take them to Tybee. But just after you called, we got another call from Tom Caldwell. He works for the Savannah police department. In fact, he's related to your neighbor here, Lula Carson. Tom and his wife have invited us out on his boat but Tom's wife can't stand John and Henry. Could you look after the kids for us? We'll be back in time for supper."

"I'd love to help...but..."

"That's great. My boys are a lot of fun. Full of surprises."

"I bet."

From the foot of the stairs, they could hear Joyce screaming. "Would you get a move-on? We're late as it is."

"Shut your fat lip, bitch," Brian yelled, opening the door and calling down. "I had to take a crap." He shut the door and pulled Phil to him. "See that bed over there," Brian said. "Tonight in that very bed I want you to go all the way with me. Show me some of those tricks you learned up in New York or out in California."

Phil was trembling. He'd never been this close to Brian's lips before although he'd had intimate contact with other body parts—but never the mouth. He could smell the cop's sweet breath. "Oh, Brian," he whispered in his ear. "I need it, I want it. I promise there won't be an inch of your body I won't make love to."

Brian's lips were only inches from Phil's face. "I've never done this with a man before. But I guess it's just like kissing a woman. You just open your mouth, stick out your wet tongue and hope that it'll get sucked on the other side."

Phil's fingers dug into Brian's back as he tasted his lips for the first time. He voraciously sucked Brian's tongue and wanted the world to go away.

Even Joyce's screeching voice calling for Brian to get downstairs at once did not succeed in breaking their connection for a long time.

*****

Still furious at Jason, although not quite certain what they'd fought about, Lula didn't want to write this morning. She kept looking into their shared patio, hoping Phil would come out for coffee so she could join him. She needed literary companionship this morning, and she just knew Phil could provide that.

To her great surprise, she heard children running and screaming next door. Surely Phil didn't move into their adjoining house with kids in tow. That disturbed her immensely. Even as a child, and except for Jason, she preferred the company of adults. The sound of kids running and screaming was one of the worst noises she'd ever heard, and she feared if this kept up she'd never write another page of *The Tireless Hunter.*

Taking her mug filled with badly brewed coffee, she decided to go out into the patio whether Phil was there or not. Perhaps he'd see her and come and join her.

Seating herself in the center of the patio, she enjoyed the hot sun, although she knew she could not stay out in it for long. But right now she imagined that it was restoring her health and energy. She'd been too tired to write. Now she remembered what she'd fought with Jason about. It was inevitably over money. She couldn't leave any money around the house. Jason would search for every penny, then rush out and spend it. He had no concerns whatsoever about how they were going to live tomorrow or the next day after the funds from her grant were exhausted.

The back door to Phil's porch was suddenly thrown open, and a nude boy, about eight or nine years old, ran out onto the porch and stared down into the patio. "Where in the hell is Phil?" he asked. "There ain't no God damn towels in our bathroom."

"I haven't seen him," she said in astonishment, staring up at the boy.

At that point, Phil opened the door and tossed a towel to the boy. "Here, sport, dry off and you'd better put some clothes on." He looked down, smiling helplessly at Lula. "This is John. John, Lula. As you can plainly see, he's a boy."

"Pleased to meet you," she said to the boy who was now drying his wet body.

"I left a towel in the hallway," Phil said to the boy. "Take it up to Henry. Get your clothes on, and I'll take you boys for some burgers. I'm starved."

Racing back into the house, Phil emerged with a tray with a coffee pot and two cups. "It's going to be another scorcher. Don't you think that Savannah should be evacuated in August?"

"I'm so used to the heat of the Deep South," she said. "Our family never had air conditioning. When it got so hot you couldn't move, we just sat out on the porch and fanned ourselves until we got too tired to do even that. God meant for people to sweat. It's good for our pores."

"Maybe, but spring and fall are my favorite times of the year. I don't like extremes in temperature."

"You're a real poet," she said, reaching over and stroking his arm. "The spring bringing renewal, the autumn sweet decay before the harsh winter descends. In spite of it being the dog days, I feel both of us are in our spring renewal period. At the peak of our creativity. You'll probably become the highest paid screenwriter in Hollywood, and I'll not make millions, but will go on to literary glory."

"I wish that for both of us." He sipped his coffee and seemed to be casting a steely eye at her. "About the other night. That kiss with Jason. I want to apologize. I got carried away."

"You're welcome to feel him up at any time," she said. "Frankly, he enjoyed it. I'm not interested in Jason's body. I want his companionship." She sighed in the scalding heat.

"He's a very attractive man. Very sexy."

"If you like a big brute of a man. Actually my fantasy man would be a lean poet. One who wears glasses and walks with a delicate step.

Raw masculinity in all its raging fury never warmed the cockles of my heart. Perhaps you'll disagree."

"Let's agree to disagree on something," he said, smiling affectionately at her. "We're such kindred spirits otherwise, but I've never met a man too big for me."

"I understand your attraction to men like Jason," she said, wiping the sweat from her brow with a napkin he'd left on the tray. "But I didn't know you moonlighted as a baby-sitter."

"I can explain all this. John and Henry are the kids of Brian Sheehan. He's an old school buddy of mine. He's down here in Savannah for the day. In fact, Brian and his wife Joyce are going boating with your cousin, Tom, and his wife. The policeman."

"Oh, I see," she said. "When you live in the South, the world gets mighty intimate. Everybody is the friend of somebody else, if they are not, in fact, related."

Still naked, John barged through the door again, the towel wrapped around his neck.

Phil looked up at him. "I thought I told you to put on some clothes, big boy."

Seeming to ignore him, John came down into the patio and plopped down in a chair next to Lula.

"Daddy lets us run around the house naked all the time. The moment he gets home, he pulls off all his clothes. Mama says daddy is proud of what he's got. He likes to show it off every chance he gets."

"Your daddy and my husband, Jason, have a lot in common," Lula said, pouring herself more coffee at Phil's invitation.

"My daddy's real big," John said to Lula. "Do you think I'll ever grow big like my daddy?"

"That's a question I've never pondered," Lula said, lowering her glasses and staring intently at the boy's equipment. "I would say that for a..." She paused. "How old are you?"

"Nine."

"For a boy of nine, you look like you have great potential," she said. "At least he didn't circumcise you. I like that. I've always believed in the natural male. What about you, Phil?"

"I've never encountered any part of a man I didn't like," Phil said. "As for foreskin, that gives you something else to nibble on."

"You've got a point there," she said.

John looked puzzled, like he wasn't following the train of thought.

"I'm not sure this is a fit and proper conversation to be having in the presence of infants," Lula said.

"I'm no God damn infant," John said, rising to his feet. "I can get hard and I stick it to Henry all the time. My kid brother walks around with a sore ass all the time." After saying that, he turned and ran inside the house.

Lula laughed at Phil. "I fear we are not following the baby-sitter's manual."

"We can play many roles, but I don't think we'd ever make it as parents," Phil said.

John called down to them from the upstairs window. "Henry's ready now. I'm putting on my clothes. You promised us those damn burgers, mister."

"Duty calls," Phil said, getting up. "Want to join us?"

"Perhaps next time," she said. "I'm not a McDonald's type of gal."

"Okay," he said, reaching down and kissing her on the cheek very tenderly. She gently ran her fingers though his raven black hair, wishing that she'd married a man like Phil instead of a nut like Jason.

"I'll be out at the barbecue tonight," he said. "Maybe you'll join us when Brian and Joyce get back from their boating thing. For all I know, they'll bring your cousin Tom and his wife."

"That sounds nice," she said. "I have a head of cabbage. There's only one dish I know how to make—and that's cole slaw. In Columbus I was rather celebrated for my cole slaw. I have a secret ingredient. Never told anyone."

"We'll see you later."

After he'd gone, she sat alone in the patio waiting for Jason's return, not knowing if he would indeed come back today. It seemed he had some other place to go that extended far greater hospitality than she offered him.

The persistent ringing of the phone disturbed her reverie. At first she thought it was coming from Phil's house. Then she realized it was her phone ringing. Whoever was on the other end of that line desperately wanted to talk to her. Fearing the worst, she ran up the steps to her porch and into her house, picking up the receiver of the still-ringing phone.

"Is this Lula Carson?" a woman's voice asked.

"This is she," Lula said rather formally.

"Thank God I got in touch with you. It's Lavender Morgan. I'm in deep shit."

*****

On the beach at Tybee Island, Tango sat up and took notice as Jason made his way across the beach in a white bikini. She also couldn't help but notice that a lot of other people—both men and women—carefully appraised Jason's assets. That white boy could sure attract a lot of attention. When she'd picked him up, he was clad only in a pair of shorts and he looked mad. He'd explained that he'd just had a big fight with Lula and wanted to sleep over at her condo for a day or so until things cooled down. That was good news to her ears as she didn't have to dance at the club tonight and could be with him.

She didn't know where Danny was, as he hadn't come home after leaving the club with Lavender Morgan's party. She suspected that Gin Tucker had captured him as a trophy and taken him home, but she couldn't be sure. With Danny, she could never be sure where he was. Right now as Jason came closer carrying two milkshakes, she couldn't mess up her mind with Danny Hansford. She had bigger and better things to deal with.

Half blinded by the brilliant yellow sunshine, Tango scooted over and made room for her handsome blond hunk. Adjusting her red bikini, she smiled at him. "Welcome back, sugar," she said to him, taking the cold milkshake offered. "Vanilla, my favorite flavor. How did you know without asking?"

"I figured you like your shakes just like you like your men. White and thick."

"You got that right, sugar."

"Personally I prefer a little chocolate now and then."

A half-hysterical whimpering sound came from her. She moved her bikini-clad body closer to him. Moistening her lips, she kissed the biceps of his left arm, much to the horror and annoyance of a fat white couple on the neighboring beach blanket. A wild panic was in her eyes. She didn't know if she could stay on this beach much longer, as she didn't want the sun to turn her skin any browner than it was.

He reached for his beach bag and pulled out a book.

"You're going to read, sugar? You so bored with me you need to read about people getting it on and not get it on yourself?"

"Nothing like that," he said. "I'm going to become your theatrical agent."

"What in the fuck is that supposed to mean?" She sat up, looking at him with a steely glance.

"I finished this novel last night. It's called *Butterflies in Heat*. I want you to read it too."

"Honey, your mama here is not much into reading. I'm strictly a gal of action—not the library type at all."

"This book is going to be made into a movie. Shot right here in Savannah. The screenwriter, Phil Heather, lives next door to me."

She shrugged. "Exactly what does this have to do with me?"

"There's a part in it for you. The role of Lola La Mour. This part is a hell of a lot more fun than The Lady Chablis playing herself in *Midnight in the Garden of Good and Evil*."

Suddenly he had captured Tango's undivided attention. A certain nervous agitation came over her. The prospect he was holding out was so deliciously tempting that she wanted to grab that book from him and start reading it right away. She'd skip over all the other parts and read only the scenes with Lola La Mour.

A frown crossed Jason's brow. Was it the sun in his eyes or was there some awful catch?

"There is one problem."

"What's that, sugar?" she asked skeptically.

"The part of Lola La Mour is that of a drag queen." He winked at her. "Do you think you could convince movie audiences that a red-hot blooded female, all-woman kind of gal like you could impersonate a drag queen?"

There was an awkward embarrassment and silence in the air. A gnat seemed to be eating her flesh. She slapped at it. When she turned to look into Jason's face, he was smiling in that little half mockery way of his, his eyes dancing with delight as if he'd pulled off some big surprise.

"You think you're pretty smart for a white boy, don't you?" she asked, sitting on the blanket and propping herself up on her sand-encrusted elbow.

"I'm not so dumb I can't tell if it's a man or a woman I'm fucking."

"Someone told you," she said.

"I figured it out for myself. You're all woman and everything but I know you're a man too. I just sensed it. Not that I got to see your front part."

"Well, I've got a front part and I'm not having it cut off just to please you."

"It's okay with me, baby, although I have to warn you, I'm not much of a cocksucker."

"You don't have to be around me. There ain't much to suck. In case you didn't detect it, I cum while I'm getting fucked up the ass."

"That's just fine with me. We'll be very compatible."

"I've got to meet this Phil Heather. I don't care what he looks like, he sounds like my kind of man."

"I'm jealous already and I haven't even introduced the two of you."

"You're certain, sugar, I can play the part?"

"You've got everything it takes to play the role of Lola La Mour, except there's one big drawback we've got to work on."

"What's that?" she asked in panic, growing increasingly alarmed, feeling her one big chance was setting with the afternoon sun.

"As written, the part could be played better by The Lady Chablis."

"Fuck that! I can out drag-queen that drag-queen any day. The bitch fucked up the Midnight film. I can't believe producers would give her a chance to ruin another film. She's box office poison."

"It's not that. The part of Lola is that of a middle-aged queen. Her getting old and starting to lose her looks is all part of the story."

"Honey, that ain't for me. I'm young and beautiful, the youngest and most beautiful woman in all of Savannah."

"That's true. But there's a way out of this. I want you to meet Phil at his house. I suspect after meeting him, we can convince him to make the screen Lola a lot younger. In fact, I bet we can convince him to tailor the role especially for you."

"I'll go for that but first let's get back to the condo and let me start reading this Lola character. I've got to figure out what kind of black pussy she is."

"Just like you, baby. Just like you." He ran his eyes slowly from her ankles to her dimpled chin. It was a girlish body with graceful legs, and she could tell by the look on his face that he approved.

"Something tells me before I start in reading all about the adventures of Lola La Mour, we're going to have an adventure of our own." She picked herself up from the beach and elicited a whistle or two as she shaked her way across the sands, with Jason trailing her. On her screen billing, she'd just use the name "Tango." Within a few months, she felt the entire world would know who Tango was.

Back at her condo, while her mind was lusting for both Jason and the role of Lola La Mour, the desk clerk handed her an urgent message. Only Matt Daniels from the club knew how to reach her.

She tore open the envelope to read that her daddy, Duke Edwards, was at the club demanding to see his daughter.

*****

In the back of the boathouse at the marina, Lula confronted Lavender. Up to now, Lavender had had no use for the writer, until Gin had convinced her that Lula was the only person who could help her out of this present mess. Lula, at least according to Gin, who was never wrong about these matters, had tremendous influence over the arresting officer, Tom Caldwell. Apparently, Tom was Lula's cousin, or some such shit.

In her lavender riding outfit, Lavender stood nervously in the presence of Tom, extending her heavily ringed hand to Lula. "I've always been meaning to invite you to one of my literary soirées," Lavender said apologetically, "but Gin always insisted you don't go to cocktail parties."

Shaking Lavender's hand gingerly as if it were a foreign object fallen from the sky, Lula then turned to Tom. She walked over and kissed him on both sides of the cheek. In the distant corner of the boathouse, she spotted Danny Hansford sitting forlornly and staring at them. "What's the problem, Tom?" Lula asked.

Lavender felt herself blushing, and she didn't embarrass easily. She dreaded to hear Tom recite the charges.

He glanced first at Lula, then at Lavender, and finally at Danny in the distance. "When Brian Sheehan, a friend of mine, his wife Joyce, and my own wife, Ethel Mae, walked into this boathouse, Mother Time here was going down on that underage kid over there. Not only that, but after a search I found they had drugs on them."

Lavender braced herself as Lula turned to confront her.

"Surely that's not true," Lula said.

Lavender shuddered, wondering if the story of her arrest would appear on the tonight news and eventually on the NBC documentary on her life. Although stories of her affairs had been fodder for the press for years, there was nothing in her long and lusty life that had equaled this.

"I can explain," Lavender said.

"What is there to explain?" Tom asked. "You were caught right in the act. A woman of your age. You should be ashamed of yourself."

"You've got to help me," Lavender said, turning in desperation to Lula. "I'll do anything." Based on her long experience as a resident of the State of Georgia, Lavender could be certain of one thing: Southerners could be bought. Everything rested on the way the various payoff was offered.

Turning to Tom, Lavender asked, "Before you arrest me—and Danny too—could I speak privately with Lula?"

"Okay, my gang left on the boating trip without me. You've already ruined my fun."

Taking Lula's hand, Lavender steered her over to a far corner of the boathouse. She looked over at Danny who met her gaze with a sullen look. "I would be disgraced if this got out. You've got to help me!"

Lula eyed her carefully. "When Tom wants to arrest someone, he can be mighty determined."

Lavender gently ran her long fingers along Lula's bare arm. "I'm going to have to approach this matter without my usual subtlety. Normally I have expensive lawyers negotiate things like this for me. But today I'm on my own."

"What is there to negotiate?" Lula asked, looking somewhat puzzled.

"I'll be blunt and to the point. How unlike me. But I'm really in the frying pan, as we say in Savannah. Gin tells me that your literary grant is running low, and that you're desperate to raise cash to complete what I hear is a masterpiece of world literature, each sentence with a touch of divinity."

"Yes," Lula said, somewhat defiantly. *"The Tireless Hunter* is going to win me world acclaim."

"I'm sure it will, my dear, but first it's got to be written, and you and your husband have got to be able to live in the meantime until this masterpiece is completed."

"You've got that right. Exactly where are we going here?"

"I'm on the board of directors of certain foundations," Lavender said, edging closer to Lula and speaking very softly. "I'm sure that within the month one of those foundations will be making another literary grant to you."

Lula's eyes sparkled, and it was at that moment that Lavender knew she had bagged the writer. There remained only the policeman.

"That would take care of me," Lula said. "I'll make any sacrifice for my art. What about Tom?"

Lavender stood straight up with a stiffening back. "Find out what he wants. Surely he could be bought. As everybody knows, I'm a woman of considerable means."

"I see." Lula looked over at an increasingly impatient Tom, cast another steely eye at Lavender, then walked over to Tom where she began a hushed conversation. In about five minutes she returned.

"Tom has agreed to forget the whole thing if you'll go to the bank tomorrow morning and pay off the rest of his mortgage. It comes to twenty-eight thousand dollars."

Lavender smiled and glanced nervously over at Tom. He returned her smile. "I'm glad you got him to agree to it."

"It took a little persuasion but he came around. When he balked at first, I reminded him that his wife doesn't know that he likes to receive blow jobs from black drag queens at various clubs around town. After I said that to him, he was very quick to agree to anything."

"You're a very clever girl," Lavender told Lula. "I think you and I are going to become very close friends."

"I'm sure we are and my biographers will surely record your important role in the behind-the-scenes maneuvers that led to the release of my masterpiece."

"They will indeed," Lavender said, "but perhaps we can leave out some of the more sordid details." She eyed Tom carefully. He was wearing a tank top and tight shorts. "That is one fine specimen of a man," Lavender said. "If I were a bit younger and I had met him under different circumstances, I think we might have become friends. At least intimate."

Lavender observed him walking over to Danny. Tom said something to the boy who reacted with a certain violence, as if he were going to strike the policeman. Danny yelled, "Fuck that! Like hell I will!"

"What's going on?" Lavender asked Lula. "Your cousin's not going to arrest Danny, is he? I thought the deal was that both Danny and I go free."

"Danny's been in trouble with the law several times since he hit town," Lula said. "Hustling. Drugs. The usual."

"What is Tom going to do with him?"

"Tom told me he got really horny watching you give Danny a blow job. If there's one thing Tom Caldwell loves more than his liquor it's a blow job. His wife won't take the plunge and he has to get serviced whenever a chance presents itself."

Lavender peered in astonishment as Danny got up. He looked defeated and turned and followed Tom to the men's room at the back of the boathouse.

"I can't believe your cousin is doing this," Lavender said.

"Welcome back to Savannah where all things are possible," Lula said. "You've been gone too long. In Savannah we still play the dirty games. We just don't talk about them the next day."

Lavender felt extra hot in her vinyl riding suit. "If for no other reason, I have returned to the South to renew my sense of horror."

*****

The cop, Tom Caldwell, thought he was humiliating the boy, but Danny's own revenge was sweeter. He was enjoying every inch of Tom, sucking out his sweet juices. It was his favorite thing, although very few people on this earth, except Danny's own daddy, knew this. Tango certainly didn't know it. Lavender Morgan would probably be shocked to learn the truth.

Danny fastened his lips around the big cock and deep-throated it just like his daddy had taught him when he was only nine years old. He pulled Tom's foreskin back tight, as Danny's tongue worked its way around Tom's cockhead. He went back to licking up and down the shaft, bringing Tom closer and closer into his power. A warm and wonderful feeling came over Danny. As he enjoyed the penetration and taste of Tom, Danny had left Savannah and was drifting into celestial space.

As Danny voraciously sucked Tom, he stroked the cop's legs and felt his thighs, his hands eventually wandering upward to feel Tom's hairy, powerful chest.

Tom was already the man Danny wanted to be one day, but Danny knew he'd never live to become Tom's age. Tom's grunts of delight mingled with Danny's own moans of pleasure. Tom exuded masculinity in all its abundance. Danny sucked and slurped, withdrawing a bit for air as he licked the cop's fat, round balls.

Tom suddenly grabbed Danny's hair as he plunged into the boy's velvety throat. Danny knew it wouldn't be long now, and already he was dreading when Tom would withdraw from his mouth and force Danny to return to reality.

As he continued to slurp and suck, Danny knew that Tom couldn't hold back much longer. Danny sucked Tom's cock all the way down his throat. Tom's cock got hot, harder, and bigger until he exploded, filling Danny's mouth with his thick, salty cum. Danny devoured what seemed like an endless orgasm. Tom had to pull away and force a withdrawal from Danny's mouth. He was determined to get the last milky white drops before letting Tom go.

"That was some action, kid," Tom said, stuffing himself into his tight shorts. "Something tells me you and me are going to be seeing a lot of each other. You're as good as it gets for me."

Once he'd finished, Danny stood up to face Tom. Danny was embarrassed that Tom had learned his secret passion. But Tom had known all along, Danny was certain. That's why the cop had invited him to go to the back of the boathouse in the first place. Tom must have sensed some desire in Danny's eyes or else he might never have demanded that he be serviced.

Up real close, Tom looked into Danny's eyes. He could smell Tom's sweet breath.

"You want me to kiss you, don't you kid?" Tom asked. "I've never kissed a man before. But you're prettier than most girls."

Danny closed his eyes and parted his lips slightly. He felt Tom drawing closer and closer. As Tom's tongue penetrated Danny's lips, he reached out, digging his fingers into Tom's back, holding him closer and closer as he slurped his tongue the way he'd so recently done with Tom's cock. He knew Tom would soon withdraw from him and be on his way, but he wanted this moment to last forever.

In minutes Tom was gone, the taste of him lingering. When Danny cleaned himself up and finally emerged from the men's room, Lula Carson was gone too. Only Lavender Morgan waited for him by his new motorcycle. He knew Lavender would never speak of what had happened in the men's room. And neither would he.

The ride to Lavender's was in silence. His remaining days on this earth were dwindling to a precious few, and he resented this aging matron's presence on his bike. He wanted to be free of her and her sexual demands. Right now he wanted to be riding on Tom's own police motorcycle. He resented the way Lavender's fingers tightened into his chest. Thank God Tom didn't take his stash from him. He'd need drugs or something before he faced Lavender in her bed again.

He let her off in the back of her home and told her he'd see her later. He wanted to go for a ride by the beach to clear his head.

An hour later he didn't know where he was. The day was almost windless. In the distance the sounds of barking dogs filled him with an ominous sense of dread. Was he an invader about to be attacked by these mad dogs?

After the dogs quieted down, a silence came over the hot, heavy day. A wind finally stirred, causing a little rattle in the palmetto fronds.

A stiff, clean sea breeze parted and then reparted Danny's long blond hair. The breeze seemed to refresh his soul, and in the distance he could see a silver glistening from the water.

All of a sudden he knew where he was. Without meaning to, he was riding toward the house of Erzulie, the voodoo queen. He had urgent business with her. Of all the people in the world, only Erzulie knew his secret—that the dead soul of Danny Hansford, murdered by Jim Williams—still had not left the world and still inhabited the second Danny Hansford's body.

As Danny's motorcycle pulled into Erzulie's dirt frontyard, two chickens went cackling for cover at this sudden invasion. Wearing a saffron yellow robe, Erzulie herself came out onto the front porch.

"If you didn't bring money, white boy," she shouted at him, "I can't summon the spirits. Those spirits send me bills every day. I've got to live too."

"I've got money," he said reassuringly, as he got off his bike.

"Then I've got time to mess with some white boy," she said, heading back into her ramshackle house. Through beaded curtains she led him into a back room. "I knew you were coming today. I just knew it. I was so sure you was coming and that you'd have some money you made whoring that I went to the graveyard at midnight. I learned some powerful shit in that graveyard." She glared at him. "How much money have you got on you?"

"A hundred dollars."

"That's a lot of money. A lot of money. I don't think I've seen that much money at one time in all my life."

"There's more where that comes from," he said, reaching into his pocket and pulling out a hundred dollar bill he'd gotten from Lavender.

With her long fingers painted a brilliant shade of scarlet, she felt the money as if not believing it was real. "These niggers who come to me for help can hardly spare a five or ten. A hundred-dollar bill! I think I'll save that." She fondled the money again. "A hundred dollars!"

"Quit playing with the fucking money and lay the heavy shit on me."

"Okay, okay," she said. "I'm not gonna take that as an insult. I know who's really talking to me. That's the real Danny Hansford in there talking. Not you, white boy." She stuffed the one-hundred dollar bill into her ample bosom before turning to confront Danny again. "Do you want the good news first or the bad news?"

He sighed in disgust at life itself. "The bad news. All my life I've gotten the bad news first."

"That boy is still living inside you and he ain't gonna let go until you're dead. There's no way out. Nothing I can do."

"For that I give you my hard-earned hundred dollars?"

"There's more, white boy. A real strange thing the demons in the graveyard told me."

"Out with it!"

"Before you die, you're gonna come into big money. Not only big bucks but you're gonna be famous too."

"Shit, you've become like some God damn fortune teller at a circus. Telling all the redneck suckers they're gonna be rich and famous one day." He practically spat out his disgust before storming out of her shack.

She ran after him, screeching into the hot day. "You'll come back. Erzulie always sees, knows, and tells the truth."

Danny spat into her dirt yard, started the motor of his cycle and stirred up a trail of red Georgia dust as he headed off down the highway.

*****

Tipper had entered the back door of the club. She could not bear to see the promotional materials or even the star billing she'd received out front. All she knew was that Gin's picture of her in The Black Widow costume was on prominent display, along with beefcake photographs taken so long ago of all the beautiful young men who'd been her husbands when they weren't out making love to other men.

Tonight she felt strangely at peace about exploiting her own notorious past, including the murder or suicide of Taylor Zachory. On looking back, she didn't know why she'd objected so violently to appearing as The Black Widow.

Even as a young entertainer, she'd always been outrageous. She'd told her first interviewer, and the remark was widely published, that she felt the vagina and the penis ought to be located in the neck. "Why?" the incredulous reporter had asked her. "That way," she'd said, "when friends embrace they could copulate at the same time!"

Tonight she hoped to capture some of the allure of her early appearances when she was hailed as an entertainer who "Blues the Vamps and Vamps the Blues."

She'd been practicing all afternoon, and, at least in her judgment, her velvet-contralto voice had never been in finer form. She was known for crooning forlornly in a stirring, husky voice. She'd decided she would definitely add the throaty "Can't Help Lovin' That

Man of Mine" to her act, as all her friends assured her she'd done that better than Miss Helen Morgan herself.

Tipper knew Frank's club was cramped and poorly lit and far too overcrowded. The stage was tiny and the piano was sadly out of tune. Even though the house was sold out, she knew most of the audience tonight was sadly disappointed at first. Coming into the club carrying copies of *Midnight in the Garden of Good and Evil,* the night clubbers really wanted to see and hear "The Lady of Six Thousand Songs," Emma Kelly, featured in both the book and the Clint Eastwood film. But Dale told her there had been no cancellations when the audience learned that she'd be appearing while Emma was on a much-needed vacation.

Emma attracted mainly an older crowd, and these same fans knew who Tipper Zelda was too. Many of them had come into maturity years ago and were weaned on headlines about her various love affairs and allegedly murdered husbands. The disappointment among fans, or so she'd been told, was quickly erased when audiences learned that she was the scandalous headliner. It was easy to forget about Emma and her six-thousand songs when you had pictures of a notorious figure like Tipper Zelda appearing. After all, sex and scandal—perhaps a murder or two—always did better at the box office than routine night club music.

Earlier in the day she'd obtained the address of Phil Heather and had personally invited him to come to her opening night. She'd paid a neighbor's boy to deliver the handwritten invitation to Phil. She had to see for herself if indeed he did look like Montgomery Clift.

Before leaving her dressing room, she'd learned from Dale that Phil had accepted her invitation and had asked to bring a guest which Dale had agreed to. The excitement of getting to meet Phil Heather momentarily overcame her disappointment in learning that he'd be here with a guest. She was hoping Phil would be at the club alone and that they might meet privately after she finished her act.

Although long past her youthful beauty, she applied all the artful makeup touches—some learned from Joan Crawford—to the image staring back at her in the mirror. Even at the peak of her beauty, she'd never been a Grace Kelly. She was known for her sexual, sensual appeal more than for her beauty. She wanted her appearance tonight to recapture some of those sullen, sexy rhythms of yesterday, a journey into nostalgia for a female troubadour who lamented through smoke and tears the man who got away.

She sucked in her breasts and stared again at the mirror. She remembered when she'd been likened to rare, ripened fruit by one columnist. She was always getting written about in those days. Reporters knew they could count on her for good copy. Once she told a reporter that men, even the handsomest of men, fascinated her only for as long as it took to down a dry martini.

She wasn't entirely bantering with the reporter. To some extent, her remark was true about all the men in her life. Her passionate involvement with a lover deteriorated after only a short summer. That was true of all her lovers and husbands—all except Montgomery Clift, whom she'd loved to the very end of his life, long after he'd lost his youth and beauty.

Now Monty had returned in the shape of Phil Heather. She'd asked Dale to point out what front-row table Phil would be seated at. She planned to sing especially to his table. The real Monty had told the press, "She's my steady girl. I think she's *fantastic.*" Though Monty had said that long ago, Tipper hoped that some of her old allure would still be there—enough to enrapture Phil Heather. If Phil looked only a quarter as good as the picture published of him in the newspaper, she knew he'd be a beauty just like the young Monty.

A knock on her door jolted her into reality. She realized The Black Widow had only fifteen minutes left before she went on stage to tantalize her audience who would not only be listening to her songs but asking the inevitable question. Did Tipper Zelda really murder all those beautiful young husbands she'd married?

She opened the door to stare into the face of Dale Evans. "Phil Heather is backstage," Dale said. "He asks for just a minute of your time. He wants to thank you for the invitation and give you his wishes to 'break a leg' at tonight's performance."

"Show the young gentleman back," Tipper commanded. *"At once."*

Dressed as The Black Widow, Tipper stood alluringly in the doorway of her dressing room. In the dimly lit corridor, it was a box of black orchids Phil had brought that she first spotted. Slowly her eyes traveled up his chest as his face came into full view under an exposed overhead light bulb.

Her eyes met those of Phil's. A gasp came from her sultry throat. Montgomery Clift, in all that youthful beauty that had once ignited fires on the silver screen, had come back into her life. He was moving rapidly toward her with those black orchids.

"Monty!" she gasped. "Oh, Monty!" She raced toward him for a long overdue embrace. Monty had returned from the grave.

The black orchids cascaded to the backstage floor.

*****

After kissing Tipper Zelda good-bye, Phil joined Brian Sheehan at a ringside table. Even now, he couldn't believe what had transpired between Tipper and himself. In The Black Widow costume, she did indeed look like a murderer. Maybe the stories were true. Perhaps she did kill all those beautiful husbands. For one brief moment as she kissed him right on the mouth, he felt he was experiencing the sting of the spider itself. Would he be her next victim?

Such thoughts disappeared as he became enraptured with her music. Tipper Zelda was an artist of major talent. The sound of her voice seemed to have its origins in Harlem. On stage as she crooned her lament to lost love, Tipper seemed to excite the audience, especially with her killer spider costume. The question that remained unspoken at the end of all her love songs was simply this: Did she kill her young husbands? From the hush, even the awe, Phil sensed from the audience, it was obvious that the jury had convicted her. She was guilty on all counts. At least in the unspoken view of the jury, her audience, she was definitely guilty of murder.

Between acts, Brian whispered in Phil's ear. "I bet the bitch did it. As a cop, I can tell when somebody's guilty. The old cow is as guilty as Lee Harvey Oswald, and he was before my time. What do you think?"

"I'm not sure," Phil said, placing his under-the-table hand on Brian's muscular thigh and dreaming of traveling much closer to the goodies during the second act. "But I have a great idea. Let's go backstage after the show. I've come up with a fantastic idea for a book. I want to write the story of her life."

"Do you think she'd ever admit to all those murders?"

"She might but it'll take some doing." He sipped his drink slowly as his mind began to spin. He needed an idea for a new project after finishing the screenplay, *Butterflies in Heat.* The story of Tipper Zelda was going to be it. Thank God he looked more like Montgomery Clift, her long-lost love, than Monty himself. That is, Phil looked like Monty Clift before the accident. After the accident, even Monty Clift didn't look like himself.

Rounds of loud applause followed by a standing ovation at her encore greeted the end of Tipper's act. It was clear to Phil that The Black Widow costume novelty, the pictures of the four handsome but dead husbands outside, the tremendous newspaper coverage, were all Tipper needed to sell out every performance.

Whoever was advising her was right. She'd rescued a career in the doldrums by capitalizing brilliantly off her own notorious past.

An overweight Savannah lady, sitting directly behind Brian and Phil, said to her equally overweight woman companion, "I wouldn't have murdered one of those beautiful men. I'd have invited all four into my bed at the same time."

Dale Evans appeared to usher Phil and Brian backstage after the show.

"Is that your real name?" Brian asked. "Dale Evans. The Queen of the Cowgirls."

"Yes, it is," Dale said, appreciatively eying Brian, especially below the belt. "Except I'm not Queen of the Cowgirls. I'm merely the Queen." He turned and headed for Tipper's dressing room, as Phil and Brian trailed him.

As agitated as a cat on a hot tin roof, Phil stood at Tipper's door, waiting to be ushered in by Dale. Phil's scheming mind was spinning out of control. He always felt this way at the birth of a new project. Dale went in first and came back out two minutes later. "Tipper is a little emotional after her performance," Dale said. "She can't see all her well-wishers. Only you, Phil."

"I'm honored," Phil said, thinking how convenient that would be for the plan already formulating in his head.

"That's okay with me," Brian said. "I need to see a man about a horse."

Dale looked him up and down with a steely appraisal. "In your case I'm not so sure who the horse is. I need to go to the men's room too. I'll show you the way."

With trepidation Phil watched Brian disappear around the corner en route to the men's room with Dale. Tipper's show wasn't the only one Dale was going to enjoy before the evening ended.

As Tipper opened the door to her dressing room and ushered him inside, Phil momentarily forgot about Brian and Dale.

In her dressing robe, Tipper eyed him seductively. "Even now I can't believe your resemblance to my beloved Monty."

"More important than that is that mesmerizing performance you gave tonight." He was growing acutely uncomfortable at her staring at his face.

"Oh, that," she said, lighting up a mentholated cigarette. "Just a few songs I've collected in my day. Songs sung in the cotton fields. In jails. By members of the chain gang. In whore houses."

"Your songs are real Americana—not just the blues. You've got anger in your voice before it gives way to passion. I love that!"

"As you could tell, I don't spare my vocal chords. Sometimes my tones are hideous but with a reason. I do so in my attempt to express anguish in its pure tone."

"You do it brilliantly."

"I was the only woman in Monty's life," she said, puffing deeply on her cigarette."

The change of subject was abrupt, making him feel that all their conversations would without warning shift to Monty.

"Once, and for just a brief period, when I was just a teenage girl singer, I had competition for Monty's love from another woman. It was 1955 and the woman was considerably older than me."

"Who might that have been?"

"Greta Garbo. When she wasn't praising the glories of the goods at Hammacher-Schlemmer, Garbo dated Monty for a few times. He had an amazing schoolboy crush on her. He called her his mysterious Sphinx. He even got to kiss her good night on one occasion but found her lips chapped."

Phil leaned forward and gently kissed Tipper on the mouth. "My lips aren't chapped," he said.

Tenderly she reached out and ran her fingers through his hair.

A sharp rap on the door and Dale Evans was in the room, his eyes no doubt still dancing up and down over the sight of the glory of Brian Sheehan in the men's room.

"Tipper," he said in a queenly but commanding way.

"This boy is definitely a dominant bottom," she said to Phil, eying Dale with disdain. "I thought I told you I'm not to be disturbed."

"Darling," he said sarcastically, "*Time* magazine is here tonight. They want to take your picture and do an interview with you." He walked over to her dressing closet. "This is fantastic publicity. Back into The Black Widow costume."

She reluctantly sighed and gently kissed Phil on both cheeks. "Come over tomorrow after eleven. Dale will give you my address. We'll talk then."

"It's a deal." Phil embraced her. "A great show." He turned and left only to discover Brian waiting outside, looking somewhat the stage door Johnnie.

Later that night as Joyce slept in the next room with John and Henry, Phil got what he'd lusted for for years—a long, deep penetration from Brian. It was worth waiting for.

The manly aroma of night club smoke and whiskey was on Brian's breath as Phil voraciously sucked his tongue. Steely hard, Brian's cock had never felt bigger than when buried deep within Phil. Scissoring his legs around Brian's waist, Phil gleefully accepted the battering as it was driving him wildly toward his own climax.

Brian fucked fast, hard, and deep but it wasn't painful. Having him at long last dissolved any pain for Phil. Brian's arms slid up across Phil's belly to tweak his tits, and Phil figured this is what he did with Joyce. Brian licked the stream of salty fluid from Phil's neck, causing Phil to moan until Brian muffled his sounds with his mouth.

A kind of savage animal growl of passion came from deep within Brian's throat, and Phil knew it wouldn't be long for either of them. Phil could take it: whatever Brian wanted to give him.

If Brian's mouth had not been covering his, Phil felt he would have screamed. Brian's blast deep into his guts and his own eruption were almost too much for one man to handle without screaming a primal rant of pure joy.

Phil found himself licking any part of Brian he could reach. It was as if he wanted to devour the man. But it was more than that. It was a compelling need to acknowledge the pure physical pleasure he'd received from this man who'd sent them both over the top.

In the hour that followed and after a long lukewarm shower, where Phil got to explore every crevice of Brian's body as he bathed and licked him, Brian snuggled into the cool bed with Phil. In spite of the steamy Savannah night, the room was perfectly air conditioned.

"Let's get into some pillow talk," Brian said, inserting his tongue in Phil's left ear, causing him to squirm.

"Let's," Phil said, fondling the muscles of Brian's back with his one free hand. The other hand had descended to capture Brian's balls which Phil lovingly caressed and fondled and didn't plan to abandon for the rest of the evening.

Brian inserted his mouth over Phil's and gave him a deep, penetrating kiss. "I want to marry you, old buddy."

Startled, Phil broke away. "You're already married."

"Me and Joyce are breaking up. We've been breaking up for the past two years. The bitch can't satisfy me—I think she's lez oriented anyway. She's going to give me John and Henry. How would you like to be known as Uncle Phil?"

Before Phil could answer, or even formulate a true answer, Brian's mouth was on his again. "Don't answer my proposal right away. Let me ask the question of you again but only when I'm in the saddle. Only when I'm about to fuck the cum out of you. Only when my tongue is about to enter your mouth. Only when you finally come to your senses and wake up to the fact that you've got what you've always wanted ever since that day you spotted me buck naked years ago at school in the shower room."

As Brian descended over Phil, he opened both his body and his mind to receive the object of his schoolboy fantasy. Even before he felt Brian's massive invasion of his body, Phil knew what his answer would be.

*****

In the morning sun before the Savannah heat became too unbearable, Lula removed her halter, letting the bright light of day warm her breasts. She'd always wanted breasts like those of Marilyn Monroe but feared she'd ended up with breasts more like those of the late Audrey Hepburn. Of course, she'd never seen a picture of Ms. Hepburn's breasts but Lula imagined that they looked much like her own.

She greatly admired physical beauty in women but had long ago stopped wishing for glamour herself. She knew the good Lord decided to give her literary talent instead—and that was gift enough for anyone. In spite of her lack of sex appeal, she'd managed to snare the handsomest man—and the sexiest—in the State of Georgia. Although after meeting Brian Sheehan last night, she felt the Darien policeman gave Jason serious competition. Brian had even complimented her three times on her cole slaw she'd brought to the barbecue. Even more than people praising her literary talent, she liked praise for her cole slaw, the only dish she knew how to prepare.

The barbecue last night had been a big success, and she hoped that Phil would make cookouts a regular event in their communal patio. When a Southern boy like Phil knew how to cook, he could do so better than any Yankee. That Phil was a master of Georgia barbecue.

She was a little sorry that Phil and Brian had not invited her to Tipper Zelda's opening but Phil claimed he had only two tickets and the performance was sold out. She'd accepted his excuse but still felt excluded. In fact, she felt like Frankie in Carson McCuller's *The Member of the Wedding,* a little teenage girl who wanted to go on the honeymoon.

There was something going on in that house next door, and Lula had the novelist's instinct and the curiosity to find out. She'd believed Phil when he'd told her that he'd gone to school with Brian. That certainly provided the excuse for Brian to visit Phil and bring his wife, Joyce, and their two kids. With her trained eye and knowledge of the human heart, Lula had quickly seen beyond that screen even if Joyce were being retarded about what was going on with her husband.

Lula had controlled her drinking last night to better observe her new friends and to understand them. She was the only one in control. Phil and Brian drank a lot. So did Joyce. So did Lula's policeman cousin, Tom Caldwell, and his wife, Ethel Mae. The way the boys, John and Henry, were running about, they might as well have been drunk too.

As the evening wore on, inhibitions gave way. Phil had served Brian barbecue before offering it to anyone else. Phil had seemed to hover over Brian, seeing that his glass was filled and that the policeman had everything he wanted. The telltale clue came when

Phil had taken a napkin and wiped sauce from the corner of Brian's succulent mouth. That suggested an intimacy between them. No man would do that to another man unless they were very, very close. She suspected Phil and Brian were lovers. Brian looked about as ungay as you could get, but she'd long ago learned that obvious signs of homosexuality meant nothing. After all, Jason appeared to be the straightest man walking in Georgia, but her husband was bent in ways she could only imagine.

Right now she shuddered to think what bed Jason might be in and what he might be doing. He didn't come home last night—in fact, she hadn't seen him since their last argument over money. With the cash she was going to get from Lavender Morgan's literary grant, their money problems were now over, at least temporarily. With this influx of cash, she probably had enough to live on while she finished *The Tireless Hunter*. After its publication, she fully expected to draw royalties from the title until her death, the way J.D. Salinger was doing with *The Catcher in the Rye*.

Her morning reverie was suddenly interrupted by the appearance of her cousin Tom in her patio. He was dressed in his cop's uniform and ready for work. "Cousin Lula," he said, "any woman with breasts as tiny as yours shouldn't expose them to the public. As a matter of fact, I would suggest you wear falsies every time you go out on the streets of Savannah."

"You don't have to look. In the privacy of my patio I can do what I want. Sometimes Jason and I lie out here in the nude. Why don't you come and join us?"

"I might," he said, sitting down opposite her and pouring himself some coffee. "That is, if you wouldn't go comparing the size of my dick to Jason."

"Can't measure up to the competition?" she asked, eying him provocatively.

"Hell, I'm known as having the biggest dick on the police force in Savannah. But that fucking Jason isn't a man. He's a God damn horse. And a faggot I might add. You married yourself a real faggot."

"You like to get your dick sucked, so don't point fingers at anybody else. If I recall, you've been getting your dick sucked by gay men ever since you were fourteen years old."

"I have to turn to men because women won't do that shit, especially Ethel Mae. She thinks it's dirty. She won't even let me go down on her."

"For a policeman making arrests for so-called sexual offenses, you're incredibly naïve. Many women are highly experienced in the art of fellatio."

"I guess that's what you call cocksucking."

"As a writer, I always prefer to give the proper name to things."

"Speaking of cocksucking, I need my dick sucked right now. I need it bad. That little Danny Hansford only whetted my appetite yesterday. I've got to have something—now, not later!"

"Don't look at me. I was never a specialist at sucking men's cocks. They always made me choke—even the small ones."

"What about Phil Heather?"

"What about him?" she asked, closing her eyes again and absorbing the sun. She wished Tom would go away. He always wanted to talk about sex all the time, and she preferred to discuss more spiritual matters this morning.

"I kept noticing him last night at the barbecue," he said. "That's one pretty white boy. Looks just like Montgomery Clift. So confess. Does he suck cock?"

"What is this? A police line-up? Am I under interrogation? How in hell do I know what Phil does in bed?"

"He slept with my old buddy Brian last night. Do you know that?"

"I'm completely unaware of the sleeping habits upstairs."

"I drove Brian into Darien this morning so he wouldn't be late for work. He had one happy smile on his face, and I know who put it there. Phil Heather. That guy has one hot mouth. Just thinking about what Phil could do to me is giving me a hard-on."

"If you want Phil, why not go upstairs and state your desires? His back door is unlocked. I heard John and Henry running around the house this morning."

"You mean just go right up to his bedroom?"

"That's right. If he's not turned on by you, he'll kick you out. Nothing ventured, nothing gained."

"Should I take off my clothes? You're a writer. Tell me what I should do to create some sexual fantasy for him."

"Be as obvious as possible."

"What in hell does that mean? Would you fucking spell it out for me?"

"Okay, if only to get rid of you. I don't know about Phil but many gay men have fantasies about sex with cops. Obviously Phil likes cops. He was in bed with Brian all night. Just appear at his door. But before going into his bedroom, take out your dick and let it hang out of your cop's uniform. If he's a cop-sucker, that's all the invitation he'll need."

"It's gonna be hard when I take it out."

"For God's sake, go on. It'll bring you some relief and get you off my patio so I can enjoy the sun before it gets too hot."

"Hot damn!" he said, making his way across the patio toward Phil's back door. "I'm really going to like this."

Relieved that horny Tom was gone, Lula settled back in her chair, shutting her eyes and trying to think about *The Tireless Hunter* and where she was going to go with the next chapter. But her mind wandered to Brian and Tom instead. Why did men like that marry women? Why didn't they just accept their nature from the beginning instead of making their families unhappy?

When about fifteen minutes had gone by and Tom hadn't come down from Phil's bedroom, and she hadn't heard any violent shouting, she realized that her cousin had scored again. Phil obviously was getting to experience a type of sex that Tom's wife, Ethel Mae, rejected. She only hoped that Tom would be discreet about the mid-morning encounter. Perhaps Brian was the jealous type.

As Tom's stay in the upstairs bedroom went on and on—he was already late for work—Lula let her thoughts drift. Gone was the memory of Jason. Gone was her imagined sexual encounter between Tom and Phil. Gone was her own unrequited love for no one in particular. She was floating in astral space, trying to get inside her characters as she plotted their next moves.

She was jolted awake by hands on her breasts. At first she thought they belonged to a man. Surely not Tom. Certainly not Phil. Then she realized they were the tender, delicate hands of a woman. She whirled around to stare into the lusty face of Joyce Sheehan.

"I've always liked a woman with small, perky breasts," Joyce said, continuing to fondle and gently squeeze. "My jugs are as big as a cow's."

Before Lula could respond to this sudden invasion, John and Henry ran out the back door buck naked and raced down to the patio.

"We want some breakfast," Henry demanded of his mother.

"Hey, we're hungry," John said.

Lula looked first at his little boy cock which was practically in her face, and not that little, then at Joyce who had straightened up after her tantalizing feel of Lula's breasts.

"Get in that house, you naked jaybirds," Joyce said. "Put your clothes on, and I'll fix you some cream gravy and ham biscuits."

At that moment Tom emerged through the back door and stretched his arms on the patio before heading for work.

Lula noticed a satisfied grin on his face. She looked up at the sky.

Another morning in Savannah had begun.

*****

Leaving Jason to recover at her condo after a lusty marathon, Tango drove at once to the Blues in the Night Club. She could hardly contain her excitement, and almost felt she'd pee her pants. How could a black gal get so lucky? She'd miraculously obtained the man of her dreams, Jason McReeves, and he'd practically sworn in her ear that he'd never go home to Lula Carson ever again.

Now she was about to meet her daddy for the first time. All her life she'd dreamed of having a white daddy, and that dream was only minutes from coming true. Duke Edwards—the very name evoked a sexy, macho stud, the kind black drag queens fantasize about. A choking sensation suddenly descended in her throat. It was as if strong fingers had gripped her neck and was threatening to cut off her air supply. Surely Duke couldn't be old, fat, and ugly. Not her daddy. In her heart she just knew he was still youthful. His genes were passed on to her, and all of Savannah knew what a gorgeous pussy she was. The man who created her just had to be the prettiest thing strutting his stuff along Riverwalk.

Pulling up in front of Matt Daniels' club where she'd gone from poverty to a well-paid entertainer, she just knew the man in the white T-shirt encasing a muscled physique and in a pair of tight-fitting jeans that left an undeniable bulge was her own daddy, Duke Edwards. He was just as she'd fantasized him night after night in her dreams.

Dirty blond hair. Perhaps forty but looking much younger. He had that trashy white Southern look that really turned her on. In some ways, he was an older version of Danny Hansford without the classic beauty of Jason but making up for it in raw animal magnetism.

Getting out of the car, her red high heels hit the sidewalk with a clanking sound as she rushed to his arms. "It's you!" she said, reaching out her arms for him.

He hugged her close and kissed her real hard right on her pouty lipstick-coated red mouth. His breath smelled of tobacco and whiskey. Breaking away, he looked at a poster Matt Daniels had plastered outside the club. "I knew you from that pretty picture. You're my daughter. Even though you're black, you look like me."

"Duke, it's really you." Her fingers snaked along his strong, muscled arms. She wanted to feel him to make sure he was real and not the fantasy of her endless dreams when she'd always awaken to empty arms longing for her daddy.

"I'm real, baby," he said a bit smugly. "Anyone who ever came into a close encounter with Duke Edwards knows it's real, sweet cheeks. You are one pretty mother-fucking black pussy even if I do say so. A hell of a lot prettier than your mama."

"How did you ever find me?"

"I stopped off in that hell hole in South Carolina where I first met your mama. Somehow I heard tell you were writing every fucker in town trying to locate your daddy. I had wrote down your address. I'm passing through Savannah heading for Miami. Thought I'd look you up. I went by your apartment but you were gone. Your pictures are all over town."

"Yeah, sugar, your little gal has become a big star. The toast of Savannah."

"I met your boss, Matt Daniels. He said you were off tonight, but he knew how to get in touch with you."

"I'm so glad he did." She hugged him again, noticing that he held her perhaps a little too long. She could feel the bulge in his jeans pressing into her, and the touch and smell of him sent shivers racing up her spine.

"Let's get out of this God damn blazing sun and go some place cool," Duke said. "Like your apartment. You got air conditioning, don't you, baby girl?"

"I shore do and I can keep it real cool for you."

He looked her up and down and smiled seductively. "Or real hot."

Without thinking about that remark, she ushered him into her car and sped off to another part of town. On the way there, he said, "Honey baby, I've been a little bit down on my luck lately. Could you stop and go in and buy me a little bottle of rotgut bourbon? I'm low on cash."

"I don't need to stop," she said. "I've got that at home."

"Having a reunion with my long lost daughter after all these years has put me in the mood for a good slug of whiskey."

"I hear you talkin', sugar."

In minutes she was entering her apartment which Duke carefully appraised, looking around as if he might settle in for a while. She certainly hoped so. There was no sign of Danny Hansford. He obviously hadn't been home in a while. She figured he was probably hanging out at Gin Tucker's. He was due to go on as her partner tomorrow night at Blues in the Night, so she sure hoped Danny hadn't skipped town. But right now she couldn't mess up her mind with that young white boy. She had an older white man—her own daddy—to deal with, and nothing could make her happier than that. At her little bar, she poured her daddy a bourbon.

"Just straight, baby," he said. "No ice and no branch water."

"I'll have one with you, sugar."

As he downed his whiskey, he was already fumbling with her air conditioner, turning it up full blast. "This is a nice little place you got here. I noticed you have an extra bedroom. I'm sure you won't mind if I stick around a little while to get to know my own daughter."

She squealed with delight. "There's nothing on God's green earth I'd like more."

He downed the rest of the bourbon in his glass and indicated to her he wanted a refill. "Tastes real good. I had a bad night."

"What happened, sugar?" she said, heading to the bar to refill his glass.

"I made it as far as Atlanta before I ran out of dough. I wanted to get on down to Savannah to see my little gal. To pick up some cash real fast I had to sell myself to these two old faggots who wanted to lick and eat every part of me."

"Oh, sugar!"

"If there's one thing in the world I can't stand it's a faggot. I'm a pussy man myself." He looked her up and down and smiled seductively. "Chocolate pussy is my specialty."

"How you talk!"

"You're a hell of a lot prettier than your mama ever was. Or did I tell you that?"

"I'm glad you like what you see."

He smiled at her again. Or was it a leer? "I like it a lot."

She handed him his newly refilled glass of bourbon. As she did, his hand brushed hers, lingering longer than necessary. "You don't mind running me a bath, do you?"

"I'd love to," she said, breaking away and feeling acutely uncomfortable.

"I want to wash that faggot slime off my body and forget about last night."

"I'll run your bath," she said, avoiding his intense glare. She was beginning to feel distress and a slight fear.

"I noticed you had a washer and dryer in your kitchen," he said. "Mind washing my clothes while I take a long bath? I hit Savannah without a change of clothes."

He slipped off his T-shirt and for the first time she could see his muscled chest. He had just the beginning of a beer belly but somehow it made him look even sexier. He kicked off his loafers and reached to unbutton his blue jeans. "I don't wear briefs," he said. "I stuff what I've got into a pair of tight jeans. The way I figure it, if a man or woman wants to stare at Duke Edwards' crotch, and that turns them on, what the hell."

As he began to lower his jeans, she turned abruptly and headed toward the bathroom to run the water in the tub for him.

She stopped up the tub and tested the water to make it the right temperature for Duke. At a sound at the door, she turned and looked up at her daddy. He was stark naked. Without really meaning to, she stared long and hard at his dangling equipment. Her breathing came in gasps. Perhaps it was the steam from the hot water. It was all she could do to avert her eyes from his crotch and concentrate on getting him some soap.

"Your mama used to get really turned on when old Duke dropped his jeans!"

She didn't say anything at first, not really knowing what to do. She wanted to flee from the bathroom yet felt compelled to stay.

He tested the water with his left foot. "It's just right. You sure know how to please a man."

"Thanks," she said, straightening up. As she attempted to ease by him, he gently, almost caressingly, took hold of her arm. "Your mama used to bathe me. All over. I figured my own daughter could at least stick around and wash her old man's back for him. What do you say?"

"Sure, Duke, whatever you want."

"That's my gal. My own little black beauty." He eased into the tub and leaned into the engulfing water.

Taking a sponge from a nearby shelf, she soaked it and began to wash his back.

"I like that," he said. "My little black beauty's got a real nice touch." He opened his eyes and looked yearningly at her. "God, you're one beautiful pussy. How about taking off all your clothes and joining me? Really get to know your daddy well."

She dropped the sponge and with a slight cry headed for the bathroom door, shutting it firmly behind her.

"What the hell!" she heard him yell. "Get back in here, you black prick-teasing bitch. I've got a fucking hard-on. A hard-on you gave me and a hard-on you're gonna take care of if you want your God damn teeth to stay in your head."

She stood trembling with her back to the door. At first she was tempted to flee from the apartment, running into the streets. She'd drive back to the condo and the safety of Jason's arms.

But another more compelling attraction loomed before her. She wanted to be a good girl but she couldn't resist. A force larger than her self-control was consuming her body. That force made her open the door to the steamy bathroom.

In the tub he looked up at her. "That's my gal. Come and feel what your daddy has for his little girl. Come and swallow it like your mama did night after night and never could get enough of it."

No longer in charge of her own mind, she felt paralyzed as her body, taking on a life of its own, moved toward the bathtub and the naked Duke Edwards.

Her hands reached out to him as they had so many other lonely nights in her dreams.

"I'm stunned," Lavender said, welcoming Phil Heather to her cocktail party where he was the guest of honor. "You look absolutely like Montgomery Clift in *Red River*, only prettier."

"I'm honored to meet you and be at your home." Phil took her hand, bent slightly and kissed it.

"My," Lavender said, impressed with this young man and his charm. "You may have the looks of your father, Monty, but you have all the charm of John F. Kennedy Jr."

"If I had my choice, I would have looked like him instead of Monty."

"Perhaps in your next life you will." She took his hand and guided him through her party of men. He took each of the hands, even the sweaty palms of her guests, as he made eye contact and accepted each of their tributes to his late so-called father.

In the corner, one fat queen, who resembled an iguana, Jay Garon, a literary agent from New York, said, "I hope you don't suffer from your father's curse."

Knowing instinctively where he was heading, Lavender interceded in a vain attempt to change the subject.

But Phil held his ground. "Exactly what does that mean?"

"The tiniest dick in Hollywood," Garon said.

Phil smiled. "I must have taken after my mother's side."

"Just like JFK, Jr.," Lavender said, relaxing now that she saw that Phil wouldn't be insulted. "I knew his father's equipment well," she said boastfully. "Regrettably I never got an opportunity to audition his son. A slight age difference." She paused to sip from her drink. "However, one night at a party at Georgetown, I felt I might have had a chance. JFK, Jr. stayed at my side all evening. I think he was enraptured with the idea of going to bed with a former mistress of his father. But as the night wore on, he regained control of his senses, kissed me good night, and left the party. No doubt to the arms of another woman. I later found out that other woman was Madonna of all people."

Rescuing Phil from the clutches of Garon, Lavender directed him to Gin Tucker who was moving in on Phil like a Mesozoic reptile hungry for lunch. "Monty Clift has returned from the dead," Gin said, extending a sweaty, limp, but heavily manicured hand with polished fingernails.

"Son of," Phil lied. "I'm not like my father at all."

"Thank God for that," Gin said, panting at the sight of Phil. "You won't let drunken car accidents spoil your beauty or drugs take your life."

"That is not my intention."

"Phil will live a long and happy life," Lavender said reassuringly. "Unlike me," she said, "his beauty will last for another forty years. At least."

"Thanks," was all Phil could manage to say. He looked acutely uncomfortable.

"I didn't know Monty," Gin said, suddenly interjecting himself as Lavender attempted to steer Phil away. "But I once went to bed with Marlon Brando. Some queens in Savannah dispute my claim, but it's true. You can't make up things like that."

"I hope you enjoyed the experience," Phil said.

"It wasn't memorable at all," Gin said, still looking disappointed. "I was expecting Stanley in *A Streetcar Named Desire.* Marlon fell far short of the mark. He called it 'my noble tool.' It wasn't very noble and certainly wasn't much of a tool."

"Maybe you'll get lucky next time. If that's the case, stay away from Brad Pitt and go for Tom Cruise instead."

Lavender was determined to rescue Phil from an increasingly gin-soppy Gin Tucker. But Gin had latched onto Phil's arm and didn't seem to want to let go. "Is it really true that Elizabeth Taylor was in love with your father? I heard she is a size queen. How could she possibly have settled for little old Monty Clift? And we're talking little. Put it in italics if you quote me."

"I don't know that Ms. Taylor is a size queen. It's true she married Nicky Hilton and Eddie Fisher, men of considerable endowments, but she also married Richard Burton twice, and he was hardly the winner of any pecker checker contests. She also married Larry and his appendage, I hear, is only six inches at the max. That is, if we can believe the tabloids."

Gin smiled. "I see you know your Hollywood history, my darling."

"You must excuse us," Lavender said in way of a reprimand to Gin. "This darling young man here will think all we do at my literary gatherings is talk about penis sizes."

"You know we always do," Gin said. "After all, isn't that the most fascinating conversation in the world?

"I suppose," she said, finally rescuing Phil from the clutches of Gin.

As she guided him across the room to his next encounter, Phil turned and smiled at her. "Aunt Bice has told me so much about you. Thanks for inviting me."

"You are most welcome," she said.

"And speaking of Aunt Bice, I've been calling her all morning. I'm getting worried. There's been no answer. I was thinking of calling a policeman friend of mine to go by her house and check up on her."

Lavender stopped in her tracks. "Forgive me, but your darling Aunt Bice called early this morning. She told me to tell you she's gone on a little motor trip. A sort of reconnaissance mission."

"Whatever does that mean?" He looked startled. "At her age she doesn't take motor trips."

"This one she felt was very important but she wanted to keep it a surprise from you."

"All of this sounds very mysterious. I hope she'll be safe. She drinks and drives, you know. Just like my father."

"She'll be fine. I think you'll be very happy when you get your surprise."

Seemingly coming out of nowhere, Danny Hansford appeared. She'd never seen him look more alluring in a trashy kind of way. She felt he'd deliberately made himself up as a hustler, although a very sexy one. In fact, Danny looked like what hustlers want to look like but so rarely do.

"Phil, this is my houseguest, Danny Hansford," Lavender said.

Phil extended his hand and Danny shook it firmly, holding it for longer than usual. "Glad to meet you," Phil said.

"Glad to meet you too," Danny said, ignoring Lavender and concentrating all his attention entirely on Phil. "I know you're the bastard son of a famous movie star and all that, but what interests me is this screenplay you're doing, *Butterflies in Heat.*"

"What I'm doing in Savannah has already spread across town," Phil said.

"You got it. The role of the hustler, Numie Rowan." He looked smugly at Lavender. "I could really play that. Except." He paused. "Couldn't you write the part a little younger for me? After all, I'm hardly over the hill."

Phil smiled vacantly as Lavender felt uncomfortable. "You have hardly begun to climb that hill, I would say," Phil said. "Danny Hansford. Wasn't that the name of the young hustler written about in *Midnight in the Garden of Good and Evil?*"

Anger flashed across Danny's face before he softened his features. "We have the same name."

Wanting to interrupt this male-bonding ritual, Lavender gently placed her fingers on Danny's left arm. "Please go and tell that lazy Norma Dixie that we have the guest of honor standing here without a drink."

Anger flashed through Danny's eyes again, and she knew he didn't want to be treated as a servant, but she felt she had to break up this liaison between Danny and Phil. She'd always been a woman of powerful intuition, and her instincts told her that a meeting between Phil Heather and Danny Hansford could only end in disaster.

"When Tipper Zelda sees you, she'd going to fall head over heels in love," Lavender said. "Monty was the love of her life—or so she says. I always suspected they were nothing more than drinking buddies."

"I've already met Tipper. I was at her opening last night. She does indeed think I look like Monty. She's invited me over."

"Keep your pants zipped up," she cautioned. "Even at her age, that Tipper is one lusty old broad."

"I feel sorry for her for having suffered so many tragedies."

"My sympathy is with her dead husbands. They're gone. Wiped out at the peak of all their male beauty."

"Wiped out?" He looked astonished. "Surely those were accidents?"

"Some day when you get me really low down and drunk, I'll blab and blab some more. After all, I was in the murder house the night her first husband, Taylor Zachory, was shot to death."

She could tell she'd captured his total interest. Before she could toss out a few more provocative remarks, she was interrupted by the appearance of Norma Dixie. The maid had worn a red dress a few sizes too small for her. Her large breasts seemed on the point of bursting out of their tight prison.

"As I live and breathe, it's Montgomery Clift," Norma said. "Back from the dead."

"Pleased to meet you," he said.

"This is Phil Heather," Lavender said rather sternly to Norma.

Norma ignored her, latching onto Phil's arm as she led him to the bar. "Did I ever tell you I used to be the maid for Mae West? Mae was originally offered the part of Norma Desmond in *Sunset Boulevard*. She was to play opposite Montgomery Clift. Both Mae and Monty turned down the parts that went eventually to Gloria Swanson and William Holden."

Lavender stood alone in the room. Although the hostess, she felt she was bonding with no one. In the far distance of the foyer, she spotted Danny in a heated talk with Gin Tucker. It was as if they were negotiating something. What in the world could her new lover, Danny, have to negotiate with Gin Tucker?

At the bar, Norma seemed to have captured Phil's undivided attention with her tales of Mae West, real or not. With Norma, one never knew.

Lavender sipped the rest of her drink, recalling a grander day when she was often surrounded by six or eight men at parties. Those younger days were sadly gone. She felt strangely left out as she wandered to her patio, there to anchor into a peacock chair. She'd sit here until discovered by one of her guests. Surely someone would come and talk to her, the hostess of the party.

*****

In his squad car, Tom Caldwell had taken Danny to a deserted spot outside Savannah. The cop told him some drug dealers lived nearby, and it was highly unlikely they would approach a police squad car.

"I don't have much time," Tom said with a certain disdain as he looked at Danny. His eyes seemed to make one thing clear: there was no love here. Tom had picked Danny up to service him because he had certain needs. Danny had willingly accepted the ride because he wanted to be with Tom and do his bidding. Danny wanted so much more from Tom. He'd never been attracted to a man like this before. With Tango, Danny was the man who was serviced. But Tom had completely reversed the roles for Danny.

As he unzipped Tom's uniform, and reached inside to feel and fondle the beautiful contents, he wished Tom would take him away for a long vacation to some remote spot. Once he had Tom alone in some hotel room, he dared to dream of all the possibilities. He would do things to Tom and let Tom do things to him that he'd never done with any man before. There was nothing he would refuse Tom. Yes, not even that. He'd punched men in the mouth who even suggested they'd like to fuck him. But he wouldn't punch Tom. If Tom wanted him there, in his most private place, he was more than willing to give in. As he pulled Tom's hardened cock from its confinement, Danny looked up longingly into Tom's eyes. The disdain was gone. There was a look of caring and compassion he found there. It came as an unexpected discovery.

Tom ran his fingers through Danny's hair. The cop had a gentle stroke. Seemingly taking a life of their own, those fingers traveled down Danny's back until they reached the top of his jeans. The jeans were too tight. Tom couldn't insert his big hand inside and settled for cupping each of Danny's buttocks instead. "I know you want it, kid. Real bad. I saw that look in your eyes. I'm the guy to feed it to you. Real soon. In the meantime, I want you to taste all of me. Every bit. Go at me like a hungry boy who hasn't eaten in days."

Danny plunged down on Tom, tasting and devouring each inch. He moaned when Tom entered his throat, and he gladly opened for the cop without choking. Danny's wanting the man so made penetration easier. Otherwise, Danny with his lack of experience felt he couldn't handle Tom or give him fully what was wanted and needed.

As Danny's fingers gently reached for Tom's nuts, there to fondle and squeeze, he felt Tom's body twisting beneath him.

"You love it!" Tom shouted. "God damn it, how you love it. Fuck! I think you're in love with me. Not just my thick piece of meat. Me, God damn it. You're in love with me, you little cocksucker. You're sucking with love."

Danny didn't respond or couldn't respond. First, he was too busy bringing Tom to climax. Secondly, he couldn't confront the truth of what the cop was saying. It couldn't be true. Or could it?

Danny knew that Tom was getting close. He both wanted to suck the essence from the man yet feared his withdrawal at the same time. He desperately needed this session to last forever but nature itself had another idea.

Tom's body jerked as the first wave of his juicy sperm hit the back of Danny's throat. He'd never tasted anything as good as Tom. He swallowed the first load and returned eagerly for more, wanting every drop the man could deliver. Some of it spilled out of Danny's mouth and drooled down his chin.

In complete contentment, Tom looked down into Danny's face, taking some of his own semen and rubbing it across Danny's chin. "God damn it, you little cocksucker, you're turning me queer. I've got to get to work."

Danny moved off the man but as he did Tom grabbed him by his blond hair. "You're not going anywhere until you give me the juiciest kiss of your life. A kiss where I can taste my own cum."

Feeling morbidly dejected at the loss of Tom even for an hour, Danny stood outside Gin Tucker's house and watched the squad car head off into the morning. Tom had brought out a side of him he'd never experienced with anybody before. No one must know this. It was a secret they shared between them.

But Danny couldn't live comfortably with this new reality of who he was. Danny Hansford was all image, and for the few short weeks that remained in his life Danny wanted that image protected.

He was the stud of Savannah. He needed confirmation of that. Somehow in his mind Gin's modeling job was just the sort of proof he needed. The idea of all the closeted men in Savannah getting fucked by a Danny Hansford dildo appealed to him immensely.

As he rang Gin's doorbell, he was ready, willing, and able to accept the photographer's proposition.

From the moment Gin with his lusty lips opened the door until the mold was cast, Danny instinctively knew how the scenario would play out. Gin took him to an upstairs room which had been completely blacked out. Once here, Danny was invited to strip off all his clothes in front of Gin's appreciative eyes. As he stripped, Danny had tried to ignore Gin, pretending he wasn't even in the room. He'd peeled off before in front of men. It was an old routine for him. Gin had seen him dancing practically nude at The Tool Box so Danny didn't think his strip act would reveal anything Gin hadn't already seen before.

He'd begrudgingly accepted the modeling job, but as he got more into it another feeling came over Danny. Gin had known and seduced the original Danny Hansford. As the camera recorded his nude body, the faux Danny kept looking into Gin's eyes for approval of what he was seeing. Danny was deeply rewarded.

As he photographed Danny, Gin seemed mesmerized and totally enthralled with his subject. Danny didn't need an oral commitment: he already knew that he was a far greater sexual allure than the original Danny Hansford, and this was very important for him to learn. The original Danny's murder may have saved the tourism industry of Savannah and been the cause of millions of dollars being spent by the public on both the book and film, *Midnight in the Garden of Good and Evil,* but the second Danny knew in his heart he was better than the first Danny. Somehow he had to do something to make the world realize this before he died.

Getting cast as the lead in the film, *Butterflies in Heat,* would be a chance to earn immortality. The original Danny left no significant photographic record, much less a film. The actor who played him in the film made the real Danny appear totally psychotic, and the appearance of the hustler character in the Clint Eastwood film was only fleeting.

With a full movie role, Danny knew he'd earn world acclaim. In his heart he believed the camera would lovingly record every beautiful inch of his body. That camera would make love to him the way it once had to Marilyn Monroe.

In some of hiss dreams, Danny imagined he was a male Marilyn Monroe. Back in the 50s female beauty dominated the media. But it was a new era. Now the male, preferably stripped, enjoyed national attention. He fully suspected that if a national vote were taken, more people, both men and women, would rather possess a full frontal nude of the late John F. Kennedy Jr. than they would the same photograph of Nicole Kidman. The hour of the male in his full glory had finally arrived by the end of the millennium and the beginning of a new one.

As Gin photographed closeups of Danny's genitalia, the boy began to plot carefully in his mind how he would seduce Phil Heather and make him fall in love with him. Danny was good at making people fall in love with him. Phil looked like an easy conquest. When he'd first met Phil at Lavender's home, he noticed that the screenwriter kept glancing frequently at Danny's crotch fully outlined in his tight blue jeans. Phil had been subtle about it, taking furtive glances but Danny didn't miss those fleeting appraisals. He could tell that Phil liked what he'd seen. Seducing him would be easy.

In a week or two, Danny just knew that the role of the hustler, Numie Rowan, would soon be his. It would be Danny's only film, far less than the film credits of James Dean, but Danny knew if he could get the part, pictures of him would adorn the bars of the world forty years from now, just like they did today of James Dean.

Those pictures of Marilyn, often in the same bars, would still be there at the mid-21st century but James Dean would be long forgotten. Fans as yet unborn would deck the walls of their bedrooms in the future with pictures of him. The Marilyn Monroe nude calendar and the Danny Hansford nude calendar would surely be among the best-selling novelty items of 2040 and far beyond.

Lost in his daydreams, Danny suddenly became aware of the presence of Gin Tucker. "My pictures will turn out fabulously. The best I've ever done. I tried repeatedly to get the murdered Danny Hansford to pose nude for me but he always refused. I know why of course. He never possessed your incredible sex appeal which I just know my camera has captured. You're a natural."

Danny closed his eyes. He liked hearing Gin's words. They were unnecessary because Danny already knew the truth of them, but he wanted to hear them anyway.

"I'm ready to take the mold," Gin said.

"That means I'd better rise to the occasion." Danny reached down and began to jerk himself to a full erection.

Gin pulled his hand away. "Men don't come to a full erection when jerking off. I want to capture your penis in all its extended glory. Only a lusty cocksucking mouth like mine can bring out that final inch in you."

Danny closed his eyes and rested his head as Gin licked his lips preparing for the descent.

"It's your party," Danny said as he felt inch after inch of himself disappearing down the talented and much experienced throat of Gin Tucker.

Gin raised up for air before taking the final plunge to the ultimate depth. "If only Marlon had had something like this. Talk about a noble tool. Marlon, eat your heart out!"

As Gin brought him to life, Danny drifted into some sort of ecstasy. All he was thinking as he was thoroughly sucked was that the Danny Hansford dildo that Gin would create would be used to penetrate unknown asses way into the future when the fabled Jeff Stryker dildo would be only a distant memory to an older generation of graying gay males.

*****

As Phil sat across from Tipper in her garden courtyard, she was enthralled. In spite of her many problems, not only the financial ones, but the rapid aging process and loss of beauty, she felt young and lovely again the way she had at her peak when men like the tobacco heir, Taylor Zachory, had wooed her.

"Monty and I were hell-raisers," she was telling Phil. "I was ridiculously young when I met him—actually no more than thirteen. I fell madly in love with him. He was a wonderfully funny man, terribly perceptive."

"I've seen all his movies," Phil said. "He was my idol. Perhaps it was a narcissistic attraction since I've always been told how much I look like him."

"You not only look like him, you are him!"

"I wouldn't go that far."

"You look beautiful, vulnerable, and sensual—just like Monty."

"You must have been of great comfort to him."

"I was at times. The advice of a young teenager wasn't always good. I even advised him to turn down certain roles. Norman Mailer's *The Naked and the Dead*. A script of *Look Homeward Angel*. And *High Noon* which went to Gary Cooper. What did I know about movie scripts? If the script bored me, I told Monty not to do it."

"I thought of Monty as a black Adonis," Phil said. "It's fascinating to contemplate how he would have been in those pictures."

"We were never faithful to each other. There were many separations because of his film career. At those times, we drifted into other often very passionate liaisons. But we always came back together."

"Did his relationship with men bother you?"

"Certainly not. I have always understood such things. All my beautiful young husbands—now dead—had intense and passionate liaisons with other men. They also had a lot of those ships that pass in the night type relationships too. I think Monty really loved women. But he preferred to have sex with men."

"I think I can understand that. What a screenplay your life would make."

"You could certainly play the Monty character."

"I never thought of acting on the screen. Only writing for it."

"Perhaps you should," she said, eying him provocatively.

"Exactly what are you suggesting?"

"What if I told you I would for the first time ever be willing to cooperate on a screenplay based on my life? Of course, I had a memoir in mind instead."

"Your story is sensational. With all this national publicity you'll be getting, especially when *Time* magazine comes out, I think we might sell both."

"I need money. Frankly, I'm broke."

"I'm sorry to hear that. All those tobacco millions got away from you?"

"Everything got away from me. Now I have only my life to peddle for a few bucks." She felt she looked pathetic in front of him, so she straightened up and belted down the rest of her drink with a certain bravado courage.

"If you're serious about this, I'd like to pursue it."

"I'm very serious," she said. "If I can go out on that stage in that God damn Black Widow costume, I can certainly tell you the story of my life."

Phil slapped at a mosquito that had landed voraciously on his neck. A long silence fell over the patio as if both were contemplating the commitment they were making to each other. He cleared his throat.

Sensing his discomfort, she said, "I know what is on your mind. You are wondering how far I will go in revealing the mysterious deaths of my husbands."

"I've read numerous stories. Up to now you've been pretty silent. I understand that you don't recall one single event that happened on the day, much less the night, that Zachory Taylor was found shot with a bullet in his head."

"The day is a total blank. I can't remember anything."

"That's not going to help me sell the screenplay, much less the memoirs."

"I know that, and it's a great obstacle. I will be more candid about how the rest of my husbands died. But with Taylor it will be a blank page."

"That's too bad. The deaths of the other husbands were mysterious and tabloid friendly. But the death of Taylor Zachory is crucial to the plot."

"All is not lost. There is one person who can fill in the blank pages. Lavender Morgan. She was at our home in Winston-Salem the night Taylor was found shot."

"Do you think she might tell us what she knows?"

"She might if I consented."

"I would rather hear the story directly from you but if you don't remember we'll have to work around it."

"In this case, we'll have to," she said

"If Lavender knows some important information and was an eyewitness to certain events, it might be the way out. It all depends on what she knows and what she saw."

"There is one larger question, and you and I both know what it is," she said.

"Okay, I'll come out with it," he said. "If you did murder those husbands, a memoir would be a confessional. The confessions of a serial killer. I don't know the criminal liability here. But surely you must have other options than earning money by confessing to serial killing."

Tipper paused a long time, saying nothing. An idea was formulating in her head. She'd always been an actress and she felt she could pull this one off too. With a sad look, she hesitated briefly the way she'd seen Joan Fontaine do in a movie once. "I would never have agreed to this until today. But early this morning I received some very bad news."

"What's the matter?" he asked, a look of concern growing on his face.

At this point she believed he would follow her anywhere, regardless of where her deceptive mind led him. "This must not be known except to a potential publisher. But I was informed by my doctor this morning that I have incurable cancer. I have only months to live. Knowing how long it would take you to write the book and how many months it would take to get it published, I know I will be dead before the book comes out. Once it's published, it will be a sensation. But I won't be here to experience the condemnation."

"Oh, shit. What rotten luck."

"It's where a lifetime of smoking will lead. In many ways, it's Taylor Zachory's revenge on me. That tobacco peddler strikes back from his grave."

The same stillness that had settled over the patio before came back. Only it was more deadly than before. The stillness was so pronounced that you could almost hear it.

Before her eyes, Phil was sweating. She knew she'd given him more information than a brain could handle in one hour. Softening her features and staring at him less intently, she said, "The book should not be just about dead husbands. It could be about Monty too and all the fabulous people I have known in my life including my involvement in a long affair with Tallulah Bankhead when I was but a young woman."

"So it's true," he said. "You've walked on both sides of the waterfront."

"Yes, in addition to marrying beautiful and famous men, all of whom died mysteriously, I was a young Eve Harrington just like the character in *All About Eve*. I pursued famous older actresses, all of whom were past their prime. Many had retired from the screen or stage."

"Could you throw out some names? I mean I've got to pitch this to a publisher."

"The list will astonish you. Greta Garbo, Marlene Dietrich, Barbara Stanwyck, Joan Crawford, and once, and only once, Marilyn Monroe. I also pursued Katharine Hepburn too but she turned me down."

"That's amazing. This is sensational."

"There's a lot more. I might be dying but I still have my memories, my life to sell. I was even involved in the civil rights movement. I've slept with some of America's greatest leaders."

"Do you care to throw out names?"

"John F. Kennedy for openers. I was introduced to him by Lavender. She'd had an affair with him but even then Lavender was getting a bit long in the tooth for Kennedy." She paused. "There's more."

"Slap it to me," he said, the excitement in his face growing by the minute.

"Martin Luther King Jr. I was walking right behind him in some of those marches. What the press didn't know is that I wasn't always behind him. Sometimes late at night I was under him. As a preacher, he always preferred the missionary position. How so unlike Monty who often preferred me on top, with a dildo, of course."

He slammed down his drink. "I don't know what to say. I've committed myself to writing *Butterflies in Heat*, the screenplay. But I'm itching to get onto this too."

"Perhaps you can do both. Write the screenplay in the morning, and tape me and my remembrances in the afternoon. After all, I can't stand more than two hours of taping a day. And I don't work Saturday and Sunday."

What followed was a long drunken hour in which Phil held out the many possibilities that awaited the future of such recollections. Sensitively, just like Monty, he interspersed his excitement with lamentations about her upcoming demise.

Before he left her home, he had almost assured her that her money problems would be solved. The advance from the publisher would take care of that.

After she'd stood at her doorway and kissed him on the lips and held him with all the passion she dared reveal at this point, she closed the door behind her and retreated to the deep recesses of her house. She stepped into her bedroom which was like a comforting womb.

She felt a kind of pride in freeing herself from the financial noose tightening around her neck.

Phil would get the advance from a publisher—no doubt a heavy cash outlay. He'd even write the memoirs. She'd tell him everything. She might even tell him what really happened the night Taylor Zachory was shot. She'd save that for the very end of her revelations.

But she'd keep one major secret from Phil. He must never know.

Her memoirs would never be published.

# Chapter Five

Lost in space, Phil resisted waking up even though there seemed an urgent reason to do so. Someone seemed to be shouting his name from his back porch but he couldn't be sure. Perhaps he was dreaming it.

Waking up abruptly, he sat up in bed. He recognized the voice. It was Brian calling up to him. "Get your ass out of that bed, Phil. Let us in and God damn it make a key for me today."

Phil raised the window and peered down. There in the early morning sun stood Brian in his cop's uniform with John and Henry tugging at him. Even though angry at not arousing him easily, Brian had never looked handsomer. It was then that Phil knew he was in love.

"I'll be right down." Rushing for his shorts to cover his total nudity, he ran barechested down the stairs to the back of the house where he took off the night latch.

Brian gave him a quick but rather passionate kiss on the mouth, then went into the house. "I've got to take a leak."

In the early morning light, Phil confronted a sleepy John and an even sleepier Henry.

"Daddy broke up with our mama this morning," John said. "It was the fight to end the century."

"Daddy got us," Henry said. "Mama don't want to get stuck with two kids around the house. She didn't want boys anyway. She wanted girls." Trailed by John and Henry, Phil led the way into the kitchen where he went over to the counter to put on coffee.

"I'm hungry," Henry said, tugging at Phil's shorts.

"I'll fix breakfast," Phil said.

As he put on the coffee, Brain walked up behind him and in front of Henry and John kissed Phil's neck, playfully biting it. Phil felt embarrassed to have Brian come on so strongly in front of his sons but Brian didn't seem in the least bit shy.

"We didn't hit each other but me and Joyce had one hell of a fight," Brian said. "I'm going over there today and move out my stuff. The last thing I told that dyke was that me and her would be out competing for the same pussies in the weeks ahead."

"What does that mean?" John asked.

Brian looked down at him. "Go up to your room and wash up for breakfast." He turned to Phil. "They like their eggs scrambled. It's easy over for me. We like sausage instead of bacon, and I hope you know how to cook biscuits. If me and you are getting hitched, I've got to have biscuits in the morning. Biscuits with sausage gravy—my favorite."

Heading for the refrigerator to get the makings for breakfast, Phil turned and looked at Brian. He was thrilled to have him move in but still a bit hesitant. In minutes he'd gone from bachelorhood to a daddy with a readymade family. "It's a little sudden."

"Sudden, my ass," Brian said, easing his tall, muscular frame into a chair at the kitchen table. "You've wanted me ever since the first day you laid eyes on me. You were practically drooling."

"You're right about that," Phil said, finding the eggs. "Thank God he'd bought sausage. Normally he preferred bacon but he was in the South.

As John and Henry headed for the bedroom upstairs, Brian called after them. "Did you kiss your daddy good morning?"

"Not yet," John said, heading over to Brian as Henry trailed him.

"Not me, you little fucker," Brian said, pointing over to Phil at the stove. "Did you kiss your other daddy?"

"I didn't," John said. Phil leaned down as John dutifully kissed him on the cheek.

"Not on the cheek, asshole," Brian called after him. "On the lips like you kiss your mama and me."

John then kissed Phil on the mouth. Henry followed his lead.

"He's your daddy now too," Brian said. "He gets a full lip kiss from both of you, or else I'll paddle your ass."

"I like kissing Phil," John said. "He's a real pretty boy." He smiled at Henry. "And I'm a man who likes pretty boys." He patted his brother on the ass.

"What did you mean, our other daddy?" Henry asked, walking over to confront Brian. "You're our daddy."

"I still am," Brian said. "Except now, you lucky little bugger, you've got two daddies. As soon as your mama and me get divorced, I'm marrying Phil. We're going to live together like man and wife. Except you can't call Phil my wife or your mama cause he's a man."

"I didn't know men could marry men," Henry said. "You can only marry a woman."

"That's true," Brian said. "After all, this is the State of Georgia. Me and Phil will be married in every way except in the eyes of the law."

"You mean you'll do to him what we spied on you doing to mama," John said.

Phil took his eyes off the frying eggs long enough to look over at Brian who blew him a kiss.

"You got that right," Brian said. "Except with Phil here, I'll be doing it a hell of a lot more. I'm in love with Phil. I wasn't in love with your mama."

"Will you cornhole him like John does to me?" Henry asked.

"You bet your sweet ass I will," Brian said, reaching up to stroke Phil's hand as his coffee was served. "As often as he wants it." He squeezed Phil's wrist. "More to the point, as often as I want it which will be quite a lot."

Seemingly satisfied at their new living arrangements, the boys turned and headed upstairs to get ready for breakfast.

"I've got to drive to work," Brian said, as Phil handed him his breakfast plate, offering toast instead of biscuits.

As Brian hungrily devoured his meal, Phil placed his coffee cup on the table and joined Brian. "Everything's happening pretty fast around here," Phil said.

"I didn't have to get down on my knees and beg you to marry me," Brian said. "All I had to do was look into your face as I was fucking you. You were in seventh heaven. It didn't take no detective to tell me you'd found the man of your dreams."

"You're right," Phil said. "I'm in love with you."

"We were always in love with each other. Right from the first. But things were different when we were in school. Everything's more out in the open now." Wiping the grease from his mouth, Brian leaned over to kiss Phil's mouth. "I love you, guy. I guess I always did. Had a hard time admitting it. Would you believe that for years I convinced myself I was straight."

"I was never that convincing," Phil said. "I always knew what I wanted."

Brian leaned in closer to him. "I hope what you're wanting is this handsome cop stud you see before you. What you see is what you get."

At that moment John and Henry came back into the kitchen. Phil jumped up to serve their breakfast.

"You'll have to mind the kids today," Brian said, glancing nervously at his watch. "I'll be home at five." In front of the stove, he gave Phil a lingering good-bye kiss before kissing his two sons and heading for the door.

He turned to issue a final warning to his boys. "Don't you fuckers drive Phil crazy today. He's a screenwriter and needs time to write—not to chase after you bad boys."

"We'll be good," Henry promised. John made no such commitment.

John and Henry ate their breakfast with the same gusto Brian had. As Phil poured each of them a glass of milk, the phone rang. It was Jerry Wheeler from New York. "Are you writing copy hot enough to singe the wings off any butterfly?"

"Hi, Jerry. The screenplay's going great," Phil said, lying. "Just great. But I want to make a few changes before I read it to you."

"Forget that! I'll read it in the flesh. I'm flying to Savannah. I've raised all the money for the film. You won't believe this. But I actually got financing from Safeway."

"The grocery store?"

"One and the same. We're going to start shooting three months ahead of schedule. I've got to get to Savannah to scout locations and cast the film. I've decided to star all unknowns. Bring in no big names. I'm announcing in the papers tomorrow that I'm casting the film among the local talent. It'll bring us a lot of publicity. Not since the search for Scarlett O'Hara."

"Let's not get carried away here," Phil said.

"I'm setting up a casting couch for the role of Numie. Any guy in Savannah who thinks he can measure up to that part has to prove it first to me. I may even direct the film myself."

"That sounds fabulous. When are you getting into town?"

"In a day or so, after I look around a bit, I'll rent a house from Arlie Rae Minton. Sounds like a really nice guy but a little dumb. Do you know he's got this sexual fantasy about Linda Tripp? That dog. I don't even know a second-rate kennel that would take that hound."

"It'll be terrific having you here while I work on the screenplay. You'll help me, of course."

"I've got plenty of ideas. But I want to have time for some fun and games too. I've had every man worth having in New York City, and I'm salivating at the prospect of devouring some grade-A prime Savannah meat."

"I'm sure you'll find an entire meat market at your disposal here," Phil said. "At least that's my first opinion."

"I'm wanted on another line," Jerry said. "Get back to you later, sweetheart."

No sooner had Phil put down the phone until it rang again. This time it was Lavender Morgan.

"I apologize calling so early in the morning," Lavender said in her carefully modulated voice. "But I have news from your Aunt Bice."

"What is it?" Phil asked, a sense of panic growing within him. "She's not been injured, has she?"

"She's fine. In robust health. She's got a big surprise for you. It's your lucky day."

"You can't let me in on it, can you?"

"And ruin her fun? No way. Come over at noon. It's very important. Aunt Bice will be here. With your surprise."

"I can't imagine what kind of surprise she's come up with."

"A delicious one, I can assure you. And I'm a good judge of these matters based on my long experience in the field."

"I'll be there," Phil promised. Before ringing off, he remembered he was the custodian of John and Henry. "In case I can't find a babysitter, is it okay to bring two young boys? Eight and nine."

There was a long pause on the other end of the phone. "If you must. But try to get a sitter. I usually like my men a little older, although I could make an exception. The eight year old sounds just too young. But the nine year old. It could be. I've heard stories."

"These boys are very experienced and worldly, I can assure you. They play adult games."

"I see. Considering the surprise, a babysitter would still be a good idea. Perhaps I can entertain your young men some other time. See you at noon." She abruptly hung up the phone as if suddenly distracted. Phil distinctly heard a male voice in the background.

Was it true? Could Lavender at her age be carrying on an affair?

John and Henry were running screaming through the house, seemingly trying to tear it apart. It sounded like a game of cowboys and Indians. As if that weren't noise enough, there was a loud pounding on his back door.

Clad only in his shorts, Phil rushed to open the door. There in the fast-rising dawn stood Lula Carson, a look of great pleading and concern on her face. "You've got to help me," she said. "There's serious trouble. It's Jason."

*****

In her desperation, Lula kept reaching for Phil's hand which she squeezed as hard as she could, even though he was driving quite fast to the condo on Tybee Island where her cousin Tom, the policeman, had restrained Jason. According to Tom, a drugged Jason had gone wild and wrecked the condo, and the landlord was demanding Jason's arrest.

"This is the only way I have of finding out about Jason's private life," Lula said. "He's gone wild like this before—he can't help it. If I didn't have my cousin working on the police force and bailing Jason out time and time again, I think my errant spouse would rot in jail."

"But you always take him back," Phil chided her, as his car turned into the driveway of the condo where Tom had directed them. A feeling of dread anxiety seemed to cross his face. "I shouldn't have left John and Henry alone in my house. They will probably wreck it."

"The boys will be just fine," Lula said. "I'm sure John is cornholing Henry right now, and they'll be too involved in that to do any damage to your house. Besides, you left the TV blaring at full blast, and plenty of junk food. That's all they need." She cleared her throat. "Right now we've got more important things on our mind."

No sooner had they entered the office of the receptionist than Lula confronted a sweating, balding horror, Jefferson Purdue. "You the wife of that maniac?" he said as a greeting.

"I'm Lula Carson. I'm a writer. I don't identify myself as wife."

"You married to the bastard or not?" Jefferson demanded to know.

Phil interceded. "Yes, this is Mrs. Jason McReeves. What can we do to help?"

Jefferson stared long and hard at Phil. "I think I've seen you somewhere before. On second thought, aren't you the movie star, Montgomery Clift? You're the spittin' image."

Phil smiled as Lula stepped aside, thinking it would be far better to have Phil handle this instead of her. Jefferson seemed to be a real movie fan.

"My father is dead. I'm his son."

"Pleased to meet you," Jefferson said, extending a soggy palm. "Your daddy was always my favorite actor when I was a kid. What I mean is, he was my favorite after James Dean died. Up to then, I always got off watching James Dean."

"I'm glad you came around," Phil said.

"How's my husband?" Lula asked impatiently.

"He's okay now," Jefferson assured her. "Tom Caldwell's up there with him now. He's restrained the psycho."

"What happened?" Lula said.

"He went wild," Jefferson claimed. "I used my pass key to get into the condo. He broke several things, and I'm going to have to press charges. I called the police. My buddy Tom took the call. I think he's related to Jason in some way."

"How much damage did he cause?" Lula asked.

"I'd say in the neighborhood of five-thousand dollars."

"That's a lot of damage for a fleabag like this," Lula said, growing angry. Remembering the literary grant so recently bestowed on her by Lavender Morgan, she said, "If I agree to present you with three-thousand dollars in unmarked bills, would you agree to drop all charges?"

He eyed her skeptically, then turned to look at Phil. "Would this here movie star's kid back you up on that offer?" He smiled at Phil. "Your daddy must have left you millions. Those movie stars really make top bucks."

Phil reached to shake Jefferson's hand. "I'll back her up."

Lula affectionately rubbed Phil's arm. "Thanks." She turned to Jefferson. "May we go up to see my husband now?" A sudden thought crossed her mind. "Who's the owner of this condo?"

"Tango—you may have heard of her," Jefferson said.

"You mean the black drag queen who's replaced Tipper Zelda at the Blues in the Night?" she asked.

"One and the same," Jefferson said. "Normally, I don't rent to niggers. They always cause too much damage. But you know with all these new laws about discrimination."

"And all the litigation," Lula chimed in.

"I know, I know," Jefferson said impatiently. "Tango's the only nigger in this building. Now look what has happened."

"But it wasn't Tango who caused the damage, now was it?" Phil asked.

"Indirectly she did," Jefferson said. "She was the black pussy who brought that Jason McReeves here in the first place." He turned and flashed anger at Lula. "After we get him out of here, you'd better keep that husband of yours on a tight leash."

"Good advice," Lula said, following Jefferson along with Phil into the elevator and up to the door of the condo.

Jefferson knocked and Tom opened the door immediately. "Glad to see you guys," Tom said, letting them in.

"I'm out of here," Jefferson said. "I don't want that homicidal maniac attacking me."

In the apartment, Lula quickly surveyed the damage, noting only some broken sliding glass doors leading out onto a balcony overlooking the water. She'd seen scenes like this before. In his drugged state, Jason had apparently tried to break out, no doubt fearing he was trapped in a cell. She was a bit sorry that she'd agreed to spend three-thousand dollars of her literary grant to replace these broken windows. Jefferson certainly came out with the better end of the deal. But the prospect of Jason going to jail was more than she could stand. She'd turned to confront Tom. "Where's Jason now?"

"He's subdued and resting in the bedroom," Tom said. "I'd let him sleep it off a little more before going in there to wake him up. It's always this way. After he sleeps it off, Mr. Hyde disappears and he becomes the sweet guy we all know and love."

The tension on Lula's face subsided a bit. She could even feel her muscles relaxing. She just knew she'd be able to extricate both Jason and her out of this latest trap. She feared newspaper publicity. It was important to her to maintain her prestige when she went to accept literary awards in the future. If there is one label she abhorred, it was the fear that she'd be called a trashy white Southerner. In New York she always maintained with her friends that her parents were Southern aristocrats. She suggested that they were planters and lived on a vast plantation far greater than Tara in *Gone With the Wind*. She'd left out that their house was purchased for eight-thousand dollars, was falling in, and consisted of only two rotting bedrooms, a small living room, and a combined dining room and kitchen.

Completely absorbed in her own thoughts, she belatedly became aware of the dynamics going on between Tom and Phil. She recalled the last encounter of the two men when she'd given advice to Tom about how he could seduce Phil.

"It was great," Phil was saying reassuringly to Tom. "In fact, among the best ever. But there can't be a repeat performance. Brian and I are together now. He's left Joyce. He's got John and Henry. They're living at my house now."

Tom looked dumbfounded. "You mean that faggot buddy of mine has finally admitted what I've been telling him all along. That he's as queer as they come."

"Something like that. Anyway we're together now."

Tom turned to Lula. "My balls are just as big as Brian's. Hell, he flashed them at me enough times. If he had the balls to leave that dyke wife of his, it gives me inspiration to leave Ethel Mae. I can't stand the bitch. Don't even want to come home no more."

"Don't do anything rash," Lula said. "But I can't be a hypocrite. All the characters I write about follow the dictates of their heart. My only advice to you is that you do the same."

"I want to come over and see you and Brian for dinner," Tom said.

"That's fine with me," Phil said.

"Good," Lula chimed in. "We'll have another cook-out in the patio. With Phil's fantastic ribs. Who knows? I might even be persuaded to make my own celebrated cole slaw again."

"I've really got to talk to you guys," Tom said. "I need some inspiration. Perhaps I'll end up using you guys as my own role models."

A sound from the next room aroused Lula's interest. "I've got to look in on him," she said to Tom.

"Go on," he urged.

With trepidation, and followed by Phil and Tom, she slowly opened the bedroom door of the condo.

There sprawled completely nude on his back was a sleeping Jason. The golden morning light of Tybee Island made him look even more spectacular. But the light was only the gilding on the lily.

Jason in any light was one of God's specially conceived creations.

"Hot damn!" Tom said, grabbing Phil's hand and placing it on his crotch. "Feel that hard-on that's about to jump clean out of my pants."

Lula turned to stare into Phil's face. He seemed mesmerized. "What do you think?" she said to him. "Of my old man."

"When I was a little boy," Phil said in a hushed tone, "my Aunt Bice told me that all men were created equal." At no point did he take his eyes off the sight of the spreadeagled Jason. "When I meet up with my Aunt Bice again, I've got to tell her that God showed favoritism."

*****

Lying in bed recovering from the assault, Tango even now couldn't believe the sudden turn of events. The arrival of Duke Edwards in Savannah had complicated her life more than anything that had come down before.

She was glad that he'd gone out to a bar with money he'd just reached into her purse and taken, without even asking her permission. She needed time to sort out her own feelings. Right now she couldn't figure anything out. Did she love Danny as before? What did the mating with Jason McReeves mean? Or had she fallen hopelessly in love with her own daddy after his assault on her on the bathroom floor?

These three sexy men could certainly mess up a gal's mind like hers. If she could just admit the truth to herself, she wanted all three of them but knew that might be hard to pull off.

Her body still ached from the encounter between Duke and her. Forcing her into the tub, Duke had ripped off her panties only to discover she was a boy. Obviously fantasizing about something else, he'd reacted violently, shouting at her, "You fucking little drag queen faggot. You had me fooled, you bitch!"

Lurching from the tub, he'd slapped her hard, knocking her down on the tile floor. He'd been raging hard. Her face had fallen against the tiles, and her nose had been bleeding when his assault on her came. Without warning or preparation, he'd plunged into her, causing her to scream.

"You won't be the first black pussy faggot I've fucked in the ass," he'd shouted in her ear before biting into it, causing her to scream out in pain again. "Those black hungry tails in prison used to line up to get fucked by Duke Edward's mighty inches."

After the initial assault, her fear had subsided a bit. At first she'd thought he was going to kill her. She'd forced herself to relax her rectal muscles to the point where he could slide all the way up her. She'd known he'd achieved full entry when she'd felt his thick pubic hair pressing against the smoothness of her butt. At first he'd plunged so violently into her that she'd emitted cries but as he'd worked his magic on her those yelps gave way to moans of pleasure.

"Oh, fuck," he'd cried out to the cold tiles. Her anal canal had seemed to go into a spasm around Duke's mighty prick. "I'm coming," she'd shouted to no one in particular, not even to Duke. As she'd erupted, he'd kept plunging. He'd known he was in the saddle and had seemed determined to make his ride last long and hard.

He'd created the most exquisite pleasure in her, far greater than Danny and even Jason, and up to then she'd thought Jason was the best of all. But Jason lacked the power and fury that Duke so clearly had mastered.

As he plunged into her, his strokes had grown faster and more violent. In his passion he'd descended on her neck, biting it harder and harder as he'd driven deeper and deeper into her. Her hips had jerked beneath her daddy, and she'd thought his attack would never end. She hadn't wanted it to end. *Ever.*

"Oh!" she'd gasped, as if not believing it herself. Recklessly he'd driven her toward another rapidly approaching orgasm, and this had never happened with any other lover in her life, even the best of them.

She'd given out a half-scream and had reached around to claw at him in her mounting excitement. Driving deep and fast, he'd been caught up in the thrill of his own rapidly approaching eruption. As his own cum had spurted hot and wet deep within her gut, she'd let out a bellow. Never in her life had she known such a climax. She'd bucked her slender body up against his heavy one, her hips writhing. A whirlwind of desire had blown through her mind. She belonged to this man forever. She'd do anything for him. He'd slid his cock deep into her convulsing channel and there in her torrid hole had plunged violently in stroke after stroke, releasing himself. Her gut full, she'd gasped as she'd erupted one more time herself, wanting this moment to last forever.

Wave after wave of sheer ecstasy had swept over her. Even when he'd bluntly pulled out of her, her entire body had continued to throb. "Now suck my tongue, bitch," he'd yelled at her, turning over and mounting an assault on her red lips almost as violently as that of her ass.

She'd sucked his tongue as if it had contained the essence of life itself. Long after he'd had his fill, he'd lain on the floor with her, biting and caressing her slender young body and licking and sucking her silicone breasts which he'd found endlessly fascinating. "I don't know why it is, but I've always gone for fake tits on you drag queens instead of those of a real woman."

Finally, releasing her, he'd felt the water in the tub. "You let the water get cold, black bitch. Empty it and run my bath again."

"Yes, Duke," she'd said, fearing him, and most willing to do his bidding.

He'd gone into the living room to watch television. When his new bath had been readied for him, she'd called to him to come back to the bathroom. He'd barged through the door at once, standing for a long time there, his arm resting on the frame as if posing like a Greek statue. She'd known men with more perfectly formed bodies, and that included both Danny and Jason, but she'd never known a man as sexy as her daddy. She'd stared long and hard at the capped penis dangling between his legs and the low hangers. Even though his assault on her had been so recent, she could not imagine how such equipment could provide her with the most exquisite pleasure she'd ever known in her much experienced life.

"Listen, and listen good, bitch," he'd said. "The next time I work up a big fart, you know where your mouth is going to be. You got that?" He'd stared long and hard and with great fury at her.

"I'll do anything for you."

"Your mama used to say the same thing." He'd stared at her one more time, as if asserting his dominance over her. "Now I'm getting in that tub, and I want you to bathe every inch of my body. But before I get in, I'm gonna bend over it. There's one part of me that I don't want a washcloth ever to touch. That special part of me in the future will be cleaned only by your hot little pink tongue."

"Okay," was all she'd said as he'd moved toward the tub and had spread himself for her as he'd promised. Her tongue darting out in feverish delight at the prospect of such a meal, she'd moved on to him as if he offered sweet nectar after a long journey through a bleak desert with Sahara-like winds.

Not able to rise from the bed, she fretted over all the things she should be doing before Duke returned. On the top of her list was hunting down Danny Hansford. Had he left her for good? For all she knew he was so irresponsible he didn't plan to return to the act as her tango-dancing partner. She just might find herself being announced at Blues in the Night and having to go on as a solo. She could do that and had performed by herself before, but she knew audience attention—especially the male contingent—would diminish without Danny and those very revealing tight pants he wore nightly.

She also knew she had to get back to Tybee Island and Jason whom she'd abandoned in the condo. She couldn't leave a man like that alone forever. He'd wanted her to come over tonight so he could read her the parts in *Butterflies in Heat* that featured the character, Lola La Mour. Jason had wanted her to be as well versed in the role as possible before meeting Phil Heather. Jason had assured her that Phil was just beginning the screenplay of the novel, and the character of Lola La Mour could be reshaped for Tango if she impressed Phil enough.

She heard footsteps coming up her stairs. They were too light and delicate to be those of Danny Hansford. She didn't expect Duke to return for hours, and he'd surely be drunk. She wondered who it might be, as no one visited her in her private apartment.

Reaching for her robe, she was nearing the door at the sound of the first light tap. She adjusted her wig so that it fitted properly, and checked her appearance in the mirror before opening the door. After all, a star, even if attired in a robe, had to be ready to face the paparazzi at any moment.

To her surprise, when she threw open the door, she was greeted with the frail, tiny figure of Lula Carson.

"You are, I presume, the cabaret entertainer, Tango," Lula said.

Tango eyed Lula skeptically, her eyes traversing her slim physique. Even though Jason's wife, she couldn't imagine such a large man making love to this little pint-size woman who was just as pale white as Tango was nut brown. "What you see is what you get!"

"You don't have to practice typical Savannah hospitality and invite me in," Lula said, arching her back as if bracing for a fight. "Since I arrived here unannounced, I'll be brief. Don't you ever see my husband again. If you see him coming down the street, you cross over on the other side. Is that understood?"

"Since when do I take my commands from the likes of you?" Tango asked. "If there's one thing Tango doesn't stand for, it's taking her marching orders from a white woman." She leered at Lula. "White men, now that's another tale to tell."

"I'm not in the habit of repeating myself," Lula said. "As a great writer, my initial communications are crystal clear for most people." She stared defiantly. "Even to the most retarded of God's children."

"If you don't get out of my doorway and stop messing up my mind with your shit, I'm liable to do something most unladylike."

"And if you ever see my husband again, I'm liable to take a gun and shoot that red wig right off your head." Lula smiled. "Since I'm not William Tell, I might miss. Instead of your wig, the bullet might lodge in your brain."

Tango's throat constricted. "I just reckon you might do that. You're crazy enough."

"Jason belongs to me. With him, the elevator doesn't run to the top floor. I have to take care of him. A black slut like you can find other men. Leave Jason alone! You know nothing of mental illness and how to care for a man like Jason. You're out of your element here. Stick with your little hustlers like Danny Hansford. I'm sure he's psychotic enough for you."

"No man, especially no white man, is ever worth dying for. You must love Jason very much if you're threatening to kill for him."

"He's more than my husband. He is my friend. My lifelong companion. We grew up together. We will always be together. You were just a fling. I can't even fight you like a woman. You're not even that. You're an illusion."

"Listen, dyke face, I'm more woman than you'll ever be."

"That remains to be seen," Lula said, backing away. "I'm going now. The smell of cheap perfume has always offended my delicate nostrils. I like to smell only fresh flowers—nothing artificial. You are merely the mock, my dear."

"Why don't you just go along and write some little stories? I'm sure your characters are as dead and lilywhite as you are. If you want to write about something, write about this." On a sudden impulse and half out of her mind, Tango threw open her robe, revealing her ample breasts and her small penis which always did appear underdeveloped, more like a tiny finger instead of a cock.

Lula's face tightened as she took in the sight. "Even your own body is caught in the twilight world between the sexes. I can clearly see why Jason would be temporarily amused by you. He's always been confused sexually. You offer a glimpse of both sexes."

Suddenly Tango felt exposed and vulnerable. She wrapped the robe tightly around her slim body, covering her naked parts and humiliated that she'd revealed them in the first place.

Before walking away, Lula turned and stared into her eyes intently. "I issue only one warning." With that pronouncement, she headed down the creaking stairs, her delicate feet descending rapidly as if her mission had been accomplished.

Tango slammed the door, her mind in chaos. She braced her back against the shut door, as if that gave her some protection. But she knew the thin wooden door didn't offer her a respite from her fear. For a moment, she imagined that crazy white bitch on the other side of the door pointing her gun at it, waiting to blast Tango into hell.

She fled to the bathroom but it brought memories of Duke's attack. She didn't know where to go and what to do. Finally, she decided to get dressed in one of her more flamboyant outfits and parade through Savannah looking for Danny Hansford. She had a few things to settle with that white boy.

*****

The moment Lavender welcomed Phil Heather back to her parlor, with its valuable paintings, she sensed an uneasiness about him. No doubt he had experienced surprises from his Aunt Bice before. When she'd called to invite Phil over and to tell him that his Aunt Bice had mysteriously reappeared from her strange mission, Phil had said, "Oh, my God, what now?" Nonetheless, he had accepted her invitation, mainly, no doubt, because he wanted to be assured that his favorite aunt was all right.

"Thank you for asking me over again," Phil said, kissing Lavender on her heavily made-up cheek. "I love this room—and these paintings are thrilling."

"I'm so glad you like them."

After taking in the beauty of her art, he looked with trepidation around the parlor. "Is Aunt Bice hiding somewhere in the potted palms?"

"She's just arrived and is upstairs applying her warpaint. As we fading glamor gals of yesterday get older, we still look the same. It just takes us much longer."

"I see." Phil hesitated. "And the surprise?"

"She'll be down with the surprise. And we're not talking a necktie here."

"On the way over here, I tried to conjure up what kind of surprise Aunt Bice would have for me. I think I know. She's rounded up my long alienated sister, Bleeka, and we're going to have a family reunion after all these years."

"A reunion, perhaps," she said, deliberately enigmatic. "But not such an immediate family member."

"But it's something on the hoof?"

"Alive and breathing I would say. But I managed only a cursory examination."

At that moment Aunt Bice barged into the room, looking at least twenty years younger and even more heavily made up than Lavender. Lavender immediately spotted the old Balenciaga that she herself had presented to Aunt Bice ten years ago. Lavender was always amused at how women gratefully wore discards from her wardrobe and even managed to look surprisingly good in them. "Great clothes never go out of style," Lavender always said when presenting one of her tired outfits to one of her friends.

"Phil, my darling boy," Aunt Bice said, racing across the parlor to kiss him on the mouth.

"You had me just a little worried," he said, his face appearing to scold her although that was masked by a look of genuine devotion.

Lavender could tell that Phil truly adored his aunt. After all, younger men sometimes do like older women, unlike the case with her own Danny Hansford. With him, Lavender practically had to ask Norma Dixie to count the silverware each day after he left to pursue whatever activities he desired after he'd left her. Although she wanted to, she didn't dare ask what Danny was up to when he wasn't with her. He always rode off on his bike, and after that regrettable encounter with the policeman, Tom Caldwell, Danny never invited her to go for a ride again.

With great apprehension, Phil glanced toward the doorway that led to the main hallway. It was obvious he was expecting his surprise.

"Oh," Aunt Bice said, seemingly aware for the first time that she did indeed have a surprise. "Guess what I brought back for you?"

"It might be better English to say guess *who* I brought back for you?" Lavender cautioned.

As if on cue, an older Terry Drummond appeared in the doorway, beaming at Phil.

Lavender looked first at Terry's happy, expectant face, then at Phil. She had always prided herself on her ability to detect disappointment in people's faces, even though artful dodgers cleverly concealed their letdowns. It was only a flash before he camouflaged it, but Terry Drummond was about the last person on the planet Phil wanted his Aunt Bice to deliver to him. Before arriving with this surprise, Aunt Bice had filled in Lavender on all the details, including how Phil had run off with Terry to live in heavenly bliss on the very day Terry was slated to marry Phil's sister, Bleeka.

As a woman of the world with broad international experience, Lavender was only too aware of many similar events that had happened at various weddings she attended around the world. Even so, she knew that Bleeka must have been seriously pissed and still bore a bitter grudge even to this day, regardless of the passing of a decade. Sisters tend not to forget doublecrosses such as that by their very own brothers.

Terry stood with a certain embarrassment before Phil. "Hey, guy, it's great to see you again."

"It's great," Phil managed to say a bit awkwardly before bending over and giving Terry a light peck on the cheek.

Again, Phil seemed expert at masking his true feelings, but Lavender sensed that the present corpulent Terry Drummond wasn't the one Phil had fallen for a decade ago. She imagined Terry didn't carry around as much weight as he did today, and surely he must have had more hair.

"You're looking good," Terry said to Phil. "The years haven't changed you." As if suddenly aware of his own blubber, Terry said,

"I might have had one too many meals of grits and country ham in Mobile."

"You're fine," Phil managed to say, glancing not at Terry but awkwardly at Lavender as if she might rescue him. "What brings you to Savannah?"

Terry looked bewildered, then turned with a kind of desperation to Aunt Bice. "You didn't tell him?"

"I wanted you to be a surprise," Aunt Bice said defensively. "Only the other night Phil was sitting on my porch and we were growing nostalgic. The way my boy spoke of you I just knew he wanted you back."

"You should have told him," Terry said. "I'm sorry, Phil. I thought you knew. I thought you'd sent for me, and I was only too glad to return. I should have never left in the first place. Until Aunt Bice arrived to rescue me, I was dying in Mobile."

"Since Aunt Bice and I last talked, there have been some changes in my life," Phil said.

Before Phil could explain those changes, Lavender invited all of them to her patio where she called for Norma to serve tea, the way she'd done when she'd last entertained George and Barbara Bush. She always offered tea to Republicans and hard liquor to Democrats, much preferring the company of Democrats.

"There is method to my madness," Aunt Bice said, sipping the tea Norma offered. The maid seemed strangely demure today, not her usual flamboyant self. Before her guests arrived, Lavender had warned her not to take over the proceedings, Lavender was even considering forcing a moratorium on Norma's Mae West stories, especially the attention-getting one about the screen legend being a man. Lavender had her own stories to tell her guests, and how could anyone possibly compete with tales of life with Mae West, even if that life were just imagined, as she suspected was the case with Norma.

After a sullen Norma had left, Aunt Bice turned to Phil and affectionately stroked his hand. "This dear sweet child here." She smiled at Terry before reassuming her explanation. "This lovely boy, Terry, is the key not only to your own personal bliss but the key to get you back into the good graces of Big Daddy and Sister Woman. Reunited once again with your own loving family."

"Running off with Terry was what caused the rift in the first place," Phil protested. "Why would hooking up with him now make any difference? It'd be like rubbing salt into a very bad wound."

"I've had a long talk with Sister Woman," Aunt Bice said. "She's willing to forgive you and intercede with Big Daddy to allow you to return to the house. But only on one condition."

"What might that be?" Phil asked, his attention riveted to his aunt.

"She wants the marriage to Terry to go through just like it was planned ten years ago. You can even be Terry's best man."

In astonishment, Phil stared intently at Terry. "And how do you feel about all this?"

"Aunt Bice explained it wouldn't be like...you know, a real marriage. I wouldn't have to do anything. Bleeka just wants to have a husband in name only before she eats herself into an early grave with those chocolates. I mean, we'd sleep in separate rooms." He smiled at Phil. "I mean, I'd be free to be with you. My only duty would be to take Bleeka to church every Sunday morning so she could show me off in front of the congregation."

"I see," Phil said.

His hesitancy did not pass unnoticed by Lavender. She suspected Phil wanted to get up and leave this tea party as quickly as possible and get on with his own agenda. "Phil, darling, why don't you think about what Aunt Bice is proposing? It would be a good way to get back into your family's graces. If Sister Woman lives up to her promises, she wouldn't be crawling into bed with Terry at night. You also need to make up with Big Daddy. The last time I saw him, he looked like he'd avoided the Grim Reaper for the last time. Go along with this plan. In a few years—maybe only two—you'll be back in charge of your ancestral home. Makes perfect sense to me."

"I don't know," Phil said. "It all seems a bit mad to me."

"You're in Savannah now where plotting such schemes is a way of life," Lavender said.

"I need a little time to think this one out," Phil said. "Everything's happening so fast. Since I just got into Savannah, my life's speeded up. It's like everything's in fast motion."

"I understand," Aunt Bice said. "In the meantime, I can stash Terry at my place and you can come and visit with him any time you like."

Terry frowned, turning to Phil. "I sorta thought you might have room for me right here in Savannah."

"Right now I have a full house. Even two young kids staying with me. Friends, you know. We'll work something out, I'm sure."

To Lavender, Phil sounded completely unconvincing.

The sudden appearance of Danny Hansford in the garden patio distracted everyone, as all eyes, including those of Lavender's, were glued to his sheer white bikini. Without a greeting to anyone, he jumped into the pool and swam three laps as no one talked but focused on his swimming.

When he emerged from the pool, his bikini clung to his groin like a see-through, clearly outlining the shape of his penis and balls. Even his flesh tones were apparent.

Aunt Bice and Terry appeared mesmerized. Lavender took the event calmly. To her jaded eyes, this was just one of a series of exhibitions she'd been a party to around the world. She noted in Phil's face that he too had seen the likes of such acts before.

"Danny, why don't you wrap a towel or a sarong around yourself and come and join us for tea?" Lavender called to him.

Norma appeared with a towel which she rather disdainfully handed to the young man.

After treating the tea party to a final view, Danny came over to join the party. Lavender introduced him to Aunt Bice and Terry but his center of attention was focused only on Phil. Taking a seat opposite Phil, Danny draped the towel over his shoulder and opened his legs for inspection. "I finished reading *Butterflies in Heat* last night. The title role of Numie was written just for me. I don't only know how to play the part, I've lived it."

Phil seemed to give the young man a thorough appraisal. "You might be right. I think you'd be a sensation on the screen."

Long after Danny had gone upstairs to their bedroom and her guests had departed, Lavender from her upper-floor veranda overheard Aunt Bice talking to Phil.

"Let's go some place to chow down on some real Savannah vittles. Lavender and her fancy teas! Tasted like Kool-Aid to me. She could have poured some rotgut bourbon in it to make it palatable."

She watched the three of them disappear and could only imagine the fate that awaited them

*****

Before Phil had left Lavender's tea party, Danny had slipped him a note. It read: "It measures 8 1/2 inches long and it's thicker than a can of Bud—and it's all yours any time you want it. Your buddy Danny."

That same note, presented to dozens of people in all walks of life, always worked for Danny. To date, no one had turned down the invitation. The part of the hustler, Numie Chase, in *Butterflies in Heat*, was all but his. Unlike his other conquests, Danny fully expected the sex with Phil would be great. He was one good-looking guy—not as handsome as Danny, nor as young, but one appealing man, nonetheless.

Of course, no one was as hot as Tom Caldwell. Tom had given him the sex he really wanted. With Tom, he could be himself and satisfy his real desires. With all the others he had to play-act at being the stud hustler. But Tom had sensed what his true desires were and had set about to fulfill those fantasies of Danny's as no other person ever had. He eagerly awaited his next session with Tom who had promised that their love-making was going to be "extra special."

Responding to an earlier phone call from Gin Tucker that morning, Danny found himself on the photographer's front porch, urgently ringing the doorbell.

In a Japanese-style red kimono, Gin answered the bell, throwing open the door to welcome Danny. "My favorite photographic subject," he said, reaching for Danny's arm to guide him inside.

At Gin's touch, Danny cringed slightly, remembering their last encounter. The pudgy, balding photographer wasn't his type at all.

In Gin's studio, Danny was relieved to find that business—not seduction—was the order of the day.

In the middle of Gin's desk lay a remarkably lifelike dildo modeled from Danny's own penis. It was odd for him to see this formidable instrument independent of his own body. The sight of it thrilled him. It looked larger and more awesome in its detached state than it did on his own body.

"After trying this on for size, the gay world will assign the aging Jeff Stryker to dildo oblivion," Gin said. "You're the new kid on the block."

"A dildo that thick can really injure somebody," Danny said.

"That's not our problem. Our biggest headache will be going to the bank to deposit all the loot we're going to make off this whopper."

"What in hell does that mean?"

"My contact in Atlanta wants to market these. He's already ordered ten thousand. He's taking out ads in *Mandate, Unzipped.* All the major sex mags."

"How do I figure into this?" Danny asked, growing skeptical and fearing he was going to be exploited without profit.

"Whatever I make I plan to split fifty-fifty with you." Gin smiled. "Isn't that fair enough? Of course, I'll need your name on a contract. I come from a wealthy family so I'm hardly doing this for the money. More a hobby, actually. As you can see from this grand house, I'm hardly destitute."

"Fifty-fifty sounds fair," Danny said. "After all, it's my dick. I'm entitled to half."

"Thank Zeus we won't have to pay for hospital bills. Guys will surely get this monster stuck up their tight butts and will end up in emergency wards throughout this great country. Some queens, though, will have such loose canals they'll probably buy two and stuff both of them up their butts."

"That would be one wide receiver!"

Gin looked first at Danny, then at the golden dildo, then at Danny again. "It's a deal, partner?"

"It's a deal. I'll sign the fucking contract. When do we get our money?"

"When my friend gets the contract in Atlanta, he's obligated to send us an advance. I think the first ten-thousand will sell fast. There will be a lot more orders. He plans to distribute this baby worldwide. Your dildo will be fucking every faggot from Tokyo to Greenland."

"I feel really funny about this," Danny said. "I mean funny good, not funny bad. On any given night I might be splitting ten-thousand guys. Hot damn! What a feeling."

"As for myself, I tried to fuck someone only one time in my whole life. When the shithead asked if I had it in yet, I withdrew from the smelly hole and never attempted that form of sex again."

"You don't know what you're missing," Danny said.

"I'm the fuckee—not the fucker." He moved menacingly close to Danny, who backed away, fearing another come-on. "I've got to tell you something," Gin said with a smirk. "Your dildo really works. I tried it out on myself last night. Oh, mama! I won't be able to sit down for a week."

"Glad you enjoyed it," Danny said, eager to sign the contract and get out of here. "I've got to go. Let's get our business over with. Danny Hansford is wanted all over Savannah today."

Crossing Whitefield Square on the way to Tango's apartment for a showdown, Danny spotted a familiar car. He recognized both the car and its occupant at once. It was Steve Parker, the guy he'd hustled for and for whom he'd acted in the porno flick with the hooker with big tits.

Steve called out to him, but Danny ignored him, hurrying across the square. Now that he was installed at Lavender's and was headed for big bucks, he didn't need to prostitute himself for a hundred bucks before some repulsive john.

"I've got to talk to you," Steve called out to him, huffing and puffing to keep up with Danny. "Big bucks!" Steve yelled after him.

The sound of those two words were like magic to Danny's ears. Even though on the road to stardom, Danny felt he had the time at least to stop and listen to Steve's pitch.

"I've been here every day waiting for you," Steve said, somewhat petulantly as Danny came to a stop. "Have I got a deal for you."

"It'd better be good. My price has gone through the ceiling since our last little film session. My dildo's about to go national. I'm going to be the biggest attraction to hit this country since Marilyn Monroe."

"That's great, and I'm really glad you're finding all this success," Steve said, mopping the sweat from his brow with the back of his hand.

"I've shown your film to some Jap business clients of mine in Atlanta. They went ballistic. They've got to have you for a private session and a private filming. There's five of them."

"Five?" Danny paused a minute. "What's in it for me?"

"Each one of them will pay one-thousand dollars for a group session. All caught on film, of course, by me. How about it?"

"For that kind of work, I've got to get three thousand per Jap. They've got the money. If they want what I've got, and want to put it on film too, that's my final offer."

"That's a lot of money. They never paid that much money before." He hesitated. "I'm not so sure."

Danny spat near Steve's feet. "Mister, you're taking up my time, and time ain't something Danny Hansford has much of." He turned and walked away, heading across the square.

Hardly recovering his breath from his last chase of Danny, Steve ran after him, desperately trying to catch up. "It's a deal! Fifteen thousand. No more. Fifteen thousand was going to be their top offer. You're not the only hot blond stud in Georgia."

Danny stopped in his tracks. He turned around, flashing the hustler smile. "I thought you'd see it my way. Those guys may never have paid fifteen thousand before, but they never had Danny Hansford on the auction block. Let's talk turkey and strike a deal. I'll even give you my phone number."

Glad to shake off the lingering aura of both Gin and Steve, Danny hurried to the apartment he'd once so recently occupied with Tango. He was going to pack his clothes and get out of there. Lavender had urged him to abandon all his possessions, claiming she'd buy "newer and better of everything," but he wanted this final showdown with Tango.

That lady had become too grand for her own good, thinking she was the star of the show. It's true: she could dance the tango and do it better than any hoofer north of Argentina. But what the black bitch didn't seem to get into her thick skull was that all the queens of Savannah weren't flocking to the club to see her damn dance. They were coming to see what was showcased so enticingly in Danny's tight, tight white pants and to marvel at his golden chest and muscles.

When he'd been broke and down and out, having to take sex jobs from people who made him sick, Tango had seemed like a hot meal ticket. At least she was good looking, and he didn't really mind that she was black. He wasn't bigoted like his parents who hated niggers and blamed them for everything that had gone wrong in their own poverty-stricken lives. Besides, Tango looked more like she had a suntan than a real black person.

With her, he'd been forced to play the extremely butch role, demanding to be serviced. The queens liked that, and he was good at the part. But he was only play-acting. Tom Caldwell knew the real Danny Hansford. He cared so much for Tom that maybe one day he'd reveal the boy behind the Danny Hansford mask: the much confused and lonely Jeff Broyhill of Clinton, Georgia, who grew up in a decaying house that Sherman's soldiers accidentally hadn't burned down in the Civil War and one on which no repairs seemingly had been made since.

Born poor, he'd remained poor all his life. But his luck was about to change. The second Danny Hansford wasn't going to be like the unfortunate original Danny Hansford, who single-handedly saved the tourism industry of Savannah and didn't get a cent for it.

The original Danny Hansford was a miserable wreck of a human being, forced to beg for and be denied a twenty-dollar bill from the antiques dealer and his john, Jim Williams. That wasn't going to happen to the second Danny Hansford. He not only was going to be one of the most highly paid sex performers in America, the subject of fantasy, but he was going to become a multi-millionaire if those paintings in Lavender's parlor were real and not fakes. With Lavender you never knew. Everything about her seemed to be fake, especially the color of her lavender hair. Even her pussy hair had been dyed lavender.

Bounding up the steps two at a time, he wanted to pack his clothes, what few he had, and let Tango know he was through with her. He'd already rehearsed his good-bye speech to her. "I don't need you now, bitch. I'm on top of the world. For me, you were just a mercy fuck." He knew he'd have to be careful, though. After he told her that, she might take a butcher knife and stab it into his heart.

He had a hard time fitting the key in the lock, and at first feared she might have changed it. But eventually it went in, and he stepped with trepidation into the darkened room, as if fearing at any minute Tango might rush out from behind a door and stab him.

The apartment seemed empty. Slowly he made his way across the living room, heading toward their bedroom. There in a band of light coming in through a torn window shade, he took in the awesome body of a nude man sprawled in the middle of the bed.

Danny quivered at the sight of him. He was built amazingly like Tom. Danny didn't know who this new man was but felt a powerful attraction to him. The stranger no doubt was Tango's new boyfriend.

He was probably old enough to be Danny's father, but he looked youthful in the golden light sneaking its way into the otherwise darkened room. A distant memory of his home in Clinton came back to him. His own daddy would sprawl across the bed just like this stranger was doing. When Danny's mama was gone, his daddy would call out for Danny to come to his bedroom. Danny always knew what his daddy wanted. Far from feeling abused, Danny welcomed those sessions with his daddy, sucking and licking him and bringing him the most exquisite pleasure. His own daddy had thought he was forcing his son to do something against his wishes. What his daddy hadn't suspected was how eager Danny had been to do this bidding. He could lick and suck on his daddy all night if he wanted him to. Until he'd met Tom nothing had given him more joy in life than that.

This stranger stirred those same feelings within Danny. He felt he had to have this man even if it exposed him to grave risks. Seemingly with a mind of their own, his feet slowly walked toward the bed he'd once shared with Tango. The sight of the stranger's penis mesmerized him and he was eager to taste it.

As he approached the bed, the stranger suddenly became aware of a presence. He slowly opened his eyes and took in the sight of Danny.

"What have we here?" the man said. "A right pretty blond boy. Maybe the prettiest I've ever seen."

When Danny met the stranger's eyes, he knew it was okay to proceed. The nude man was virtually inviting him to go ahead and do what Danny felt compelled to do.

A knowing smirk came over the stranger's face. "It tastes better than it looks."

\*\*\*\*\*

It was clear from reading the accounts in the press that Tipper was fast climbing the ladder of success again. With a wicked exploitation of her past, she was in the news once more, no longer a fading cabaret entertainer of yesterday but a media headliner.

Physically, emotionally, and creatively, she was at the peak of her power. She loathed being a has-been like some Norma Desmond in *Sunset Boulevard.* If exploitation of her notorious past was the key to her present success, then she'd unlock that past.

Applying a new makeup which she planned to try out tomorrow night, Tipper studied herself closely in the mirror. Not being truly glamorous, she was immensely pleased at how she'd been able to create the illusion of glamor. "It's all in the greasepaint, kid," she said out loud to herself.

She smiled at the enigmatic reflection of herself in the mirror. The world had always been immensely concerned about her past. Was she a murderer? Only she knew that. In spite of all the lurid speculation and the circumstantial evidence, no one had ever proven that she murdered any one.

Nor would they. She was much too clever for that. When The Black Widow attacked, she left no clues. It was ironic that she planned to write a confessional memoir with Phil. She'd spent her entire life covering up her past.

At that moment the telephone rang. It was Phil. "Great news!"

"Oh, Phil, darling, it's wonderful to hear from you." She tried to sound as coquettish as possible. With a little imagination, she could believe it was Monty's voice on the other end of the phone.

"I met this agent at one of Lavender's cocktail parties. I was totally repulsed by him. His name is Jay Garon, and he looks like an iguana."

"Oh, dear heart, you know ugliness in a man repulses me. All my husbands were extremely beautiful men and you know how Monty used to look."

"If we can get beyond his reptilian face, I think we may have a crude but effective guy to do the memoir pitch to the publishers in New York. I called Lavender and learned he's leaving Savannah very soon. He was down here about some movie deal with John Grisham. Another film set in Savannah."

"He's the agent for John Grisham?"

"That's the one. I called Jerry Wheeler in New York. He's the producer of *Butterflies in Heat,* the screenplay I'm doing. He claims Garon is hot. For a buck, he'll do anything. Hyman's attack on her mommie dearest, Bette Davis. Shit like that. He was James Leo Herlihy's agent, the guy who wrote *Midnight Cowboy.* You get the picture. Garon's sold everything, even porn. I hear he made big bucks off a book called *Copsucker.* But that was in his distant and notorious past. Right now he's stealing all of Grisham's millions that he dares to get away with."

"Do you really think this is the agent for us? Perhaps someone more respectable."

"If you want money, Garon's our boy. If you want prestige, I can call Bertha Klausner. If Gertrude Stein were alive today, she'd use Klausner."

"In that case, get the iguana!"

"I'll call him and try to set up a meeting with the three of us before he leaves town. That okay with you?"

"I'll be here all afternoon and evening. Any time." She paused. "I can't wait to see you again. You are adorable. Just like Monty."

"I may look like Monty but that's where the resemblance ends. He and I are not alike at all. I'm not the moody, brooding type. I believe in having fun in life—not letting life eat out your guts."

"You're a liberated Monty. That's what I always urged for him. You're what Monty could have been had he not been haunted by his demons. If anything, I'm looking forward to a great friendship with you even more so than I had with him."

There was a long pause on the other end of the receiver. "I can't replace Monty."

"Now, now, we'll worry about that later. In the meantime, track down this reptile before he crawls out of Savannah. I'll go to my cupboard and look up a recipe for iguana pie."

"People eat iguanas?"

"A delicacy in some parts of the world, my dear. Talk to you soon, my love."

"Bye for now."

As she put down the phone, she was left with a strong feeling that he was glad to get off the phone. That wasn't like Monty. Monty would call her at any time of the day or night and in his drugged and drunken stupor talk for hours.

That thought was banished from her brain at the sudden ringing of her doorbell. Whoever was on the other side of that door obviously wanted her immediate attention, and for that reason she deliberately delayed answering it, studying her appearance long and hard in the mirror in the foyer. For all she knew, paparazzi were lurking on the other side of that door now that she was back in the news again.

After a disappointing concert tour that had to be canceled, Tipper Zelda had pulled it off again. A media headliner once again. She smiled at her reflection in the mirror as she daintily adjusted a curl. "There's life in the old gal yet."

A petulant Dale Evans attired in pink shorty shorts and a white lace shirt greeted Tipper as she opened the door. "I thought you'd never answer," he said, not disguising the irritation in his voice as he barged into her foyer uninvited. "We've got to talk."

"The aggressive bottom herself," Tipper said, deliberately mocking Frank Gilmore's lover. She despised the real Dale Evans and disliked this namesake even more. Still reeling from Dale's past insults, she shut the door behind him and followed every mincing step of Dale's into her living room.

"Got anything to drink other than some rotgut shit?" he asked.

"Perhaps a Scotch?"

He eyed the bottle skeptically. "Not my brand at all. My Frank buys only the best for me. But I guess it'll do. Everyone in town knows you've fallen on bad days, so what can I expect?"

"Listen, queenie, and listen good. I'm not in the mood for your insults. Right this very minute John Grisham's agent is coming over here. Before this day ends, I may be offered a million-dollar deal for my memoirs."

"Not bloody likely, bitch," he said, taking the bottle of Scotch from her and pouring his own drink. A stiff one. "Even if you do dupe some publisher into releasing your memoirs, you know you won't tell the truth about all those murders. Christ, you could get arrested if you confess. There is no statute of limitations on murder. Did you know that? Have you ever thought about that?"

"I've thought about everything. Don't worry your pretty little dyed head. Tipper Zelda's always got her ass covered."

"Even that's not true," he said, belting down a strong one. He might act like a queen but when it came to hard drinking Dale could hold his own with the toughest lumberjack. "My Frank is covering your ass yesterday and today. Your checks are bouncing all over town, and someone's got to cover them."

"I am momentarily embarrassed financially but quickly climbing back to the top."

"Even if you swindle some publisher, you'll need money in the meantime, and that's why I'm here today." He plopped down on her aging sofa, desperately trying to find a comfortable spot. He sighed. "I want to become your theatrical agent. We can meet in Frank's office and sign the contracts tomorrow."

"Don't make me laugh," she said, going to the liquor cabinet and pouring herself a stiff drink too. *"Time* is about to feature me. I hear *Newsweek* is going to come out with something. I just got a call from *Vanity Fair.* I haven't returned the call yet but maybe a cover story might be in the offing."

"Maybe." Dale settled back, finding the comfortable spot on the old sofa. "You're certainly a sensation at the club. We're sold out for the week, and getting calls for reservations next week. I don't know what we're going to tell Emma when she comes back from her vacation. You're outdrawing her two to one in spite of *The Book.*"

"Perhaps all this new business will be reflected in my paycheck," she said. "I should be getting a percentage of the gross."

"We'll talk about that later. I've got a deal for you. It's big. I checked with Larry at the bank. The deal's big enough to pay off your mortgage."

"What do I have to do?" she asked skeptically. "Get up on stage every night and confess to murdering all four husbands."

"Nothing so drastic. You've got the memoirs for that. I told you, Frank and I planned to open the first gay night spot on the Redneck Riviera itself. Old Myrtle Beach, land of family values, country music, and good, clean fun. I want you to headline the show."

"Savannah was a bit of a comedown for me. I'm more San Francisco, New York, London."

"That was yesterday. You'll be a sensation. The mayor is already threatening to close us down. There's going to be a Gay Pride Parade that day. The major TV networks will probably cover the event. Several elected officials are sending their wives and kids to the Up Country until the festivities die down. Myrtle Beach can be turned into a media event, and you can be the star. It'll represent the clashing cultures of America today. Even Al Gore and George W. will be forced to make comments on it. You'll be at the very center of the flame. What do you say?"

She belted down another stiff drink and eyed him skeptically. For such a miserable little rat, he could be effective at times. After all, his idea of The Black Widow act had put her over the top again. She couldn't dismiss his proposals even though that was her first impulse. "Let me think about it and get back to you tomorrow. Of course, until this week my gay fans have been all that have kept me going these past few years. I guess I owe it to them."

"Bullshit! You owe it to yourself. You'll get your mortgage paid off. Your appearance at the hysteria we're going to create at Myrtle Beach will get another $250,000—at least—added to your memoir price tag. Think about it." He looked at a Mickey Mouse watch he wore. "I've got to go. Frank will want me home in bed, freshly showered and pre-lubed, at four o'clock." He rose impatiently. "I don't know why it is. But he always insists on penetrating me every afternoon at four. Three won't do, and five is definitely out of the question. Only at four. This has sometimes led to some awkward encounters, especially when we were flying to Miami. But somehow we always manage, even if airborne."

"That's comforting," she said, showing him to the door.

"I know you're going to get real sensible and take my offer."

"We'll talk later." She gently shut the door behind him, already mentally preparing herself for her invasion of Myrtle Beach.

In the foyer she appraised herself in the mirror once again. "Who would think that I, Tipper Zelda, would ever end up working Myrtle Beach?" Her appraisal of herself was interrupted by the ringing of the phone. She went over and picked it up.

"Hi, babes, it's Phil again. I just talked with The Iguana. He can see us around four. He's leaving town at seven and it's now or never. I threw the bait to him and he bit it."

"That's good," she said. "I'll expect you guys real soon. Let's run these memoirs up the flagpole and see if anybody salutes them."

*****

In the taxi heading for Tipper's home, Phil tried to sit as far away as possible from The Iguana to avoid both his dragon-fire breath and his endless cigarette smoking. But the whole car seemed polluted.

Getting rid of Terry for the night was more difficult than he'd contemplated. He finally got the young man to agree to live temporarily with Aunt Bice until their relationship could be more fully clarified and the mock wedding with Sister Woman planned. Phil's mind was in total chaos about the whole mess, but he planned to pursue some of his favorite aunt's agenda if it meant he could be reinstated in the good graces of Sister Woman and Big Daddy.

The note from Danny Hansford still burned in his pocket. Danny was like his sexual fantasy come true. Only days ago he would have taken the hustler up on his invitation at once—in fact, would have locked him in his bedroom. But the offer was too late.

In his heart, Phil knew that with each passing hour he was falling more and more in love with Brian. He cursed their own silliness for waiting ten years to begin what he knew was the love affair of his life. From the very first time he'd spotted Brian at school, he'd known that Brian was always the one. The others were only distractions because he couldn't have Brian. He almost hated Joyce for the chances she had to paw all that golden flesh for an entire decade.

Phil knew there would be no more encounters with studs who presented themselves, like his most recent session with Tom Caldwell. He should have sent the cop on his way when he came upstairs to Phil's bedroom uninvited. The policeman had been so incredibly sexy and alluring that he'd found it impossible to say no at that time. But if such a situation happened again, he was definitely going to turn down the offer, regardless of how enticing as in the most recent case with Danny Hansford.

Phil almost fled the smoke-filled car as it stopped in front of Tipper's door. Bounding up the steps, he rang the bell as the fat Iguana trailed him, already in need of another cigarette.

"This had better be good for me to haul my overripe pussy over here right before I've got a plane to catch," Garon said.

"It'll be hot," Phil promised him, looking back only once. The less he had to face The Iguana, the better. "We'll make some big bucks so you can stuff them into that big vagina of yours."

"It takes quite a lot to fill up my snatch. The only actors in Hollywood who could do it were John Emery and John Ireland."

"I've heard of Ireland but who was Emery?"

"Tallulah's one and only husband."

At that point in The Iguana's biography of Hollywood passion, Tipper—looking quite stunning and heavily made up—threw open the door.

"Tipper Zelda," Garon said, licking his lips at the prospect of another tasty morsel, "I must say you're still one of the most beautiful women in show business. I said that to Loretta Young just the other night. In her case I didn't really mean it, but in yours I do."

"Thank you, Mr. Garon, and welcome to Savannah. Hi Phil." She reached over and gave Phil a slightly wet kiss on the lips, no doubt as she'd done repeatedly with Montgomery Clift.

In her living room, she posed as enticingly as she could in front of The Iguana, pouring him the Scotch he requested and trying to appear as a character in Noël Coward's *Private Lives*.

Settling into his seat and accepting the drink from her, The Iguana looked deeply into her eyes. "I've heard you sing many times in New York and once in London but I never came up to introduce myself. I was once known as the prettiest boy in Hollywood. George Cukor, who had his pick of all the pretty boys, chose me. I was quite celebrated."

Already Phil was noticing that The Iguana had the disconcerting habit of interrupting social chitchat or business to interject highly tainted and suspicious autobiographical data.

"Since I know you don't have much time, I'll cut to the chase," Phil said, suddenly business-like. "As you know, Tipper has not cooperated with the press in divulging the details of her—forgive me—notorious life. But in this memoir she'll tell all." He looked over at Tipper who had seated herself with a drink opposite them. Noticing the slight hesitation on her face, Phil felt he'd overstepped the boundaries of where Tipper was willing to go.

"That's divine," Garon said, polishing off his Scotch with such rapid fire Phil feared he'd need liquid reinforcements soon. "I've followed each delicious murder of your handsome hunk husbands. It's been like one of those old movie serials I used to watch as a kid growing up in Fall River, Mass. You're not using the memoir as a confessional, are you? It's been done before."

"Actually, Mr. Garon," Tipper said, assuming a regal pose, like the cruel, callous, and rapacious bitch, Regina Giddens, in Lillian Hellman's *The Little Foxes.* "I hate to disappoint you and others, but I didn't murder any of my husbands. Not a one, not that they didn't give me good cause."

The Iguana sank deeper into the sofa and deeper into his disappointment. He turned angrily to Phil. "There went the one-million dollar advance." As if Phil were a servant, he gruffly signaled him to replenish his Scotch. "Innocent of everything?" he barked sarcastically at Tipper. "Perhaps we could call your memoirs *The Continuing Adventures of Rebecca of Sunnybrook Farm.* I'm sure Shirley Temple is just dying to make a comeback—that tough little slut."

Still maintaining her regal pose in spite of The Iguana's talk, Tipper said, "I'm no fool, Garon. I know publishers want red meat, even a fat iguana like you delivered on their platter from time to time. After all, no publisher was interested in Gloria Swanson's memoirs until she agreed to write about her affair with Joseph Kennedy."

"And just what is it that you're prepared to serve up to a scandal-hungry world?" Garon asked.

Phil sighed and headed for the liquor cabinet himself, this time eager for a drink of Scotch for his own parched throat. So far the encounter between Tipper and The Iguana seemed headed for disaster.

"In the memoir, I'll name the real murderer," Tipper promised. "A celebrated figure, no less. Fortunately, now deceased so she can hardly sue."

The Iguana leaned forward in his seat, as did Phil. Tipper seemed to relish their undivided attention, and, like the skilled performer she was, deliberately prolonged the suspense of the moment.

"The insanely jealous Greta Keller murdered each and every one of my husbands," Tipper said in such a matter-of-fact tone that it was hard to challenge her accusation.

"The legendary Greta Keller!" Garon said. "What old queen doesn't know of her?"

"I'm not an old queen but I've heard her voice," Phil said. "It was used in the movie, *Cabaret*."

"One and the same," Tipper said. "When I met Greta, she was a bit long in the tooth and I was virgin meat as far as lesbians was concerned. But she fell for me and in a big way. She pursued me everywhere, and I was flattered by her attentions since she remains my own favorite chanteuse. I have all her records."

"So did Hitler," Garon said. "I understand she used to be his favorite singer. Even his mistress until he discovered she was a Jew just like me."

"She fled Berlin just as the hangman was coming for her," Tipper said. "No time to even go back to her apartment for her sable coats. Sailing to America, she had an affair with Ernest Hemingway. Greta was a much experienced woman before she met me. Her most regrettable affair was with Marlene Dietrich. Marlene stole Greta's persona. The blonde hair. The sultry looks and husky voice. Greta was the star in Vienna when Marlene was in the chorus line. Greta scored her first big hit with 'Lili Marleen.'"

"I like the sound of this," Phil said, looking over at The Iguana for approval. The lizard-like face of The Iguana remained without expression or commitment.

"Greta wanted me just for herself," Tipper claimed. "I kept falling for and marrying guys, but she stalked them and eventually murdered every one of them. She eventually killed Montgomery Clift, but that's another story and a very different kind of death from my other men who were violently murdered in each and every case."

"Forgive me, but I think Tipper's story has more holes that a piece of Swiss cheese," Garon said, downing the last of his drink, glancing nervously at his watch, and literally heaving himself up from the sofa although in dire need of assistance. He turned to Phil. "Have an outline of all this bullshit in my office in New York by Friday. It's so stupid that I think it'll sell. The talk shows will eat it up. I'm practically licking Oprah's pussy. She'll go for it especially if I promise her a hot one with Grisham, and a few other things. I think we're staring $750,000 in the face. How does that sound to you two gaping pussies?"

"That's great!" Phil said. "I'll go for that. How about you Tipper?"

"I think it's worth more but if that's the going rate these days..." Tipper said.

"Let's face it: you're a has-been," Garon charged. "Many years ago I could have gone for the top dollar on this one."

"But I'm coming back and coming back big," Tipper said, a little too defensively. The Iguana had clearly angered her, and it was obvious she detested this exploitation of her life, even though moving fully ahead with it.

"Murder and sex always sell," Garon said. "Especially if we can blame the death of those long-gone hunks on a faded celebrity of yesterday, even a faded one like Greta Keller. I wish it had been Dietrich instead."

In the foyer, he gave Phil a repulsive wet-lipped kiss before planting one on Tipper's much-used mouth. "I'll be seeing you girls at contract-signing time. If there's one thing this great big pussy knows how to do, it's how to sell books." He paused on the landing, surveying the still-waiting taxi that was to haul his enormous butt to the airport. "Dyke copy is hot now. I didn't get Stanwyck to write the ultimate dyke book, but this one should be sensational. It'll be great for your career. It could even relaunch Greta's career."

"But she's dead," Phil protested.

"That's a good point," Garon said, opening the cab door, "but I haven't always let that stop me. Two of my best-selling romance writers died several years ago, but I haven't told that to their publishers. I just hire hacks to write the books for them."

"Neat trick," Phil said, waving a faint good-bye to The Iguana.

"Good day, Mr. Garon," Tipper said, assuming her regal pose.

Phil took her outstretched hand and held it tightly, as they watched the taxi pull away from the curb and head for the airport. He wasn't entirely certain what he had committed himself to. From the bewildered look on Tipper's face, he knew she also wasn't sure of her commitment. He turned and headed up the steps to her main door, still holding her hand.

A slight hesitancy came over him about entering her home alone with her, but he went inside and shut the door behind them, as if that would keep out the prying eyes of an increasingly tabloid world.

*****

After Jason came out of the bathroom, encased in a rather dirty and battered terrycloth robe, Lula invited him into the kitchen for a cup of tea. She didn't always brew it to his satisfaction, but kept offering the drink any way. At least it was better than her coffee.

"I don't know what to say," he told her, not looking her in the eye and sitting down opposite her at their littered kitchen table. "I'm fucked up in the head. Always was. In fact, I was known for having a screw loose back in Columbus." He finally looked her in the eye. "But you knew that back then. You knew that the day you married me. Why did you marry me?"

"Why not?" she asked with a certain bravado. "We were two lost souls. I felt a great bond with you. All my life I've been the subject of ridicule. You didn't make fun of me. You accepted my eccentricities as perfectly natural. You have a wandering nature. But so do I. I've always followed the dictates of my heart—and so have you. We belong together."

"You do have a forgiving nature, and I've always admired that in you."

"It would be silly for two artistic souls like us to ever have a conventional marriage. God knows I'm no suburban housewife. You're hardly the nine-to-five husband returning home at night to the wife and kids and the TV dinner. That's not us."

"At least you have an art form. You're a novelist. As for me, I have all these feelings I'm trying to get out of my system. I want to express myself in some way, but I don't know how. I can't write, paint, sculpt, act, sing, play an instrument, and the list goes on and on. But I've got something to express. When I can't find an outlet, I just go crazy like I just did with that tango-dancing black drag queen."

"You've done much worse than that before, and, if I know you, you'll get into even more horrible shit in the years ahead."

He reached over and gently took her hand in his, caressing it like it was the most delicate of treasures. "You'll always take me back, won't you?"

"I've always told you we were soul mates and I mean that. I've never wavered in my commitment to you, and I never will." She looked deeply into his eyes. There was no false sentiment in her heart this morning. She truly believed what she was saying to him, and planned to honor her commitment to him. She feared if she cut him loose to leave him dangling in the world that he would be dead in a few months. He wouldn't commit suicide but it would be a fast death nonetheless.

His soul wandered daily and especially nightly into a self-destructive valley where the vegetation was cannibalistic. She knew that in time he would destroy himself and never live to an old age. But she was determined to keep him alive as long as possible. Even though she might keep him alive, she knew it would be all but impossible to force him to lead a useful, productive life. That was beyond him. He had no such goal and couldn't possibly understand what a productive, creative life was. He was a man who blindly followed his instincts with no regard as to where he was going or what the consequences of any of his actions would be.

The air in the kitchen had grown stale, and she knew she should get up and open a window to let in what she hoped was the only breeze that might be stirring in the fiery hot furnace that was Savannah in August. But she didn't want this moment of bonding between them to end. Without having to say too much to each other, or spell out any horrendous details, they were coming together again as a union, a couple, perhaps a duo from hell, but a man and a woman nevertheless.

Outside their door, life was moving on, and she couldn't escape from it for very long. Their solitude and moment of bonding came to an abrupt end with a loud pounding on her kitchen door. She looked at Jason one more time before slowly getting up from the kitchen table to answer the urgent summons. Whoever was on the other side of that door seemed not to want to rap gently but to knock so furiously the glass panels shook in their frames.

Even though fortified with tea, she was hardly ready to encounter Savannah's voyeur and all-around psycho, Arlie Rae Minton. At first she wanted to slam the door in his face until she'd remembered he was the caretaker of the property, even though he never came around and any repairs had to be done by the tenants themselves. A handsome young blond boy, apparently in his early 20s, stood awkwardly behind Arlie Rae.

"I have come to make a citizen's arrest," Arlie Rae shouted angrily.

"Now, now, let's simmer down," she said. "Exactly who do you plan to arrest?"

"Who is in charge of looking after those two little perverts next door?"

"They're the sons of Brian Sheehan. They live with Phil Heather. He had to leave for a bit, and I promised to look in on the kids." She paused, looking back at her kitchen table. "Except I got all involved in talking to my husband."

"Is that no-good Jason back at your house?" Arlie Rae asked skeptically. "Just the other day I saw him getting into the car of that black drag queen, Tango. That nigger bitch should be run out of Savannah, going around corrupting white men."

"That's no concern of yours," she said firmly. "Just what brings you to my kitchen door today? I know it's not to sample my cooking."

"That's for God damn sure. You're known as the worst cook in Savannah. This boy here." He looked over at the young man who appeared to be acutely embarrassed to be in Arlie Rae's company. "He tells me he's not a pervert."

"I'm no God damn pervert," the angry young man said. "I'm trying to find Phil Heather. He told me to look him up when I got to Savannah."

"Well," Arlie Rae said, eying the boy skeptically. "As you can hear, he says he's not a pervert. But I can't believe any boy that good looking hasn't been hit on by queers. Why, look at that bulge in his jeans. That bulge alone is pure queer bait." He turned to Lula again. "Look what he's got in his jeans and look what I've got—or not got. Fuck, I'm a perfect concave."

"I'm sure you guys aren't wasting my morning talking about what you have or have not in your crotches. My husband, Jason, has you both beat by a country mile." She impatiently placed one hand on her hip. "Exactly what in hell do you want?"

"I'll file my charges with the police—they'll hear all about it—when I haul you down to the station on a citizen's arrest."

Fearing the fool really meant what he was saying, Lula called to Jason back in the kitchen. "Get Tom on the phone. Tell him to get over here right away. Tell him to bring his handcuffs. We'll see who's going to get arrested."

"Don't you threaten me," Arlie Rae said. "I'll go to the press and air my charges against you."

"What fucking charges are you talking about?" she asked.

"Corrupting the morals of minors."

"Just what minors have I corrupted?"

"When I came here with this young boy—who may or may not be a pervert—the front door of Phil Heather's house was unlocked. I went in and heard noises coming from the upstairs bedroom. I tiptoed up the stairs and spied on what was going on. The boy who calls himself John was fucking the butt of that little pussy Henry."

She said nothing, emitting a little sigh of despair. "Arlie Rae, you are known for certain voyeuristic tendencies. How long did you stand at that door looking at these boys?"

"That's hardly your business. But I did stand there for a little bit until I could fully determine what was going on so that I could give the police an accurate description."

"That's not exactly what happened," the young man interrupted. "I came upstairs and saw this redneck fart. He was concealed behind the door playing with his tiny dick while he watched the boys go at it."

Lula stared long and hard at Arlie Rae. "Is this young man telling the truth?"

He lowered his head. When he looked up at her, a tear had welled in his eyes. "I can't help it. I've got this affliction. Everybody picks on me. God made me the way I am. Now I ask you, if God didn't want me to do what I do, why does he make me do it?"

"Right now God is telling you to forget all about this and go back home to your bedroom. And those pictures of Linda Tripp on your bedroom walls."

Looking defeated and filled with despair, Arlie Rae left the porch and headed up the driveway.

Lula walked across the porch and extended her hand to the young man. "I'm Lula Carson. I'm a novelist."

"I'm Chris Leighton. I'm a dancer/actor."

"What brings you to Savannah?"

"Phil Heather told me to call him but he didn't know his phone number at the time. He gave me Arlie Rae's number. He said I could come and live with him if I ever came to Savannah."

"I see." She gently touched his arm directing him inside her kitchen. "Phil's got a full house right now. Why don't you wait here in my kitchen with my husband and me? I'll fix you some breakfast. You look hungry."

"I'm starved. I haven't had any food since I left Key West."

"Come on in then." In the kitchen she introduced Chris to Jason.

Jason stood up to shake the hand of the young man, but as he did his robe became undone and he stood completely exposed before Chris.

Chris stared in seeming disbelief at Jason's appendage. "Pleased to meet you," Chris said, looking down and not making eye contact with Jason.

Still holding the young man's hand, Jason moved closer to Chris. "Do you want me to deep kiss you?" He glanced up at Lula. "It's okay with my wife."

She came over and unlocked Jason's grip on Chris. She fastened Jason's robe for him and gently eased him back into his chair.

"Sit down, Chris," she said firmly like a school marm. "How about some country ham, biscuits, and scrambled eggs?"

"Hey, that would be great," Chris said, looking bewildered.

Jason smiled at Chris. "Wait till you taste Lula's cooking. She's known all over Savannah for her cooking. She's a God damn good writer too."

"Just a little correction," she said, pouring Chris some tea. "I'm a great writer. When my first novel is published next year, I'm going to win the Pulitzer Prize."

*****

Finding the front door unlocked, Tango entered the apartment slowly, being as quiet as possible, in case she came upon a burglar. Her neighborhood was being victimized by more and more robberies every week. Crime was definitely on the rise in Savannah.

The noise coming from her bedroom didn't sound like any burglar she'd known. At first she'd thought that Duke had picked up some hooker in one of the local bars and had returned with her to the apartment. Almost insanely jealous that her daddy would turn to another woman so soon after their first sexual encounter, she headed toward the door to their bedroom. She fully planned to yank out every dyed hair in the hooker's head. That would teach her to stay away from Duke.

To her shock, surprise, and astonishment, Danny was going down on Duke who obviously was approaching orgasm. He held Danny's head down on his raging penis, and Danny seemed only too willing to do his bidding.

This was not the Danny she'd known, the macho boy who loudly claimed in front of almost anyone, "I'm no God damn cocksucker." He was not only a cocksucker, but a skilled one at that. At the sound of Duke's moans and groans, Tango closed her eyes, not wanting to see her boyfriend swallow Duke's offering. Read that *former* boyfriend. During the short time she'd lived with Danny, she hadn't known him at all. Apparently, Duke had managed to break through to reveal Danny's secret desires quicker, faster, and more efficiently than she had after spending weeks of nights with him.

Turning from the lovemaking on her bed, she headed for the closet off the living room. Piece by piece, she took each item of Danny's clothing and threw them on her living room floor. He didn't have that much, and what little he had she wanted out of her apartment and out of her life. Their show business performances together were over too. Tango & Danny were no longer a team. Since she was the star, she felt she could quickly find another dancer to take Danny's place. The whole act revolved around her anyway. If she couldn't find a replacement as generously endowed as Danny, she'd merely stuff his crotch. His clothes piled on the floor, Tango confronted Danny as he emerged from the bedroom after having serviced Duke. He was clad only in a pair of tightly fitting jockey shorts and had a full erection ready to burst out. He might have satisfied Duke, but her daddy certainly hadn't satisfied Danny.

He seemed shocked to see her in the living room. He looked first at his clothes piled on the floor, then into her blazing eyes. "You saw it, didn't you, black bitch?"

"I saw what a cocksucker you are," she said. "You had me fooled into thinking you're a real man."

"You never had me fooled into thinking you were a real woman," he said angrily and defensively. "I knew you were the world's poorest excuse for a man, even less a man than The Lady Chablis. As a woman you're a joke too. When I want a real woman, I'll get me one. I don't have to turn to some bad imitation."

"I'm more woman than you can handle, you little faggot."

"Faggot?" he shouted at her. "Look who's calling who a faggot?"

"Would you queens pipe down in there?" Duke called from the bedroom. "Haven't I satisfied both you pussies? I need my sleep."

"Sorry, Duke," she called in to him. She motioned Danny to follow her out onto their back terrace.

He went first to his pile of discarded clothing and slipped into a pair of blue jeans. Out on the terrace, he turned to her with bitterness. "Thanks for packing my clothes so neatly," he said sarcastically. "I only came here to pack 'em up and get 'em out of here. That is, before I got distracted."

"That is," she said, placing her hand on her hip and mocking him. "That is, before you saw a big cock you wanted to suck."

"You tell anyone about that and I'll cut that tiny dick of yours off and make a real woman out of you."

"Don't worry. I'm telling no one. I'd disgrace myself. Tango is known for collecting real men—not faggot cocksuckers."

"I'm known for capturing the hearts of real women—not pathetic nigger drag queens."

"Shit, there you go. In any relationship between a white and a black, the nigger word gets used."

"You're not even a good nigger. Your own race is ashamed of you. You...you're a mistake of nature."

"Listen, white boy, get out of my house and get out fast. I can't stand looking at your lilywhite face no more. It takes a real man to satisfy me. As you should know, that real man is lying in my bed in there. You might suck his cock, but he fucks me up the ass. He practically swore a signed oath that it was the best piece of ass he ever had."

"I'm out of here." He went back to the living room and started throwing his clothing into a black plastic garbage bag.

"Not that I'm interested," she called after him as she trailed him into the living room. "But what's your new address? Gin Tucker's no doubt. Just your speed. Savannah's biggest faggot cocksucker."

"For your information, I'm moving into the most spectacular house in Savannah. With one of the richest women in America."

She paused as if her ears weren't working. "Don't bullshit me."

"I'm gonna have more money than you ever dreamed about. Not only that, but I'm headed for big stardom. I don't need to tango dance with some nigger drag queen."

"You're telling me you're moving in with Lavender Morgan? The old hag of Savannah. A woman at least a hundred and thirty-seven years old!"

"And she's got a million dollars for every one of those years. I'm gonna be hauled around town in a fucking limousine. If I see you going by, I'll toss a dollar bill your way. But even that would be more than a two-bit hooker like you are worth."

"Get out!" she shouted on the verge of tears. He'd hurt her. No man walked out on Tango. When Tango was through with a man she left him. Danny was playing a cruel joke on her.

Grabbing his clothing, he headed for the door, slamming it behind him.

When he was gone, the tears flowed from her eyes. He'd humiliated her. She'd try to think of some way to get even with him. No white man hurt Tango like that and escaped without having to pay. She didn't love him any way. Never had. He was just a dumb kid from somewhere in central Georgia, from a place no one had ever heard of. Jason had been a far better man and a greater lover than

Danny Hansford could ever be. Danny's idea of lovemaking was to lie back in bed and call out to her, "Go down on me, bitch."

She didn't need to put up with that kind of shit any more. Even if she'd recently lost Jason too, she still had Duke asleep in the next room. She wanted him more than all the others, she finally decided, and was determined to have him. Duke was more man than either Jason or Danny put together.

Not only that, it was time she started to perform solo. After all, she was a star, the biggest star in Savannah, bigger than Emma Thompson or Tipper Zelda. She didn't need to share the spotlight with Danny any more. Her worst enemies claimed that the queens didn't come to see her act, but came to see Danny shirtless and wearing those revealing tight white pants.

Tonight Tango would go out as a solo star performer and prove all of her critics wrong.

Before morning, she'd be the true queen of Savannah. Forget about The Lady Chablis or Lavender Morgan. Tango would soon be laughing and screaming at them, "Eat my pussy, bitches."

*****

Up to now, Lavender had resisted repeated calls from her New York attorneys, instructing Norma Dixie, her maid, to tell the greedy hounddogs that she was sick and couldn't come to the phone. Finally, she was able to stall the bastards no more and was forced to listen to how bad her financial situation was. It was rapidly deteriorating.

Although she'd requested more time to enjoy her precious art collection, that period of grace was at an end. She'd been bluntly informed that her paintings, including Picasso's *Mother and Child*, had to be sold to raise needy cash. One of her attorneys informed her once again that the Picasso would not fetch the $25 million she was asking. "We've got Picassos backed up in our warehouses," the attorney had said. "Why did he paint galleries of shit?"

As she wandered through her living room, tears welled in her eyes. She loved each and every one of her paintings. She was celebrated for her collection and her taste in art. She smiled bitterly, recalling a better day when *L'Express* in Paris had called her "a cross between Lady Hamilton and Moll Flanders." *Le Figaro* had pronounced her, "A veritable heroine from a novel" in a story that ran with a glamorous picture of herself on its frontpage.

It was during those heady days that she'd acquired each and every one of these paintings from the private collections of some of the richest men in the world. She'd never paid one dime for any of the paintings, including the most valuable, the *Mother and Child.*

Knowing her passion for paintings, from Monet to Matisse, each of the paintings had been given to her as a gift of love by the men to whom she'd brought so much sexual satisfaction. Suzy in the *New York Post* had called her, "A femme fatale of the first order, catnip to men, a fascinating woman who has been loved by some of the world's most powerful moguls." The paintings were a tribute to her.

Of course, some of the men in her life, especially John F. Kennedy, gave nothing, seemingly feeling that she should be the one honored at having his penis inserted in her. It was she, in fact, who'd given money to Kennedy in the form of campaign contributions.

She could not bear the humiliation of having to sell these paintings, and warned her lawyers that the sale had to be done discreetly. She shuddered at the prospect that word of the sale would leak to the producers of that upcoming documentary on her life produced by NBC. In addition to the massive invasion of her private life that she was going to have to suffer, she couldn't stand the idea that the exposé would also reveal the news of her financial difficulties and dwindling assets.

A Savannah matron, Jessie Porter-Newton, had issued a bitter warning when Lavender had resettled in town. "Now listen to me, Miss Scarlett O'Hara. I remember what we used to call you. The society of Savannah will forgive a man or a woman any indiscretion—even murder in the case of that queer, Jim Williams, who killed that young hustler, Danny Hansford. They'll even forgive an international whore. That is, they'll forgive you if you're rich. But if you're poor, Savannah ain't in no forgivin' mood."

As a silent Norma fixed her some strong coffee, Lavender made the dreaded call to New York and the office of her attorneys. She agreed to have her paintings crated and heavily insured within forty-eight hours. They would be shipped to New York where the attorneys hoped to dispose of them quickly. "And with as little noise as possible," she'd cajoled them.

Sitting down at the breakfast table, Lavender collapsed in tears, and was comforted by Norma. "Now, now, Miss Morgan, many great woman go through tough times. Take Mae West. She—or should I say he?—wasn't as rich as people thought she was. There were times when the wolf was at her door. But she always rallied and staved off the salivating beasts. You'll do the same, Miss Morgan. I have faith in you."

"Thanks, Norma, I'm feeling a little low today." She surveyed the breakfast room, looking for telltale signs that Danny had gotten up early and had had his breakfast. He hadn't been in her bedroom when she'd awakened this morning. "Where's Danny?"

As if on cue, he came in through the kitchen door, looking far too untidy for her tastes. "Morning, ladies. I've been out polishing my bike. I'm real proud of it."

"Sit and have coffee with me," Lavender said. "I want to tell you something."

"You think I'm out riding my bike too much?"

"It's not that. I've received some bad news." She had no intention of telling this little hustler that she was experiencing financial difficulties. She hardly expected him to understand her precarious situation. Even with her mounting debts, she knew she'd still be fabulously wealthy in his eyes. He probably thought anybody with ten-thousand dollars in the bank was among the filthy rich.

She doubted if Danny's family ever had more than one-hundred dollars in their shack at one time, whereas she had dined, romanced, and seduced men who looked with disdain on "mere millionaires." Since she didn't want word to get out about her troubles, she'd decided to tell him a convenient lie. "I just talked with my attorneys in New York. The company that insures my paintings is threatening to cancel my policy if I don't ship my paintings out of Savannah."

She was amazed at the shocked look that came over Danny's face. To her surprise, he seemed almost mortified. Up to now she didn't think her precious collection meant anything to him. She wasn't even certain that he'd heard of Picasso. "Why in the God damn hell? Can't you do something about those fuckers?"

Continuing to lie, she said, "The company determined that the security is too weak for a collection that at its true market value might be worth as much as one-hundred million dollars. The *Mother and Child* alone is worth twenty-five million. Also this torrid climate is ruinous to paintings. I'm going to have to ship every one of them to New York."

Slamming his coffee down, he jumped up and glared at her. "How many times do I have to ask? What are you going to do to stop this? I want those paintings here. I'm proud of you for collecting them over the years. Real proud. I don't want to see you lose them. If you ship those God damn paintings to New York, those crooked faggot lawyers up there will figure out some way to steal them from you or sell them at one-quarter of their worth."

"The boy's right about that," Norma said, plopping some fried eggs and liver mush down in front of him."

"Right or wrong, the paintings have got to go," she said firmly in the face of their opposition. "I can't risk it. I've got to take their advice. Besides, I feel nervous sleeping upstairs over one-hundred-million dollars worth of art. The whole damn town knows I own these paintings. I feel I'm setting myself up for a major robbery. I could get knifed in bed."

"You're forgetting one thing," he said defiantly.

"What, pray tell?"

"I sleep in your bed. No one's going to knife anybody with Danny Hansford in bed to protect you."

"That's very sweet—and all," she said a bit hesitantly, still shocked at what she viewed as his overaction to the shipping out of her paintings. "But my mind is made up. I must do this for my own protection. If I refuse their demands, and something happened to the paintings, I could be out one-hundred million dollars and with no insurance."

Without saying another word, he got up from the table and stormed out the door.

"I don't understand why he is carrying on so," she said, turning to Norma. "Do you know what's gotten into that boy?"

"I don't know, Miss Morgan. But then I don't understand why you've taken up with a little hustler like that in the first place. 'Cept he's mighty cute."

She beckoned Norma to pour her more coffee. "Surely after all those years living with Mae West, you aren't surprised to learn that older women often don't say no to a young man, especially a man with the considerable endowments of Danny Hansford."

"I know all about that. 'Cept Mae West wasn't an old woman. Mae West liked the young boys, but Mae West was a man. An old faggot. What old faggot hasn't had his head turned by a young man in tight jeans, especially one with as much stuff tucked into those jeans as Danny Hansford?"

"Maybe he's proud to live in a house where his girl friend—namely lavender-colored me—owns one-hundred million dollars worth of paintings. I bet he grew up in a shack that couldn't even afford to buy Christmas cards, much less paintings."

"I'm sure it's something like you say, m'am."

To Lavender, Norma sounded very unconvincing. Leaving the breakfast table, Lavender wandered back into her living room. She was going to spend the rest of the day studying each painting closely and reliving the memory attached to each acquisition. Presidents, royalty, movie stars, and some of the world's leading politicians—a parade of greats—had been enthralled by her paintings. Now one by one each one was going to disappear forever from her life.

If anything, each painting meant more to her these days than it did when she'd first acquired it. Their loss would diminish her greatly.

She sank into her sofa, no longer able to bid adieu to her paintings, at least for the moment. Each painting had become like a year in her life. When you're twenty, you're sometimes anxious for a year to pass, especially if you have major plans for the upcoming year. But when you'd reached her stage in life, you held onto each day as if it were your last. You didn't even want to throw away an afternoon, much less a day.

Opening her eyes again, she surveyed her gallery of paintings. Perhaps they would bail her out of her present financial jam. That were like savings you stash away for a rainy day. The rainy day was here. But the raindrops were bitter, like sulfuric acid peppering her face. Each possession, removed from her, would be gone for good and no longer replenished as they were back in the days when she was the belle of the world.

She rose from the sofa and began her long, long farewell to her paintings. She feared it wasn't just the paintings she was losing, but an entire epoch of her life. With such a thought, the torrid August day in Savannah moved in on her alabaster skin like a sirocco.

His mind in disarray, Danny was plunged into chaos on hearing the news that Lavender planned to crate her multi-million-dollar art collection and ship it to New York—no doubt never to see it again. Up to that moment, he felt he had plenty of time to plot a course of action. Forgetting his upcoming stardom for the moment, those paintings were his ticket to a fortune.

Once the art was out of the house, he didn't know how he would sell the collection. But he'd once read in a magazine that certain private collectors around the world paid big bucks for stolen art. Of course, they could never display the art publicly, and could never sell it except to private collectors like themselves. But there was still a market out there.

He wasn't so stupid that he expected the full one-hundred million for the art, but he hoped to get at least ten million. The idea that a little boy growing up in Clinton, Georgia, with the name of Jeff Broyhill might one day end up with ten-million dollars boggled his mind. If only his parents could see him now. They'd be right proud of their son, even if disappointed that he'd abandoned the family name to take on the persona of the late but hardly lamented Danny Hansford.

Danny knew that the rest of his life might be numbered in mere months. The real Danny Hansford who inhabited his body and soul wanted him dead, and it was but a matter of time before that wish would be granted to the trapped and murdered Danny. Jeff Broyhill, masquerading as Danny Hansford, would soon be gone. But with those millions stashed away, he was going to live out his final days in grand style.

After stealing the paintings from Lavender, he would continue to stay with her but only for a few more weeks. He couldn't dump her too soon after the art theft. That would be too suspicious. But he could "fail" to get a hard-on. He just knew her interest in him would wane soon after that. Lavender Morgan was one lusty old broad. After repeated failures to satisfy her sexually, her hots for him would soon become an Artic chill.

He feared he couldn't think clearly today. He had only hours to make big decisions. Before Lavender made arrangements to crate the paintings, each and every piece of art had to be out of her house. He didn't even have a place to hide the paintings once he stole them.

The day was moving in fast on him, and each step had to be thought out. Trouble was, he didn't have time to think. His redneck mind had never worked with rocket speed. He had to sit and ponder just like his mama did back in Clinton. Sometimes it would take her days to plan even the simplest move. Deciding what to cook for supper was a monumental undertaking. That is, if his daddy had left her any money to buy any food for supper at all. Usually he didn't. The women he shacked up with fed his daddy so he didn't have to worry how he was going to fill his belly at night. The only time his daddy showed any interest in Danny was when he wanted to get sucked off, and that was only when his women friends couldn't get away from their husbands for the night.

Not even thinking where he was going, he found himself in the men's room where he'd been picked up by that porno freak, Steve Parker, from Valdosta. Once when Danny was in the men's room on a particularly hungry day, with his meat dangling in front of a urinal waiting for a salivating customer, he had noticed a small window above the urinals. On tiptoes he'd stared into the darkened window that looked like it'd last been washed in the 1920s.

Zipping up, he'd gone around to the back of the urinals where he'd discovered an old rusty door. He pushed it open and the creaky sound sent a chill through him. Stepping inside the room, he discovered what had appeared to be a utility room that had long since been abandoned. In the rear among the spiderwebs were two old-fashioned bathtubs, now yellowed by time, resting on claw feet. Apparently this toilet had been a very different type of facility back in the 20s when somebody used to come here for baths.

Hearing a noise, he'd frozen in his tracks. Somebody had entered the men's room to take a piss, but the man had left soon after. Shutting the door securely behind him, Danny had gone back to the urinals.

Today he remembered that secret hiding place. It seemed that no caretaker had gone into that room for decades. It truly was a room that time had forgotten. He decided after removing the paintings from Lavender's home he would stash them in that abandoned toilet until he could think of a way to get the art out of Savannah.

Disposing of Norma for the night had been easier than expected. Just flash one-hundred dollars for the night at a gin mama, and she'd be out of the house in no time.

Except even with his generosity, the former maid to Mae West was still filled with curiosity. "Just what is going on in that white boy head of yours resting under all that hair with no real color in it at all? I've seen chicken shit with more yellow in it than your hair."

"Forget about my God damn hair for one night," he told her. "I want one real romantic evening with Lavender without you butting your black face in the living room to ask us if we want something. Men and women like to be alone sometimes without the household help watching."

"That's bullshit and I know it. You've got something going on. I can't believe a white boy hustler like you is getting all that romantic over a grandma ten times your age."

"Haven't you ever heard of young guys falling for older women? I mean young girls fall for older men all the time. I know they're looking for sugar daddies in most cases, but sometimes it's genuine love. It's real love I feel for Lavender."

"It's love of her money—and that's it."

"What do you care what it is? I fuck her, don't I? I'm sure you hear her screams of passion. When was the last time you heard screams of passion in this fucking museum?"

"When I got fucked by the garbage man when Miss Morgan was away in Washington."

"Go have yourself a good time and don't haul your fat black ass in here again until after the sun comes up." With that, Danny shut the door behind her. He knew Norma was heading for the bar around the corner. Drinks there were two for one during happy hour, and the bar had the longest happy hour in Savannah. She'd be smashed in no time and out of his way for the rest of the evening.

Alone at last with Lavender, Danny had already inspected the paintings. They were merely hanging on the wall. On several occasions she'd already told him there was no security system in the house.

"I grew up in a different era," she'd once told him. "If you owned a Matisse, you hung it on the wall. There was a time that some of the greatest paintings in the world were left virtually unguarded."

The talk was not of art but of love. He poured her a glass of champagne and one for himself. The living room was lit by candlelight, and the paintings took on an eerie glow. In the flickering light, they were almost ghostly.

"You look especially beautiful tonight," he told her, caressing her ear and fondling one of her breasts. "I gave Norma the night off, and I'm feeling very, very horny."

She responded to him the way he knew she would. She pulled him closer until her tongue could dart into his cherry-red mouth. He tried not to gag. Gently breaking away after she'd had her fill of him, he got up and headed for the champagne bottle although he felt he needed stronger juice to get through this night. "I've got to tell you something."

"What is it, Danny?" she asked, glowing with affection for him.

"When I first met you, I was impressed with your glamour, your money, your fame—all that shit. But I've got to confess. I've never known a woman who's satisfied me like you have. All this making love to me has created this awesome thing." Champagne glass in had, he turned around and stared at her with all the sincerity he could muster. "I've fallen in love with you."

"Oh, Danny." Getting up slowly from the floor, she approached him, then gently fell down on the deep carpeting of her living room. She unzipped his pants and pulled out his penis. Skinning the head back, she devoured it with hunger as it lengthened to an incredible thickness in her mouth. Although she'd sucked some of the most famous dicks in the world, and was surely a world class sword swallower, it wasn't her expertise in fellatio that was turning him on.

As he drank the champagne and noted her lavender-colored head bobbing up and down below his belt, he looked around at the world class masterpieces staring back at him. Before the night was over, each of these paintings would be his, if only temporarily, before he found a new home for them. At least for one night little Jeff Broyhill of Clinton, Georgia—now the second Danny Hansford—would possess millions of dollars worth of art.

He was staring at a Paul Klee when he erupted in her mouth. But by the time of his final and violent eruption, a masterpiece by de Kooning had captured his eye.

Getting Lavender thoroughly intoxicated—almost drugged— would be the easy part. It would take all his skills as a hustler to give her the sexual thrill of her life. Before the night was over, she'd be swearing that he was a better lover than John Kennedy, Onassis, Prince Aly Khan, Elie de Rothschild, Edward R. Murrow, Frank Sinatra, Ernest Hemingway, Gianni Agnelli, and all the others she constantly raved about, although the only names he recognized were Kennedy and Hemingway.

Tomorrow morning the much-fucked Lavender Morgan would have sexual memories of him that would last her the rest of her life. In fact, he truly felt that tonight would be the last royal fuck of her life. For all he knew it might be the final fuck period. She'd have all that, a gift from him.

What she wouldn't have was a living room filled with world masterpieces.

\*\*\*\*\*

Her new theatrical agent, Dale Evans, was being fondled by his lover, Frank Gillmore. Tipper leaned out the window of a black limousine as they neared the club in Myrtle Beach where she was tonight's headliner.

Suspecting violence, some of the local media were also lured to the event. If a riot ensued, Tipper Zelda would almost certainly grace the cover of *Vanity Fair*. At the very least, she expected to appear on every major news network. CNN cameras, or so Frank had told her, were already at the club.

Even though she'd lived in the South, Myrtle Beach had always been a place you drove through rapidly en route to somewhere else. Corn dogs and cotton candy, it was a land of silver Spanish moss, salt marshes, petulant crabs, tidal flats, the Shag, campgrounds, amusement parks, miniature gold, a frenzy of theaters, and miles and miles of pasty-skinned rednecks in bathing attire. Along the Grand Strand, wearing a thong bathing suit was illegal.

In such an unlikely place, filled with Bible thumpers and their kids, Tipper arrived with Dale and Frank at the new gay dance club, with the unlikely name of Mountain Mama.

The next few hours passed as in a blur. Something had gone wrong with her contact lenses, and she'd forgotten to take her spare set. Without them, she was technically blind. Now that he was her theatrical agent, the aggressive bottom, Dale Evans, took complete charge of her, telling her what to do and when, how to look, what to say, and how to arrange herself before the camera. He'd even selected her songs for the evening, including "Forever Young." That Bob Dylan favorite was not a song she normally included in her repertoire, but Dale had insisted it would be the crowd pleaser of the night.

Even before she was to go on, right-wing protesters had formed. She'd heard there was violence at the Gay Pride Parade, and forty-two people had been arrested. Three young men had been seriously injured, having had their heads bashed in by neo-Nazi skinheads.

Dale directed Phil and Brian back to her dressing room so they could embrace and show their support before she went on. Even though she couldn't make out Phil's features, she could see enough to know that he looked like Monty in soft focus.

"It's a circus out there," Phil said. "I know how awkward this must be for you. But we've heard that the *Vanity Fair* cover is almost definite. I just talked with the Iguana, Jay Garon. He's delighted. He thinks it's all but a sure thing that he'll get big bucks for your memoirs, especially if we make them hot."

Phil might look like Monty but he certainly didn't sound like him. When she'd first met Monty he'd been enraptured by her personality and perhaps even awed a bit by her young beauty. Her celebrity hadn't impressed him at all. After all, he was far more famous than she was. He'd seen the woman who resided behind her facade, and, even though a homosexual, had embraced that side of her, finding warmth, love, affection, comfort, and yes, even sex, at her womb.

Her nightmare fear of Phil was that he saw only the commercial possibilities of exploiting her. She suspected he wanted to suck off her fame and not give her the man's loving that she desired. She certainly didn't want to create a relationship with Phil where it was always assumed that he'd arrive on her doorstep with Brian as his escort.

Like Lavender, Tipper had known only the most celebrated people on earth. Although some of these rich fans of her might have "dated" policemen on the side, these cops were to be defined only as tricks and not paraded out into polite society. One of her former best friends, Clifton Webb, fell in love with his chauffeur. But Clifton never invited his driver into the society parties he attended. To those, he escorted his domineering mother, leaving the chauffeur waiting in the limousine outside. To Tipper, this was the way it was in polite society, and she feared that Phil was either unaware of this social rule or else was deliberately flaunting convention.

"Are you worried about going on tonight?" Brian asked. "I mean, thinking someone might attack you with all those hotheads out on the street protesting."

At first she decided she wasn't even going to answer the question. But out of politeness to Phil, she turned to Brian. "I'll be fine. But thank you for your concern."

"Me and Phil are seated right at a front table," Brian said. "If something goes wrong, I'll jump up and clobber them over the head."

"That's reassuring," she said rather disdainfully before turning her attention to Phil.

As Phil went to kiss her good-bye, it was obvious he was aiming for her cheek. But she'd diverted his kiss instead and it had landed right on her lips, just the way Monty used to kiss her in those heady, glory days of long ago.

When the men had left, she'd retreated to her mirror where she had to pick up her thick glasses every few seconds to see if she were applying her makeup properly.

The noise coming from the front of the club where she was to appear was like a drunken biker's convention. The sounds of beer drinking, loud shouting, and blasting dance music assaulted her ears. This was not the proper venue for her. Already she regretted having signed Dale as her theatrical agent. But she desperately wanted to pay off the rest of her mortgage and protect the roof over her head.

To accomplish that, she was willing to do almost anything, even appear at this riotous club where she'd been told that an angry crowd of "born again" Christians had been assembling since Myrtle Beach's first Gay Pride Parade had ended hours ago. Dale had told her that some of the protesters were being hauled in by bus from some of the more redneck towns and villages of South Carolina.

"South Carolina started the Civil War," Dale had said. "Now they're trying to launch the culture war against gay rights."

Alone at last, Tipper faced the truth about herself. She no longer cared about political movements, especially sexual politics. She'd supported Martin Luther King Jr. and the civil rights movement of the 50s and 60s. As far as she was concerned, she'd done her duty for social equality. Today's political agendas—straight, gay, or born again Christian—didn't touch her heart at all. She wanted no part of attaching her name to any cause any more, except her own. Her survival now meant more to her than any other cause that had captured her fancy in the past.

At that point Dale had barged into her dressing room. He had a review of her Savannah night club act that had appeared in *Variety* and was eager to share it with her. She knew she'd been at her best in Savannah, and was eager to read a critic's confirmation of that.

"The shithead has killed us," Dale said, his face covered with despair. He read from the paper. "Tipper Zelda's appearance suggests a mummy and salutes the limitless possibilities of makeup. Of her battered gin mama voice, we had best remain silent, as that voice is now a parody of herself. She appears like a ghost, a shadow of herself that hints at what used to be. Her publicized role as The Black Widow, exploiting the deaths—perhaps murders—of her young husbands is one of the century's most tasteless show biz acts. We hope she's getting big bucks. Surely the only reason she's prostituting herself is for the money. The cost to the legend of Tipper Zelda is painful to imagine."

Like a sadist trained deliberately in the inner chambers of hell, Dale Evans had completely destroyed her confidence minutes before she was to appear on stage. He might as well have taken a sledgehammer and beaten her head in. He'd done something worse: he'd grabbed a knife and plunged it into her heart.

His introduction of her was clearly heard backstage. "One of the all-time greats of the cabaret world—a name that evokes the most glamorous heyday of Garland and Dietrich—is with us tonight. Tipper Zelda, like the rest of us, has been a survivor. We came through the parade today. We're queer—and we're here to stay in Myrtle Beach."

Catcalls and loud cheers rose up from the audience.

Dale went on. "Tonight we're in here having a hell of a gay old time. Tipper Zelda has long been a friend of gay people. After all, she was Monty Clift's red hot mama, and all her husbands were gay. Although we can't promise you Tipper will reveal all tonight, she's appearing as The Black Widow. So that might at least suggest who killed all those gorgeous young ex-husbands of hers. Did Tipper do it? The riddle is buried in one of her songs. Listen carefully and you too might be Miss Marple and hear the clue. When Tipper goes off stage, we're going to conduct a straw poll. You can vote on whether you think Tipper is a murderess or not. To all you hot men from the Carolinas, I give you the one—the only—Tipper Zelda."

Not really seeing well behind the darkened curtains, and horrified at such an introduction, Tipper staggered toward the spotlight on the small stage to the sound of deafening applause. That loud clapping and shouting temporarily overcame her fear that her appearance was mummified. At one point she almost stumbled but quickly regained her regal bearing.

With a kind of swoony decadence, she stepped into the spotlight. Almost in a whisper-quiet voice, she began her first song selected by Dale. He'd wanted her to sing "Just a Gigolo" from Marlene Dietrich's last and most ill-fated film she'd shot since achieving world stardom. The words seemed self-mocking to her, especially the last line: "Life goes on without me."

The only reason she'd agreed to do the song was because of the German lyric which ends "...people pay, you keep on dancing." She'd changed "dancing" to "singing." That's what she was doing tonight. Keeping on singing.

After all these years, she was determined to give these men—many of them newly liberated—the performance of her life. They deserved nothing less. She knew the press was here, and she had to do something to counter that asshole's review in *Variety*.

Near the finish of her first number, her performance was interrupted by the sound of crashing glass. Protesters outside were breaking into the club. In minutes, the strong arms of Brian Sheehan were rescuing her from the stage and hustling her to safety at the rear of the club.

It was only the next morning when she'd read the papers and listened to the morning news that she realized the riot at Myrtle Beach was hailed as the first major step toward gay liberation in the South. One announcer for NBC came on with the pronouncement that the club, "Mountain Mama," will one day be synonymous with the Stonewall riots in Greenwich Village of the 1960s.

# Chapter Six

When Phil went back to his house, he confronted Lula Carson in his living room watching television with John and Henry. Apparently, Brian hadn't returned from work yet.

"It's been a day," she said. "Can I get you a beer?"

"That would be great," he said, accepting kisses from Henry and an especially wet one with tongue from John.

When Lula had left the room, John snuggled closer to Phil. "Any time you want to drop my old man in favor of a younger stud, I'm your boy."

"Cut the shit," Phil said. "I don't want to hear you talk like that again."

Looking sullen, John rejoined Henry on the sofa to watch more television.

Going back into the kitchen, Phil was just in time to accept a cold beer from Lula who had also decided to have one for herself. "Arlie Rae Minton—I'm sure you remember him, he's unforgettable—came by on a mission. He slipped upstairs and caught John and Henry going at it. I think Arlie Rae jacked off during the session, then came over and threatened to have all of us arrested for corrupting the morals of a minor."

"From what little I know of Arlie Rae, that sounds typical. Any serious threat here?"

"Not at all. The crank is probably home beating his tiny meat surrounded by pictures of that hound dog between pukes, Linda Tripp."

"She's a trip all right. So is Arlie Rae."

Lula sipped her beer. "Every time I've been over here the phone has been ringing. Jerry Wheeler. Terry Drummond. Lavender Morgan. Danny Hansford. That black drag queen bitch, Tango. I slammed down the phone on her. Gin Tucker. It seems all of Savannah wants to get cast in your movie."

"That's good, I guess. I mean to have so much interest."

"Even the mayor called. He said that after Clint Eastwood came down here and made the entire city look like a cesspool of filth and perversion, he was glad to learn that a film crew would be descending to portray Savannah in its true light."

"My God, he hasn't read *Butterflies in Heat*, has he?"

"Surely not. He is aware of the title, though, and wants you to retitle the film—*Savannah, a Great City of the Old South.*"

"Real catchy title," he said sarcastically going out to their shared patio, hoping to catch any breeze that might be stirring.

Lula trailed him. "There's more. I'm not going to let you off so easily. When you leave me in charge of your household, expect fun and adventure at every turn."

"Surely the Arlie Rae episode was enough for one day. Jason's got into more trouble?"

"Jason is sleeping for the moment. He's come back to me filled with remorse and guilt. He says he will never betray me with another woman ever again."

"If Tango can be called a woman. I note he left out betray you with another man."

"He did that deliberately and conveniently, I'm sure. But Jason isn't the only one who can attract prospective bedfellows of the same sex. Only this afternoon I received an offer to indulge in fornication myself."

"Not from Arlie Rae?"

"No, he's too committed to Linda Tripp. The offer came from Joyce Sheehan. She claims that during the brief few minutes we spent together, she's fallen madly in love with me."

"So Brian is right. She's a dyke."

"Appears so."

Taking a big gulp of cold beer, he confronted her. "Are you going to get together and bump pussies in the night?"

"Colorfully put. I'm thinking about it. Only as a literary experiment, nothing of passion. It's a coincidence but I'm confronting a very similar situation in *The Tireless Hunter*. I'm not sure I've achieved the proper verisimilitude in the scene. Perhaps if I play out a real life human situation and confrontation, I will know if what I wrote is true and good."

"Good luck. Sounds a bit risky, though. Actually I'm relieved. It removes any guilt from me that I broke up a happy marriage. If Brian wants a man and Joyce is after a woman, then I may have done them both a favor."

"I think you did. Brian told me that he's madly in love with you. He said he doesn't know how he managed to go home to Joyce during a wasted decade of his life. A very vital one for a young man—his golden twenties."

"I love the big bruiser more every time he comes to my bed. I really care about the guy. Up to now I've been a slut. No more. That encounter with Tom was my last time at the rodeo."

"I'm glad to hear that. You and Brian make a lovely couple."

Even though she was saying soothing words to his ears, he sensed an apprehension in her face. She wasn't clever about concealing her feelings. "Is there something else you want to tell me?" he asked with a certain trepidation.

"You have a visitor. It's a matter of the heart."

"Oh, my God. Terry Drummond left Aunt Bice's house and has come here. Brian will shoot him if he comes near me. I'm just beginning to find out how jealous my new husband really is."

"It's not Terry Drummond. It's an extraordinary handsome young man by the name of Chris Leighton. He says he's an actor and dancer if you want to believe that. He's not something you'd discard with the dishwater. Actually he's the type of young man you'd dress in silk pajamas and lay on velvet sheets covered with red rose petals and rare black orchids."

"That sounds very intriguing but I'm a married man, a faithful married man as of now. Besides, I've never heard of a Chris Leighton. Probably some hustler who wants to play the role of Numie in *Butterflies in Heat.*"

"I think he might be a hustler but a very tender and sensitive one. A person who's still new to the game. One who has received only the minor burns of life. Not the full funeral pyre. I've been talking to him all afternoon. He fled Key West. Ran into real trouble down there. He said he thinks you fell in love with him during a night spent at a motel in Marathon."

Phil slammed down his beer on the patio table. "That Chris Leighton. I do know him but I had forgotten all about him. I did invite him to come and live with me in Savannah but that was back when dinosaurs roamed the earth. My life has completely changed since that drunken night I picked him up."

"All invitations, especially invitations of the heart, should be extended with a cut-off date. I think you owe it to him to see him. He's just next door waiting for you to come home. I sort of explained the children at your house, but I didn't tell him about Brian. It wasn't my place to do that."

"Then I'll have to come clean with him. Of course I'll see Chris. I invited him to Savannah, didn't I? I'll give him some money. Help him out somehow."

"Good," she said, getting up. Apparently, she'd had more than the beer, perhaps an afternoon of brandy drinking now that she'd gotten the money for that grant from Lavender Morgan. "Come with me. We'll surprise Chris." As he trailed her, she turned her head to confront him. "If you don't want this beautiful boy, I'm sure Jason would love for him to move in with us. Jason has already made repeated moves on Chris today. I'm sure my husband has stuck his tongue down the boy's throat several times, if not done some other unimaginable horror to him."

In Lula's decaying living room with its flea market furniture, Phil took in the sight of the beautiful boy with whom he'd shared a night of sex in the Florida Keys. Relaxed and without the anxiety of playing the hustler role, Chris looked sweet and vulnerable, not a battle-trained veteran of the sex-for-pay world he'd so recently and reluctantly become a part of.

Some inner radar seemed to signal Chris that he was under observation. Very slowly he opened his eyes, appearing not to know where he was. He took in the sight of Phil hovering nearby. It was clear to Phil that Chris didn't even recognize him at first. Their time together had been so fleeting.

Sitting up abruptly and with a certain fear, Chris opened his eyes wide as if remembering Phil for the first time and registering his promises and invitation back in Marathon in that motel parking lot. "I came to you just like you wanted me to. Just like you begged me."

"Chris, it's good to see you," Phil said awkwardly. "Are you okay?"

Before answering, Chris glanced nervously at the presence of Lula. "Can I get you guys something?" she asked.

"Some tea, please," Phil said to her, hoping to have a few moments with Chris to sort things out.

When she was gone, Chris turned to him. "Everything you warned me about in Key West came true. Only worse. I was taken by boat to a deserted island. I was held down and fisted by three guys. It's all on video."

"I'm so sorry." Phil didn't really know what to say.

"They kept me there. They did terrible things to me. I think they were going to kill me. I really do. Do you know what a snuff film is?"

"Regrettably I do. You don't think."

"Hell, yes, I think. If two guys in a boat, Bill Johnson and Johnny Frels, hadn't come by, I think those sick bastards would have killed me. These guys were out boating and landed on the other side of the island. I wasn't under heavy guard or anything. What was I to do? Swim twenty-five miles through shark-infested waters? Bill and Johnny believed my story and took me aboard and brought me to safety in Marathon."

"Did you go to the sheriff's office and report what happened?"

"Are you crazy? If word of this leaks to the newspapers, my career as an actor and dancer would be ruined forever. Besides, I was too embarrassed."

"I'm sorry all this happened to you. I really am. But I'm real glad you're safe now. Is there anything I can do to help you?"

"Hell, yes. You can keep your promise. Move me into your house and make me your lover."

"You see, a lot has happened since Marathon. My life's changed. I meant what I said at the time, but..."

Phil was interrupted in mid-sentence by the sudden appearance of Brian who came into the living room. By the look on his face, he'd obviously heard part of their talk. "If you've got any important business with my lover here." He looked possessively toward Phil. "Any business at all, you talk to me. I wear the pants in this family."

An awkward silence fell over the room interrupted only by Lula who came in carrying a tray with freshly made tea for all.

*****

With dismay, Lula looked on as no one drank her tea even though she thought it was one of her more successful efforts. A silence had come over the room.

Brian sat glaring at Chris, and Lula feared that physical violence was near. She abhorred brutality of any sort. Looking on in dismay, Phil sighed. To show his loyalty, he reached for Brian's hand. The policeman's large palm encased Phil's smaller hand and held onto it tightly.

"Looks like I took you up on that invite a little late," Chris finally said, breaking the deafening silence.

"Listen," Phil said, "I could lend you some money. Help you get back home. Shit like that."

"Hell with that crap!" Chris said defiantly. "When I left that mudhole where I was born I was God damned determined never to go back."

"You can't stay with Phil," Brian said. "That's for sure."

"He doesn't have to stay with Phil." The words came from the stairs. Jason had descended from the upper bedroom. "He can stay right here with Lula and me." With a dog's trust, Jason looked over at Lula. "Is that okay with you, sugar?"

She knew her husband so well and was totally aware of what he was plotting. She had to make some strong, hard decisions for the survival of their marriage. She didn't want to make them, but they were being forced upon her.

In her bewilderment she hesitated before answering, "Are you sure?" she asked Jason. "I mean, you just met him."

"We exchanged a little spit when he came upstairs to the bathroom," Jason said. "I like this boy a lot. He's real pretty, and I was always a sucker for a pretty face."

"At first when I felt Jason I couldn't believe it was real," Chris said. "But I figured if I could get fisted on an island in the Florida Keys, I could handle Jason." He hesitated. "I mean when I heal up back there and everything."

Phil looked first at Brian, then at Lula. "This is all a little sudden. I mean moving Chris in and everything so soon."

"Phil might agree to put you up somewhere," Brian interjected. "In a motel or something until the dust settles. Give everybody a little more time to make up their mind."

"That sounds like a good idea to me," Phil said. "I'll go for that."

Lula still wasn't sure. In one part of her brain the idea had occurred that if Jason had a live-in toy boy like Chris, he might not go running off all the time. He always got into trouble and would probably end up in jail if he carried on as he was. If Chris could tame Jason, it might be worth it having the handsome young man move in with them. With the two of them upstairs carrying on, doing God knows what, she might at least have the peace and tranquillity she needed to finish *The Tireless Hunter* now that she had the money from Lavender Morgan to support them.

"As you know, Jason," Lula said, moving closer to him and fondling his cheek. She was only slightly embarrassed that her husband was still in his white jockey shorts with their prominent bulge. The way she figured it, everybody in the room was probably intimately acquainted with Jason any way, so it didn't really matter. "I have always believed that a man—or a woman for that matter—should always follow the dictates of the heart. For me to deny you the comely charms of this succulent golden youth would make you so frustrated you'd extract your revenge on me somehow. The human heart doesn't want to be denied what it craves. For all I know, you'd sabotage my writing. Perhaps even burn *The Tireless Hunter*, even though it is my only copy."

"I'd get even—that's for damn sure," Jason said. "When I see what I want, I go for it. I can't remember getting turned down by no one. When people—men or women—see what I've got, they go for me in a big way."

"I'm sure these gentlemen know you aren't making idle boasts," Lula said, going over and sitting beside Chris on the sofa. She offered her hand, and he extended his, enclosing it in hers. "Welcome to our happy home. You'll find we're not a conventional married couple."

"I'm not even sure I know what conventional means," Chris said. "Does that mean average?"

"Something like that," Phil said.

"I just want to stay somewhere where I'm not abused," Chris said, smiling into Lula's face.

"We'll treat you with great kindness," Lula said. "Feed you too. I'm a pretty good cook. At least I'm celebrated for my cole slaw, and I'm learning to make other dishes as well."

Everyone turned when they heard the sound of loud feet on the back porch. Tom Caldwell came into the living room through the back kitchen door. He was trailed by John and Henry. "Hi, gang," he said. "Looks like you assholes forgot you asked me over for dinner tonight."

"My, God," Lula said, "I did forget all about it."

Brain stood up and hugged his longtime friend, Tom. "I hear you're giving up pussy too, boy."

"You got that right," Tom said. He patted Brian on the ass. "Think you can take stretch exercises until you can take it?"

"Fuck that!" Brian said. "I'm a top. Ask Phil. He's all the witness I need."

"Is that true?" Tom asked Phil. "Deep in the middle of the night, doesn't Brian beg for it just like a horny woman?"

"Brian's telling the truth," Phil said. "He's all man and all mine."

Brian gave him a light kiss on the lips before going out to the backyard to get the barbecue going.

As Tom came into the living room, Lula got up from the sofa, releasing Chris's hand, and turned to Tom. "Cousin, I want you to meet our new boarder. Tom Caldwell, Chris Leighton. Chris is going to be staying with us for a spell."

Tom looked astonished. "Up until this very day, I thought that Danny Hansford was the prettiest boy in Savannah. Now I'm not so sure. You both look alike. Blond and everything."

"Glad to meet you," Chris said, getting up from the sofa and shaking his hand. Tom held onto Chris's hand for so long Lula intervened and separated them. "I don't normally hang out with cops," Chris said.

"I'm your friendly, understanding type of cop," Tom claimed. "Not all of us cops are big brutes clubbing the shit out of some poor victim." He moved closer to Chris. "I'm more the loving type of cop."

At this point Jason intervened, putting one arm possessively around Chris. "Cousin, you'd better stick to that cocksucking, tango-dancing Danny Hansford and leave this one here for me. I saw him first."

Tom turned with a flash of anger toward Jason. "You might have two inches more than me, but then you've got two inches more than anybody in the world. In love and war, it's not who sees them first, it's who captures them."

Lula noted that Chris seemed to beam at this attention. He was a homeless outcast a few minutes ago and now he was being virtually fought over. Without her noticing it, Phil must have disappeared into the backyard to help Brian with dinner.

"I want you two guys to know that I'm not a fucking size-queen," Chris said. "After getting fisted in the Keys, I'm not sure I want anything too big up there again. At least that's how I feel until my tissues become human again."

"That would rule out me," Tom said. "Certainly Jason here. I can't tell you how disappointed I am."

"There may be one part of me out of commission," Chris said. "If you look carefully, and you guys have looked very carefully, there's nothing wrong with this cherry-red tongue of mine and the world's most adorable cupid lips."

"How you talk, boy!" Jason said. "You're turning me on. When I first met you, you were acting so butch."

"That's just an act," Chris said. "I play that tough macho role because that's what most johns want. But that's not my true nature. Deep down, in my real true heart, I'm more like a female kind of guy. I've done drag and everything."

"You are fucking getting me hot," Tom said, groping himself. "You're just the kind of blond treat I go for. Once I've got to have it, I can't wait. Hell with kissing on the first date. I fuck on the first date."

"Listen, I told you I saw him first," Jason said.

"You listen," Tom countered. "You owe me a lot of favors. I've gotten you out of some big jams. You could have ended up in jail, asshole, if it weren't for Cousin Tom here. I want the boy, and I want him now."

"Forget it!" Jason said bitterly.

"Gentlemen, and I trust you are Southern gentlemen about matters of the heart," Lula said. "Let's don't talk about our lovely guest as if he didn't exist. Doesn't he have a mind of his own— certainly a heart of his own?"

"That's right," Chris said. "I can make up my own mind. After all, I'm free, white, and twenty-one." He paused. "Maybe not twenty-one yet, but I'm getting there."

"What do you want to do, Chris?" Lula asked.

"M'am, could I open up and be honest with you?" Chris asked. "I mean, tell you my real gut feelings?"

"I have always been a repository of the secrets and desires of my fellow human beings," she said.

"Tom here and that handsome hunk of a husband of yours are my alltime fantasies," Chris said. "Back home I would cut out pictures of guys like them in magazines and hide them in my room at night. I'd dream about them. Except for Phil, who's a real handsome guy, most of the men I've had to sell myself to have been fat, ugly, old, and balding creeps. These guys are really hot. I want both of them." He hesitated for a brief moment as if not daring to make his final request. "Preferably both at the same time."

Jason looked at Tom, then winked. "I think Cousin Tom here and I can arrange that." In his strong, muscular arms, Jason picked up the much smaller Chris and tossed him over his shoulder as if he were but a mere bag of potatoes.

Tom patted Chris on his sore butt and trailed both men up the stairs.

In despair, Lula turned from the sight of them. She didn't even want to imagine what animal passions that would be satisfied, the deep cravings of human desire, that would be acted out in that upstairs bedroom. Jason and Tom would no doubt fulfill some primal need within them, and Chris would be getting to live out a fantasy he'd merely dreamed about before.

She was relieved not to be a part of it, believing that love should only be a gentle undertaking, a sharing of the souls, a rubbing, caressing, fondling, kissing, and embracing of the flesh—not some plunging, devouring machine of a human being taking out his lust on another person without regard to what pain it caused.

At the barbecue Lula was amazed at how perfectly in charge Phil and Brian appeared. They were like a married couple who'd been doing this culinary routine for years. Brian had made himself master of the actual barbecue itself, whereas Phil was boiling the fresh corn ears and baking the canned beans in the outdoor oven. John and Henry were already into their fifth Coca-Cola of the evening.

She was also amazed at how affectionate John and Henry were with Phil, gravitating to him more frequently than to their own daddy. Henry tugged at Phil until he was picked up and thoroughly hugged, and at one point John came over to Phil tugging his leg and holding on as if in desperate need of love and attention. Phil ran his fingers along John's cheek before reaching down to kiss the boy on the top of his head.

Lula feared that at any minute Joyce Sheehan might barge into this cozy domestic scene, but realized she, Lula, had more to worry about from Joyce than did either Brian or Phil. This mother didn't seem to put up much of a battle for either her husband or her children, and Lula suspected that Joyce was relieved to be free of the burden.

About an hour later Tom came downstairs to join them at barbecue. "How about one of those cold beers, Phil?" he called out. "I've worked up quite a thirst."

"Where's Jason?" Lula asked.

"He's coming right down," Tom said. "Him and Chris are cleaning up."

"You must have had one hot time," she said.

"The boy's hot," Tom said. "He's got the morals of an alleycat. Will do anything." As Phil handed him a beer, Tom said, "You're getting rid of a hot piece there, boy." He looked over at Brian. "But my old buddy here will keep you satisfied and begging for more."

"With Brian, I don't have to beg," Phil said.

"You've got that right," Brian said, turning over the ribs. "I made him wait for ten long years. Don't you think that's enough?"

The sound of a branch falling echoed across the backyard patio. The screech of a man could be heard. Tom ran over to the sideyard to see what was the matter. With a thud the branch hit the ground, bringing someone down with it.

Lula trailed her cousin to see what was the matter. On the ground outlined in the light of the porch was Arlie Rae Minton.

"You okay, boy?" Tom asked, picking up the young man.

"I guess I'm okay," Arlie Rae said. "Nothing seems broken except the tree branch. The ground was real soft."

"Did Jason and Tom and that new boy you brought over give you a real eyeful?" Lula asked.

"That was the hottest God damn sex I've ever witnessed in my life," Arlie Rae said. "I didn't know people did things like that. I always get major entertainment around this house of perverts."

"Not from me," Lula said, helping him to his feet. "Brian and Phil almost have the barbecue ready. Why don't you come and join us? Everybody knows how much you like barbecues."

"I love barbecue, and I *know* my barbecues," Arlie Rae said. He looked up as Jason and Chris came out the kitchen door into the night lights of the patio, then he turned to Lula again. "If there's anything I like even better than Linda Tripp, it's barbecue. 'Cept I hope it's not that Carolina barbecue. I eat only Georgia barbecue."

*****

Even now Tango couldn't believe the humiliation of the past hour. Very reluctantly Matt Daniels, owner of the Blues in the Night Club where she'd danced with Danny Hansford, had agreed to let her perform solo.

"Tango dancing is for two people, bitch," he'd yelled at her right before curtain call. Although nervous and highly agitated by his lack of faith in her, she'd defended herself mightily against his attacks. "I'm a star," she'd told him. "Stars can go on alone. They don't need chorus boys."

How wrong she was. When the mostly male audience learned that Danny wouldn't be appearing, they had booed her. After five minutes the occupants of several tables got up and walked out the door. Before the end of the first act, the room was largely deserted except for a few tourists who'd wandered in by mistake, thinking that she was The Lady Chablis written about in Berendt's *Midnight in the Garden of Good and Evil.*

Her second act just didn't happen. Matt Daniels ordered his DJ to play dance music instead, although there were hardly any patrons left to dance. "You bombed! Those faggots out there come to see Danny's big cock in those tight white pants. It's a beefcake show. You're the supporting player. Danny was what sold tickets—not some little nigger drag act."

"Go to hell, you prick," she'd shouted at him before storming out of the club. He'd called after her, telling her her show was canceled unless she got Danny back or a replacement. Than he shouted that he was temporarily booking some clones of Peter, Paul & Mary.

Blinded by tears and wandering the streets of Savannah alone at night, she ignored the whistles and catcalls from some young black men. For all she cared, they could grab her and rape her in some back alley, give her AIDS, or whatever, and she wouldn't give a damn. She wanted to die. Hating Matt Daniels, she wished that the son-of-a-bitch with his tiny dick would rot in hell. She doubted very seriously if The Lady Chablis would allow herself to be treated in any sort of way. She'd heard that when The Lady Chablis didn't like the way a club owner parted her hair, she would storm out the door. Only yesterday Tango was the toast of Savannah, the hottest gal in town. Now she was fired and without a commercial act to sell. The Lady

Chablis would once again occupy the throne as the queen of Savannah. The Lady's dethronement by Tango, or so it seemed, had been only fleeting.

Wandering into Club One on Jefferson Street, she was dismayed to see crowds of young men flocking to see The Lady Chablis, who'd apparently come here from Columbia, South Carolina. What could The Lady Chablis possibly be doing performing in reactionary South Carolina?

There were dozens of straight couples in the audience, and to her shock and surprise, the actress Demi Moore. She might wonder why The Lady Chablis was in Columbia, but Demi Moore's appearance in Savannah and at Club One puzzled her all the more. Even without Bruce Willis, Demi surely had something better to do than go to see The Lady Chablis perform, boycotting Tango's show instead in favor of Club One. She must certainly have become bored with Leonardo DiCaprio real quick, and from what Tango had heard there wasn't much there to get bored with.

On stage The Lady herself was exchanging banter with her mostly male audience. Tango was immediately jealous of Chablis. Of course, Tango knew she was far younger and more beautiful than Chablis had ever been or ever could be, but what she didn't have was the black diva's sass.

"Show us your tits, Chablis," a young college boy called out.

"That's The Lady Chablis to you, child! Oooo, if you want to see a strip show, go elsewhere. I only show my delectable boobs to some pretty blond white boys, and then only in the privacy of my boudoir. They're real too—not silicone."

"You look pretty good for a man," the companion of the college boy called out.

The Lady Chablis came to an abrupt halt on stage, placing both hands on her hips. "No, no, no, honey, who are you calling a man? I just had my estrogen shots today, and my candy has shrunk so much I thought it had fallen off at first. But I'm a showgirl. Don't you ever go calling The Lady Chablis a man. The Doll is all woman! Think you can handle a real woman?"

Turning her back on the performance and heading for the door, Tango was sickened by The Lady Chablis's success. Tango resented the fact that she couldn't exchange gay repartee with her audiences, and could only dance. She was a great dancer, but she feared these audiences didn't want major artists but silly drag acts with talk of tits and ass.

Relieved to be out of Club One, she headed for friendlier and more comfortable terrain, Harlot's Box. Her black diva friends, especially Maybelle and Laurie Mae, hung out there. Although jealous of Tango's star billing, they always treated her like the bigtime diva she was. Tango only hoped that Laurie Mae and Maybelle hadn't heard that her solo act had bombed at Blues in the Night, and she'd been fired until she could find a hot white boy replacement for Danny.

Entering the club, she pretended not to be aware of several white boys eying her. She knew she could have any of them any time she wanted. But with her darling daddy, Duke, warming her bed, she hardly needed male companionship this evening. In fact, she was just wandering around waiting for Duke to sober up, hoping he'd be ready for another round before she turned in for the night.

At their usual table, Maybelle and Laurie Mae were sitting with a large black woman. This big mama was drunk and getting drunker and Tango wondered if she knew her. The fat bitch looked real familiar. Suddenly, Tango recognized Norma Dixie, the maid to Lavender Morgan who always went around town claiming that she'd been the "household engineer" for Mae West and that the late actress was actually a man.

Tango felt humiliation because she knew that Norma obviously was aware of all the details about how Danny Hansford had left Tango to take up with that granny, Lavender Morgan.

Recognizing her, Laurie Mae called to Tango to join their table. At first Tango had wanted to retreat from the club but, once spotted, reluctantly agreed to go over to the table. She felt embarrassed to be presented to Norma Dixie.

Maybelle jumped up from the table to give Tango a kiss on the cheek, as did the more masculine Laurie Mae. "Tango, I want you to meet Norma Dixie," Maybelle said. "She knew Mae West and a lot of show business greats."

Norma hardly acknowledged Tango. "That's not all the story. I not only knew Mae West, I designed all her gowns and wrote a lot of her best oneliners. I was actually a star myself in Harlem. I was a headliner at Norma's Room. All the big stars turned out to see me in those days. Lena Horne, Louis Armstrong. Everybody. Most of 'em were there to steal my material."

Tango sat down opposite Norma, and feared a confrontation with the desperately inebriated woman. "Show business is a very cruel game. One day you're up there on the top, and the next day you're working as a maid for some white woman. I've always said, though, it's better to be a has-been than a never-was."

"Who in the fuck are you calling a has-been, you little black drag queen bitch?" Norma said, almost forcing herself up from the table. "With all my connections, I could be a star today if I wanted to. I could get plenty of offers in night clubs."

"Now, now," Laurie Mae interrupted, fearing Norma might strike Tango in the mouth. "We're here to have fun. Not fight."

"My son books some of the biggest acts in Atlanta," Norma said arrogantly. "He's always begging me to headline a show there. I have a very large following. My fans are eager to see me again."

"Oh," Tango said, ordering a Pink Lady from the waitress. "I was a big headliner in Atlanta myself before I got hot, hot offers in Savannah. I know all the top people who book shows in Atlanta. What's the name of your son? Perhaps I know him."

"Domino Dixie," Norma said proudly. "A wonderful son. Very handsome, very macho. Not some fucking nigger drag queen like you pussies I'm hanging with. He's a real lady killer."

Tango gasped. "Domino Dixie. I know Atlanta is a very big place, but my best friend there is Dominique Dixie. The name is so similar. Dominique is hardly macho—handsome, perhaps, although the bitch claims she's a ravishing beauty, even more beautiful than me, as if that were possible. Dominique Dixie is the biggest drag diva you'd ever want to meet. In fact, the bitch was supposed to send me my gowns and stole them all for herself. When I go back to Atlanta, I'm going to pull every hair out of that cunt's head."

"I don't know about any God damn Dominique. My son's name is Domino Dixie, and I'm proud of him. A credit to his race." Norma bolted down the rest of the bourbon in her glass and called loudly for another one. "I've got a picture of the good-looking stud here in my purse." She reached into her handbag and retrieved a wallet, pulling out a picture of her son.

Tango took the picture from Norma and studied it carefully. "Christ, I was with the bitch when this picture was taken. It was one of the few times I've ever seen Dominique—or Domino as you call her—as a man. Domino Dixie and Dominique Dixie are one and the same pussy."

As the waitress placed Norma's replenished glass of bourbon on the table before her, Norma picked up her drink and tossed it into Tango's face.

Tango screamed as the liquid rained down on her made-up face. She jumped up from the table, ready to tear into Norma with claws and fists until she realized that the maid was an old, fat, and drunk cow.

At the door to the club and in front of all the other patrons, who had grown strangely silent, Tango placed her hand on her hip. "Any time you want to catch your drag queen son performing, head for the Rainbow Room in Atlanta." She turned and left the club.

The night hadn't gone at all like she'd planned it.

*****

Through a deep, drowsy awakening, Lavender Morgan stirred to light. The room was hazy, as if filled with an early morning dew. But it couldn't be early morning. A drapery was left open, and the brilliance of the noon-day sun of a Savannah August streamed through into her boudoir.

Her lavender-colored domino completely removed, she noticed two things: the nude body of the blond and beautiful Danny Hansford lying by her side and the fact that Norma had not served morning coffee. Noticing the latter filled her with fury. Norma always served morning coffee unless she'd gone on one of her legendary binges. If she'd done that, Lavender didn't expect to see her maid until six o'clock in the evening when Norma would be filled with apologies and remorse. On such occasions, Norma always claimed that she'd "had a bad burger." Lavender could only conclude that Norma was either lying or else there must be a lot of tainted burgers served in Savannah.

Instead of that fat, drunken maid of hers, Lavender had rather think of the luscious golden boy beside her. She fully understood that Danny would be her last love. In some ways he'd been the most spectacular of all of them. Not since Karl in those long, foggy, half-remembered decades of yesterday had a young man thrilled her so.

Danny was an expert love-maker. He knew all the right places to massage either with his lips or his remarkable penis which always seemed to be rock hard and ready for any challenge. She loved the taste, size, and thrill of that penis. She'd never known such pleasure. It was amazing that such a young boy had far more lovemaking skills than those who'd devoted a lifetime to seducing women, and that included John Kennedy, Frank Sinatra, and Nelson Rockefeller, among countless others. Men like Sinatra and Kennedy had viewed women as objects of their own pleasure, whereas Danny had been different. He'd wanted to please her and satisfy her. Surely there must have been some pleasure in it for him. After all, he'd climaxed three times. But at no point did she ever feel he was seeking his own gratification but trying to give her the sexual thrill of her lifetime.

She knew that in time Danny would eventually leave her bed and go on to other pleasures and pastimes. It was for that reason that she planned to treasure every moment here with him. If he were going to be her last lover, and at her age that was a distinct possibility, she wanted to suck him dry. In spite of all their lovemaking of the precious evening, she desired more from him this morning. She hoped to rise from her prone position and hover over Danny, taking his young manhood in her mouth and devouring it as a prelude to another glorious day with this creature.

Her lusty lips also wanted to descend on his balls and lick, suck, and caress until she'd had her fill which would take far longer than an hour. If there was one pleasure she loved more than most in life, it was licking a man's balls. Perhaps she'd always wanted to have a pair herself and sucking those who had been so blessed was as close as she could get to fulfilling her own dream.

She attempted to rise from her satin pillow, but settled back uncomfortably. A vague anxiety came over her. She wasn't certain what had actually happened the night before. It was as if she remembered part of the evening, but not all of it.

She knew better than to have drunk so much champagne. But it'd been a special evening, and she secretly wanted Danny to think she could drink just as much as he could. She'd been foolish to try to keep up with a young man. If she remembered correctly, she must have passed out at some point. She still felt drugged. Her doctors had warned her that she'd have to give up drinking so much, but she paid them no mind. Her head resting once again on her pillow, she felt the room spinning out of control. It was as if she were still drunk. It would be hard chastising Norma for drinking too much when Lavender herself had been an equal offender.

Slowly, very slowly, she pushed herself up from her pillow into the brightness of the new day. The stillness of her house was almost deafening in its silence. Oral sex or any other kind with Danny was definitely out. If anything, she felt so sick she wanted to vomit. She looked once more at Danny sleeping peacefully by her side. He, too, must have passed into oblivion with so much drink. "Damn it!" she said out loud, realizing her entire household, including Norma, was completely hung over. It would be a day of grumpy tempers and headaches. At three o'clock the bonded movers from Atlanta would arrive to cart off her precious paintings. She wanted to shower and sit in her parlor, enjoying her final hours with her treasure trove of art.

At this moment she had no idea what she would hang on the wall to fill the ugly gaps left by her beloved paintings. She knew if she continued to have her teas for the bachelors of Savannah, she would have to offer some explanation for the loss of the paintings. She didn't dare let word get out that she was going through a period of financial distress.

In the shower she began to come to. Before Danny got up, she wanted to be fully bathed and completely made up. At the most glamorous stage of her latter cabaret career, would you truly want to confront the aging Marlene Dietrich as she emerged from her morning shower? The same could be said for Lavender.

In front of her vanity in the side room off her huge bathroom, Lavender confronted her old and decaying face in the mirror, and her bedraggled hair. She'd definitely need that wig today. Like the time-hardened trouper she was, she began to work on her face, applying generous make-up, touched off by the final coup de grace, lavender colored lipstick. Within a half an hour she felt she'd taken a decade—maybe more—off her years. She was ready to wake up Danny now.

As she stood looking down at him, she felt that in the innocence of sleep he was more beautiful than ever. When he was up and about, she felt he had to assume some bravura. Under the protective shield of sleep, he could revert back to being the golden boy he was in real life.

As if suddenly aware that he was being observed, Danny opened his eyes. Upon seeing her, he smiled. "Good morning, baby," he said, rubbing his perfect nose into the pillow. "You sure do know how to show a guy a good time. I didn't know women did that to men."

"Women do everything to men," she said, bending over and giving him a kiss although she still felt drugged and dizzy. Turning from the bed, she moved toward the heavy black draperies, pulling them back to let in the sun-dappled day. "That damn Norma," she said. "I don't know why I keep her on. The black bitch didn't even bring coffee this morning. Probably drunk in her bedroom. I should fire her."

Bounding up from the bed, Danny moved toward her. He was fully nude. She took in the splendid sight of him. The boy was a work of art, not destined for street hustling at all but meant for the most elegant boudoirs, the most expensive yachts.

Taking her in his arms, he kissed her tenderly and deeply. "Last night was one of the most important of my life. When I was cuddled in your arms, I felt I was getting all the love I was denied as a child."

"Oh, Danny," she gasped, hoping he didn't view her as a substitute for a mother. Lavender Morgan didn't want to be anybody's mother.

"Let me have a fast shower," he said enthusiastically. "I'll be down in a minute." Heading toward the bathroom, he turned and winked at her. "That was some workout. It'll keep me content until about five o'clock today." He pivoted around, waving his ample cock at her. "Then junior here is going to want a lot more loving."

"How you young people talk," she said. "In my day, we did it. We just didn't talk about it too much, especially the next morning."

"Times are a changing, woman. Now get me that coffee, and how about some chocolate doughnuts too? I really love chocolate doughnuts." He disappeared into the bathroom, shutting the door behind him.

Slowly she made her way down the steps, taking one step carefully at a time. She didn't want to slip and fall. A broken hip would ruin everything for her now. She'd try to get the drunken Norma from her bed to make that coffee, but Lavender wanted it served in her parlor. There with Danny she could enjoy the first coffee of the day surrounded by her precious paintings which would not be hers for much longer.

Even before going in to wake up Norma, she headed for her parlor to have one more look at her art. It might be the last chance of the day to be completely alone and surrounded by her paintings. The sunlight coming into the parlor was so strong and vivid that at first she suspected the lighting was artificial.

In the center of the room her eyes adjusted to the blinding light. She didn't understand this because she always tried to keep the room slightly dark to protect her paintings from the harsh Savannah sun.

She stood before two giant French doors opening onto a wrought-iron balcony leading to the street below. The draperies had been torn from their brackets, and the windows were wide open, a slight wind making the white sheers billow in the breeze.

Even before her eyes darted around the room, she instinctively knew her paintings were gone. In her heart she also realized she'd never see them again.

Had the movers come far ahead of time? That couldn't be. They weren't due until three o'clock. All her paintings had been stolen last night. Millions and millions of dollars worth of art, and that included Picasso's *Mother and Child*, had been looted from her home.

The scream that came from her parched throat startled even her. She didn't recognize the voice as her own. It was the screech of a victim heard right before a long sharp knife goes into a delicate throat.

*****

"At first I wanted to beat the shit out of you," Tom Caldwell was telling Danny as they sped out of town to the remote Crab Shack where they knew they could talk privately down by the river. "Then I got it into my head that this might be the luckiest day of my life."

"I knew you figured out I stole the paintings when Lavender called the police," Danny said. "You were really going after her, but the way you looked at me, I could just tell you knew I was the one."

Tom smiled. "Where did you stash them?"

"In the storage room behind the men's room at Whitefield Square."

"I know it well," Tom said. "I used to dangle my meat there hoping to entrap faggots, but we don't do that no more—'cept maybe sometimes when we don't have much else going on."

"The way you interrogated the old bitch, you made it seem like she stole the paintings herself."

"That was the whole point. I wanted the guys working with me to know what I'd learned about Lavender Morgan. This is a small town and word travels fast. I think the rumor was spread by a drunk Norma Dixie who overheard something. I don't know what Lavender told you about why she was getting rid of those paintings, but I know the truth."

"Hit me with it."

"The old bitch is being forced to sell them. That's why they were going to be crated and shipped to New York. To raise money to pay off the cunt's debts. She's overspent by millions, and her creditors are moving in real fast."

"That's hard for me to figure. I thought she had millions."

"She does and I know for poor white Southern trash like us it's hard to comprehend, but sometimes multi-millionaires can be deep in debt. It's like they've got assets, but the goodies are tied up in non-liquid things. The wolf is sometimes at their doors, and they've got to sell off quick—even if at a loss."

"I still say a millionaire is a millionaire. When you grew up in Clinton, Georgia, and you saw some months where your whole family didn't even have one-hundred dollars to piss on, Lavender Morgan is still one rich woman in my eyes. I saw her fucking jewelry once. She keeps it in a safe. That sparkling stuff alone must be worth millions. Some of the richest men in the world gave jewelry to her when she was an international whore."

"The God damn jewelry would be a hell of a lot easier to get rid of than these fucking paintings, even though they're worth millions. When you stole those paintings, how in the fuck did you expect to dump them and what kind of money are we talking about here?"

"I know me and you don't know an ant's fart about art, but I've been lying awake at night doing some mighty serious thinking."

"How about sharing those thoughts with me?" Tom asked. Pulling into The Crab Shack, Tom led Danny into the seafood joint and told the waitress to fetch them two cold beers to be served at one of the tables down by the river.

Once seated at a wooden table and noting that the nearby places were empty at this time of day, Danny leaned back enjoying this sudden tranquillity after all he'd been through. Lavender, a world class drinker, could handle a lot more booze than he'd ever imagined she could do at her age. But then in her heyday she'd managed to match Sinatra drink for drink.

Danny had gone to his voodoo queen, Erzulie, and told the "Haitian Venus" that he had to have one of her potions to knock-out this woman he wanted to fuck, not actually naming Lavender, of course. For all he knew, the money-hungry Erzulie could be a double agent, although he didn't know for whom.

The mistress of voodoo never told anyone what was in her potions but Danny knew they always worked. Both men and women from the highest society folk to the lowest field nigger came to Erzulie for her potions. No one ever claimed they didn't work.

Erzulie's knock-out potion had done the trick. Lavender's fall into oblivion had come soon after Danny had slipped the potion into Lavender's champagne. This passing out had come none too soon for him. If he had to make any more of that perverted love to her, he feared he might throw up. As a hustler he considered himself top rate. How many guys his age could still keep it hard while making love to a woman one-hundred and ninety-nine years old?

Tom didn't say anything until after the waitress had delivered their beers and had headed back to The Crab Shack. He tasted the beer and from the look on his face, Danny could tell Tom liked it a lot. He licked his lips and downed a lot more of the beer. "Before we got to this dump, I asked you a question, and I really want an answer. How in the fuck does a kid like you think he can dump all those paintings? They must be worth a hundred million dollars. Maybe a lot more. I've heard a lot of rumors."

"I've got a Jap connection in Atlanta," Danny said with more confidence than he'd actually felt.

"And just how does a little redneck boy from Clinton end up with a Jap connection?" Tom stared at him intently.

"I made a porno for this guy, a creep from Valdosta named Steve Parker. He showed it to these Japs in Atlanta—business associates of his—and they went ballistic. You see, in their country they only have men with tiny dicks. They go ape-shit when they get to see a Southern white boy with big meat."

"Well, it might work. I've heard that the Japanese often buy stolen art from Europe and America."

"They'll pay top dollar."

"Just what kind of money are you talking about? How much do you plan to charge for paintings worth at least one-hundred million?"

"That's one-hundred big ones on the open market. At a real sale. I can't get that kind of money but I've got a figure in mind."

"Lay it on me," Tom said, downing the rest of his beer and signaling the waitress on the back porch of The Crab Shack to bring them another round.

"Ten-million dollars. Ten million fucking dollars."

"You're going to share this loot with me," Tom said. It wasn't a question. "You get five million. I get the other five million. That's my reward for covering up this crime for you and protecting your ass. I'm taking a big risk myself. We both could end up in jail for a very long time."

"I don't think I have a long time to live," Danny said enigmatically.

Tom looked at him as if he didn't understand, but from the expression on his face decided not to pursue that subject.

"Five million is a lot more money than I plan to spend for the rest of my life," Danny said. "No problem in my sharing it with you. When I come into my millions, you'll find I'm very generous."

"You'd better be or I'll kick your ass," Tom said, lowering his voice as the waitress approached with another round. After she'd gone, he tasted the cold beer and looked out at the slow-moving river. "All the good people of Savannah dream one day of getting rich. In Savannah this is a more important dream than power. Having a lot of money. If you've got a lot of money in Savannah you can get away with anything. Even murder. Take Jim Williams, for example. Killing that little streak of sex Danny Hansford and getting away with it, although it took a little bit of trouble, a jail term, and considerable legal bills."

Danny winced at the mention of the real Danny Hansford. He too sipped his beer and eyed Tom carefully. The Savannah cop had become more than just a sexual partner. At The Crab Shack their agreement had been reached. They were no longer mere lovers, but partners in crime as well.

Looking across at Tom, Danny was growing increasingly agitated. In the Savannah summer sun, the cop had never looked handsomer or more virile. It was at this very moment that Danny came to feel he was hopelessly in love with Tom Caldwell.

Danny's mind might be on a sexual encounter but Tom's concern was obviously on those long-dreamed-for millions. "We've got to get those paintings out of Whitefield Square. No one might have gone into that room in a quarter of a century, but they could at any time. After all it's public property."

"I didn't know where else to put them," Danny said. "I loaded them in a rented van and stashed them there. I was real careful that no one saw me. I didn't see a soul stirring on the square."

"I've got an idea." Tom leaned closer to him. "I've got this fishing shack. It's on a remote island. A cop friend of mine, Brian Sheehan, and I go there but that's about it. I can slip the paintings out tonight and take them in my boat to this shack. I'll leave them there until I get the word from you to haul them off to Atlanta. We've got to be God damn careful."

"That's great! I'll feel a lot safer with those paintings out of that stinking men's room."

"God damn, I'm taking a risk."

"But look at the rewards. Where in the fuck is a Savannah cop or a manure-spreading boy from Clinton, Georgia, gonna get their hands on five-million dollars each?"

"You've got a point, boy." Tom seemed to be eying him in a different way. Neither man said anything. Each sat looking intently in the other's eyes.

"I guess we won't draw up a contract between us, partner," Tom finally said, breaking the silence. "But there must be some way to cement our deal."

"I know a way," Danny said.

"What have you got on your mind?"

"I want to leave this joint right now with you. I've got a certain itch and only you can relieve it."

"And what kind of itch is that?" Tom asked, raising an eyebrow, a smirk on his face.

"I want you to go where no man has ever gone before."

*****

The call from Norma Dixie came in just as Tipper was devouring all the press coverage of the "cultural war" at Myrtle Beach. Most of the press coverage was favorable to her, and it was definitely certain that she would now be featured on the cover of *Vanity Fair* in an article called "The Comeback of The Black Widow."

After years of neglect and abuse, the press had discovered her again, and the local paper carried a story that she'd been offered a week-long series of concerts in Atlanta. If those performances were successful, Tipper expected to parlay her success there into a nationwide tour that would be remarkably different from her last failed attempt.

As she chatted with Norma, the world looked rosy. "I got urgent business in Atlanta," Norma said. "It's about my son, Domino. I read in the paper that you need to get over to Atlanta too. Probably to sign a big fat contract."

"That's right. I was going to call Phil Heather and see if he would drive me. I'm not much into flying."

"Forget about that white boy. I'll take you over there. In fact, I want you to meet my son. He's like a theatrical agent. Maybe you'll let him read your contract before signing it. He knows how all those hot shots in Atlanta can slip you a fast one."

"We'll see," Tipper said enigmatically, although eager to have Norma drive her. At least Tipper could be entertained with Mae West stories during the long, boring drive.

Two hours later, Tipper was attired in her smartest black outfit with a red scarf. Her high heel shoes were also red. When Norma appeared in her driveway, she was dressed entirely in red. As Tipper got into the car, she informed Tipper that, "Mae West always told me I should wear red when going to the big city. It's my best color."

As predicted, Norma entertained her with her Mae West stories when she wasn't talking about the macho qualities of her son, Domino. "He ain't like those nigger drag queens in Savannah at all. I ran into that Tango bitch last night at Harlot's Box. The little pussy that replaced you at the club."

"I can't stand her," Tipper said. "I hardly need Matt Daniels and his dumb club any more. My audiences are growing so big I'll require an arena."

"You're on the way to a big comeback. I feel it in my gut. Real big. Mae always wanted to come back. *Myra Breckenridge* and *Sextette* didn't exactly polish her reputation none. I was with her during the shooting of *Myra*. She couldn't have done it without me. At first when the script arrived, Mae thought she was being offered the lead role of *Myra*. The pay was only $100,000, and Mae was furious. 'Tell those fuckers the salary is a joke,' Mae instructed me. Later we learned that Mae was being offered the part of the sensuous talent agent Leticia. Mae demanded that the character's name be changed from Le*tit*ia."

"Even then, $100,000 was a bit cheap."

"She finally got Fox to agree to pay her $350,000. But there was a big problem. For insurance purposes, she had to submit to a physical. The doctor, obviously, would have discovered she was a man."

"How in hell did you get around that?"

"Mae made some sort of compromise between her own private doctor, who was privy to the real situation, and the doctor for the insurance company. I never knew what it was. Because her blood sugar level was high, she ate nothing but salads days before, and at the actual appointed time I was able to sub my urine for hers. It was not a complete physical, and she passed."

After checking into a suite with Norma at the Ritz-Carlton in Buckhead, the fat maid retreated to a king-size bed, claiming she was still recovering from one of the world's most massive hangovers. Norma said she'd need her sleep if they planned to go out tonight with her son, Domino.

Taking a taxi to the offices of the lawyers for her concert backers, Tipper was delighted at how smoothly the negotiations went, unlike her first humiliating encounter with Dale Evans. She was so pleased, in fact, that she'd thrown in a couple of extra demands, including a chauffeured limousine during her stay in Atlanta, the suite where she was currently staying at the Ritz-Carlton, and an increased budget for advertising announcing her appearance in the city. Tipper told the lawyers, "After all, Mae West always said if you hit town, don't keep it a secret."

Back in a taxi again, with her contract signed, Tipper directed her driver to take her to the Martin Luther King Jr. Center for Nonviolent Social Change on Auburn Avenue. She wanted to keep her second mission of the afternoon a secret from Norma.

In her briefcase Tipper held private letters and memorabilia from Dr. Martin Luther King Jr., with whom she'd had an affair. Although making no attempt at blackmail of the Kings, she felt the center, especially Coretta, would be eager to acquire these artifacts, including the letters. Tipper recalled how she'd financed the trip of Dr. and Mrs. King to India in the early days, and it seemed altogether fitting that they might help her now.

Tipper had wanted to have a direct meeting with Coretta but when she reached the center a secretary informed her that "Mrs. King is feeling ill" and could not see Tipper, although she sent her fondest regards. Tipper learned that her meeting had been rescheduled with Dexter Scott King, her son. Tipper had met Dexter twice before and on each occasion had taken an instant dislike to him, as he no doubt had to her. Perhaps Dexter had resented her involvement with his daddy.

As the afternoon moved closer to twilight, and still no summons from Dexter, Tipper grew increasingly agitated. After all, she was a star but wasn't being treated like one. She couldn't help but notice that persons arriving with later appointments got in to see Dexter, and she didn't. By six o'clock it had become all too apparent that Dexter had no intention of seeing her and that she was, in fact, being humiliated by having to wait such a long time in the corridor. Without saying anything to the secretary in the far distance, Tipper left the center and got another taxi between Boulevard and Jackson Streets and headed back to her suite at Buckhead. Selling the documents would have brought her some much-needed cash but with all her new commitments, and with a fat contract in her purse, the sale was not as vital as before.

Back at her suite, Tipper was surprised to see Norma completely dressed and ready for a night on the town. "I've made reservations at the Rainbow Room for us."

"What kind of place is that?" Tipper asked, coming into the living room and laying the Dr. King memorabilia down on the sofa.

"It features drag acts."

"What an odd choice for the evening," Tipper said, heading for the liquor cabinet. "I thought we were going to see your son. Why some drag acts?"

"I can't go into all the details, but there's a rumor I've got to check out. To put the record straight, so to speak."

"Whatever you think best," Tipper said. "But I was looking forward to meeting your son. He sounds real nice. You must be proud of him."

"Time will tell," Norma said, heading to pick up an urgently ringing phone as Tipper settled in on the sofa with her newly made drink. She couldn't fully determine what was going on, but Norma seemed boiling mad and getting madder. "You motherfucking, cocksucking asshole," Norma said into the phone before slamming it down.

"What's the matter?" Tipper asked, sitting up on the sofa and growing increasingly concerned.

"I told you about the theft of Lavender's paintings."

"I know. It's amazing. I once told Lavender that she shouldn't allow millions of dollars worth of paintings to hang on her walls unguarded like that."

"Lavender hears only what she wants to—just like Mae West. But that ain't the half of it. I'm due back in Savannah tomorrow for some hot questioning about the theft. It's like the scumbag cops think I'm in on it somehow."

"You? How ridiculous."

"Crap or not, I've got to defend myself. The God damn cops aren't gonna pin this on me, especially when I know who made off with all those paintings."

"You do?" Tipper felt bewildered. "Spill the beans."

"Danny Hansford, that no good white hustler. He even gave me the money to go out and get drunk. He wanted me out of Lavender's house last night so there would be no witnesses."

"You can't prove that, surely."

"I can't prove it but I know in my gut it's true."

"You know what I think of Mr. Hansford and his dancing partner, Tango. But neither one struck me as a major art thief. Lavender's collection was well known. Those paintings could have been stolen by anybody. Even a gang from New Jersey. How would little Danny Hansford know how to dispose of that much art?"

"I have always found that good-looking, blond-haired white boys with big dicks can do pretty much what they want in this world."

After leaving Norma and retreating to her own bedroom, Tipper found she had three hours alone and she welcomed the respite from the talkative maid with all the stories of Mae West, Lavender's stolen paintings, and her macho son, Domino.

Before she'd gone to lie down, Tipper had at least learned why they were going to the Rainbow Room. Apparently Tango had informed Norma that she knew a drag queen in Atlanta by the name of Dominique Dixie. Tango had even suggested that this transvestite might actually be her son, Domino, who in his performances became Dominique.

As Tipper rested before her night out with Norma, Tipper thought not of the maid's problems or her most recent humiliation by Dexter King, nor even of her juicy contract, but of Phil Heather. How she longed to be alone with him. She knew that the long interviews he'd conduct with her for her memoirs would give them the chance to bond.

She was hoping to recapture the love she'd had with Monty. With Phil, it would not be easy to make him fall in love with her. It hadn't been easy with Monty either. He hadn't loved her at first sight. Their relationship grew over many a season, and she was confident that in time Phil would come to love her as Monty had.

Later, after having rested and fallen asleep dreaming of Phil, Tipper dressed and headed in a taxi to the Rainbow Room with a heavily perfumed Norma. They were about the only women in a room filled with men and were given a ringside table. Norma had been hoping to see a picture of Dominique Dixie outside the club or at least in the program. But the waiter told her there was no program. "Whatever queens show up for the night is whatever bitches go on," the guy told Norma.

After several rounds of drinks and some really bad drag acts, Norma braced herself when the MC announced the appearance of Dominique Dixie. "Let's give one of our favorite queens a big round of applause," he told the audience. The clapping was lackluster.

The lights dimmed and when a spot went on, it was turned directly on Dominique who appeared dressed entirely in mauve with a pink boa and black high heels that towered dangerously high.

"Y-e-e-e-s, my possums, tell your mothah how glad you are to see the bitch," Dominique beseeched her audience, getting them to applaud just a little more enthusiastically. Dominique wore long orange earrings with a wig of tight blonde curls. Lip-synching a song and shaking her body like a high roller, she danced around the center, coming up to a table of young men.

In her low-cut gown, with her breasts half exposed, she came on strong to a handsome young Italian male who looked like he was still in college. "They're real, honey," she said, taking his hand and directing it into her cleavage. "C'mon and get it, honey," she sang out, forgetting to match the voice on the sound system.

Stopping next at Tipper's table, Dominique squinted her eyes. "I'm too vain, possums, to wear glasses and I could never afford contact lenses but as I live and breathe I think we've got two real ladies in the audience tonight. One's white and the other's so black I can't make out her face in the dark. But from the size of that red dress, I think Hattie McDaniel's come back from the dead."

Raising her massive bulk from her chair, Norma moved menacingly toward Dominique. In one sudden move, she ripped the wig from her son's head.

The stage manager shut down the lights. The club became very, very dark.

*****

The rather corpulent Terry Drummond seemed petulant and a bit angry at Phil as he drove him and Aunt Bice to the Heather plantation for a long-awaited reunion after an absence of a decade.

"I thought you'd come over last night," Terry said with a slight whine in his voice. "I waited up until 2 a.m."

Phil hadn't noticed that whine before. He really wondered what he'd seen in Terry in the first place. Back then with Brian holding out no prospects for a future, the seventeen-year-old Terry had looked mighty good to him. But a boy that young, eating country ham and buttered grits for a decade, can change a lot. He'd also noticed that Terry had grown increasingly feminine.

Phil didn't really answer Terry's question but Aunt Bice did. "Phil had house guests and those darling boys, Henry and John, to take care of."

In silence, seated beside a sulking Terry and a chain-smoking aunt, Phil drove through the gate heading for the Heather plantation. Motes of dust danced in the car as reflected by the morning sunshine. The sun was rising high on another impossibly hot day, and Phil feared all of them would be sweating profusely at the plantation. The Heathers had never believed in air conditioning. Phil just hoped those old wooden ceiling fans hadn't given out their last dying spin and could still stir up the hot air.

Dizzy and with a hole growing at the pit of his stomach, Phil took in the sight of the old plantation house. It wasn't Tara but still evoked antebellum splendor, although it looked as if repairs hadn't been made since the Yankee soldiers departed with what they could carry off.

Getting out of the car and trailed by Aunt Bice and Terry, Phil headed with trepidation across the rickety veranda to greet Big Daddy sitting in his familiar peacock chair surveying the cows in the fields below. It's a spot where he'd sat for the last forty years until the chill of a late autumn day always drove him inside for the winter, where he usually took to his big four-poster bed, still draped in rotting mosquito netting put there in the 1920s.

Phil signaled Aunt Bice and Terry that he wanted to approach Big Daddy alone. "Go into the parlor. I'll come in later after I talk to Big Daddy."

Coming face to face with Big Daddy, Phil met his penetrating stare and, as he did, tried to conjure up the long-ago handsomeness that had graced his father's face. It was hard to find in the premature wrinkles and the jowls that sagged with the weight of the decadent years.

Phil had been born when his father was nearing fifty. What he now faced was not the robust man he'd known but a rotting memory of that tiger. The graying hair had thinned, and the gold teeth that had once looked macho and raffish now looked merely like the flawed repairs of a backwoods dentist. The face was ruddy and crinkled, the eyes mired in crow's feet. His eyes were slightly popped but still radiantly blue and ready to meet the shattering gaze of Satan. The once famed belly laugh was gone. The voice that emerged through all that blubber was weak with a slight gurgle as if strangulation was at hand. Big Daddy's smiles and raucous roar seemed but a distant memory as Phil confronted him on the porch.

"My faggot son has returned," Big Daddy said. "You look so fucking pretty you should have been born a girl. I always told Big Mama that I made a real big mistake the night I fucked her without protection and she gave birth to you."

"I'm not your faggot son," Phil said defensively. "I'm your son and I've come back, and I'm mighty grateful you allowed it."

"Who would ever believe that Big Daddy, the biggest womanizer this country has ever known, would sire a faggot?"

"I'm a man in my own right, and I want you to be proud of me. I've reformed. I need to be back here with you and Sister Woman. We're family. You need me at your side."

"Don't bullshit me. You've come back hoping I'll put you in my will. You can look at me and know I'm dying. You smell money, don't you? Or is it both death and money you smell?"

"I've come back because I love you. I'm your son. You're my daddy. Your seed brought me into this world."

Big Daddy looked with total condemnation at Phil. "I've got to ask one question, and I want the truth. I lie awake at night asking this question."

"What is it?"

"When you get into bed with a man, do you become the woman or the man?"

"Always the man," Phil said, lying.

Big Daddy breathed a sigh of relief. "That puts an old man's mind a bit at rest. Thank God you told me that, and if I ever find out you just lied to me, I'll go into the living room, take my shotgun and blow your brains out before I turn that shotgun onto myself."

"It's the truth, Big Daddy! I swear it on Big Mama's grave."

At this point Aunt Bice, trailed by a still sulking Terry, appeared on the veranda and walked forward to embrace Big Daddy.

"Get away from me, woman!" he shouted at her. "The stench of rotgut bourbon on your mouth always turns me off."

"If I recall," Aunt Bice said, looking insulted and injured, "you and I polished off quite a lot of that bourbon before you grew too decrepit to drink your liquor like a real man."

"Don't lecture me on what a real man is," Big Daddy said. "I'm still a real man. I guess I need to joggle that senile brain of yours but I recall one night after I'd fucked you three times in a row you said it was the greatest ride of your life."

Phil looked at Aunt Bice but didn't detect embarrassment in her. His aunt confronted Big Daddy. "I lied to you, you bastard. If truth be known, it was one of the lousy lays of my life."

"You fucking bitch," Big Daddy said. "If I could get out of this chair, I'd rip off one of your sagging tits."

"Now, now," Phil said, interceding. "This is not the time to go down memory lane. We're here for a happy family reunion—that is, just as soon as we round up Sister Woman." He looked apprehensively at her upstairs bedroom window.

"Hello, Mr. Heather," Terry said hesitantly, stepping up to Big Daddy and tentatively extending his hand.

Big Daddy brushed it aside. "I don't shake hands with faggots. In the good old days, we'd run white faggots out of the county after tarring and feathering them. Nigger faggots we'd string up to a tree and hang by the neck." He chuckled at some distant memory. "That is, after we played a few fun games with them."

"How ghastly," Terry said, backing away.

Big Daddy eyed the boy skeptically. "Father Time ain't been good to me, but it's rotted you, too, boy. You look like shit. A little butterball if I ever saw one. But wait until you see Sister Woman. She eats a box of chocolates a day."

"You're not one to talk about anybody's weight," Aunt Bice said. "How many tires have you got around that stomach of yours? The last woman you were known to have fucked, Viola Craven, told me she couldn't find your dick. It was buried in too much blubber."

In his heart, Phil prayed that this acrimony between Aunt Bice and Big Daddy wouldn't lead to his getting ejected from the plantation again. Then he remembered that Big Daddy and his aunt always talked this way to each other. They seemed to get off on such insulting banter. Even so, he looked for some way to rescue the morning.

A screech not quite human came from the front door. The screen door opened and out emerged Sister Woman. Phil was appalled at the sight of her. She must have gained one-hundred and fifty pounds in ten years. A dim corona of blurred lipstick circled her mouth. She had put on a house dress that billowed in the early morning breeze like a flapping tent. Her reddish hair stood on end like a rubbed cat. There was an unhealthy pallor about her skin, reminding Phil of the slimy green linoleum that used to cover the kitchen floor in the rear of the house, and was probably still there.

"Sister Woman," Phil managed to say, moving toward this figure of condemnation and spite. "Come and give your brother Phil a big welcome home kiss."

"Get away from me, you bastard," Sister Woman said. "A kiss is not what I'd like to give you right now. The only way I agreed to let

Bice bring you back to this house was for one reason and one reason only."

"And what might that be, little darlin'?" Phil asked.

"I am God damn determined to proceed with what was scheduled ten years ago," Sister Woman said. "Namely my marriage to this no good Terry Drummond here." As if for the first time, she looked over at her former fiancé. "Christ, Terry, if you keep eating you'll get as fat as me."

"Bleeka," he said awkwardly. "It's been a long time."

"Far too long," she said. "Phil here could have every man he wanted. He even got Brian Sheehan one night, and every woman in the county wanted Brian. With Phil's good looks, which unlike the rest of the family he's still retained, he could have had any man he wanted. I had only one. You. I know you're a pathetic excuse for a man, but I want that wedding planned a decade ago to proceed as if the last ten years never happened."

"Well," Aunt Bice interjected, "that is exactly why we're here. To talk over arrangements."

"We'll talk over arrangements, all right," Sister Woman said, her voice growing bitter and shrill. "But we'll do it inside the parlor and not on the front porch like a pack of niggers. And we'll do it after I hear an apology from Terry here for running off with my faggot brother and disgracing me in front of everybody of any importance in this county. I've never been able to leave this house since that day."

"I'm so sorry," Terry said.

"It'll be okay," Phil said. "We've got to work out terms." He glanced over at Big Daddy to see how he was reacting to all this mess. Snoring peacefully, Big Daddy's head was bent at an angle onto his shoulder.

"Before we discuss my wedding plans, first things first," Sister Woman said.

"Exactly what business of the day do you want to dispense with first?" Phil asked.

Sister Woman glanced with unconcealed hostility, first at Phil, then at Terry, then back at Phil again. "Tell your former little fuckmate to get his cocksucking tongue over here and nigger lip me good. I want to taste male spit and male tongue—something I haven't had in so many God damn years I've forgotten the taste of it."

Terry hesitated, looking at Phil hopelessly, like some trapped animal in a jungle rite.

At first Phil didn't say anything. He wanted to retreat from this whole scene like Big Daddy had done, to imagine this drama wasn't taking place on their front verandah. His face contorted, Phil turned to Terry but avoided his eyes. "Would you get over there and perform what Sister Woman is demanding? Like she said, Sister Woman's been denied long enough."

*****

In the fiery heat of a Savannah August, Lula heard the sounds of John and Henry screaming in the back yard, apparently hosing each other down. She regretted being the baby sitter again, but wanted to help Phil, knowing how important this Heather family reunion was. Jason had gone to bed upstairs with their new boarder, Chris Leighton. In her heart, she didn't object to this mating of Jason and Chris. Perhaps with Chris under the roof, Jason would stay home more and not wander off to get into serious trouble, at which point her cousin, Tom, always appeared to bail him out.

Even though that grant had come in from Lavender Morgan, work on *The Tireless Hunter* had died like this hot, hot afternoon in Savannah. It was hard for Lula to concentrate on fictional characters when her own heart and emotions were churning. She felt she owed it to herself to go mating to pay Jason back for his dalliance with this Leighton boy.

She had no prospects in mind. It seemed disloyal to Phil to call daggle-tailed Joyce Sheehan even though she knew the invitation for a romantic get-together would be quickly accepted. At least Brian had ended his marriage, and in all likelihood Tom would be breaking with Ethel Mae as well.

Perhaps Lula should bring a halt to hers too, although she felt so fiercely protective of Jason she didn't think she could abandon him to the size-queen vultures of Savannah. For all she knew, Jason would be performing live sex shows at The Tool Box bar if she left him, forcing him to survive without her *largesse*.

What she didn't tell anyone, and rarely admitted even to herself, was that she didn't like the actual sex act with men or women. She wanted to be held, caressed, and cuddled. The only person who really understood that was Norma Dixie. All the others, male and female, wanted to attack her sexual organs. She didn't like that at all, finding sexual intercourse with a man, especially Jason, painful. She felt her own vagina was something to be loved and caressed in the most genteel of fashions. It wasn't meant to be a receiver of a gigantic organ plunging into its delicate cavity and causing bleeding in her.

Jason didn't so much fuck her but invaded the walls of her vagina, ripping and tearing. Yet, and this she didn't understand, that seemed to be what most gay men and straight women wanted in a man. The brute strength, and an overdeveloped organ that was a plunging, devouring instrument of pain and torture. She much preferred the tender lips of a man or a woman on her most private parts. Such a form of love-making was soothing to her. Anything else, even though she permitted the act to take place, was like rape to her.

Her vagina monologue was interrupted by a loud pounding on her front door. No one in Savannah seemed to telephone any more. They just showed up at your doorstep and started pounding. An unpleasant memory of having done just that at the door to Tango's apartment rushed through her head, but she dismissed it. In a battle for the love and possession of a man—in this case, Jason—social graces could never be a consideration.

To her astonishment, Tango stood on the front veranda, her garish make-up melting in the heat. "Don't let your pussy hairs stand up," Tango said. "I'm not here to fight with you over Jason. You can have Jason. I have my own lovin' man now."

"Then what does bring you to my doorstep in that ridiculous, vulgar drag outfit? Even as a Saturday night whore, you'd have trouble in that little get-up. A boa, no less. A pink boa in Savannah in August."

"Listen, you skinny little bitch with the tight pussy," Tango said. "I'll have you know I'm known for my tasteful wardrobe. In case you never read any books other than that stupid shit you're always writing, I'm made up as the vulgar, demented, and narcissistic Lola La Mour in the novel, *Butterflies in Heat.*"

"I'd say you were perfect for the part. You fit all those qualifications marvelously."

"Don't sass me, white bitch. I have read this novel—actually I didn't read all of it, only the Lola scenes. I am destined to play Lola.

The part must have been written with me in mind. If you let me meet this screenwriter, Phil Heather, I'm sure he will agree that he's found his Lola."

"Phil's not here at the moment. Screenwriters rarely cast films any way. But I happen to know the producer of the film, Jerry Wheeler, is likely to arrive in Savannah at any minute. He's the guy you've got to meet if you want to get cast in the film, although I hear he's coming to Savannah to audition The Lady Chablis for the part."

"Fuck that nigger bitch with her bad teeth and sagging tits. She's old and ugly. I'm young and beautiful."

"You are quite pretty at that," Lula said. "When you're not made up like some revolting drag queen."

"I told you, and I ain't telling you again, I'm made up this way 'cause that's what the part calls for. They call it dressing up to play a role."

"You are sure dressed up. If that short little skirt was any shorter, you could see all the way to Honolulu."

Barging past her without an invitation, Tango entered Lula's foyer and headed for her living room. "Where is this Phil sweetheart? His big mama Lola owes him a wet, sloppy kiss."

Trailing her into her own living room, Lula said, "I'm afraid Phil's gone to a family reunion at the moment. He doesn't live here. He lives next door."

The sound of screaming boys assailed Tango's ears. In rapid strides and on dangerously high heels in red patent leather, she walked toward the kitchen and peered out at John and Henry in the back yard. "Who are those two cute little boys?"

"Phil's children. I'm babysitting."

"I didn't know he had children. I thought he was gay."

"Both could be true."

For the first time today, Tango relaxed her facial muscles. "How true, how true. Look at Jason. In fact, I think most of my lovers have been married." She looked contemptuously at Lula.

"In the Old South they'd call you a home-wrecker. But I think that term isn't used any more now that everybody's home seems to be wrecked in one way or another."

"I can't help it if married men flock to my little honeypot. The Lady Chablis refers to hers as candy. I'm one up on her. I call mine the honeypot. Candy is something sweet, artificial, and unhealthy. It also rots your teeth, and that's one thing The Lady Chablis has plenty of—rotten teeth. Honey is something natural, healthy, and far better tasting than candy."

"I'd say so. I always like honey. I'm not a candy-eating woman."

Tango placed her hand on her hip, assuming a stance of imperial bearing, like a caricature of Lola in *Butterflies in Heat.* "Since Phil isn't around to pucker up for mama, how about introducing me to that Jerry Wheeler stud? After all, you owe me one for not taking Jason away from you."

"I guess, Miss Honeypot, you can't hear too well. Beeswax in your ears, no doubt. I just told you that Jerry Wheeler isn't in Savannah at the moment. He's on his way here."

"How can I get to meet him?"

"I think I can set that up. Aside from our own little personal conflicts over Jason, I can also be objective—artistically objective, the way an artist should be. I think you'd make a perfect Lola. Just the right touch of insanity. The incredible vanity. The aura of psychotic self-enchantment spinning around her at all times."

Tango stared at her. "Although I'm just a simple gal at heart, I can extend my range as an actress to play Lola La Mour. Me and Lola as personalities have nothing in common. Lola can't accurately access her fading charms and is in self-delusion, thinking she is far more alluring than she actually is. Being artistically objective like you said, I can also size up my charms. I've always known I'm hot stuff. A midnight gal in a nine o'clock town."

"The best way for me to introduce you to Jerry Wheeler, whom I haven't even met yet, is to invite Phil and him to join me at ringside at your show. When he sees you dancing with that Danny Hansford, he will surely agree he's found his Lola La Mour."

"That's a great idea even though I didn't think it up myself. Usually when it comes to my career, I have to come up with all the ideas." A sudden frown crossed her perspiring face. "There's just one problem."

"What might that be?" Lula asked, anxious to end this second encounter with Tango. At this point, Lula felt she would promise to do anything for her just to get Tango out of her house.

"Danny quit the show. He's moved in with the old hag, Lavender Morgan, instead. Matt Daniels says he won't reopen my act until I find a dancer to replace Danny. Where in Savannah can I find a male tango dancer?"

Seemingly coming from out of nowhere, her question was answered. "I ain't no God damn tango dancer, but there's no better male dancer in the State of Georgia than yours truly."

Tango seemed mesmerized by the youth who stood in the living room clad only in a pair of tight-fitting white jockey shorts. Knowing her husband, Lula imagined that just minutes ago those jockey shorts were on the floor beside their bed. Chris looked like he'd been thoroughly worked over by Jason.

"Tango, this is Chris Leighton," Lula said. "He just moved in with Jason and me. That is, until he gets established and finds a place of his own."

"I see," Tango said, smacking her lips. "White boy, how good are you at learning a new dance step?"

"There's no dance step on God's green earth that I can't learn in just one hour." He smiled at Tango. "With the right teacher, that is."

"Boy, would you like to jump-start your career and go on with me at the Blues in the Night Club?"

"Fine with me. I'm between engagements. I just got in from Key West where I did a film."

"I don't know what kind of film a white boy like you makes, but what I'm offering is a live audience."

"I'm all ears," he said. "Or since you're a dancer, I'm all feet."

"You're something else too," Lula interjected. "Why don't you go upstairs and put on your blue jeans and a T-shirt and run off to have a dance rehearsal with this actress here?"

"Okay with me," Chris said. "I'm open to all offers."

"Yeah," Tango said, her eyes traveling carefully up his body, beginning first with the feet. "I bet there isn't too many offers a boy like you turns down."

"Don't sass me," Chris said. "Besides, before I go off with you, I've got to ask you a very big question."

"I'll answer truthfully like you're the writer to whom I was dictating my memoirs."

"I've just got to know one thing. Are you a man or a woman?"

Anger flashed across Tango's face. "I'm all woman, baby. More woman than a white boy like you can tame."

"Okay, 'cause I'm not going to be seen on any stage dancing with a nigger drag queen."

Lula sighed, going over to the stove to turn on the tea. Perhaps before the afternoon faded she'd get some writing done on *The Tireless Hunter*.

"You don't mind, do you?" Tango was asking, although Lula hardly seemed aware of her voice. "My make-up's running something awful in this heat. I guess you never heard of air conditioning. I need to slip away into your powder room and make myself look more alluring. That is, if I could possibly do that. I'm such a natural beauty I don't need make-up. You do have a powder room in this dump, don't you?"

"The toilet's out in the hall," Lula said. "Help yourself." Back at her stove, she looked out the window to see that John and Henry had removed their bathing suits and were doing some heavy kissing.

Turning from the sight and wanting to give them their privacy, she realized the boys weren't entirely protected from prying eyes. Surely, Arlie Rae Minton lurked behind the fence somewhere.

*****

Rushing home to make arrangements to begin rehearsals with Chris Leighton, Tango was excited and thrilled to have found a new partner. Chris bore a remarkable resemblance to Danny except Chris seemed like a sweet boy who wouldn't cause the trouble for her that Danny had. Danny was competing against her for all the attention, and the way she figured it Chris would be no more than a chorus boy, allowing her to grab most of the acclaim.

As she came into her apartment, she was thrilled to see Duke sitting in front of her television set, drinking a beer. He was watching a baseball game on television.

She rushed over to kiss him but he pushed her away. "When I'm ready to fuck or have you suck me off, I'll tell you, okay?"

She backed away, though still delighted to have her daddy living with her, even if he humiliated her. "I've got a new dance partner to replace Danny. We're going to start rehearsals at Blues in the Night. I'll soon have my old job back with big money coming in." She hoped the latter promise would tempt him to stay in Savannah.

"I'm glad to hear that," he said, "'cause I've got plenty of other offers. I was thinking of heading down to Florida. One day at some fancy resort on Miami Beach, parading around in the tightest bikini the law allows, and I'll have some rich old hag begging for it."

"Don't go Duke," she said, going to the refrigerator to get him another cold beer. "I'll be making real big money soon. And I'm up for the lead in a major motion picture about to be filmed here."

He looked at her skeptically, not sure she was telling the truth. "Glad to hear that, 'cause I've got expensive tastes. If all these big bucks are going to come in, I think I'll stick around." He stood up in front of her, taking the beer from her and slamming it down on a coffee table. "I'm going to become your business manager," he announced in his harshest of voices. "You got that straight? Your fucking business manager. I'll collect the money and put you on an allowance. You nigger drag queens spend all your money on gowns any way. You need a real man to manage money."

"I'd love it if you managed my career," she said. "I think you'd be great."

"Who knows?" he said, sitting back down on the sofa and reaching for the beer. "I might do for you what Colonel Parker did for Elvis."

After watching the game, Duke got up and headed for the bedroom, announcing he needed to catch up on his sleep. She was there dressing for her first rehearsal with Chris. Matt had turned over the club to them for the late afternoon, and she was eager to see if her new partner could actually learn the tango.

She still had thirty minutes before she'd agreed to meet Chris at the club, and she wanted to talk to Duke about something before he fell into one of his beer-induced slumbers which could last for hours. God, that man knew how to sleep. When awake, he also knew how to make love, and she wanted to keep him around for that, regardless of how he managed her career.

"I was hoping to ask you something before you fell off to sleep," she said tentatively.

"What is it, woman?" he asked. "You know I don't like to be bothered by small talk."

"It's about my mama. I was wondering why you took up with her in the first place. Your being white and she being black."

He raised himself up in bed and adjusted his ample crotch. "Back in that shitass town where we lived, there were plenty of white gals who'd let me plug them. But as you know from our brief acquaintance, ol' Duke Edwards likes a gal to do a lot more things to him than plug 'em. A lot more things. Your mama had a reputation for doing anything any white man requested of her." He settled back into the pillow. "I must say that bitch lived up to her reputation."

"Didn't you love her, just a little bit?"

"Fuck that!" he said. "She was a nigger. No white man in that town fell in love with a nigger gal regardless of how pretty she was. It just wasn't done. Nowadays you can fall in love with anybody."

He'd made her angry. "You shouldn't talk about my mama like that. I'm sure she was nice."

"Would you get the fuck out of here and get to that rehearsal? I'm real sleepy and I ain't in no mood for talk. If I ever want to talk, I'll let you know. Duke Edwards is known as a man of action, not a man of words." He turned over, burying his face in the pillow.

She stood looking down for a long moment at his long, sexy body. If he were awake and able, she desired him right now. She felt if he'd made love to her, it would make her dance all the better. Suppressing that feeling, she gathered up her garb, stuffed it into a bag, and headed for Blues in the Night.

At the back door to the club, Matt Daniels was smoking a cigar. She just hoped he also didn't want a blow job. Wrapping her mouth around Matt's stubby dick was not how she wanted to begin rehearsals with her new boy dancer, Chris Leighton.

"We've got a problem," Matt said, grabbing her roughly by the arm.

"Unhand me, rat turd," she said. Matt felt if you worked for him at his club, he owned you. "Slavery was outlawed, even in Georgia, a long time ago."

"Not in show business, baby."

"What's the God damn problem?"

"That boy you picked up. A hustler, no doubt. Who else would go with a nigger drag queen?"

"Would you cut the crap about nigger drag queen? I can't stand that expression. I'm all woman!"

"Bullshit! Not the last time I reached down there and grabbed that little piece of okra."

"Enough of that. The problem, man?"

"Your boy's a good sub for Danny. Real great body on him. I'm straight as they come but even I am considering plugging his cute little butt. He's wearing a pair of tight white pants Danny left behind before running off with the old cow, Lavender Morgan."

"That's fine. You don't have to spend more money on wardrobe."

"All well and good. The boy has a generous dick. I mean really generous and almost as big as Danny's. But he doesn't have Danny's big balls which really helped fill out those white pants."

"What am I supposed to do about that?" She was growing more irritated with Matt by the minute.

"In all my years in show business, I never had to go up to a male performer and tell him to stuff his crotch. But you drag queens know all about crotches. If we're to get the size queen crowd we enjoyed when Danny was appearing here, you've got to be the one to stuff Leighton's crotch."

"Easier said than done. Most guys don't like to be told they need a sock put in their crotch. I'm the last person to stuff a crotch. I've spent half my life hiding my crotch from view. Even in the tightest pants, I look like I have a perfect concave and a sweet juicy clit."

"I know, bitch, I know. I also know this. If you don't stuff that boy's crotch to resemble Danny Hansford's basket, I'm not booking either of you." He deliberately blew cigar smoke in her face. Matt turned and walked away toward his office to answer an urgently ringing phone.

Tango stamped her foot on the wooden floor. In her fury she spat in the direction of Matt. If she didn't desperately need white men as her bed partners, she would find it easy to hate them.

As the late afternoon faded into early evening, and the rehearsals continued, Tango was delighted with Chris's performance. He hadn't misled her. He was a great dancer. Unlike Danny Hansford, Chris could take direction. Although he'd never danced the tango before, he learned the steps quickly. His topless body seemed to glide into hers. Although he accidentally kicked her ankle once, causing her great pain, he was extremely apologetic and such a mishap never happened again.

She liked him more and more as they learned the dance steps. If she figured correctly, she'd be able to appear on stage with him in a week if rehearsals continued to go as smoothly as they were.

Although she didn't like to drink when she was rehearsing or performing, Tango went into Matt's office and returned with two cold beers. The bastard had cut off the air conditioning before leaving the club.

"It sure is mighty hot," Chris said. "But I'm taking to this tango, don't you think?"

"I think you're doing great. Real great. We're going to make a fantastic team."

"I saw pictures of Hansford. He does look like me. One hot guy."

"You dance better than Hansford. With you as my partner, there will be two real dancers on that stage. With Danny, they just came to see his body and that crotch bulging out of those tight pants."

"I was gonna bring that up but I was a little gun-shy. I mean, I think my body's just as pumped up as his is. But either he stuffs his crotch or he's got a lot more meat down there than I do."

A sudden inspiration came over her. "I wasn't really going to bring that up either, but there is a way on opening night that you could be—shall we say, an even bigger sensation than Danny Hansford."

"Fuck to hell, I'd like that! I want to be bigger and better than Danny Hansford in every way. 'Cause I just know people will be comparing us."

"I'm not really an expert on such matters, but there is one Savannah queen who is the world's expert on crotches. He's probably got every device known to mankind in his townhouse. He can outfit you in a pair of tight pants, using whatever trickery he employs, and he'll make you a sensation. Would you like that?"

"I'd like it. Who's this queen?"

"Gin Tucker, Savannah's resident size queen."

"Let's call him up and get me to him. How about it?"

"It's a deal. Sure you won't mind some queen putting his hands into your crotch?"

"Not at all. After all, it's show business, and isn't all of show business an illusion? I mean you're pretending to be some beautiful black dancing female, but you ain't, are you?"

"You know, don't you?"

"When not blowing cigar smoke in my face, or cruising my ass when I changed into Danny's tight white pants, Matt Daniels told me. That's one wierdo. I felt he really wanted to fuck me."

"I'm sure he does. You might succeed where even Danny Hansford failed."

"What do you mean?"

"Bringing Matt Daniels out of the closet."

"No, thanks. I'll take a raincheck on that one."

"You're smart." Tango kissed his cheek and headed for the office of the club manager. She knew Gin Tucker could easily handle this assignment.

As she made her way across the darkened backstage area, she felt a slight flutter in her heart. Only days before she'd been in love with Danny Hansford before giving her heart to Jason McReeves. But after her daddy, Duke Edwards, came into her life her heart belonged to him.

Now she dared to imagine the unthinkable: she was growing extremely fond of sweet little Chris Leighton and for one moment was dreaming of his tender embraces instead of the sexual brutality Duke inflicted on his partner.

*****

Alone and dejected, Lavender sat in her living room staring vacantly at the empty walls where her precious treasure trove of art had once hung. A haunting fear tormented her brain. Even if she didn't want to really admit it to herself, she knew the truth. Danny Hansford had drugged her last night.

The whole seduction, the champagne, the tender words, everything had been but a prelude to knock her out so that she would sleep through the early morning theft of her art. She'd rented a van for him because he'd told her that he'd have to leave for a few days to visit his sick mama in Clinton, Georgia. That might be true. Redneck Southern boys seemingly always had a sick mother stashed away somewhere. But in her heart she also knew that the van was used to transport her stolen paintings to some unknown location where, no doubt, they would be sold at a fraction of their value.

Throughout the day her phone had been ringing without stop. She knew that her New York lawyers were calling when the first news broke of the stolen paintings. She'd read two stories already and listened to the television news. The story was going nationwide, maybe even international. After all, she was a fabled figure known on various continents. The theft had all the makings of a good story: mystery, intrigue, stolen art, a famed courtesan living in seclusion with the illicit multi-million-dollar acquisitions of another day. The theft was all the incentive the media needed to dredge up her former affairs and broadcast her notorious past to a new generation of Americans who might never have heard of her.

One element was missing from the stories already published or broadcast—and that was Danny Hansford. For reasons that surprised her, Tom Caldwell, the investigating officer, had agreed not to release information that Danny was in her bed or at least under her roof at the time of the theft.

She was caught in a complete and total dilemma. Although she suspected beyond a reasonable doubt that Danny had stolen her art, she could not reveal her suspicions to the police. All she needed to humiliate herself even more was news to be broadcast that she was shacked up with a teenage boy. That media portrait would make her grotesque. At least in the past, her name had been linked to the movers and shakers of the world, including President Kennedy. For all she knew Danny could be underage. If news broke of her romantic involvement with a boy young enough to be her great-grandson, she would never be able to appear in public ever again.

She was a proud woman and wanted to end her life with some dignity. She'd survived enough scandals for a thousand headliners and didn't need this final one.

Another fear that gnawed at her was that news would also leak out about her financial distress. She'd enjoyed being known as a woman of great financial power. To lose that reputation would be too much of a strain on an already overburdened heart.

Tom Caldwell had kept his word and left Danny out of his police report. "It just wouldn't look right, m'am," he'd told her. "What with you being an older lady and all. People would get the wrong idea."

"Tell me about it," she'd said to Tom. "I'd be not only the laughing stock of Savannah, but the world."

"It's the best thing I could do for you, m'am," Tom had said. "There are those in these parts who consider Danny a little hustler. It might not set well with the public to learn that one of the alltime big glamour gals has resorted to paying for sex from teenage hustlers."

She'd breathed heavily fearing a stroke might be forthcoming. "I hate to ask this, and it's a little embarrassing to bring it up, but do you happen to know Danny's age?"

"Yes, m'am, I do. He just turned sixteen."

"Oh, my God," she'd said, sinking back into her chair. "Talk about robbing the cradle! I'm even embarrassed for you to know I've been involved with this boy."

"M'am, the police force in Savannah are very understanding in these matters. In the course of a day, we see many things that the public doesn't hear about. The stories I could tell you. Your little dalliance is safe with me. You see, I'm what you might call a man of the world."

"Your discretion is greatly appreciated." Lavender's heart had been broken far too many times for her to give in to tears. But on this miserable, wretched day she wanted to have a good cry. Any woman could understand that. The moistening of her eyes told her she was on the verge of tears. But before the first teardrop fell, she was stunned to see Danny barging into the living room.

"I hope the cops get those God damn thieves," he said. "If there's one thing I hate in this shitass world, it's a fucking thief."

She sat up abruptly, for the first time a little afraid to be alone in the house with him. "I was wondering where you'd gone."

"I had a little business to take care of."

He was always mysterious about his comings and goings, and she didn't want to press him any more on his whereabouts for the past two hours. "The police found no sign of forcible entry."

"That don't mean much. They got in through the French doors. It's easy to do. You can practically walk into this house. There's no security."

"The doors weren't broken in to."

"It might have been my fault. Last night I'd had too much champagne and I opened one of the doors to go out on the veranda to get some fresh air. I thought it might clear my head. Maybe I didn't shut the door when I came in." He smiled seductively at her. "I was a little anxious at that point to get upstairs and make love to my gal."

He was a little charmer and even though she didn't believe a word he said, she was still enchanted with him. If he asked her and in spite of all the love-making of last night, she would still gladly accept his invitation for another bout of marathon sex. All he had to do was extend the invitation and she'd be trailing him up the steps and into the bedroom for more of that special kind of love-making he'd shown her last night. The boy had never been more skilled or thrilling to her, and she'd been made love to by studs of international repute.

"I'm gonna ask you to do one special favor for me," Danny said. "It's the most special favor I could ever ask, and I just know you won't turn me down."

"What's that?" she asked skeptically.

"I just read that Jim Williams's Mercer House is being put on the market by his sister, Dorothy William Kingery."

"I know it well," she said. "I used to go to Jim's parties—that is, before he murdered the real Danny Hansford."

"I know, I know," he said impatiently, flaring with anger at her reference to the real Danny Hansford. Ever since she'd known him, she'd never really understood why he wanted to take the identity of a murdered hustler. You'd think he could find some more aspiring role model.

"I know Dorothy very well," she said. "What do you want me to do? Call her up and offer to buy the place? I hear she's asking way too much. Besides, I have this town house."

"Of course, you do," he said, his eyes sparkling at some upcoming prospect. "You don't have to buy it—just pretend you're interested. Call her and tell her you're afraid to live here any more after your robbery. You think Mercer House is more secure. But you want to spend one night in the house alone to sorta get the feel of it. She'd buy that, wouldn't she?"

"I'm sure she would. We've always known and liked each other very much. She'd certainly view me as a serious bidder instead of an idle thrill seeker."

"I want one night in that house," he said, his voice rising. He looked seductively at her. "If you think last night was special, wait until you see what I can do in Mercer House."

In spite of all her reservations, and regardless of how her good judgment told her not to, she rose from her seat to go to the telephone and call Mercer House.

*****

There were grander *palazzi* in the world, but the Victorian mansion of Mercer House was still the pride of Savannah, even if Jim Williams did shoot the original Danny Hansford to death within its walls. Some of the paintings, antiques, and silver had been sold off to pay Williams's legal bills in the various trials that followed the fatal shooting of Danny. But the place was still the most richly embellished that the second Danny Hansford, or little Jeff Broyhill of Clinton, Georgia, had ever seen. Up to now Lavender's town house was the most spectacular roof he'd ever slept under, but Mercer House had even that beat.

From tree-shaded Monterey Square, it rose up just like in the Clint Eastwood movie—an Italianate mansion with ornate iron balconies and red brick. Behind a cast-iron fence, it looked foreboding, and tourists passed by outside at all hours of the day and night to look at the "murder house."

Danny knew that no doors in Savannah would ever be open to him, except those owned by horny men or women who wanted his body. With Lavender, it was different. If she went to Washington, Bill and Hillary would probably let her sleep in the Lincoln Bedroom. He liked being around someone rich and powerful, even if her painting collection had been diminished last night.

He'd decided that his early plan of dumping Lavender or showing her total indifference so she'd abandon him was wrong. He might have need of her in the days ahead. He might even take her home to show her off in Clinton, Georgia. What fun that would be, arriving with a rich woman, even if old, in a fancy limousine. At least all the people who claimed he'd amount to nothing would have to eat crow. He'd have to warn his mama to pretend to be sick and ailing, but since she usually was in that condition anyway, that wouldn't be difficult to pull off.

In the living room of Williams's former mansion, Lavender and Danny sipped Madeira, an old Savannah custom, although he'd much rather be drinking a cold beer. But he wanted to be fancy like his aging mistress.

After finishing her drink, Lavender announced she was feeling dizzy and wanted a long, hot bath and perhaps two or three hours of sleep before meeting him "for dinner and romance."

He was only too willing to agree to that. He had big plans for the time he would be free of her demands, both sexual and otherwise. After she'd gone, he went over to the phone in the hallway and dialed Tom Caldwell.

Later, in the same bed where the original Danny Hansford had sodomized Jim Williams, the second Danny breathed in deeply and prepared himself as best he could to receive the first penetration of his life. It was to come from the man he'd fallen in love with, after a young life of vowing he'd never come under anyone's spell, male or female.

In spite of all of Tom's instructions, it hurt like hell as the long, thick cock penetrated virgin territory. Suddenly Tom's body slammed against Danny with a jarring force that caused him to cry out. He hoped Lavender didn't hear him and come to investigate. Tom pushed roughly down until he had Danny completely impaled. Danny squirmed and tried to break free, feeling he'd faint from the intensity of the pain if he didn't. But Tom held him firmly in his clutches, although not moving inside him, letting Danny slowly get used to the invasion.

The searing, intense pain ebbed faster than Danny realized it would, and an almost indescribable sensation of unendurable, sensual joy surged through his body, like Tom promised. The hot, widespread head of Tom's prick plunged as deep as it could go inside Danny as Tom began his ride to the finish line. Covered in sweat, Danny moaned and gasped in an ecstasy of passion.

Tom's groin slammed more and more forcefully and deeper and deeper into Danny, and at first he panicked. He realized he was but a teenage boy and he'd placed himself in the position of satisfying the sexual appetite of a grown, mature, and very inflamed man. Danny's fear was that he was not up for the challenge and would faint from the repeated jabbings in spite of the pleasure it brought him.

Regardless of these fears, Danny began to meet Tom's lunges with a powerful thrust of his own. He was raising himself up off the bed to welcome each of his older lover's assaults. Guttural, muttered syllables were coming from Tom. These were punctuated with moans, gasps, and heavy breathing. It was as if the intensity between them would ignite into fire.

Totally buried within Danny, Tom erupted from somewhere deep within himself. Danny felt that incredibly powerful bursts of hot juicy cum was spewing inside his guts. Using all the power and force he still had left in his body, Danny tightened around Tom's cock, and, as he did, he erupted himself in the most powerful orgasm he'd ever known in his life. Blow-jobs were nothing compared to this.

Slowly, very slowly, Tom withdrew his spasm-wracked prick from Danny's guts, even though the boy held onto him, not wanting to feel him slide off. The moment Tom was freed of him, Danny felt an incredible sense of loss.

Without warning, Tom descended on him, pressing his tongue deep into Danny's mouth. Danny sucked it with all the power and force left in him. He clasped his body tightly against the older man's and wanted this moment in their lives to last forever.

When Tom had had his fill, he withdrew his tongue from Danny. "I've got to go. I don't want your old hag to come in and find us here. I'm moving the paintings tonight, partner."

Without any further good-byes, Tom pulled up his pants, adjusted his uniform, and headed quietly out the door, planning, as agreed, to slip out the back way.

Once out of the house, Tom, if he kept his promise, would haul Lavender's stolen paintings to his remote fishing shack.

Before going downstairs again, Danny silently opened the door to the bedroom Lavender was occupying. Fresh from her bath, she was sprawled nude on the double bed, her unpainted mouth open and snoring. Without benefit of all the artifice she applied to her face and hair, she looked like a pathetic old woman.

At the moment he could not believe that he had made such passionate love to her. It was even harder to comprehend that the press had hailed her as the 20th-century's greatest courtesan.

Seeing that she was knocked out—this time on her own steam or lack of it—Danny retreated to the room where the fatal shooting of the real Danny Hansford had occurred. The pretend Danny stood where he imagined the real one had been facing Jim Williams across a desk. Closing his eyes, he stepped back in time. Jim Williams was sitting across from him. The unarmed Danny could see him as real as if it were life.

Collapsing onto the floor, as the original Danny had done, the pretend Danny clutched his chest as if that would offer some protection from the imaginary bullet that had penetrated his skin. Face down on the floor, where he'd deliberately fallen and bloodied his nose, Danny closed his eyes as tight as he could. It took little imagination to conjure up Williams getting up from the desk and firing at him two more times, both at point blank range. Danny screamed out in imagined pain as one of the bullets entered his skull just behind his right ear and the other penetrated his back.

It was there, an hour later, that Lavender found him still sobbing with his face buried into the floor.

"Danny!" she shouted. "What's the matter? What happened?"

Even with her bending over him and turning his head to reveal a blood-soaked face, he still couldn't stop crying.

He knew he'd soon be dead, lying in a pool of blood like the real Danny Hansford.

*****

On the way back to Savannah, Norma was behind the wheel with her son, Domino, in the seat beside her. Tipper rode in the back seat, listening to Norma's endless harangues of her drag queen son who was now dressed in blue jeans and a T-shirt, looking very much like an ordinary young man and not the flamboyant Dominique of last night at the club.

"If I'd wanted a girl, I'd put you in a dress instead of pants," Norma angrily told her sulking son who sat as far away from her as possible, practically edging out of the right side of the fast-moving automobile.

Norma was so furious that Tipper feared she might run off the road, because she frequently took her chubby hands off the wheel to make defiant gestures at Domino.

"Norma, it'll be okay," Tipper said reassuringly. "You of all people should understand this. After all, didn't you live with Mae West and wasn't Mae West a drag queen?"

"That's right, mama," Domino butted in. "Your talking about Mae West all the time, and all her drag outfits, was what put the whole thing in my mind in the first place."

"So, now I'm to blame, you little faggot."

The rest of the ride was mainly in silence even when they stopped to refill the car with gas and have a cup of coffee. A dismal mood had descended.

Near the outskirts of Savannah, Norma announced her plan. "After I drop you off, Tipper, I'm gonna take queenie here to Lavender's and see if she'll hire him as a yard man."

"I'm no yard man," Domino protested.

"Listen, bitch, and listen good," Norma said. "You're on probation. The courts turned you over to me with the promise we'd live under the same roof together and that I'd look after you. Do you want me to get the judge on the phone and tell him you're living in Atlanta illegally and performing nightly as a drag queen? And, more to the point, do you want to go back to jail?"

As Domino hung his head low, Tipper knew Norma had won this battle, although Tipper suspected that it wouldn't be long before he was in a gown again.

Happy to be free of Norma and her son, Tipper gratefully retreated to the safety of her house, confident that her mortgage had been paid and she wouldn't be forced out on the street. Before she could even change into something more comfortable, she heard the urgent ringing of her phone.

Thinking it might be Phil Heather wanting to come over to discuss her memoirs, she picked up the receiver.

The heavy breathing of the Iguana could be heard on the other end. He was calling from New York. At first she thought he was going to announce a prospective deal on the sale of her memoirs. But he had something entirely different in mind.

"I've heard of the visit to the King Center in Atlanta," he said.

"My, news travels fast."

"I've got a buyer for the King papers. I hear your letters are hot."

"Martin and I did have a rather torrid affair," she said. "Of course, I was a little young and inexperienced thing back then."

"Don't give me that bullshit. I know all about you. You were fucking everyone in sight, from Martin Luther King Jr. to Monty Clift."

"I was trying to learn about life," she said a bit defensively.

"Yeah, and that's why I sucked so many cocks. To learn what each one tastes like."

"You don't have to be vulgar."

"Don't be ridiculous. I'm a literary agent. What about it? I might get at least two million, maybe three for your stuff. His other papers might be bought by the Library of Congress. I hear they're asking thirty million."

"That would be a fantastic deal."

"You mean the government deal or my deal?"

"Your deal," she said.

"Great!" he said. "Make copies and express them to me tonight. You'll get some lovely green bambinos coming your way."

"I'm just curious. Who's willing to pay that much money for my papers and letters?"

"None of your business. The buyer wants them. Once she gets them, she plans to destroy them."

"Oh, I see." She paused in hesitation. "Any news on my memoirs?"

"Yeah, I've talked it around. But I can't offer anything to any publisher until you get me a proposal. Get in touch with Phil right away. Tell him to get onto it fast. You're hot news again. A cover in *Vanity Fair* coming up. Now's the time to strike."

The Iguana, she'd heard, didn't say good-bye. He merely put down the receiver and took his next call, no doubt from John Grisham.

Even before she'd had a chance to go to the bathroom, she rushed back to answer a loud pounding on her back door. Opening the door, she encountered Erzulie, the voodoo queen of Savannah, standing on her door stoop attired in a saffron yellow robe. Although Tipper did not know the voodoo artist, she recognized her from her pictures in the paper.

"Forgive me," Erzulie said, "but I'm from the Old South. Back in the good ol' days, no fat nigger gal came knocking on the front door of any upper-crust white female person such as yourself."

"I'm Tipper Zelda," she said, rather astounded at the encounter. "And you must be the famous Erzulie."

"Oh, I'm known in the little briar patch of Savannah among some good folks, but my fame is nothing compared to yours."

"You flatter me," Tipper said. "Won't you come in and have some tea?"

Erzulie said nothing but barged past with lightning-like speed, rather amazing for a woman of her corpulence.

In the middle of the kitchen floor, Erzulie stood her ground, checking out everything in sight. "I'd like to take a raincheck on that tea. After all, no one ever accused me of being the queen of England. Got any bourbon?"

"As a good old lady of the Deep South, I do indeed," Tipper said, heading for her cupboard. "I stash away some Southern Comfort here for these late night visits to the kitchen."

Without being asked, Erzulie sat down at the kitchen table. "Wet my gullet with some of the stuff."

Pouring her a stiff drink, Tipper confronted her. "And to what honor do I owe the pleasure of your company?"

"I have come here with awesome news for you—some good, some tragic," the voodoo queen said.

"For God's sake, what is it?"

Downing a hefty swig of Southern Comfort, the voodoo queen said, "Erzulie has bills to pay. It is not my custom to go around dispensing free information to white upper-crust women, unless I see some little greenbacks on the table."

"How much do you want?" A frown crossed Tipper's brow. "This isn't some sort of scam, is it?"

"I want one-hundred dollars for hauling my fat ass over here in this August heat," Erzulie said. "When I tell you what I've got to tell you, you'll be having me back for a lot more hundred dollar visits."

"Okay," Tipper said. Even though she feared Erzulie was the ultimate con artist, she felt her revelations would be entertaining enough to justify the expenditure of one-hundred dollars, especially now that Tipper felt millions were on the way after long years of financial hardship.

Going up front to retrieve a hundred-dollar bill from her purse, Tipper returned to find Erzulie pouring another drink from the bottle of Southern Comfort. "Here's your money," Tipper said, placing the bill in front of the voodoo queen who fondled it most affectionately before stuffing it in her ample bosom.

"God knows, other than a big dick on a nigger man, I love the sight of one of those greenbacks. A joy to my poor old eyes."

"What do you have to tell me?" Tipper said, growing impatient and feeling she was being had.

Erzulie slammed down her drink. "Listen, you overblown white bitch. Don't get smart-ass with me. I want you to know that I'm just as good as you are."

Deeply offended, Tipper ordered her from her house.

Erzulie didn't budge but sat in the chair defiantly, her large buttocks spilling over each side of the chair.

"I said, get out!"

Erzulie through cloudy eyes looked up at Tipper who stood over her. "Listen, Black Widow, I know that you killed each of those husbands of yours. Just to show you that I'm real and no fake, do you want me to describe in great detail exactly how you bumped off each of them—and for what reason?"

"No, no," Tipper said, going over to the sink and pouring a little water into the glass. She went back to the kitchen table and sat down opposite Erzulie, reaching for the bottle of Southern Comfort and pouring herself a stiff drink as well. "I can't relive any of those scenes. Even if your vision is strong, say nothing of it." After downing her drink, Tipper got up on wobbly legs and headed for the front parlor while Erzulie finished off what was left in the bottle.

In minutes Tipper returned with a five-hundred bill, all that was left in her purse from her trip to Atlanta. "Here," she said, handing the money to Erzulie.

Erzulie studied the bill carefully. "Land of Goshen, I've never seen five-hundred big ones in all my life."

"Tell me the news you came here in the first place to tell me," Tipper demanded.

Very slowly a drunken Erzulie pushed her massive weight from the too small chair. "I'll make it very brief but very clear. The good news is that you're going to make a powerful comeback. It won't last long. Maybe no more than three years. But it will be a comeback and you'll get national attention."

Tipper smiled, believing Erzulie for the first time today. "Now the bad news."

"Your role as The Black Widow isn't over yet." Erzulie paused at the kitchen door before opening it to the back porch.

"What are you talking about? I'm not married any more."

"That's right. Any gal who kills off all her husbands is eventually going to be left with none."

"Yes, yes," Tipper said, growing increasingly alarmed. "Then how can I continue to be The Black Widow except in my night club shows?"

"You are going to be the one who leads to the death of both Danny Hansford and Phil Heather. With that pronouncement, Erzulie was out the door.

On unsteady feet, Tipper felt faint, her world growing blacker and dimmer as the voodoo queen's words still resounded in her ears.

# Chapter Seven

Big Daddy ate collards for lunch and dinner, and tonight the cook had prepared a big batch of them for this family reunion dinner. "My doctor says I'm courting death every time I consume masses of pig fat," Big Daddy said. "To hell with him. If I go out, I'm gonna go out giving my belly a good time. I'm just as addicted to pig fat as I am to rotgut bourbon and Sister Woman here to chocolates."

As much as he longed for a family reunion, Phil felt trapped. He didn't belong here. This might be his actual family but he felt no real love, loyalty, or bond with either Big Daddy or Sister Woman. He was different from the rest of them.

As he noticed Sister Woman moving her chair closer to Terry as if he were a tasty morsel and she was some spider about to spring, Phil shuddered. He feared what might be lurking for Terry in spite of the initial assurances that Sister Woman would settle for a marriage of convenience, one for appearance's sake only. Terry was sweating profusely and looking as if he wanted to run out the door, the way he'd escaped with Phil a decade ago.

Aunt Bice bit her heavenly painted lips together. Even after smacking down on the collard greens, enough lipstick remained to make her look like a brazen streetwalker. She surveyed the family dining room. "The meals, the family meals that must have taken place here. This room has withstood the Civil War and other wars too—not that close to home. It's a family house for the ages."

"Cut the shit, Bice," Big Daddy said. "If the termites stopped holding hands, the place would fall in. It's older than any of us. When I'm dead and gone, they'll probably bring in bulldozers and turn it into a housing development."

Phil longed to be with Brian and the kids tonight wondering if they were getting a decent supper. "My God," he thought to himself. "I'm becoming a housewife." He kept glancing over at Terry until he could stand to look at the pathetic boy no more. Of this he could not be sure, but he felt that Terry was gradually giving in to the reality of the situation.

The young man had nowhere to go, as options for a fat boy were limited. He had no money, no talent, no prospects. Phil felt that Terry's face was beginning to dawn with a reality that he might be better off here at the Heather plantation than he would facing an uncertain future—perhaps that of a night janitor in a turnpike motel in the wilds of north Florida.

Dropping her overly buttered cornbread for a moment, Sister Woman reached for Terry's hand, encasing it in a tight grip. "It's gonna be the biggest wedding this county has ever seen," she announced. "Even if Big Daddy here spends every last cent he's got."

"Now, now, Sister Woman," Big Daddy cautioned. "We don't want to get too carried away. I mean if you and this faggot boy were a little prettier and not grossly overweight. I mean you won't make the loveliest bride and groom. There's no store that has a wedding dress ready made for you unless they can sew two dresses together."

Sister Woman slammed down her fork, crashing it against her plate. "If I'm overweight, it's because my family has driven me crazy. I've been made to feel undesired." She cast a look at Terry as if personally accusing him for all the misfortunes in her life.

As she bounded up the steps, on the way to another crying jag in her room, Big Daddy called after her. "Is tonight gonna be a three chocolate box night?"

A long silence came over the table during which Phil examined his own motives for being here. It was strictly for the money. He wanted Big Daddy to restore him to his will. Phil felt if he could return to the family fold, it would not be to enjoy the dubious companionship of Big Daddy and Sister Woman, but to feel free to come and go to this house where his bedroom was still intact. He'd seen to that when he went upstairs to use the bathroom. It was the same bedroom where he'd once kissed a younger, handsomer, and much thinner Terry. Some of Phil's rotting and yellowing clothes from ten years ago remained in the room.

When a large black woman came in to refill Big Daddy's tall glass of overly sweetened tea, he pushed it aside. "Get me some rotgut bourbon and be quick about it. These family reunions are taxing on a man's heart."

"It's good to be back," Phil said weakly. "I've really missed the place."

"No you haven't," Big Daddy said. "You haven't missed it at all. I remember all those years of your growing up here. Buying those body beautiful men's magazines and slipping them up to your room to whack off. Lusting after that Brian Sheehan every chance you got.

You don't know that I know this, boy, but I heard that when Brian used to go out on dates, you'd follow him to dance halls and bars and stay a discreet distance away but watch him all evening to see what that stud was up to with the gal of his choice for the evening."

"Those were just rumors, Big Daddy," Phil said defensively.

"Bullshit!" Big Daddy said, launching into a coughing spasm after downing a hefty dose of bourbon.

At the end of the meal which Phil feared would never terminate, he drank his coffee and ate sweet potato pie with the best of them. The old cook sent word that he made the pie just like "little boy Phil" used to like it. What Phil never told the cook was that of all the vegetables in the world, the sweet potato was his least favorite, especially when served coated with sickeningly sweet melted marshmallows.

In the living room, Big Daddy turned on the old record player from the Fifties and invited Aunt Bice to dance to the tunes of Doris Day, Frank Sinatra, and Judy Garland. Phil had never known Big Daddy to dance in forty years, although once he was known as the best square dancer in southeast Georgia.

Not wanting to dance, Phil asked Terry to join him for a moonlight walk on the veranda. Terry eagerly accepted but when he reached to enclose Phil's hand, he withdrew it. Terry looked dejected and disappointed.

"Ten years is a long time," Phil said. "Perhaps we could have made a go of it—maybe not. We'll never know."

"You mean I haven't a chance with you?"

"Not a chance. I'm in love with Brian Sheehan."

"The straight stud Big Daddy was talking about tonight?"

"The same guy. I've always loved him. Except he's not so straight."

"So, God dammit, I'm left here to marry your fat cow of a sister. You're off with your hot fucking stud. I've been had."

"You left me, remember? I didn't leave you. I thought I loved you at the time. It took a long while to get over you."

A screech almost like a wild animal came from the throat of Big Daddy, resounding across the veranda. Phil turned and ran toward the big parlor, with Terry waddling behind.

In the glow of the chandelier, Phil let out his own howl of despair as he confronted the scene before him.

Aunt Bice had fallen on the floor. Drunk and bewildered, Big Daddy hovered over her as if that could bring life back to her still body.

*****

An urgent call from Phil had brought Lula rushing toward his side at the home of his Aunt Bice, who had been delivered to the funeral parlor. Although reluctant at first to accompany her, Jason had agreed to drive her to Darien. He'd really wanted to go to the beach with Chris, but Tango had insisted that Chris needed all the time for rehearsals for their upcoming gala opening. As their battered old car neared Aunt Bice's crumbling but still shabbily elegant home, Lula was amazed at how she'd so quickly integrated herself into Phil's chaotic life. She knew in her heart that she'd be better off writing the pages of *The Tireless Hunter* but found real life more fascinating and endlessly intriguing for her than her fictional characters could ever be.

As the car carrying Jason and Lula pulled into the backyard of Aunt Bice's house, Phil ran out the door and helped Lula out of the car. Removing himself from the driver's seat, Jason got out and walked around to embrace Phil and kiss him on the mouth. Phil gave Jason his right hand, extending his left to Lula, and together they walked toward Aunt Bice's back veranda.

At the top of the steps Phil turned and looked into Lula's eyes. "I loved my aunt," he told her, tears welling in his eyes. "She was the only one in my family who loved me and understood me. I'll miss her something awful."

"I know you will," Lula said, summoning a real compassion from her heart. For one brief moment she wished she'd been married to a man with Phil's sensitivity and not Jason. With Phil, she'd met a kindred spirit. With Jason, she'd met the child she'd never have in real life. Lula knew she would not make a good mother. The idea of Jason as a father was too preposterous to contemplate.

The back door was thrown open, and John and Henry rushed out and into her arms. Without meaning to, she was becoming a surrogate mother to them. This was about the last item on her agenda. After hugging and kissing the boys, Lula greeted Brian as he emerged from Bice's kitchen wearing one of her old yellow-stained aprons. "I've whipped up some chili," he told her. "Life goes on."

"Hi, Brian," she said, kissing him on the cheek.

Jason moved toward Brian to kiss him on the mouth, but Brian moved his head. Jason got the cheek instead. "Sorry, sport," Brian said, smiling. "From now on, only Phil here gets to taste the succulent cherry-red lips of this stud hoss."

At the table she was seated between John and Henry. "It's so much nicer living with Phil," John volunteered. "Mama never liked us."

"She bitched all the time," Henry said.

"Not only that but she paddled our butts every day," John said, "whether we deserved it or not."

"And I'm the kind of boy who likes his butt treated with tender, loving care," Henry said.

"You can say that again," John said, reaching over and patting his brother on the back.

After lunch, Lula joined Brian on the back porch as Phil and Jason drove over to the funeral parlor to make the final arrangements for the departed and dearly beloved Aunt Bice. If Lula had known that Brian was going to make chili for lunch, she would have brought along her fabled cole slaw. In her view, a good Southerner never served chili without cole slaw. It just wasn't done. But Brian was so sweet and charming she could easily forgive him.

"I'm happy for the first time in my life," Brian said to Lula, sucking in the first real breeze of the day from Aunt Bice's verandah. "Joyce made me so unhappy. We fought all the time."

"Didn't you both take delight in the kids? They have their peculiarities but are really wonderful boys?"

"I think Joyce always resented having kids. She said I made a cow of her. Surely no woman in all the world bitched as much through pregnancy as she did."

"My novel, *The Tireless Hunter*, is about women and men who follow the dictates of their heart. To see you doing that, to see my cousin Tom doing the same, or about to do the same, is all I could hope for. Sometimes I've wanted to follow the dictates of my own heart and flee from Jason, but we always come back together."

"Have you ever thought that maybe you and Jason really love each other? Unlike Joyce and me."

"I've thought about it a lot," Lula said. "The more Jason and I hurt each other, the more we stay together. Maybe the marriage is about emotional sadism."

Brian seemed to remember something. "Better put on some coffee." It was obvious he didn't like to pursue such conversations. "I don't even know what emotional sadism is, unless it's about the shit me and Joyce lived through for ten whole years. With Phil, our marriage is about love and bringing up the kids, and sort of having a good time together just being with each other."

"Do you feel incomplete without him?"

"I feel incomplete that I let him out of my life for a whole mother-fucking decade. I knew a long, long time ago that Phil loved me, and loved only me. I'll kick myself forever for not giving him my love when I knew how much he needed it. I needed him just as much as he needed me, but I married Joyce instead."

"At least it produced two wonderful boys."

"That's for damn sure." A frown crossed Brian's face. "You've seen it for yourself. My boys are a little mixed up. I mean, sexually. Oh, shit, you know what I mean."

"Of course, I do."

"Before Phil and Jason get back, could you have a little talk with them? I mean, about them growing up and leading their own lives and not being totally dependent on each other."

"I'll see what I can do. If your boys want to come and talk to me, I'll be down wandering through Aunt Bice's peach orchard. Georgia is fucked up in more ways than I care to recite, but at least it grows great peaches."

"See you later." Brian headed for the kitchen presumably to have a rendezvous with Aunt Bice's old coffee pot.

Later, joined by John and Henry, she took their little hands and led them through the orchard where the smell of the ripening summer fruit gladdened her heart.

"Daddy wanted us to talk to you," John said, "and I'm not as dumb as I look. I know what it's about."

"I do too," Henry chimed in.

She stepped cautiously. "Right now you think the two of you are the most important people on earth. I know you mean everything to each other."

"I belong to John—and that's that!" Henry said defiantly. "It will always be that way."

"But you must not miss out on the adventure of life," she warned them. "There's a whole big world out there. God did not plan for us to spend our whole lives with family members. I understand where you are right now. But you must grow and change in the months ahead. You need to meet other people, both boys and girls until you fully determine the one person you want to spend the rest of your life with. But that can only come years from now. After years and years of experience."

"We want to have what Daddy and Uncle Phil have," said John. "They're in love. They're happy. Me and Henry are in love too. Why can't we have what Daddy's got?"

"Brian and Phil arrived at whatever it is they have after many a summer. They tried many different lifestyles. They experimented with various relationships until they fully determined what they wanted."

"Why should we go through all that shit when we know what we want right now?" Henry asked.

"Yeah," John said, growing surly. "We're happy now. We've trusted you until now. But I think you're trying to break us up and make us unhappy."

"No, no, no," she protested. "I want you to make your own decisions. I'm just trying to suggest the other possibilities of life."

"We don't want your fucking suggestions," Henry said, bursting into tears and running toward the house.

John's eyes spat fire as he glared at her. "See what you've done? You've hurt the boy I love. I'm gonna go after him. He needs me."

As she watched John flee after Henry to comfort him, she was miffed at Brian for putting her in this position in the first place. For all she cared John could love Henry as much as he wanted to. Perhaps the boys were right. Let them love each other. Of course, in time conditions would change. Life would see to that.

Fearing she'd lost the boys' trust, she headed back to the house after gathering a few of the ripest and most succulent peaches.

In the distance she could see an old pink Cadillac roaring up the dirt road to Aunt Bice's house.

At first she'd thought Jason and Phil might be returning from the funeral parlor.

But it wasn't Jason and Phil driving the pink Cadillac. With screeching brakes, the car came to a sudden halt near her, alarming her so much she dropped two of her ripest looking peaches.

A corpulent woman slowly emerged from the car which looked like a leftover from a garage sale of Elvis. "Where in the fuck is my faggot brother?" she demanded to know of Lula.

Noticing a chubby young man in the seat beside this monster, Lula smiled demurely before returning to this perspiring mass of blubber.

"To whom am I speaking?" Lula inquired.

"I'm Sister Woman."

"Then you must be related to Phil."

"To my ever-lasting regret. See that boy sitting up there in front of this Cadillac with me?"

"His presence has been made known to me," Lula said with all the Southern charm she could muster in a situation like this.

"His name is Terry Drummond," Sister Woman said. "Before he got fat, he was going to marry me at a big wedding ten years ago. But my faggot brother arrived home and proceeded to steal the groom right from my snatch. Isn't that right, sugar?"

Seemingly embarrassed, Terry nodded in shamed agreement.

"I see," Lula said. "A little domestic tift."

"Fuck that! A major betrayal."

"I know Phil," Lula said. "He's not here at the moment. How can I help?"

"We're waiting for him right here at Aunt Bice's," Sister Woman said, ordering Terry from the car.

"Please come up to the verandah, and I'll get you people something to drink," Lula said.

"Thanks a hell of a lot," Sister Woman said, heading for the verandah. "Phil thinks he's gonna be tied up with this God damn funeral."

"I'm sorry to learn of the passing of your aunt," Lula said.

"My aunt was a God damn alcoholic slut," Sister Woman said. "The bitch should have died years ago."

"It's important that Phil make the funeral arrangements," Lula said. "He's gone to the funeral parlor with my husband, Jason."

"That's just fine," Sister Woman said. "But there is gonna be one major complication to this funeral."

"And what's that?"

"All the clan, all the people of the county, are gonna be gathered for Aunt Bice's funeral. I couldn't stand the bitch but everybody loved her. There may even be a few thousand."

"I'm glad so many people are coming to pay their respects."

"As soon as the old whore's six feet under, I want Phil to invite them to my wedding that same afternoon. A crowd like that won't assemble more than once. I've got to strike while the iron's hot."

"You probably have a point there. A funeral and a wedding on the same day."

"I can't hang out here much longer," Sister Woman said. "Me and Terry are going back home. I'll call that Phil, and he'd better listen." She waddled back to the Cadillac and left with her tires screeching.

In the distance she spotted Phil's car coming at a much slower speed up the dirt road. "My, oh, my. I always said it was risky to be up and stirring on a hot afternoon in August in Georgia."

*****

As she prepared her face to go before her public on opening night, Tango couldn't believe how fast Chris Leighton had learned to tango. He was an amazing dancer, and she felt she was falling in love with him.

That didn't mean she'd fallen out of love with her daddy, Duke Edwards. She loved him too but in a different way. He brought the violence to sex she desperately needed. Chris in contrast had a tenderness to him that appealed to her heart. Life couldn't be about sexual violence all the time. You needed someone to go on a picnic with after a walk through the woods. There had to be those tender moments too.

Staring back at her in the mirror was the most gorgeous woman she'd even seen. In spite of all her troubles, she still had her looks. Even Dominique had confirmed how great Tango looked when he'd arrived at the club earlier and had gone backstage to greet her and wish her well. Dominique said that Danny Hansford would be returning the gowns Tango had left in Atlanta before she'd fled to Savannah.

She'd been startled to see Dominique dressed as a man. Her friend told her all about what had happened when Tipper Zelda and Norma Dixie had visited the club in Atlanta to see his drag performance.

Norma now knew the truth, and Tango feared retribution from Dominique for alerting Norma that her son was a drag queen. The young man was strangely forgiving, saying he was going to work temporarily as a gardener on the property of Lavender Morgan. "That's better than going back to jail," he'd told Tango.

Tango feared that Dominique would soon be pursuing the in-house stud there, her old flame Danny Hansford. But she couldn't mess up her mind with that prospect tonight. All she could think about right now was fitting into that slinky red dress cut up to her carefully concealed crotch.

Her return to the club was a big event in Savannah, or so Matt Daniels had just informed her before leaving her dressing room. He was so excited at the prospect of lots of business that he'd demanded his usual blow-job. She'd refused, claiming, "I'm too big a star to do that any more." Matt had left in a huff.

Tango knew all the town's gossips would be there. Most of the audience, except for some stray tourists wandering around with copies of *Midnight in the Garden of Good and Evil*, would know her performance well. Chris Leighton would be the big mystery guest of the evening. Would he fill out those tight white pants as well as Danny Hansford? Surely that was the question of the night. Only Gin Tucker knew the truth, and he'd sworn a vow of secrecy about what he'd stuffed into Chris's pants. Of course, she couldn't trust that old Truman Capote clone for one minute.

Lavender Morgan would no doubt be sitting ringside with a jealous Danny Hansford and her usual entourage. She'd be a few million dollars poorer after the loss of all those paintings, but what the hell? Lula Carson and Jason would be there, as would Phil Heather and his new companion, Brian Sheehan, the cop from Darien. Tango had even heard that Tipper Zelda would make an appearance at the club, her former stamping ground where she—not Tango—had been the star. Tango wanted to be especially good if Tipper were in the audience. That was one white woman she wanted to make real jealous.

After checking her make-up for the hundredth time, Tango approved of what was staring back at her. She'd knock them dead tonight. Going next door, she tapped on Chris's dressing room which was no more than a small broom closet.

When she opened it, she approved mightily of what she saw before her. If anything, Chris looked far more succulent a morsel than Danny Hansford on his finest night. Gin Tucker, she feared, had been a little too generous in stuffing Chris's pants. In comparison to Chris, Danny looked like Princess Tiny Meat. But somehow the whole package held together. Chris was sweet and charming, whereas Danny was usually hostile and belligerent, even in front of an audience. Chris had a younger, fresher appeal than the more jaded Danny, and Tango felt the gay males in the audience would eat that up. Or, more to the point, they'd want to eat Chris. He was fresh meat. The new kid on the block. She was fully confident that he'd forever wipe out the memory of Danny once he appeared before a live audience.

Chris eagerly grabbed her hand and pulled her inside. "I don't want anybody to see me before I go on."

She shut the door behind her and took in the full glory of the young man, forgetting for the moment the more jaded and experienced charms of her old man presumably waiting for her back in their apartment, although with Duke you could never be sure he'd be home when you got there. She'd invited him to watch Chris and her dance but had no way of knowing if he'd show up.

"For a white boy, you look mighty good," Tango said. "Too damn good if you ask me. With all those glistening muscles and in those damn white pants, no one is gonna look at the star of the show." She placed her hand on her hip in a defiant pose. "Namely me, baby."

"Surely they will," Chris said reassuredly, checking his makeup. "You're a star. After tonight and with me as your partner, your star will grow brighter and brighter. We'll make it big. I just know it. There's probably some talent scout out there in the audience waiting to sign us up with a big, fat Hollywood contract."

"Your mother here ain't exactly sure that's how it's done anymore." She flashed a smile at him, showing her amazing pearly white teeth. "But we can dream, can't we?"

Chris smiled back at her but a growing concern came across his face. He seemed nervous and she detected a slight shake in him. "I'm okay," he said, noting her concern. "Opening night. My first time out as a professional dancer. Why wouldn't I be a little nervous?"

"Baby, if a performer ain't nervous, she ain't no good, I always said. When I first started performing, I used to puke before going on."

"God damn, I hope that doesn't happen to me."

"It ain't gonna to, sugah. Trust this gorgeous pussy standing before you."

"You're the hottest bitch in Savannah."

"Thanks." She burst into a near hysterical laughter.

"What's so damn funny?"

"The two of us. I've spent half my life hiding my crotch. The Lady Chablis called her crotch her sugar, and hides hers too. But it looks like you're hiding nothing. Nothing at all."

"I want to give the queens their money's worth."

"You'll do that and more."

He took her arm and gently leaned over, planting a gentle kiss on her cheek.

At first she jumped back the way she always did before going on, fearing that he might mess up her makeup. But then a different impulse came over her. "Chris, dahling, us swamp bitches don't go in for cheek or hand kissing." She'd heard that line somewhere. It wasn't original. "I'm a gal who likes it on the mouth. Right on my hot red lips or not at all."

He hesitated a moment, then stuck out his tongue to wet his lips. He leaned over and planted a long, lingering kiss on her petulant mouth.

She thrilled at the taste of him. If she didn't fear she'd wreck her costume, she'd have this white boy on the floor, begging him to fuck the hell out of her. But as a true professional show business lady, she knew that was out of the question. They were due to go on in just three minutes. Breaking away from him, although it took all her will power, she ran to the mirror. "That was good, sugah. Real good." She quickly reapplied the makeup he'd kissed away. Satisfied that she was ready for her closeup, she noticed he still had some of her lipstick on his mouth. She grabbed a tissue and wiped him clean just as Matt Daniels pounded on the door.

"Hey, gals," he called out. "Show time."

Backstage as she stood with Chris waiting for the curtain to rise on their tango, he took her hand in his. "Thanks, Tango, you're the first person who ever gave me a chance before. I won't let you down. Believe me, I wouldn't do that to you. I'm no Danny Hansford."

"I'll be real proud of you after tonight's show. I just know it."

The next forty minutes passed as in a dream. The opening night audience had greeted their first number with thunderous applause. When Chris had appeared in those white pants, he'd gotten a standing ovation from most of the gay males in the audience. She noticed that one male at Lavender Morgan's table wasn't standing. Could that be Danny Hansford?

New to the tango, Chris danced it like a real pro from Buenos Aires. It was amazing how he'd picked up the number as if he'd been performing the tango all his life. At one point he feared she might kick him with her high heels or he'd kick her ankles, but no accident happened. She felt they were magical together, with far more excitement generated on stage than when she'd appeared with Danny. Unlike Danny, Chris was a true partner. Even though dancing in a duet, Danny always seemed removed from her and slightly out of step with her rhythm.

When the curtain went down for the first act, the thunderous applause that had first greeted them resounded even louder within her head. She took five bows before Matt Daniels dimmed the lights. He'd called a thirty-minute intermission, which was rather long. Matt knew the audience was filled with heavy drinkers, and he wanted to hustle his rotgut bourbon.

Backstage Tango was perspiring heavily, and so was Chris. He was sweating so profusely he told her he was going to grab a quick shower to cool off before changing into a new pair of tight white pants.

"You did good, baby," she assured him.

"We're going to go to the top," he said, his eyes lightning up. "You and me, baby."

In her dressing room she was startled to encounter Duke Edwards. She rushed toward him expecting a congratulatory kiss from her daddy. He slapped her instead, knocking her to the floor. "You God damn slut! A whore just like your mama."

"Duke, what's wrong?" she asked, rubbing her face from the impact of his open hand. Her whole cheek stung like it was on fire. "The audience loved it."

"I ain't gonna have no nigger daughter of mine out there behaving like a whore with that asshole white boy."

"Chris is great. The audience loved him, too."

"Tell this fucking Matt Daniels you're gonna go on solo for the second act. The stupid kid is stealing the show from you." He helped her up. "Don't you get it? You're my meal ticket. The kid is going to be the star, replacing you. That means I'm not eating next week."

"No, no, Duke, you've got it all wrong. We're fabulous as a team."

"Do you want me to take my fist and plow it into your face this time?" he asked, standing menacingly over her. "I will. You're not gonna go on with that fucking faggot again."

"I don't want to defy you, daddy, but I'm gonna go on and it's gonna be with Chris Leighton."

"You mean that, don't you?"

"God damn right, I mean it," she said defiantly. "God damn right."

"Okay, bitch, we'll see about that. Your mama defied me. And she's regretting it from her grave."

"What do you mean?"

"I killed the bitch. That's what I mean." Heading toward the door, he slammed it behind him.

Her heart in total chaos, she stood paralyzed in her dressing room, not aware of the passing time until she realized the intermission was almost over. Hurriedly, she changed her costume and made up her face one final time before the finale. Long before Matt arrived to rap on the door, she gave her face and her costume one final appraisal before rushing next door to check up on Chris.

Earlier she felt she'd heard him call out to her because the wall between their dressing rooms was thin. But Matt had turned on disco music from the seventies and it was so loud she couldn't even hear herself think.

When Chris didn't respond to her knock, she opened the door, finding it unlocked. Maybe he was still in the shower. If so, she'd better warn him to hurry up. They didn't have much time.

Upon entering the cubicle, she found the lights out, which struck her as real strange, sending fear through her body. What performer got dressed in a room without lights?

She fumbled for the light switch, finding it to the left of the door. She flipped on the bulb and turned around.

A screech not quite human emerged from the depths of her throat. The sound was really coming from her heart.

Covered in blood, Chris lay sprawled nude on the floor. He'd been disemboweled.

*****

Lying in her bed unable to sleep at three o'clock in the morning, Lavender played back the events of the past evening as if it were a movie spinning through her head. Her first impulse had been to say no when Gin Tucker called, inviting her for the opening night of Tango's new act in which she'd found a hot new dancing partner to replace Danny. Too tired and concerned with her own problems, Lavender had little desire to traipse off to Blues in the Night. She was still suffering the loss of her paintings and dreading the upcoming television documentary on her life. That, combined with her mounting financial woes, was enough to keep any woman in bed.

Hidden behind a red satin domino, she searched for Danny's body in her bed but he must have gotten up in the middle of the night and was wandering about somewhere. After all that questioning by the police, he was hardly in the mood for sex. For the first time in her life, neither was she.

It had been Danny who had vehemently insisted that she go with him to the night club. Naturally he'd been curious as to who had replaced him in Tango's act. All over Savannah comparisons would be made, and Danny was eager to see who he was being stacked up against. "Who in hell is this Chris Leighton?" he'd demanded to know from Lavender.

"I've never heard of him. Darling, I don't spend all my time hanging out with all the flotsam and jetsam drifting into Savannah."

Her remark, though intended as a put-down of Chris Leighton, had been interpreted as a direct attack on Danny. "Who in hell are you calling trash?"

"I didn't mean you," she had weakly defended herself. "If I thought you were trash, would I invite you into my bed? Would I let you share my home?"

"Guess not," he'd said but he'd still seemed angry.

Watching Chris Leighton dance with Tango had not soothed Danny's anger. If he were mad when he'd arrived at the club, he'd grown even more bitter as he'd watched Chris dance.

It had been obvious to Lavender. Chris was a far better tango dancer than Danny ever was. Not only that, but Chris had brought a more wholesome and fresh-faced look to the act. The young man had been charming, incredibly sexy, and a charismatic show business personality. In almost every way, Chris Leighton as a performer had Danny beat.

Under Lavender's keen and much experienced eyes, she'd recognized that Chris's crotch was even bigger and more prominent than Danny's bulge. Danny was more than adequate—in fact, most men could only dream of having what Danny possessed. But unless Chris had artfully stuffed his crotch, he was the biggest act in Savannah, perhaps even a rival of the legendary Jason McReeves.

At the thought of him, Lavender had turned around and waved meekly at the next table at Lula Carson and Jason. She hardly knew Lula and had only met Jason, but apparently the literary grant to Lula had come through because Georgia's literary sweetheart had been all smiles.

Lavender had shuddered to think of their last embarrassing encounter. But there wasn't a household in old Savannah that didn't cover up some scandal.

When the club had learned of the fatal attack on Chris Leighton before the curtain was supposed to go up on the second act, Lavender had been stunned and shocked. She'd feared involving herself in another scandal. She'd suspected that the television documentary on her life would have to be rewritten if she continued to mix herself in one notorious event after another. She'd been horrified to learn that she'd have to go to the police station for questioning.

Her experience at the police station with Danny had been humiliating, and someone had photographed her as she was entering the main hall of the precinct. She'd wondered where that photograph would appear. Before arriving at the station, she'd asked Danny to walk some thirty feet away as she didn't want the paparazzi to link them romantically.

As far as suspects, Lavender had been out of the loop except for her involvement with Danny. One of the prime suspects, Danny had sat at her table and had excused himself to go to the men's room at intermission. The men's room was only ten feet from Chris's small dressing room. It had been learned that there had not been a lock on Chris's door. Anyone could have gone into that small cubicle and knifed Chris before returning to either the men's room or else the main room of the night club.

If Lavender recalled properly, and with the liquor and the late hour she didn't trust her memory, Danny had been away from her table for about twelve minutes. Of course, when she'd given her report to the police, she'd claimed he was away from table less than five minutes, just enough time to go to the urinal, a long walk away, and to return to sit beside her.

Later when they'd gotten home, she'd asked Danny where he'd been that other missing time, and he'd claimed that he'd gone into the alleyway for a smoke and to breathe the air. When she'd asked him if anybody had seen him in the alleyway, he'd grown belligerent and had headed for the liquor cabinet. She had chosen not to question him any more.

She feared being in the same house with Danny, and knew she had to plan a way out of this obviously doomed relationship just as soon as possible. Had he stolen the paintings? Had he murdered Chris Leighton out of pure jealous spite? She'd be on the phone with her attorneys in the morning. Danny's case was looking better because he'd walked out on Tango and her dancing act. If he'd been fired, and had been replaced by Chris, it would have been a more troubling turn of events.

Before she'd left the police station, she'd learned a lot of other gossip. A mysterious stranger had appeared. Matt Daniels had seen him storming out of Tango's dressing room during intermission. Apparently, he was in a jealous rage over Chris Leighton At the moment, if she'd heard right, this outsider was the prime suspect.

But then other rumors surfaced. Even Jason McReeves was somehow involved. The word was, Jason himself had been involved intimately with Tango, and, if gossip could be believed, Tango had dropped him in favor of Chris. As the whole town knew for a fact,

Jason was crazy and seemed capable of doing anything to anybody at any time.

There were two or three other suspects but Lavender couldn't mess up her mind with more speculation. Chris had been seen leaving the house of Gin Tucker only that afternoon. Had there been something going on between Chris and her good friend, Gin? Possibly. She'd noted that Gin had excused himself and had been back at the urinals in the men's room longer than anybody. But, or so she'd been told, Gin spent a lot of time at the urinals of Savannah, so that had come as no surprise to anybody.

When Danny eventually returned to bed, she lay silently, her eyes protected by her satino domino. She didn't want to talk to him right now, fearing the drift of their conversation. From now on, there would be a lot of words left unspoken between them.

About an hour later, when he'd been snoring very softly and seemed in a deep but troubled sleep, she eased herself from their king-sized bed and slipped downstairs. All night at police headquarters she'd heard about a missing murder weapon, a giant knife like a machete. Danny had been disemboweled with a very large knife. But where was the murder weapon? A search of the club and all the suspects had been ordered but no murder weapon had been found. Even her touring car had been searched. Nothing had been discovered. The person who had brought the murder weapon into the club had done so rather artfully. No one had seen anybody with a giant knife or certainly no one but poor Chris Leighton had actually seen the weapon that night. No one, that is, except the murderer himself.

As she made her way down the carpeted steps of her town house, she noted that she'd said "himself." Could the murderer actually be a woman? It never seemed to occur to anyone but maybe Tango herself had murdered Chris. Tango had been seen coming and going from his dressing room more than anybody. Had he spurned her advances? Anything was possible. Lavender was amazed at how Tango was not even considered a suspect yet she was in the best position to have murdered the young dancer and concealed the weapon.

All this night of talk about knives had sparked a buzz in her brain. She possessed a machete, a very famous weapon, presented to her by Ernest Hemingway, one of her many and former lovers. He'd taken it on one of his safaris to Africa. According to her unreliable former pal, the author had once used the machete to stab a wounded tiger who'd entered their safari camp in the middle of the night and had attacked two native guides. Like everything else Hemingway told her, you couldn't totally rely on his tall tales. But the machete was capable of killing a tiger or even a lion and most definitely a young dancer such as Chris Leighton.

She'd once mentioned this machete to Danny, and he'd been fascinated by the story, and had demanded to see the weapon. In his hands, he fondled it and tested its sharpness. He'd even play acted taking the machete, as Hemingway claimed he had, and plunging it into the heart of a ferocious lion.

Before her cabinet of souvenirs, Lavender opened a drawer where she kept Hemingway's safari machete. It was the most prominent souvenir in the drawer. She picked up its sheath and saw at once the weapon was missing. She quickly shut the drawer, knowing it was no use to search through the cabinet for it.

The machete, like her paintings, was out of her house, and she knew she'd never see it again.

*****

When Danny woke up, Lavender had already left the bedroom, and for that he was grateful. No hot young stud wanted to confront a two-hundred-year-old woman first thing in the morning. He'd have plenty of time to shower and get dressed before having to face her across the breakfast table.

Secretly he suspected that she believed he'd stolen her paintings. He'd have to be real careful of her and not say anything that might give him away. He also suspected that even if Lavender believed he'd stolen her art, she wouldn't go to the police, fearing a scandal that would certainly be broadcast on that upcoming television special about her life. He felt clear-headed and actually quite good today, although something troubled him about last night. Something had happened at Blues in the Night, and that something involved him but he wasn't quite sure in what way.

For the first time he knew an awful truth. Every day the real Danny Hansford living within him was growing stronger and stronger. Yesterday was the first time the real Danny had overcome him as if he were overpowered in a wrestling match.

Even before leaving for the club, the real Danny had told him to bring the machete. Nothing from Norma's kitchen. Only the safari machete given to Lavender by Hemingway would do. That weapon had killed lions and tigers in African jungles.

As he was stealing the machete, Danny couldn't understand why the real Danny Hansford living within him wanted Chris Leighton killed. It was as if Chris was emerging as a possible third Danny Hansford, and Savannah had room for only two Danny boys even if they inhabited the same body.

Danny hadn't understood the voice that was urging him on. No reason was given for anything. Only commands were received. Nothing was explained. He was merely told to do something and he felt compelled to carry out the orders. The real Danny, the voice urging him on, didn't tell him how he was going to go into the club and stab Chris Leighton to death. The voice left Danny to figure that out for himself.

Danny didn't know what to do until an opportunity arose with Domino. Danny had learned that Norma was taking Domino to the Blues in the Night so that he could see the show of his former friend, Tango. Domino had brought to Savannah several of Tango's drag outfits that she'd been forced to leave in Atlanta when she fled town.

Hearing this, Danny had volunteered to put the box of gowns in Lavender's limousine and to deliver them to his former partner, Tango, in person. Norma told Domino that she didn't want him seeing Tango backstage, so she'd readily agreed to let Danny deliver the gowns.

"Besides, I need to clear the air with Tango any way," Danny had told Norma and Domino. "Bringing back all this drag crap will win a few points for me. After all, I just walked out on her. Very unpro of me."

This morning Danny couldn't recall many of the events of the past night. He did remember stealing the Hemingway machete and concealing it in the box of drag outfits. He even remembered going to the club with Lavender, Norma, and Domino where they were joined by a group of Gin Tucker's friends.

Excusing himself, Danny had gone backstage where he ran into Matt Daniels, his former employer. "You fucking asshole," Matt had yelled at him. "Walking out on the act just when I was starting to make big bucks. What are you doing back here, shithead?"

"I'm sorry," Danny had said, trying to appear as meek as possible. He hadn't wanted to infuriate Matt any more than he already had. "I've got a box of Tango's gowns from Atlanta. They're in the back of Lavender Morgan's limousine. She's spent a lot of money on these gowns, and I want to give them to her."

"Put them in the back room," Matt had barked at him. "I don't want you going into her dressing room and upsetting her on opening night. You've fucked up her mind enough."

"Fair enough," Danny had said.

"When you've done that, then got the fuck out of here," Matt had said. "I've had it with you. You've got a big cock but little talent."

Danny remembered moving the gowns from the limousine to the back room as instructed by Matt. He even remembered returning to Lavender's table. He especially recalled how charismatic Chris Leighton had been performing with Tango before the same audience that had once thrilled to his own dancing and tight white pants.

If it could be possible, Danny had been stunned to see that Chris was getting more applause than Danny ever had. Could Chris not only be a better dancer, but fresher and better looking? Until he saw Chris perform, Danny had always prided himself on being the handsomest and sexiest stud to walk the streets of Savannah.

Danny had frowned and grown increasingly agitated as he'd watched Chris perform. That meat showing in Chris's pants couldn't be real. No one had a cock that big. Danny had shown real flesh but he suspected Chris was faking it.

As Chris had entered his final number on stage with Tango, Danny had been tempted to get up from his chair, head for the stage where he'd rip Chris's tight white pants off and reveal to the audience how he was really hung. Then in his fantasy Danny would whip out on his own dick and show this God damn jaded audience some real meat.

None of that ever happened, of course. And Danny was completely uncertain what had taken place at intermission. From the moment he'd excused himself to go to the men's room, his mind had become a complete and total blank, as he'd confessed to Tom Caldwell at the police headquarters last night.

He just couldn't remember. His earliest recollection had been when he'd returned to Lavender's table and had waited and waited for the second act to begin. He remembered the lights going on to reveal Matt, informing the audience of an "accident" back stage. The club owner told the patrons that the Savannah police had surrounded the club and no one was to leave the building until officially cleared by the police. As one of the suspects, Danny had been taken to the police station where he'd been questioned endlessly. The questions had been tough, and not the kind, forgiving questions that his friend Tom had asked about Lavender's stolen paintings.

Tom was coming by this morning to take Danny to police headquarters for more questioning.

In her breakfast salon, Lavender was drinking endless cups of coffee and scanning the local newspaper with its lurid details of the Chris Leighton murder. "Are you mentioned?" he asked her.

"Thank God, no," she said. "But you are. Fortunately confined to a back page with a picture of you and Tango dancing at the club. You look good."

He took the paper from her and glanced briefly at Gin Tucker's photograph. He certainly looked better than Tango in the news photo.

Before Danny had even drunk his first cup of coffee of the day, Tom had come into the breakfast salon, ushered there by Norma Dixie who had said very little all morning.

"Morning, m'am," the cop said to Lavender. "Hi, Danny."

"No handcuffs," Danny said mockingly.

"Cut the shit, boy," Tom said, perhaps more to impress Lavender with his toughness than to intimidate Danny.

"Time to go?" Danny asked.

"Yeah, get ready," Tom said with a harshness in his voice. He turned to Lavender. "I'm sorry we're not making headway about your stolen paintings, but this Leighton murder has got everybody tied up."

"I understand," she said. "A human life should always take precedent over someone's artistic view."

"Glad you see it our way, m'am."

"Be kind with Danny," she cautioned him. "He's a very sensitive boy in spite of his macho facade."

"Like hell, I am," Danny said in rebuttal. "I'm plenty tough."

"Would you get ready?" Tom said, turning on him in real anger this time before looking back at Lavender. "Excuse me, m'am, for using such vulgarity in the presence of a fine lady like you."

"Good day, gentlemen." Lavender got up and left the room.

When her back was turned, Tom winked at Danny. "C'mon, sport," he whispered. "We got other fish to fry today. No more police headquarters—at least not for today."

As Tom's car sped away from the city of Savannah along Route 20 to Atlanta, Danny knew he wasn't going to police headquarters, at least not today.

As planned and arranged before the Chris Leighton murder, Danny had to meet with some Japanese businessmen in Atlanta. Steve Parker, the middle-aged John, had made all the arrangements. Danny had a few sexual services to perform and a few paintings to sell.

It was going to be one hell of an evening. The hottest time in Atlanta since General Sherman burned it down.

*****

After a night of troubled sleep, Tipper Zelda woke with a sense of impending doom. The events of last night raced through her brain which was still in a sense of denial. Just as she was about to regain her place on the world stage, that dark, demented side of her human heart—suppressed for years—was returning. She knew she could not stop her descent, even though money and prestige seemed to be appearing on the horizon for her.

She'd gone to Blues in the Night alone last night, although when Phil Heather had spotted her, he'd invited her to join his table. As always, he seemed to be accompanied by his policeman friend, Brian Sheehan. It seemed she could never get Phil alone, although that would surely change when she started dictating her memoirs to Phil. Memoirs, incidentally, she planned to fill with lies, distortions, and a total misrepresentation of her life. The story she would dictate to Phil would not be the epic of her life as it was actually lived. It would be how she would have preferred it to be lived if she'd been in complete control, which she never was.

At fno point must Phil ever learn of her dark side. She'd always been a woman who stood on the side of the right and just, championing the politically correct causes and contributing to all the right charities. She was an entertainer known to lending her talents to the proper fund-raising events. Even now, she didn't understand how forces beyond her control could take over her body and lead her to commit acts she would never even contemplate in the normal course of a day if her brain were functioning properly.

Even as a little girl, her mother had detected this dark side of her. She was the sweetest and prettiest little girl in all the world until one day she wasn't. She could not remember what had driven her when she was eight years old to take her mother's lipstick and write, "Fuck, fuck, fuck," all over the bathroom mirrors and walls. She didn't remember doing it, but she must have. Her father didn't do it, and her mother most assuredly did not. It could only have been her. When she'd written that, she wasn't even certain what fuck meant.

She'd been sent to child psychologists but they had been of no help. That's because they'd only seen the sweet side of herself. In all her sessions, the dark side never emerged. She'd managed to keep it buried from the psychologists regardless of how deeply they'd probed.

Last night at intermission, Phil and Brian had excused themselves to go backstage to congratulate Chris before he went into his second act dancing with Tango. She'd taken the opportunity to go out into the alleyway for a much-needed smoke.

Shortly before the curtain was to rise on the second act, she'd stamped out her lit cigarette onto the cobblestones and had started to walk back from the rear alleyway to the main stage door where she'd arrived so often when she had been the headliner at Blues in the Night.

Instinctively she'd stepped back into the shadows when she'd seen Danny Hansford dart out the door carrying a machete. He'd rushed to a nearby garbage bin and placed the weapon in one of the trash bags. Then he'd carefully checked his clothes in the light over the stage door, as if looking for some telltale clues. Perhaps blood. Indeed there had been what had looked like a blood stain on his shirt. He'd ripped off his shirt. To her surprise, he'd worn an identical shirt underneath the one he'd ripped off. Grabbing the soiled shirt, he'd gone back to the garbage bin and concealed it within the same trash bag as the machete.

When he'd gone back inside, Tipper's body had assumed a will of its own. It had been as if she weren't directing her own actions. She'd rushed to the trash bin and removed the soiled shirt and the machete.

At first not knowing what to do, she'd held the shirt and weapon in her hands. She'd been afraid that someone might enter the alley at any minute and catch her with it. Had Danny murdered someone? Was she standing here foolishly and recklessly holding a murder weapon?

In a few minutes she'd known what to do. She remembered that in the rear of the club was an old slave kitchen from the antebellum days in Savannah. The club had been built over the site of a once private home. In those days the kitchens were constructed away from the main building as a protection against fire. All the cooking had been done in this brick-built structure.

Over the years some of the bricks had fallen down, and the entire structure was in a state of disrepair, but kept by the city as a sort of historic relic.

Rushing to the old kitchen, she'd taken the machete and blood-soaked shirt and dropped them through loose bricks behind the fireplace and down into the murky old chimney. The police would virtually have to tear down the structure to find the murder weapon if they even thought to look here too carefully. After having done that, she'd felt she had artfully concealed the murder weapon and the blood-stained shirt.

At the stage door, she'd adjusted her gown and as she'd stepped into the hallway she'd touched up her makeup in a dimly lit mirror that had been streaked by time. She'd made her way back into the main hall of the club to see the second act.

At that point in time she didn't even know who had been murdered or if anybody had been killed. If somebody had been murdered, she'd been in a complete fog as to why she'd protected Danny Hansford from justice.

She didn't like Danny and had resented his act with Tango from the very beginning. What could her possible motive be in protecting such a little hustler who'd shown nothing but contempt for her and had contributed to her being booted out of Blues in the Night? She'd hardly owed that one any favors. Yet she'd protected him and that formed one of the mysteries of her life.

It was like all the other mysteries about herself that she didn't understand. All those murdered husbands. Had she really killed them? In the cool light of a sane day, she could honestly say she didn't remember. Even if she could remember, she knew it was The

Black Widow and not her. How could she be blamed if she didn't actually commit an act of atrocity?

If dark forces took over a human life, and compelled that person to commit evil, then the person momentarily inhabited should be absolved of all wrongdoing. That was her firm position, and she'd never seen anything wrong with maintaining that.

Rejoining Brian and Phil at table, she'd thanked Brian for his rescue of her at Myrtle Beach. She didn't dislike Brian but viewed him as a major obstacle in her relationship with Phil Heather.

All her dreams at night had told her one unmistakable truth. Phil Heather, whether he knew it or not, was the reincarnation of Montgomery Clift.

At first she'd not been certain of that. But as the hours and days had passed, she became more firmly convinced. During their collaboration on her memoirs, she knew he'd reveal himself to her. With his increasing awareness that he was actually Montgomery Clift, she just knew he'd leave Brian and those dreadful children of his and come back to her to resume the life that she and Monty had been destined to lead before the furies dictated otherwise.

Phil had been reborn to fulfill a destiny with her that Monty's tragic death had prevented happening. Monty had been meteoric and had left a fragmented life, denying at times his own identity. He was a darling guy but a tragic mess. Monty had been a lost orphan who'd turned to her. She'd been too young to know and understand him and had failed him. When he'd rejected her, she'd responded in a jealous but controlled fury, tragically leading him to his ultimate death. She'd helped ease him on down the road with his disposable syringes and all that Demerol. At least Monty had thought he was taking Demerol. Only her dark side, The Black Widow, knew what the actor was really taking. Under her "care," she'd watched his decay. If Monty could not live the existence she'd imagined for him, he had to pay.

And pay he did. Before her eyes, he'd slowly turned into a physical wreck. Although still relatively young, he was becoming an old man. His body was covered with varicose veins. He complained of constant pain, especially in his back. At times he had not been able to walk. His hyperthyroid condition had seemed to worsen by the day.

On the last day of his life, July 22, 1966, he'd refused to see her, locking himself in his bedroom in his New York brownstone. She'd learned later that he'd eaten a goose liver sandwich and had retreated for the rest of the day, until discovered dead the next morning at six.

His death might have surprised others but it hadn't come as a shock to her. She'd known it was coming. She could almost have predicted the hour. When she'd left the brownstone for the final time that morning, she'd known then she'd never see Monty again.

That is, until now. Rising to help her into her chair was the smiling Phil Heather. Even if he didn't know he was Monty, he soon would. She would guide him ever so gently back into his past life and once he'd rediscovered his true identity Phil would no longer be Phil but would be Monty.

This Monty would be different from the one before. This Monty would exist for only one reason and that was to bring her happiness. He must be made to realize that at the very beginning. If Phil didn't become aware of him, the same fate might await him that had lurked out there to snuff the life out of her former husbands.

But Phil would understand. He'd be there for her and only for her. Brian and all the others would have to go. Phil had to exist for her. His own life and aspirations weren't that important. She firmly believed that Phil had been placed on this earth for only one purpose, and that was to love her and to devote his life to her. She'd be a big star again with lots of money. He'd give her the adoration that Monty had failed to. Monty had been neurotically trapped in his own tormented life. Phil would be free of that burden and could serve her as neither Monty or any of her husbands had done.

She envisioned Phil making love to her for hours. Phil would not see the physical, aging wreck she'd become. In his eyes, she'd be in full bloom like the young girl who had captured the heart of the first Monty.

"It's taking a long time for the curtain to go up," Phil had said to her. He'd looked like he was growing increasingly impatient. "My Aunt Bice died, and I've got to get back to Darien. The funeral's in the morning."

"My God!" she'd said in astonishment. "Why are you here?"

"It was because of me that Chris Leighton is in Savannah," Phil said. "He begged us to come. I don't mean to show any disrespect for my Aunt Bice but there's not much I can do to help her now."

"I know it doesn't look right," Brian said. "I mean, our being here."

"It's fine," she said. "It'll all be over soon and you'll be back in mourning in Darien."

"If that curtain doesn't go up soon, I'm out of here," Phil said. "We've already visited Chris in his dressing room. I even ran into Tango. She's dying to play the part of Lola La Mour in my screenplay, *Butterflies in Heat.*"

"She's too young and pretty for that part," Brian interjected.

At that moment the lights had gone on on the stage, and Matt Daniels had announced the accident backstage.

In moments, Tipper had learned that Chris had been disemboweled with a huge knife. Someone had seen Tipper going into the alleyway outside for a smoke.

Later that night she'd been questioned extensively by the police. She'd firmly maintained that at no point during her cigarette break from the show did anyone enter that alleyway. She'd claimed steadfastly that she'd been alone in the alleyway during the entire time. No one, she'd said repeatedly, had come or gone from the stage door until she'd returned to table.

After her interrogation, Phil and Brian had driven her home from the police station and long after they'd kissed her good night at her front door, she still had not been able to understand why she was protecting Danny Hansford from a murder rap and even putting herself at risk. With all that she had going for herself in her reincarnated life, why would she take such a chance for a young man who held her in obvious contempt?

There was a reason, and she was certain in the days ahead that reason would become painfully clear to her.

*****

As Aunt Bice's body was lowered into the grave and the Southern Baptist pastor spoke of "dust to dust," a streak of thunder tore across the August sky. As if Aunt Bice herself were speaking from the heavens, a sudden cloudburst opened up, drenching the mourners.

Claiming his legs were bad today, Big Daddy was overseeing the burial from his old Cadillac, where he remained safely dry. But Sister

Woman and Terry Drummond got soaked as they ran toward Big Daddy's car that used to be the terror of the roads in this part of the county.

All the mourners scattered, even Lula running away with John and Henry. Only Phil remained at the graveside, accompanied by Brian. Brian had taken off his raincoat and lovingly covered Phil with it. He'd also bravely held Phil's hand in the presence of the other mourners who may or may not have noticed, and who may or may not have cared.

At the end of the ceremony, Phil, along with Brian, shook the hand of the preacher before kneeling for one final adieu at the graveside of his cherished aunt. Back in the car with Brian at the wheel, Phil cuddled in the back seat with John and Henry. Lula rode up front with Brian as he steered the car along too familiar roads on the way back to Aunt Bice's house.

Once inside, Phil and Brian changed into dry clothes. Before heading downstairs, Brian reached for Phil, holding him close. "I was there for you today. I'll be here for you always."

Phil kissed Brian passionately and held him as tight as he'd ever held him. "I let you get away once. I won't let you get away again."

Brian gave him a final tender kiss on the lips. "That's one promise I'm gonna hold you to."

They joined Lula on the back porch where she stood overlooking the torrential rain. "I found some of Aunt Bice's bourbon," she said. "What's a Southern funeral without bourbon?"

"Aunt Bice sure loved her bourbon," Phil said. "I used to sit out here with her at night listening to the cricket concerts and finishing off many a bottle with her."

"I've known Aunt Bice ever since I was a little kid," Brian said. He smiled, looking out at the downpour. "Gotta fix that drainpipe," he said as an afterthought.

His saying that reminded Phil the house was now his. Aunt Bice, the only relative he'd ever loved, was gone forever. He walked over to Brian and cradled himself in the cop's protective arms. "I'll miss her so much. She loved me regardless of who I was."

"She sounds like a fine Southern woman," Lula said. "I wish I had known her."

With his arm still around Phil, Brian looked out over the farmland. "I was just thinking. Maybe you'll keep that little townhouse in Savannah as long as the movie deal's on. But when it's finished, I think we should bring John and Henry here. It's a better place for them to grow up instead of being pulled up in some city. This place is a bit cluttered but a real home. There's farmland and everything."

"We'll have enough money now for you to quit your job and come and live here," Phil said.

"I'm for that," Brian said. "I don't get off chasing people down and giving them speeding tickets or hauling in drunk drivers."

"That sounds great, fellows," Lula said. "Except I'll be lonely and destitute missing you guys. If you go that will leave only Jason and me. Perhaps Arlie Rae looking through the window hoping to catch Jason with his jockey shorts off."

"Speaking of Jason, where is he?" Phil asked. "I didn't see him at the funeral."

"Me either," Brian said.

"Jason's run off again," she said. "He was never much for funerals even when we were growing up in Columbus. I don't know where he is. We'll probably get a call."

"Tom wasn't at the funeral either," Phil said. "I thought he might show up."

"I called him to meet us here," Brian said.

"He seems to have disappeared too," Lula said. "Oh, my God, don't tell me Tom and Jason are going to hitch up. They shared the bed with Chris Leighton. Could it be that while making love to Chris they fell in love with each other?"

"I doubt that," Phil said. "They're too similar in type."

"You know what I think?" Brian said. "I think Jason was so torn up over Chris's death that he went to a bar. Since Savannah is only a small village, and Jason's reputation as a cocksman has preceded him, I think he was picked up. He's probably in some apartment right now getting serviced."

"Perhaps," Lula said. "That's an old pattern that keeps repeating itself endlessly."

One of Aunt Bice's dearest friends, Viola Victoria Purdue, was preparing some lunch for them. She called back to Phil on the verandah. "It's Sister Woman. She wants you to come to the phone."

Excusing himself, Phil went into the kitchen and picked up the phone. Without so much as a greeting, Sister Woman said, "The wedding's at two o'clock at the Darien First Baptist Church. Terry wants you to be the best man. God knows why."

"Will Big Daddy be up on his legs long enough to give the bride away?" Phil asked.

"Big Daddy will be just fine. He just didn't want to get caught in a cloudburst at that funeral."

"We'll be there, my little darlin'. I can't believe you're getting married at last."

"That's right, faggot," Sister Woman said. "And you're doing nothing to disrupt the wedding this time. If you're getting pumped nightly by Brian Sheehan, you don't need little Terry Drummond any more. Not that my future husband is so little."

"My precious, let's don't go calling anybody else fat."

"You cocksucker!"

"Now, now," Phil said. "Let peace and harmony reign in the land. One final question. Just the other night I learned that before you started eating all those chocolates and gaining all that weight—in other words, while you were still mobile—you used to chase after my Brian. Is that true, little darlin'?"

"Hell, yes, I chased after Brian, joining every other horny woman or male cocksucker in this county. Brian has the biggest dick in a county whose men are known to have tiny meat. Who wouldn't go for those mean inches?"

"Very well put and you do have a point."

"I don't want to think about it," Sister Woman said, seemingly furious on her wedding day. "You get the prize and I end up with Terry Drummond who I don't think will be of much use to me. During your short and ill-fated affair with him, what was he? A top or a bottom?"

"A bottom."

"Oh, Gawd. That's what I thought." She cursed to the side and had seemingly stuffed something in her mouth. "Be there at two o'clock, you fucker." Sister Woman slammed down the phone.

After kissing Viola Victoria on the cheek and thanking her for preparing lunch, Phil called to John and Henry. They were in Aunt Bice's living room watching television. John was complaining. "A black and white TV?" he asked, completely puzzled.

Phil ran his fingers through the boy's hair. "My Aunt Bice was an old-fashioned woman. She liked black and white better."

Henry came up to him, giving him a kiss on the cheek. "I'm sorry your aunt died. I bet she was real nice."

"The finest aunt a guy like me could ever have."

The hours ahead passed quickly for Phil. It was like watching a movie of his own life. The wedding was a disaster. It should have been filmed.

The first horror had begun when Big Daddy's legs had given out as he was walking Sister Woman down the aisle. That giant of decaying flesh had just collapsed, falling on the floor. Phil and Brian had rushed to the rescue, and with the aid of two ushers, had managed to get Big Daddy back into his Cadillac. The stench of rotgut liquor had been strong on Big Daddy's breath.

In the meantime, Sister Woman had been left abandoned in the middle of the aisle, facing the stares and even condemnation of all the invited guests. When Phil had seen her face, he'd known at once how humiliated she was. As the wedding march resumed, he'd linked his arm with hers and had proceeded to go up the aisle with her where Terry, in an ill-fitting tuxedo, awaited them. Terry had looked like he was at the wrong party, wanting to escape as he wisely had a decade ago.

Before the ceremony could be concluded, two other disastrous events had occurred. One had been the arrival of a drunken Joyce Sheehan, who'd stormed down the aisle toward Brian. Even as the pastor had officiated at the wedding, Joyce had barged in screeching at Brian.

Escaping from the hold of the ushers, she'd run down the aisle toward Brian and her children. "I heard you were here, you faggot asshole," she'd yelled at Brian. "I've come for my kids. I won't have them raised in a queer household." She'd reached to pull Henry from his seat, but John had risen suddenly and punched her in the face, causing nosebleed.

Sitting beside Brian, Lula had reached over and offered comfort to Joyce. "Now, now," she said. "We'll handle this tangled mess later. But, first, there's a wedding." She'd led a crying and staggering Joyce from the church.

Phil had closed his eyes, not daring to look out into the congregation. When he'd opened his eyes, he'd stared into Brian's face, admiring his bravery to sit there proudly through that horrible scene with his wife.

As the wedding had resumed, Phil had looked out over the audience, fearing perhaps that someone might be ready to throw rotten tomatoes. To his horror, he'd spotted Jerry Wheeler, his producer from New York, entering the back of the church. He'd been accompanied by Arlie Rae Minton.

With a face as grim as Terry's, Phil had managed to survive the rest of the wedding. Even though it'd been a short ceremony, it had seemed to drag out forever.

He'd stood with Brian watching as Sister Woman and Terry had gotten into the back of the honeymoon station wagon that was going to take them to Orlando for a real Disney good time. Phil had tried to ignore Jerry's pleadings to show him how much progress had been made on the screenplay, *Butterflies in Heat*. What he had been unable to convey to Jerry at that time was that he did not have one acceptable page of that script committed to paper.

He'd deal with Jerry later. Right now a comment that Sister Woman had made to him kept ringing in his ear. Before getting into the back seat with Terry, she'd whispered something to him.

"I tricked you cocksuckers," the bride had said. "It's not going to be a marriage in name only. I'm going to make Terry fuck me nine times before the cock crows."

Phil had looked with dismay at Terry's face. As Sister Woman had managed to squeeze her corpulent body into the back seat with Terry, he'd looked back at Phil in desperation as if he could manage to rescue him from this clutching, devouring woman as he'd done a decade ago. But the passing ten years had been a long time. Phil had turned from the sight of Terry as he'd walked back to Brian's car.

Back at Aunt Bice's house, the wake had gone smoothly as he greeted each and every one of his dead relative's friends and thanked them for coming to show their respects. Although all of the guests had attended the wedding, no one spoke of it. It was a marriage that never happened, as far as the other guests seemed concerned.

When Phil had managed to get Jerry drunk, the producer had stopped pestering him to produce copies of the screenplay.

The only disturbance came when two policemen friends of Brian's extracted Arlie Rae from the downstairs bathroom. One of the cops had caught Arlie Rae hiding behind the shower curtains where he could spy on people, both men and women, using the toilet.

Viola Victoria had graciously taken Arlie Rae to the back porch where she offered him some potato salad and Southern fried chicken.

Looking everywhere for Brian, Phil found him on the front porch. He came out onto the porch just as Jerry was offering Brian the lead role of the hustler, Numie, in *Butterflies in Heat.*

\*\*\*\*\*

It was her first chance to talk to a bigtime Hollywood producer like Jerry Wheeler, and Lula Carson zeroed in on the inebriated arrival who released his clutches on Brian only when Phil called for Brian to come and help him with something.

Rushing to replenish Jerry's drink, Lula sat down beside him. Jerry looked disappointed that Brian had mysteriously vanished. "I'm Lula Carson," she said. "I can't rightly say we've met before, although I assure you the pleasure is all mine."

"Hello," Jerry said a little informally. "You sound Southern."

"I am," Lula said proudly, although on second thought she didn't really feel that being born Southern bestowed any special gifts on one, except for mendacity and exaggeration. "Born and raised in Columbus, Georgia."

"There's only one thing I like about the South," Jerry said.

"What might that be?" she asked, urging him to taste from the replenished drink she'd offered.

"Incest."

She looked startled. "Incest? My, oh, my."

"I'm a great believer in incest," Jerry said. "My daddy had a ten-inch dick and a gay son."

She looked at him again in disbelief until deciding he was only joking to test the limits of her tolerance. "Although I have never pursued it myself, I'm a great believer in incest myself. It brings a family closer together." She smiled as she looked at him. Now he appeared startled. "In fact, incest plays a large part in this literary masterpiece I'm struggling with. It's called *The Tireless Hunter.* "

"What's it about?

"It's about the way of twisted love of the human heart. Twisted love. Twisted bodies."

"Sounds like a great story," he said with a slight condescension in his voice.

"It's my masterpiece," she said. "I'm sure it'll bring me fame and fortune."

"Can I see a copy of it?"

"As soon as it's finished," she promised. "Perhaps I'll sell you the film rights."

"Who do you see in the cast?"

"All unknowns. I don't write parts for stars. I write only for real people. People who actually have hearts even if sometimes those hearts don't always beat in the right places."

"I'm thinking about using only unknown actors for my film, *Butterflies in Heat*. Phil, as you know, is doing the screenplay. I'm in Savannah scouting not only for locations but for supremely talented natural actors."

"That I can see," Lula said. "I didn't mean to eavesdrop but I heard you offering the part to Brian. Of course, he's superb for the role. Just the right age, and, as I'm sure you noted, he fills out his clothes just right."

"When he sat down—right in the same chair where you're seated—and his pants bunched up around his crotch, it looked like meat for the poor."

"I hear Brian is very well endowed as are several other men in Savannah. Not all of our men but a few. Each in his own way is quite celebrated in Savannah for their endowments. Not that I personally care about such things."

"Other than making movies, it is all I care about," he said.

"You must have fun casting a part."

"The most fun in the world. But never as much fun as casting *Butterflies in Heat*, especially the role of Numie, the..."

"I know," she said, interrupting him. "The well-endowed hustler." Now, of course, you've promised the part to Brian, and the search is over."

"Hardly. To date, I've promised at least two dozen boys in Hollywood and another two dozen in New York the role. Producer's right, you know. Even though the casting couch ain't what it used to be back in Zanuck's day, I still believe in it."

"I'm not so sure I believe in a human being prostituting oneself to get a part in a mere movie."

"I don't believe in it either, but as long as it's done, I'm taking full advantage of the system. I've always believed in taking full advantage of every opportunity that comes my way." He paused reflectively. "Even some chances that don't come my way."

"Mr. Wheeler, I am honored to meet you, and I have a feeling you're going to be just the right producer for *The Tireless Hunter.*"

As the rain stopped and the clouds parted slightly, a golden streak of sunlight cut through the sky, illuminating Jerry's face. She thought he was a very handsome man, blond like Brian and Jason and very well built, more of a swimmer's body than a Stallone. He looked amazingly like Tab Hunter in the Fifties at the time he was dating Tony Perkins. She was going to comment on the likeness to Tab Hunter, but decided against it. She doubted if Jerry or anybody else for that matter knew who Tab Hunter was any more.

As she sat silently watching the sun stream across Aunt Bice's fields, she felt a warm feeling for Jerry. They were so different yet she felt a strange bond with him as if she understood him, even though he probably stood for all the glitter and artificiality in the world she despised.

"You're not kidding me," he finally said. "*The Tireless Hunter* is really good?"

She took his hand in hers and pressed it against her breast. "It's really good," she said, reaching over and kissing him tenderly on the cheek.

He looked off reflectively into the fields. She wondered how many cow pastures he'd ever seen. "But, first things first," he said. "I've got to find the right actors for *Butterflies in Heat.*"

"I know the novel very, very well," she said, "and I can assure you that every part in the film can be played by some of our great talent already living in Savannah. They come cheap too."

"That's wonderful news to my jaded ears," he said.

"You've already found your Numie in Brian."

A frown crossed Jerry's face. "Trouble is, I just promised the role to a big blond hunk this morning."

"Oh," she said with growing alarm.

"Brian's hot and I bet he has big meat but this hunk I met is not only good looking, he has my daddy beat, and I used to think dear old dad had the world's biggest dick. I don't think that anymore. Not after getting banged by this guy. When he got it all the way in, I thought the damn thing was coming out my throat."

"I know the feeling well," she said, sighing.

"You've had one that big too?" he asked, his eyes lighting up.

"I'm married to a guy like that. His name is Jason McReeves."

"Isn't that a coincidence?" Jerry said. "The guy asleep in my motel room is also named Jason McReeves."

She sighed again, downing the rest of her drink and needing a restocking of bourbon in her glass at once. "I'm sure there must exist a number of Jason McReeve types in the South with that very same name. But it would be rare indeed to find one who is blond and with a twelve-inch dick too."

Jerry slammed down his glass. "Oh, shit! Oh, fuck! Oh, no!"

She patted his hand. "Don't worry about it. It happens all the time. It's okay. Jason and I have an open marriage. An understanding about such things."

"I feel like I've just been invited to the Queen's garden party at Buckingham Palace, and just as I was bowing low I let out this great big fart."

"It's not quite that bad. If there's a size queen hitting Savannah, Jason has inner radar. Can track them down in two seconds."

"Just like he did me. The moment I hit town, Jason was coming on to me like gangbusters."

She got up on wobbly feet. "Let's slip away from this confusing and depressing event. Frankly we don't know whether we're mourning the death of Aunt Bice or whether we're celebrating the wedding of Sister Woman and Terry Drummond. Take me to Jason. I bet he's drunk. We'll sober him up and maybe you'll help me get him back home."

At Jerry's motel, where clothes and sheets were scattered all around the room, along with soiled towels, Lula took in the golden body of Jason as he lay completely nude on the top of the bed. All sheets and blankets had been kicked off.

In silence she stood with Jerry taking in the sight of this magnificent specimen, as she had done so many times before in so many other motel rooms.

"The guy's not to be believed," Jerry said. "Unlike many guys with big dicks, Jason has a pair of balls to go with it."

"That he does," Lula said with a resigned weariness as she went over to wake up Jason.

She gently shook him as he awoke from a deep sleep after a morning of passion. "It's time to go home, dear," she whispered in his ear, gently kissing his forehead like a loving mother.

"Lula," he said, sitting up in bed. He wiped his eyes and looked around the room. "Jerry."

"I hope you guys had a good time," Lula said, searching for her husband's blue jeans. "But the maid's outside waiting to clean up the room." She surveyed the mess. "And does it ever need it."

"I'm sorry," Jason said, rolling over and heading for the bathroom. "It won't happen again," he promised.

"Yeah, right," she said.

"It's just that Jerry was so God damn attractive, and he did promise me the lead in his new movie, and I know how we're always needing money and..."

She cut him off. "Get in that shower and be quick about it."

"Thanks," Jerry called after him as he shut the door. "You do know how to show a guy a good time, but I won't be able to walk for a week."

On the way back to Savannah to drop Jason off, Jerry looked over in the back seat. A fully clothed Jason had fallen asleep. Jerry smiled at Lula. "You know what, sister?"

"What's up?" Lula asked.

"We've shared our first man together." He winked at her. "I know it won't be our last."

*****

Lula Carson kept her promise although Tango never believed she would. When the call first came in from Lula, Tango had been despondent. Duke had found the money she'd hidden in the empty sugar bowl in the kitchen and had disappeared. He'd been gone all night and she was nearly hysterical.

She'd rushed for the phone, thinking it was Duke calling. Perhaps he'd had an accident. Surely he would have come home last night if something bad hadn't happened to him. After all, he was her daddy and he loved her above all others.

"It's Lula Carson," said the light voice on the other end. "I'm here with Jerry Wheeler. You're in luck. He's casting unknowns in *Butterflies in Heat*."

"Can you get me an audition? Let me meet Jerry. I'm sure he'll be impressed with my beauty and my looks."

"I'm sure he will, my dear," she said. "Sorry I couldn't give you much notice, but he's ready to meet you now."

"My gawd, I'm not ready," she said.

"It's a bit complicated. Jerry is set on casting Phil Heather's father, Big Daddy, in the role of the Commodore in the book. I'm sure you know who the Commodore is in the novel."

"Yeah," Tango said a bit skeptically. "I only read about him 'cause he's in all of my scenes. He's my lovin' Sugar Daddy even though he's old and repulsive."

"We're driving up to Big Daddy's plantation a few miles from Darien," Lula said. "Jerry wants you to ride with us and meet Big Daddy. He wants to see how the two of you react together. To see if there is any chemistry there."

"You've got yourself a nigger bitch," Tango said gleefully. "Give me thirty minutes before you come by. Just ring the bell downstairs. What will emerge on those steps is the one and only Lola La Mour, the real star of *Butterflies in Heat*." She put down the phone.

In half an hour, Jerry's car pulled up in front of her apartment house. Tango still had seen no sign of Duke. Dressed as Lola La Mour, she raced down the steps, nearly tripping on her red high heels, real Joan Crawford "fuck me" shoes.

She was astonished at how handsome Jerry Wheeler was, as he got out of the car. He looked just like Tab Hunter did in the Fifties. Tango's first reaction was that Jerry would be a natural to be cast as the fading blond actor if any producer wanted to make *The Tab Hunter Story*.

"Fuck!" Jerry said as way of any greeting. "Just as David O. Selznick realized he'd found his Scarlett O'Hara when he met her against the movie set where Atlanta was in flames, I realize I've met my Lola La Mour."

"Hot damn!" she said. "I don't need movie flames. I'm a gal who turns men into burning bushes right in front of me."

"You're one hot pussy—that's for sure!"

"More woman than any man can handle," she said, pursing her lips provocatively. "Although, big boy, you look like you could handle what I've got to offer."

Jerry backed away. "Count me out. I'm a strict bottom. I like big dick up my ass."

She looked up at him skeptically. "Is there any fool left in the world who doesn't?" She smiled at him, licking her red lipstick. "If you're not going to be my top, we'll be sisters then. Okay?"

"It's a deal," he said, helping her into the back seat.

"Afternoon, Lola," Lula said. "Or is it Tango?"

"Whatever time it is, baby, all of our clocks are ticking, and I've waited long enough to become a bigtime movie star," Tango said. "*Midnight* didn't do anything for The Lady Chablis. I haven't exactly heard of any Oscar-winning performances she's made since. But *Butterflies in Heat* is going to get me an Oscar. I can feel it in my bones. I can wrap my twat around that black pussy role better than any other bitch in Georgia or the entire fucking South for that matter."

"You are a formidable woman," Lula said. "I can well understand why my husband was attracted to you." As Jerry got back into the car, she reached over and touched his arm. "You, too, Jerry."

"Christ, does that mean you've had Jason McReeves too?" Tango asked.

"I'm guilty," Jerry said, starting the car. "It's a miracle I can even sit behind the wheel of this car. I should be in the hospital."

"You can say that again!" Tango cried out from the back seat.

"Both of you may have possessed Jason's body," Lula said, a bit defensively, "but only I have known his heart and soul."

"Honeychild," Tango said, "you can take that heart and soul and shove it where the sun don't shine. Give me those twelve inches any day."

The rest of the ride to Big Daddy's plantation was mostly in silence. Lula had arranged with Phil to set up a rendezvous with Big Daddy who would be at the Heather mansion alone now that Sister Woman was off trying to seduce poor Terry Drummond.

At first Phil had been astonished at Jerry's casting idea. "Hell, it might work," Phil had said. "The part was originally thought of for Orson Welles. But that was long, long ago. Nobody in Georgia looks more like the Commodore than my Big Daddy."

As Jerry's car pulled into the driveway, Tango said, "I'm dying to meet this Big Daddy. Anybody named Big Daddy is a friend of mine. Of course, I have my own Big Daddy waiting for me back at the apartment. He could play the role of Numie. Gawd knows, my Daddy has all the equipment."

"I'd like to meet him," Jerry said, his interest sparking. "Hell, does every man in Savannah have a big dick?"

"Apparently not," Lula said, smiling. "At least five of them do. That includes my Jason, Brian Sheehan, Danny Hansford, and one or two others. Otherwise, it's deprivation time for some."

Big Daddy was sitting in his usual spot on the front veranda sipping either Southern Comfort or rotgut bourbon. At this point it was entirely possible that Big Daddy didn't know what he was drinking. It appeared that both a funeral and a wedding on the same day had taken its toll on Big Daddy."

Before meeting Big Daddy, Tango wanted to repair her makeup and adjust her dress after the car ride, and Lula wanted to use the toilet.

Jerry walked over and reached out to shake Big Daddy's hand. "Hi, I'm a friend of Phil's. He's a great guy. You should be proud of him. Real talent."

"What kind of talent?" Big Daddy asked, eying Jerry as if he were a glowing lunar rock just deposited fresh from somewhere in the solar system and just newly landed on the front porch.

"Talent as a writer. He's really good. I wanted the best for *Butterflies in Heat.*"

Big Daddy snorted. "You look like a butterfly in heat yourself."

"I'll take that as a compliment," Jerry said proudly. "I've always been up front about who I am. I'm a faggot, queer, cocksucker. I take men's cocks up my ass and in general show them a good time."

Big Daddy looked flabbergasted. "I thought I'd seen it all but I've never heard a man talk like that before in all my born days."

"Get used to it," Jerry said. "We're queer and we're here to stay. No more hiding in closets."

"There isn't a closet big enough to hold you—that's for sure."

"Thank you," Jerry said. "You did mean that as a compliment."

"I don't know what I mean no more," Big Daddy said. "All this queer stuff is getting to me. At the same time I'm beginning to relax about it. I've been watching some TV shows. I think the whole fucking world's going queer, and if I want to stay in this world and be a part of it I'd better start engaging in some queer stuff myself.

Trouble is, at my age I don't know how to go about it. Not too many cocksuckers have been hitting on me lately."

"The first thing you can do is let us run a test on you as the Commodore in *Butterflies in Heat,"* Jerry said.

"Yeah, Phil told me something about it and explained the role to me. Seems odd casting me as a faggot."

"The Commodore isn't exactly a faggot," Jerry said. "He's a moral degenerate. He'll fuck anything that moves. That doesn't make him a faggot. A pervert certainly, but not a faggot. Actually, he was quite a man, even a whoremonger, in his day, but his day is fading as he's getting older and more desperate."

"Now that's a part I can relate to," Big Daddy said. "Except I don't understand perversion."

Jerry moved closer to Big Daddy, until his eyes were only inches from the old man's face. Jerry bent over Big Daddy's chair as if he were staring him down. "Don't kid a kidder. When the roll call is sounded in hell, and they ask for the biggest pervert in the State of Georgia to step forward, guess who that is going to be?"

Big Daddy breathed heavily for a moment before saying anything. Then he sighed, as if giving in to Jerry. "You got me, boy. There have been things I've done, especially when I was younger, that I'm not exactly proud of, but I've done them nevertheless. There are things I've done that will send me directly to hell once my heart stops beating. Things so horrible that I lie awake at night trying to convince myself that I didn't do them in the first place. That I only imagined them."

Still not moving away from Big Daddy's face, Jerry said, "I know, I know. I knew the first time I saw you today. I knew I could go to central casting and try to get some dumb actor to play one of the most degenerate characters in modern literature, or I knew I could go directly to you and confront you eye to eye and ask you to play the role you were born to play."

"You fucking little cocksucker you," Big Daddy said, still breathing heavily. "I can see those pink lips of yours right now. I can smell that sweet candy breath of yours. If I got that God damn tongue of yours in my fucking mouth, I'd suck on it for an hour before letting it go. Then I'd demand that it be stuck up my asshole to do its dirty work for another hour. Then I'd fuck you all night. Cum three times in you and still not pull out."

Fresh from using the bathroom inside, Lula and Tango emerged on Big Daddy's veranda, just as Jerry removed his face from Big Daddy's and backed away. "Let me introduce Lula Carson," Jerry said. "Except for your son, she's the best writer in the modern South."

"I'm working on my masterpiece," Lula said. "It's called *The Tireless Hunter*. It will bring me fame and fortune. I'll send you one of the first copies."

"I never wasted time reading books," Big Daddy said. "I was always a man of action. Books will be written about me."

"I'm sure they will, and even as we meet I am already envisioning working you into *The Tireless Hunter*," Lula said. "You look like a refugee left from a fading and dying South. A male Blanche Du Bois. Even the character of the fictional Big Daddy in Tennessee Williams's *Cat on a Hot Tin Roof.*"

"I don't know whether to grab you and feel your tits," Big Daddy said, "or be insulted."

Lula stepped back, as if fearing that Big Daddy might suddenly heave himself from his chair. "This is Tango," she said awkwardly.

"Correction, please!" Tango butted in. "The one and only Lola La Mour."

"My Gawd," Big Daddy said, motioning for Lula to stand aside so his tired old eyes could take in the full impact of Lola La Mour.

Tango smiled demurely and even petulantly at Big Daddy, even though she felt he was the single most repulsive man she'd ever encountered.

"If there's one thing I can smell a mile away it's nigger poontang," Big Daddy said. "It was always my favorite thing on earth. I fucked white women but it was always a mercy fuck. It was poontang I craved back then and poontang I crave now. The younger the better."

"What you see is what you get," Tango said, hand on her hip. Before she knew what was happening, Big Daddy had reached out for her and pulled her down on his lap. His bourbon-sour tongue explored her tonsils, and his left paw attacked her silicone breasts.

"We've found our Lola La Mour and our Commodore," Jerry said to Lula.

Tango did not break away. She felt she was already auditioning for the part, and she gave herself over to Big Daddy in every way she could. Not even Duke Edwards himself was going to get to devour this much of her.

"You feel it getting hard, bitch," Big Daddy called out to her as he came up for air. "It ain't been hard in years but it's getting hard for nigger cunt." His hand went to her pants where he felt around for a moment. "That's the biggest clit I've ever felt on a nigger woman, and I've felt clits that protrude out so much they are like little cocks. That really turns me on." He kept fondling Tango who squealed in delight. "When I get my mouth on a clit that big, I'm not coming up for air until they tell me it's the Fourth of July."

"Let's excuse ourselves and go for a walk in the meadow," Lula said to Jerry who readily agreed.

After they'd gone, Big Daddy was breathing so heavily Tango felt he might expire. "You've got to help me inside. We can't do it on the front porch, and I don't know how long this hard-on of mine is going to last, bitch."

"C'mon and get it, honey," Tango said to Big Daddy as she jumped up and with surprising strength helped ease his body out of the peacock chair where she managed to propel him to the front door and into his house. Seeing a sleeping parlor off the main living room, she steered him to that bed, feeling time was wasting and she might not be able to get him to the master bedroom.

She was about to have sex with the world's fattest and most repulsive man, and that was exactly what the script called for. She actually welcomed the upcoming deflowering by Big Daddy, knowing it would toughen her character and make her play the part of Lola La Mour even better, having so recently lived it.

She'd heard lots of stories about how Marilyn had become a star. "If Marilyn can do it, so can Tango," she said to herself. She knew she'd have to get on top of Big Daddy and not the other way around. Otherwise he could crush her.

"Make it work, God," she whispered to herself, hoping their plumbing would connect in some real and vital way and that she'd bring him the sexual satisfaction obviously denied to him for so long. If he could achieve orgasm today, she knew it would no doubt be his last.

As for her, she'd do anything to become a star. Regrettably she opened her eyes as Big Daddy was dropping his pants and pulling down his soiled underwear. She decided to close her eyes for the rest of the act that would transpire between the two of them.

With her eyes closed, she could imagine and dream and make love with abandon. No white man could take her dreams and fantasies from her, and she would rely on all of them to get her through the upcoming hour. It would be a cleansing moment of truth for her, and she was the gal to pull it off.

*****

Lavender Morgan kissed Brian on the cheek as she was shown into Aunt Bice's small library to meet privately with Phil. She was filled with excuses as to why she couldn't make it to the funeral. She claimed that she'd gotten lost since she was without a driver, and Danny Hansford had mysteriously disappeared. The actual truth was that she couldn't abide to go to anybody's funeral.

After Kennedy died, she'd never appeared at funerals even when her presence was almost dictated. Throughout her life she'd always managed to summon up the flu on demand. Whenever it was mandated that she attend a funeral, she became violently ill and couldn't get out of bed, sending flowers and her condolences instead.

She kissed Phil tenderly and offered her heartfelt sympathy to him, as she knew he was genuinely in pain and suffering over the loss of his favorite aunt.

"The loss is not quite the same," he said. "There will never be another Aunt Bice. But I was so sorry to hear about your paintings. I was told that each and every one of those paintings was like a child to you."

"They were," she said, as tears welled in her eyes. "In my heart I just know I'll never get them back. God only knows where they'll end up. Probably one of them will surface in some auction house thirty years from now, and my estate will move to reclaim it. As for me, I won't be there. I'll be resting peacefully with Aunt Bice."

"You've got many good years left. You know that." He guided her into Aunt Bice's favorite chair where she always read her magazines to keep up with what was going on in the world.

"I know this is an awkward time to ask you to see me privately," Lavender said. "But Aunt Bice, right before she died, made me promise to tell you something."

"Oh, God," he said, "I don't know if I want to hear this."

"You must listen, my dear. It's for your own good. All of Gin Tucker's crowd knows that Jay Garon is in New York hustling Tipper's memoirs for big dollars, and that you've agreed to write them after you've finished *Butterflies in Heat.*"

"It's hardly a secret."

"Aunt Bice fears that you're getting into a trap and she didn't want you to get involved with Tipper and her memoirs."

"Why didn't Aunt Bice speak to me about this herself?"

"She felt that you were a Heather and a stubborn one at that, and that if she told you not to, you'd go ahead and do it anyway."

"She's right about that. We Heathers are a determined lot. We are rarely known for listening to advice regardless of how well meaning."

"Your aunt knew that. She's always known that I was in the house with Tipper the night Taylor Zachory was murdered."

"You say murdered. Not a suicide?"

"No one can be absolutely certain what happened that awful night. Only Tipper knows the truth. Tipper and Peter Paul."

"Peter was Zachory's companion, wasn't he? Friends since boyhood."

"One and the same. One can only speculate about the depth of that relationship. It was so close that Taylor took Peter on his honeymoon. He occupied a spare room in the bridal suite."

"That's pretty close," Phil said.

"Before you get sucked into Tipper's fantasies about her life, you must know that she is a notorious liar. I've known her for decades. The story of what happened to her always changes every day. In the seventies she had a different version from what she was saying in the eighties."

"Not a good subject for biography, is it?"

"Exactly and that's why your Aunt Bice didn't want you to become Tipper's ghost writer. Bice felt you could embarrass yourself in the publishing world and that your career as an author would be seriously damaged. Tipper would sucker you into writing a bogus biography. Trust me on this."

"I think you may be right. I've already talked to Brian. All on my own, before you even said anything, I've been seriously questioning if I want to get involved with Tipper. I don't feel comfortable around her. We're definitely not compatible. Deep down I think she suspects I'm the reincarnation of Monty Clift, and that whatever she had with him—and God only knows what those two sickies were up to—she wants to recapture with me. That is out of the question, of course."

"If I were you, I'd go to Tipper and tell her that you're not the guy for the job. I'd call Jay Garon and tell him to find another writer. Get John Grisham."

"I think I will. I just don't have the heart for it. I'm going to be tied up for several months with *Butterflies in Heat.* After that, I need to get this place in shape. Brian and I may move the kids in here. I may take a few months off from writing and get my new life in order. I've got to deal with Big Daddy, too. I'm back trying to claim my rightful place at Tara and that's going to take some fancy footwork."

He went over and poured Lavender Aunt Bice's favorite brandy and handed it to her without even asking if she wanted it. He just knew she did.

She accepted it gracefully. "Before I leave, I'm going to do something I haven't done in years. As a tribute to Aunt Bice, I'm going to break decades of silence and tell you what I know about what happened that night Taylor was killed."

"Because I'm so intimately involved at this point, I would really like to hear it," he said.

"Over the years I've jokingly referred to Tipper as a murderess at cocktail parties. But I always left open the possibility I was joking."

"But what you're about to tell me now is no joke, right?" he said.

"No joke at all," she said. "Peter Paul was only nineteen years old at the time Taylor was killed. Taylor wasn't much older himself. Peter and I had been drinking a lot on the day of Taylor's murder. But Taylor hadn't joined us. There was so much tension between Tipper and Taylor that each of them stayed in their bedrooms. Although not married very long, it was understood from the beginning they would have separate bedrooms."

"Do you think Peter was in love with Taylor?"

"I've always thought that. He was a very petulant boy. Very jealous. He even selected what underwear Taylor was going to wear on any given day."

"That's a real valet."

"The night of the murder there was a big party at the tobacco mansion. Mostly relatives and friends of Taylor's. Tipper didn't know many people in the Deep South and that's why she'd invited me as a house guest. Out of sheer boredom. Wanting someone who could talk her own language."

"That's one party I would love to have attended."

"It was some party all right. Everybody getting drunk, especially Tipper and Peter. Yes, and Lavender Morgan herself. Taylor didn't drink much. He seemed to be sipping from the same cocktail all evening."

"Could you sense the hostility between Tipper and Taylor?"

"Even though drunk, anybody could. In the early evening Tipper had been the life of the party. She'd come downstairs in red satin lounging pajamas. She'd been vivacious and had even sung two of her biggest hits for the guests. As the night wore on, Tipper got drunker and drunker. She is the only one in the world who can drink more than me. But about ten o'clock she mysteriously disappeared. She would not reappear until in the early hours of morning when all the guests were gone."

"From what I've read, no one ever figured out where she'd gone. She still claims to have no memory of that evening."

"That's her claim all right. Shortly before midnight I was fed up with all the rednecks Taylor had invited, and excused myself and went to bed. After all, the hostess herself had departed from her own party. About half an hour later I came down to the kitchen to warm me up some hot milk because I felt I needed a coating on my stomach after drinking so much hard liquor."

"Had Tipper come back?"

"I don't know. I never saw her. But I looked into the library where I heard voices. I was going to join Peter and Taylor until I witnessed something strange going on. Neither man ever seemed aware of my presence. For some reason Taylor was ordering Peter to strip, although the young man was allowed to retain his underwear. I spied on them—I know I shouldn't have—as a drunken Peter got up in front of Taylor and stripped down to his briefs. I remember his briefs were so sheer that his genitals were clearly outlined and on view for Taylor's inspection. I felt this was some strange ritual going on between them. It was designed to humiliate Peter and show Taylor's dominance over him. I knew at once that stuff like this must have been going on for years."

"Did you manage to slip away without being detected?"

"I did. As I was leaving, Taylor was ordering Peter to sit across from him and spread his legs in a lotus position."

"My God, this should be Jerry Wheeler's next movie."

"After going back to my bedroom, I was awakened around one o'clock by what sounded like a boisterous Peter and Taylor going past my door and into the master bedroom. Taylor slept in the master bedroom. Tipper's bedroom was down the hall. After they'd gone past, I opened my door into the darkened hallway. There was just enough light for me to see Taylor, still fully clothed, enter the master bedroom. Peter followed him in. Except this time Peter was completely nude, having lost his briefs somewhere along the way."

"It doesn't appear they were going into that room to read Bible verses."

"I'd always known that Taylor was a closet case. Is Tipper capable of marrying any other kind? Peter was an extremely beautiful boy. Much handsomer than Taylor. Taylor treated Peter with great cruelty and always liked to humiliate him, especially in the presence of other guests. When I returned to bed, I could only imagine what was going on in that master bedroom."

"S&M?"

"A whole lot, I'm sure. I think I drifted off to sleep again, and when I woke up at least an hour had passed. I heard Tipper from the hallway screaming at Taylor in the master bedroom. I don't know if Peter was still in there or not. Tipper was calling him faggot and cocksucker, lovely terms of endearment. I've always believed that Tipper returned from her mysterious disappearance and found Taylor fucking Peter."

"What happened next?"

"I'm not quite sure. I didn't hear Taylor at all. Tipper went screeching down the corridor to her own bedroom and then there was silence. I almost decided to stay up the rest of the night, fearing I wasn't going to get much sleep. But I was still slightly drunk and I fell asleep once again. At 3:45am—I'll always remember the time exactly—I was awakened once more with what sounded like a gunshot. That was followed by the sound of Tipper screaming. I jumped out of bed and reached for my lavender robe. All I could hear at that point was Tipper calling for Peter."

"You decided to come to the rescue?"

"Of course. I raced down the hall. I saw Tipper standing in the hall outside the master bathroom. Taylor had to go out into the corridor to get to his bathroom. The bath couldn't be entered from the master suite. When Tipper saw me, she called out, "Taylor has shot himself.""

"At that point you didn't know if Taylor were dead or alive.""

"Tipper didn't make that clear, only that Taylor had shot himself. I rushed into the master bedroom where I found Peter lying there almost in a state of shock. He was still naked. I looked for Taylor's body but saw nothing. I asked Peter what had happened. I wanted to get to Taylor. But he looked at me with a blank gaze. He said nothing. The kid didn't even seem to know who I was at that point.""

"Then what?""

"I went back to the corridor where a shell-shocked Tipper was still standing outside the door to the bathroom. For the first time I noticed blood on her peach-colored gown. Darting past her, even though she tried to restrain me, I went into the bathroom. I remember it was covered with white tiles. But some of those tiles were blood red. When I looked into this gigantic bathtub, Taylor was lying face down in a pool of blood. I didn't see a gun anywhere. I rushed to his side and turned him over. Half of his face looked shot off. I'm no doctor but I knew he was dead. When I got up, Tipper was standing before me. She no longer appeared shell-shocked. If anything she was in complete control. She ordered me back to my bedroom. She told me she could handle this herself, and I was to tell the police that I'd slept through the whole thing.""

"You agreed to that?""

"I did. On looking back, I know I shouldn't have. But I did.""

"What about Peter?""

"He suddenly emerged from the master bedroom. Since his own clothes were in a different part of the house, he'd dressed in one of Taylor's business suits. It didn't fit. In spite of the gruesome circumstances, he looked a bit like a clown. I did as I was told. I retreated to my room where the police knocked on my door three hours later.""

"In other words three hours went by before the police were summoned. No one called an ambulance?""

"Obviously not and that's all I know. Tipper and I have never spoken of it again even though we've known each other for decades.

Her official position at the coroner's inquest was that she didn't remember a thing. I've never believed that. Any woman in that much control—moving a body and mopping up blood—would remember every detail."

I know the story from now on," Phil said. "I've read the newspaper accounts, and everything about her recollections appears tainted."

"Hell, yes! Taylor's body was dragged to a sun porch. This is where Tipper claimed she found him—not in the bathroom. Why they dragged his body there I don't know. Someone, probably Peter, mopped the blood up from the bathroom but wasn't that thorough. The police still found blood on the white tiles."

"One thing I never understood was that when the police found Zachory's body there was no gun," he said. "A shooting suicide with no gun?"

"The case has a million contradictions like that, and would indeed take a movie or a book to explain it more fully. The sun porch was completely searched for a weapon. The police could find nothing. About three hours later, long after the body had been removed, the sheriff came back onto the sun porch and noticed the gun lying in the middle of the floor on a carpet. It was about eighteen feet from where Taylor's body was discovered shot."

"It would have been impossible to have overlooked the gun after a thorough search," he said.

"By all means. Someone obviously placed the gun there. But who? There were a zillion other problems with the cover-up story by Peter and Tipper. I thought both of them were going to go to the electric chair. The police didn't even find the bullet that exited through Taylor's head. Imagine not even finding the bullet although they searched everything with a fine tooth comb."

"From everything I read, it was murder, and that was the biggest hurdle I was going to face in writing Tipper's memoirs."

"It was murder. But the tantalizing question is how they got away with it. The answer was always obvious to me. The Zachory family was one of the most important in North Carolina. Real tobacco barons. A great deal of the state's economy depended on them. For some reason, they didn't want Tipper and Peter prosecuted."

"Did you know any reason why? You'd think they'd want revenge."

"I think it was more complicated than that. The Zachory family were the biggest homophobes in the world. Taylor's death was scandal enough. They didn't need a courtroom hearing evidence that their favorite son was a homosexual involved with a nineteen-year-old boy. There were many other reasons too. The family also learned that Taylor had never put Tipper in his will and all his millions were going to go to his younger brother. I think that cinched the decision for the Zachory family. Taylor was dead. They couldn't bring him back. But they could keep the bitch from getting his millions. Case closed."

"And so it was. But it remains a tantalizing mystery."

"One that your Aunt Bice didn't want you to get involved in."

"I'm not. I'm going to set up a meeting with Tipper and tell her the deal is off. She won't be needing the money any more. She's going to be making big bucks on a number of deals, I'm sure. So the wolf won't be knocking at her door."

At the door Lavender kissed him good-bye and promised to be in touch real soon. "I loved your Aunt Bice," she said, reaching for his hand.

"I loved her too. I'll miss her something awful."

"Like me, she was a lusty old broad. But our days are numbered. She went before me. I'm next."

"You're still carrying on. That Danny Hansford. That's one hot little streak of sex."

"He is and I'm ashamed of myself for it. It's my last fling. I figured I might as well enjoy it." A sudden fear come over her.

"What's the matter?"

"With Danny Hansford, I fear there is going to be an awful price to pay. I'll not get out of this affair very gracefully and without tremendous costs. It's not just the money. Not just the stolen paintings."

"You don't think Danny had anything to do with that?"

"I think plenty," she said, reaching for the doorknob. "But I've told you too much already. If I'm not careful you'll be writing my memoirs."

"Now that's a writing job I'd really go for."

She smiled at him. "Some day. If you think Tipper has a hot story, wait till you hear my tall tales."

"I bet your revelations would make headlines around the world."

"You're right about that. One night in Washington in 1963 I personally altered the course of history, but that's another bedtime story." Lavender blew him a kiss before heading out the door into the stifling heat and humidity of an August afternoon in a world without Aunt Bice.

*****

Totally nude and completely exhausted, Danny lay in the king-size bed Steve Parker had arranged for him in an Atlanta hotel. He didn't know where Tom Caldwell was. They weren't supposed to meet for another two hours.

Danny would need all this time to recover from the two-hour ordeal and sex marathon he'd just been through with the Japanese businessmen. Steve had taken the unprocessed film that recorded the event to a photo lab. There, it would be developed and multiple reproductions would be sent to happy family-value homes in or near Tokyo. Copies of the film would be surreptitiously watched, probably again and again, by each of the Japanese men who had devoured him

Before meeting with Tom, Danny needed sleep to recover from all the energy spent. He tossed and turned in his bed with its rumpled sheets. He couldn't escape from the memory of those devouring mouths.

A cameraman had recorded every lascivious move of the Japanese men as each of them at the same time had tasted every inch of his body, licking, sucking, and slurping every secretion and flavor left on his skin. No shower could have bathed him more thoroughly. The sucking mouths and lapping tongues, penetrating every crevice, seemed hungry enough to cannibalize him.

He'd been a paid whore but he'd never lived through anything like that before. Each man was physically disgusting to him, and one was hideously overweight. But he'd given each and every one what was wanted and desired: a pound of his flesh. Even that had hardly satisfied them. It was as if each one wanted his blood instead.

Even when he'd risen from the bed and had headed for the bathroom, the overweight businessman followed him. At first Danny had thought the man wanted to watch him urinate. But it soon became clear that the pathetic-looking creature was begging Danny to use his open, gaping mouth as a toilet bowl. Reluctantly Danny had inserted his cock into the man's eager mouth. The man had swallowed every drop, continuing to suck and drain even when Danny had fully relieved himself. Finally the man had gotten up from his kneeling position and in front of Danny had licked his lips, savoring the final taste.

Danny had returned to the bed and the camera. The eager, hungry mouths had descended again. Their prodigious talents in fellatio had brought him to the brink time and time again. Finally he could hold back no more, even though each of his attackers had wanted to prolong the session. As his first scalding spurt of jism had exploded, a mouth had withdrawn itself suddenly so that all of them could be a witness to the explosion, especially the camera. After he'd delivered his last blast, mouths had fallen on him again to taste the hot sweetness of the sperm.

As he lay gasping for breath on the bed, the men had turned him over, prying open his ass cheeks for their amusement and to reveal his most private spot to the camera. Even though they'd drained him in front, these same mouths had descended once again on him, licking, tasting, and probing with their tongues.

The fat man had clamped his lips on Danny's anus and had inserted his tongue so deeply into Danny he felt he was getting fucked. After five minutes of this, two of the other, younger men had pulled the man away so they could have their turns.

The climax of the long ordeal had arrived when each of the men had lined up on the bed, demanding to be penetrated by Danny. He'd serviced all of them, never losing his erection. As kneading, stroking hands worked his body, he'd entered each of them, fucking wildly and brutally, not caring whether he hurt or not. He'd been inflamed and his cock seemed to follow a life of its own, making each cry out at the enormity of his penis.

He was no longer their hired whore. He was their master, and they were forced to receive him. As he'd plunged for a final time, the fifth man had screamed when Danny had penetrated him. He'd begged Danny to take it out. For him, Danny had fucked all the harder, screaming at his final orgasm of the day.

Danny thanked God he was alone at last in bed. Soon he would have so much money he would never have to prostitute himself again.

When Danny woke up, Tom Caldwell and Steve Parker both were standing over him. Tom reached for his blue jeans and tossed them to Danny before turning to glare at Steve. "Get dressed, kid," Tom said. "I think this queer here and his slimy Jap friends have made you earn your keep for the day. I've already collected the money from him. I'll keep it in a safe place for you."

Steve glared back at Tom. It was obvious the two men had been fighting. "I'll join you bloodsuckers in the living room," Steve said.

After he was gone, Tom turned to Danny. "I'm sorry for what they put you through," Tom said, stroking his forehead. "And I'm sorry I made you do it."

"It's okay. It's over now." Danny got up and slipped into his clothes. His entire body ached, all his muscles strained.

"Sport, I know I'm sort of a hero to you and everything," Tom said. "But I've got a fatal flaw. A flaw I share with a lot of my fellow Southerners. When it comes to money, I go crazy. I think I'd sell my beautiful white daughter to a pack of horny nigger men if they paid enough. I'm sick. But only about money."

"I said it's okay," Danny said, reaching to kiss him. "At least my lips are clean of those bastards. No one touches my lips unless I give them permission. From now on, they belong just to you."

Tom held him close, kissing Danny and fondling his abused body. "When we collect the big bucks, I'll take you out of Georgia. We'll spend the rest of our lives together just making love on the beach."

In the living room, Steve stood by the liquor cabinet. He looked up as Danny came into the room, pointedly ignoring Tom. "I'm afraid I've got some real bad news for you guys."

"What is it, faggot?" Tom asked, moving menacingly close to Steve.

Steve continued to ignore Tom, focusing on Danny instead. "Your friend here is outrageously demanding ten million dollars for Lavender Morgan's stolen paintings. This poor flatfoot doesn't seem to get it through his head that stolen paintings, especially famous stolen paintings, are virtually worthless on the world market. Even the mere possession of them can get the owner thrown in jail."

"Yeah, yeah, pussy boy, we know all that," Tom said, still standing close to Steve as if to intimidate him by his mere presence.

"What's their offer?" Danny asked Steve. "If not ten million, then what?"

"One million dollars in cash and not another penny," Steve said flatly.

That pronouncement was followed by Tom's fist plowing into Steve's face. The impact knocked Steve to the floor where no one volunteered to help him up. Steve picked himself up and raced to the bathroom.

When he was gone, Danny turned to Tom. "You didn't have to do that."

"Bullshit! Those Japs probably offered Parker five million. He plans to give us one million and pocket the other four million as his commission."

In moments Steve was back, rubbing his face with a wet cloth. "You can strike me down, even beat the shit out of me," Steve said.

"You'd probably love it," Tom said.

"Take it or leave it, boys," Steve said. "That's all they will go. They'll have to smuggle the paintings back into Japan, and that's also very risky. Something could go wrong along the way."

"We're out of here," Tom said. "We'll find another buyer who'll meet our price." He grabbed for Danny's arm.

Steve called them back. "I've got the money. All in twenty dollar unmarked bills." He went behind the bar and retrieved two large bags. "Count it for yourself."

"Holy hell!" Danny said. "I thought I'd never live to see one-million dollars in my own rotten life."

Tom plowed through the money on top of the bag. "Is this for real?" he asked Steve.

"It's real," Steve said. "Every green bambino in there is for real. Lovely green, like the first grass of summer. Beautiful green stuff. More than a person would ever need in a whole lifetime."

Tom looked haplessly at Danny who looked back at him with the same exasperated emotion. After the long marathon sex session and after this temptation, Danny felt drained, not knowing what to do. He looked to Tom for guidance.

"You fucking, cocksucking bastard," Tom said to Steve, looking as if he could punch him out again. "I'll have the paintings delivered anywhere you want them before midnight tonight."

"I'll give you the address of a warehouse in Jacksonville," Steve said matter-of-factly as if arranging only a routine business deal, perhaps a minor insurance policy.

Hours later in Lavender Morgan's townhouse, where Danny was waiting for the phone to ring, one of his favorite sports programs was interrupted with a news bulletin.

Driving a rented truck, Tom Caldwell was instantly killed when rammed by a larger truck which had spun out of control as the policeman had neared the approach to Jacksonville. The TV news report claimed that Caldwell was transporting all the stolen art except Picasso's *Mother and Child* that had been removed from the Savannah townhouse of Lavender Morgan.

*****

Just arrived from New York, Jay Garon, the literary agent known as "The Iguana," read each and every one of her letters from Dr. King. He said his client was waiting outside her door in a limousine. Once Tipper peered out the window but the limousine's windows were tinted, and she couldn't see who was in the long black car.

"These are hot!" Garon said. "Really hot. Too bad I can't publish them. I could make a killing."

"Are you buying them for that purpose?" she asked tentatively.

"Not at all," he said. "Not at all." He looked over at her. "Here's the deal." He sounded as if he were negotiating a Hollywood deal on a film based on a Grisham novel. "My client—who shall be nameless, by the way—will offer two million dollars. Of that, I take half a million. The rest is yours."

She felt she should hold out for more money, but actually the offer was far greater than she'd ever imagined. Garon must not know this, but she'd been willing to sell the letters for a top price of one-hundred thousand dollars when she'd visited the King center in Atlanta. Nonetheless, she didn't want to appear overly eager. "I was hoping for more."

"Bullshit you were," Garon bellowed. "This is a deal of a lifetime. I know you're broke. You're not only broke but aging and falling apart. It's your last chance, cunt."

"Okay," she snapped. "You don't have to call me names, you fat butterball of faggot scum. I'll take your God damn deal."

He reached into his briefcase. "Here's a cashier's check made out to you for one and a half million big ones." As he handed her the check, she examined it carefully. She breathed a sigh of relief. Her financial woes were over.

Garon rose abruptly from her sofa. "Do you have a barbecue out back? All Southerners have a barbecue out back. I figure you do too."

She looked astonished. "At a time like this you want barbecue?"

At her old barbecue, covered in burnt charcoal, Garon reached into his pocket and pulled out a cigarette lighter. He said nothing but methodically burned each and every one of the King letters before her astonished eyes.

She stood back in horror watching the written memory of one of her past loves vanish before her eyes. At first she'd wanted to protest but said nothing. With the check in her purse, it was all too obvious that the letters no longer belonged to her.

As the last letter burned, she became acutely suspicious that Garon's client sitting out in the back of the limousine was none other than Coretta King. Who would want the letters destroyed more than Mrs. King herself? But that was only her suspicious mind at work. For all practical reasons it didn't matter who put up the two million dollars. The letters were now destroyed and would live on only in her memory, and she feared that wouldn't be that much longer. A few years perhaps, and that would be it for her.

In her foyer, Garon seemed impatient to get out of Savannah and back to the airport. "I've been trying desperately to get in touch with Phil. Where is he?"

"At a funeral, I think," she said.

"What in the fuck is he doing at a funeral at a time like this?" Garon said, licking his iguana lips. "Funerals are for dead people. We've got live ones to deal with."

"What do you mean?"

"I've got a hot deal going on your fucking memoirs," he said. "But I've got to have a proposal in my office in New York in forty-eight hours." He glared at her, looking deep and almost frighteningly into the depths of her eyes, as if peering into the hidden recesses of her soul. "And, yes, Ms. Black Widow, we've got to deal with Taylor Zachory's murder. In the memoirs you can no longer get away with that crap about how you can't remember a thing. Blame the murder on somebody, Greta Keller or whomever. But get me a murder, bitch."

Totally confused as how to respond to him, she stood looking dumbfounded. "We'll see what we can do. I have a message in for Phil. I think he'll be back in Savannah this afternoon. I left word that he's to see me right away on urgent business."

"Fine, handle it." Garon threw open her front door and bounded down the steps. "We'll talk," he called back to her. "Enjoy your money." He opened the back door to his limousine himself, as the driver didn't budge from the wheel. As the door opened, Tipper caught sight of a heavily veiled woman. Garon slid into the seat beside her, barked something at the driver, and the limousine disappeared up the street as Tipper stood watching it speed off.

At the foot of her stoop, she heard her phone ringing, and she rushed to answer it. It must be Phil. "Oh, God," she said out loud, as she hurried inside and slammed the door behind her. "Make it Phil. It's got to be Phil."

It was Phil and within the hour he was sitting across from her in the same seat so recently vacated by The Iguana. To her consternation, he appeared slightly nervous being alone with her in her townhouse. At least he'd left Brian at home. She'd been upset at first when he'd asked if he could bring Brian over with him. She'd flatly denied the request, claiming they had very personal information to discuss.

He accepted her drink. As she offered it to him, she ran her fingers over the smooth skin of his hand. He had beautiful skin, just like Monty. With money in her purse for the first time in years, and with Monty in the reincarnation of Phil with her, her life was on target again. With Phil, she just knew she'd find all the happiness denied her until now.

"I told you over the phone what Garon wants," she said, settling across from him so she could enjoy his male beauty, which he possessed in amazing doses like the young Monty itself. She had experienced too much of the aging, tired, and burnt out Monty and was thrilled to go back and meet the younger version that had been denied her. When she'd first met Monty, he was already in deep decline.

"That's what I'm here to talk to you about," he said, sipping from his drink as if it were poison. "I can't meet Garon's deadline. It's impossible. I'm overly committed. The producer of *Butterflies in*

*Heat* is in town demanding to read the first pages of my script. There is no script. I don't have one acceptable page of dialogue. I've got to bow out on the memoirs thing."

She bolted forward in her seat, as if not truly hearing him correctly.

"I don't know how to write the memoirs either," he said. "The most sensational thing in your life was the murder of Taylor Zachory. And you remember nothing. Or so you say."

"Just one God damn minute," she interrupted him. "Perhaps you could have said the suicide of Taylor. How do you know my husband was murdered?"

He stood up. "I don't know if he was murdered or not. I don't know what happened to any of your husbands. Not only that, I don't care to know." He put down his drink. "I've got to go. I'm sure you'll find plenty of writers eager for a chance at your memoirs."

"God damn you, you little faggot!" she shouted at him. "No one walks out on Tipper Zelda."

"Perhaps I'll be the first." He headed for the foyer.

She was so furious at his rejection that if she had a knife she would have plunged it into his heart. Monty was slamming the door shut on her for the second time in her life.

As if picking up on her thoughts by some inner radar he possessed, he said. "And I'm not Monty Clift either. I have a relationship. It's with Brian Sheehan, the man I love. There will be no relationship between us." He stared back at her. "Stop thinking I'm Monty. I'm not. He died in 1966. I'm Phil Heather. A separate human being who's going to walk out that door and get on with his life. Please don't call me again." He opened the door and raced down the steps to the street.

She stood on her stoop watching him go until he turned the corner and disappeared from view.

A small gust of wind stirred the otherwise dead afternoon. Her whole body started to shake, and she knew what that meant. She rushed back into the house to shut the door, as if that would keep out the demon. But no door would ever stop the demon.

The demon lived inside her heart and she could never escape from it.

Without his knowing it, Phil had unlocked the door to let out the demon.

# Chapter Eight

Back in his rented house in Savannah, Phil had a troubled sleep even though in the arms of Brian. Throughout the night he'd tried to comfort Brian over the loss of his best friend, Tom Caldwell, in that trucking accident in Florida. For part of the night Brian agonized not only over Tom's death but his theft of Lavender Morgan's art as well.

"I've known that guy most of my life," Brian said. "We even grew up together. There was nothing to indicate Tom was a thief. A rogue maybe. A sexual predator certainly. But not a thief."

"We never know anybody, do we?"

"I know you, babe," Brian said, reaching out and pressing Phil against his nude body. "You won't betray me, will you?"

"Never! I'm committed to this relationship."

"You'd better be, God damn it. You're all I've got." As if remembering something, he said, "You and the boys."

"I want you to call the station in Darien," Phil said. "Speak to the chief. Quit your job. Our life's getting too complicated. Besides, I think your job is too dangerous. Neither of us has to work any more if we don't want to. Aunt Bice has provided for us."

Brian ran his fingers through Phil's dark hair. "You're so beautiful. But my career goal in high school wasn't to become a kept man. I've got my pride."

"Don't worry," Phil said. "There's plenty of work to do fixing up Aunt Bice's old house. After we get our lives in shape, we'll do things to make money. I don't mean just my writing. We'll get into some business. We'll do something together but it'll take time."

"I know we will, and I'm behind you all the way. Whatever we decide to do."

"We've got to think of John and Henry too," Phil said. "Do what's right for them too. I'm calling a lawyer today and making a new will. My present will leaves everything to Aunt Bice. My new will will leave everything to you and the boys."

"You don't have to do that," Brian said, "but it's a commitment somehow and I respect that. After all we can't get married in the eyes of the state so it's good to have something on paper, something that recognizes us as a couple."

"We're a couple all right," Phil said, nuzzling his nose into Brian's well-developed shoulder.

From the kitchen below came the sounds of John and Henry trying to get breakfast for themselves. "We'd better get up and get downstairs," Brian said, "before our boys wreck the kitchen. I bet they already woke Jerry up."

As Phil bounded out of bed and headed for the bathroom, he was pleased to hear Brian refer to John and Henry as "our boys." He did feel like a daddy to both boys and had come to love them dearly.

In front of the mirror he confronted his unshaven face, as the bad memory of Tipper Zelda came back to haunt him. That woman made him feel creepy. About the last thing he wanted to do in the whole world was to write her memoirs, and he was glad to be out of her spider's nest. He feared a woman like Tipper could cause a lot of trouble for him.

Suddenly, as he heard Brian getting out of bed, the dread of the day was moving in on him. He couldn't believe it but he had to attend another funeral, that of Tom Caldwell. His wife, Ethel Mae, wanted Tom in the swampy Savannah grounds as soon as possible. Normally when a police officer died, even if not in the line of duty, there was a big funeral in Savannah with all the department showing up for the burial and the ceremonies.

But Brian had told him that only a few officers, all loyal to Tom, planned to show up. Brian would be the chief mourner, feeling Tom's loss more than Ethel Mae would. After all, Ethel Mae had already lost Tom. He'd died a scandalous death, and most of the people of Savannah who knew him wanted him buried and forgotten. The saga of Tom Caldwell would become just another chapter in the torrid lore of this muggy Southern city.

Brian told Phil he'd get breakfast for the kids while Phil dealt with Jerry. The producer didn't want to stay at a hotel so Phil had offered him the front bedroom downstairs opening onto a sun porch. Jerry had his own entrance where he could come and go. When Brian and Phil had returned home last night with the boys, Jerry had announced that he had a list of clubs and was going out for a night on the town to "discover some local talent." He promised to be up early in the morning to start working on the screenplay with Phil. When Jerry had learned that Phil had not made a lot of progress on the script, he'd announced he was going to be the co-author of the screenplay himself, taking top billing, of course.

When Phil heard voices from the bedroom, he rushed back to the kitchen, kissed Brian on the lips, John and Henry on the cheeks, and headed with two cups of scalding black coffee to Jerry's bedroom. The producer had obviously found some fresh meat during his shopping expedition last night, and Phil was prepared to greet the trick with a morning wake-up call, hoping he'd soon depart so he and Jerry could get to work on that screenplay. Phil had a lot of ideas and thought about the script most of the time. He just had not had time to sit down in front of a computer.

When Phil knocked on the bedroom door, it was immediately opened by Jerry clad only in his jockey shorts. "Morning," he said, "we could sure use this coffee."

"Hi," Phil said, coming into the guest bedroom where discarded clothes were tossed all over the floor. In the middle of the bed, with his nude chest exposed, was a strikingly handsome man with dirty blond hair. He could easily be forty but he was one of the sexiest men Phil had ever encountered, and he had known the best. Phil's first thought was that if the stranger had been ten or fifteen years younger he would be perfect for the role of the hustler, Numie, in *Butterflies in Heat.*

"Phil Heather, meet my new love, Duke Edwards."

Duke reached to shake Phil's had. "How's it hanging, partner?"

"Long and low," Phil said, offering coffee.

"Duke and I met last night at Club One," Jerry said. "It was love at first sight. It was certainly love at second sight." With that pronouncement, Jerry pulled the sheet from Duke revealing a large uncut penis and a massive set of balls. "This is one hung Georgia boy."

Phil checked out the merchandise, then averted his eyes in embarrassment. Duke, however, didn't seem ashamed at all—not that he had anything to be ashamed of. Exposed, he drank from the black coffee Phil had offered.

Phil headed for the door. "I'll catch you guys later."

"Wait a minute," Jerry called after him. "I want to ask you a big favor, and you owe me a lot of favors for not firing you as the screenwriter who doesn't have any script."

"What's on your mind?" Phil asked.

Duke answered for him. "I want to move in here with Jerry. I think I've got a better chance here than in my present situation. Jerry thinks he can get me to lose a few pounds and turn me into a topnotch model. A mature look but not all that mature if you know what I mean."

"I think that's a great idea," Phil said, feeling no enthusiasm at all. "You're a good-looking man and you'll go far."

"Of course, with a dick like that he'd be fantastic for porno, but I want to get him into more legit work," Jerry said.

"You're welcome to our happy home," Phil said. "I hope you don't mind kids making a lot of noise. Be warned."

"I can deal with it," Duke said, reaching for Jerry's hand. "Just so long as I've got this hot stud here to service me. Jerry's the hottest sex I've ever had, and until I met him I thought I'd had the best."

Jerry put down his coffee and moved his body over Duke's, taking his penis and skinning back the head before plunging down on it.

"Excuse me," Phil said, shutting the door and rushing back to the kitchen.

Two hours later, after Duke had consumed a huge breakfast cooked by Phil, he returned to the guest bedroom to watch television. Jerry headed for Phil's computer to record his ideas for the opening scenes of *Butterflies in Heat*.

Brian and Phil promised to return in three hours from Tom Caldwell's funeral.

At first Phil had been reluctant to leave John and Henry in Jerry's care because the producer didn't have many baby-sitting credentials. Brian thought it would be all right.

Just as an added protection, Phil called on Lula Carson next door and asked her to look in on the boys in an hour or so. She readily agreed. Phil was growing increasingly fond of Lula, as she was always there for him when he needed her. He hoped that one day he could return the favors to her as she'd bestowed so many on him.

Later, in a little church on the Isle of Hope, the pastor who was going to preside over Tom's funeral spotted Brian and Phil and ushered them into the back room of his parish. There Phil encountered the angry face of Ethel Mae, Tom's wife. Brian had known Ethel Mae for years and had once dated her before she started going steady with Tom. He'd attended dinners and barbecues with her and had gone on boating and vacation trips with Tom and her. It was only natural and proper for him to approach her and offer his condolences.

"No one is as sorry as I am about Tom's death," Brian said, bending over to kiss her on the cheek.

She pulled back from him and slapped his face real hard. "Get away from me, you faggot. You're slime." She turned to Phil with equal hatred. "You're slime too, you dirty queer."

"C'mon," Brian said, rubbing the sting off his face. "Tom's dead now. Let's get through the funeral and let bygones be bygones."

"I'll get through the funeral," Ethel Mae said. "I'm still Tom's wife. He would still be my husband and alive today if he hadn't got messed up with you faggots. You're responsible for his death just as much as if you'd taken a knife and plunged it into his heart."

"You know that's not true," Brian said, in a rather soothing voice, hoping to cool her fury.

"I know it's God damn true," she said, "and if you don't leave this church, and take your cocksucking boyfriend here with you, I'll call the cops and have you evicted."

Brian looked at her in shocked disbelief, then turned to Phil. "We'll come back later and pay our respects to ol' Tom," he said. "Let's get out of here so Tom can be buried in peace." He turned and glared at Ethel Mae. "Something he never had with you."

In the churchyard, Phil noticed that Brian was shaking. "This has been a hard day," he said getting into their car on the passenger side.

Phil remained in the car with Brian until the short service ended. A light rain misted the graveyard but the sun came out shortly thereafter, as the few mourners scattered in all directions.

When everybody had gone, Brian got out of the car and reached inside for the bouquet of white gardenias he'd brought for Tom. Phil trailed him as he went to his longtime friend's grave, where he knelt in a silent prayer and placed the flowers on the newly dug site. As he got up, Phil saw tears welling in Brian's eyes.

"Good night, ol' buddy," was all Brian said as he headed back to the car.

Phil said a silent little prayer when Brian had gone, surveyed the graveyard, and headed back to the car too. An ominous feeling descended over him, a kind of foreboding. Chris Leighton had been murdered. Tom Caldwell had been killed in an accident.

"Oh, God," he said out in a soft whisper to himself. "Don't let there be anybody else." He wanted to be with Brian and their boys.

Suddenly, fleeing from the graveyard, he was filled with fear.

*****

In Gin Tucker's studio, Lula Carson was preparing herself to be photographed for the book jacket of *The Tireless Hunter.* The commitment had been made some time ago, and she'd brushed the idea from her mind. But as of late she'd developed a writer's block. She felt that if she went ahead with a photograph for the book it might release her fears so she could start writing again. As of now she was making about as much progress with her novel as Phil Heather was with his screenplay, *Butterflies in Heat.*

Gin wanted Lula's photograph to cause as much comment and controversy as did Harold Halma's picture on the dust jacket of Truman Capote's *Other Voices, Other Rooms* in 1948. Capote claimed that the camera had caught him off guard.

Like many of Capote's stories, this was untrue. He had posed himself in the provocative position of a late teenage-like male Lolito. He was totally responsible for both the picture and its succulent baby mouth, seemingly ready to give someone a blow-job, and the subsequent publicity.

Fashioning her hair into bangs, as Capote had done, Lula looked at her face in the mirror. It was a look of prenatal sorrow. She appeared freshly emerged from the womb and not totally comfortable with the world she'd so recently joined. She also looked maliciously bitchy and definitely a quail, as some of her lesbian friends liked to call young women.

Her only fear was that such a provocative photograph would trivialize her work, and readers would concentrate more on defining her identity by her look than by her writing. If she kept writing, she realized she might be known more for her personality than for her actual words. After all, who had ever read any of the works of Gertrude Stein, although everybody, even the unwashed of today, seemed to know of Ms. Stein and her lady love, Alice B. Toklas.

Before Gin's camera, Lula assumed some of her most provocative poses, as if deliberately courting literary notoriety. Once launched into her posing, she could not hold back. There was always something of the dramatist and actress in her. She might appear half-way normal in an everyday street encounter, but once a camera was turned on her she believed in performing. She just knew that in all the pictures Gin was taking, at least one would be sensational. She closed her eyes, imagining her photograph appearing in every major literary review in America, not to mention *Time, Newsweek, The New York Times,* and all the major dailies.

At the finish of the shoot, Lula rose from the sofa only to confront Danny Hansford standing at the doorway. "The back door was opened," he said to Gin. "I just let myself in. After all, you did call for me."

"Hot damn!" Gin said, eying the boy. "You and those tight jeans are welcome here at the House of Sodom any time."

Lula did not know the boy, although she'd encountered him briefly that day Tom was threatening to arrest Lavender Morgan and Danny. Her last memory of him was when her late cousin was taking Danny into the back of the boathouse where she'd later learned Tom had demanded oral sex from the boy.

Gin excused himself and invited Lula to have a drink while he conferred in private with Danny.

Relieved to be finished with the shoot, Lula poured herself a bourbon and waited for Gin's return. Memories of Tom came rushing back to her. She'd been furious when she'd learned that Ethel Mae had excluded Phil Heather and Brian Sheehan from the funeral. They were friends of Tom's too, especially Brian who had been his lifelong companion. Ethel Mae was playacting at being the mourning widow, although people closest to the family knew the marriage was winding down and would have eventually led to divorce. But Ethel Mae was trying to collect all the money she could from Tom's death, and was threatening to sue everybody. She'd refused to talk to Lula about why Tom was transporting Lavender's stolen paintings to Jacksonville. As far as Ethel Mae was concerned, those paintings did not exist.

When Gin returned, Danny trailed him. "We've got something to show you. Something both Danny and I are real proud of." He held up a dildo for her inspection, then offered it to her.

She studied the dildo carefully, presuming it to be one modeled from real life by Danny. Jason had told her that Gin made these as a hobby. According to Jason, Gin had pestered him every time he saw him to pose for a dildo. Her husband had claimed he'd refused every time the subject came up, but with Jason you could never be sure he was telling the truth.

Fingering the dildo, Lula looked over at Gin and smiled, casting a glance and a faint smile at Danny too. He seemed not in the least embarrassed that his most private part was on exhibit. "I'm not sure what I'm supposed to do with this," she said. "It's mighty impressive and all, and I wouldn't take that away from it at all, but both of you good ol' Southern boys must remember that I have Jason McReeves as a live-in." She smiled again at both men. "Case closed."

"Listen," Gin said, temporarily angered at her seeming put-down. "That's not why I'm showing you the dildo."

"Then why for God's sake?" she asked. "Either you want me to be impressed with its length and thickness or else you expect me to put it to use."

Standing hostile and silent, Danny looked at neither of them.

She stared at Danny several times, because she'd heard more and more rumors that the young man had been deeply involved with her cousin, Tom. She wanted to ask all about that relationship, and was especially eager to learn of any events that might have happened during the last days of Tom's life. But from the look on Danny's face, she could tell she would be getting no information out of him. She suspected that Danny knew all about how Tom came to be hauling Lavender's stolen paintings to Florida.

Gin went over to the liquor cabinet and poured himself a drink to join Lula. He offered one to Danny but he refused. Slurping deeply from the drink, Gin had a petulant look on his face when he turned around again. But, knowing Gin, that came as no surprise to her. He nearly always had a petulant look on his face.

"Do you know who J. Hue Dornan is?" he asked.

"Of course, everybody in Georgia knows the shithead," she said. "He introduced legislation banning same sex-marriage. He's the red-haired psycho of the Senate. Foaming at the mouth about Bill Clinton day and night. The president said J. Hue reminded him of a maddog with rabies."

"Get this! That creepy homophobe is going to be living in this house for two days."

"I thought it was your house," she said.

"Well, I guess I exaggerate from time to time," Gin said. "It's actually owned by my rich parents. They are making me move out and turn the place over to J. Hue for two nights. Naturally, I'd have to leave. Surely you couldn't imagine J. Hue and me under the same roof for two nights."

"I'm flabbergasted," she said. "You'd better get rid of all your porno and all the dildo crap."

"Not so fast," he said.

She looked over at Danny, who was still saying nothing but stood glaring at them instead as if he really didn't want to be here. But regardless of where Danny was, she suspected he didn't want to be there.

"I'll leave," Gin said. "But I'm planning a little surprise for J. Hue and I need your help."

"I'd like to help but I don't know how I can be of much use," she said.

"I'll give you all the photographs you need for your dust jacket and press campaign for free," Gin promised. "As many copies as you want. I'll even help you mail them out. I saw what a great actress you were when I took pictures of you. What I'm going to ask you to do is some acting in the presence of J. Hue. In other words, pretend to be my maid."

"None of this is making sense," she said.

"Danny has already agreed to play his part," Gin said. "Lavender keeps him on a tight leash. He's always in need of money, and I'm paying him generously."

"What do I have to do?" she asked.

"Sit down and have another bourbon," Gin said. He motioned for Danny to sit down too.

Danny took his dildo and sat down with it, admiring it.

"You might not believe this, but J. Hue is a closeted homosexual," Gin said.

"All you guys claim your worst enemies are homosexuals," she said.

"That's often true," Gin said. "Some of the worst homophobes in America have been gay themselves. Joseph McCarthy, for instance."

"How does my being a maid fit in with all this?" she asked.

"My dear, you are about to find out," Gin said, seemingly smacking his lips at the upcoming dirty tricks he was about to unleash on the senator. "J. Hue was the first one to report me to my parents that I was gay. Christ, you'd think they could have figured that out for themselves. It led to my getting kicked out of their house and shipped off to the more tolerant shores of Savannah."

Completely confused as to what was going on in the devious mind of Gin Tucker, Lula sat back on the sofa.

"How'd you like to participate in a major sting of J. Hue?" Gin asked.

"I'll commit to it without knowing any of the details," she volunteered. "If there's anything I like better than writing *The Tireless Hunter*, it's striking back at right-wing homophobes like J. Hue."

"That's my gal," Gin said. "I knew I could count on you. Now here's what both of you must do, and I know you'll pull it off brilliantly. If my plan works, J. Hue will lead off the tonight news and be the laughing stock of America."

*****

Tango used to get up when the roosters started crowing in South Carolina, and this morning was no exception. Wild and frantic, she was up before the moon had left the world.

Duke hadn't been home all night, and she feared he'd left her forever. It'd been too good to last. Her reunion with her daddy had been one of the abiding dreams of her life but, faced with the reality of it, it was hugely disappointing. Physically, he was everything she could hope for in a man. But Duke had personality problems, and she felt in many ways they were as severe as those of Danny Hansford.

In her bathroom and in front of her mirror, she felt she looked awful. Did all movie stars wake up to such a disastrous face before having to transform themselves?

Her session with Big Daddy had been the most humiliating of her life. Going down on the repulsive Matt Daniels had been a mere prelude to the degradation and humiliation Big Daddy had forced upon her. She'd known some pretty disgusting men in her day, but none as evil and wicked as Big Daddy. To achieve sexual satisfaction, Big Daddy required his partner to perform acts on him so perverted that the mere thought of them revolted her so much she wanted to puke.

Big Daddy was demanding that she return soon and perform the same acts on him. She had to meet with Jerry Wheeler and tell him that she couldn't possibly go through with it. The only way she'd go to bed with Big Daddy again was if Jerry himself personally demanded that she do that, and that her casting as Lola La Mour required her to service Phil's father in the way she had. She prayed that she could act the part of Lola without having to give in to Big Daddy's revolting sexual excesses.

Both Duke and Danny Hansford had humiliated her in Savannah, and, even thought attracted to them, they repelled her in a way. The only man who'd ever genuinely loved her and treated her like a decent human being was Jason McReeves. To show Duke what he'd lost, or else what he was neglecting at night, she was tempted to go and find Jason in spite of any promise she'd made to Lula Carson. Did promises to "the other woman" really count? She didn't think so.

Romance wasn't all that was on her agenda. Matt Daniels had called her frantically at midnight, demanding that she continue with her act. He said that since Chris's stabbing at the club, the telephone had not stopped ringing for reservations. It seemed that every tourist in Savannah, even though carrying copies of John Berendt's *Midnight in the Garden of Good and Evil*, wanted to visit the site of this new murder.

To most of them, especially after the release of the Clint Eastwood movie, the murder of the original Danny Hansford by the antiques dealer, Jim Williams, was pretty stale news. It had happened so long ago. A voyeuristic public demanded a new murder, and people had found that in the slaying of the young and handsome Chris Leighton.

Matt claimed that the public was so curious about seeing Tango appear that she didn't have to do anything but just show up. They wanted to get a good look at her. Of course, many in the audience tonight would think that she might be the murderer. In that respect, Tango felt she was eerily aping the show business act of The Black Widow herself, Tipper Zelda.

A sudden inspiration came over Tango. There was no way she could train another male tango dancer in Savannah before tonight's performance. But she remembered that when she'd appeared with Dominique in Atlanta, their duet had been a sensation. She and Dominique possessed a huge repertoire. It would be more than enough material for tonight's show, or even tomorrow night's performance.

Regretfully she'd learned that Norma Dixie had forbidden her son to appear in drag ever again.

Putting on her red wig and covering her swollen and sleepless eyes with large dark sunglasses, Tango got dressed in a pink pants suit and headed out the door, pointing her feet in the direction of Lavender Morgan's house. She had no idea if Danny would be there or not. But she wasn't going over to see that white boy but to have a showdown with Norma.

Tango wanted Dominique for her act tonight, and Tango felt she could be mighty persuasive around Norma, although she didn't want to get into a push and shove match with that one. All Norma had to do was sit on Tango's slim, frail body, and Tango feared she'd never dance again.

It was not Tango's custom to go to the back door of white women's houses the way some members of her race did even today in Savannah. But when faced with the awesome prospect of Lavender Morgan, Tango felt it was in her best interests to cut through the back alley and appear in the rear where Norma was likely to be. She knew that Norma's cottage was in back, and on this particularly foul morning Tango didn't want to confront either Danny or Lavender.

To her surprise, she found Dominique working in Lavender's flower garden. Tango knew at once that those coveralls were selected for Dominique by Norma herself. In his heyday in Atlanta, Dominique would never appear like a common laborer. Tango was surprised at how meek and almost innocent her friend looked as a man. Dominique needed makeup and a woman's gown and costume jewelry to assert a true identity.

"Girl," Tango called out to Dominique. "Get out of that male drag and into a dress. I want you to go on with me in my show at Blues in the Night. I'm talking tonight, Girl."

Startled, Dominique looked up. "There's no way Norma's gonna let me appear there—so forget it. She'll have me thrown back in jail."

"Bullshit she will," Tango said mockingly. "She'll have to deal with me first."

Norma emerged from her sideporch. "I heard that, black bitch. What you got to say for yourself before I knock your teeth in?"

"Norma, I didn't know you were up and stirring," Tango said. "It's mighty nice to see you looking so well on this fine summer morning."

"Bitch, I'm giving you about ten seconds to get off the property of Miss Morgan," Norma said in her most threatening way. "After that, only the Good Lord can be responsible for your welfare."

Dominique rushed over to Norma. "Don't hurt her. She's my best friend. We've been through a lot together."

"You mean spread your assholes for a lot of men to fuck, isn't that right?" Norma asked.

"It was more than that, much more," Dominique said.

"I need a backup performer, and I want to offer the job to Dominique," Tango said defiantly.

"There is no amount of money or enticement that will get me to change my mind," Norma said. "My son has dressed up like a woman for the last time in his life."

"It pays one-thousand dollars a night," Tango said to Norma. "And I'll give all the money to you. You can be Dominique's agent, collecting the money. Many of the patrons also give us tips. *Big* tips."

Norma paused on her porch, the threatening look on her face gradually giving way to a more mellow glow. "Get in my house, gal," she called to Tango. "I don't want the neighbors hearing all this scandalous crap."

Seated comfortably in Norma's living room, Tango negotiated the terms with Norma. Dominique wasn't allowed to sit down because he had dirt on his gardening clothes.

"I was in show business myself," Norma said, "and I understand the demands of the marketplace. When I appeared at Norma's Room in Harlem, I had planned to sing only Gospel hymns. But management took another view. They selected the songs for me, and certain other acts I was forced to perform. I had to make a living and keep my child here from starving to death."

"We all understand that," Tango said. "Now let's get down to business. We don't have much time. Norma, since you're so well versed in show business, maybe you'll come over to the club today and direct us. At least point out what we're doing right and doing wrong."

"That I can do, child," Norma said rather gleefully considering the rigidity of her previous position. "Mae West didn't make a move in show business without seeking my advice first."

"Mama," Dominique said to her rather sternly. "Let's level with Tango. She's my friend. Just as you found out my deadly secret—that I like to dress in drag—so I have long known about yours. Tell Tango, mama."

"We've got work to do, child," Norma said, growing defensively.

"I said tell Tango the truth," Dominique said in a most masculine and commanding voice.

Tango was startled, not knowing Dominique could be this forceful as a man. Up to now Tango suspected that Dominique only became a powerful personality as a woman, never as a man.

"We don't need to air our dirty linen in public," Norma said. "My son feels I have exaggerated my connection with Mae West."

"There was no connection," Dominique said. "You never worked for Mae West. You never, in fact, knew Mae West."

"God damn you, you little drag queen bitch," Norma said, rising to her feet. "You take away a person's illusions, you stab away like a knife at the story of their life, and that person ain't got nothing left. It's like cutting into their soul." She burst into tears and ran from the room as fast as she could waddle.

"Go comfort her," Tango said to Dominique. "She'll help us now. We don't need to rub anything in."

"Sure thing," Dominique said. "She's my mama with all her faults." He headed back to the bedroom in the rear where Norma could be heard sobbing.

Sighing, Tango turned from the sight of him going down the hall. Her eyes focused instead on two figures emerging from the rear of the house. Clad completely in lavender, Miss Morgan was making her way down the garden path to her limousine. She was propped up by none other than Danny Hansford.

*****

Danny had several carefully wrapped packages including three large ones which he put in the back of Lavender's limousine. She had agreed to ride up front with him enroute to Clinton, Georgia, his birthplace. She didn't know why she'd agreed to accompany him to

Clinton—a village she'd never heard of—but a call from her lawyers in New York made her decide to leave town for the day.

Her paintings were going to be returned, as ownership had been determined. A lot of the press, including major TV news people, would be swarming around her home today, and she felt she couldn't stand the media attention. When Danny had invited her, perhaps to show her off in Clinton, she'd said yes, if only to escape Savannah until the heat died down.

On the dreary road to Clinton, she took time to wonder why a young man would want to show off a grandmother anyway. But she just assumed he'd be presenting her as this rich and powerful friend he had—not his mistress.

"The shitheads I grew up with in Clinton always said I'd amount to nothing," Danny told her. "When they see me arrive today in this fancy car, they'll know God damn different."

"Are you sure we should be going to Clinton?" she asked him. "Why don't we go to Buckhead and check into a suite at the Ritz-Carlton instead?"

"Fuck that," he said, pressing harder on the gas. A very determined look came across his face. "I want to see my mama. As for my old man, I don't ever care to run into that bastard again as long as I live."

She did not press him for more biography, assuming that his father had been very abusive to Danny.

"By the way," he said, "in Clinton I'm known as Jeff Broyhill. Don't you go calling me Danny now, do you hear?"

"I hear fine, and I won't," she said. "I promise."

Since Danny didn't want to talk, she thought about her paintings. Actually she had a lot to talk over with Danny but there was no communication with him. She wanted to ask him about his relationship with Tom Caldwell and Danny's involvement in the theft of her art. Danny knew plenty, but she realized she'd only get a tight lip from him.

She was relieved to have her paintings back though troubled that her most valuable art, Picasso's *Mother and Child*, was still missing. She wondered if Danny knew where that one was, and suspected he was hiding it somewhere. She could only imagine how Tom had acquired her paintings, and who it was that arranged to receive them when he tried to deliver them to Jacksonville. She was almost certain that Jacksonville wasn't the final resting place for her paintings and could only wonder what foreign port they would be shipped to.

As they neared the approach to Clinton, Danny seemed to take on the pride of a hometown boy, informing her that it had been Georgia's fourth largest city in 1820. She surveyed a ruin of a town. Sherman's armies had marched through here in 1865, and the town never recovered and was never rebuilt.

She saw the remains of some early 19th-century structures, many of which were falling in. They passed the Old Clinton Barbecue. "They serve the best barbecued pork in the South," he assured her, a woman who'd spent much of her life eating foie gras and drinking only vintage champagne.

"I guess you'd call this place Southern Gothic," she said. "A bit frightening, actually."

"You've lived in too many places," he said. "It's about time you saw how down-home folks live." He turned up a bumpy, unpaved dirt road that led to a small and dilapidated clapboard sided house down a country lane. A skinny cow grazed about two hundred yards from the front porch, where an old washing machine evocative of those made in the post-war era stood along with a rusty swing.

As Danny brought the car to a stop, almost hitting the front porch, a pale-faced, stringy-haired woman emerged, throwing open the screen door. "Jeff," she called out to him. "Thought you weren't due here till hog-killing time."

"Mama," he shouted, racing up the steps to give her a kiss.

She backed away, "Where'd you pick up all those big city ways? You know this is a family that don't go in for all that kissin' and fuss."

Emerging from the passenger seat, Lavender stood firmly, even proudly, in the debris-littered yard.

"This is Lavender Morgan," Danny said. "She's a rich woman from Savannah. She's had a lot of affairs. Even John Kennedy, the president of the United States. Lavender, this is my mama, Hazel."

"Pleased to meet you," Lavender said. "What Danny...I mean, Jeff meant was that I once worked in public affairs with the president."

"I heard him the first time," Hazel said, a bitter, almost steely, look of disapproval settling across her burnt-out face. She turned to her son. "Why did you bring this brazen Jezebel to my house? I saw her for the whore she was the moment she got out of that fancy car. In Clinton we can spot a whore a mile away. In this case a very old whore."

Lavender's heart sank with the afternoon. So much for family reunions in Georgia. If at all possible she wanted to turn and leave right this minute and never set foot on Danny's doorstep, not that anybody was inviting her to do so.

"Now, mama, Lavender is my girl friend," Danny said. "We're going to be married next week in Savannah. That news came as a complete shock to Lavender.

"Since she's so much older than I am, in just a few years— maybe very few—I'll inherit all her money," Danny said. "Give it to you, mama."

"If she's gonna be your bride, and she has all that money you say she does, I guess the least I can do is invite her to come inside and have some buttermilk with us."

Lavender smiled faintly. "Dan...Jeff has brought presents for you."

"I always did take to presents," Hazel said. "Not that I've seen many of them in my life."

In the battered old living room with a sofa that might have been new before the depression, Lavender tried to drink some of the warm buttermilk.

At one point Danny jumped to his feet to go to the toilet. When he was gone, Lavender turned in her most gracious manner, which she usually assumed when meeting royalty, and smiled faintly at Hazel. "I know it must seem strange to you to see Danny arrive here unannounced and accompanied by a lady of shall we say? A certain age."

"You look seventy-five years old to me," Hazel said flatly. "Maybe a lot older. You got on so much makeup I can't tell. And that purple color. I thought only whores dressed in purple. Even your hose is purple. Not to mention those high-heeled shoes."

"It's actually lavender. Like the lavender of the fields. It's always been my favorite color."

"When did you start molesting teenage boys?"

"Well, I wouldn't put it so graphically..."

Before she could complete her answer, Danny returned, fastening his thick belt buckle. "When me and Lavender get married, I'm gonna get you some indoor plumbing," he said to Hazel.

Lavender gasped. She was in desperate need of going to the bathroom herself and couldn't hold back any more. "May I use your outside john?" she asked, dreading the experience.

"Go ahead," Hazel said. "You'll find an old Sears & Roebuck catalogue in there. Me and my husband don't believe in wasting good money on toilet paper."

As Lavender made her way through the weed-infested backyard, she confronted the rotten outside john with a half moon carved on its rickety door. She shuddered to think what awaited her inside. Even before she opened the door, the smells from this john on a hot August afternoon overpowered her, and she felt she might be better off taking to the open fields.

She opened the door and braced herself before entering the foul-smelling hell hole. As she was finishing, she reached into her purse to find some tissue to wipe herself. It was at that moment she saw something slither on the seat beside her. She threw open the door, the light streaming in to reveal a large rattlesnake in a coiled position.

Jumping from the seat, she ran hysterically toward the house, adjusting her clothing as best as she could.

Danny was on the back porch at once. "What in fuck are you hollering about?"

"A rattlesnake!" she shouted. "It's in the john."

He dashed for the kitchen and emerged with a shotgun. He raced toward the toilet and in moments she heard gun fire. In a minute Danny could be seen walking through the backyard holding up the largest rattlesnake she'd ever seen. She screamed at the sight of it and retreated inside the house. Even Hazel and her hot buttermilk were better than that outside john and some monster reptile.

Completely shaken from the experience, she came into the living room just at the moment Hazel was kneeling on the floor in front of the sofa. "Come here, woman," Hazel commanded her. "Get down on your knees and pray."

Not knowing what else to do, Lavender bent over and kneeled on the floor, even though she felt too stiff to be getting down on a wood surface. The prayer seemed to go on into eternity but eventually

Hazel finished and released her grip on Lavender. She braced herself and pulled herself off the floor.

"Mama, I left that snake on the kitchen table," Danny said. "It looks like it'll make real good eatin'. Papa will love it."

"You're gonna eat that creature?" Lavender asked.

"Why not? We're not rich like you. We don't waste around this household. Rattlesnake tastes even better than chicken. You and Jeff should stay for supper. I'll fry you up a batch."

"Thank you but Jeff and I have to get back to Savannah, and it's a long drive."

"I see," Hazel said. "Thanks for coming. I hope you and my son will be real happy in your marriage. If Pa and I don't make it to the wedding, it's that we don't travel much. I've never been out of Clinton in my whole life. One time my daddy was going to take us to Atlanta. He talked about it as the years went by, but he never did."

"I'm so sorry," Lavender said. "It's been nice meeting you." She extended her hand to Hazel but the woman made no motion to shake it.

Retrieving her hand in mid-air, Lavender headed for her limousine. "I'll be outside in the car," she said to Danny. "Good afternoon, Mrs. Broyhill."

"You be good to my boy, you heah?" Hazel called after her.

"Oh, yes, of course," Lavender managed to say as she hurried across the front porch toward the waiting limousine.

Danny came out onto the porch with his mama. "Ain't you forgetting something?" Hazel asked Danny. "I mean, there was talk of presents."

"Oh, God, yes," Danny said, "I forgot all about them." He went to the back of the limousine and carried several large presents up to the front porch where he deposited them around Hazel. He picked up a large crated package and disappeared inside the house with it. Back on the porch he whispered something to Hazel and once again tried to kiss her. She gave the boy her hand instead.

At the old Clinton Barbecue, he said he wanted to show her off to his friends and invited her in for some good pork. She thanked him but declined, claiming she had a vicious headache which was true. She found that visiting the Broyhill homestead was more than she could handle with ease. Getting out of the car, he warned her he might be at least an hour, maybe two or even a lot more.

She told him she'd brought a blanket and would rest in the roomy seat at the rear of the car.

"Okay, if you want to miss out." He slammed the car door and went inside. The blasts of country music came from the rear of the building.

Getting into the back seat she decided to take some of her special medicine. Her doctor always prescribed it for her. She didn't know what it was but it always made her feel good.

As she went to retrieve her purse, she realized she'd left it in the living room of Hazel's house. She didn't want to disturb Danny so she got behind the wheel of her limousine and drove it back to the Broyhill homestead. This time there was no one at the front door when she knocked loudly. Finding the door unlocked, she went inside. "Mrs. Broyhill," she called out.

Unwrapped packages littered the living room where she'd so recently kneeled to pray. From a back bedroom, Hazel emerged. "It's you again," she said in a rather disappointed voice.

"I'm so sorry to barge in like this, but I forgot my purse," Lavender said in her most apologetic manner.

"Now that you're here," Hazel said, "I want you to come and look what Jeff hung in his old bedroom. He told me he wanted to keep it here for safekeeping."

Her suspicions aroused, Lavender trailed her to the rear and Danny's old bedroom.

"Look what he hung on the wall," Hazel said. "I think it's demon possessed. I'm gonna chop it up for kindling."

To her astonishment, Danny had hung Picasso's *Mother and Child* over his old iron bedstead. "Oh, no, no, don't do that," Lavender said, her panic mounting. "I love the painting. It's just a cheap reproduction but I've always wanted one."

"You like this heathen stuff?" Hazel asked in astonishment. "A woman of your years."

"I do indeed," Lavender said. "I have ten one-hundred dollar bills in my purse. Let me give that to you. You were going to use the painting for kindling anyway. You would have to explain its loss to Jeff eventually."

"One-thousand dollars," Hazel said. "I ain't seen that much money in my whole life. It's yours."

"I have a special compartment in my limousine where I can conceal big things," Lavender said. "Jeff doesn't know about it. The deal on the painting will be our little secret."

"And the money will be our little secret too," Hazel said. "If pa knew I made this much money, he'd beat me within an inch of my life." She reached out and affectionately touched Lavender's hand. "We women must have our secrets from men."

"I've spent a lifetime keeping secrets from men, but now I must go." Lavender crawled up on the bed and removed the painting, carrying it to the back of her limousine where she carefully concealed it in a hidden compartment.

She waved good-bye to Hazel and drove back to the parking lot of the barbecue joint.

Danny still hadn't emerged and didn't until three hours later. He found her asleep in the rear.

*****

Danny was going on with his life, but his heart was broken over the death of Tom. That handsome cop was the only person he'd ever loved in all the world, and now even that pleasure was denied him. No one must know that he was in love with Tom. That would be his secret that he'd take to his early grave, which seemed to be coming up even faster than he'd expected.

When he was alone, he'd cry over the death of Tom. He felt responsible for his lover's death. Danny knew if he hadn't been so greedy and hadn't stolen Lavender's paintings, Tom might be alive even today. All the get-rich-quick schemes had turned to failures for him.

Even the fifteen thousand dollars he'd made with the Japanese perverts in Atlanta had disappeared. Tom had taken the money to hold for Danny. Apparently it had not been found on his body, and even if the mysterious money turned up it would now belong to Ethel Mae, his wife. And that was the hardest money Danny had ever earned.

To survive, Danny was still dependent on Lavender's generosity. He'd planned to ditch her, but now felt he had to hold onto her to support himself in the last few months of his life.

The only money he could expect to come in was from Gin Tucker and the sale of the dildo. Gin had assured him he'd make at least twenty-five thousand dollars from the dildo—maybe a whole lot more. Interest in the dildo, at least according to Gin, had been running high.

When Gin had asked him to participate with Lula Carson in the sting against J. Hue Dornan, Danny had reluctantly agreed, although he had no taste for politics at all. Gin obviously had some deep grudge against the wacky politician, and Danny agreed to play his role but with no enthusiasm.

It was just a temporary gig along the way. With his hopes for really big money drying up by the moment, Danny even considered calling Tango and asking to be taken back into her act now that Chris had been murdered. He'd heard that bookings in the wake of Chris's murder at Matt Daniel's club had been heavier than ever. The public always had a great curiosity about a murder scene, as witnessed by the continuing interest in Mercer House where the original Danny had been shot.

Every now and then some vague memory of Chris and the club resurfaced in Danny's brain but he quickly assigned it to the dark recesses of his mind so that it wouldn't trouble him. As each hour went by, he remembered less and less about that night at the club. His only memory at this point was that he'd accompanied Lavender there. There was nothing else to recall.

If he had anything in the "bank" at all, it was Picasso's *Mother and Child.* That had been retained from Lavender's stolen art. But there was too much heat on the art right now. He'd wait awhile before approaching Steve Parker again to sell it. It was, after all, Lavender's most valuable painting, and it was in a very safe place. No one would think of looking for the painting in his old, rotting bedroom in Clinton, Georgia, whereas Tom's fishing hut on the remote offshore island would no doubt be searched thoroughly.

After giving Lula Carson, the "maid," final instructions, and elaborately informing Danny, the "houseboy," of his duties, Gin fled the premises before the arrival of the notorious national homophobe, J. Hue Dornan. J. Hue's hysterical, foam-at-the-mouth attacks on President Clinton and on homosexuals in particular made even Senator Jesse Helms of North Carolina look like a reasonable statesman. J. Hue proclaimed his only real purpose was to rescue

America from godless perverts and save it for the typical American family, which he envisioned as a God-fearing man and woman with two adorable children, one boy and one girl.

Both Lula and Danny were a little skeptical of Gin's claim that J. Hue, in fact, was a closeted homosexual. Lula had pointed out that gays often attributed homosexual tendencies to their enemies whether it was true or not.

Nonetheless, Danny was determined to carry out Gin's little fantasy game with J. Hue, though Danny still remained skeptical if the sting would work. In spite of his rabies, J. Hue was probably a sly old Southern fox that would not easily succumb to their manipulations.

Lying in bed wearing the briefest of sheer white bikini underwear, as mandated by Gin before he left, Danny heard voices coming up from the foyer downstairs. Apparently J. Hue had arrived. Danny had been told that J. Hue would be occupying the master bedroom upstairs, whereas Danny had been assigned a smaller adjoining bedroom where the bathroom was mutually shared.

He heard Lula coming up the steps with J. Hue to show him the master bedroom and to deposit his luggage. The reason J. Hue was in Savannah was not entirely explained to either Danny or Lula, except that J. Hue often visited key cities in Georgia, hoping to beef up his right-wing support and perhaps raise contributions for his upcoming senate race, as his six-year term was coming to an end. He'd already announced his intentions for re-election.

Before Lula went downstairs, she explained that Danny, the houseboy, would be available to help unpack his luggage and secure anything for the senator that he so desired while he was a guest at the Tucker residence.

After Lula left, Danny rose from the bed briefly and turned up the music in his room, knowing it would irritate J. Hue who was constantly ranting against rock stars, especially Mick Jagger and Sting. Before lying down, Danny adjusted his basket so that it showcased his endowment at its finest. He also fluffed himself up in the way a male porno star might do.

Before he'd been on the bed thirty seconds, J. Hue barged in through the bathroom door and into his bedroom. "God damn," J. Hue screeched. "Turn off that fucking music so I can get some sleep. I've got a big speech tonight."

For the first time J. Hue became aware of Danny lying seductively on his bed. At the sight of such male beauty in such a state of undress, J. Hue nearly gasped. "I mean..." He paused, as if not knowing what to say. "What I mean is... You big boys. You young big boys like your music loud. I understand that." His eyes remained glued on Danny's bulging basket of goodies.

Danny jumped up from the bed and turned off the music. "Hi, I'm Danny," he said. "Are you the new guest?"

J. Hue studied him closely. "You don't know who I am, do you?"

"Nope, but I'm here to serve you whoever you are," Danny said adjusting his crotch.

"I'm a Mr. Dornan," he said. "An insurance salesman from out of town."

Danny smiled and shook his hand, delighting in the fact that J. Hue had decided to conceal that he was a U.S. senator. Perhaps Gin knew what he was doing after all in using Danny as bait to bring J. Hue out of the closet.

"You're something else," J. Hue said. "You should be in the movies."

"I am in the movies."

"Perhaps I've seen some of your films," J. Hue said, his eyes still glued to Danny's basket.

"Not unless you watch gay porno flicks."

"Gay porno?" J. Hue coughed slightly. "I can't say I've ever seen one of those."

"You should see me in action," Danny said. "I'm a top. My dick when it gets hard is really big. Lordie, lordie, Miss Maudie, I can fuck and fuck some more. Guys love to get fucked by me."

"I see. It looks like you're something else. Something else indeed."

"I'm here to serve you but I thought I'd take a bath first," Danny said. "I've been working out in the yard and I'm a bit sweaty. It's so damn hot up here and there's no air conditioning."

"Please, go ahead."

Right in front of him, Danny pulled down his briefs and gave J. Hue the frontal view. The senator sighed, as Danny willed the blood into his cock, making himself semi-hard.

"I've never seen a cock that big on a kid your age," J. Hue said. "In fact, I've never seen a cock that big on men twice your age. I'm real small myself." He nervously chuckled. "My former wife—the God damn swamp bitch—used to tell people I had the smallest dick in Georgia."

"Even a man with a small dick can still be of use to me," Danny said.

"I don't rightly understand what you mean," J. Hue said.

"As long as the guy's mouth is big and his asshole can take it dirty and deep, I'll go for him. I'm horny all the time."

"I see," J. Hue said, practically choking on his words.

The sexual tension in the air was so great that Danny decided it was time for his bath. "I'm taking that bath now. Come on in and talk to me. I like an audience when I bathe."

The next few hours proceeded as in a dream sequence for Danny. J. Hue had not only watched Danny take that bath, but had volunteered to wash his back for him. The senator had been so efficient as a bath assistant that he'd even gone lower, coaching Danny into a full erection which wasn't difficult to do since he was always ready and raring for action.

For a man who loudly denounced homosexuals, J. Hue turned out to be extremely skilled in gay action, exploring every inch and crevice of Danny's body with his talented tongue.

When Danny threw J. Hue back on the bed and gave him a long, deep penetration, it was only too obvious that the senator was accustomed to this kind of servicing before. Danny's penis had gone in too easily. J. Hue had known all the right moves to make to bring Danny to a spectacular climax.

It was later in the evening that disaster, as script written by Gin Tucker, had occurred. After a few drinks, Danny had brought out the dildo he'd modeled. He'd begged J. Hue to let him insert it as a prelude to another penetration from Danny of the real thing. J. Hue had gladly consented, almost begging for it.

Danny had told him that he had to put some lube on it first because of its size and thickness. Using the lube that Gin had left for him, Danny slowly had entered the senator.

The lube had turned out to be some crazy kind of glue. The dildo had lodged itself deep inside the anus of the senator and wasn't coming out. When J. Hue had attempted to pull out the dildo himself, it had caused tearing and bleeding to such a degree he'd screamed in pain.

The screams had sent Lula the maid rushing upstairs to see what was the matter. When confronted with the scene, Lula had screeched in horror before dashing to call an ambulance.

Even as J. Hue had loudly protested against summoning help, he'd been eventually rushed to the hospital where two doctors had removed the dildo from his battered anal canal.

Some unknown party had called the press, and photographers had quickly gathered at the hospital. The local television station in Savannah was the first to broadcast the news.

Within fifteen minutes CNN had led off with a bulletin, by which time the news was being broadcast around the world by NBC and CBS. ABC was the last network to carry a bulletin.

Early risers in London who tuned in to the BBC had been startled to find J. Hue Dornan's "hospitalization" the lead item on the news of the day.

President Clinton, in nearby Hilton Head, was interrupted during a speech and given the handwritten bulletin. "So far I haven't gotten many laughs with my speech today," Mr. Clinton said. "I have some new material. Let me try this one out on you."

*****

Shaking violently, Tipper headed for the liquor cabinet and some Southern Comfort to steady her nerves. She wasn't herself any more. Just at that moment in her life when everything was looking good again, the dark force was moving in on her. This evil side had brought her such pain before, always at the moment she was about to bask in glory, money, and happiness with a man.

When she'd landed Taylor Zachory, she felt she'd had it made. A handsome lover. A fabulous mansion. Thirty million dollars in the bank. Thirty million that would be so much more today. Maybe ninety million or even a hundred million.

The force had become jealous. Tipper had unwisely provoked the force because of her own initial happiness with Taylor. If only she had not aroused the jealousy of her evil side, Tipper might easily be living a carefree life today.

Phil had rejected her, and for that he would have to pay the ultimate price. Phil Heather himself meant nothing to her. He was merely a carrier. The real rejection had come from Monty himself.

She knew that Phil no longer inhabited his own body. It was Monty. The actor's initial rejection of her, widely reported in many books and the stuff of movie lore, had been humiliating enough.

What was unforgivable was that Monty had come back to mock her again and to deny his love. As the years had gone by, she was getting over the first rejection. Then without warning she'd seen the picture of Phil and had known at once that Monty was back to taunt her. Why had he not gone on his way and allowed her to recover from her initial pain?

Of course, what Phil—really, Monty—had done to her could not go unpunished. The evil force had decided that, and Tipper knew she must carry out the wishes of The Black Widow. If she didn't she feared she'd taste the sting of the spider's bite herself. To preserve her own life and sanity, Tipper always had to do the bidding of this evil force.

In her own life, she had never wanted to harm anybody, much less take an action that led to their deaths. She'd always considered herself a good woman. She wanted love, the good, pure, honest love of a decent man. But all the men who'd come into her life had been evil and twisted.

All her husbands and even Monty himself had wanted to lie with men and not with her. They had gone through the emotions of love with her but Tipper always knew their hearts weren't in her bed. She'd always feared that when making love to her, these perverted men were reaching their climax by dreaming of other men.

For their sins, they had to be punished. And they were. The same fate awaited Phil. Regrettably, The Black Widow always made her wishes known to Tipper but never gave her a clearcut map as to how Tipper was to carry out her demands. Tipper was left with her own ingenuity in having to come up with various schemes to achieve the deepest and darkest desires of The Black Widow.

To destroy Phil and ultimately Monty would be horrendous enough to carry out, but The Black Widow had come up with a new stipulation that made the plan almost impossible to achieve. Finishing the Southern Comfort in her glass, Tipper poured herself some more. The Black Widow's second demand appeared an almost hopeless undertaking. But Tipper knew she had to heed the command and carry it out some way. But how?

The Black Widow had fallen in love with Danny Hansford, even though Danny himself was possessed of an evil spirit. Once Tipper learned that from her dark force, she'd known why she'd concealed the bloody machete Danny had used to kill Chris Leighton and had hidden not only the weapon but the blood-soaked shirt.

Tipper would have no reason to do that. But if The Black Widow wanted Danny's legendary lovemaking, then he had to be spared. He couldn't be locked away to rot in some jail or sent to an electric chair, his beautiful golden body to burn away.

Not knowing what to do next, Tipper was in tears. If she didn't figure out a way to accomplish these monstrous goals, she herself would be done away with by The Black Widow who no doubt would go on to inhabit another soul, as she was eternal.

Tipper felt very mortal today. Even with money and a renewed career on her horizon, it would mean nothing if these horrible deeds were not carried out to the perfection demanded by The Black Widow. What would the money and the fame mean to Tipper if she weren't around to enjoy it?

Like an answered prayer, there was a knock on her back door. It was Erzulie, the voodoo queen. Eagerly Tipper showed her into her kitchen and quickly offered her some Southern Comfort.

"White woman, I'm glad to see you up and about," Erzulie said. "The minute all my kinfolk heard I had bagged some green ones, they came rushing to me for a handout. Know what? I'm out of money today and was hoping I might be of some service to you. Something in my bones told me that you were in dire need of my special services today."

Seated across from Erzulie, Tipper eyed the voodoo queen with a keen, appraising eye. "I need your help."

"I reckon you know I get paid for my services," Erzulie said, sampling the liquor.

"Do you do small jobs or big jobs?"

"Both small and big. I adjust my fees accordingly. For a really big job, I would have to get all of one-thousand dollars."

Tipper paused for a long moment. "What about twenty-five thousand dollars?"

Erzulie slammed down her liquor. In seeming panic, she heaved her body up almost as if trying to rise from her chair. "I might get somebody else to get rid of someone, but Erzulie don't actually do the killing herself."

"Who says you personally have to murder anyone?" Tipper asked.

"Honeychild, Erzulie wasn't born yesterday. For twenty-five thousand big ones, I know the party of the first part had to do the actual killing."

"Not at all."

"Then spill the beans, child."

"How well do you know Danny Hansford?" Tipper asked.

"I know that white boy better than he knows hisself. He ain't himself. He's taken on the identity of Danny Hansford even though he's actually Jeff Broyhill from Clinton."

"That's a conceit, of course, isn't it?" Tipper asked.

"Child, I don't know nothing 'bout no conceits. The real Danny Hansford—that little white hustler murdered by the antique dealer, Jim Williams—lives within the body of this Jeff boy. When Danny Hansford says he's really Danny Hansford, and not Jeff Broyhill, he means it."

Tipper started to protest yet stopped at the same time, knowing that evil forces—in her case The Black Widow—do possess other bodies and even other souls.

As if reading her thoughts, Erzulie smiled before taking another swig of her drink. "You of all people know what I say is true."

Tipper sighed. "How right you are about that. How can Jeff free himself from this Danny Hansford?"

"That is a very, very hard thing to do," Erzulie said. "An almost impossible feat. In most cases, the host body has to actually die hisself before the spirit can be set free."

"But in a few cases." Tipper leaned in closer to Erzulie. "In a few cases..." She paused. "Go on. Tell me."

"It's very rare and it takes a lot of special potions and magic. In a few very special cases—and this ain't likely to happen often—the victim can free hisself by allowing the evil force to escape into the body of another person."

"Listen, and listen good," Tipper said, her voice so forceful it was as if The Black Widow herself was actually speaking to Erzulie. "I want the soul of Danny Hansford to leave Jeff Broyhill's body and inhabit the soul of Phil Heather. Phil is already inhabited by Monty

Clift. Once the soul of Danny Hansford moves in too the dual occupation of his body will surely lead to his death."

"Only one evil soul can live in a body at the same time," Erzulie said. "There ain't no room for two."

"Then I'm right. The host body will die. I know that to be true."

Erzulie nodded in agreement. "Have you got a picture of this Phil Heather?" she asked. "I've got to see what he looks like."

"Yes," Tipper said. "Come up to my living room. I'll show you his picture and I'll also direct you to where he lives."

"That has to be done. I've got to see the boy in the flesh."

In Tipper's living room, Erzulie studied the picture closely. "I can tell from just looking at his picture that this ain't no Phil Heather living in that boy. It's someone from long ago. Someone famous. Maybe a person in show business."

"It's Montgomery Clift," Tipper blurted out. "Like I said."

"I don't know anybody with a name like that, but I know someone is inhabiting that boy."

"You've got to help me. You've got to free Danny."

Erzulie smiled, a rather lascivious grin. "I know that The Black Widow that still lives within you is one horny bitch. She wants the big, thick white meat of Danny Hansford for herself. But to get him, like I know she wants him, we've got to get Lavender Morgan out of the picture."

"How would we do that?"

"I have my ways. Believe me, for twenty-five thousand dollars I could bring Jesus Christ hisself back from the dead."

*****

Back in Savannah, Phil waited with John and Henry for Brian's return from Darien. At police headquarters, Brian planned to quit his job and retire from the force to devote his life to taking care of Aunt Bice's farm. As soon as Aunt Bice's will was probated, and Phil inherited the house, he planned to put Brian's name on the deed as a co-owner with joint rights of survivorship. Already they were becoming a family, if not in the eyes of the state, at least on legal documents.

As he'd entered the house and had stood under the light of the back porch, Phil had thought he'd detected a movement in the shrubbery lining the driveway. At first he feared it might be Arlie Rae Minton spying on the house. Among Lula Carson and Jason, and Brian, John, Henry, and Phil living in the other house, Arlie Rae could find no more interesting house in Savannah for his voyeuristic instincts. Phil had to admit to himself that these various households put on a good show for Arlie Rae when he got tired of looking at his cheesecake pictures of Linda Tripp.

But it wasn't Arlie Rae. The shadow in the shrubbery was much larger and darker. Phil had detected the smell of some strange smoke. It wasn't a marijuana cigarette—that aroma he knew well, especially from his younger days. It was a smoke almost like incense. He'd quickly gone inside the house and from his darkened living room had peered out at the bushes. But whatever was there, if only a figment of his imagination, seemed to have disappeared. Perhaps it had been nothing at all.

Phil was sitting in the kitchen drinking a Budweiser when he heard a light rapping on the back door. He'd come to recognize the delicate sound. It was Lula Carson on one of her endless visits. Although he adored her, she did come calling a lot, apparently to ease her loneliness. Obviously, like Arlie Rae himself, Lula found life in his household more interesting than sitting in front of her computer facing the blank pages of *The Tireless Hunter*.

Apparently, Lula was making no more progress with *The Tireless Hunter* than Phil was with his script, *Butterflies in Heat*.

Jerry had left three pages of the film script on the dining table before disappearing somewhere with Duke Edwards. Now that Jerry had discovered Duke, he wasn't as interested in the film as he'd been before.

With Duke apparently satisfying all the sexual fantasies Jerry had ever dreamed about, the producer—or so it could be assumed—would not be dusting off his casting couch to audition studly young men for the role of the hustler, Numie Chase, in *Butterflies in Heat*. Considering the trouble Jerry might get into in a Southern town with those auditions, Phil thought it was just as well that he'd settled on Duke right at the beginning before some local daddy arrived with a shotgun to blow Jerry's head off. After all, as liberal as Savannah was when stacked up against the rest of rural Georgia, the city was still firmly planted in the Deep South.

Lula looked very happy as she came in through the kitchen door. "I just found out there's a big carnival-style party at the school ten blocks away. There will be prizes. Junk food. Everything. I'd like to take John and Henry."

"That's great," he said. "They were getting too house bound."

"When I heard about it, I knew they'd love to go." She paused, looked over at Phil, and smiled. "Do you think I want to be a parent after all?"

"Perhaps," he said. "That was the last thing on my agenda. But I'm getting into it. I love the boys dearly."

"So do I," she said. "Do I have your permission to kidnap them for a few hours?"

"Permission granted." Just as she headed for the living room to pick up the boys, the phone rang in the kitchen.

It was Brian, telling him he'd not be back in Savannah before midnight. The men on the force had wanted to throw Brian a spontaneous farewell party and he'd accepted. "After all," Brian said, "I might be driving drunk one night and one of the boys might pull me over. I'd better suck up to them tonight if I don't want to get a ticket."

"Have fun," Phil told him, "and drive carefully back to my loving arms. I miss you something awful. Savannah at night seems downright spooky without my big guy around the house. Lula is taking John and Henry to a party at the school."

"Hell, that will leave you alone unless Jerry and Duke are there."

"They disappeared early in the day—God knows where—and I don't know when they'll get in."

"I'm a little afraid to leave my baby alone in Savannah," Brian said. "There are so many studs wanting a piece of you."

"I'll be fine," Phil said. "Enjoy your party and hurry home. The bed will be warm."

"I love you, guy." Brian put down the phone.

After fixing himself a turkey sandwich, Phil decided to study Jerry's script to *Butterflies in Heat* and pick up the action from where Jerry had left off. Perhaps he could write three pages himself before John and Henry returned. As he headed for the dining room to retrieve the script, the phone in the kitchen rang again. Thinking it might be Brian calling back for some reason, Phil rushed to pick up the receiver.

"Baby, you've bowed out of the party and are heading home right now," Phil gushed into the phone.

There was a long, almost deadly silence on the other end. *"Baby!"* came a mocking voice, sounding like that of a young man. "I'm not bowing out of any party. In fact, the party could just be beginning for us."

"Who is this?"

The voice on the other end seemed miffed that it wasn't recognized at once. "Who in the fuck do you think it is? Hillary Clinton? God damn it, it's Danny Hansford."

"Oh, hi, Danny, I remember meeting you at Lavender Morgan's house."

"Yeah, and I remember slipping you a note," Danny said with barely controlled fury in his voice. "An invitation, asshole, to suck my big dick. Danny Hansford isn't used to getting turned down by anybody, man or woman."

"Yes, I got that note," Phil said in a businesslike voice. "You're very attractive and all..."

Danny interrupted. "Very attractive. Are you out of your God damn fucking mind? Attractive. A freshly mowed pasture is attractive. I am very, very, *very* good looking. Listen, sweetheart, don't kid me. I'm the best looking blond stud in the State of Georgia."

"I'm sure many will agree with that assessment," Phil said. "But I've got my own blond stud, and for my money he's got everybody else in the world beat. Besides, I'm in love with him, and I don't plan to suck anybody else's cock, regardless of how tempting."

"I'm six feet tall. My waist is slender. I've got big, broad shoulders. A dildo I modeled for Gin Tucker is about to become the hottest selling item in America. My dick is so thick it's more than five inches in circumference. You can choke on it, bitch."

"I'm sure it's a very, very impressive dick and will bring a lot of happiness to a lot of people. But not me. I've got my own lollipop."

"What a cunt! I know you're lying. You're so attracted to me you were slobbering at the mouth when you met me at Lavender's. You couldn't take your eyes off my crotch. You probably have never seen a crotch that big in your whole rotten life."

"Keep your crotch, damn it," Phil said, growing angry. "Okay, I took a look at it. So what? Gay men always check out other men's crotches, especially when they are so blatantly on display like yours was. But it didn't mean a thing to me. I've seen bigger and better. Believe me."

"How dare you put me down, you scumbag little faggot you."

"If you think this is going to get you the lead in *Butterflies in Heat*, you're sadly mistaken. The role has already been promised to my boyfriend, Brian Sheehan. Better luck next time. Why don't you do porno? Sounds like you could make a living in that. Especially if your dildo attracts all the attention you think it's going to get."

"You asshole! You dirty rotten piece of shit!"

"I've heard about all the endearments I care to hear for one night," Phil said. "I don't like to hang up on people. But I'm putting down the phone."

"Wait!" Danny cried out. "Wait until you hear one more thing."

"What is it? I've got to go."

"For the rest of your days, which I can assure you are numbered, you will regret treating me like this. You'll pay an awful price. You've just signed your death warrant." Danny slammed down the phone.

Phil also hung up the receiver. If Tom had been alive, he might have called him for advice about what to do with Danny. If Brian were here, he'd know what to do. For the moment, Phil decided to do nothing. He didn't take Danny's threat seriously. Just another psychotic kid trying to break into show business. He'd encountered that type on both coasts.

Two hours later the kids hadn't returned with Lula. Phil had managed to write two pages of the film script, and he was feeling pretty good.

From his window the night breezes were blowing in. Since hardly a breeze had been stirring for days, he decided to go down into the kitchen, take a beer from the refrigerator, and enjoy the night air in the backyard he shared with Lula and Jason.

Jason, according to Lula, had disappeared again. But that was hardly news. The way Phil saw it, Jason would disappear on the day he was supposed to be buried.

Outside, as Phil sucked in the night breezes, Danny's words came back to haunt him. Was their recent phone conversation more than just an idle threat?

An ominous feeling came over him, and he turned and headed quickly back into the house, locking the door to the back porch, although he usually kept it open.

*****

Lula Carson was writing again. Her participation in the scandal involving J. Hue Dornan had been the impetus she needed to get her writing again. Changing the senator's name, and even the city in which the dildo incident occurred, she'd written an entire chapter about the sting. It was, perhaps the best piece of writing in *The Tireless Hunter*. The only problem was, it didn't seem to fit into the rest of the narrative, and was, at best, a wild detour.

After finishing her chapter, she went upstairs to add it to her growing manuscript but couldn't find it. She always kept the manuscript by her bed in case a sudden inspiration came late at night. Sometimes she kept it under her bed when she retreated there to escape from her demons.

She'd seen Jason with her manuscript yesterday before he'd disappeared to God knows where. He'd been reading from it and this had led to one of their major fights.

"You've ripped off my soul in the manuscript," he'd charged. "First you've made me lame brained, the village retard, and then you've exposed all my most personal secrets. Things I told you on the pillow in the middle of the night. How can you do this to me?"

"I must write from my own experiences," she'd told him. "Straight from my heart."

"But you've taken everything from me in this novel. You've left me with nothing." He'd burst into tears just like he used to do as a little boy growing up in Columbus.

"I didn't mean to, really I didn't," she'd said. "Once the novel is published, once it's out there, it'll bring fame and fortune to me. You'll benefit from that."

With tears running down his cheeks, he'd looked down at her. "You don't understand. I wanted to write my own story. Now you've taken it from me. My innermost thoughts. Now there is nothing left for me to write about."

"You're no writer. I'm the writer in the family."

"How can you say that? How do you know I can't write? I must be given a chance. You can't steal my soul?"

"Hell with that! I'm writing my own life experiences, and if a great deal of those experiences happened to be with you, then I'm entitled to use them as a source of literary inspiration."

He turned from the sight of her, heading for the kitchen having deposited her manuscript back on her writing table. She followed him. "I can't let you do this to me. You've exposed me to the world in a very cruel way. If this novel is published, people will ridicule me. You've left no skin on my bones. With your pen, you've pierced all the way to the depths of my heart."

"Don't you think you're being melodramatic? Besides, I didn't use a pen. I used a computer. Writers don't use pens any more."

"It was just a matter of speech."

"I don't give a God damn what you say. I'm finishing *The Tireless Hunter*, and I'm going to publish it. I refuse to allow a publisher to change one word of it. It's a masterpiece. It will bring glory to me after all these years."

"What years? You were just a fucking teenager not that long ago. You haven't struggled. You haven't even paid your dues yet."

"Living with you is tantamount to paying dues from hell," she'd said.

"We could change that," he'd told her, looking at her more sternly and more severely than he'd ever had in his life. "I could be out of your life. Out of your damn novel."

"You may get out of my life," she'd told him. "In fact, I think I'd welcome that. But what I have written about you in my book remains. Exactly as I wrote it. It's true: I hardly painted a romantic portrait of you. But it was etched in glass. The reason you can't stand it is you can't bear to face the truth about yourself."

"Lula Carson," he'd said, "I've known you since I was a little boy. We've shared some very secret, very private moments together. You've spent all those years telling me what's wrong with me, how inadequate I am, how dumb I am, how I have failed you in a million ways. In my book, I will set the record straight. My portrait of you will put you in the hospital."

"You wouldn't dare," she'd said to him. "My book will come out first. I'll be famous then. The only way you could sell your book is to cash in on my fame. An exposé of me. You'd be cannibalizing my flesh."

"We'll wait and see how this little drama plays out," he'd said threateningly. "You've always had it your way. I'm taking back my life. I'm not going to let who I am be encapsulated in *The Tireless Hunter*. The whole novel is your poison pen letter to me. Now I know why you've put up with me all these years. All my philandering. My drinking. My drug taking. You weren't doing that because you loved me. You were doing it so you could drain my life's blood and put it all in the pages of that book from hell you're writing."

He'd stormed upstairs, presumably to change his clothes and search for money. But she'd hidden her house money in a place so secret he'd never find it. It was buried in a tin can under their back porch. In a few minutes she'd heard him leave by the front door, which he'd slammed behind him. Usually he left by the back door.

With that hideous memory of her confrontation with Jason haunting her every move, she searched the house in desperation for her manuscript.

Within her house there wasn't much furniture and almost no hiding places for something as large as a manuscript. When she couldn't find her hard copy, she nearly screamed in panic as she raced to her computer. The empty screen stared back at her. Jason had erased her manuscript from the computer.

It was gone. The manuscript was gone. *The Tireless Hunter* had disappeared from the face of the earth. Of this she had no doubt: Jason had destroyed the manuscript. All her precious words and observations. Her very life itself. All destroyed.

The reality dawned. In her heart she knew she'd never write it again. She couldn't go back and recapture what she'd already put on paper. There was something blocking her from doing that. The recipe for the book was forever destroyed.

Hearing footsteps on the stairs, she spun around to stare in Jason's face. His expression told her all she needed to know.

"It's gone," he said. "I got in a boat down by the boathouse and rowed it way out. Once out there real good, I released each page of it to the water. It's now shark bait!"

She didn't really hear his words as her brain plunged into a chaos from which she thought she'd never recover. Her heart was beating so wildly she felt its thumping was like the sound of a drum beat.

"There's nothing left," she said to him. It was as if she were reporting on a fact and not asking a question.

"My goal is to record my own life," he said. "Destroying that manuscript was like getting my own soul, my own life back. The next time you sit down to write a novel, make it your own life. Your own experiences. Don't have the entire God damn manuscript be about me and your projection of my soul. You don't know what in the fuck I'm like. You never understood me. You just thought you did."

"Until this very moment I never knew how much you hated me," she said through a barely audible voice.

"Until I read *The Tireless Hunter*, I never knew how much you hated me. It's amazing how you could live with somebody as long as you've lived with me, and hate them as much as you do."

"I never hated you. I don't even hate you now. Even after what you've done to me. Destroying a masterpiece of world literature."

"It wasn't a masterpiece, honey. It was a pile of shit. You're hopeless as a writer. Find some other profession. Perhaps be a waitress in a diner."

"At last you've found your tongue if only to use it viciously on me."

"By destroying that hideous crap you called a novel, I can do something with my life. As long as I was with you, you were making me an emotional cripple. I'm better than that. Much better."

"Jason," she said in hopeless despair, "you've got two things: a big dick and a retarded brain. Perhaps that is all you'll need to get through life. Up to now I've felt sorry for you and carried you on my skirttails. No more. Please pack your clothes. You can fit everything you own into one battered suitcase. Please go right now." She turned and headed down the stairs. She didn't want to see him ever again.

Within less than thirty minutes, she heard him coming down the steps. He left again by the front door as he had before. This time she assumed he had a suitcase packed with his meager belongings.

"So that's it," she said as she wearily went to make herself some black coffee. "That's how a marriage ends. That's how a lifelong friendship ends. The packing of a suitcase. The walk out the door."

The day loomed before her. She didn't think she could get through it. But there must be a way.

\*\*\*\*\*

When Jerry Wheeler called with an invitation to have lunch at Clary's Cafe, Tango eagerly accepted. She felt tired and didn't look her best, as she'd been up all night waiting for the return of Duke Edwards. He'd never come back even to get his clothes, and she feared he'd left Savannah, perhaps hitching a ride on the open highway heading to Florida.

Until that phone call from Jerry, the only good news had come from Dominique. It seemed that Norma had had a total change of heart. She had not only agreed to let her son perform at Blues in the Night, she was busy getting him a drag outfit, since he'd left all his gowns in Atlanta.

Fortunately Lavender Morgan had come through with just the right item in her overstuffed closets. Dominique had assured Tango the outfit was sensational. The only problem was, Tango feared if Dominique were too sensational, he might overshadow her own performance, and Tango was, after all, the star of the show.

When she arrived fashionably late at the cafe, Jerry was seated at a table in the rear. As best as she could on short notice, Tango had dressed up like the whorish Lola La Mour, the black diva in *Butterflies in Heat*. From now until the film was wrapped, Tango didn't want to appear out of character and, in fact, planned to work the role of Lola into her act at Blues in the Night.

At her approach, Jerry got up from the table and treated her like a real lady. "Is it Tango today? Or is it Lola?"

"From now on, child, it's gonna be one and the same," Tango said. "Strutting my stuff down the street on the way to meet my gorgeous producer, I had three cars stop. The gentlemen driving those wheels made the lewdest propositions to me. If I didn't have this bigtime movie career looming in front of me, I know how I could make my living. All I'd have to do is walk down the street and shake my moneymaker."

"That's great!" Jerry said, glancing nervously back toward the men's room. "I hope you don't mind, but I've recently acquired a new assistant. He's joining us for lunch. A fantastic guy. I've put him on the payroll at a big salary. He's been hired to give me an insight into the role of the Southern hustler. He's so terrific that I'm tempted to cast him in the part himself. He'd make a great Numie. But Phil has convinced me to go with Brian. Brian Sheehan is about the hottest thing walking around in a uniform in Savannah. Wait until you meet him. You guys will be terrific together."

"I just can't wait to meet this Brian Sheehan," Tango said. "I've already met one of the characters cast in the film." A frown crossed her face, followed by a look of total revulsion.

"Sorry about that," Jerry said, looking mournful. "I was just glad it was you and not me that Big Daddy took a fancy to."

"What is your assistant's name?" Tango asked, not really caring.

"Duke Edwards," Jerry said nonchalantly. "He's hung like a horse. Real handsome in a trashy sort of way. He fucked me four times last night."

In total shock, Tango said nothing as she spotted Duke coming out of the men's room.

"Here he is now," Jerry said.

At the table, Duke extended his hand when Jerry introduced him to Tango. Tango looked deeply into Duke's eyes but said nothing. "I'm not a gal into handshaking," she said with all the bravado she could muster. "When I meet up with a stud, I like his tongue down my throat or else I like him to unzip so I can see if it's worth messing up my mouth with."

Duke laughed. "She'd make a perfect Lola," he said to Jerry. "If what you told me about Lola is hot and true, you've got the right pussy here for the part."

Tango glared at him, and for the first time in her life she felt she really hated another human being. Even now, sitting across from her daddy at a table, she couldn't believe the romantic crush she'd developed so suddenly on him. He was nothing when stacked up against Danny Hansford, a much younger and sexier man. At least that was her new viewpoint. And there was no man in town who could match the talents and beauty of Jason McReeves, even Brian Sheehan himself, although she admitted she was rushing to judgment in regards to Brian.

"I hope you don't mind," Jerry said, signaling the waitress they were ready to order, "but for insurance purposes I've got to ask you an important but personal question."

"Fire away," Tango ordered. "This beautiful black bitch has got nothing to hide. Nothing she's ashamed of."

"Are you a man or a woman?" Jerry asked. "Transgendered perhaps?"

A contemptuous smirk crossed Tango's heavily made-up face. "For the stupid purposes of your little insurance company, you can put down that I'm a man. But, and I'll lay this one on you, I'm about as much of a man as Sharon Stone. As Madonna. As Marilyn Monroe. Get it!"

Jerry smiled, affectionately rubbing Duke's hand as the waitress approached to take their orders. Duke ordered enough for three men, Jerry preferring a simple hamburger, and Tango opting for a salad with lemon as a dressing.

"We gals have got to keep our girlish figures," she announced to the overweight waitress.

The tension in the air between Duke and Tango was almost unbearable for her, although Jerry seemed totally unaware of their connection. At first Tango had wanted to shock Jerry and announce that his new lover—stolen from her own love nest—was none other than her daddy. But wisely she decided that this Yankee producer should only gradually be exposed to Southern decadence and not get the full treatment all at once.

Seemingly Duke had no intention of revealing the link to his newly acquired lover, and had obviously decided that he'd get a lot more in life hanging out and fucking Jerry than he would fucking her. This surprised her because Tango felt she was virtually at the doorstep of international stardom, and Duke, if for no other reason, would stick around to collect her future millions. But Jerry must have convinced him that there were even more millions to be made by sleeping in his bed.

As if the day could get any worse, Tango looked up only to confront The Lady Chablis. Believe it or not, The Lady was heading directly for their table.

"You must be Jerry Wheeler," The Lady said, ignoring Duke and Tango. "The manager told me who you were, child."

"You are no doubt the celebrated Lady herself?" Jerry said, getting up and extending his hand. "You saved Eastwood's movie, and did it ever need saving. Without you in the film, no one would have bought a ticket."

Tango stared up at The Lady Chablis. Duke got up to shake her hand, but The Lady continued to ignore him.

"Child," she said to Jerry, "if you want a real actress for the part of Lola La Mour, you can cast me. I read *Butterflies in Heat* last night, and if ever there was a role I could play, it's Lola La Mour. I am Lola La Mour. I know that pussy. I can play her."

"I'll keep you in mind as the script is written," Jerry promised somewhat weakly.

The Lady reached into her purse and gave Jerry her card. "I want you to call me tonight and come on over. I'm a great cook. You ain't tasted nothing yet, baby, until you've had my..." She paused provocatively for a long time. "My collards, child."

"I'll call you tonight."

"I'll be sitting by the phone waiting for it to ring," The Lady said, before turning her back on the table and prancing off into her day, whatever that was.

Tango could not imagine what The Lady Chablis did during the daylight hours. She seemed like such a creature of the night.

Sitting down again, Jerry turned to Tango, "You know I didn't mean it. I was just saying that to pacify her."

"Of course, The Lady Chablis and Lola are the same age," Tango said. "With a beauty like me, they'll have to paint wrinkles on my face."

"You'll be fine as you are," Jerry said. "We can win greater audiences by having you and Numie younger and fresher than called for in the novel. Books are one thing, films another."

Back home alone, she retreated into her bedroom and for one brief moment was tempted to throw herself on the bed and go into a crying fit. But the very moment she was about to do that, she stopped herself. Duke Edwards wasn't even worth ruining her make-up. He was just a cheap, aging hustler, and she couldn't understand why Jerry bothered with him.

Brian Sheehan was off-limits to Jerry. Apparently, Phil had wrapped that stud up and locked him away. But there were plenty of handsome young blond studs to play the role of Numie in *Butterflies in Heat,* and Tango knew Jerry could have them all. There was even Danny Hansford. That kid would look dynamite on screen.

There was one man who would be even better. Jason McReeves. He had everything it took to be a sensation, especially if there was a nude scene. She shuddered to think of the possibility of a nude scene on screen between Jason and her. They would need trucks to carry in the fan mail. Jason and she could be big international stars. Another Dolph Lundgren and Grace Jones act, except, *much* better.

Six hours later at Blues in the Night, Tango knew that she was still the Empress of Savannah. The Lady Chablis at Club One had become a stale act. All the tourists in town with copies of Berendt's *Midnight in the Garden of Good and Evil* had booked all the tables from Matt Daniels. Every one had come to gape at her.

There was speculation that Tango herself had murdered Chris Leighton. When she'd first appeared, the audience had virtually swooned as if getting a look for the first time at the black diva murderess herself.

Backstage Tango had confided in Dominique. "Tipper Zelda thinks she can be big with that Black Widow spider number. But those gay husbands of hers were murdered years ago. No one remembers them except some old queens over seventy. But the Chris Leighton murder—that's new and hot. That's what the public really wants. Even that Danny Hansford murder back when dinosaurs roamed the earth is pretty old today. I'm the hottest thing in town. I'm at the center of the latest murder. Perhaps there will be another book written about Chris's murder. In that book, I'll be the fucking star—not the snaggle-toothed Lady Chablis!"

In a shocking pink gown and towering red high heels, Tango knew she looked sensational. With all this applause and approval, what did it matter that she'd lost a lover who was over the hill any way? She wanted adulation more than lovers. She knew she could have any man in the club if she wanted him.

At ringside, Norma had applauded louder than any one, especially in the two numbers that Tango did with Dominique who appeared attired entirely in lavender, one of the cast-offs from the wardrobe of Miss Morgan herself. Apparently, Norma was settling into the role of the mama of a black drag queen diva. Tango suspected that what had really won Norma over was the prospect of money coming in. Even with all her dough, Lavender was said to be mighty stingy when it came time to paying staff.

All through her first and final acts, a couple looking something straight out of Gothic America, dressed in cheap clothing, had sat at a ringside table next to Norma's. Through her entire act, they had anchored there with sunken faces, not laughing at any of her jokes and not applauding any of her numbers. Both the man and woman had stared at her with tight-lipped venom as if they could kill her.

Tango felt they had wandered into the wrong club. More properly they might be at a Southern Baptist revival meeting. At first she was going to come on to the man, making lewd sexual jokes and perhaps sitting on his lap and running her long, tapering fingers through his graying hair. But as she'd approached the table, she'd backed away. The vibes they'd given off warned her to stay clear of the couple. Fearing an embarrassing encounter, she'd avoided them, playing to more hospitable patrons at the other tables, including Norma.

As Tango was taking her final bow to thunderous applause, the hostile woman in the bad-fitting dress rose suddenly from her table and lurched toward Tango only a few feet away. She ripped off Tango's red wig and plowed her fingers into Tango's face, almost seeming to dig into her flesh for her very blood.

Tango screamed and backed away from the woman. Two men rose from a ringside table and rushed up to protect Tango and pull the screaming woman off her. Tango had fallen to the floor, as the hostile bitch kicked her in the face.

"You God damn nigger whore!" the woman shouted. "You killed my son. You fucking queer!"

It was only later when Tango was being rushed to the hospital, accompanied by Dominique and Norma, that she'd learned that the man and woman at ringside were the parents of Chris Leighton.

*****

At three o'clock in the morning, as she slept in the same bed with young Danny Hansford, there was a loud pounding on her bedroom door. Removing her satin domino, Lavender Morgan called out. "What's the matter?"

It was Norma Dixie. "It's the *po*-lice. They want you to come down at once. They're tearing up the house."

"Oh, my God," Lavender said, rising as quickly as her aching back would allow. "Tell them I'll be down as soon as I get dressed."

"You'd better hurry up or they'll come up here for you."

"What in the fuck's the matter?" a sleepy Danny asked, turning over in bed, the covers slipping from his nude body.

"The police are searching the house," she said, rushing toward the bathroom.

"Shit, I've got dope stashed in the library downstairs." He jumped up from the bed too and reached for his clothing.

"That's great!" she said. "Just great." She turned from the sight of him and headed toward the bathroom. It was all too clear to her now. She should have kicked the boy out long ago before tomorrow morning's headlines. In her bathroom, she desperately dialed Slim Roberts, her balding local lawyer. He wasn't the best or the brightest, but she demanded he get out of bed and come at once. She also told him to wake up her law firm in New York and alert them to what was happening. Roberts claimed he'd be over right away and that she was to say nothing until he got there.

Seated in her living room with Danny on one side of her and her attorney, Slim Roberts, on the other, Lavender confronted the police. Led by Johnnie Stockwell, a corpulent officer in a uniform too small for him, two other policemen stood glaring at the strange trio in front of them.

"Miss Morgan, I'm very embarrassed to have to bring up some things," Stockwell said. "But the law's the law, and I've got to enforce it. An anonymous tip led me to your house at this ungodly hour."

"Exactly what are the charges against Miss Morgan?" Roberts asked. "I've seen the search warrant. I know you have a right to be here. But what are the charges?"

"Possession of dope," Stockwell said. "And that's for openers."

As Lavender remained silent, Mr. Roberts said, "Miss Morgan is an eminent citizen of the world. She does not take illegal substances. Nor does she allow them in her home."

"They were found in her fucking library," Stockwell said, growing angry.

Lavender cast a brief and rather hostile glare at Danny who had assumed a face of total innocence.

"Need I remind you that Miss Morgan has many political enemies," Roberts said. "Someone could have easily planted those illegal substances here. She is known for having many cocktail parties in the late afternoon. These parties are often attended by many men unfamiliar to her. They are brought as guests of her friends. There is no security. Anyone could have planted those drugs."

"Perhaps," Stockwell said. "A thorough investigation is in order."

"Might I also remind you that some of Miss Morgan's worst foes are right here in Savannah tonight," Roberts said. "They flocked into town to hear a speech by Senator J. Hue Dornan. And we know what happened to him."

One of the policemen laughed until confronted by the stern face of Stockwell. The policeman quickly shut up.

"I don't know who put the dope there," Stockwell said. "But we'll find out. We have also found something very alarming in our search of the property."

Lavender felt her heart beating almost dangerously. "No," she said to herself, "it cannot be that."

But it was. "I also had my men search Miss Morgan's limousine. We found the painting by Picasso she had reported stolen from this very living room we're sitting in."

Roberts turned to confront Lavender in astonishment, but quickly regained his composure. "Those paintings were uninsured," the lawyer said. "Why would Miss Morgan want to steal one of her own paintings and report it stolen if it were uninsured?"

Lavender glanced briefly at Danny. Up to now he'd remained rather stone-faced. But even he had become jittery. She knew he found it almost impossible to believe that Lavender had that painting in the back of her car. She suspected he must be wondering how she'd retrieved it from his bedroom in Clinton where he'd left it.

Stockwell cleared his throat. "The paintings discovered in that truck wreck that killed Tom were uninsured. Try this on for size. The only painting insured was *Mother and Child* by this Picasso fellow. It was overly insured if you ask me. I saw the painting. My twelve-year-old boy could do better."

"I find it unbelievable that Miss Morgan would leave that Picasso in her car," Roberts said. "It too must have been planted there by some enemy."

"We found it carefully hidden away in a concealed apartment," Stockwell said. "We policemen in Savannah are pretty smart when it comes to concealed compartments on limousines. We have our drug dealers here, and plenty of 'em too."

For Lavender, the next two hours passed as in her worst nightmare unfolding. Even at this early hour, the damn photographers were waiting to take her picture arriving for questioning at police headquarters. She'd tried to conceal her face as best as possible, but just knew her photograph would be splashed all over the newspapers tomorrow morning. To her horror, she noted a TV news crew filming her arrival at the station. Danny made no attempt to conceal his identity, staring at the cameras with a certain kind of glee. This notoriety would no doubt make him famous. It would make her more infamous than she already was.

She learned that the TV documentary of her life as a courtesan was slated for broadcast this coming Tuesday. No doubt NBC would rewrite the ending of their script. She feared other major stations would also air retrospectives of her notorious life. At the end of this ordeal, she suspected she could no longer live with comfort in Savannah or even America for that matter. She would seek some anonymous place where no one had ever heard of her. Perhaps Patagonia. She would indeed run to the end of the world, depending on how events in the next few days played out.

While her lawyers battled with the police outside, Danny and Lavender were left alone in a closed door waiting room.

Danny turned to her and smiled. "So this is it?"

"What do you mean?" she asked.

"This is where me and you split up. It seems we weren't very good for each other."

"Young man, need I remind you that you got me into this shit in the first place? Stashing all that dope was a dumb idea."

"Bullshit! You bought dope for me. You're just as guilty as I am. Trying to corrupt the morals of a minor."

"Don't give me that crap," she said angrily. "The moment you popped out of your mother's womb, you were thoroughly corrupted. The only decision you had to make in life is how wicked you wanted to play the game."

"Maybe I am corrupt," he said. "But there were a hell of a lot of people out there only too willing to cash in on the corruption. To get a piece of the action." He smiled again, even more smugly than before. "I'd list Lavender Morgan, grand empress of Savannah, as one of those despoilers of youth."

"Don't rub it in. I'm mortified that I took up with you in the first place. I must have been out of my mind."

"No, you just wanted to get fucked by a big dick. A big young dick."

"That you did and that you have. I can't take that away from you. But on looking back now it hardly seems worth it."

"You loved it, cow. I just know it'll be the last great fuck of your life. Even if you bought someone, I doubt if he could get it up for you—even with the lights turned off."

"Considering the mess you got us in, gratuitous cruelty hardly becomes you."

"Don't we know all the fancy words?" he said with utter contempt in his voice. "When they take your mugshot, you'll look just like a bag lady caught shoplifting."

"Thanks for the encouragement," she said sarcastically. "If you're trying to make me feel more awful than I do, or give me any more insecurity, then you are succeeding beyond your wildest hopes."

"I just have one question to ask you," he said. "When I went into that barbecue joint, what alerted you to go back to mama's and retrieve that painting? Had you suspected all along?"

"Right from the beginning I thought you'd stolen my paintings," she said, "although I doubted if I could prove it. I had no idea you had left my Picasso at your mother's. When I discovered my purse missing, I drove back to your house. You were still inside swilling down beer."

"So that's it. On looking back, we would have been better off leaving it where Jesus flang it."

"Hardly. Your mother hated the painting. She was planning to burn it for kindling."

"Oh, shit!"

Slim Roberts came into the room to tell both of them they were to be questioned separately. Roberts would accompany Lavender to her questioning, and he had arranged for one of his law partners, Peter Copeck, to be with Danny while he was interrogated.

Reluctantly, but having no other choice, Lavender rose from her seat and headed for another room where Roberts directed her. In the corridor, a man introducing himself as Jerry Wheeler, the producer of the upcoming film, *Butterflies in Heat*, ran up to her. At first Roberts tried to brush him off, thinking he was a reporter.

"I've just heard the news of your arrest on TV," he said. "First thing this morning. You're fantastic. They showed pictures of you.

You film great. You were dynamite yesterday. But you're even more fascinating as an older woman."

"What do you want with me, young man?" she said rather imperiously.

"I'm offering you the role of the dress designer, Leonora de la Mer, in *Butterflies in Heat*," Jerry said. "It'll be your one chance at immortality. Captured on film, you'll be greater than Gloria Swanson playing Norma Desmond in *Sunset Boulevard*."

Roberts took her arm and gently pulled her away from Jerry, directing her down the long corridor.

She looked back at his urgently pleading face only once.

"Let's lunch," he shouted after her.

\*\*\*\*\*

When Danny was released from police custody, he'd just assumed that Lavender Morgan had posted his fifty-thousand dollar bail. To his surprise, the newly wealthy Tipper Zelda turned out to be his benefactor. Up to now, he'd assumed that she despised him. When they appeared on the same bill at the club, she wouldn't even speak to him. Now, to his complete disbelief, she was willing to post bail.

Even when he agreed to get into her car and drive over to her house, Danny was nervous in her presence and suspicious of her motives. At the very beginning, she informed him that her friend, Norma Dixie, was packing his clothing and moving his stuff from Lavender's house into her guest bedroom.

"But why are you doing this for me?" he asked. "I'm grateful and I need a place to stay. But I didn't think you cared for me this much."

"I think you're innocent," she said. "I don't believe you stole those paintings at all. Lavender stole her own Picasso. It's clear to everybody that she's the guilty party. As for a little dope, you wouldn't be the only teenage boy in the State of Georgia who indulges a bit in that."

"You're very understanding," he said.

The rest of the ride was in silence. When Tipper got Danny home, she invited him back to her kitchen where she fixed him some scrambled eggs and country sausage. "I hope they weren't too rough on you at the jail."

"They were pretty tough, but I've been interrogated by the police before. When the paintings were stolen, Tom Caldwell questioned me about the theft. He was much nicer than any of the shitheads I met up with tonight."

"Tom Caldwell," she said. "Wasn't he the cop killed in that truck accident? Caught with all of Lavender's paintings except one."

"That's the guy." A mournful sound echoed in his voice. He felt he was on the verge of tears but he couldn't let Tipper know how much he cared for his friend Tom. God, he missed that guy. If things had worked out differently, he felt he could have run away with Tom and started a new life together.

Looking over at blousy Tipper Zelda, he felt he'd gone from the frying pan into the fire, as his mama used to say. One broken down old hag to another. He shuddered at the prospect that Tipper might be viewing him as a sexual object.

Tipper got up suddenly when she heard the urgent ringing of her front door bell. Dawn was breaking across the Savannah skyline as Norma Dixie appeared on her doorstep. "I got his clothes in the back of my car," she told Tipper. "But I need the white boy to help me bring them in. My son Domino is on the way. He's riding over here on Danny's motorcycle. Lavender wanted Danny to keep the bike as a going away present."

"How nice," Tipper said, ushering Norma inside her foyer.

"I don't like no one riding my cycle but me," Danny said with a certain hostility in his voice. He brushed past Norma and went to her car where he unloaded his two suitcases and carried them up the stoop into Tipper's foyer.

"The guest room is upstairs," Tipper said. "Second on the right."

As Danny deposited his clothes in his newly acquired bedroom, he heard the familiar sounds of his cycle coming up Tipper's driveway, heading for her back yard. In a panic he rushed downstairs and out the back door, there to confront Domino getting off his cycle.

"It's okay?" Danny asked. The cycle meant everything to him. He couldn't stand the idea that Domino might have had an accident or even scratched its finish.

"It's just fine, blondie," Domino said. "One of my former boy friends was the greatest motor cyclist in the State of Georgia. We rode all over the state together. I learned everything there is to know about these bikes, honey."

Assured that his cycle was in mint condition, Danny turned to Domino. "Thanks. I'm glad that bitch Lavender is letting me have it. That stingy cunt might have taken it back to the showroom and demanded her money back."

"She sure is one cheap old hag," Domino said. "She pays my mama virtually nothing."

As if for the first time, Danny became aware of Domino as a person in his own right. Although technically they'd lived in the same house, he had paid no attention to Domino. He'd heard from Lavender that Domino had been a drag queen in Atlanta appearing as "Dominique." As far as Danny was concerned, he gave drag queens wide berth after his ill-fated experience with Tango.

"I'm sorry we didn't have a chance to get acquainted better," Domino said in his most provocative, seductive voice. "Unlike my sister queen, Tango, I don't normally go in for white boys. Over the years I've found that they don't normally have enough hanging between their legs to mess up my mouth with." He moved closer to Danny. "In your case, blondie, I might make an exception. If you thought Tango was good, you ain't seen no action yet. I taught that black bitch everything she knows." He smiled into Danny's face. "But I didn't teach her my special sexual secrets. What say we go out some time and I demonstrate some of my exotic talents on that beautiful body of yours?"

"That sounds like a real tempting offer," he said, backing away. "I'm a little busy right now. But when the heat is off, I'll be calling you. Sounds like you've got some special surprises just for me. And after a night with me, you'll know that it ain't just black boys that have got something hanging between their legs."

"I know, I know, sugah," Domino said. "Tango has given me a blow-by-blow description of every inch."

Domino was interrupted by the sudden appearance of Norma on Tipper's back porch. "Get in that car out front, youngin," she shouted into the early morning air at Domino. "Get away from that white boy. It's boys in tight blue jeans that has always got you into more trouble than I can handle for you."

Domino reached for Danny's hand, giving it a light brush before heading up the driveway toward Norma's car parked out front on the street.

When Norma had gone, Tipper offered Danny more coffee at her kitchen table. "You'll be real comfortable here," she assured him. "I've come into some money, and I can help you."

"But I still don't get it. When we worked at Blues in the Night, I thought you couldn't stand me. Once or twice when I spoke to you, you never said a word back at me."

"That was then and this is now," she said.

"You sure have changed."

Tipper looked out at the new light of day streaming in. "I have a confession to make as well. When you were dancing at the club, I felt the audience was coming to see your act and not mine, and I was real jealous."

"That's decent of you to admit it," he said.

"It's true," she said, "but things are different now. As I said, I've come into some money. I've got offers of big contracts. I've got engagements. There may be a television show on me just like there is going to be one on Lavender Morgan. Things are really looking up in my career. I'm even getting offers to write my memoirs."

"You can't do that," he said.

"And why not?" she asked.

"You'd have to write about all those husbands you killed."

She seemed to bristle at the remark, and he feared he'd angered her by being so blunt. "What makes you assume that I murdered those husbands?"

"I don't really know for sure," he said. "But you're billing yourself as The Black Widow—and everybody says you murdered them. That's what Lavender told me too. She once told me she was in the house the night your first husband, Taylor Zachory, was murdered."

Tipper's face grew pale. "That Lavender. She was indeed in the house that night. But she didn't witness the fatal shooting of Taylor. My young husband could indeed have killed himself. No one knows for sure. As for me, my memory of that night is a complete blank."

For the first time he understood Tipper a bit more. He believed what she said. His memory of the night of Chris Leighton's murder had also become an almost blank page. These things happened.

The way Tipper was looking at him made him think that she was understanding a lot more about him than she was saying.

In some distant corner of his brain, he did remember coming into the alleyway after Chris had been stabbed. He didn't know why at the time but he was holding the Hemingway machete. Foolishly, he'd put the weapon in the garbage where it could easily be found by the police, and had taken off his shirt which had blood on it. Miraculously he'd known enough to wear a matching shirt underneath the soiled one.

He'd been vaguely aware of some presence in the alley observing him that night. He'd remembered a cigarette that had quickly fallen to the ground, its burning tip stomped out.

Going back to the club, he had remembered nothing of the incident and wasn't even certain that if there had been a presence in the alley or not. Now, sitting across from Tipper at her kitchen table, he did feel that she had been there, seeing and observing everything.

If that were true, he had to be real nice to this fading star. Given his present troubles, she could make even bigger trouble for him. She knew too much.

He'd have to be extremely careful around her, listen closely to her wishes, and follow them. At this moment, and not sure of all the details, he was convinced that Tipper Zelda held the power of life and death over him.

He was comforted by the fact she'd posted his bail and had taken him in now that Lavender had made him homeless. He also knew that Tipper wasn't doing this out of the generosity of her heart. She wanted something from him, and wanted it big.

In the hours and days ahead, he had to find out what Tipper's agenda was, and he just knew in his heart she had one. He shuddered to think what it might be.

*****

Summoned by Tipper Zelda for an early morning meeting in her kitchen, Erzulie arrived right on time. Tipper thought she looked hung over and a bit tired today, but Tipper too had had a restless sleep. At times she was both excited at the prospect of having Danny upstairs asleep in her guest room and at other times she was terrified of housing this murderer. Just like he killed Chris Leighton, he might turn on her in the middle of the night and stick a knife into her heart.

"White woman," Erzulie said, "you've made me a rich woman, and I suspect there are more green ones on the way as your demands for Erzulie's services will surely grow when you see what I can do."

"We've talked everything over last night," Tipper said, growing impatient. "I'm going to wake Danny up, and you've got to convince him what you say is true."

"Don't worry," Erzulie said. "The Haitian Venus knows her stuff. While I'm waiting for this white boy, do you have any Southern Comfort to relieve a tightness in my throat?"

"Help yourself," Tipper said, "but don't get drunk. We've got work to do."

At the top of the stairs, she tiptoed toward Danny's bedroom. Last night she'd heard him go downstairs toward the kitchen, no doubt to get something to drink. In the past few days, Savannah had been so hot and humid that all its denizens were walking around with parched throats. Apparently when Danny had come back to his room, he'd left his door partially open.

She knew she shouldn't spy on another human being in an unguarded moment. It just wasn't right. But that dark force who lived within her was propelling her silently toward Danny's door. By the time Tipper had reached his door, the force had completely taken over and she was at her mercy.

Before her hungry eyes, the nude body of Danny Hansford was sprawled on the bed, having kicked the sheets aside in the intense heat that had seemed to defy her meager air-conditioning system last night. He was a sleeping Adonis, the most beautiful young man she'd ever seen, and all her husbands or lovers such as Monty had been beauties. But no one had matched the broad shoulders and the golden skin of Danny. He evoked a panther asleep after a jungle prowl. There was a salacious smile on his face, as if inviting rape from an intruder.

In sleep, his huge uncut cock was standing tall against his belly and throbbing in its demand for relief. With the force in complete control, she moved silently into his bedroom and toward his bed.

His eyes opened wide by then and his mouth clenched hard in a grimace of surprise. But she was too quick for him. In just a moment, she'd fallen onto him, taking all of him in her mouth with the skill and intensity she didn't know she had within her.

Her lips, tongue, and hot throat descended for its meal. His penis felt like a recalcitrant snake being pulled up and out of his balls. He twisted and struggled with a kind of joy, showing her that she was satisfying him as he had probably rarely been fulfilled. The force was such a better seducer than she was.

When his explosion came, it seemed to half blow her head off. She licked, slurped, and sucked until she was certain it was all gone. She kept his penis in her mouth until it had grown flaccid, then withdrew her lips from it, kissing the head.

"Did anyone ever tell you you give the greatest blow-job in the world?" he said, his voice still sounding sleepy. "And I've been worked over by experts."

"Please get up and get dressed. Come to the kitchen. Erzulie is here. We have a nice surprise for you."

"A surprise?" he asked, looking puzzled. "I don't like surprises."

"I think you're going to like this one immensely," she said. "It's a good surprise. It will save you."

With that provocative announcement, she turned and left. In the hall she stopped and came back to his room as he jumped up from the bed, his manhood bouncing in front of him.

"In case no one ever told you before," she said, "you have the sweetest cum in all the world."

An hour later, as Erzulie downed her third glass of Southern Comfort, Tipper felt the voodoo queen was finally reaching Danny with her scheme.

"Why didn't you tell me this before?" Danny asked, still deep in his suspicion.

"Because I doubted my own power to pull it off," Erzulie said. "But lately I've been having strange visions."

"It's astonishing," Tipper said. "But Erzulie has had a breakthrough. It could save your life."

"You're telling me that Jim Williams has moved into the body of Phil Heather," Danny said. "That must be why he's treated me so shitty."

"Exactly," Tipper said. "He hates you."

"That explains everything," Danny said. "Otherwise, I would have had the faggot eating out of my hand. After all, the whole fucking world is turned on by Danny Hansford."

"It don't work in all cases," Erzulie said, putting her glass on the table, "but if you can get rid of this Phil Heather, you will be getting rid of Jim Williams. His spirit still remains on this earth. Once you kill Phil Heather—you'd really be killing Jim Williams—the spirit of Danny Hansford that lives within your soul will also be free to go. Both spirits—that of Danny Hansford and that of Jim Williams—will go straight to hell where both of them belong. You can go back to being that boy you was in Clinton before that demon took over your soul."

"Do you mean that?" Danny asked, his excitement growing.

"You could live here in this fine house with me," Tipper said, glowing with enthusiasm. "It would be a new start for you. You're a terrific looking boy with immense talent. The world would be yours."

"Do you think I could become a big star like you used to be?" Danny asked, turning to Tipper.

"I think it's not a question of could you," she said, "but when you'll become a big star."

"This is going to be no easy piece of shit," Danny said, a bitter frown crossing his beautiful face. "I'm already under suspicion by the police. I have a potential drug charge hanging over me. The cops think I was involved with Tom Caldwell in the theft of those paintings. They even think I might have killed Chris Leighton."

"Don't worry about it," Tipper said. "Erzulie and I will help you. Phil is vulnerable. We can come up with something. We can lead Phil into an ambush. At the time of his death, we will establish a perfect alibi for you. We can do this."

He looked at her hopelessly. "How in the fuck?"

"Don't rush us, white boy," Erzulie said. "These things take time. But we'll come up with a way. There must be a way."

In a flash move, Danny grabbed Erzulie by the arm, jerking her closer to him. "Listen, black bitch, and listen good. You think of a fucking way. This is my chance to live my life. Get rid of that asshole Jim Williams and his boy Hansford in one swift move. It would free me. There's a great future out there for me, and I want to live it. You can do it!"

"Simmer down, child," Erzulie said. "I'm going back to my broken down old house this morning. Once there, I'm gonna brew a special tea. It may drive me insane for a few hours or even a few days depending on how potent this tea is. But once I come out of the trance I will know the way."

"You mean that?" he asked, releasing her arm.

"I don't talk shit, blondie," Erzulie said. "When Erzulie says something, Erzulie means it."

"She means it!" Tipper said, her voice rising as she started to shake violently at the prospect of what was coming up. She thought she'd freed herself of her own dark forces but was wrong. Perhaps it would be the same with Danny. He might never be free of the dark force who had control of his soul.

The ringing of the phone in her hallway sent Tipper scurrying to answer it. A lot was happening in her life right now. It had started to move again. Every phone call meant change and excitement in her life now that it was rolling again.

Picking up the receiver, she heard an unfamiliar voice that had a rather eerie ring to it. "I want to speak to none other than Danny Hansford."

"May I ask who is calling please?" Tipper said.

"No, you may not, cunt. Put Hansford on the phone."

"I'm putting down the phone. I refuse to be addressed in such a way."

The voice grew angry and threatening. "Tell the faggot Hansford that I want to talk to him about the murder of Chris Leighton."

At the mention of Chris a panic swept over Tipper. She felt at once this was a blackmailer. All her life she'd been pursued by blackmailers, each one pretending to have evidence that she had murdered one of her husbands. She'd faced each and every one of her blackmailers.

She knew at once that Danny had to talk to this psycho. He might indeed know something. Maybe he was at the night club when Chris was murdered. Perhaps he'd seen something.

When she came back to the kitchen, Erzulie was gone and Danny was looking slightly glassy eyed as he drank his coffee.

"There's someone on the phone," she said softly, trying not to alarm him. "He insists on speaking to you."

"Unless it's the cops, I don't want calls from fans," Danny said arrogantly. "You gals have given me enough to think about for one morning."

"Please take the call," Tipper said. "I think he knows something about the stabbing of Chris Leighton."

It was subtle but a slight recognition passed between them like a hidden secret that two very close friends refuse to speak of, although each in his or her heart knows how black it is and realizes that each other is a party to it.

"I gotta take the call, right?" Danny asked, slowly getting up from the table, a weariness descending on him she had never noticed in one so young before.

"Whatever it is," she said, "we will handle it. I'm right behind you all the way. I have ways of dealing with blackmailers."

"You're pretty sure it's a blackmailer," he said.

"I've spoken with enough blackmailers in my day to know one when I hear one."

"It's odd the bastard wants to talk to me about the murder of Chris Leighton," he said.

He stared her straight in the eye with an innocence so incredibly believable that she wanted to make what he said the truth, if only she had the power to do so.

"I had nothing to do with the stabbing of Chris Leighton." His shoulders slumping, he slowly made his way up front to answer the urgent phone call.

# Chapter Nine

Hand in hand with Brian, Phil walked the land he'd known as a boy. He recalled how Aunt Bice had always saved the ripest peaches for him when he was a boy.

"You must miss her something awful," Brian said.

"I do," Phil said. "There will never be another Aunt Bice." He squeezed Brian's hand. "Thank God I have you and the boys."

"And I have you," Brian said, taking his hand and putting it to his mouth where he pressed his lips against Phil's palm. "For the first time in my life I'm happy. It took so long. My entire youth."

"You're still young and handsomer than ever," Phil said. "Pretty soon you'll be starring in a big movie."

"Do you think so?" Brian stopped in his tracks and looked over at the sea beyond. "Don't you think that Jerry is full of shit? At least at times."

"Jerry is always full of shit, but he seems rather sincere in wanting unknowns for all these roles. He feels established stars are too set in their ways. I think he sees himself as a Josef von Sternberg creating a Marlene Dietrich."

"Whoever he was."

Phil walked in silence with Brian down to a little stream. "I'm glad the Yankees left the place standing but I don't think my aunt has made repairs in thirty years."

"That's what I'm here for," Brian said. "I really want to fix the old place up. A place for you, me, and the boys."

"I've come to love John and Henry," Phil said. "I'm still very disturbed how they just live for each other."

"I'm not too worried about it," Brian said. "School will start soon. They'll meet new friends. Maybe even some girls. Find other interests. You'll see."

Sitting on a bench by the stream, Brian took Phil in his arms and gave him a long, passionate kiss. "I've found my mate," he whispered in Phil's ear.

"And I've found mine," Phil said. "Actually I found him a long time ago."

"Sorry about that," Brian whispered. "I didn't know my own nature at the time. It took a little while for me to decide I want to be a faggot."

"Even if you dressed in a gown, there's no way you will ever be a faggot," Phil said, licking Brian's lip to savor its taste. "You're all man. I know that better than anyone."

"With one, I am. I never gave of myself to anybody else, especially Joyce. We'd go through the mating ritual with virtually no passion on either side. It was like a duty we felt we had to perform with each other. Eventually we no longer felt duty bound."

Giving Brian a quick kiss, Phil got up and stretched. "I've got five pages of script to show Jerry when he comes up here today with that Duke friend of his."

"That's a real piece of Southern white trash," Brian said.

"Just the kind Jerry likes," Phil said. "Years ago he could have had me." He turned to Brian and smiled. "A real class act."

"For my sake, I'm real relieved he didn't get you," Brian said. "I let you get away once. I don't plan to make that mistake again."

"Nor I." Phil bent down and washed his hot face in the cool spring. "Big Daddy called before we left the house. He wants me to drive up to the plantation. He's alone there. He's either lonesome or else wants to have a come-to-Jesus meeting with me."

"Sounds ominous."

"Anything with Big Daddy is ominous but I've got to go see what he wants. I'll probably be back by four. Jerry and Duke won't be here for dinner until some time after six."

"I'll miss you," Brian said, joining him by the stream where he too splashed cold water on his face. "Want me to go with you? To protect you from Big Daddy."

"Thanks for the offer, and I'd really like that. But Big Daddy wants this to be a one-on-one."

Just thirty minutes later, Phil was seated on Big Daddy's veranda, sharing some bourbon and branch water with him.

Big Daddy looked at him seemingly with x-ray vision. "Glad you're here, boy. Actually I almost wanted to call you back and request that you bring that yallah gal with you. What was the bitch's name? Tango. Some made-up crap like that."

"Jerry Wheeler wants you to play a major role in *Butterflies in Heat*. That doesn't mean you have rights to bed Ms. Tango whenever you want her."

"If you fancy boys told me right, she's supposed to be my black bitch in the story. Since I'm not a trained actor, I can only get into the role by doing it."

"I'll let Jerry deal with this one. He's the producer."

"I've known a lot of women in my life, both black and white. But I've never met a woman as hot and as skilled as that Tango cunt. That is one hot pussy."

Phil sighed and sipped his bourbon. He didn't want to spoil Big Daddy's illusions and tell him that Tango was a man. If Big Daddy didn't find that out during their hot time together in bed, Phil would be the last to let him in on Tango's secret.

"Guess you figured I didn't bring you here today to discuss nigger pussy," Big Daddy said, accidentally letting a big fart that Phil pretended not to notice.

"I figured you might have something else on your mind," Phil said.

"I might as well let you have it." He looked long and hard at Phil. "You're not my fantasy come true of the son I wanted. What I really wanted, was a heavy-drinking, cow-shit kicking stud hoss who'd fuck every woman in the county and rip up their pussies with his big dick."

Phil smiled. "What you see is what you get."

Big Daddy frowned. "What I see is a real pretty boy. Everyone always said you should have been born a gal. No man should look as pretty as you look."

"You're my daddy. I take after you, although mama was pretty too."

"I was handsome. There's a God damn country mile between handsome and pretty."

"Since I have your genes, you sure can't fault me for the way I look," Phil said defensively. "Actually I like the way I look, although I don't know how Montgomery Clift got in there. Did he visit mama one night when you were away?"

"Don't sass me boy. Several members of my family looked pretty much like you do. The same penetrating eyes. The pretty, pouty lips. The dark hair. The intensity. It's not bad to look like a fucking movie star, even if that actor died years ago on a drug overdose. Don't let that happen to you."

"I don't take drugs. I smoked some pot when I was a kid. Snorted some coke. Never heroin. But I gave that up a long time ago."

"But you haven't given up sucking cock, have you?"

Phil was stunned by Big Daddy's bluntness. "I make love to Brian. He makes love to me. I'm not going to lie to you."

"Good. If there's one thing I can't stand in a youngin of mine, it's mendacity."

"Daddy, I love you, and I want back in your life. But I can't come back lying to you. I will never get married, at least to a woman. For all practical purposes, Brian and I are already married. We've even got kids to prove it."

"Yeah, right! But those kids didn't come out of your asshole, did they?"

"They did not, but they're still our boys. They belong to Brian and me and we love them dearly."

"Bring those boys up here as soon as you can," Big Daddy said. "I want to spend a day with them."

"I'd be glad to," Phil said, "but why the sudden interest in John and Henry?"

"Because long after I'm dead and gone, long after you're dead and gone too, John and Henry will be the owners of my old plantation. The Heather plantation. My land. My family land. Land that has always meant more to me than either you or that mess of blubber known as Sister Woman."

"I don't understand."

"Just this morning, my jackal lawyers have departed this house," Big Daddy said. "I've drawn up a new will. I've willed this land to you. All my property. My money. My stocks and bonds. The only request I've made is that you're to take care of that idiot daughter of mine until the bitch overdoses on chocolate. At the rate the cow is going, I'll outlive her."

"That's very generous of you, and I'll honor your request. I'll keep the property as long as I live."

"That's when John and Henry will probably get it," Big Daddy said. "I finally decided that since you and Brian can't produce, I'm stuck with the boys. I want to pass the land on to some future generation."

"Do you think Terry and Sister Woman might have a kid?"

"Don't kid a kidder," Big Daddy said with contempt. "First, if Terry ever confronted Sister Woman in bed, he'd find a hole—at least from what I've heard—as big as a tunnel. That faggot son-in-law of mine would just fall in."

"Daddy, I know I've not turned out to be what you expected or even wanted, but I am your son and thank you for taking me back. Believe it or not, I'm a fine and decent man, and it's important to me to have a family of my own. It's not the kind of family you might have wanted for me, but it's what I want. We're what you've got. And I want you to love us."

Like a beaten dog, Big Daddy sighed. "I don't think you've taken notice that my glass of bourbon is drying up, and a big man like me gets real thirsty on a hot August day like this."

"Be back in a second." Phil rose quickly from his chair. But as he headed back across the veranda, Big Daddy jerked his arm and pulled him down onto his fat lap. Aging but still powerful arms forced Phil's face close into Big Daddy's unshaven jowls from which rose a stench of bad alcoholic breath. Big Daddy crushed his lips against Phil's and inserted his tongue deep into Phil's throat as his mouth had unexpectedly come open at the sudden attack. After Big Daddy had swirled his tongue around Phil's mouth and drained all his son's saliva, he released him and pushed him away.

In stunned disbelief, Phil stood looking down at Big Daddy as he rose to his feet again. He didn't know what to say. He couldn't even believe that such a scene had taken place.

"Don't stand there looking at me like some dumb country fool," Big Daddy said.

"Why did you do that?" Phil asked.

"I did it because I've realized too late in life that I've had a pretty boy faggot son, and I never really took advantage of the situation," Big Daddy said. "Now stop standing there looking at me like some dumb nigger hired hand for the day. Get me that bourbon." Big Daddy chuckled to himself. "You're not the only one that's had desires." He sighed. "For me now, it's too late. Get on your way."

\*\*\*\*\*

To wander along without Jason was not what Lula had envisioned for her glorious future, which she had imagined would be spent coping with the demands of literary fame and fortune. Even greater than the loss of Jason was the destruction of her precious manuscript, *The Tireless Hunter.* If only she could swim out into the ocean and retrieve every page. In her heart she knew she could never record on paper the story she'd written. A recreated version, she felt, would be weak lemonade. She owed it to the memory of *The Tireless Hunter* never to attempt to write it again.

"I feel like somebody has peeled my skin from my flesh," she said out loud in her kitchen. She was an oyster without a shell. With no novel upstairs, she would wander defenseless into the world.

She'd written of isolation, estrangement, and loneliness, and that was her condition now. She feared it would be her condition forever. After Jason there would be no one. Her link with him was always strange but forever special, dating from her earliest childhood memories. She had no memory bank with anyone else, and never intended for anyone in the future to get that close to her.

On an impulse she decided she'd go for a walk through the town. She went upstairs to the bathroom and pulled off all her clothes. Then she went into the bedroom she'd shared with Jason and removed three of his large handkerchiefs left behind in his hasty exit from their house. Slowly and deliberately she fashioned a homemade bikini and then left by the front door, not bothering to lock it. Whatever there was left in the house was of no value, now that her manuscript was gone forever.

When two schoolboys started to follow her, she knew what a sight she must be. She was so skinny with her skeletal arms and pipestem legs that she must look like a prisoner just released from Dachau in 1945. For some reason she'd wanted to expose as much of her body this morning as the law would allow. She invited the world to look at her shrinking body, knowing the insults were soon forthcoming.

"Hey, scarecrow," one of the boys called to her. "It's not Halloween yet."

Spotting a beauty parlor, she decided to go inside. There were three empty chairs and no customers on this hot day. Two beauticians were standing idly by. Each looked at her with barely concealed disgust. "Can I help you," the fatter of the two said. She wore a pink dress with stains on it. At Lula's approach, the skinny beautician wandered off to the back.

"I want my hair dyed the brightest color of orange in this shop," Lula said.

"Are you sure?" the beautician asked. "Orange is such a vivid color. Halloween, really."

"Halloween," Lula repeated. "That's it. That's what I want."

"If you insist, but I have to warn you that orange is the color that many black drag queens select as their shade."

"I feel a great affinity in my heart for black drag queens."

"You do?" The beautician seemed amazed. "There's a drag queen who comes in here for us to work on her wigs. They're red—not orange."

"Could her name be Tango?" Lula asked.

"That's the one."

"I know her well. She's been having an affair with my husband, Jason McReeves."

"Oh!" The beautician seemed shocked and a bit leery of Lula. Before asking her to sit in the chair, she requested that Lula put on one of her beautician's gowns to cover her body. "I don't want anything to drop on your bare skin."

Lula agreed, knowing full well that the real reason was to cover her hideous nakedness in case any other customers came in.

"Tango is due here this morning," the beautician said. She checked her calendar. "She'll be here in thirty minutes. Just in case you don't want a confrontation with her, you could leave now and come back later long after she's gone."

"I'd love to meet up with Ms. Tango," Lula said, flashing a crooked smile and showing slightly gnarled teeth.

"There won't be any violence?" the beautician asked, growing alarmed.

"No violence," Lula said. "We're rivals—that's true. But friendly rivals."

When Tango in a red wig arrived, carrying two boxes of other wigs, Lula was deep into getting her hair painted a bright orange.

At first the drag queen diva didn't recognize her, and Lula did not rush to identify herself. As if sensing an adversary was in the parlor, Tango peered closely at Lula. "You're not Lula Carson?" Tango asked.

"I am the writer herself," Lula said looking up at Tango. If anything, she looked cheaper and more whorish than ever.

Sensing that Lula was evaluating her critically, Tango said, "Please don't think I would dress this garish in my private life. I've dressed the role of the hooker I'm going to play in *Butterflies in Heat*. She's Lola La Mour, a woman—that is, a woman of a kind— who's a bit Saturday night trash. But sexy."

"My darling, Jerry Wheeler could have found no better person for the role. In fact, knowing the character as I do, it will not be a stretch for you to play Lola."

"I hope that's not an insult, because if it is, I might snatch all that orange hair off your skinny head and you'd be one bald freak."

"No violence," the beautician cautioned.

"Nothing like that," Lula promised. "I'm sure Tango here was only speaking metaphorically."

"Whatever that means," Tango said, literally spitting out her words.

"Actually, I was planning to go over to see you today," Lula said.

Tango looked astonished. "You've already been to see me once. That was enough to last a lifetime."

"It's about Jason."

"You already got him back," Tango said. "I shouldn't have let him go so easy."

"Actually I don't have him back," Lula said. "He's left me. For good this time. I just know it."

Tango's face brightened. "Jason's up for grabs. Why didn't you call me?" She turned to the beautician. "Her husband's got the biggest cock in Savannah, maybe in the State of Georgia. Perhaps the Southeast."

"That must be one big dick," the beautician said. "I wish I could trade him in for my husband. Talk about tiny meat."

"Jason's mine!" Tango said with glee, dropping her wig boxes. "I'll be back for these later. Actually, I'm wearing a blonde wig as Lola La Mour."

"I don't know where Jason is," Lula said. "He's got no money. Unless somebody takes him in, he'll be homeless."

"Don't you worry, honey," the beautician assured her. "Any man with a dick like that will not be wandering alone on the streets of Savannah for long."

"I've got to get him before some other queen gets her mouth on him," Tango said. "Where is he?"

"I haven't a clue," Lula said. "All I know is he's gone."

"See you later." Tango hurried from the beauty parlor and into the hot streets.

Later Lula, with her new orange hair, emerged from the beauty parlor. With her large great eyes that seemed to suck in the world, Lula wandered the streets of Savannah. Although she found stares whenever she encountered anyone, no one called her names. They just looked and judged.

In the heat of the day, she began to feel that Jason might have done her an enormous favor in destroying the manuscript of *The Tireless Hunter.*

An old playwright mentor of hers had warned her, "It takes a tough old bird to work in the theater." The same could be said of publishing novels. You gave it your heart, and then published it, often to have the world reject it bitterly. Even indict your heart. Maybe Jason was protecting her from the onslaught that might surely have followed publication of her book.

Very few of the masses would be prepared to endorse her view of sexual morality. There were those, and she was certain they existed in great numbers, who were set to attack her violently. The attacks would be personal, and of that she was thoroughly convinced.

Knowing her frailties, was Jason actually trying to save her from the barbs of the world, fearing the knives waiting out there to stab at her heart would be fatal?

She didn't know what to do today. There was nowhere to go, no one to see, no one to love or be loved by her. There was no book to write. No fame or glory waiting out there to decorate her future.

Passing by Gin Tucker's house, she wanted to go inside and have him rephotograph her. She no longer wanted to look like a clone of Truman Capote on her dust jacket. She wanted to look like Greta Garbo instead.

But that was not to be. There would be no dust jacket. No publication of *The Tireless Hunter.* There would not even be a Jason McReeves, and she could hardly remember life without him.

Once she'd read that Mary Pickford in the last years of her life retreated to her bedroom and never left it. Even though years apart from the silent screen star, Lula felt she should use Pickford as a role model. She planned to go back to her rented house, there to retreat to her lone bedroom upstairs.

If the world wanted her, people would have to break in and find her, and she'd be in bed. It was the only sensible solution, she felt.

Entering her kitchen through the back door, she heard the phone ringing. Thinking it was Jason, she rushed to pick up the receiver.

It wasn't Jason.

"I'm Jay Garon," came the voice on the other end. "I'm the hottest literary agent in New York, and I'm in Savannah on a secret visit. I also represent John Grisham."

"Then you must be making millions if you represent him," Lula said. "Why would such a million-dollar agent be talking to lowly me, Miss Lula Carson of Columbus, Georgia?"

"Because Gin Tucker said you have a manuscript at your house, *The Tireless Hunter,* that is going to make you world famous. A literary celebrity overnight. A new Carson McCullers, or even a Truman Capote."

"That Gin," Lula said in her most coquettish voice. "He's always going and telling tales out of school."

"I want to read that God damn manuscript," Garon said. "I sold *The Firm.* I've sold some of the biggest deals in Hollywood. Before I kick off, I want some prestige. I want to represent a writer who is going to win the Pulitzer Prize. Gin told me where you live. I'm coming over with or without an invitation."

"But, Mr. Garon..." Before she could complete her sentence, he'd hung up the phone.

*****

At a knock at her door, Tango braced for a confrontation, even though she didn't know who it was. Could it be Danny Hansford? Duke Edwards? Perhaps Jason McReeves himself. She felt so lonely and frustrated today she might have welcomed any of the three, especially Jason.

Checking her wig and makeup, she silently prayed it wouldn't be Lula Carson before she threw open the door. Standing there, staring back at her, was Duke Edwards. He was carrying some costumes on his arm.

"What do you want?" she asked defiantly. "We're not giving out freebies around here no more."

"Fuck that!" he said, barging past. "I don't throw mercy fucks to black drag queens no more. I've got myself one hot-shot Hollywood movie producer who is promising me the world."

She stepped back and slammed the door, barging into the living room to confront her daddy. "That hot-shot movie producer is gonna make a big star out of me, bigger than The Lady Chablis could ever dream of."

He turned to face her with a smirk. "Then we've both found our pot of gold at the end of the rainbow."

"Honey, I've found mine." She glared at him. "I don't know about you. Jerry might find you amusing for a week or so—I doubt more than that. You're over forty with a tire around your waist. You've got a big dick but Hollywood is full of young, *young* men with great bodies and big dicks. Did you hear what I said? *Young!*"

His sudden slap sent her sprawling across the sofa. "I've still got it. Jerry can have his pick, and you know that, queenie. He picked me. Me, Duke Edwards. I'm the guy he wants fucking him at night."

"You bastard!" she shouted at him. "Slap me one more time and I'm calling the police."

"Listen, I've got more important things to do today than bicker with some demented nigger bitch," he said, tossing the clothes in her face. "Jerry wants you to try on these outfits. See that everything fits. If they don't, rush out and get some alterations made."

"What in hell are these tacky outfits?" she asked. "I wouldn't be caught dead wearing this shit. I doubt if The Lady Chablis herself would put on one of these atrocities."

"Speaking of Chablis," he said, grinning with contempt at her, "Jerry is right now testing her for the role of Lola La Mour in *Butterflies in Heat.*"

She jumped up from the sofa with enough fury to tear into his flesh. "You're lying. He promised the role to me."

"What does the word of a Hollywood producer mean? Not a God damn thing. Before he left New York and California, he promised the role of Numie to three or four guys. I'm not even sure he'll go with Brian Sheehan. Depends on how he tests for the part. For all I know, I might take off a few pounds and have him give the role to me."

"It would be type casting. A sleazy hustler. That's all you've ever been and all you'll ever be."

"I'm out of here before I beat your face to pulp," he said, heading for the door. "It's my last time here. You can keep my clothes. Jerry has bought me new duds."

"Loved your visit."

"Jerry told me to tell you to haul your ass to Gin Tucker's studio today at two o'clock. He wants to make some tests of you. If you fuck up, you're out the door."

"Even if I don't get to play Lola, I'm still a big star. For your information, I'm playing to standing room audiences at Blues in the Night."

He opened the door but paused and looked back. "Do you think for one moment they're coming to see you dance your stupid tango? They're coming to see the scene of a crime. They're coming to gaze at what they think is a crazed black drag queen murderer."

In rapid strides, she walked to the door to the apartment, slamming it behind her, hoping to shut Duke out of her life forever.

Hours later, after Tango had emergency alterations made to Lola La Mour's film wardrobe, she took a taxi to the house of Gin Tucker where an assistant cameraman showed her to the rear to Gin's notorious studio and dildo factory. Grotesque pictures of Lula Carson, looking like a young dyke, lined one side of the wall.

The assistant motioned for her to go to a dressing room at the far corner of the studio where she was to change into Lola's sultry red number for a song, "The Last Resort," one of the lyrics which went, "When you're at The Last Resort, why not try an indoor sport?" The song had been sent to her last night, and she'd learned the words. Jerry wanted to test her voice. Even if he didn't like her singing, she still might get the role. Her voice could always be dubbed. Throw in an old Eartha Kitt number.

Suddenly the door to the dressing room burst open and out emerged The Lady Chablis, looking like she'd just been voted Ms. Gay Dixieland, wearing a black and red dress and red high heels. There was a saucy bounce to her walk, and her hips swung like the pendulum of a clock.

"*Oooo,* child, am I pissed off at you," she said, spotting Tango. "*Yayyiss, yayyiss,* I am seriously pissed off at you."

Tango stiffened her back, imagining how Joan Crawford might do it when confronted with Bette Davis. "What have I done to displease her ladyship?"

"Child, don't give me no sass," The Lady said. "*No-no-no,* honey." Eyes sparkling and an almost olive skin glowing, Chablis turned with a venom. "The Doll has got the role of Lola La Mour all in the bag. I am pissed off that you are here testing for the part that rightly belongs to The Lady. I don't like no woman interfering with my white boys, and I don't like no woman trying to get movie roles that belong to me. As I told Clint Eastwood, if he didn't cast me as The Lady Chablis, playing myself, and not that Diana Ross who wanted to be me, the City of Savannah might go up in flames if he tried to shoot his film here without me."

"You've got a better tongue than I have," Tango said, "and you can deliver all the sass. But I've got the looks and talent. Besides, I won't have to be making up all the jiveass dialogue for Lola. That's the job of Phil Heather, the scriptwriter. I just have to deliver the lines and look like a black bitch in heat, and that I can do better than anybody else in this fucking city. Get ready to move over. I'm announcing to the newspaper that there will soon be a new empress of Savannah crowned, and you're looking at her, baby. I also have bigger tits than you."

Chablis licked her luscious red lips. "Y'mama is gonna be Lola La Mour. So *Miss Thing*, I suggest you buzz your skinny ass outta this town. Savannah belongs to The Doll, and that's me, honey. Yeah, *girl!* Yeah, *bitch!*" Like an uptight pussy debutante, The Lady Chablis glided full breasted and narrow shouldered across the room. She waved at the cameramen who'd just tested her. "I caught you guys looking at my pussy," she shouted to them. "I wrote down my private and very special phone number in Gin Tucker's toilet back there, and I expect to be hearin' from all you white mother fuckers pretty soon. The Doll will show you what it's like to fuck a real pussy." And with that promise, she faded from view.

Coming in from the rear where he'd broken his huddle with Gin Tucker, Jerry went over to Tango and gave her a kiss. "You look terrific. You are truly Lola La Mour. If Big Daddy were on the set today, he'd grab you and impregnate you for sure."

"A prospect from hell," she said rather disdainfully, barely concealing her jealousy at his having tested The Lady Chablis.

"Don't worry about my having Chablis here," he said. "I had to make the test for diplomatic reasons. Actually, The Doll didn't know it, but I was actually testing her for the role of Dinah, Lola's sidekick in the film. It's just a minor part but the boys and I thought she'd be terrific in the role."

"Maybe you're right," Tango said, warming a bit more to Jerry. "But I can't imagine The Lady agreeing to such a lesser part."

"Don't worry," he said reassuringly. "If the money's right, I can talk her into it. I mean, she once told John Berendt that men had offered to pay her money to have her walk over them in high heels. With offers like that coming over the phone, I'm sure she'll be receptive to the role of Dinah."

"I'm glad to hear you say that," Tango said, "because I was ready to walk right out of here when I saw that Chablis emerge from the dressing room."

"You'll be the star, sweetheart, Chablis merely a supporting player."

Called to the set, she was nervous when she encountered Duke standing there watching her. For the first time, Jerry's face revealed that he seemed to sense that Duke might have known Tango before he introduced them at the cafe.

Tango was visibly shaken by her daddy's presence, and she felt she could not give her best performance with him watching.

Instinctively knowing that, Jerry asked Duke to go get Big Macs for all the crew. Duke's face flashed violent anger at being treated like one of the hired hands on the set, but he reluctantly turned and headed out the door.

Gin Tucker detained Duke momentarily, no doubt trying to negotiate a contract for a dildo modeling session. Gin had advanced radar to detect men who'd make it as a model for a dildo. Duke brushed Gin aside and left hurriedly.

"I get the funny feeling," Jerry said, turning to Tango, "that you've known Duke for some time."

Tango put her hand on her hip. "From day one, darling. You see, Duke Edwards is my daddy."

Jerry appeared flabbergasted. "You're kidding. Your daddy? Your real daddy?"

"You got that right, sugah," Tango said, smiling defiantly like Lola La Mour might do. "And I must say I'm real surprised at a hot-shot, jiveass motherfucker like you."

"What do you mean?" he asked, still looking stunned.

"Taking up with a daddy fifty years old. I would think that a good-looking guy like you could have done better or at least got someone younger."

Jerry was gasping for breath. *"Fifty?"*

*****

Lavender Morgan had stayed up most of the night reading *Butterflies in Heat*, paying close attention to the scenes with the fading dress designer, Leonora de la Mer, a sort of American Chanel who lived with her dying dreams in a house in the Florida Keys, romantically called Sacré-Coeur. Lavender found it easier to concentrate on the troubles of the fictional character than she did her own nightmarish life.

Shortly before dawn, she sat up in bed and removed her satin domino. The bed was empty. She regretted not having the golden body of Danny Hansford beside her. The youth might have stunning looks and magnificent equipment but he had also brought nothing but trouble to her.

She gasped, breathing deeply, as the day with all its horror seemed to descend on her at once. She faced scandal. She'd be in the newspapers and on the television news. "What the hell!" she said, getting up from her restless bed. She'd known nothing but scandal all her life. Why, she asked herself, with all her experience, did she fear it so now? It'd been easier on her when she was young to read about her scandalous life in the dailies. It'd been romantic and glamorous.

Somehow revelations about her financial trouble, her involvement with a teenage boy, and participation in the stolen paintings were not the stuff of headlines to give her comfort or thrills. It was pure humiliation. Involvement with a teenage boy—and at her age—was not the same as rumors about her being the young, beautiful mistress of some of the world's most powerful movers and shakers. Legends about her incredible wealth, regardless of how she'd accumulated it, were hardly the same as revelations about her mounting financial troubles. Feature stories documenting how she'd acquired some of the world's masterpieces of modern art were hardly the same as implications that she'd stolen her own art to collect the insurance money to pay off her mounting debts.

Fresh from her shower she tried to make herself as glamorous as the beautiful face that used to stare back in the mirror at her when she was young. It seemed a hopeless undertaking but she attempted it anyway. She'd canceled her afternoon teas with the bachelors. Perhaps she'd never stage them again. Those teas with all the gay young blades seemed a part of her past.

Instead of her usual teas, she'd decided to let Jerry Wheeler come over and make a pitch to her about playing the role of Leonora. At first when he'd approached her at the jailhouse, she thought he was a maniac. But after checking with Gin Tucker, she found that Jerry Wheeler was indeed a producer and that the plans to shoot *Butterflies in Heat* were moving rapidly along in spite of an unfinished script. She'd been offered many gifts in life but never a starring part in a feature film. She was flattered. Many people in her youthful past had told her that she was so beautiful she should be in films, but no role had ever been presented to her. She almost wanted to say, "Until now when it's too late." She looked at her face very intently in the mirror, fearing she resembled Tallulah Bankhead on a bad night.

Tallulah was always saying "Press on," and had even requested those words be written on her tombstone. She'd taken her long ago friend's advice and pressed on with the day. Before Jerry arrived with his assistant, Duke Edwards, she had to receive the police in her home. She wished that she could be questioned by Tom Caldwell. He was so kind and easy with her, unlike the rest of the Savannah police. But Tom was dead, along with her stolen paintings, many of which had been destroyed in the crash of his truck near Jacksonville.

By two o'clock that afternoon, Norma Dixie had brought her a refreshing bourbon with a sprig of mint. Lavender was visibly shaken. Up to now she'd tried to protect Danny from the police but she no longer felt any loyalty to the boy who'd shared her bed.

"Throw his white ass to the dogs," Norma had told her before the police had arrived. "Mae West would have done that. Mae believed in saving herself. If that boy hadn't stolen those paintings, you wouldn't be in all this shit."

Lavender had taken Norma's advice, detailing to the police how she'd acquired Picasso's *Mother and Child* from Danny's homestead in Clinton, Georgia, and how Danny's mother had been planning to burn it for kindling. At this very moment the police were probably questioning Danny's mother to see if Lavender's story were true. Lavender also told the police that she'd hidden the painting in the car and had planned to go and report its discovery as soon as Danny left her house that morning. She feared if Danny learned she had the painting, he might become violent and might even kill her. She'd claimed that fear of Danny had kept her silent until now.

Actually the police, though a bit skeptical, seemed to believe her story. One of the officers found it far-fetched but it was creditable enough to be checked out. Everything, it seemed, depended on what Danny's mother might say in Clinton. She was such a devout born-again Christian that she probably would bluntly tell the police what had transpired and refuse to lie for Danny or anyone else. But Lavender could not be sure. Her suspicion of born-again Christians had always been strong.

At the agreed upon time of four o'clock, Jerry Wheeler had arrived with the most extraordinary and sexy-looking older man, who he introduced as his assistant, Duke Edwards. Duke smiled and gently shook her hand, holding it for what she thought was an extraordinary long time for a handshake. He'd flattered her outfit and her looks, and she'd stared deeply into his blue eyes. He had a mesmerizing quality about him, and was no doubt Jerry's hustler. How fortunate for Jerry, she thought. Duke wore a white shirt and white pants, his feet encased in sandals, and he was deeply tanned, which only accentuated the deep blue of his eyes. Lavender felt an old hag like herself could loose herself in the deep blue sea of those eyes.

Norma brought drinks to her guests by the pool where Jerry made a long and very convincing pitch to her about why she'd be great in the part of Leonora de la Mer.

In her straw hat which protected her from the fierce sun, she leaned back and laughed softly, trying to imitate the actions of Leonora in the novel she'd so recently read. "What makes you think I can act?"

"You've been acting all your life," Jerry said. "I've seen the newsreel footage of you. You're fantastic, and you'll be even greater in the film."

"It is an interesting proposition," she said. She turned to Duke and smiled demurely. "And I'm one woman who has received her share of propositions."

"I bet they are still coming in like gangbusters," Duke said.

She smiled again before turning to Jerry. "The role is extremely provocative. I fear there are many actresses around who would be dynamite in the part. Lauren Bacall comes to mind. There are others, of course, but Bacall would be the best."

"I want you," Jerry said, reaching for her hand and holding it gently. "Of course, you'd have to test for the part. We've rented Gin Tucker's studio. Would you agree to do a test?"

"I'd insist on it," she said. "I too want to see what I look like on the screen. In color no less. I have no intention of making myself out to look like a horse's ass unless I, too, am pleased with what I see on that screen. A test would be great."

"It's a deal." Jerry turned up his glass and finished the last drop.

Norma arrived with fresh drinks, bourbon with fresh mint. "I'm a Scotch man myself," Jerry said, "but that bourbon tasted good."

"I brought some of my cheese balls," Norma said, serving Duke before Jerry and Lavender.

"I bet they're great," Duke said. "I hear you black mamas can really cook."

"Don't sass me, boy, with that black mama shit," Norma said. "They're not casting *Gone with the Wind*. They're casting *Butterflies in Heat.*"

"I didn't mean to make you mad," Duke said.

Ignoring him, Norma turned to Jerry. "I too have read *Butterflies in Heat*. There's a role for a fat woman in that movie. Tangerine Blanchard from Atlanta, Georgia. I was born to play the role of Tangerine."

"But that part calls for a white woman," Jerry said. "With orange hair. Real Southern white trash."

"Honey, the role could be rewritten for a black woman," Norma said. "I wouldn't be the first black woman cast as a maid. I'm already the maid for Miss Morgan here. We could just play ourselves."

"I don't know," Jerry said with obvious doubt on his mind. "Grand ladies with black maids sounds a bit Thirties to me."

"You don't know this, but I was Mae West's personal assistant. I advised her on all her roles—not that she had all that many when I came along—and even wrote some of her material."

"We'll see what we can do," Jerry said. "But I was planning to offer the role of the blousy Tangerine to Tipper Zelda and convince her to appear in an orange wig."

"Tipper Zelda!" Norma said with a gasp. "I've got more talent than Tipper will ever have."

"I think Tipper would be ideal as Tangerine," Lavender said. "The two of us would be a sensation on the screen. I know you want unknowns in the parts, but Tipper and I could give the film some name recognition, but what the hell."

"Miss Morgan," Norma said with mounting fury, "are you trying to get me denied my big break on the screen?"

"Why don't you go fry some oysters for the boys?" Lavender asked. "Norma makes the best fried oysters in Savannah."

Without another word, Norma turned her back on the trio and headed for the kitchen, carrying the same small tray she'd brought the drinks in on.

Duke looked over at the pool. "It's so hot I'm frying. I'd sure like to jump in that refreshing pool of yours, Miss Morgan."

"By all means," she said, motioning with her hand. "Check in the bathhouse over there. I'm sure you'll find a swimsuit to fit you."

"Thanks," Duke said, easing his muscular body from the chair and heading for the bathhouse.

When he was out of hearing distance, Lavender turned to Jerry. "I don't know where you found him but, daddy, buy me some of that."

"There's a real problem in the relationship," Jerry said.

"He's too much for you?" she asked. "I couldn't help but notice how he filled out his pants."

"It's not that," Jerry said. "Duke has the equipment, all right, and that's one stud who knows how to use it."

"Then what's the problem?" she asked. "This is Savannah. We're very understanding of various attachments."

"I just learned that Duke is fifty years old."

"And what in the fuck is the matter with fifty?" Lavender asked. "I'd love to be fifty again."

"All my life I swore I'd never take up with a man who was even close to fifty, much less actually fifty. It's a firm rule. Now that I know how old Duke is, I've got to get rid of him. I can't stand to have a man of fifty touch me."

"You're being silly," she said, "even if you're my producer and in theory my boss, I should be more discreet with you. Duke doesn't look more than thirty-five. Frankly, I think he looks stunning."

"My mind is made up," Jerry said. "He's got to go."

"If you're kicking him out, why not toss him my way?"

"You want him?" he asked, looking astonished. "You could be seen with an older man better than you could with Danny Hansford. It would raise fewer eyebrows."

She hesitated before answering. Wasn't her life messed up enough already? Did she really need to take up with another hustler?

As if answering her own question, Duke emerged from the bathhouse in an almost sheer white bikini just like Danny had worn. The golden light of the afternoon bathed his body. It wasn't the world's most perfectly formed body, and it revealed he'd had a few beers in his day, but for some reason he was the sexiest man she'd ever seen.

As he moved toward them, she leaned back in her chair breathing deeply. Thank God her large sunglasses covered her eyes which were zeroing in on one part of Duke's anatomy. She closed her eyes, imagining that later in the night she'd be on the receiving end of one of the deepest and most satisfying penetrations of her life.

\*\*\*\*\*

Tipper Zelda had agreed to drive Danny to within a block of Arlie Rae Minton's apartment. She'd convinced Danny that he had to go upstairs to the psycho's apartment and hear his demands. "He may have something on you," Tipper was saying, as she slowed her car down and parked it in an obscure alleyway. She turned off the lights.

"But you know I didn't kill Chris Leighton," Danny protested.

For a moment Tipper remained silent. When she finally spoke her once fabled throat seemed hoarse. "You don't really remember what happened that night at the club, and you know that's true. It's like when my first husband was killed. I simply don't remember the events leading up to his death. I will never know whether I killed him or he took his own life."

Danny remained silent for a long time too. One part of his brain wanted to recall what happened that night at the club, but the other side of his brain refused to release the information. The battle between the dark force and himself was being waged to a violent degree within his own skull, and at any moment he fully expected to feel the impact of his head being blown off.

He turned and with pleading eyes looked over at Tipper who was staring back at him. "You know what happened the night of Chris Leighton's murder, don't you?"

She hesitated a long moment before speaking. "I know."

That was all he needed to hear. He didn't want details. "I must go and see this Arlie Rae Minton."

"You have no choice."

"I'll be back soon," he said, getting out of the car.

"I'll be here waiting," she said. "Be very, very careful. You could be walking into a trap."

He easily found the address he'd been given. In front of Arlie Rae's door, he waited almost five minutes before knocking.

In seconds the door was thrown open by Arlie Rae. "I knew you'd come. Get in here. I don't want any Peeping Toms hearing what I've got to say to you."

Without saying a word Danny was ushered into a small, cramped apartment. Everything—the kitchen, the living room, and the bedroom—was in one area. Danny noted various pictures of some horsy-looking woman plastered all over the walls and ceiling near Arlie Rae's bed. Not knowing what to say, he asked, "Who is that ugly bitch?"

"Watch your tongue, boy," Arlie Rae said in a burst of anger. "That's Linda Tripp. She's hot. The sexiest woman in America."

"You gotta be kidding," Danny said.

"I'm not kidding, and ordering you here is no joke either," Arlie Rae said.

"What's on your mind?" Danny asked.

"Plenty," Arlie Rae said. "Sit down."

"I'd rather stand," Danny said. "The way I figure it, we can make this meeting brief."

"I said sit down." Arlie Rae's command was so sharp Danny felt he should heed it.

Seated at the kitchen table, Danny turned with a steel-faced determination to Arlie Rae. "If you're like most guys, you brought me here to suck on my big dick. Forget it! Even at my most desperate, I wouldn't give you a mercy fuck."

Arlie Rae glared at him but said nothing. He went into his bathroom and emerged within a minute with a blood-soaked shirt and a machete.

Danny immediately recognized the machete. It was Lavender Morgan's safari machete, presented to her by none other than Ernest Hemingway. "You stupidly hid these in a garbage can outside the night club. Tipper Zelda was in the same alleyway watching what you did. After you'd gone back inside, that Zelda cow went over and retrieved the shirt and the machete and concealed them behind bricks in an old oven left over from the Civil War or some such shit."

Danny was breathing heavily. At first he wanted to grab the machete and shirt from Arlie Rae and run from this apartment where he felt the air was growing staler by the minute. It was unbearably hot, like an oven really. "So what do you want?"

"I'm sure we'll work out a deal."

"I'm not much good at dealing with blackmailers."

"I'll make it easy for you," Arlie Rae said. "I'll spell out my terms."

"Spill the beans."

"For some reason Tipper is covering for you. Maybe she's fallen in love with you. I know she's put up bail for you. She's installed you at her house. She's got plans for you."

"There's nothing between Tipper and me, you little faggot."

"Watch who you're calling a faggot," Arlie Rae said, clutching the murder weapon and the shirt to his chest. "Danny Hansford shouldn't be calling nobody in Savannah a faggot."

"I'm no faggot, shitface," Danny said, rising to his feet. "You got that? Or do I have to rearrange you face?"

Arlie Rae didn't say anything for a moment. "Tipper Zelda was poor as a church mouse a little while ago. But suddenly she's got money. If she's taken it upon herself to hide your crime, for whatever reason, you're gonna be a costly toy boy."

"Exactly how much are we talking here?"

"I want one-hundred thousand dollars up front, and after that a nice cool ten thousand a month for as long as I live. I'm God damn tired of being a janitor and cleaning up people's shit."

With a face as cold and bitter as an Artic night, Danny stared deep and hard at Arlie Rae. "I'll pass along your blackmail request to Tipper. When it comes to her money, you'll have to negotiate directly with her. In the meantime, I'm taking back the machete and my shirt. They belong to me." He moved toward Arlie Rae to retrieve his possessions.

"Not so fast, asshole," Arlie Rae said, backing away from Danny. "The deal is, I hold onto these little souvenirs."

"No way!" In a sudden move Danny grabbed the possessions from Arlie Rae. He easily overpowered the weaker man, took the shirt and machete, then punched Arlie Rae in the nose, as blood spurted all over his face. The janitor fell back and toppled over on his battered sofa.

"God damn you!" Arlie Rae shouted. "I'll get even with you. I'm calling the police."

As Arlie Rae crawled toward the phone, the battle in Danny's brain seemed to have ended. His head was at peace and no longer churning. Everything seemed calm now. It was the way it was when a violent hurricane sweeps over the land, followed by the quietest, most tranquil sunny day.

Reaching the phone, Arlie Rae dialed for the police. Danny encased his fingers around the handle of the machete. The grip felt familiar. The second time was easier.

In one sudden move he plunged the machete into Arlie Rae's back. There was a moan, like a little shriek, but it wasn't powerful at all. Blood gushed from Arlie Rae when Danny stabbed him again. Even though Danny knew Arlie Rae was dead, he kept stabbing at his back, and Danny didn't really know why.

When he left the apartment, Danny carried the bloody machete and shirt with him. He didn't bother shutting the door because he didn't want to leave fingerprints.

At the door he paused silently. On an impulse he wanted to look back. But then he asked himself why. He knew Arlie Rae was dead. No one could have lived through that. He didn't need to waste time rubbernecking to see what a blood-soaked body looked like after it had been knifed. A sight like that could give a man nightmares.

Danny decided he already had enough nightmares without adding Arlie Rae to his dreams at night. He did pause long enough to look at a big blow-up of Linda Tripp over Arlie Rae's little dining table.

Tripp's eyes seemed to be accusing him.

With his possessions, he hurried out of the apartment and down the street to Tipper's car.

*****

In Tipper's darkened back yard, she held Danny's arm in a tight grip. "We can't take the machete or shirt inside the house. You may be a suspect. With all this shit spinning around you, my house could be searched."

"I'll drive somewhere and throw them away," he said.

"We'll hold onto the machete," she commanded. "I'll burn the shirt in the barbecue." Taking the shirt from him, she covered it with lighter fluid and set it on fire on the grill.

"I feel my life's blood is going up in smoke," he said, staring at the flames, the only illumination on the grounds as she'd turned off all the porch lights before driving him to Arlie Rae's.

She grabbed him and planted a long, deep kiss on his mouth, inserting her tongue although she felt a slight revulsion on his part. Perhaps she'd imagined it. Like the trained hustler he was, he quickly warmed to her passionate kiss and let her taste his tongue and drink fully of his succulent lips.

Breaking away, he asked, "What are we gonna do with the machete?"

"For the moment I'm hiding it next door," she said, walking across the yard, trailed by him. "The place is up for sale and no one has lived there for three months."

In the back yard of an old and decaying 19th-century house, she buried the machete in that neighbor's barbecue, carefully concealing it in ashes. "No one will find it here."

"Don't be so sure," he cautioned.

"In the morning I'll give it to Erzulie," she said. "She'll hide it for us until the time is ripe."

He looked puzzled. "What do you mean, ripe?"

"She'll carry it to Bonaventure Cemetery."

"You mean, give it a proper burial?"

She stopped and stared at him in the darkness. "Something like that. In time, when you're ready, I'll tell you what we're going to do. We'll have a grand party—a real farewell—in that cemetery."

"Am I invited?" The sound of a voice from the darkened corner of her back porch startled her.

She whirled around. For a moment she didn't recognize that familiar voice. Then the identity of that voice came to her like a bolt of electricity going through her body.

It was Dale Evans.

For a long moment, a deadly silence fell over the yard. She didn't know what to say. Recovering slightly, she said, "Of course, you are. Actually considering what you must have heard, you're invited to all our parties from now on."

"Glad to hear that," Dale said.

Danny stood peering into the darkness and was apparently totally confused.

"Danny Hansford, meet Dale Evans," Tipper said.

Still Danny said nothing.

"I'm really looking forward to getting to know you," Dale said to Danny. "I've heard great stories about you, and I hope all of them are true."

"To what do we owe the honor of this visit?" Tipper asked. "In the middle of the night and unannounced."

"You learn more interesting things in Savannah calling on people unannounced in the middle of the night," Dale said.

"I'm sure you do," Tipper said. "But before we're overheard by anybody else, let's get the God damn hell back to my house and turn on the lights." She unlocked her kitchen door and ushered both young men inside her kitchen.

In the glow of light, Dale seemed to be not only giving Danny an intense appraisal, but from the look on Dale's face he heartily approved of what he saw.

"So, what do you want?" Danny asked, not concealing the hostility in his voice.

"Although I may have heard a great deal about you," Dale said to Danny, "you may not have heard much about me."

"I don't know who you are," Danny said.

"I'm Tipper's business manager," Dale said.

Going over to pour herself a drink, Tipper spun around. "If I recall, we haven't gone into contract yet. There are still details to be worked out."

"Oh, my darling," Dale said. "Perhaps you don't understand. After what I've heard, after what I know, I dictate all terms of our business arrangements in the future."

"You bastard!" she shouted at him before pouring a stiff drink. "Does Frank know you are here?"

"Frank doesn't know where I am," Dale said. "He kicked me out three hours ago. He caught me engaged in a rather embarrassing position with one of the waiters at the club. I'm out the door. From now on, you're my meal ticket." He smiled provocatively at Danny, pursing his lips. "You and this hot blond stud standing before me in those tight jeans that leave little to the imagination."

"You might have your claws into Tipper," Danny said, "but you don't own an inch of my flesh."

"That remains to be seen," Dale said. "I've got you by the balls, baby, and I know what impressive balls they are. Gin Tucker has already sold me one of your dildos."

Again, a long silence descended among them. Tipper didn't know what to say. She'd already labeled Dale an aggressive bottom, and right this moment she realized how accurate her appraisal was. Once again, she was confronting a blackmailer. She'd dealt with them before, some more powerful and in the know than Dale. In a theatrical way, as if on stage, she smiled at both Dale and Danny. "Let's be civilized," she said. "Let's all adjourn to my parlor and discuss our new terms."

"What fucking terms?" Danny asked.

"The terms—obviously—where I will be living under Tipper's roof," Dale said. He raised his eyebrows. "And sharing your bed."

"I'm not sleeping with you," Danny protested. He looked first at Tipper, then at Dale. Neither said anything. "Oh, shit!" Danny finally said before trailing both Tipper and Dale to her living room.

Without being asked, Dale walked over to Tipper's liquor cabinet and poured himself a bourbon. "Can I get one for my man?" he asked Danny.

"I'm not your man," Danny protested. "But get me a tequila. Straight."

"Your wish, hot stuff, is my command," Dale said, reaching for a bottle. "And sit in the chair across from me, and don't cross your legs. I want to see what I'm going to be enjoying for the rest of the night."

"You fuck..." Before Danny could finish his sentence, Tipper interrupted.

"Do what he says," she told Danny. "From the way I see it, Dale's in the driver's seat."

"In more ways than one," Dale said, handing Danny his tequila and settling on the sofa across from him. "I don't know what fun and games you guys were up to tonight. I'm sure I'll read all about it in tomorrow's papers." He paused. "Unless you want to tell me now."

"We did nothing," Tipper said.

"Yeah, right!" Dale said. "You would think murdering Chris Leighton would be enough for one year. Surely a murder a year is enough to satisfy the Black Widow Spider herself."

Tipper remained silent, only staring at Dale. He had arrived on her back porch at the wrong moment. He wasn't part of her plans. His intruding himself into her life at this moment was a big mistake. Dale was an absolute fool to come up against the dark force who lived within her. His intrusion would no doubt be fatal.

She'd deal with Dale in good time, or rather the dark force would. She'd let him enjoy his momentary victory over her. She'd even sacrifice Danny to his desires. There was no way out.

She was certain that Dale would have his date with her dark force. She shuddered to contemplate what fate might await him.

In the meantime, she sat back and tried to relax and consider the circumstances. Knowing that she'd have the ultimate revenge allowed her to tolerate the overweening presence of Dale in her living room. What remained was for her to convince Danny that he too had to go along with Dale's scheme.

Dale sipped his drink, his eyes darting first at Danny and then at Tipper. "As your business manager, I have wonderful news for you," he said to Tipper.

"What, pray tell?" she asked.

"I ran into Jerry Wheeler today," Dale said. "He's in town casting *Butterflies in Heat*."

"I know," she said. "All of Savannah knows."

"Don't be a smart-ass," Dale said. "What you may not know is he's going to offer you the role of Tangerine in the film. Have you read the book?"

"Yes, I have," she said. "I recall the character. It's a fucking sloppy maid with a red wig. A legs apart, over-the-hill fat broad. Tipper Zelda is associated only with glamor. I could never play such a farty part."

"Too bad, little dah-ling," Dale said. "I've already accepted for you."

She slammed down her glass. "You have no right."

Dale leaned forward in his seat, glaring at her. "Listen, you murdering bitch, as of tonight I have a right to do about any fucking thing I want around this dump."

"Okay," she said rather calmly considering the circumstances. "Tell your friend, Mr. Wheeler, that I'm delighted he's considering me for the role. Perhaps it is only appropriate that I go against type. Who knows? I might win a best supporting actress nomination."

"You might, indeed," Dale said. "With me calling the shots around here, I might even keep the two of you out of the electric chair."

"We've done nothing," Danny protested.

"You don't have to convince me of a thing," Dale said. "I'm not the judge. My job will be to keep the police off your hot little asses."

"And how do you propose to do that?" Tipper asked.

"In case you are a suspect in this latest escapade—whatever in the fuck it was—I'm here to establish an alibi," Dale said. "We were here all night. Neither you nor Danny went out all evening. You've been with me all the time. I rushed over here when Frank kicked me out."

Tipper breathed heavily. "That would be a very good story to maintain."

Danny sighed. "Yeah, that would be great."

Dale put down his drink and rose from his chair. "All of us have much to talk about in the morning. But right now I'm going to go upstairs and run a bath."

"A bath will do you good," Tipper said.

"The bath's not for me," Dale said. "It's for Danny. I figure he must have worked up quite a sweat doing what he did tonight, and a long relaxing bath will be just the right tonic."

Danny started to protest but Tipper signaled him to go along with Dale's desires.

"You don't have to scrub any part of that luscious body of yours," Dale said to Danny. "I'm here to take care of everything for you."

*****

After only twenty minutes in his Savannah kitchen, the telephone rang. At the sink, with his hands wet, Phil was preparing breakfast for Brian and the boys. After a day of work on the screenplay with Jerry, he planned to drive them to Aunt Bice's where all of them had been invited up the hill for a family reunion dinner with Big Daddy following the return of Sister Woman and Terry Drummond from their honeymoon. Drying his hands, he picked up the phone.

"It's Tipper Zelda," came the voice. "Phil."

His voice was cool and detached, although polite. "Good morning. I'm real busy right now, but how could I help you?"

"I want you to forgive me for my outburst the other night," Tipper said. "I'm real sorry. I'd been drinking."

"Let's forget it, but my mind is made up. I'll not be working on the memoirs. As I said, I'm sure you'll find many eager and talented writers who'd like the job."

"There will be no memoirs," she said flatly. "That's not what I'm calling about. My manager, Dale Evans, said that Jerry Wheeler is considering me for the role of Tangerine, and I'm interested."

"It's a great part for somebody," he said. "You're far too glamorous, perhaps."

"But I can make myself unglamorous," she said defensively. "I wouldn't be the first performer who's done that."

"Indeed you wouldn't."

"I know my getting the role is still tentative," she said, "but I wanted to repair any damages in our relationship."

"That's fine with me," he said. "A little misunderstanding. I'm willing to forget all about it."

"Could we seal it with a drink?" she asked. "An old Savannah custom."

"If you wish," he said. "But it's really not necessary. I have to leave town tonight but I'll be back in the morning."

"I want you to come and have a martini or two with me at the Bonaventure Cemetery," she said.

"You mean like Mary Harty did with John Berendt in *Midnight in the Garden of Good and Evil*?" he asked.

"Exactly. I'd like to relive that scene with you."

"That's intriguing. There's a cemetery scene in *Butterflies in Heat*, and I'd like to check it out."

"I want it to be at eight o'clock tomorrow night," she said. "I've done this many times before. It's a lot of fun."

"I don't know about the fun part, but I'm game. It appeals to the dramatist in me."

"I'll meet you at eight along Bonaventure Road at the entrance," she said. "I'll have the martinis and everything."

"Can I bring Brian?" he asked.

"Don't bring anyone," she said. "This is a little make-up session for the two of us. It's very important. We'll be there for only an hour. I don't want you to tell anyone you're meeting me. It's our secret."

"Why are you being so mysterious?"

"Our make-up toast with each other is just one of the reasons I'm meeting you."

"What's the other one?"

"Since you're not going to write my memoirs, I want to tell you how each of my husbands was murdered," she said.

"My God," he said. "You're serious."

"I've never been more serious in all my life," she said. "But there's one condition."

"Let me have it."

"You can't reveal or write about what I'm going to tell you until I'm dead."

"That's fair enough."

"Good," she said. "Until tomorrow night at eight."

Putting down the phone, he rushed to the stove to check his poached eggs, now overly poached. What writer wouldn't go for the bait she was dangling in front of him? The tabloids had speculated for decades about how Tipper's husbands were killed. Even though he'd have to wait until she died to reveal the murderer, he was fascinated at the prospect that tomorrow night he would learn the true story.

The martini meeting in the graveyard sounded a bit corny but it would be following the custom promoted in Berendt's book. Phil would tell Brian that he had an errand to run and that he'd be back soon.

Without his being aware of him, Brian came up behind Phil and wrapped his arms around him. "I'm one hungry husband," Brian said. "The boys will be descending on us any minute."

He turned and kissed Brian on the lips. "That was real special last night."

"I loved it," Brian said. "You grow more responsive to my needs all the time. We've got all the passion like the first time but there is a tenderness here we didn't have before."

"Some people call it love."

At that moment John and Henry rushed into the kitchen, demanding to be fed.

That same night at the Heather plantation, Big Daddy was amusing Brian and Jerry with stories of the Old South. Back from her honeymoon, Sister Woman was upstairs getting ready for the dinner two black cooks in the kitchen were preparing. Big Daddy had insisted on all his favorite foods tonight. Each dish had been forbidden by his doctor.

Terry had demanded to see Phil in the back yard, and Phil replenished his drink and headed out to meet him near an old swing. "Hey, guy," Phil said. "How was the honeymoon?"

"The nightmare of my life," Terry said. "I can't go through with this marriage."

"What happened? Or should I ask."

"You bastard!" Terry said, turning on him in fury. "You set me up for this. There was supposed to be no sex. But sex was all she demanded on that so-called honeymoon. What a fuck-up! She even insisted I go down on her at one point. I've never been so disgusted in my whole life."

"Oh, shit! What are you going to do?"

"I'm not staying here—that's for damn sure," Terry said. "You've got Brian Sheehan. With all his muscles to paw every night, you certainly don't want fat me."

"I don't know what to say. I'm real sorry how things worked out."

"I'm the one who's sorry," Terry said. "But I'm leaving. Right now."

"I don't get it."

"What that fucking cow, Sister Woman, doesn't know is that I've packed all my clothes in a rented car I've got parked in that garage down the hill. I loaded up this afternoon when Sister Woman was asleep upstairs and Big Daddy was in a drunken stupor on the porch."

"You really mean this, don't you?" Phil asked. "When are you going?"

"Right now." Terry reached into his pocket and produced a key, dangling it in front of Phil.

"You're sure this is the best career move for you?" Phil said. "Sister Woman is revolting. But she's an heiress."

"Sister Woman can take this plantation and all her stocks and bonds and stuff them up her overripe cunt."

"I'm sure they'd fit," Phil said.

"I want you to kiss me good-bye, like you used to, but I think I've kissed my last Heather," Terry said. He turned his back to Phil and headed down the road, his fading figure lit only by the moonlight.

"Good-bye, Terry," Phil called out. "I'll remember the good times."

Jerry called to Phil from the back porch. "Come on, guy. Dinner's ready. Big Daddy is looking for you and Terry. Sparking up an old romance?"

"Nothing like that," Phil said, walking in rapid strides toward the back porch.

"Where's Terry going?" Jerry asked. "Dinner's ready."

"Terry's getting the hell out of here," Phil said. "He's had it with Sister Woman. The first time he ran away with me. This time he's going on his own steam."

"He wouldn't be a bad looking kid if he slimmed down," Jerry said.

"It's going to be some dinner," Phil said. "You haven't experienced hell until you've seen Sister Woman seriously pissed off."

"You're family," Jerry said. "You'll have to break the news to her."

"I know. That's my job. What fun."

"Speaking of break-ups," Jerry said, "you haven't asked where I stashed Duke Edwards."

"I was too kind."

"I gave him away to Lavender Morgan."

"You what?"

"You heard me," Jerry said. "I found out he's far older than I thought, and I've got my youthful standards to uphold. Incidentally, he's Tango's daddy."

Phil paused at the doorway, looking long and hard at Jerry. "I've heard about all the news I can handle for one night."

"Phil," Big Daddy shouted from the dining room. "Get your ass in here for dinner. Sister Woman's got herself all dolled up special for the night. She's so happy in her new marriage that she promises to give up chocolates. Tell Terry to get his fat ass in here too."

Jerry looked at Phil before heading in for dinner. "Good luck. I don't envy you."

Phil sucked in the aroma of the Southern cooking coming from the dining room. The moment he entered, Sister Woman—a mass of green cotton—yelled at him, "Where in the fuck is Terry?"

Phil swallowed hard. "Before we begin this festive dinner, I have an announcement to make."

*****

With the arrival of the literary agent, Jay Garon, in her modest home, Lula didn't know how to dress or even behave. She was aware that Phil knew Garon and had called Phil earlier for advice, but he was not next door or even at his Aunt Bice's house. Neither was Brian and certainly not John and Henry.

At first she'd wanted to cancel the meeting with Garon but had decided to go through with it anyway. She really wanted to know what he'd heard about *The Tireless Hunter*. Only Jason and she knew that the manuscript no longer existed. She didn't want word of the novel's loss to get out, especially to people, including Lavender Morgan, who had presented her with the literary grant on which she and Jason had been surviving.

All day she'd expected Jason to call her or just to show up on their doorstep. But not one word from him.

It didn't make a lot of sense—in fact, it might mean she was insane—but somehow she felt meeting with Garon and talking about her masterpiece would somehow bring the novel back to life. Could Jason have stolen her hard copy and presented it to the agent? That might be possible although she had grave doubts.

Nonetheless the meeting with Garon gave her something to live for, because since the loss of her manuscript and her abandonment by Jason she didn't see much in the way of a future for her.

Losing the manuscript dramatized to her that she had nothing to replace it with. There would be no follow-up, no series of masterpieces coming from her pen. The reality was that she could not sit down and recreate *The Tireless Hunter*, much less attempt another book.

As he fled from their home, Jason had taken her life's blood. She'd loved him in her way but knew now that her love wasn't enough to save Jason and certainly not herself.

For her meeting with Garon, she put on a simple gingham dress and sandals. She'd worn the dress in college, and it was made of durable fabric. She turned on a fan in the living room, as the day was unbearably hot. As John Grisham's agent, Garon, she just knew, could afford air conditioning wherever he went, including in his chauffeured limousine.

When he knocked on her door and was ushered inside, Garon startled her by his appearance. She hadn't known that he looked like an iguana. He immediately requested some vodka which she rushed to the kitchen to procure for him. Seated across from him on her battered sofa, she found his smell overpowering. He'd covered his corpulent body with Chanel No. 5.

He flashed a smile at her, and she was intrigued by his large mouth. No doubt entire armies had deposited their semen in that gaping mouth. Most of his smile was toothless. She was certain that should he so desire, the Iguana could buy a dental clinic but he preferred to keep his original rotting teeth.

"I'm so thrilled that an important agent like you would even consider a manuscript from little ol' me, Miss Lula Carson of Columbus, Georgia."

"Who loves ya, baby?" he asked before lighting a cigarette without requesting permission. She didn't have any ashtrays so she took the saucer from the bottom of a flower pot and placed it next to him.

"I've got radar when it comes to latching onto a hot property," he said. "Without me there would be no John Grisham."

"I'm mighty impressed with your achievements in the literary world," she said.

"I've fought every step of the way," he said, puffing mightily on his cigarette. "I've had to sell everything—mostly crap. Porno like *Copsucker*. Shit like that."

"Launching oneself into the field of publishing, or so I'm told, is an undertaking of awesome proportions."

"Quaintly put," he said, eying her skeptically. "Do you write like you talk?"

"Not really. When I write I find that I have a different voice. A special voice." She paused theatrically for effect, leaning closer to him. "A unique voice." She giggled nervously. "Perhaps I'm being immodest."

"Don't worry about it," he said, crushing his cigarette in the ashtray. After downing a hefty swig of vodka, he immediately lit another cigarette and started puffing away. "If you've got talent, fuck modesty. I never had modesty. Back when I was the prettiest boy in Hollywood..." He paused to cough violently.

Startled by his spasm, she could offer no help. She couldn't even in her wildest imagination conjure up the Iguana as the prettiest boy in Hollywood.

"I had offers from everybody to become their boy, but I chose the director, George Cukor." He looked over at her, searching her face, perhaps to determine if he should identify Cukor. "Through Cukor I got to know all the big stars of the day—Tallulah Bankhead, Bette Davis, Marlene Dietrich, Joan Crawford. Talk about egos!"

"I agree with you," she said in a soft voice. "If you believe in yourself, you've got to convince the world of your artistic worth."

"Fuck that!" he said. "That's why you've got me. I'll peddle the manuscript. I'll do all the promotion. You sit in a loft somewhere and turn out the crap. I'll even accept the Pulitzer Prize for you."

"Thanks anyway, but that I'd like to do myself. It would mean so much to me."

"Whatever." He was growing impatient. "Where's the God damn manuscript? I don't have all day."

She felt the suffocation of the day moving in on her. "I don't have it right this very minute. But I'm having a copy prepared for you. It'll be ready at six."

"I can't wait around for it," he said, crushing out another cigarette. "Can you deliver it to my hotel tonight? I'm staying at the Hyatt."

"It will be there before seven," she promised. "Do you think you'll have time to look at it tonight?"

"I'll look at it when I get back from my nightly rounds," he said. "Every night I have to suck at least three big cocks before falling to sleep. Now that I have all that delicious Grisham money, I can buy almost any cock I want. Last night I met this handsome hunk wandering along the waterfront. I couldn't believe the bulge I saw in his jeans, and I can assure you this pussy sitting before you doesn't mess up her mouth with tiny dicks."

"Was he blond?"

"Yeah, how did you know? He said his name was Jason McReeves. When I got him back to the hotel and pulled off his jeans I discovered he had the biggest dick in the Southeast. You wouldn't believe the size of that thing. Big balls too. I gave the stud five-hundred dollars, and it was the best investment I've ever made. I wanted to shack up with him tonight but after I gave him the money he just disappeared from the hotel room. He didn't steal anything. Just took the money and ran."

A headache descended suddenly on her, and her heart felt heavy. She looked at the Iguana but didn't really see him. Her mind was on Jason. "That definitely sounds like Jason McReeves," she said. "He's well known in Savannah. You hit the jackpot with him. I'm afraid that after Jason it will be downhill for you. The other men you are likely to meet tonight on your prowl probably won't measure up."

"You're right. This Jason hunk has sure spoiled me for future encounters."

Abruptly changing the subject, she said, "I'm honored that you'll read my manuscript."

"I won't actually read it," he said. "I never read manuscripts. I couldn't even read *The Firm*. Actually I read a few pages of it and hated it but I was still able to sell it to Hollywood. I just take a manuscript, feel it, maybe look at a paragraph or two, and sort of absorb it."

"That's a marvelous talent," she said. "I could never do that. I read every line and often stop to contemplate what the author meant."

"I don't have time for crap like that," he said, rising slowly to his feet. "I've got to go. Get that manuscript to my hotel tonight. I need prestige. I've made all the money I'll ever need, although I'm not turning down any wheelbarrows of gold arriving at my penthouse in New York. But the literary world has laughed at me too long for being too commercial. I've got to have prestige at this point in my life. A National Book Award, shit like that. I'll show the fuckers who laughed at me."

"Mr. Garon," she said, rising and shaking his hand. "It's been a pleasure having you in my home. I hope *The Tireless Hunter* will not disappoint."

"It'd better not," he said almost like a threat before bidding her adieu and heading out the door where she noted a long dark limousine waiting to take him to his next feeding ground.

In the white heat of summer Savannah, she put on a straw hat and decided to spend the rest of the day walking the familiar streets and squares of the city, absorbing the daily life, even though not a lot was stirring today. It was just too hot for most people to be outside.

She passed by the First African Baptist Church on Montgomery Street, the first such church in North America. She went by Mercer House, "the envy of Savannah," where Jim Williams had shot the real Danny Hansford so long ago. She paused to look at the house at 230 East Oglethorpe Avenue where Conrad Aiken, the American poet and critic, had lived. He'd won a Pulitzer Prize, something that would never happen to her.

She even went by Flannery O'Connor's childhood home on Charlton Street. Once Lula had dreamed that she would join the pantheon of Miss O'Connor and Carson McCullers as a trio of literary sweethearts from the State of Georgia. Now Lula knew that was only to be dreamed, never realized.

With the Savannah River at her back, she walked to Johnson Square, Wright Square, Chippewa Square, Madison Square, and Monterey Square before pausing for a brief rest at Forsyth Park. Apparently she'd been walking too fast, and her clothes were soaked in sweat. Her heart seemed to be beating irregularly.

Once back in her kitchen she poured herself a large pitcher of water and carried it upstairs to her bathroom. Her irregular heart beat continued to pound dangerously within her frail body.

She decided to go to her medicine cabinet and take something for her condition. Nothing in the cabinet was particularly prescribed for an irregular heartbeat but she'd swallow the capsules anyway, regardless of what they contained.

Someone somewhere in the world had made the powders filling these capsules. Presumably the powders were manufactured to help people. In that case she would swallow all of them in case there was some magical power encapsulated within that would bring her renewed energy and vitality, that would restore her life.

Feeling faint and very dizzy after she'd swallowed all of the capsules, she stumbled toward her bed. The heat was oppressive. The room was like a hot attic on a Georgia summer with no ventilation. She was trembling all over as she collapsed on the unmade bed.

Perhaps she should leave Jason a note if he ever came home. But she felt too weak to do that.

Lying prone on the bed, she closed her eyes and folded her hands over her heart. In that position she fell asleep at once.

As she drifted off, she found it was the most peaceful and untroubled descent into sleep of her entire life.

The burden she'd known since the crib lifted miraculously from her.

*****

Though facing movie stardom, Tango still felt depressed and apprehensive. She'd been so close to having the top studs of Savannah, Danny Hansford and Jason McReeves, and even her daddy, Duke Edwards, and now all the men were gone. She couldn't cuddle up with a career at night. Being loved by a hot man was vital to her. When all three men walked out on her, it left her feeling very insecure.

She checked her appearance in the mirror. Staring back at her was the most gorgeous black pussy she'd ever seen in her life. How could a man leave her?

It was more understandable why Duke or Danny had abandoned her. They were the cheapest of hustlers willing to follow the flow of money. The most appalling desertion was by Jason. She'd liked him the most. When stacked up against Lula Carson, Tango just knew any man in his right mind would go for her and not the skinny and—let's face it—downright disfigured Lula Carson. Maybe she could write, and Tango didn't know that for sure. But Tango doubted that Lula knew how to fuck.

On the other hand, Tango was born to fuck. She remembered the first time a man had fucked her. She'd been twelve, the guy a field hand of twenty-three. He'd been white, naturally. Tango wasn't going to take it up the butt from no nigger man. Nigger men, as everyone knew, fucked too rough. When the guy had entered her, she'd never had such a thrill. Even though the man had been plowing into virgin territory, he'd entered her easily. There had been no pain on her part, only the most delicious feeling of pure ecstasy. Her walls had closed in on his cock, conquering it. She'd wanted to entrap it forever inside her guts. Before she'd finished with him, he'd cummed twice within her, and even when he'd pleaded he couldn't go another round, she'd held him firmly, not wanting to release the exquisite feel of his penetration of her lower depths.

From that day forth, Tango had decided she wanted a man to penetrate her at least two or three times a day. Her body demanded it. She also felt constant fucking was good for her complexion.

The telephone rang, and she rushed to pick up the receiver. It was Jerry Wheeler wanting her to come over to Phil Heather's house and read four pages of dialogue he'd written for her last night. "I'll be frank, honey," he said. "I think you're absolutely right for the part. But I've got to deal with the money boys in New York. I've got to be absolutely sure."

"Is The Lady Chablis still up for Lola?" Tango asked.

There was a long pause. "Yeah, but not in my view. The suits in New York want Chablis because of the name recognition. I'm completely opposed to it. It would invite comparisons with her performance for Eastwood. That's why I'm voting your ticket. A new fresh face. I'd think you'd be dynamite on the screen, especially when paired with that sexy blond Brian Sheehan. I'm telling the suits that you and Brian will be the next Grace Jones and Dolph Lundgren. They're sorta digging that at the moment."

"Please go to bat for me," she said. "I've just got to play Lola La Mour. I was born to be Lola."

"I know that, sweetheart, and I'll do my best," he said. "Could you get ready and be over here in an hour?"

"It's a deal," she said. "I'll show up as Lola herself in all her finery." She was hesitant to ask the next question. "How's Duke?"

"I haven't brought you up to date," Jerry said. "But after what you told me at Gin's studio, I dumped him. Fifty-year-old men aren't my scene."

A panic shot through her body. "Where is he? Back on the streets? Why didn't he come back over to my place?"

"Don't worry," he said. "Ol' Duke is living in the lap of luxury. His new patron is none other than Ms. Moneybags herself, Lavender Morgan."

"Oh, shit, that great-grandmother is pawing my daddy."

"I'm sure she'd doing more than pawing," he said. "I hear she gives the greatest blow-job in the Western world. Even better than Nancy Reagan who in the late forties was known as the fellatio queen of Hollywood."

"Duke and Lavender Morgan," Tango said. "That's the most disgusting thing in the world."

"It all depends on your viewpoint," Jerry said. "There are those who might find you and Duke disgusting."

She said nothing and didn't want to respond to that. Had Duke told Jerry that he'd fucked her? With Duke, you never knew. "I'll see you soon," she said. "I've got to get myself ready."

After she'd hung up with Jerry, she headed for her bathroom and her big mirror. But before she reached it, there was a knock on the door. She opened the door to stare into the face of Jason. "My God, it's you," she said, reaching out and taking his arm. "Get inside my house, child, before some size queen kidnaps you and sells you to a male bordello."

Inside her apartment, Jason shut the door and reached for her, kissing her long and hard and inserting his tongue.

She clung to him passionately, never wanting him to go. "You've come back to me," she said. "The answer to my dreams. You're the best. The best ever for me."

He pulled away and headed for the living room. "I've been thinking all morning about it. I'm tired of one-night stands. My time with you was the best ever. Everybody else I meet treats me like a piece of meat. You seemed to have genuine feelings for me."

"That's because I love you," she said. "I think I fell in love with you the first time I saw you." A sudden chill came over her. "What about Lula Carson?"

"I've left Lula. For good. I don't want to go back there again. I can't go back there again. Besides, I've done the most evil thing I've ever done in my life. Up until I did this thing, I never thought of myself as mean. Now I think I'm the world's greatest shithead."

"You killed Lula?"

"Hell, no! Nothing like that. Although you might say I stabbed her in the heart." He turned and looked helpless when confronting Tango. "I destroyed the most precious thing in her life. Her manuscript to *The Tireless Hunter*. I doubt if she'll ever write again."

"That's bullshit," Tango said. "If she's a real artist, like this lady standing in front of you, Lula will suffer for weeks, then bounce back. If she's a true artist, she'll overcome any setback. No doubt there were problems with her novel. Her second version will be even better than the first."

"Thank you for saying that," he said, going over and kissing her lightly on the lips. "It makes me feel just a little bit better, though I don't think I'll ever forgive myself for tossing away that manuscript."

Suddenly remembering her appointment, she said, "We've got to go over to Phil Heather's house to meet Jerry Wheeler. I want you to come as my escort."

"I don't want to go over there," he said. "I might run into Lula."

"I'll call Jerry and meet him inside," she promised. "I'll tell him you and Lula broke up. That you're with me now, and you don't want to encounter Lula Carson ever again."

"I don't hate her or anything like that," he said. "It's just..."

"You don't have to explain," she said, racing toward her bathroom. "I've got to get into my Lola La Mour drag."

In Phil's living room, Tango dressed in her Lola finery, a little red polka dot number that Jeff Chandler might have worn if he could have fitted into it—she dazzled Jerry with her reading of the script. It was the scene where she confronts Numie, the hustler, as he's walking out on her for good. After her rendition, she wasn't quite sure, but she detected a misty tear in Jerry's eye. Tango felt she'd played it to perfection.

Jason was filled with compliments as well. "You're one hell of a black diva," he said. "I'm real proud of you."

She detected a nervousness in Jason. Perhaps it was being so close to Lula again. He kept looking apprehensively at the back door, as if Lula would barge in on them at any minute.

After complimenting her performance for the third time, Jerry turned to Jason. "I think Tango is due for another compliment."

"And what might that be?" Tango asked, placing her hand on her slim hip, the way the character of Lola La Mour might do.

"Jason McReeves here is the best thing since Victor Mature was photographed nude on an army cot during World War II," Jerry said. "It led to an immediate Nazi surrender. No German soldier could compete with that."

"You're very kind," Jason said. "I'm flattered."

"If I ever decide to film *The Victor Mature Story*, I know who can play Victor," Jerry said.

"Believe me, dahling," Tango said, "it's real. I've climbed that mountain, and I can testify."

Jerry turned to Tango with a slight smirk on his face. "I've climbed that mountain too. It's the Mont Blanc of dicks."

Her face flashing anger, Tango faced Jason. "Is there anybody in Savannah you haven't fucked?"

"It was just one time," Jason said. "Jerry picked me up on his first night in town before he met Duke Edwards at Club One. It was just a brief fling." He confronted Jerry. "It was good too. So good you promised me the role of Numie in *Butterflies in Heat.* What about                                                                                      that?"

"It was just a promise," Jerry said. "You know me when I get drunk. To suck a dick as big as yours, I'll promise the world. The next morning I forget all my promises."

"Thank God I didn't take you seriously," Jason said. "Otherwise, I might pound your face in."

"No violence," Jerry said, backing away. "If you can act, you'd make a great Numie. Both you and Brian are ideal for the role. What's a gay size queen like me to do? I can't let every stud I meet play the part."

Suddenly, Jason seemed to resent being treated like a piece of meat. He stood up and walked toward the rear of Phil's house, as if remembering something. Tango felt a rising sense of panic. She realized she'd made a mistake showing off Jason in front of Jerry. The producer might take Jason away from her the way he had Duke Edwards. She also feared bringing him here so close to Lula. He might go over there and have a reconciliation with her. Apparently, his running away, then getting back with Lula, had occurred countless times.

When Tango sensed Jason was heading out the back door and going over to Lula's she called after him. "Stay here with me."

He stopped momentarily and looked back at her. "I'd better look in on Lula. It's only fair. She's still my wife. I destroyed her manuscript. It's the right thing to do."

"Don't go..." Tango's words died down to just a whimper.

"You can't stop him," Jerry said. "He looked mighty determined. If he wants to be with you, he'll come back. If he doesn't want to be with you, you're better off without him. Although, based on my own close encounter with him, you'll never find the likes of Jason McReeves roaming the streets of Savannah ever again."

Fifteen minutes must have gone by as Jerry discussed the role of Lola La Mour with Tango, telling her how he thought the part should be played. She could hardly concentrate on the producer's words, as she kept glancing toward the rear of the house waiting for Jason's return. At this point she didn't even know if he would come back.

A shrill bellow came from the back porch. Tango jumped up from the sofa, and trailed by Jerry, fled outside to see what was the matter.

There in the bright Savannah sun, Jason was standing forlornly, holding the dead body of an orange-haired Lula Carson in his arms and looking up at the sky as if someone there could bring her back to life.

*****

Tennessee Williams had it right when he wrote his novel, *The Roman Spring of Mrs. Stone.* Lavender had recently seen the movie on the late show starring Vivien Leigh as the aging actress and Warren Beatty as the miscast Italian gigolo. In the book and in the movie, Mrs. Stone had started to "drift" into the world of hustlers, and that was exactly how Lavender felt after retreating from a two-hour session in bed with the sex expert, Duke Edwards.

Whereas Danny had been a mere boy, Duke was a skilled womanizer who knew what to press, feel, suck, and penetrate. In his life he must have known countless women, and in fact must have spent most of his years making love to women. His skill as a lover was almost incomparable, and she'd been made love to by some of the world's most famous lovers, including Porfirio Rubirosa himself when she'd managed to lure him away from Barbara Hutton and Zsa Zsa Gabor during a trip to Paris.

It was inevitable at her age that Lavender had "drifted" to purchasing hustlers. Danny had been her first, Duke her second. But she felt neither one of them would be her last. She had hoped that after a lifetime of affairs she would settle down and take up knitting. But that was not to be. If anything, she was as horny now as she was when she was twenty and could have all the sex she wanted for free. Back in those salad days, she had to turn down offers from men, often as many as ten in one day. Today she was reduced to paying by the inch.

Over breakfast Duke was most attentive, unlike Danny who usually ignored her. "I was wondering," Duke said, looking over at her with a seductive smile. "Why don't we get the fuck out of Savannah in August and go somewhere where it's nice and cool? Maybe the Alps."

"That's a great idea," she said. "I'm dying here." She paused as if remembering something unpleasant. "Of course, I have a few personal matters to take care of. Still a little trouble with the police, but I hope everything will be resolved soon."

"I hope so," he said. "It's too hot and humid here. I always wanted to travel. I mean, travel in style. Not stand on the fucking road and hitch a ride with some fat, bald pig who'd have me for supper before he'd buy me supper."

"That kind of life on the road I don't know about," she said. "Thank God. It sounds nightmarish."

"You don't know the half of it."

Norma Dixie came in, cast a contemptuous eye at Duke, then informed Lavender that Phil Heather wanted her on the phone. "That boy says it's an emergency."

"Oh, my God," Lavender said, rising from her chair in alarm. At the phone she picked up the receiver with trepidation. "Good morning."

"Sorry to call so early," Phil said. "It's Lula Carson. She's committed suicide."

A little shriek escaped from Lavender's throat. It wasn't that she knew Lula well or was even that friendly with her, although she had gotten her the literary grant for reasons Lavender had rather not think about this morning. "I'm so very sorry to hear that." These days the death of anyone she knew, regardless of how slightly, stabbed at Lavender's heart, evoking her own mortality.

"She overdosed on pills," Phil said. "I don't know why. Jason had walked out on her, but he's done that before."

"Then there must be some other reason," she said. "Do you know how *The Tireless Hunter* was coming along? In my talks with Lula, her novel—she called it a masterpiece—meant more to her than Jason. More to her than anybody or anything."

"I don't think she was writing much lately in spite of your grant which saved her financially," he said. "Even if her writing slowed down, I think she would have regained her inspiration. We writers have various periods of productivity. I doubt if she killed herself over *The Tireless Hunter.*"

"I'd really like to see the manuscript," Lavender said, "after hearing so much about it. Maybe she was close to finishing. The greatest gift to Lula might be for me to get it published."

"That had crossed my mind too," Phil said. "But a strange thing. I've searched the house with Jason. We can't find the manuscript. Jason said she had a hard copy and, of course, it was on her computer. The novel's been completely erased. It's vanished."

"She may have destroyed the novel before killing herself," Lavender said. "Maybe she thought it was lousy and couldn't bear to let the world read it, after having given it so much self-promotion."

"You mean announcing how great it was and everything to everybody months before anybody read it?" he said.

"Exactly," Lavender said. "We must hold that out as a possibility. Who would destroy the novel—erase it completely—but Lula herself?"

"You may be right," he said, sounding despondent.

"What about the funeral?" Lavender asked.

"I called her parents in Columbus," Phil said. "They had already been contacted by the police. Her parents want no part of the burial. Once they learned Lula killed herself, they said they're washing their hands of the whole matter. They'll not come to the funeral or participate in any way. Apparently, to her parents suicide is a bigger sin than abortion. They're fanatically religious."

"Then Jason will have to bury her," Lavender said. "Even if he walked out on her, he's still her husband."

"Jason will do what he can," Phil said. "He never has any money. I'll pay for the funeral and arrange the burial myself."

"Let me help," Lavender said. "You were kind not to ask me, but I want to participate. I have a plot of land in Bonaventure. It's just there waiting for me to die. I could arrange to have her buried in my family plot since her own family doesn't want her in Columbus."

"I'm sure Jason would agree to that. You're very kind to make the offer."

"I want to do my part," Lavender said. "Just between you and me there have been too many deaths in Savannah. Chris Leighton. Tom Caldwell. Now Lula Carson."

At the mention of those dead people, Norma interrupted. "People are dropping dead like flies around Savannah. Who knows? We could be next."

Lavender brushed her aside and directed her back to the kitchen. She didn't need Norma's dire speculations today.

"I'm spooked out by it all," Phil said. "Lula was my newest friend on earth but she was quickly becoming one of my dearest. Our boys loved her. John and Henry are crying their eyes out. They don't understand death."

"Do any of us really understand?" Lavender said. "I'll be over at your place soon if that's all right with you. We'll make the arrangements."

"Lula's body is at the morgue," he said. "The police may want to order an autopsy."

"No one thinks Lula was murdered, do they?" Lavender asked. "It seems there is enough investigation going on for murder around here—I mean the Chris Leighton thing."

"I've heard no talk of murder," he said. "The police interviewed me. Jason apparently was with Tango when Lula killed herself. Jason discovered the body. I don't think the police seriously think Jason killed her."

"I don't think he did either," she said, preparing to hang up and get ready. "If there's one thing I know how to do in all the world, it's arrange a funeral. I've had vast experience."

The next day, since everyone was anxious for a fast burial, Lula's body was released in the custody of Jason who ordered it sent to one of the local funeral homes. The police decided that it was obviously a suicide and no autopsy would be performed.

Lavender planned with Phil to have Lula buried at dawn at Bonaventure. Only a handful of people attended, mainly Phil, accompanied by Brian and his two sons. Norma Dixie was there, proclaiming her undying love for Lula. Even Gin Tucker showed up but Tipper Zelda turned down an invitation, claiming she hardly knew Lula. Out of respect, Jerry Wheeler showed up.

Jason came with Tango which Lavender found an outrageous stunt, because Phil had told her that Jason had only recently taken up with the dancer. If Tango had any taste at all, she'd stay home. But, with Tango, what did one expect?

Lavender artfully concealed her feelings about Tango's presence because Jerry had told her that it was highly likely that Tango would appear opposite her in *Butterflies in Heat*, Lavender playing Leonora de la Mer and Tango her arch rival, Lola La Mour. For the good of the film, Lavender smiled and greeted Tango as Lula's body was being lowered into the bog.

Lavender stood before Jason and shook his hand. His eyes were red from crying. "I loved her, Ms. Morgan. I truly did. I know it doesn't look like that this morning, but there will always be a special place in my heart for Lula."

Lavender graciously offered to allow Jason and Tango to ride back to town in her limousine. Duke didn't seem too keen on the idea but said nothing. Once in the car, Tango reached into her purse, pulled out a compact, and checked her make-up. "A gal has got to look good even at a funeral."

"I had to bury so many people I keep a wardrobe just for the occasion," Lavender said.

"I see you're wearing black," Tango said. "Black don't look good on me and that's why I showed up in beige. I hear you always wear lavender."

"I always wear lavender—it's my favorite color, my namesake, obviously—but at funerals it's basic black for me."

"La-de-dah," Tango said, leaning back and seemingly enjoying the luxurious upholstery of the limousine. "My daddy sure struck it rich this time." She looked over at Duke. "He sure got himself a fine rich lady to haul his ass around Savannah."

"Shut your fucking mouth," Duke snapped at her.

Lavender was puzzled. She looked first at Duke, then at Tango.

"You didn't tell this fine rich lady," Tango said provocatively before turning to smile into Lavender's stunned face. "Child," she said, addressing Lavender in a rather imperial manner, "this stud hustler who you have took up with is none other than my daddy."

*****

Dawn had hardly broken, and it found Danny in the Greenwich Cemetery at plot G-19. He stared down at a small granite tile.

Danny Lewis Hansford
March 1, 1960
May 2, 1981

Before the day was over, the second Danny—namely Jeff Broyhill of Clinton, Georgia—would know if he were to join the real Danny Hansford in this grave or would be set free to roam the world as he chose. Today would be the most important day of his life. It would be the day on which future days would depend, if there was any time left for him at all.

Right now he couldn't be sure. Far from being nervous about this evening, he felt strangely at peace. Of this he was certain: after tonight his trials and tribulations would be over. He would be either dead or else set free of a troubled soul refusing to leave the earth.

Coming out of her trance, Erzulie had convinced him that he had to kill Phil Heather. It was the only way. He wouldn't be striking at Phil himself but at Jim Williams. No matter what happened tonight, Jim Williams would die brutally, the way he should have died after killing the real Danny Hansford.

The time just spent with Dale Evans was going to be Danny's last as a prostitute. He wanted no more sucking, devouring mouths descending on him to take his life's blood. Dale had been insatiable, his tongue exploring every crevice of Danny. Dale simply couldn't get enough of Danny. But Danny wanted to be free. No more Dale Evans types in his life. No more Gin Tuckers. No more Tipper Zeldas.

What he really wanted was for Tom Caldwell to return. If Tom wouldn't come back to earth, perhaps Danny would go off to join him in some celestial place. There Danny could be happy.

All his life he'd known nothing but pain and trouble. He hadn't lived many years on this earth, but the time had been one of brutality and hurt. There had been no real love until that faint glimmer of it with Tom. Danny had been used by everybody he came into contact with, whether it was Tango or Lavender Morgan. The parade of names didn't really matter. All of the people who'd come into his life had wanted a pound of his flesh, and he'd usually delivered.

Regrettably, Danny had delivered too much. He'd given so much to strangers he didn't save enough for himself.

He bowed and said a silent prayer at the grave of the real Danny Hansford. He prayed that this Danny would no longer inhabit his soul after today and would go on his way, wherever that was.

Getting up from the grave site, the second Danny looked down forlornly at the marker, knowing that he might be occupying some such site in Clinton, Georgia, if the day didn't go right for him.

He dreaded going back to Tipper's, fearing that she would be there goading him on in his act of violence, aided by Erzulie and her voodoo.

Dale was an unknown factor in the household. Danny felt that if Dale knew what was in his best interest, that he would flee from Tipper's doorstep and never darken it again. Each hour that Dale spent in that household, he was implicating himself deeper and deeper into murderous plots. Danny felt that Dale didn't know the extent of his involvement. A man could spend years in jail for being an accessory to such things. But Danny decided not to tell Dale anything. He was fully responsible for his actions, and if he chose to force his presence into the lives of Tipper and Danny, Dale must pay the consequences.

Before going back to Tipper's, Danny headed for Mercer House after leaving the cemetery. On Monterey Square he'd watched as Clint Eastwood had directed scenes from the movie, *Midnight in the Garden of Good and Evil.* Lighting a cigarette, Danny stood looking at the facade of Mercer House where Jim Williams had fatally shot the original Danny Hansford. No sign of life could be detected within this house where Danny and Tom had spent some time, Tom's presence unknown to Lavender Morgan.

As Danny dropped his cigarette at his booted feet, sharp pains shot through his body. It was as if Jim Williams were pumping bullets into Danny's body. He could feel them. The impact caused him to fall down in the square as if shot.

No life was stirring on the square this morning, so there was no one to rush to his aid. Danny didn't know how long he lay on that square as if dead. But when he came to he felt that some time had passed. Maybe some people had passed him by, but paid him no mind, thinking he might be a drug addict in a coma after a night of substance abuse. In Savannah people often let you alone.

Although it was dangerous to go near the murder site, Danny headed for Arlie Rae's apartment after leaving Mercer House. The police had not contacted him today, although he thought they might. If he were a suspect in the Chris Leighton murder, maybe he might be a suspect in Arlie Rae's murder. What he feared was that Arlie Rae's telephone records might be investigated. If the police learned that Arlie Rae had called Tipper's house from his home phone, Danny was in deep shit.

An empty squad car stood in front of Arlie Rae's apartment, and the police had cordoned off the area but there was no sign of life, either outside or from within the building. Danny hurried on his way, heading for Tipper's. He didn't want to think of those final moments with Arlie Rae. Wherever he went, Linda Tripp's accusing eyes seemed to follow him.

In the kitchen he encountered Dale pouring himself some freshly brewed coffee. "Like a cup, stud?" Dale asked.

"Yeah," Danny said, not making eye contact and embarrassed at the intimacy of last night. What had happened to a hardened hustler like him? Since when did he get embarrassed at intimacy?

"I've heard stories about you," Dale said, placing the cup in front of him, "and I thought the local queens were exaggerating. But after last night I've joined your fan club. You were terrific. I don't know why I put up with that stubby dicked Frank Gilmore all these years when I could have had a hunk like you."

Danny tasted his coffee and then slammed down the cup. "You did it for money, bitch. The same way I've done it." He paused and glared at Dale. "Or else because I'm being blackmailed. It's only because you've got something on me that I'd go to bed with you at all. You make me sick!"

Not even bothering to look again into Dale's stunned face, Danny headed up front to the living room where he heard Erzulie talking with Tipper. Upon seeing him, Tipper jumped up and shut the door behind him. "Dale knows enough about us. I don't want him to hear any more."

"White boy," Erzulie said, "today is the day you're gonna be set free."

"How do you know that?" he asked skeptically. "A million things could go wrong."

"They ain't gonna go wrong," Erzulie said. She smiled at Tipper. "I've worked it out with the spirits. The spirits are gonna help you tonight."

"Phil is to meet me at sunset at Bonaventure," Tipper said with a malicious glee. "He thinks it's for a martini at the Aiken grave site. That's an old Savannah tradition."

"Yeah, I know about it," he said.

"The machete will be given to you at the right time," Tipper said. "Remember it won't be Phil you're killing. It will be Jim Williams. The moment Phil departs this earth, thanks to you, you're free."

"You're gonna be free, boy," Erzulie said. "Freedom. That's a wonderful word. I was descended from slaves. We wasn't free. Right now you're just as much a slave as my ancestors. Freedom, boy. It's mighty delicious."

He looked first at Erzulie, then at Tipper. He wanted to believe them but something told him not to. Maybe Jeff Broyhill of Clinton, Georgia, still lived somewhere within. Jeff wouldn't hang out with either Tipper or Erzulie, and Jeff would have punched Dale Evans in the face. That Jeff part of him wanted to flee from this house and never see this unholy trio ever again.

But could he? He was in their power. Whether he fully believed them or not, he felt he had to do their bidding. That other part of him, the real Danny Hansford who inhabited his body, wanted out, and Jeff was clearly being told that the only way to get Danny out of his soul was to kill Phil.

He was annoyed at himself for not being fully convinced. Up to now he'd put his faith in Erzulie, and he had no real reason not to continue to give her his trust.

The disturbing link was not with Erzulie but with Tipper Zelda. When he'd looked into her eyes, he'd been deeply disturbed. That was no sane woman looking back at him. Even though Tipper cleverly disguised it, he felt she was crazy. There was madness there, and he was moving deeper and deeper into her orbit.

"I'll do what you want," he blurted out in a voice he didn't recognize as his own. "Just tell me what you want done." He stood in the room, not making eye contact with either of them.

"I'm glad you'll help us," Tipper said. "We're doing it for you."

"Yeah," he managed to say in response but the word hardly escaped his throat.

"Freedom, boy," Erzulie said, heading for Tipper's liquor cabinet. "It's the greatest sounding word in the world. Hallelujah! Hallelujah!"

\*\*\*\*\*

The sun was setting as Tipper spotted Phil Heather walking among the Tillandsia-draped oaks to keep their rendezvous. Earlier when she had spoken to him to confirm their date, he'd told her that he had lied to Brian about where he was going. "It's the first time I've ever lied to him, and I detected something on his face, like he didn't believe me. But you're insisting on secrecy, so okay."

"A little surprise I have for you," she'd told him in her most reassuring voice.

Before agreeing to meet Phil at Bonaventure, she'd read up on the history of this cemetery bordering the Wilmington River. Sometime in the late 1760s the land was settled by John Mulryne, a British colonel.

He decided to call the place Bonaventure, and he ordered the construction of a brick plantation house here in time to celebrate the marriage of his daughter, Mary, to Josiah of the Tattnall family of Charleston. In the late 18th century the plantation burned to the ground in a spectacular fire. The fire started while a formal dinner with liveried servants was under way. The butler told the host that the roof was on fire and the house could not be saved. The host ordered the servants to take the tables and dinner plates outside in the front yard. The regal dinner was consummated by the light of the raging fire. At a final toast each guest tossed a crystal goblet against an old oak tree. The dinner party laughter and the sound of shattering crystal are said to still echo throughout the graveyard on a windy night. After a tumultuous history, Bonaventure was purchased in 1850 by Captain Peter Wilberger who turned it into a cemetery. By 1907 the City of Savannah had acquired the land along the waterfront.

As Phil walked up to Tipper, he asked her what was in the basket she was carrying.

"It's a basket of martinis," she said. "You know. You've read *Midnight in the Garden of Good and Evil.* I even have the silver goblets."

"Martinis at the grave site of the Aikens," he said. "I hear after Berendt's book, it's become a tradition, even with tourists."

"It's a wonderful Savannah custom," she said, leaning over and kissing him on the lips. "I still can't believe how much you look like Montgomery Clift."

"We've been over that," he said in a firm voice. "I'm not Montgomery Clift. He's dead. He's not coming back. We'd better get over dead lovers of yesterday and move forward. How about that?"

Although his words infuriated her, she masked her annoyance and gently took his arm, directing him along the pathway to the Aiken grave.

He graciously offered to carry her martini basket which she gladly surrendered to him.

At the grave site, she pointed out the double gravestone. It bore the names of Dr. William F. Aiken and his wife, Anna. Both died on the say day of February 27, 1901. "Conrad Aiken was only eleven when Dr. Aiken shot his wife, then killed himself."

"The book said she went to too many parties to suit his taste," Phil said. "Do you think Dr. Aiken really killed his wife because she went to too many parties?"

"It sounds ridiculous, but that's the legend. Like most Savannah legends, don't study it too closely."

"Where's Conrad Aiken buried?" he asked.

"On this bench where people can sit," she said.

"A gravestone constructed like a bench?" he asked.

"Aiken wanted people to visit this lovely spot long after he was gone," she said. "To come here and down martinis in silver goblets and just watch the ships move up and down the Wilmington River."

"On the bench," he said, "I just noticed it. It's inscribed COSMOS MARINER, DESTINATION UNKNOWN."

"That's us," she said, reaching into her basket and pouring him a martini in a silver goblet. "This is the best martini you'll ever taste for the rest of your life."

"If not that," Phil said, "the most dramatic martini I'll ever sip."

On the second drink from the martini, she proposed a toast. "To our working together on *Butterflies in Heat*. To our making a great film."

"To your eating up the screen as Tangerine," he said. "Winning an Oscar as best supporting actress."

"If that is held up as a possibility," she said, "I must insist that you down the rest of the martini in one gulp. That way, you'll make it come true."

"Here's looking at you, kid."

She held back, not drinking the toast with him. His head was turned up to the sky which suddenly grew darker almost the moment the sun sank below the horizon.

She couldn't drink. Not now. If she had her head raised drinking a martini from a silver shaker she might not have noticed what happened next.

From out of nowhere a machete swung through the air, lopping off Phil's head, sending it rolling across the floor of the cemetery. Blood gushed from Phil's uncapped neck like an oil gusher newly released. The rest of Phil's body collapsed on Conrad Aiken's grave site.

Like a monster whose face was frozen in wax, Danny looked first at Phil and then at Tipper. She'd never seen such a ghoulish look on a human face. He gazed down at Phil one more time. Blood was still running from his neck but not at the same velocity. Danny faced her squarely. Still holding the machete, he seemed to menace her, making her fear for her own life. Was he truly insane? Would he now turn on her? His body seemed to grow larger and taller.

"You tricked me," he said. It wasn't Danny's voice but another sound coming from somebody else. The voice also didn't seem to emerge from Danny's throat but deep from the recesses of his bowels.

She was afraid of him. Backing away, she stumbled and fell across the bench, ending up on the ground, her large eyes staring into those of Phil. His wide open eyes seemed to be accusing her, as if knowing she was The Black Widow responsible for his murder, as she'd been the killer of all her four husbands. Before she could pick herself up from this ghoulish encounter, the machete cut into her neck sending her head rolling. Her body now gushed blood like a fountain with a powerful spray.

What no one tells you is that the brain continues to live for at least five seconds after your head is separated from your body. You see and know everything that's happening for one brief moment before oblivion.

Tipper lived long enough to see a figure in the darkness grab the machete from Danny and chop off his head.

# Aftermath

Three years later, dusk was settling over Aunt Bice's meadow before the first frost. Brian sat on the back porch before going in to fix dinner for John and Henry. His sons were going out on their first double date with two girls, both twins, who lived three miles from the Heather plantation.

He always sat here in the early evening twilight, enjoying a drink and thinking of Phil. He remembered the good times, the promise of what might have been, or what should have begun thirteen years sooner but was delayed by his own failure to recognize his nature.

Sometimes he would tremble with fear, but he sat out here every night, regardless of wind, rain, or chill. He could think out here and ponder what to do with the rest of his life.

The only thing his brain wouldn't let him think about was what happened during that final hour Phil Heather spent at Bonaventure Cemetery.

# If you've enjoyed this book,

## Please consider these other fine works by
# Darwin Porter

from

and

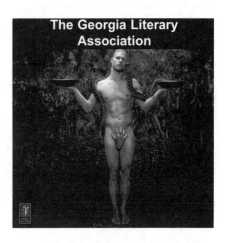

**Blood Moon Productions**

Biographies that change
the way America interprets
its cinematic past.

**The Georgia Literary
Association**

Sophisticated,
provocative entertainment you
wouldn't necessarily expect
from the Deep South

# www.BloodMoonProductions.com

# BLOOD MOON PRODUCTIONS

### & its affiliate, The Georgia Literary Association.

**Current and Backlist Titles, arranged
in their order of publication, Autumn, 2006**

www.BloodMoonProductions.com

## *Brando Unzipped* by Darwin Porter © 2006
ISBN 09748118-2-3  Hardcover  $26.95

"Lurid, raunchy, perceptive, and certainly worth reading."
*The Sunday Times (London)*

"Yummy. An irresistably flamboyant romp of a read."
*Books to Watch Out For*

"Astonishing.   An  extradordinarily  detailed  portrait  of
Brando that's as blunt, uncompromising, and X-rated as
the man himself."
*Women's Weekly*

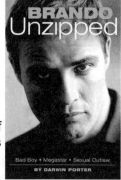

## Blood Moon's Guide to Gay and Lesbian Film (First Edition)
ISBN 0-9748118-4-X © 2006 Softcover $19.95

"Authoritative, exhaustive, and essential, *Blood Moon's
Guide to Gay and Lesbian Film* is the queer girl's and
queer boy's one-stop resource for what to add to their
feature-film queue.  The film synopses and the snip-
pets of critic's reviews are reason enough to keep this
annual compendium of cinematic information close to
the DVD player.  But the extras--including the Blood
Moon Awards and commentary on queer short films—
are butter on the popcorn."
*Books to Watch Out For*

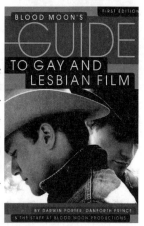

## Blood Moon's Guide to Gay and Lesbian Film (Second Annual Edition) Available February 2007 © 2007

More of the reviews which filmmakers, both domestic and international, find
useful, informative, and compelling.  Hot, provocative, and unique, it's loaded
with reviews and commentary on recently released GLBT films, both feature-
length and shorts. It includes reviews of many films scheduled for release during 2007.  Lavishly illustrated, and endorsed by the directors of several major
GLBT Film festivals, it's the second in a successful series already praised by
the gay and lesbian press as "indispensable."

## Howard Hughes, Hell's Angel

by Darwin Porter ISBN 0-9748118-1-5 © 2005.
Hardcover. $26.95

"Darwin Porter's access to film industry insiders and other Hughes confidants supplied him with the resources he needed to create a portrait of Hughes that both corroborates what other Hughes biographies have divulged, and go them one better."
*Foreword Magazine*

"Thanks to this bio of Howard Hughes, we'll never be able to look at the old pinups in quite the same way again."
*The Times* **(London)**
*Publisher's note*: This title was _nominated_ for *Book of the Year 2005* by *Foreword Magazine,* and _awarded_ *Book of the Year 2005* by *Senior Life and Boomer Times*

## The Best Gay & Lesbian Films: The Glitter Awards 2005   ISBN 0-9748118-3-1.

Softcover © 2005 Compiled and released in cooperation with THE GLITTER AWARDS    $23.95 *Publisher's note*: This title was awarded a _Silver Meda_l in **Foreword Magazine**'s Book of the Year Awards 2005.

## Katharine the Great: A Lifetime of Secrets Revealed

by Darwin Porter. ISBN 0-9748118-0-7 © 2004. Softcover $16.95

The appearance of this book within six months of Hepburn's death in 2003 led to an avalanche of commentary, and some derivative works, that at last weren't afraid to discuss this "phobically secretive" diva's role as a bisexual in Hollywood. *"The door to Hepburn's closet has finally been opened. This is the most honest and least apologetic biography of Hollywood's most ferociously private actress ever written."*
*Senior Life/Boomer Times*

"Behind the scenes of her movies, Katharine Hepburn played the temptress to as many women as she did men, ranted and raved with her co-stars and directors, and broke into her neighbors' homes for fun. And somehow, she managed to keep all of it out of the press."
*Dallas Voice*

### The Secret Life of Humphrey Bogart: The Early Years (1899-1931) by Darwin

Porter ISBN 0-9668030-5-1 © 2003. Softcover  $16.95

"Darwin Porter uncovers scandals within the entertainment industry of the 1920s and 1930s, when publicists from the movie studios deliberately twisted and suppressed inconvenient details about the lives of their emerging stars."
**Turner Classic Movie News**

"Exceptionally well-written."
**Hollywood Inside**

### Hollywood's Silent Closet by Darwin

Porter ISBN 09668030-2-7 © 2000. Softcover. $24.95.

"A steamy but historic account of the pansexual intrigues of Hollywood between 1919 and 1926, compiled from eyewitness interviews with men and women who flourished in its midst. If you believe, like Truman Capote, that 'the artful presentation of gossip will become the literature of the 21st century,' you'll find this a juicy and highly irreverent read."

"A brilliant primer for the *Who's Who* of early Hollywood."
**Gay Times (London)**

### Blood Moon by Darwin Porter. ISBN 0-9668030-4-3.
(Abridged edition). © 2002 Softcover. $10.99.

"Blood Moon exposes the murky labyrinths of fanatical Christianity in America today, within a spunky context of bisexual eroticism. If you never thought that sex, psychosis, right-wing fundamentalism, and violence aren't linked, think again, and read this erotic spellbinder. Blood Moon reads like an IMAX spectacle about the power of male beauty, with red-hot icons, a breathless climax, and erotica that's akin to Anaïs Nin on Viagra with a bump of crystal meth."
**Eugene Raymond (*After Dark Magazine*)**

### *Rhinestone Country* by Darwin Porter
ISBN 0-9668030-3-5 © 2002. Softcover. $15.95

"The *True Grit* of show-biz novels, *Rhinestone Country* is a provocative, realisitic, and tender portrayal of the Country-Western music industry, closeted lives south of the Mason-Dixon line, and three of the singers who clawed their way to stardom."
**Advance Reviews**

"Written with a deep respect for the changing face of The South, it's like no other novel I've read. An American original."
**Alex Zucker**

### *Butterflies in Heat* by Darwin Porter.
ISBN 0-877978-96-5 © 1976 and now in its 15th reprint. Re-released in 1998 in cooperation with the Florida Literary Assn. Softcover. $12.95.

"A well-established cult classic of the bizarre, the flamboy-ant, and the corrupt. How does Darwin Porter's garden grow? Only in the moonlight, and only at midnight, when man-eating vegetation in any color but green bursts into full bloom to devour the latest offerings."
**James Leo Herlihy, author of *MIDNIGHT COWBOY***

### *Jacko: His Rise and Fall*
#### The Sexual History of Michael Jackson
by Darwin Porter. ISBN 0-9748118-5-8 © 2006.

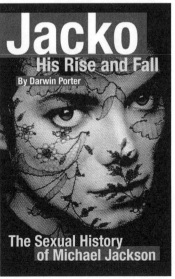

Inside the Wacko World of MJ: An overview of the tribulations of an entertainer whose fame surpassed, in some corners of the globe, that of either the US President or Jesus Christ. The real story of the megastar's rise to fame is more com-plicated than you might ever have imagined--and certainly more bizarre--with "Michael" anecdotes that involve many of the best known celebrities in Hollywood. From Darwin Porter, whose work has been described by *The Sunday Times* of London as "raunchy, lurid, perceptive, and cer-tainly worth reading."